The Sutton Hoo Stories

ÆTHELING

S.T. Sonntag

ISBN: 0692420924
ISBN-13: 978-0692420928

For my Jellybean

Note

This book contains words in Old English. This is not the language of Shakespeare (which is an archaic form of Modern English), nor is it the language of Chaucer (who spoke Middle English). This is the language of *Beowulf,* which can be somewhat intimidating to the casual reader. These words appear in *italics* throughout the book. For the ease of the reader, I have included a pronunciation guide, glossary and list of characters in the appendices.

Old English Pronunciation Guide

Old English	Pronunciation	As in...
Æ/æ	[æ]	Cat, black, ash
Þ/þ or Đ/ð	[ð] or [θ]	thing OR there
Cg	[dʒ]	edge
Sc	[ʃ]	ship, shield
g	[g] or [j] or [ɣ]	grave OR year OR [ɣ] (as German or Dutch 'g' sound)

Old English Glossary

Additional Glossary in Appendices

Old English	Pronunciation	Definition
ætheling	ah-the-ling	Prince/princess, son or daughter of a king or high nobleman
Ceorl	churl	Free servant
Cwene	kway-n	Queen
cyning	kyoo-ning	King
dryhten	drick-ten	Chieftain, warlord, commander
ealdorman	ay-al-dor-man	Earl, nobleman
flyting	fly-ting	A verbal competition of wits, often involving poetic insults
gedriht	ye-drickt	Professional trained warriors
heahcwene	hay-ah-kway-n	High queen
heahcyning	hay-ah-kyoo-ning	High king
hilderinc	hill-deh-rink	Warrior
hlaford	hla-ford	Lord, chief, leader (archaic form of "lord")
huscarl	hoos-karl	Household guard, bodyguard, retainer
moot/-mot	moot	Meeting, gathering
pening/ peningas	pen-ing/pen-ing-as	Unit of currency, equivalent to about £15-20
scylling/ scyllingas	shilling/shilling-as	Unit of currency, equivalent to about £100
symbel	sim-bel	A highly ritualized drinking ceremony in a mead hall
thegn	thane	Retainers of a king or lord, similar to the later knight
wergild	ware-gild	Fine for an offense against a person (lit. "man-gold")
witenagamot	wi-tana-ga-mot	Council

Prologue

Annie waits for me at the top of the steps.

"Do we get a discount if I show them my military ID?" she asks, digging around in her passport bag.

"Nah, it's free," I say, but I push a couple of five-pound notes into the Plexiglas donation box.

It is stark white in here, and the sleek, ultramodern glass ceiling clashes weirdly with the majestic colonnaded entrances to the exhibits, but I kind of like the dissonance.

We go left first.

The huge bust of Ramses fills the room, and I start to say the first few lines of Shelley's *Ozymandias* before Annie rolls her eyes.

"You're turning into Mom," she says.

"God damn it," I say, catching myself. "You're right."

We work our way through the Egyptian sculpture, and Annie has me take a picture of her in front of the winged bulls with human heads, which guard the entrance to the Assyria exhibit.

"What do they call these?" She asks, pointing to the sculptures. "Read the signs, idiot," I tell her.

"You're supposed to know all about this stuff," Annie says, pulling me by the neck to take a selfie in front of one of the sculptures. We both pucker stupidly and she sifts through a couple of Instagram filters. She sends it with the caption, "British Museum!" and six or seven little hearts and hashtags and smiley faces. She sends the same picture to Zack and Jesse, with the caption *suck it, we're in London!*

They respond with some kind words of their own, regardless of the extra cost for overseas texting.

"I didn't study Assyriology," I say. "Besides, didn't you see this kind of stuff when you were over in the Gulf?"

"I was only there for, like, a day before I had to get on the boat," she says, glancing at a sign on one of the friezes and taking a picture of the dying cat indicated on the slab of brown stone. "After that it was a whole lot of water. I did go to a couple of the museums in Rome though. That was pretty cool."

My feet start to hurt by the time we finish the Greece and Rome exhibits, and Annie's making suggestions about heading to the gift shop. I shake my head. "We have to go upstairs."

"Ugh. If you only came for the medieval stuff, then why didn't we just go there first?"

"It's like when you save the big caramel swirl in your ice cream for last," I say.

"Ooh, we should go get some ice cream when we're done here!" she says, and we start to climb the white stairs in the center of the massive atrium.

"Well hang on," she says as I push past her. "I want to look at this stuff."

I don't listen to her. I follow the line of galleries to the end. I push my purse back onto my shoulder, wishing it wasn't so heavy. Annie follows behind me at a trot, muttering something like "nerd."

My fingers find my ponytail, like they usually do when I'm nervous. The room is blue, and the cases are angular and sharp-looking. The artefacts are green with corrosion, sitting neatly on little shelves behind the glass, with clean white signs beneath them.

I want to run around the room screaming, but I'm rooted to the spot as I look at every item before moving on to the next.

"Oh cool, I remember this from your thesis," she says, looking into one of the cases.

"I'm surprised you read it," I say.

She shrugs. "I skimmed the technical archaeological stuff that I didn't really understand, but I got the gist of the rest."

"That's the whetstone and stag scepter," I say, pointing to the long stone shaft with a stag-topped iron ring. "We think it came together to make a kind of scepter for the Bretwalda."

"The Bretwalda was the king right?" she asks.

"Not exactly," I say. "See, back in about the 600s, you have all these separate Anglo-Saxon kingdoms, like Mercia and Wessex and East Anglia and Kent, right, and they kind of do their own thing and run their own kingdoms, but occasionally there is someone mentioned called the Bretwalda. No one's really sure exactly what 'Bretwalda' means, but he acted as something like an overlord of all these little kingdoms. There were only a few of these guys, and they seem to crop up when there were periods of turmoil or transition. Think of it like a high king. A *heahcyning*, I guess it would be in Old English."

"Do you just have like an endless supply of Old English words on hand?" she asks, examining the silver nesting bowls in another of the cases.

"Pretty much," I say. "So anyway, the whetstone would have symbolized strength in battle, like how the *heahcyning* could keep his men honed and ready to fight, and then the stag is like the king of the forest, so it's an old symbol of power. That's what some people think, anyway."

"Oh cool," she says noncommittally.

She doesn't get it. She doesn't have the fluttering in her stomach, the tingle of the past catching up with her. She is just too nice to show that she doesn't really care.

I am almost afraid to round the corner. If I do, I'll see it, and then I won't be able to leave again. The cleaner will have to sweep me out, and even then, I'll only go kicking and screaming.

I tighten my ponytail again, nervously walking past the carved standing stone. My heart is pounding. My palms are sweating. I'm glad Annie isn't looking.

You can't see much of it any more. Most of the helmet rotted away in the acidic soil where it had been for the last 1400 years before they dug it up. The ancient iron looks like scales against the plain, featureless mold of the modern reconstruction. Nevertheless, the face is still there, a bird with outstretched wings that forms the nose and the eyebrows of the facemask. I've forgotten how big it was.

The sign above the helmet says, *The Sutton Hoo Ship Burial, Early AD 600s.*

This is why I hate archaeology. I get too invested. I get caught up in their lives. I'm not supposed to, but I do. I'm supposed to write papers that no one will ever read, about why this interlace pattern indicates a paradigm shift, or what we can deduce from using Raman Spectroscopy instead of XRF for elemental analysis of artifacts. That's what I'm supposed to do.

But it's why I love archaeology, too. I love the feel the dirt under my fingernails as I prod around in their world. My back aches and the sun burns my neck and flies bite my ankles. I find the broken pieces of the lives that came before me; I look at them under a microscope in a sterile lab, and I pick away the dirt that was thrown over their graves. I'm not supposed to hear them. I'm not supposed to watch their lives unfolding in front of me every time I close my eyes. It hurts. And I love it.

I take a last look at the helmet, at the scepter, at the rusted bowls and spears and swords. I feel a smile tweak my lips as I shut my eyes tight.

THE BRITISH ISLES, AD 616

Chapter One

Bricgweard

The Bridge-Guardian

The great building punctured the sky, crushing the houses, workshops, stables, and yards with its shadow. The hillock on which it stood was the highest point for miles on this side of the river, and now that it was crowned with the new hall, it seemed a mountain. Eadyth entered the hall, whose doors were flung wide to let in the light. The serving folk within greeted her with bows and lowered eyes, but she waved them back to their work.

"Gamol," she called, scanning the hall for the *ceorl.* She found the serving man's half-bald head and short, doughy frame near the back door, admonishing some girl for dropping a bucket of water. The bucket's contents soaked into the packed earthen floor, and as Eadyth approached, the girl scurried away. The serving man, always thinking himself higher than he really was, wore his usual simpering smile when he saw her and he bowed low in greeting.

"Everything is going smoothly, I hope?" she asked him, though it was not really a question, "We'll be having more men than we previously thought. I hope that you are prepared for the extra guests."

Gamol nodded. "Yes, my Cwene. There is more than enough food and plenty of space in the hall for them to sleep."

"Good," Eadyth said smartly, "I'll need you to collect the chests as well. The *cyning* plans to give out rings tonight, so make sure that the two caskets are brought out and placed next to the high seat." Gamol nodded, and she continued, "We will need to lock the doors before the ceremony, so make sure that your serving folk are out by noon. You may leave one or two to tend the fires, but they will have to use the back door."

"Yes, my Cwene," he said again, his head bobbing so quickly she thought he might have been some sort of rotund bird.

"Finally, before the guests arrive, I want you to take a quarter of the meat and a third of the rest of the food and set them aside for the slaves and freedmen serving at the feast. Bread and smoked fish and salt, and sweets for the children if they wish."

Gamol opened his mouth, scandalized. "Forgive me, my Cwene, but surely that is too much! Might I suggest a tenth portion instead? That is the usual amount to offer to slaves at a feast."

Eadyth glared at him. "I know what the usual amount is," she said coolly, "I am sure, Gamol, that you will obey your *cwene*, or your tenth portion shall be from their leavings. Perhaps that might teach you something of generosity."

His momentary insolence disappeared, replaced by its usual deference. "It shall be done," he said, meekly slithering away to yell at someone else.

Eadyth circled around the hall to check on the servants' movements, slowly chipping away the mountain of work that needed to be done. She was satisfied with their progress, really, but it was always better to pretend that she expected more of them. It kept anyone from growing complacent and lazy.

She made her way outside and was speaking with a few servants carrying barrels of mead and ale, but dismissed them when she saw two gruff looking men walking determinedly toward the drink casks. Eadyth intercepted them, and the brighter of the two swooped toward her, planting a kiss on her cheek.

"Rædwald, have you done anything at all today? Or do you plan to let everyone else do the work and tell your men that it was all your own doing?"

"I've been making sure our sons are fighting fit," Rædwald said in mock outrage. "That is hard and thirsty work."

"Well then get yourself a cup of ale, my husband," she cooed, stroking his beard before pulling the end and saying, "and then find something useful to do. Our sons have no battles to fight today."

"You don't know how beautiful you are when you order people around," Rædwald said, his eyes narrowing lasciviously. "I've half a mind to follow you into battle."

"Maybe you ought to," she laughed, "I'd bring back more treasure."

"You wound me," Rædwald said, putting a hand over his breast.

"Well, you'll have to wait to die until later," she sighed, "I have too much to do to tend to your corpse just now." She turned to the iron-haired man and said, "Ricbert, I'm glad you've come back. How have you been keeping?"

"Very well, my Cwene," the grim man said, "I've just been taking a beating from those sons of yours. They are turning into formidable warriors. Sigebryht was giving us all a lesson in how to properly handle a spear."

Yes, Eadyth thought, *Sigebryht's father was good with a spear too. It didn't stop him dying on one, though.*

"And the others?" She asked.

Ricbert chuckled, which was as good as a guffaw from any other man. "Eorwald nearly took my arm off, even with a practice blade, and Rægenhere is quick as lightning."

Eadyth grinned. "I'm sure they'll be well prepared when they see battle," she said. "And I'm sure you've both been telling them plenty of stories to make them eager for it."

"They are their father's sons," Ricbert looked at Rædwald, who was swelling with pride. She felt as if she were intruding on a gaze between lovers when Rædwald looked back at his companion.

"Well, I think my boys have a little less around the middle than their father," she poked at Rædwald's waist, and Rædwald grabbed her by the arm.

"You'll excuse us, Ricbert," Rædwald told his friend, his tone suddenly formal as Ricbert gave another of his rare smiles, "I must discipline my wife for her impudence." In a fluid motion he had lifted her from the ground and flung her over his shoulder.

She tried to tell Ricbert something, but it came out in a squeal as her husband carried her away. Rædwald flung open the door to the king's temporary residence, the largest of the ring of houses built to encircle the great hall itself. Eadyth protested, kicking her legs and beating on Rædwald's back half-heartedly.

Her feet crunched the rushes on the floor as he set her down carefully. She intended to box his ears thoroughly, but within a heartbeat his mouth closed on hers. One hand was on her back, the other snaking through her hair as she surrendered to it. Only with great reluctance did she finally pull away.

"Blast it, Rædwald," she punched his arm lightly; "I don't have time for this. There's too much to do."

"There are hours yet before sundown. We have plenty of time." He kissed her again. "You wouldn't deny your *cyning*."

"I'll deny you all I want, you great buffoon," her own arms wrapped around his neck and she bit his lower lip. "I am your *cwene* and the mistress of this house."

"Oho! I've always wanted to bed royalty." He lifted her a second time and tossed her on the furs of their bed.

He lay next to her a while later, his hand across her stomach. "Do you think you could be pregnant again?" he asked.

Eadyth smiled at him but did not say anything.

"If you were pregnant, would you want a boy or a girl?" he persisted.

"I seem to be good at making boys," she said.

"I'm sure it will happen," he said reassuringly.

"Four children well out of childhood, and you want more swaddling to change?" she asked lightly, though he seemed to sense the gloom she tried to keep out of her voice.

"We're both still young," said Rædwald. "You've got time for me to get another child on you before we are old and grey."

"I suppose," She conceded, "The gods know I'm not ready to be a grandmother yet."

"Who said anything about becoming a grandmother?" Rædwald laughed and kissed her, "Our children aren't old enough for you to be a grandmother."

"Our children are grown, and they will be starting their own families soon. There's no escape from the inevitable. Perhaps I'll just help to take care of our children's children."

"Sunni is still young…"

"Sunniva is a woman flowered and grown, and you're blind if you can't see that every man from here to the Fens wants her," Eadyth said impatiently. "My sons are grown men who have seen battle, and my daughter stopped being a child when she decided to make calf-eyes at first *thegn's* son to wink at her. What can I do if I am no longer their mother?"

Rædwald pulled her close, murmuring some gentle words that he thought would help. She let him try, more appreciative of the effort than the words themselves.

"Well, in any case I ought to finish preparing for tonight," she said briskly, getting to her feet and combing her flyaway hair back into her braid. "You are such a distraction. Off with you." She could not stifle a giggle as he patted her bottom on his way out the door.

When her husband had gone, Eadyth stripped off her working clothes and washed her hands and face in the basin. She was still flushed, but the cold water and the silence of her room were refreshing.

Milthryth, the willowy, gentle-faced serving girl, floated in a while later carrying Eadyth's freshly aired dress and lifted the impossibly soft linen over Eadyth's head. Eadyth loved the occasions when she could wear her finest clothes; the dress was dyed a deep blue, hemmed in silk ribbon and fastened at the wrists with large gold clasps. It hugged her waist and her arms, and pooled like water on the floor.

Milthryth chatted happily about her new marriage and how she hoped to get pregnant as soon as possible. Eadyth offered what expertise she could; it was up to the gods whether the girl's womb would be full or not, and sometimes the gods withheld. Milthryth would find that out for herself, though; there was no need for Eadyth to break her spirits too soon.

Eadyth pulled the bright yellow apron-dress over the top and fastened the straps with a large gold brooch on each shoulder. As heavy as the brooches were, they weighed down her shoulders even more as she slung a few strings of beads and trinkets between the pins. The baubles of glass and amber and the garnet glinted in the thin rivulets of sunlight snaking in through the cracks around the door.

On one hip rested her seax, her short sword, hanging in its stamped leather sheath below a smaller belt-knife; on the other hung her keys and an ornamental drop spindle which was too heavy not to break any thread she would have tried to spin with it. Her simple working spindle lay in a basket of fluffy wool beside the bed, wound with newly twisted thread.

"How do I look?" Eadyth asked, smoothing her dress over her hips.

"Beautiful," said Milthryth fondly. "How many people have come, my Cwene?"

Eadyth thought for a moment, ticking the numbers off on her fingers. "All but one *ealdorman*, and their wives and children are here as well, so that makes about thirty; the *thegns* and a smattering of *huscarls* are already here as well, so there will be at least five or six score, I think."

"So many?" Milthryth asked, agape.

Eadyth laughed. "It won't be crowded; you know that the new hall is enormous. Besides, crowds mean there are plenty of men who fight for my husband, and that is a good thing."

Milthryth still seemed surprised that so many people could fit into a single building comfortably, and Eadyth smiled at her in silence while the younger woman adjusted a few braids and rings in Eadyth's hair.

After a few deep, yet discreet breaths, Eadyth felt prepared to confront the throng of people who would soon surround her. While Eadyth fully appreciated the fact that her husband had the loyalty of so many retainers, the noise of loud boasts and drunken songs usually made her head ache and left her tired for days afterward. A few moments to prepare, and she could weather the flood of people more amicably.

The old hall, three miles away by the Wood Bridge, was not large enough to accommodate the numbers Rædwald was expected to host regularly, and more often than not the men were forced to sleep crammed together as though on a ship. They never complained, of course; they always were always so drunk and piled with gifts from their king that they had little time to grumble about the crowds. If Milthryth was so astounded by the idea of a hundred people, Eadyth wondered what her smooth face would look like if she knew how many the hall was built to house.

Eadyth instructed Milthryth to find Sunniva to make sure that she was ready, and then Eadyth stepped out into the weak sunshine. It was cool and damp, but the sun had burned away the mist that had lingered during the morning and left everything with a bright green smell. Eadyth could see the line of tents and pavilions on the outside of the hamlet where the early arrivals had been staying for the past few nights, and a stream of people were filing toward the great hall and crowding dutifully around the entrance.

She found Sigebryht making his way up the wide, sloping grass toward the hall. He was as solemn and stately as ever and wearing the massive cloak pin shaped like two fighting ravens, which had belonged to his father. As she watched him approach, it struck her how much he looked like his father: tall and thin as a spear, with warm brown, Eastseaxisc eyes and flecks of red in his close-cropped beard. The Englisc all seemed to have blue eyes and flaxen hair, and she saw in Sigebryht an image of her own people. She loved him for it.

He greeted her with a kiss, and was followed by Rægenhere and Eorwald, still joking about something or other. She was sure Eorwald had grown another half a foot since that morning, and he was rubbing his newly-shaved head. Only his gold beard, much longer than most men his age could grow, showed his similarities to his father the king.

Rægenhere had a light of mischief in his eyes as he turned to find his sister following them, and Rægen caught her by the neck to muss her long brown hair. She extracted herself with dignity as Rægen and Eorwald laughed. Sige tried to give his half-siblings a stern look, but a hint of a smile tweaked the side of his mouth.

"You look very pretty, Sunniva," Eadyth told her daughter, rearranging a curl that Rægen had moved out of place in his roughhousing. There were intricate braids pulling the light brown curls away from her face, woven with small gold rings and arranged into twirling, snaking patterns that would have looked at home on a brooch. The rest of her hair tumbled down to her waist in a thick waterfall that would have made a prized stallion jealous. The deep bluish-green dress she wore hugged her body, truly that of a woman now. Even if Sunniva had not been the biggest flirt this side of the River Stour, any man would have goggled at her simply for walking into a room. Eadyth did not know whether to be protective or mildly envious of her daughter's striking loveliness.

"Thank you," Sunniva said brightly, kissing her on the cheek. She bounced off after her brothers to join in their jests in a way that made Eadyth admonish the four of them for their language more than once.

The king arrived with a swagger, bedecked in as much gold as he could physically place on his body. Gold arm-rings, gold clasps for his cloak, gold and garnet beads; even the ends of the straps that held his sword in place were decorated with small gold studs. At his waist was a gold belt buckle that was as long as Eadyth's hand, ornately decorated with interlaced beasts. He looked a king in every sense of the word, a ring-giver, a loaf-keeper, a wielder of power and leader of men.

After greeting his children and his step-son warmly, he turned to Eadyth with a grin that shone brighter than his silver and gold beard.

"My Cwene," he said, kissing her hand, "let us welcome the world."

*****

Sunniva shifted from one foot to the other, a bead of sweat trailing down her spine. It was not overly warm, but the autumn sun was out and heated the dark cloak so that she felt as if she was being roasted. She looked around at the assembled people, all dressed in their finest clothes and adorned with every gold and silver ornament they owned, staring in rapt reverence at the *godeswif*.

The woman's face, surrounded by blindingly white hair, was lined with wisdom rather than with great age, and she was smiling as she looked at the assembled folk. She had brought half of them into the world, after all; Sunniva included. Lifting her long, strong arms into the air, she spoke her blessings on the great house and everyone who would be sheltered under its roof.

Sunniva felt her stomach rumble when the breeze changed and brought the scent of roasting meat down from the smoke hole in the great hall's ceiling. A gnat's buzzing distracted her as the *godeswif's* voice turned into sonorous chanting.

Sunniva caught Wynne's eye and smiled; the other girl rolled her eyes in a silent commentary on the ritual. Sunniva smirked and continued to search the crowd for faces she knew. Milthryth stood a few paces behind Wynne with her new husband, and she looked pious and willowy as usual. Milthryth's brother Anlaf was staring at Sunniva, a greedy and guilty look on his face. Sunniva winked at him, and saw him go as red as his sister's dress. She had always loved teasing him, sitting on his lap and letting him get hard, then running away to giggle with Wynne. The poor boy was a few years older than she was, around Eorwald's age, and just as infatuated with her as any other boy she knew. He asked her to marry him at least once a fortnight, seemingly unsatisfied with the kisses and looks she gave him, and of course she always refused him. She would have fun with him tonight; that was for certain.

The *godeswif* had turned from the doors of the hall and took a bowl from her assistant. The bowl was filled with the blood of the ox they had sacrificed the previous day, mixed with water from a sacred pool somewhere Sunniva had never heard of. The *godeswif* dipped a fir branch in the water and splashed a few drops on the doors of the hall. She then handed Mother the key ring, and blessed her and Father by smearing a drop of the watery blood on their foreheads.

She blessed each of Sunniva's brothers, first Rægenhere, then Eorwald, and finally Sigebryht; that they would go forth with the wisdom of Woden, the courage of Tiw, and the strength of Thunor. She thought it was unfair that Sige always came last, even though he was the eldest; it was of course because Sige was not the king's own son, and only their half-brother. The *godeswif* then turned to Sunniva and smeared a drop of blood on Sunniva's forehead, blessing her with fertility and grace in the name of Frea. She hid the scowl that threatened to cross her face at the fact that that her brothers got the strength and courage, but she knew that it would do no good to protest a ritual older than time itself.

"My honored friends," Father raised his hand as the *godeswif* retreated, "I welcome you all to my new high seat, which I name the Bricgweard!"

There was a round of approving shouts and cheers, to which the king grinned and waved his upraised hand.

"I invite you to my board, my beloved warriors, and offer you the gifts of my hearth and my hall. Let us celebrate a bountiful harvest and hope for a healthy and prosperous new year to come." He spoke with the king's voice today, all courtesy and tradition. The crowd cheered again, and with the scrape of wood on stone, Mother and Father thrusted open the doors.

Sunniva's first memories were of this hall, though the familiar scent of sawdust had been replaced by the thick aroma of roasting meat; the shouts of the workers supplanted by the murmurs of the crowd. It was her home, though she had barely stepped foot inside. Her entire life had been spent waiting for this single building to be finished. The years of toil and battle her father had spent, the loyalties he had won, were all immortalized here. Here was where he would reward his *thegns* for their service and their loyalty, here he would drink and feast in celebration and sorrow, and here would his bier lie when they said their final farewells. It was a part of him, and a part of their family. Long after they were all gone, the great Bricgweard, the Bridge-Protector, would still be there, and men would feast and drink and sing there until the end of days.

Sunniva gave her eyes a moment to adjust to the dimness of the hall. She strode between her brothers and took their hands as they entered the building. She had of course seen it during its construction, but she had not appreciated the immensity until now, as she walked its length to the high seat. It seemed as though every wooden beam was carved with figures of boars and bears and wolves and ravens. There was a torch stuck in a bracket on every post, each one aflame. The light made the carvings look almost alive, and the gold and silver ornaments on her father and brothers made them look like they were on fire.

"*Godes hæmað min ears*," she breathed, hoping that her mother would not hear.

Trestle tables, benches and stools ran along the central aisle where the floor was sunken around the long central hearth, so that at least two hundred men could sit comfortably. Tapestries and curtains hung along the walls to keep out the cold and could be drawn across the alcoves for warmth and privacy – she had never seen such a thing! The alcoves were deep enough for two or three people to sleep side-by-side, though an image flashed across Sunniva's mind of something else the private spaces might be used for…

She shook her head quickly to rid herself of the image. There was plenty of time for that sort of thing later, after all. She focused instead on the wool hangings, embroidered and woven by her mother and women from the nearby village of Wuffingham. All depicted stories of ancient heroes as well as tales of their own ancestors, the Wuffingas. Sunniva rather wished that she could have played some part in the decoration of the hall, but her deplorable weaving skills meant that her works usually ended up as horse blankets.

She saw several of the *ealdormen* entering behind them, all wearing a similar expression to her own, eyes opened as wide as their mouths and no words available to them. She felt a deep sense of pleasure at the fact that they most likely had never, and would probably never again, enter a house so splendid.

Rægen squeezed her hand, and she returned it with an excited grin. She breathed deeply through her nose and her stomach rumbled again. The scents of roasting meat and freshly baked bread filled the hall, and she caught Rægen stealing shifty glances at a pile of honey cakes being brought within an arm's reach of them.

Before the food and drink were served, the faithful *thegns* were rewarded for their service with gifts of gold, land, jewelry, and other goods. She sighed in dismay that she would have to wait to fill her growling stomach, but sipped a mouthful of mead to keep her hands busy. She knew she ought not to complain; was the natural way, after all. These men fought and sometimes died for her father and they deserved to be rewarded for their service. This ritual was performed in every hall in the world, as far as she knew. Despite the growling in her stomach, she was touched at the love they showed the king; it was one thing to fight for a man for the promise of gold and land, but they looked at him just as she did: as a father who loved them.

Rægenhere had a look in his eye which bordered on lust when the servants began to bring out the food. The trestle tables were soon heavily laden with hot fresh bread, carrots and onions floating in broth, eels, at least five kinds of fish, thick rashers of bacon, oat cakes, boiled duck eggs, baked plums, butter and honey and flagons of mead and stout beer. Sunniva and her brothers offered the first of their food to the gods, and then Sunniva tried a bite of everything. She was full to bursting by the time the giant roasted cut of the sacrificed ox was brought to the king. She had some of that too, though, and she drank enough mead to make her dizzy.

"You ought to slow down," Sige told her as she started on her third cup, "you'll make yourself sick." He was right, of course, but she would never admit it.

"I'm fine," she said with a hiccup. She had never been allowed to drink as much as she wanted during feasts, though this never really stopped her and Wynne from pilfering a jug of ale and getting drunk together. She realized that she was having trouble focusing on Sige's face, however, and decided to follow his advice.

When the food had been finished, Sunniva saw Wynne waving at her from across the hall, where a knot of girls were gossipping happily. Sunniva glanced over at her mother, who seemed to be deep in talk with Ricbert; and then at her father, who was concentrating on finishing his ale and looking very red in the face. She knew that she would not be missed, and she hurried to her friends. All were giggling loudly, more than a little red in the faces themselves.

"It's the gracious *mædencwene*!" Wynne kissed her on both cheeks, "it's so grand, isn't it? Your father is so generous to share his new hall with us."

"Your father seems pleased," Sunniva told her friend, and Wynne quickly dispatched with the honorifics.

"Oh, my love, my father is absolutely dying of happiness right now. If I thought he was devoted to the *cyning* before..." she said, rolling her eyes in an overly-theatrical but loving way. "Look," she held out a thick golden disc, hanging from a string of beads from her neck. "Father's just given it to me."

"Beautiful," Sunniva gushed, admiring the pendant and sitting down at the table to join her friends in their gossip. A serving girl had just finished filling her cup when Sunniva heard a muffled sob from the corner of the alcove behind them. "Oh, no," she said, "What's wrong with Leofdæg?"

Wynne lowered her voice conspiratorially, "It's that man of hers. You know she's been going on that he'll marry her, but that a *ceorl* could never marry a *thegn's* daughter, so he was saving to buy more land so that he could provide for her? Well, the *cyning's* given him so many gifts after the last fighting season that now he has all the rights of a *thegn,* except for the title. And what do you know?" her voice dropped to a bare whisper, "he won't have her. He told her as much just now, in front of everyone. It was dreadful," she finished with relish.

"No!" Sunniva gasped and she stole a glance at Leofdæg, who was weeping openly against the wall now. "What happened?"

"As soon as the other *thegns* found out he had land and was going to build a house of his own, they started offering their daughters up for him. He suddenly had very little time for our sweet Leofdæg, I'm afraid."

"I heard she had his bastard in her belly and that's why he had said he would marry her, because her father was going to give him half again her bride wealth." A short, stocky girl named Eoforhild appeared at Sunniva's elbow, bouncing eagerly to join in on the gossip.

"She's not got anyone's baby in her," Wynne said, turning her back on Eoforhild, "stop making up stories, and mind your own business."

Eoforhild glowered and skulked away.

"Well, she hasn't got anyone's baby in her anymore," Wynne finished in Sunniva's ear.

Sunniva clapped her hand over her mouth. "Tell me?"

Wynne shook her head, the look she usually got when she was sharing a secret slid away to be replaced with a frown. "She told him she was pregnant, and she thought he would be pleased and that he would marry her then, but he said that if she was giving herself to him before they were married she was probably opening her legs to everyone else as well, so he told her he would not claim the babe when it was born. She went to the *godeswif* the very same day and, well, you know..." she trailed off, with a pointed look at Leofdæg. "She tried to tell him before the feast what she had done, and – oh, my love, it was a disaster."

"The poor thing," Sunniva said, looking at the weeping girl. She was sitting quietly, but her face was puffy and red, and she looked as if anything could set her off. Sunniva pulled Wynne's hand, and they sat on either side of Leofdæg, who had a strong honeyed scent of mead on her breath. The girl was staring at a young man who was drinking with the other *thegns*; she could see why Leofdæg had liked him, but when he looked their way Sunniva shot a venomous glare at him.

"Calm yourself now, my love," Sunniva said, "Dry your tears. No sweet girl should have to be settled with a stupid spotty arse like him." She wiped the girl's tears away with her thumb and gave her wet cheek a kiss. "Let's have a drink and a bite of food, and in the morning we will have forgotten all about him."

They nibbled some honey cakes and talked about boys and complimented one another's dresses and jewels. Leofdæg gave some half-hearted smiles as they pointed out nice looking young men, *thegns* and serving *ceorls* alike, and flashed smiles and fluttered their eyelashes, making the men blush or wink back in their direction. Sunniva groaned as few of her companions began to sigh and fawn. Rægen had picked up the harp.

"He's so beautiful," Wynne said next to her, her chin cupped in one hand. Several of the other girls agreed in simpering voices. "And such a nice voice. I could let him sing to me all night long."

Everyone was in love with Rægen, and Sunniva had long-since given up trying to fight their infatuation. He was indeed beautiful, if that was the right word to describe a man; he and Sunniva looked so much alike that they were sometimes mistaken for twins even though he was four years her senior, and Sunniva knew that she was beautiful, because everyone constantly told her so. They shared the same light brown hair and grey eyes, and Rægen was one of the kindest people that Sunniva knew, always jesting and smiling in a way that made Sunniva's friends melt into puddles. Wynne in particular had been obsessed with him since before he had grown a beard, and it tired Sunniva to see her wasting her time.

"You know that it's never going to happen," Sunniva said.

"I can dream," Wynne sniffed.

"Why don't you talk to Eorwald? He likes you."

"He's so fierce, though!" Eoforhild piped up again. "He looks like he'd run a sword through the first person to look at him sideways!"

"You should want someone fierce!" Sunniva protested. In all fairness, Eorwald was quite fierce-looking, and it wasn't helped by how tall and broad he was, or by the way he shaved his head and left his beard long, making him look much older than he actually was. She knew that he was a dear, really, but she understood why her friends might be frightened off. "What kind of husband would he be if he were not fierce?" she finished.

"Rægen is all of those things!" Wynne simpered. "Plus he's better looking. Especially when he's not got much on." There was an appreciative round of tittering from the assembled girls.

"And no one said anything about marrying him," said Eoforhild, though there was a distinct hopelessness in her voice.

"That's right," Wynne sniffed, "a gentle man is better if all you want are some kisses under a blanket. Though I wouldn't object to something more..." she trailed off suggestively.

Sunniva rolled her eyes. "Have you actually seen Rægen without a tunic on? He looks like a shaved puppy."

"You just can't see it because he's your brother!" Eoforhild said, "And you've already snatched up Anlaf for your little plaything and he's one of the only other handsome boys here." She pouted, even crossing her arms. Sunniva wondered if Eoforhild wouldn't stamp her foot next.

Sunniva sighed. It was a lost cause. "I hope you all enjoy fighting one another for my brother, then," she said, feeling her head swim as she took a long draught of mead. She glanced around the room, pointedly ignoring her friends and looking at the new faces. She recognized a few, men from the village she had grown up with and some she knew from the nearby market town of Gipeswic. She had flirted with each of them in their turn, to be sure, but with the influx of North Folk men from the Fens and South Folk from the coast, she wondered what she had ever seen in her local playthings to begin with. Anlaf was pretty enough, a little weedy and gangly perhaps, but she liked that he was tall. She thought fleetingly about stealing him away for a cuddle, but she could not find him just then and the thought quickly fluttered from her mind.

She listened to the girls' talk, content and warm and more than a little bit drunk, when a cool draft fluttered in from the door. A man slipped in, unnoticed by most except for those sitting nearby. The man strode to the high table and was greeted by the king, and then embraced by Ricbert and then by her brothers. The men pushed him into Sunniva's vacated seat and the man laughed as Rægen told him something which made even Sige blush.

She remembered the man's face vaguely, but could not find a name to match it. She felt herself smiling as she looked at him, though, and for a moment imagined how those broad shoulders might look without a tunic covering them, how it might feel to untie his shoulder-length hair and put her fingers through it, the color of rusted iron…

Ecgric, she remembered, the dreamy smile turning into a grimace of annoyance. Ricbert's son. Of course, why hadn't she remembered at first sight? She had known him well, years ago, before he had gone to Cantwareburh. He had still been a beardless boy playing with her brothers, the last time she saw him. He had been so cruel to her back then; she had a sudden desire box his ears at the memory.

"You can't play with swords," he had once told her, so long ago now, "you are a girl, so you must play with dolls inside. This is men's work." He had been half a foot taller than Sige, with a wisp of dark hair on his lip that had looked like dirt. She had punched him in his balls, she remembered, which was about as high as she could reach at six years old. She had run away, clutching her doll, as he had doubled up on himself. Rægen had doubled up as well, but with a fit of laughter that Sunniva heard following her even now.

It was strange to think that the nasty boy who had teased her when she was little was the same one who sat with her brothers now. She knew he had been back to Wuffingham several times in the ten years he'd been fostered with his mother's people in the land of the Eota, but she had not bothered speaking with him on any of those occasions. She had not even laid eyes on him in at least five of those years. Perhaps she would take some time for him now. *Maybe he's grown into less of a horse's arse after his long time away,* she thought, *the South's certainly been good to him.*

He'd grown much taller, and harder, like he had been reforged from a thin ash spear into a brutal iron battle-axe. She found it took a long time for her to tear her eyes away as the image flashed across her mind of broad shoulders, glistening with sweat, poised above her…

She sipped some mead and watched the gathered folk for a while, pleased that the men could not take their eyes from her. She toyed with a stray curl and winked at a few of the younger men, enjoying the attention they heaped upon her. She suddenly felt bored, anxious for a bit of fun.

"Anlaf," she called to the youth as he walked past the knot of girls, "Come and keep me company. I've missed you!" She shared a devious smile with Wynne, who scooted over to make room for him. He hesitated, and his ears turned red.

"I – I'm sorry, my lady, I don't think – I must go and find my father. Please excuse me," he shuffled away. She was caught off guard at the way he addressed her; hardly anyone used such formality with her, except in front of the king. She quickly recovered her wits and watched Anlaf's retreating back, her eyes narrowed.

"I don't think my dear Anlaf likes me anymore," Sunniva turned the scowl into a pout.

"He seems to have grown weary of starting his night with a *cyning's* daughter and ending it with his palm," Wynne said sagely, swirling her drink in her cup. "Your little plaything seems to have moved on, my love."

"I suppose I will just have to find a new plaything then," Sunniva said, glancing back up to the high table.

*****

"I haven't seen so many girls in one place in years," Rægen smiled contentedly, surveying the room. Sige nodded, though without much enthusiasm. There were pretty girls, ugly girls, fat and skinny and everything in between; twenty of them at least, Engla and Seaxe alike, all gossiping happily as if they were sisters. The Engla girls were fairer, light-haired and blue eyed; common enough sights in the hall, though the dark red and brown hair and honey-brown eyes of the visiting Seaxe people were a welcome change. They flitted around, giggling and drinking their mead, flirting with the handsome *thegns* who flirted back just as heartily.

Sige listened as his two brothers had a heated argument over which one of the girls might be the most likely to go under a blanket with one of them. He was glad that Sunniva had left to sit with the other girls; she would probably give them all a good smack if she heard their conversation. Maiden ears were not meant for the brusqueness of men's words, after all. Rægen had bet on the slight maid with bright red hair and a green dress, while Eorwald favored a sweet looking girl with golden curls and doe's eyes.

"I'll have to agree with Rægen on this one," Sigebryht told his youngest brother. "Fiery hair means she's fiery down below, that's what they say."

Rægen pounded his horn cup on the table, laughing. "Truer words were never spoken," he said, "Now, little brother; I think you owe me a song."

Eorwald scowled. "I owe you no such thing. I'm too drunk to remember any songs, anyway. Go on and take my turn, and you can play me to my rest." Eorwald put his head down on the table as Rægen called for the harp. Those sitting nearby hushed as Rægen's practiced fingers danced over the strings.

Sige nearly laughed aloud at the look on the face of the golden haired girl, whom he recognized as one of Sunniva's friends. She leaned on her elbows, her eyes wide and wistful, and a bright pink flush appeared on her cheeks as Rægen winked at her.

"I may have been wrong," Sige muttered to his brother, "That other girl seems keen. You'd better go and claim your prize."

Rægen returned the grin and shook his head, absently plucking the strings, "I'll let them all stew a little longer, I think."

"Well if neither of you want to do anything about it, I'll take them both," a hand clapped Sigebryht on the shoulder. He turned to find a familiar face looming over them.

"Ecgric," he stood and embraced the newcomer. "We wondered if we would see you before morning. We thought you'd been eaten by wolves."

"Near enough," Ecgric said, poking the sleeping Eorwald between the shoulder blades, causing him to jump awake. "I'd forgotten that the greenway bridge was broken, and had to go another eight miles out of the way to the ford. I practically had to carry the damned nag across; she refused to get her feet wet."

"Your father is probably pleased you've finally come home," Sige looked round at Ricbert, who was talking with the king. "He never stops talking about you."

"Yeah, he's always going on about what a little *swines scitte* you are," Eorwald mumbled drunkenly into the wood of the table.

"I see your little brother still can't handle his drink," Ecgric said with a smirk at Eorwald. "That's too bad. He's missing the feast. Just look at those girls. Suddenly I'm not just hungry for food." A wicked grin crossed his face. "Oh that sweet little thing in the corner..." he trailed off with a suggestive groan of appreciation.

"Which?" Rægen was squinting, scanning the gaggle of girls once more.

"Over there. Look, in the alcove, two along to the right. Brown hair, you see her, don't you?" He pointed, "She must be one of the Seaxe girls, right?"

"Eorwald is right; you are a *swines scitte*," Sige said, "that's my sister you're leering at."

Ecgric stared, a mixture of shock and amusement on his face. "No… that can't be Sunniva. Sunniva hasn't got tits like that."

"Stop it," Sige smacked him on the back of the head. "She's a little girl."

"I hate to tell you this, my friend, but that is no little girl." He said it as if he did not hate to say that at all. "Last time I saw her she was a knock-kneed little brat. I have been gone a long time haven't I?"

Sige gave Ecgric a stern glance but Ecgric ignored it, still eyeing the knot of women. "Who would have thought that Sunni the little pest could have grown up so… pretty?"

"If you don't stop talking about my sister like that, I will geld you," Rægen warned.

Ecgric threw up his hands in submission. "My apologies!" he said, "I had no idea she had such fierce protectors. I'll find a more reachable goal."

Sige raised an eyebrow, sure that if the man had ever actually met Sunniva, he would know that she needed no such protection. Still, Sige was glad for the change in subject as the argument recommenced over which of the other girls might be the most likely to be Ecgric's bed warmer that night. Sige suggested that Rægen had warmed up the yellow-haired girl for him, but Ecgric decided he would simply have them all – with the exception of Sunniva, of course, he added with a bare hint of mockery. Ecgric did not make idle boasts; he was rumored to have been the lover of the *heahcwene* while he had been in Cantwareburh, and he had probably had half a hundred other women besides. Sigebryht wondered if there were any bastard children born in Cantwareburh with the same iron-brown hair.

The food was cleared away, and the harp was set aside as the noise in the hall began to dissolve into subdued drunkenness. Eorwald was slumped over the table, his head resting on his folded arms, and Rægen was trying to balance a stack of cups on his sleeping brother's head.

"Until the morning, my beloved friends," Rædwald slurred as he disappeared with Eadyth through a door at the end of the hall to where they slept. Many of the young women had departed as well, off to share their secrets and giggles in the maidens' house, or chivvied grumpily away by their mothers to their own homes in the village.

The trestle tables were pushed to the side, and serving men brought additional blankets and furs to line the wide alcoves where the visitors would sleep.

"What do you think, should we get our baby brother to bed?" Rægen asked, and clucked at Eorwald. "The poor dear. He'll be so ashamed when we tell him Sunniva out-drank him."

Sige sniggered and slung Eorwald's arm over his shoulder. "Up you get, little one," he grunted, hoisting Eorwald's bulk as best he could, "time for bed."

Eorwald struggled fruitlessly, swinging a punch at the air and mumbling something incoherently.

Rægen took him under the other arm and they departed the main hall. The Bricgweard had two adjoining rooms to the main audience hall, one small chamber for the king and queen's own use, and a separate house where the royal family spent most of their time when there were no visitors. Bolsters were set in alcoves sectioned off from one another to allow a bit of privacy, and a fire was crackling merrily in the small central hearth, flickering against the dark green curtains hung on the walls to guard against a chill.

Rægen and Sige unceremoniously hoisted Eorwald into his bed. Ecgric had remained in the main hall, his hand firmly planted up the skirt of some girl, oblivious to their words as they said goodnight.

Sigebryht wondered what the mystical secret of Ecgric's hold over women was. *Perhaps if I understood it, I wouldn't be so bloody awkward around them,* he thought. Ecgric claimed he had no secret, but Sige knew the man could talk a Christian woman's legs apart. He probably had done, for all anyone knew.

Rægenhere's charm was easy to understand, as handsome and amiable as he was. Even Eorwald had a certain appeal girls, particularly those who just wanted to watch him lift heavy things.

It did not bother him as much as it should have done; that he did not have much desire to chase girls along with his brothers, and that in itself worried him. He did not want to wait until he had married some *thegn's* daughter to make sure his cock worked properly, but every time he had the opportunity, he seemed to find some reason not to go through with it.

But that was stupid. He knew his prick worked. He had been with women, not as many as Ecgric perhaps, but he had taken plenty of girls under a blanket. He scowled at the ceiling when he remembered the last time, remembered the girl with a turned up nose and big blue eyes and yellow hair, and the look on her face. He had blamed the drink, but she had taken it as a personal slight and left in a huff. It was stupid that it did not bother him as much as it should have done.

*****

Eorwald's head pounded, and all he wanted was to go back to sleep. He had woken on his own bed, still fully clothed, a blanket tossed over him and the curtains drawn across the alcove. He dully remembered trying to punch Sige as he had ordered him to lie down, but could not recall actually following his brother's instructions.

He had only forced his way out of bed when Rægen had threatened to throw a bucket of water on him, and only stood behind his father's chair now because he knew a headache would be the least of his worries if he did not.

"...the word of Christ to your people," the black-robed man was saying. He had a thick accent that sounded vaguely Frankisc, and he had heavily lidded eyes and dark olive skin. A shield of hair was shaved from the crown of his head; Eorwald rubbed the stubble of his own hair and thought how ridiculous it was to only shave off a patch of it. Did the man have lice, perhaps, or was this just the fashion in Francland?

"...the salvation of the world, the one who died for our sins upon the Holy Cross..." the man was still talking, and Eorwald's head was still throbbing.

"...they've infected half of Eota-land with their nonsense already," Sige was saying to Rægen, perhaps too loudly.

The Christ-man shifted his dark gaze to Sige, and it turned even darker, "The Cross, my son, the holy beam on which our lord and savior Jesus Christ suffered and died for the redemption of all mankind." The man made an odd movement with his hand over his breast and Eorwald tried to stifle a snort of laughter.

"Wait, Jesus was hung from a beam?" Rægen looked confused. "I think that you must mean Woden. Woden hung himself from a Sacred Oak to learn the magic of the runes, not Jesus. Perhaps you misunderstood."

The man did the strange little motion again with his hand. "Jesus Christ did not suffer for magic, but for the redemption of all mankind from the sins of the world. The one true God, the Son of God –"

"Now this is just getting ridiculous," Rægen said. Eorwald nodded fervently, "A man can't be his own father…"

The king turned round in his seat and silenced them with a look. Father had been accepting of this Eastern god Christ before they were born, and had undergone some strange initiation ritual around the time Ethelbert had been chosen as the *heahcyning*, but no one had bothered to share the lore with any of them. Mother was the one who had taught them the old stories of the gods and how to pray, and she did not like the Nailed God of the Romans.

The Christ-man continued. "I humbly ask you, mighty *cyning,* to allow me to preach the Word of the Lord to all that will hear throughout the land of the Engla that they might bow before the one true God!"

"Yes, yes," the king said wearily. "Go then. None of my folk will hider you."

The dark man grinned and bowed his head, showing that ridiculous shaved spot to the king. "You are truly doing the service of the Lord!" he said, pointing two fingers at the king and making the same odd motion again. Eorwald stepped forward at the menacing gesture, but the king waved him away.

Father addressed the Christ-man once more, "be warned, though, you will not force any of my people to accept your god, by word or deed. If I find you have coerced anyone, or have damaged any altars to Woden or the other gods –"

"I assure you, Rædwald Cyning," said the Christ-man in a greasy voice, spreading his hands, "My fellows and I have no such intentions."

"Off you go then," the king waved him away, and the Christman left with his two companions, who spoke excitedly in some strange harsh Eastern tongue.

"Odd man, that," Eorwald mused aloud when the Christians had scurried away. "Father, what was it he meant by 'you were baptized?' What does that mean?"

"It's the way they that bring people to worship their god," he said, "they take you into a river or a pool and push you into the water, and say some Latin words and then you're a Christian."

"They did that to you?" Rægen asked, "Does that mean you are a Christian too?"

"I suppose so," Father shrugged, "I couldn't understand them when they did it. It was something to do with dying and being reborn again, because the story says that Christ rose from the dead and then became a god. I put a shrine to Christ with the other gods, but they need their own *godesmen* to do the rituals, so I haven't bothered with it much."

"So what sort of rituals do they do?" Eorwald asked. He found himself leaning in, as if he were a goodwife listening to some titillating gossip.

Sige said, "I've heard that the Christ-men carry a vial of their god's own blood and drink it on the holy days."

Father laughed loudly, "No, though not too far off the mark. They believe that wine turns into the blood of Christ when the priest says words over it in Latin, and they drink that."

"That is disgusting," Rægen said, echoing Eorwald's own thoughts. "Even if it's supposed to be magical, they still drink human blood. That's an abomination in the sight of the gods, to drink the blood or eat the flesh of human beings."

"It's just wine, really," Father reassured them, "they say their words and do their magic, and somehow we are all saved from sin that we never knew we committed in the first place."

Eorwald thought this was all getting rather absurd. He wondered why the Christian *godesmen* were so fervent about promoting their strange faith full of blood magic. Decent folk surely would never accept a god who required this of his followers.

"Why did you let them baptize you?" Eorwald asked.

"When you are in the service of a *heahcyning* who thinks that you might usurp his power," Father responded with a weary sigh, "you will do whatever you can in order to show that you are loyal. Ethelbert's wife was a Frankisc princess, and she brought her bishop with her from Francland. I was there when their missionaries were trying to gain followers, and Ethelbert let them baptize him. He told us all that if we were truly loyal, then we would submit ourselves to the Christian god and be baptized as well."

"So you only did it as a show of good faith?" Rægen asked.

"I did," Father said, "and it served its purpose. I have no reservations about this Christ; all gods can help in times of trouble, after all."

"Mother didn't appreciate it, though," Sige chuckled.

Father smiled reminiscently. "She said that it was cowardly to worship a false god simply because the *heahcyning* had lost his mind."

Eorwald grinned. The story had long-since passed into family legend, but it always amused him to hear about it.

"In any case," the king shrugged, "their cult is catching like the pox right now, and it doesn't serve anyone to forbid their priests spreading the message. It's harmless enough as long as all they do is talk. Sometimes you have to pick your battles."

There were relatively few people coming today to speak with the king, but even so it was slow going. Eorwald pressed his fingers into his eyes in an effort to stop his head from throbbing, to no avail.

A middle-aged farmer with stooped shoulders waddled toward the high seat, followed by a pretty young woman whom Eorwald assumed was his daughter. The man knelt before the high seat and immediately started pleading his complaint.

"It's like this, my *cyning*," he began, his voice crackling, "My wife Steorra here, she is new with child."

"You should be pleased," the king said.

"Begging your pardon, my *cyning*," the *ceorl* interrupted, shaking his head, "Steorra en't let me touch her since our weddin' night, near on two years past." He shot a glare back in the woman's direction, "What's more, I seen a man a-stalkin' round my Steorra in the village, and she tells me that she were raped."

"That is a serious accusation," Rædwald said, "Steorra, is it true that a man forced himself upon you?"

The girl nodded without looking up from the ground.

"Did you know the man who did it?"

She nodded again.

"He was..." the farmer began to answer, but the king silenced him with a look.

"Please tell me what happened, Steorra," Father asked the girl, not unkindly.

She glanced at her husband and seemed to flinch away from the sight of him. "He – I met him on market day; I was selling – selling some cloth that I'd woven, and he told me how pretty I was and how fine the wool was..." she blushed, "And I told him I was a woman married but he kept coming round that day." Another flinching look at her spouse, "He told me that marriages could be broken, and if I married him instead I would be a fine lady and he would get me all the best jewels and I would not have to work ever again."

Of course he did, Eorwald thought wearily.

Steorra licked her lips and shot another glance back at her husband. "Then he – well, he took me behind the tent and..." she trailed off, sounding frantic. "I tried to tell him that I didn't want to, but he told me that I ought to... I ought to be pleased that he was offering me his favors..."

The king seemed to be turning something over in his mind, and it was a moment before he spoke again. "Offering you his favors? What sort of man was he? Was he from the village?"

She nodded with another look at her husband, who was glaring at her.

"He was a *thegn*!" the husband cried, "Ceadda, the get of some North Folk whore!"

"You will control your speech in the presence of your *cyning*," Sigebryht warned the man, who shut his mouth.

Eorwald knew the one being accused, the son of some jumped-up North Folk *ceorl*, an errand rider for the king who had been awarded enough land and livestock to give him the rights of a *thegn*. If it had been another freedman, a farmer or a tanner or anyone else, the king would not even be involved in the judgment. The free folk settled their own matters of law and honor in the Folkmoot, and usually only appealed to the king when they could not make a judgment themselves. A freedwoman accusing a *thegn*, now? That was not so easily dealt with.

"Do you know where this man is now?" Rædwald asked.

"I saw him at the feast last night," Rægen said. "I'm sure he's not gone home yet."

"Bring Ceadda to the hall," Rædwald commanded Ricbert, who stood on the other side of the high seat, "he may tell his part before I render any judgment."

Ricbert nodded and left without a word.

While they waited, Father heard the other supplicant, another freedman who had lost several sheep to wolves and was begging for assistance to feed his family. He had even brought one of the carcasses as proof, a shredded mass of bones and gristle wrapped in a blanket.

"I cannot bring your sheep back from the mouths of wolves," Rædwald told him, "but you will have four months' worth of barley to make up for the lost income from the wool and from the meat you've lost, and you may supplement it as needed from the extra stores, if there are any at the end of the winter. It should get you through the next lambing, at least."

The *ceorl* bowed in thanks and left the hall.

"That's the fourth wolf attack in as many months," Eorwald noted, "I think they are getting bolder."

"Either that," said one of the older *thegns*, a grey-bearded man named Ælberht, "Or the farmers are lying to get more grain."

"The thought has crossed my mind," Rædwald said, "But I don't think so. Their recompense is not much food, compared to the silver they could have gotten by the sheep. And grain doesn't grow back as quickly as wool. It would not be worth a meager few months' grain to dispose of a perfectly good sheep, if they don't plan to eat it themselves."

The door opened and Ricbert returned with the *ceorl's*-son-turned-*thegn*. Steorra's husband had to be restrained as he shouted curses at Ceadda, who was smirking insolently.

"Do you know why you were brought here?" Rædwald asked as the sneering youth approached the high seat.

"I could not begin to guess," he said, "Dryhten," he added as a latent courtesy to remind everyone that he was a *thegn* now and that Rædwald was his commander, not just his master.

"This woman and her husband accuse you of raping her, and want compensation for the child you put in her belly and the dishonor you've brought on her." Rædwald told him. "You may speak your defense, and then my council and I will pass judgment."

Eorwald felt a strong desire to put his fist through the man's perfect teeth.

"My *cyning*," Ceadda began, "I will not deny sleeping with her, but this woman broke her own troth and dishonored herself when she flopped on her back the moment I told her she was pretty." He looked back at the girl, who was staring fixedly at the rushes on the floor. "Besides, how could she be with child if she had not enjoyed it? I believe she feared her husband's wrath and now feels remorse for her actions in seducing someone above her own position in life, and now she is crying rape to save her own hide."

Steorra was looking at the ground, tears streaming down her face.

"Is that all you have to say?" Father's voice was cold.

"May the wise counsel of your *witenagamot* prove me innocent," he said lightly. "I took nothing that wasn't given freely." He capped the speech with a wink at Steorra, who looked torn between screaming and running.

"Very well, you may all leave while I confer with my council," Father waved them away. "We will call you when we are ready to pass judgment." He then beckoned one of the house-*thegns* to accompany them; such heated tempers would inevitably lead to a fight if the parties were left alone.

"What a *swines scitte*," Eorwald said, more to himself than to anyone else, but Rægen nodded fervently.

"What say you all?" Rædwald asked the twelve assembled men.

"I think that Ceadda is in the right," one of the older *thegns* said, "I would not put it past a pretty girl with a grizzled old husband to open her legs for some handsome young *thegn*."

"It would not be the first time a girl felt remorse and accused her lover of attacking her. Jealousy? Fear? Anger?" another said.

"You can't be serious," said Rægen, "Didn't you see her? She was frightened of both of them. She's got bruises on her face, and she was crying like a river. And you saw how afraid she was of Ceadda. Either her husband beat her for getting pregnant by another man, or Ceadda was trying to keep her quiet, I'll bet my arm-ring on it."

"We aren't debating if her husband beats her," said the old *thegn*, "If he beats her, she has the right to divorce him. That is not what we are deliberating right now, my *ætheling*." He gave a deferential nod to Rægen, but Rægen ignored it with a sneer.

"She probably believed Ceadda if he told her he would take her away with him. She might have liked the attention." Eorwald thought of his sister, how she flirted and smiled at every man she saw. "Maybe it just got out of hand?"

The king listened to his council argue for a moment, pursing his lips as he often did in thought. "The truth of this lies somewhere in the middle," he said at length. "I think that Steorra might have acted inappropriately with Ceadda; I am not blind to the fact that she is clearly unhappy in her choice of spouse."

"She probably never made the choice to marry that old man," said Rægen heatedly, "flirting with a man gives him no right to rape her."

"She is pregnant," the old *thegn* said, "It is known that a woman cannot become pregnant if she is raped. She has to be stirred, the same as a man, for his seed to quicken in her, otherwise the woman cannot conceive." He nodded his head with finality.

"That's just a tale they tell to make sure you pleasure your wife, you old fool," Eorwald said, "Women get pregnant all the time without being 'stirred.'"

"Ælberht is a part of this council, Eorwald," Father scolded, "He has the right to his voice, even if you two disagree."

Eorwald scowled at the pompous old *thegn* and thought mutinously how much easier this would be if a woman could serve on the *witenagamot*. Mother would probably defend the girl, and Father almost always listened to her. He was pleased, however, that only a couple of the older *thegns* seemed to agree with Ælberht.

"Send them in," Father told Ricbert, who summoned the feuding men and the nervous woman back into the hall.

"Ceadda of the North Folk," Father said loudly, "you are accused of the rape of a free woman, and the men hearing your case have found you to be guilty. The *wergild* for this crime is a pound of silver, which you will pay immediately."

The smirk slid from the youth's face as he heard the verdict. It was a steep penalty, and Eorwald wondered if the hefty *wergild* was meant to punch some humility into the little prick.

"Furthermore," Father added, "You will pay ten *scyllingas* per year at the harvest, until the child you put in this woman's belly comes to adulthood. I hope this will make you think before you decide to turn your eyes on a married woman in the future."

The king turned to Steorra, who was smiling behind the tears. "You are not completely blameless in this," the king told her, "I will leave it at the discretion of your husband to decide if you ought to be punished for his cuckolding." Her smile disappeared, to be replaced with a look of terror as she glanced at her husband.

"I thank you for your swift justice, my *cyning*," the old man said as he steered his wife from the hall.

Rægen still looked mutinous as they took their leave of the king an hour later. He was scrubbing a hand through his beard and looked as if he might punch something when Eorwald met him outside.

"It's not fair to her," he all but shouted at Eorwald.

Eorwald raised his hands, "You don't need to tell me that."

"You know that she was a slave, don't you? That she only married him so that she could have a roof over her head and keep herself from slavery again."

"Rægen, I'm just as angry about it as you are, but –"

Rægen cut him off. "And now she will probably be beaten bloody by that swine because someone attacked her in the first place. It's not right." He was pacing now, and Eorwald could almost see a tail thrashing by the catlike way he moved.

"Don't tell me you've got eyes for her," Eorwald said, more to break the tension than to goad his brother, but Rægen rounded on him.

"I only want to see justice done, and it was failed today because old wool-headed turds like Ælberht think they know what they are talking about. I am supposed to be *cyning* someday, Eorwald. How will I be able to make sure that justice is carried out, when I see injustice happening under my nose and can do nothing?"

Eorwald ground his teeth together and scanned the yard as Rægen returned to his pacing. The Christian man and his companions were flapping down the lane like overgrown bats in their heavy black cloaks, leading a heavily laden packhorse behind them. Something made him uneasy as he looked at them, like something slimy had dropped into his stomach, but he ignored it and turned back to his brother.

"Come on," he said, "Ricbert will be expecting us. If you can't do anything about Ceadda, maybe hitting something will help." It was usually Eorwald's course when he was angry, and at the very least it would distract Rægen. It would distract them both, really. He needed a distraction.

Chapter Two

Flitan and Feohtan

Contests

he winter rains had turned the road into a sloppy, treacherous mess, and Ecgric wished that he could remain in one place for more than a fortnight before having to endure it again. He wondered why the *heahcyning* and the king of the Engla could not simply meet in person to discuss matters of state, or at least wait until the spring, but it was not his place to ask.

It was not as if there weren't pleasurable aspects of spending the winter in both Cantwareburh and at the Bricgweard. He enjoyed spending time with the *æthelingas*, his friends from childhood; they practiced their war games and went hunting or hawking, and had many a late talk about battle tactics or hounds or horses. The Bricgweard was full of the pleasures of being a man. Well, perhaps not all of the pleasures.

But Cantwareburh, now, that was a completely separate matter. Cantwareburh was the seat of that final joy of being a man. Cantwareburh was where he had become a man in the first place, fighting for the *heahcyning* by day and spending his nights with Bercta, the *heahcyning's* wife. He had been saddened when she died; she had been the one to teach him how to please a woman, after all; but even after her death the amusements of Ethelbert's hall had not diminished. There were enough girls who had come with the *heahcwene* from Francland that he never became bored. He might grow lazy drinking and swiving all day, but nights spent under a blanket with a pretty companion were more than prize enough for his indolence.

He had returned to Wuffingham the night before, and had spent an enjoyable night talking about battle tactics with Eorwald and being beaten handily at merels by Sigebryht, and telling Rægenhere about his exploits in the South. Winter nights were always long and dull, but he enjoyed the company and the homely pleasures that Rædwald's hall offered. He had even covertly watched the king's daughter, Sunniva, from across the room; once or twice she caught his eye and shot a suggestive smirk in his direction, which he considered returning for a bare instant. He thought about how her long, lithe body would look without that cumbersome dress, but he refrained from acknowledging her, as he had done for months, ever since he had first noticed her at the harvest feast. He remembered the threats of her protective elder brothers all too well, and he did not feel like being castrated for the sake of a girl. He had lasted this long, after all; he could watch her and be content, and then bury his prick between some Eotisc thighs once he returned to Cantwareburh.

Ecgric sat with Rædwald and discussed the goings on in Cantwareburh, as usual. Repeated the reports, really. No one fought wars or made alliances during the cold, damp bleakness of winter. What was the point in being an errand boy when there was nothing to report?

The king watched Ecgric for a long while before he spoke. "You won't be returning to Cantwareburh," He said at length, "I am going to have Guthwine go in your place. I think you've done about all you can there, and your presence has been rather heavily remarked upon by Ethelbert."

Of course it has, Ecgric thought, *I fucked his wife so hard I'm surprised the whole country didn't hear her. He probably was more upset when I started on his mistress, though.* He nodded briefly in acknowledgement, keeping his thoughts unvoiced.

"Yes, well," Rædwald cleared his throat, "I think that you might be more useful to me here than in Cantwareburh. I'm making you an *ealdorman*. Wigstan has died leaving no heir, and I am therefore giving you his lands around Gipeswic."

Ecgric did not attempt to hide his pleasure. "Thank you, Dryhten," he said, "I hope that I will serve you honorably."

"As you have always done," Rædwald said, "This is more than just going to war, though, Ecgric. I want to make Gipeswic a great market town, and I need help doing that. I expect you to strengthen the defenses of the *burh* there, and you will have to provide men to fight for me in times of war."

This was nothing surprising. "Of course, Dryhten."

"I'm not finished. You will act as steward of the Bricgweard when I am not here. I also expect you to keep the Gipeswic *thegns* in line. As much as I admired Wigstan, he was not a forceful leader. The landowners thought that they could walk all over him, particularly in his old age. You will have to show them that this will not be tolerated."

"I don't entirely understand how I should go about doing that," Ecgric said, "aside from the obvious," he patted the hilt of his sword, grinning wryly.

Rædwald raised a brow but nearly winked at him. "They need to be reminded that they are not above the law, no matter how wealthy they might be. I cannot keep wasting my time with them every time they have a petty argument that they refuse to settle in the Folkmoot."

Ecgric frowned, "You know as well as anyone that I am a rather impatient judge," he said slowly, still wondering at the king's decision.

"That is exactly why you are the best man for the job." Rædwald seemed rather pleased with his little scheme. "Every other man I've sent to deal with these *ceorls* and petty *thegns* has been completely useless. I need someone they won't be able to push around or bribe into taking sides."

Ecgric nodded with grim finality as he was dismissed, the delight of being raised to the level of *ealdorman* fading almost as quickly as it had emerged.

As he crossed the yard, Ecgric saw Sunniva playing knucklebones with one of the girls from the village. They sat cross-legged on the ground, taking turns to throw the bone in the air, and then giggled as they scrambled to pick up the remaining bones from the ground before the thrown one fell. Their twitters made him remember why he had never liked her in the first place. She was just a pest, he remembered. She had always followed them around when they were young; always trying to have a go at swords or to get one of them to play with her toy horses with her. She was an annoying little brat then, and he did not need the threat of castration to stay away from her now.

Even so, he felt restless. He had not had a woman in ages. He thought of Leasið, the *heahcyning's* mistress. What a sweet thing she was. So pious and gentle, and yet she was already fucking Ethelbert while his wife was coughing blood. He smiled when he thought of the way she would stuff her fist in her mouth to keep anyone from hearing her moans, and how she had always failed miserably.

It's always the pious ones, he thought, *the women who cover their hair and fold their hands so prettily to pray; those are the women begging for your cock come nightfall. And every time, they arrange their skirts and say it will never happen again, and then every night they come to you, frothing at the gash for another go.*

To relieve the tension, he decided to beat the pulp out of one of the *æthelingas* for a while. He preferred to spar with Eorwald, who was brutal and fearless, but he found Rægenhere and Sigebryht instead. Sigebryht always feinted and dodged, light on his feet but always on the defensive, and Rægenhere was similar; both circled one another, considering weaknesses, before a shout and a slash, then more circling. He watched them for a few moments, pointedly avoiding looking at their sister. Eventually he had to join in, when he grew so distracted by Sunniva and her gaggle of women that he was no longer paying attention to the sparring men.

The sun was high overhead by the time they stopped. Ecgric pulled off his battered helm by the nose piece, and tucked it under his arm. As they passed a couple of small hovels, Rægenhere waved at Sunniva, who was approaching them with her yellow-haired friend.

"Are you staying out of trouble?" he asked her.

"I always stay out of trouble," she said, "although I think that lately it's just because I've run out of silver, and the whores demand payment up front."

Ecgric could not help but laugh at the foul mouth she had acquired from three older brothers, and Sunniva turned to him in turn, one eyebrow arched. "Of course Ecgric is always up to date on the going rates of whores, aren't you, Ecgric?" She asked him.

"They usually pay me for the pleasure," he returned the crooked smile she gave him.

"Oh, do sheep carry *peningas* now?" Sunniva shot back, "That's news to me, but it's good that they pay you for your services, at least." She turned back to Rægenhere, who was nearly collapsing with laughter, smiling indulgently as she waited for him to draw breath. "Well if we are finished talking about Ecgric and his curious affinity for farm animals, I wanted to let you know that Father is looking for you, Rægen."

Ecgric watched her as she walked away. Her dress clung to her small breasts and flowed over her hips, her hair bouncing against her back as she trotted away arm-in-arm with her friend. She threw a glance over her shoulder at him, and he saw her grin before whispering something to the other girl. Both erupted in a fit of giggles that disgusted him, even as he watched the sway of her hips as she walked away.

She's half your age, he had to remind himself, *and she's the* cyning's *daughter besides. It's not worth the trouble. No matter how beautiful or clever she is, it's better to stay away; even if she is making it extremely difficult to do so.*

*****

Eadyth enjoyed the soft breeze as it rushed past her bare arms. It was warm today and she had dispensed with sleeves, though she felt sweat starting to bead on her forehead before she had gone even a furlong down the lane.

The farm which supported the royal household was only about a league from the Bricgweard, and she had Sunniva for company, so the hour-long walk passed pleasantly enough.

Eadyth knew they were nearing the farmhouse when she began to sneeze violently at regular intervals. The haymaking and the newly blooming spring flowers always made her sneeze and her eyes grew red and itchy from the dust. Eventually they arrived at the farmhouse and found Gamol ordering people about, as usual.

"You ought to go find something to do," Eadyth told her daughter. She knew that it would be easier to deal with Gamol when he did not need to bow and scrape before more than one of his superiors. Sunniva bobbed away toward one of the empty fields, and Eadyth fixed her face to look politely interested if sternly businesslike.

"I see things are going well," Eadyth said, examining the stacks of hay and the *ceorls* working in the field. "You've started the second fallow ploughing?" There was a definite line where the trodden, light-brown dirt had been churned into the thick, rich earth that would be used for planting next year. A couple of small children were making little piles of mud, and Sunniva went to speak with their mothers. It was nice to see Sunniva doing something useful; she had always encouraged all of her children to remember the poor folk who kept food on their table, and she was pleased when they took to it so happily.

Gamol nodded, startling Eadyth out of her thoughts. "And the haying is nearly complete; there should be plenty of fodder for the winter, even after the sheep got into the field and ate half of it."

"What naughty little lambs," Eadyth said, as she let Gamol lead her behind the field to where twenty sheep had been corralled in a fenced area. They were all in need of shearing, and looked like fat brown and white clouds jostling together before a storm, bleating in annoyance.

"Ah," Gamol said, "We are behind on the shearing, unfortunately. Only I just don't have the labor to spare on it yet, as we are all so busy with the haymaking and ploughing." He seemed more annoyed about the delay than Eadyth was, but she pursed her lips and nodded as a way of showing her solidarity with his frustration.

"It's still early," Eadyth said distractedly. She had seen the shaved pate of Paulinus the Christian priest, of all people, helping a *ceorl* to hold a screaming sheep still while the man sliced the thick mats of wool away with a sharp, hooked knife. When the animal had been stripped of its heavy clothing, the priest and shepherd got to their feet.

"Wulbeorn," she said to the man holding the knife, "I hope that you and your family are well."

"Aye, my Cwene, we are well enough," he said, grinning.

"I seem to remember you had a little one on the way, last time I saw you?"

"Yes, my wife had the baby a few months ago. A little *mædencild*," Wulbeorn said, beaming, "And as fat and pretty and sweet a girl as anyone could have wished."

"Have you given her a name?"

"No, no," he said, "she's not old enough yet, but when the

harvest comes we will give her a proper name. We just call her Gæten, Little Goat, for now. She does bleat like one!"

Eadyth laughed, "I'm sure it fits her quite well." Gæten was at least a sweet name; she knew half the honey-names people gave their babes stuck much more firmly than the real names ever did.

Wulbeorn smiled and returned to his shearing, murmuring gently to the sheep as he roped one to the post.

Eadyth then turned to Paulinus. "I did not expect to see you here," she said, speaking rather more coolly than she had done to Wulbeorn. "I had assumed you preferred the contemplative life to the work of the hand."

Paulinus smiled greasily. "Ah, my Cwene, but the work of the hand is indeed a form of contemplation and prayer. Anything I can do to help my fellow men, is the work of God." He lifted his eyes to the sky, as if his god sat on a cloud.

"Well, we must be in agreement there," she said. "There certainly is enough that needs doing, and your help is appreciated. Did you do much in the way of farming back in... where is it you come from?"

"Close to Rome," he said, "And no, I did not do much in the way of farming before I entered the service of the Church. My father was a *ductus*, what you might call an *ealdorman*, and I was but a third son with few prospects before the Spirit of God moved me to join a monastery."

"So they make you become a farmer if you join a monastery?" Eadyth asked. She had made a concerted effort to not learn anything about this foreigner or his god, but as she helped to pick briars and sheep dung from the sheared mats of wool, she could not help but wonder about the strange land with such strange men as Paulinus.

"Everyone is equal within the confines of the monastery," Paulinus said, "Even princes and noblemen learn to tend fields and brew ale and shear sheep, for we all have a responsibility to our brothers."

"Even the men brew ale? What, do they spin the wool and bring up the children as well?" She shared an amused look with Wulbeorn, who chuckled quietly.

Paulinus smiled patiently. "When you live in a community of men, sometimes you must take women's responsibilities. But there are nuns who help us with certain tasks, and we live in harmony with them, though they are separated from us."

"That's right," Eadyth said, "you folk aren't allowed to have sex, are you?" This was one of the first bits of trivia she had learned about Christians, and it amused her greatly.

"We take vows of celibacy upon entering the service of God, yes," he said, a reddish hue touching his otherwise browned skin, "though some men find it harder to follow than others."

"You've never found yourself yearning for the comforts of a wife and family?" she asked archly.

Paulinus narrowed his eyes. "The love of my God is all the love I shall ever require. I have little interest in women, as I wish to keep my body and my mind pure so that it can be filled with the spirit of God."

"And so you think that being with a woman will contaminate you?" She asked.

"All women carry the mark of the first sin on this earth," Paulinus said patiently. He closed his eyes as he spoke, as if she would contaminate him with her very presence. "All women are daughters of Eve, the first woman, who brought sin into the world by defying the Lord. This is not to say that women cannot be holy, but it is only when they accept that they must be inferior to men that they can come closer to God. Women must not try to speak with the Lord, for it will only lead them into ruin."

Eadyth could not help but to stare at him in disgust for a long while. "If women are not permitted to speak with the gods, then how do they do their duties? You cannot use herbs without knowing the lore behind them, and you cannot heal sick people without knowing the proper spells, or help women through childbirth without communing with the gods. Don't tell me that your priests know how to lessen birthing pains," she said, failing to keep a mocking jeer out of her voice.

"Such practices are an affront to God," Paulinus said, still in that knowledgeable tone that made her skin crawl. "Women are given pains during childbirth as a punishment for Eve's sins. It is the sacred duty of the missionaries of Christ to put a stop to these practices." His voice had the barest hint of fire behind it, and Eadyth decided it was best not to pursue the question further; it only served to make her blood boil.

"So tell me, Paulinus Priest, why did you decide to come all the way across land and sea to this place? Surely you had not planned to shear sheep for an Englisc king, when you took your vows. I am sure that there are plenty of, as you say, pagans, back where you come from, that you would not have to come all the way here." She rather wished he would go back where he came from and leave them alone.

"No indeed, my Cwene," he said cheerfully, as if he had not just criticized half of the population, "I had planned to spend the rest of my life at Monte Cassino, and devote myself to Christ in solitude and contemplation, but I was chosen by his Holiness the Pope to come and bring the light of God to the Seaxe."

"You ought to get over to where the Seaxe live, then," Eadyth said, "You're in the land of the Engla, not the Seaxe."

"You are Seaxisc yourself, are you not?" Paulinus asked, but held up his hand as if to beg for forgiveness for his slight. "Please forgive me; the language is difficult for me. We foreigners tend to call all men from this land Seaxe people."

Eadyth shrugged. "I understand. I tend to call all of you people Dirty Easterlings in any case." She smiled, and thankfully he seemed to understand it as a joke, though she knew the smile would not reach her eyes. "You are right, though. I am Seaxisc, though no one really cares much about that sort of thing, unless you get it wrong. We are all kin, in the eyes of the gods."

"My people believe the same thing," Paulinus said. "All are children of God."

Eadyth did not believe that this was the same thing at all, but gave him another very forced smile before she stood to leave him. "Well, I thank you for your help in the shearing, Paulinus, and for your… interesting conversation. Wulbeorn, please give my blessings to your wife and children."

"May the peace of the Lord be with you, Eadyth, Engla-Cwene," Paulinus cut in before Wulbeorn could do more than bob his head in gratitude, and she could not help but raise an eyebrow in amusement at the stupid hand gesture he always performed when the Christians said those words.

She left him there, trying to hide the grimace under a gentle smile, and uttered a silent prayer to Woden in thanks for the wisdom he had given her, that she was not as deluded as this priest.

Sunniva was still playing with some of the small children, her dress caked in mud from their play. The *ceorls* were waving goodbye to Sunniva and to Eadyth as Eadyth finally pulled her daughter away from the games, and a little yellow-haired girl hugged Sunniva around the waist.

"You must be a good girl now, Ælfheah," said Sunniva, "Mind you finish your spinning and do not talk back to your mother," she lowered her voice conspiratorially, "and the next time that brother of yours tries to knock down your mud house, do that trick I showed you, and he won't do it ever again!" She gave a wicked grin to the little girl, who shared it. Sunniva handed her a basket of food to take to her mother, and a bit of honeycomb. The girl gave them a wide, toothless grin and scampered away.

"You have the makings of a good *cwene*," Eadyth told Sunniva as they began their journey home, "People love a generous heart and a generous hand."

"I just want them to love me like they love you."

Eadyth laughed. "You're well on your way then," she said, "That's the benefit of being a *cwene*. You get to be their loving mother, rather than their stern father. You can offer them bread and a place to sleep when they have no home, and you don't have to punish them or deny them anything."

"But you have to be stern sometimes," Sunniva said, "I mean, you hold court in father's place when he's gone, and you don't get to be the doting mother then."

"Well, being stern is part of being a mother too." Eadyth said. "If you let your children run wild, they will end up hurting themselves, or hurting you, or wasting everyone's time. It's a fine balance, but it's all for their benefit."

"How did you learn to be a *cwene*?" Sunniva asked after they had walked a while in silence.

"Trial and error," Eadyth said, shrugging. "Mostly error, to be truthful. Again, rather like being a mother. You'll never know how stupid you are until you have a child."

"I would be completely inept at being a mother," Sunniva laughed, "I like children, but only when they've grown up a bit and can play and run about, but once they start crying I would rather hand them back to someone who knows what they are doing. I don't think I would ever want to have children, really."

"You feel differently once they're your own," Eadyth said, giving her daughter a hard look. "And unless you decide to live a life without love, you'll end up a mother eventually."

Sunniva tensed. "I don't know what you're talking about," she said.

Eadyth rolled her eyes. "Your father might be oblivious, but I'm not. If you want to go sneaking around with every boy old enough to have an arm ring, then that's your business. But you will have to marry someday, and it's best not to have a bastard hanging on your skirts when that day comes."

"You had Sige and father still married you," Sunniva said indignantly.

"Sigebryht was born to me of my late husband," Eadyth reminded her, "not the product of some youthful dalliance." She sighed. "Listen, I've realized I can't control what you do. You're too much like me, and I think if someone told me I couldn't spend a few hours under a blanket with a pretty young man, I would do it anyway out of pure spite." Sunniva had slowed her pace, and Eadyth knew she had hit the mark. "If you need your kisses behind the stables, I won't stand in your way. I only ask for a little discretion on your part."

"I don't need your permission, Mother," Sunniva said. "I'm a woman grown and I can make my own choices, though apparently everyone seems to have forgotten that fact. And I am perfectly discreet," she pouted.

"You're also a *cyning's* daughter, and as such you are not always given a choice. The time will come when you have to do your duty and make sacrifices for the sake of your family and your people. You are what the gods have made you, and you must be a peace-weaver if it is asked of you."

"Why?" Sunniva asked, "Why should that responsibility fall on me? I thought that was why we had sons in the first place, because peace is fickle and war always wins out anyway? What is the point of me marrying some fat old Mercian so that we can have a few years of feigned alliance, when we will just end up fighting them again?"

Eadyth drew a steadying breath before she responded. "What if I told you, that by securing an alliance with one of our enemies, even for a few years, you could prevent a battle? What if, by you choosing your own fun and pleasure over the duties of the daughter of a *cyning*, that battle took the life of one of your brothers, or your father, or the lover you would choose over your responsibilities?"

Sunniva glowered at the ground, having stopped walking completely.

"You know that I am right," Eadyth said.

"Of course you are right," Sunniva said irritably. "It doesn't mean I have to like it. There is no glory in preventing a war; the glory comes from fighting in one. No one will sing about me doing my duty."

"It's the lot you were given," Eadyth said, and knew the sadness in Sunniva's voice as her own. "I know you don't like it, but it's the way things are. We don't get to follow our brothers and our sons and our lovers to the halls of the gods, we have to tell their stories and pick up the pieces they leave behind. Men will not fight without the hope of renown, and yet we do it every day."

Sunniva chewed her lower lip and looked at the ground. Eadyth put her hand on her daughter's shoulder, and gave her a small smile. "If it were easy, men would do it," she said, and Sunniva could not restrain a laugh.

*****

Wynne sprawled back onto the furs, pouting, "Sunni, my love, I am so wretchedly bored. Let's go for a walk, shall we? I think the men are practicing in the yard; we could go and watch them…"

Sunniva wrinkled her nose. "You just want to watch Rægen. It's not going to happen, Wynne. He doesn't like you."

"Yes he does," Wynne pouted, "He kissed me once."

"He kissed you on the cheek, because your father introduced you to the *cyning* and we all happened to be there. If you'll recall, Eorwald and Sige kissed you too, and you don't go on about them all the time."

Wynne considered for a moment. "Sigebryht is good looking, I suppose, but he's much too old. And Eorwald… I don't know, he just likes to fight and drink. He isn't sweet like Rægen." The simpering look on Wynne's face made Sunniva want to slap her.

"You'll probably marry an old man anyway," Sunniva told her. "He'll deck you in jewels and gold and then fall asleep on top of you while he tries to bed you." She climbed on top of Wynne, straddling her. "And he'll give you dry little kisses that you'll imagine were Rægen's." She mimed a clumsy act of lovemaking while Wynne shrieked with giggles beneath her.

"Oh, my beautiful young wife," she said in a cracked, deep voice, "Oh, yes, yes, yes…" She collapsed on top of Wynne, and let out a loud snore.

"I won't have to worry about that, because I'm going to marry Rægen." Wynne said confidently.

Sunniva got to her feet, and helped her friend to hers. "Come then, my love, let's see if the sixty-eighth time trying will finally do the trick."

They found Sunniva's three brothers and Ecgric practicing their war games. Rægen and Eorwald were sparring, dodging and striking their blunted iron swords against one another's shields.

Sunniva and Wynne watched as the men whacked at each other for a few minutes, Wynne jumping in alarm every time Eorwald landed a blow on Rægen's thick leather shoulder guards. Sunniva looked over toward Ecgric, who she was pleased to find had taken off his tunic in the warmth of the day. It was not as if she had not seen a half-naked man before, but her eyes were drawn to him like dogs to meat. A pattern of interlaced beasts had been etched with ink into his shoulder and chest, circling a large Tiw rune. She had watched Sige receive such a mark after his first battle; it had taken a full afternoon for the *godeswif* to carve the raven design in his back with a needle, and Sunniva had winced on her brother's behalf when the *godeswif* rubbed in the dark dye to make the design permanent. Sige had gotten a few more after the first, and Rægen had one as well, but Eorwald had none, as he had not yet drawn blood in a battle. She wondered how many battles Ecgric must have fought in to have merited such designs. Whatever the number, they had hardened and scarred his body into something fearsome and huge that she wanted to put her hands on.

"Enjoying the view?" Wynne asked her, clearly noticing the way she was staring at Ecgric.

"You're one to talk," Sunniva snapped, "Why don't you go and ask Rægen to go to bed with you, so you can stop lusting after him?"

Wynne scowled, and returned to her doting.

Eventually, Ecgric seemed to notice a gaggle of other girls who were watching them practice from the other side of the yard.

"Ugh!" Sunniva said to Wynne, "He's trying to flirt with that cow Freida!"

"Freida the Fire-Cunt," Wynne giggled, "Careful you don't take any of her leavings; I've heard she's spread the pox far and wide, and that's why she left the North Folk and came down here."

"I wouldn't doubt it," Sunniva said, vaguely irritated that Ecgric was paying attention to a flame-headed little whore rather than to her.

"If it bothers you so much, then go and claim him!" Wynne seemed exasperated, which was usually Sunniva's occupation. "But you should know those brothers of yours have expressly forbidden him to go near you, so it might be a bit of a job."

"How did you learn that?"

Wynne shrugged. "Eoforhild heard Ricbert talking to him the other day. She didn't hear the whole conversation, but he was telling Ecgric that he needed to stop fucking his way throughout the countryside or he'd have the *cyning* to answer to. He said to stay away from you in particular."

Sunniva chewed her lip, annoyed. *So my brothers and even my father's damnable friend have decided what men I can play with?* "I'll bet I can sway him. He's a man; he'll start listening to his prick before long and forget anything he may have told my brothers."

"I'll bet my new gold chain you can't," Wynne retorted, "He's an *ealdorman* now. He's probably so high on his own honor he won't look twice at you."

Sunniva glared at her friend, and held out her hand to shake. "This will be just like the time you thought I wouldn't be able to get Anlaf to show me his prick, and you lost a ring," she said.

"You have three days," Wynne said, now grinning. "And I'll know if you lie."

"I won't need that long," Sunniva said. She pinched her cheeks to bring out the color, and found a lock of her hair to twirl around her finger. She caught Ecgric's eye a couple of times, but he looked away pointedly before she could do anything more than wink.

"And what will you give me when you fail?" Wynne mocked.

"Shut up," Sunniva hissed. What was wrong with her? Normally she only had to look up sweetly through her eyelashes or crook a finger and boys would do whatever she wanted. Had she lost her power? Or was Ecgric a new challenge altogether?

"Go and talk to Rægen and Eorwald, and leave Ecgric on his own," Sunniva told her friend. Wynne responded with a slightly terrified look.

"Oh, just go!" Sunniva commanded irritably. She waited for a few moments, and was pleased to find that Ecgric was the last to leave the yard, and she grabbed his hand as he passed, pulling him into the space between two houses.

Sunniva felt slightly weak as she looked at the strong shoulders and the iron-brown hair of his chest, and had to stop herself from touching him. It took her a moment before she regained her composure and smiled sweetly at him.

"I hope that you're not upset with me," she said in the slightly high-pitched voice she always used to get what she wanted, "for teasing you the other day. I only meant it as a jest." She looked up at him, still grasping his hand and sliding her thumb up the back of it, biting her lower lip.

"Of course I'm not upset with you," he said, pulling it away but smiling at her, "I was actually rather impressed. You ought to join in the boasting at the next feast; you'd put all the men to shame with your wordplay."

"Perhaps," She beamed, and watched him for a moment before saying, "I was glad to hear that you're back for good, now. Hopefully you're not too disappointed to be home, after the bustle of Cantwareburh."

"There are some benefits," he said after a pause. He was watching her twirl her fingers around the long lock of brown hair, and she could see the mill-wheel of thought turning in his head. Perhaps she had not lost her magic touch after all.

She took a step closer. The scent of his body made her breath catch and she looked up into his eyes, which had a glint of fire when she dragged her fingertips across his stomach. The mad idea to push him against the wall and have her way with him crossed her mind for an instant, but she held still, her fingers lingering on his skin.

"I promised I wouldn't—" he began with a pained expression, but Sunniva cut him off.

"You promised that you wouldn't try to take advantage of me," she finished for him, "but I can assure you that you will take nothing that isn't given freely."

"The *æthelingas* told me –" he licked his lips, "I don't want to defy them," he said lamely, and she could hear the raw desire in his voice and the effort he was putting into not touching her.

Sunniva's face hardened. "Am I not a child of a *cyning*, the same as they are? Why should their opinions count for more than mine?" She paused, but did not let him reply, "Please, the next time you see my brothers, tell them that they have no right to be making pronouncements on my behalf."

Ecgric seemed surprised, but took it in stride. "They know what's best for you."

She nearly slapped him, but glowered instead. She closed on him again, and this time his back was to the wall and he had nowhere to go. She had a hand pressed to the center of his chest, his skin cool from sweat under her fingers.

"I had thought that I knew what was best for me," She said in a venomous whisper, "And the next time you, or my father, or my dear brothers, or any man, decide to make decisions on my behalf, I will take this," she reached between his legs and squeezed what she found there, pleased to find it was straining against the wool of his breeches, "and I will make you eat it." She smiled sweetly at his expression, and met his eyes. She felt his heart thumping beneath her hand, faster even than her own. She felt the hair under her fingers as she glared up into his eyes, wondering if she had pushed him past desire into fury when she felt him grip her, one hand on the back of her head, the other on her back. He was kissing her, fiercely, angrily, and she let him do it, she wanted him to push her against the wall and waste her until her legs gave out, but she pulled back from him.

"I'll not make you break your word," she snarled, "but I am the only person who gets to decide how I choose to entertain myself." She rather regretted not being able to take advantage of said entertainments, but she turned her back on him and felt his eyes following her as she left to claim her new chain.

"I don't think that should count," Wynne said, clutching her jewel.

"I won the wager. He kissed me, so I win. Hand it over." Sunniva held out her hand.

Wynne glowered and pulled the chain over her head. "It's not fair; no man can resist you. I shouldn't have made that bet."

"I can't help it if you have a gambling problem," said Sunniva. In truth, Ecgric had resisted her, but Sunniva would never tell her friend that. She slipped the long chain around her neck and looked at it for a moment.

Wynne looked mutinous.

"You know, I don't think this chain suits me," Sunniva said, and pulled it off again. "I'll let you keep it. The knowledge that I've won is prize enough." She had never really intended to keep the chain in any case; Wynne's father might have been wealthy, but Sunniva's father was a king. She knew which of them would be more upset to lose that amount of gold.

Wynne smiled at her. "So how was it?" she asked, leaning in.

"Rather rough," Sunniva said, "And not just from his beard, either. I didn't want him to stop, but I needed to punish him." She loosened her braid and combed her fingers through the tangles.

"What had he done?" Wynne asked.

"He seems to be conspiring with my father and brothers to keep me a wholesome maiden forever," Sunniva rolled her eyes, "Everyone seems to be particularly interested in my virtue, don't they?"

"Your virtue is a bargaining point," Wynne said sagely. "Old men want beautiful and pure young wives, not old sluts. I've heard that the Franca check their women before the wedding to make sure they still have a maidenhead. Imagine what it would be like to have some old crone prodding your bits to make sure you haven't been spending too much time under a blanket!"

Sunniva laughed aloud at this. "That's the stupidest thing I've ever heard," she said, "If I were a man, I would want my woman to know what she's doing. My father married my mother because he knew she was able to have sons, not because she couldn't figure out where a cock was supposed to go."

"It's just what I've heard," Wynne said with a shrug, "It's all to do with their gods, I think. One of the Christian goddesses was able to have a child without having sex, so they think all women should as well."

Sunniva tried to wrap her mind around that bit of information, but it was too ludicrous. "Idiotic," she said, and shook her head. "Anyway, that's not the point. I am a grown woman, and I won't have anyone deciding who I can take as a lover."

Wynne raised her eyebrows. "You want to take him as a

lover? I thought it was just a silly little wager?"

"So what if I do?" Sunniva said, now unsure. "I should be able to make that choice for myself."

"You like him," Wynne giggled, "You do!" she squealed when Sunniva scowled at her, "You're probably wishing he would come in right now and have his way with you."

There was no denying that Sunniva wanted him. Everything about him was powerful and hard and slightly dangerous, and she felt a slight stirring below her navel when she thought of the way he had kissed her.

She felt woefully naïve about the whole thing, even though she pretended to know what she was doing. He was older than Sige by a few years, well old enough to have had a dozen women already. The extent of her knowledge was clumsy fooling about with village boys, kissing beneath blankets or behind the stables and letting them touch her breasts or her cunny on occasion. There had been the time she had persuaded Anlaf to show her his prick; he had blushed furiously when he had dropped his breeches and she giggled to see it standing straight out from the mat of dark golden curls, long and skinny like him. She had lifted her skirt on a whim to let him put it in her, just to see what it would feel like, but he became so excited at the very idea that he spurted his seed onto her thigh before he could get close. The fancy had disappeared as quickly as he had come, and she had immediately gone to tell Wynne. Poor Anlaf. Now he would never have a chance at her, now that she had decided on her prize.

"It's just a game," Sunniva said, "I was trying to prove a point."

Wynne raised an eyebrow. "Well, I don't think Ecgric's the type of man who will let that game go on for long."

"Good," said Sunniva, her mouth twisting into a grin, "Because I intend to win quickly."

Chapter Three

Eotenes Dohtor

The Giant's Daughter

ieva had not thought that she would miss waking up with Leoma's feet against her head. Leoma was always kicking and rolling about, and the last time Gieva had shared a bed with her sister she had kicked so hard that she left a bruise above Gieva's knee. That was the night that Leoma had fallen ill, when she had kicked and cried and burned in her sleep. And then she was cold, and the bruise on Gieva's leg started to fade, first purple, and then edged with yellow, and then it was gone.

Gieva smoothed the blanket across her bed and pulled on shoes. She stoked the fire, hung the cooking pot, and sat outside to spin while it warmed. The morning was cool and quiet, and the feel of the soft wool between her fingers was soothing.

Father appeared from the direction of the stream, carrying a bucket. "Is your mother up yet?" he called as he approached.

Gieva did not look up from her work, but shook her head as she picked a piece of straw out of the newly-formed thread. Mother wasn't likely to get up today. "I think she has a headache," Gieva said, as her father sat nearby and set to cleaning the eels in his bucket.

"Ah," said Father, and he whacked an eel against a stone to keep it from squirming.

Gieva pursed her lips and flung her spindle again. "She thought I was her sister last night. She kept trying to talk to me about her mother, and then she got confused and started crying, and she kept asking for Leoma."

Father said nothing.

"It's not getting any better, either," she finished with a note of impatience.

"I know," Father said after a while.

"It's been weeks and weeks," Gieva persisted, "She keeps forgetting where she is, and she..." she could not finish. She set down her spindle in her lap and watched her father tearing the guts out of the eels. He seemed to be pointedly avoiding her gaze.

"It's hard for her. She's just lost a child. You won't know what that's like until it happens to you. I hope it never does."

"It's hard for me too," Gieva said, "Can't you talk to her? Can't you make her...?"

Father tossed the last eel into the bowl and wiped his hands. "I don't think it will do much good," he said, "Your mother needs time, that's all. Losing Leoma was a deep blow for her, but she will be back to normal again."

Gieva frowned, but not at her father's words. She thought she heard something far off.

"Is that a horse?" she asked.

"I think so," Father said, squinting into the distance. "Take these inside," he pushed the bowl into her hands.

Gieva set it down on the table next to the hearth, and then stood in the doorway as she saw the weak morning sun reflect off the helm of the *huscarl* as he approached, the mount frothing beneath him. When Gieva recognized it as her cousin Ælfhelm, she retrieved a water bottle and rushed forward.

"What is it?" Father was asking.

"Cynhelm's farm has been attacked," Ælfhelm said, dismounting. "Along with several other houses along the rivers Cam and Granta. I was with Cynhelm's family when the house was raided."

Gieva handed the bottle to her kinsman, and he drained it. Several serving folk had appeared from their work, eager to see what the fuss was about.

"When did this happen?" Father asked, "You must have ridden through the night if you came from Cynhelm's farm."

"Past midnight," said Ælfhelm, "Everyone had gone to bed except for two guards. It was a quick and brutal raid; twenty or so men. We don't know who they were, but their speech sounded like they came from the North. I can't be sure, though." He gentled his horse, which was nickering and waving its head in agitation. "His wife and his young son went missing after the fight."

"Where is Cynhelm? I thought he was supposed to be in Grantabricge until Midsummer." Father said, anxiously twisting the horse's reins.

"That's where I'm headed, if you can give me a fresh horse," Ælfhelm said. "I've been sent to tell him what's happened."

"Of course you'll have a horse," Father said, and was silent for a moment, thinking. "Has word been sent to the *cyning*?"

Ælfhelm shook his head. "You know as well as anyone that Cearl is useless. I know a message was sent to Rædwald of the Engla, but who knows if he'll help us. It might've been only a raiding party from Lindsey, and nothing we cannot handle on our own if we have a bit of time to prepare."

Father nodded grimly. "I'll have my horse saddled for you," he told Ælfhelm, "but first go with Gieva and have something to eat and drink before you go; you look half a corpse."

Gieva led him to the house while Father led the sweating horse to the stable. "I'm glad you're safe," she told Ælfhelm while busying herself next to the fire; "I wonder why they would have taken Cynhelm's wife? If it is just a raid, wouldn't they be looking for gold and weapons?"

"Sometimes I forget how little you know of the world," Ælfhelm said, though not unkindly. "Even outlaws know that an *ealdorman's* wife and son are worth their weight in gold, if a little more difficult to carry off. You ought to be careful or they'll have you next."

Gieva's alarm apparently showed on her face, because he added, "It'll be well in the end, don't worry," and he began to wolf down mouthfuls of the pottage Gieva had placed in front of him. "There is a rumor that they are *wycingas,* mercenaries sent to find some contender to Athelfrith's throne who was said to be in Mercia, but they have been burning houses and attacking Gyrwas just for the fun of it, it seems."

Fear gripped Gieva, and she found herself staring at her kinsman. "You don't think there will be a war, do you?" She asked him, her voice barely a whisper. "What if they come here?"

Ælfhelm clenched his jaw. "I hope it doesn't come to that," he said. "But only time will tell. Are you protected here?"

Gieva nodded. "My father is here, and we have at least twenty men from nearby who can hold a sword. And I can use a shield," she said proudly, and Ælfhelm nodded.

"I hope you won't have to use them, but you should all be on your guard. I don't know why those men attacked Cynhelm's hall, but you might be next. You should prepare for the worst."

Father did indeed seem to plan for the worst. Within days of Ælfhelm's departure, he had sent out messengers to the neighboring farms, telling the inhabitants to make their way to the nearby village of Ealdham as quickly as they could. If Cynhelm had been attacked, how long would it be before the northern raiders started attacking the local *thegns*?

"It is best for everyone to stay together," Father said. "These *wycingas* may burn our houses and steal our goods, but our people are the priority. Ealdham is fortified, and better able to withstand an attack than scattered farms are. You have to get your mother and go to the village as soon as you can. I will take some men with me, but I'll leave a few in your company to protect you. I don't want too many going at once, or it will only draw the eye of attackers. A message will have gotten there by now and the village hall will be open for those who live in the farms. You'll be safe there."

"Aren't you coming with us?" Gieva asked him, following him outside to the stable. She could not entirely hide the note of alarm in her voice, even though she attempted to sound calm and practical.

He shook his head. "As we don't know where Cynhelm is, I will have to raise the *fyrd*." He motioned for a serving man to help him onto the saddle of Ælfhelm's horse, now watered and rested. "Last news was that the invaders were headed down to Grantabricge, and so that is where I will go. I will meet you in Ealdham as soon as things are settled."

Gieva bit her lip as her father looked down from his saddle.

"Fight bravely and die well, if die you must," she said.

Father bent down to kiss the top of her head. "It will all be well, my girl. I'll see you soon."

Gieva watched the horse trot down the path, and her father and his men disappeared from sight. She registered a rising feeling of panic, but breathed deeply to wash it away. Now was not the time to get flustered. She set about doing as her father had asked; wrapping loaves and dried meat and salted fish in bundles and packing them into a bag, gathering traveling clothes, and finally, collecting her mother.

Gieva had to shake her a few times before she opened her eyes.

"Godrinc?" Mother said, looking around the room. She was pale and thin, wearing only a shift and looking quite confused.

"Father is outside," Gieva lied, "Mother, you have to get up. We have to go to Ealdham for a few days."

Mother sat up, bleary-eyed. "Hand me my dress, then," she said, "and make sure you tell Leoma to bring her spindle when we go. She's always forgetting it. If we are to be stuck Ealdham I won't have you two being unproductive." Her voice was light and touched with annoyance, as if it were all just a minor inconvenience to be threatened and driven from one's home.

Once, Gieva might have tried to correct her, though now she knew that it would cause more grief than it was worth. Gieva helped her mother gather her things and they set off up the road to Ealdham.

*****

Ecgric plunged his horn into the barrel of mead. It was the fourth or fifth time, but he was not drunk yet, and he wished to be. The light was fading quickly, but the ring of trees was illuminated by the massive bonfire glowing in the center. A few girls rushed past him in a blur of white and gold, holding hands and giggling as they heard the sound of the harp. Rægenhere must have had a few drinks himself by now, Ecgric thought; Rægenhere's fingers always ended up on the strings of harp after his head was filled with ale.

Ecgric broke through the circle around the fire and sat down amid the throng of people, all eyes turned to the *ætheling*.

"*The mind alone knows what lies near the heart; he alone knows his spirit. No sickness is worse for the wise man than to have no one to love him.*"

"Come to me, I'll love you!" one of the maidens piped up, to general laughter from the crowd.

Rægenhere grinned at the girl, and went on, "*That I found when I sat among the reeds, and waited for my desire; body and soul the wise girl was to me, nevertheless I didn't win her.*" He frowned theatrically, and Ecgric rolled his eyes as another of the girls let out a sympathetic whimper. He scanned the pile of white-clad women, who were all gazing in rapt attention at Rægenhere and his recitation of the wisdom of Woden, when he met the gaze of a pair of grey eyes beneath a ring of yellow flowers.

"*The Giant's girl I found on the bed, sleeping, sun-radiant; the pleasures of a lord were nothing to me, except to live with that body,*" Rægenhere continued.

Sunniva did not take her eyes away from Ecgric's. She stood, leaving her friends behind, and disappeared outside of the circle. Ecgric rose from his seat and found her alone, somewhat apart from the mass of people listening to the singing. She wore a circlet of marigolds on top of her unbound hair, which cascaded down to her waist and flowed over her bare arms. Sunniva took the horn from his hand without a word, and drank.

"Blessed Eostre," she said when she had finished, a drop of the sweet liquid clinging to her bottom lip. He had to restrain the ludicrous urge to kiss it away.

"And to you," he paused for a moment. "You look beautiful."

She raised an eyebrow. "Yes, I am aware of that, funnily enough." She began walking away, and he could not be entirely sure if she was jesting or not.

"Would you rather I tell you that you look ugly?" He asked, keeping pace with her.

"No, I enjoy being told I am beautiful, just as much as any girl," she shook out her hair, "But it's hardly original."

"*He who flatters gets favors*," Ecgric said, "Or do you doubt the words of Woden?"

"The All-Father lost his eye to bring us poetry, and you squander his gift by telling me the same words a hundred other men have given before you?" She smirked in that crooked way she did when playing at riddles. He felt his head swimming, though he doubted it was from the drink.

"I could say that I have never owned a ring that could match the silver of your eyes." It sounded stupid in his head and stupider coming out, but she seemed pleased.

"Hmm, you're nearing the mark now," Sunniva said. "I think the All-Father would be pleased that you are at least attempting to make his sacrifice worthwhile."

"I am no poet," Ecgric told her, "I'm a warrior. My poetry comes from my shield and sword, not from my mouth."

"And yet I would rather have your mouth touch me than your shield or your sword," she said wryly, stopping to look at him. She leaned on one leg, her head cocked slightly to the side, making her dress curve over her hip in an effortlessly seductive way as her finger made a trail down to his belt. "I know what you want, Ecgric," she said quietly, "Why do you deny yourself something when it's offered freely?"

"You know why," he said, trying to push her away, "You're not just some *ceorl*'s daughter or a whore that I can just have whenever I please, you are a…"

"I am the daughter of a *cyning*," she said, "And I think I deserve to enjoy myself before I get sold off to some old man."

"No man will have you if you aren't a maiden," he told her, "I don't want to ruin your father's chance at an alliance in exchange for a night with you. I have some integrity." He vaguely registered that they had made their way back up the hill to the Bricgweard, but was deserted now as everyone had gone down to the bonfires.

Sunniva laughed. Ecgric followed her dazedly, and the door swung shut behind them.

"I think you'll find that ship sailed a long time ago."

He could not be certain if she was lying or not. She had drawn closer, but he did not move away this time.

Ecgric did not realize what he was doing until he had touched the bow of her lips with his own, still tasting the honey of the mead clinging to them. He was drunk on the scent of her body and the way her hands began to wander as she pulled him into one of the deep alcoves. She was trying to pull off his tunic, but he kissed her again, slowly and deliberately, which only served to make her more eager. Every time she tried to reach down his trousers, he stopped her. He delighted in the crease of annoyance that had appeared between her eyebrows as she grew more and more frustrated.

Ecgric pulled the shoulder of her dress down, kissing the arc of her neck as he revealed the small white mounds beneath, each tipped in a dark bud that hardened as he ran his thumbs over them. He touched his lips to one of them, and heard her whimper as he drew it into his mouth, lifting the hem of her skirt and searching out the soft patch of hair at the apex of her thighs. It cost him a considerable effort to pull his hand away; he wanted to bury himself in her when he felt the wetness there, but the look on her face amused him. He deliberately traced the contours of her hips, her breasts, kissing her as he felt her chest rising and falling in ragged bursts. She was annoyed, she was unsatisfied, and she wanted him.

Sunniva let out a growl of frustration. "You're toying with me," she said in a hoarse whisper.

"Now you know how I've felt all this time," he said in her ear as she squirmed against his hand. He enjoyed this, seeing a flush creep up from her breasts into her cheeks as he touched her, but she soon became too impatient to let him continue and she pulled their bodies together with surprising force for someone so small.

Perhaps it had been the long while since he had been inside a woman, or perhaps it was the torment of watching her for so long without being able to touch her, but he was spent within moments.

He wanted to sleep, but he leaned on an elbow, tracing the line of her cheek as he kissed her again. Her eyes were wide with what he hoped was surprise or excitement, but they closed again as he drew his lips along her neck and past her collarbones, moving his hand back between her legs. He held her close to him even when she tried to move away, and she bit the skin of his arm as her lithe body became taut. She gasped, let out a low, musical groan, and then she relaxed with a shudder. Everything about her was agonizingly beautiful, from the way she bit her lip to the way her back arched and she screwed up her eyes as if in pain, and the way she had sighed and closed her eyes when it was over. She rolled onto her stomach, as if forgetting he was there.

Ecgric drifted in and out of sleep for a time, a battle being waged in his mind as he felt Sunniva's body next to him. He should not have done it; he should have resisted her. It would have been for the best.

But why should he feel so guilty? It was not as if he had raped her, after all. He should not be punished for having sex with a woman who brought him into her bed willingly.

He looked over at Sunniva, who was facing away from him as she slept, tendrils of hair falling down her back and pooling onto the bed behind her. He rolled onto his side, snaking his arm over the curve of her waist and pulling her closer. He knew that shouldn't have let this happen, but as he breathed in her scent and felt the warmth of her skin against his, the words Rægenhere had sung came back to him: *the Giant's girl I found on the bed, sleeping, sun-radiant; the pleasures of a lord were nothing to me, except to live with that body.*

*****

Eadyth seemed to spend as much time fixing her daughter's mistakes as Sunniva spent making them. "You have to stop being so impatient," Eadyth told her, "There's a rhythm to it, and you have to make sure you catch every thread or it will fray. Like this," she showed Sunniva how to slide the long needle through the hanging strands of thread so that it caught each of them. "Now help me to push it up," she said, "evenly, now."

"It looks terrible," Sunniva complained, looking at the lumpy waves in the fabric where it differed from Eadyth's own work, "What if I just went back to spinning? I can spin while you weave and it will go twice as quickly."

Eadyth held back a sigh. "Big pieces like this are a two-person job, and I need your help. And don't roll your eyes at me," she scolded Sunniva, "You're going to have to learn to do it properly eventually, so you might as well practice." She watched as Sunniva started to slide the needle back through in the opposite direction. It would be years before Sunniva could even attempt to use the man-high loom on her own, Eadyth knew, and Sunniva wasn't exactly patient. A crease formed between the girl's eyebrows, and she was chewing her bottom lip in the same way her father did when he was concentrating. A feather of light brown hair had fallen over eyes and she brushed it away impatiently.

"And we push up again," Eadyth said, and they added another row.

An hour later, Sunniva had finished a hand's breadth of the fabric; it was still uneven in places and she had missed a few strands of the warp, but she was improving despite her impatience.

"I'm going outside," Sunniva said, stretching her back, "Wynne is waiting for me."

Eadyth continued her weaving as Sunniva bounced from the room, and Eadyth heard Ecgric's voice outside the weaving house. Sunniva greeted Ecgric and Eadyth heard two sets of footsteps retreat around the back of the weaving house, and her weft tangled as Eadyth was distracted, certain of what her daughter was getting up to.

She swore and picked the knot apart, as she heard the door open again. Rædwald entered and sat down on Sunniva's vacated stool, his ever-present smile sliding off his face.

"You seem upset." He was always adept at stating the obvious.

"It's just a knot," Eadyth said, finally freeing the tangled thread, but then she sighed, "And our daughter."

Rædwald's mouth set in a line behind his beard. "Ah."

"I think she's old enough that we need to try to find her a husband," Eadyth said. She saw him chewing the inside of his cheek, as he often did when he was thinking about something unpleasant.

"What?" she prompted, "Do you think she's too young? She's well old enough to be married; I don't know what we are waiting for."

Rædwald said nothing, but she got her answer.

"That girl has more men following her than a battle commander," Eadyth said. "If we don't do something she's going to end up with one of their bastards in her, and then no one will have her."

"No, Sunniva wouldn't… she's a good girl." Rædwald seemed mildly horrified, which amused Eadyth despite herself. "You don't think she's…"

Eadyth realized another knot had tangled the string, and she threw it aside. "I don't know what our daughter might decide to do, but I know what men tend to do when a woman gives them the opportunity," she said, "if she doesn't lift her skirts for one of them, eventually one of them will do it for her."

He frowned. "None of my men would dare touch my daughter," he said, "especially against her will."

You sweet, stupid old man, Eadyth thought, *you've seen so many things in your life and yet you don't think any of your men would rape our daughter half a hundred times if given the chance.* "I don't doubt the honor of your *thegns*," Eadyth lied, "I just think it is time we set up a marriage for her. She is young and pretty, and could give us a powerful alliance with one of the *cyningas'* sons, or an *ealdorman*, perhaps. Ethelbert has a son, doesn't he? Let's look into that."

Rædwald frowned. He doted on Sunniva, his sweet little girl, and Eadyth knew that he would be reluctant to send her off to some faceless man a world away. Of course Eadyth loved Sunniva as much as a mother could love her child, but that did not mean she was blind to her daughter's activities, and the girl would have to be married someday before the charm of youth and beauty wore away.

"I know it's hard for you," he said, "she's a good girl, really, but I know mothers and daughters sometimes have trouble getting along."

Eadyth sighed. "You couldn't have just given me more boys?" She asked playfully, "Boys are easy. Boys love their mothers and grow up strong and handsome, and you don't have to worry about teaching them to run a household or about their bride wealth or whether they're going to ruin everything because they are relentless flirts…"

"But boys die," Rædwald reminded her, "brave, strong sons do not always survive, even if they love their mothers."

"Women die in their own battles," Eadyth said, thinking of her own mother, who had bled to death trying to bring a son into the world. "Sunniva will fight just the same as Rægen or Eorwald or Sige."

"And you seem to be well eager to send her forward to those battles." Rædwald said sullenly.

They glared at one another for a while before Rædwald held out his hands to her. "Calm yourself, my love," he soothed, "Let's not argue. Our children are growing up, and it is a challenge on both sides."

"It would be less of a challenge if we had a daughter who actually listened to her mother," Eadyth complained.

"If she listened to her mother, I would know she was not your child," Rædwald said with a hint of a grin.

Eadyth snorted. "No, I listened to my mother. I did not hoist my skirts for every man who called me pretty."

"You did for one."

"Yes, and look where we ended up!" She said, smiling at him, "But you were a *cyning*. How could I refuse?"

"You did refuse," he said, "Often, and loudly."

"I wanted to know you would fight for me."

"My greatest victory," Rædwald said, smoothing a flyaway hair back behind her ear.

Eadyth looked at her husband for a long while. Sometimes she forgot how much she loved him, from the strands of silver in his gold hair to the beard that tickled her cheeks when he kissed her, to the little soft belly he got when he hadn't been fighting much; every part of him. He was the one who had given her two brave, strong sons and an infuriatingly beautiful daughter, and who had treated her boy as his own for over twenty years. She never knew she could have loved him when they married, but she did now.

"Does it still count as a victory if I surrendered?" she asked, and he grinned at her.

"Now," she said, leading the way out of the weaving house, "you didn't come here to watch me weave and hear me complain about our children. What have you got to tell me?"

"We've had a messenger from Grantabricge."

"And?"

Rædwald answered in a rather long, single breath, as if he were waiting for her to box his ears. "Cynhelm needs help. There have been groups of warriors starting fights and burning farms along the Granta near the *burh*, and the messenger says that they had nearly closed in on the fortress when he left."

And there it was. He was asking her permission to leave. "You're needed here," she said, not looking at him. "Send Ricbert. Or give up this farce of trying to make Ecgric your steward and send him."

"I am the *cyning*," he said grumpily, as if he had been denied a sweet. "And those are my people; I can't just force them to fend for themselves while I sit and feast and milk the cows and pretend nothing is happening."

"They're not your people, though, are they?" she reminded him, "Those are not Engla in Grantabricge, and Cynhelm is sworn to Cearl of Mercia, last I looked."

"I don't care if Cynhelm has sworn allegiance to a bloody Wæliscman," Rædwald said, "He has always been an ally to us. I won't leave him and his people to be slaughtered."

"You've already made up your mind about this, haven't you?" Eadyth asked him irritably.

"I wanted to tell you first. It won't take long; a couple of weeks at the most. I just want to see what's going on, and help Cynhelm if I might."

"Are you taking the boys?"

"They need to see battle at some point. Real battle, not those little scuffles we had before in the West. Sigebryht has already asked to come; he was there when the messenger arrived. As for the others; Eorwald has never fought in a shield wall before, and Rægenhere needs to learn to command. It will be good for both of them."

Eadyth stared at him. "Command?" she said, incredulous, "No. He's not ready. I won't have him leading men into battle when he's barely fought in any himself."

"Rægenhere won't be leading anyone yet, you silly woman," Rædwald said, "But they've both got to learn how at some point. You can't think they should sit in the back of the ranks and watch, now they're men grown? My sons will never shame themselves that way. They are Wuffingas." He said it defiantly, and with a finality that she could not overrule.

She narrowed her eyes, but nodded, and he took her in his arms again. "As your cwene, I command you to come back in one piece," she told him, "And bring my sons back safely as well."

"You have my word," he told her.

Chapter Four

Onđringa

Forward

ll stood shoulder-to-shoulder on a ridge of land near the River Granta, shields overlapping and weapons drawn, as the king met the opposing captain under a gesture of peace.

"Can you hear what they're saying?" Rægen asked beside him, squinting stupidly, as if that would help him to hear what was going on.

Eorwald shook his head. "I don't even know who they are. They don't look like any Mercian shields I've ever seen."

"They're not Mercian," Ecgric said from the other side of Rægen, "They're from Bernicia, or Deira. It's all basically the same thing, now. All Northumbrian scum." He was idly clanging the handle of his battle-axe on the inside of his shield. "Hurry up," he said under his breath.

Eorwald chewed his lip again, and glanced back to see Sige standing a few paces behind them, an arrow knocked but his bow unbent, waiting.

It was taking too long; why was Father still talking? Eorwald wanted to run at them, to hack his way through their lines. He ran his eyes up and down the wall of men, searching for a weak point as he had been taught to do. He had trained for this, practiced and sweated night and day for the chance at a real fight.

For a moment, he worried that they would not see battle; that he would go home without giving his sword a name. Rægen had named his sword Wælcyrige for the men she had sent to Woden's hall; but the blade in Eorwald's hand had yet seen no battle and had spilled no blood. It was thirsty, and he itched to give it drink; that is, if his father would stop talking and get back into the line.

The king turned back to the shield wall, looking disappointed. There would be no fighting today. Eorwald's shield arm dropped slightly, but he immediately raised it again and let out a cry as a spear flew past, nearly rustling his ear. The king's face flashed with fury and excitement, but he did not look back, and in one fluid motion he plucked the javelin from where it stuck in the ground, and returned to the center of the shield wall.

"It looks like they are unwilling to accept my terms," the king said, tossing the spear lazily to one of the men behind them, and then raised his voice. "Shields up, men!" he shouted, turning on the spot and sliding into place between Rægen and Ecgric. A shout went up, and Eorwald grinned. He saw the men opposite them through the gaps between the shields.

"Which one was it?" Father muttered, "Which one threw the spear?"

"The boar shield, with the red, in the second rank, three along to the left." Eorwald told him. He had not seen the man throw the spear, but he saw several angry Northmen staring at a sheepish-looking warrior in their midst.

The men in their line stepped forward as one, on each clatter of weapon on shield. "These men are flies!" Ecgric called, "And they tried to sting the arse of your king. What do we do to flies?"

Shouts of "crush them!" and "squash them!" rose up, along with a "Fuck them!" came from one man, which made them all laugh rowdily. They were twenty paces away, and Rædwald called to halt. "Wall!" he shouted, and Eorwald dropped to one knee as the second rank overlapped their shields with the first. "Fire!" Sige shouted from behind them, and he heard the whistle of javelins and arrows fly through the air, and the satisfying sound as a few stuck in the enemy shields. He heard a cry from behind him as an enemy arrow soared overhead, and glanced back to make sure it had not been Sige, but Sige had dived behind him, his shield a roof over their heads.

He heard the shouts of the Northerners as they edged closer, and then stopped. He looked through the gap in the shields to see them, stopped like idiots and making their own wall. He was struck with the absurdity of it, like two crabs facing one another on the beach.

"Oh this is ridiculous," he heard Ecgric voice his own thoughts.

"You're right," Rædwald answered. "Let's end this," he shouted. The back rank pulled away, and the front formed into two lines, with the point centered on Rædwald. The king's voice resounded over the shields as he shouted, "*Onðringa*! Forward!"

Eorwald followed just behind Rægen, overlapping his shield as they rushed forward, his nameless sword held tightly in his hand. "*Engelcynn*!" he shouted, and the men took up the cry as they built up speed. He felt his shield crash into the opposing wall, and thrust it up to knock the axe out of a Northumbrian hand as it tried to pull his own shield down. The slight twinge of panic in his guts was squashed as his heart beat faster, his limbs became lighter, and he could see and hear more clearly than ever before.

He stabbed his sword underneath into the exposed thigh of his attacker, wrenched it free, and pushed forward. The wall had given way, and he heard Rægen's voice call to regroup. Eorwald ran toward the voice, but felt a blade bite at his back as he ran. It did not hurt – he doubted if anything could hurt him just then – but it startled him enough to slow his run. He spun around, seeing the deformed boar's head shield. He smashed the man's shield out of the way, knocking him to the ground.

"You fucking coward," Eorwald shouted at the man, "you can't attack anyone unless his back is turned? You're no better than a criminal," he stomped on the man's hand as it reached for the sword, and kicked it away, "Filthy *wearg*."

The man swung a blow at Eorwald's leg with a belt-knife, but Eorwald kicked that away as well, driving the point of his sword into the ugly man's neck.

"Coward," he spat, stepping over the man and returning to his brothers, now reforming on the other side of the Northumbrians.

He prepared to lock his shield again with those of his brothers, but the Northumbrians were in chaos. Several had raised their hands in surrender, and Rædwald had to shout at one of the *huscarls* who was about to snick the head off of one of them. "They've submitted!" he called, and the *huscarl* stayed his blade and grabbed the Northumbrian by the back of his hair, pushing him toward the king.

Eorwald's shoulder stung where the boar-shielded man had struck him, and he could feel the cool air as it snuck through the leather and wool. He wiped the coward's blood from the blade, and realized that it was no longer nameless. He kissed the hilt of Weargbana and slid her into her sheath.

The Northumbrian leader had been slaughtered, but his lieutenant was kneeling before the king. He had a broad, scarred face and was giving the king a look that would have curdled new milk.

"Who are you?" the king's voice was dangerous. "Speak up, you sniveling *swines scitte*." He aimed a kick at the man, who grunted, "Ulfric, son of Ulfric."

"And why did you and your men decide to attack me when my back was turned?" he asked, "Is that the way you northerners fight now, Ulfric, son of Ulfric?"

"Do not hold the rest of us accountable for Wiglaf's folly," Ulfric said defiantly, though the wind had been taken out of him by the force of the king's boot.

"Yet when this Wiglaf decided to start a battle, even after terms had been agreed upon, you and your men did not silence him, but decided to fight anyway. I know that Grantabricge is a lovely part of the country, but was it really worth losing half your men needlessly?"

"We didn't come for Grantabricge," Ulfric said, "We came for the *ætheling*."

"That wasn't what your *dryhten* told me when I discussed terms with him."

"My *dryhten* had his reason for keeping the truth from you. We come for the *ætheling*, I will not deny it."

Rægen looked around, slightly breathless with a streak of blood across his face, but unharmed. "Well, you've got two of us, how about you take your pick?" he grinned at Eorwald. "I'll have you know though, my brother is much better in bed."

Ulfric spat on the ground at Rægen's feet, earning a smack across the side of the head from Eorwald. "The traitor *ætheling*, Edwin of Deira," he said, "We were on orders from Athelfrith Cyning to track him down. Rumor was that he was traveling this way. You should not have interfered."

Rædwald gave a mirthless laugh. "You're saying that I should have stood idly by while you harried my people? That I should have let you go on raping their wives and killing their greybeards while you pretended to look for some stupid boy?"

"Edwin is dangerous," Ulfric said.

"Edwin was killed years ago," Rædwald shot back, "Come up with a better lie and I might refrain from sending Athelfrith your head."

"He is alive!" Ulfric's voice had an edge of panic now. "He was in Mercia, and we had word that he was coming this way. I only did as I was bid, and that was to find Edwin and bring him back to Deira to be charged and executed."

"And you thought he might be hiding under the skirts of some woman in Grantabricge?" Eorwald asked.

"Enough," Rædwald said as Ulfric opened his mouth to retort. "I will let you live, Ulfric son of Ulfric," Rædwald told the kneeling man, "and you will take a message to your *cyning*."

Ulfric frowned. "What is the message?"

"You will tell him that the next men of his that I find in my lands will be given the Blood Eagle and their corpses dragged back to the North by goats."

"But Edwin –"

"It is not my fault that your *cyning* cannot keep track of a ghost," Rædwald cut him off. "If he is still alive, I doubt that he will come to a land that has never been friendly to his family. You might want to work on a better excuse before you try attacking my allies again. Get out."

"You're just letting him go?" Eorwald asked, when the man had been taken away, "You can't trust him; he ought to be taken prisoner like everyone else."

"I won't waste any of my men on a fool's errand to the North," Father explained, "It's not a matter of trust. He won't go anywhere else, alone and surrounded by enemies. When he arrives home with his superior dead and his army captured, he will have to explain to Athelfrith what has happened. I don't care if he repeats my words exactly; the message will be clear."

Eorwald scowled. "You should have sent his head back instead, if you only wanted to send a message."

"That would serve little purpose."

"It would tell Athelfrith not to try this again," Rægen put in, "It would show him that we are not to be challenged!"

"The gods frown upon killing prisoners needlessly," Father said, "As do I. You two have the blood-joy now, and it clouds your judgment." Eorwald and Rægen shared a look of impatience, but Eorwald knew that Father was not wrong. The smell of smoke and blood changed many thoughts.

In an act which surprised and delighted those Englisc men assembled, Cynhelm knelt before Rædwald and placed his sword upon the king's knee, as they assembled in the great hall at Grantabricge that evening.

"Rædwald Cyning," he said in a carrying voice, "I, Cynhelm, Ealdorman of Grantabricge, hereby swear to you, in front of these assembled men, my loyalty and my love from this day forward. When I called for aid, you were the only one to answer. Let me swear by the sword in my hand that I and my family will serve you and yours from this day forward, forswearing all other false oaths."

Rædwald beamed and handed the sword back to Cynhelm saying, "I accept your oaths and I hereby swear my own, that you will always have a place in my hall as my retainer and as my friend. *Wes ðu hal, Cynhelm eorl, Þegen Rædwaldes!* Hail, Ealdorman Cynhelm, *thegn* of Rædwald." Rædwald lifted a horn of mead and shared it with Cynhelm.

The king then offered his men gifts for their bravery, those trinkets and rings which they had won from their defeated foes. Eorwald cheered them as they approached and received their gifts and promises of livestock and lands, and was praised in return when his father called him forth.

Eorwald knelt before the high seat, and felt his father's hand on his head as the king's voice rang out over the crowd. "Today was my son's first battle, and he slew the coward who tried to skewer me. I wish to recognize him for his deeds," he pulled from his mathom chest a coat of burnished rings and handed them to Eorwald. "I am sure you will continue to make me proud, my son."

Eorwald grinned and received the gift from his beaming father, and thanked him. He took the coat of rings and rolled it carefully, placing it with his other gear. He wished he had been able to wear it today; if he'd have worn something other than his padded leather jerkin he might have been able to avoid the pain now dully thudding through his shoulder. He did not mind. He had earned both the wound and the coat, and he knew that both would serve him well in all of the battles to come.

"You need a woman," Ecgric said, clapping Eorwald on the back right over the cut, and it made him wince. "You never sleep so well as after a battle, and it's doubly so if your bed is warm."

Eorwald shook his head, "I don't know," he said, "I don't much like the idea of raping some girl I just tried to protect."

Ecgric grabbed the hand of one of the cup-bearers as she passed, and she giggled as he pulled her onto his lap. "You wouldn't be raping anyone," he told Eorwald, flipping the girl's hair back over her shoulder, "What's your name?" he asked her.

"Ælfflæd," the girl answered.

"That's a pretty name," Ecgric told her, and she giggled again. "Now Ælfflæd, I have a serious question to ask you, and you must answer truthfully." Her eyes widened conspiratorially as she nodded. "If our handsome *ætheling* here were to ask you to share his bed tonight, would you go with him?"

Ælfflæd raised her eyebrows as she surveyed Eorwald. "If that is what my *ætheling* wishes," she said, "I would be happy to keep him company. After all, you and your brave friends saved us all. It is the least I could do." She rose from Ecgric's lap and plopped into Eorwald's.

Eorwald felt like punching the wide smirk off of Ecgric's face, but he enjoyed the feel of the woman, and as she led him into a quiet corner of the hall, he knew that he would indeed be sleeping very well that night.

*****

Rægenhere's harp had found its accustomed place in his lap, and he hummed a song to himself. Ecgric found himself humming along as the other plucked idly at the strings, watching a group of women chatting happily with one another.

"Just pick one, and be done with it!" Ecgric groaned. "Your sweet pious devotion is driving us all mad."

"You don't just take women," Rægenhere said irritably.

Ecgric raised an eyebrow. "The last time I looked; we always take treasure when we've earned it. Otherwise, what would your honored father give his *thegns* for their service?"

"What about her?" Ecgric prompted. He felt responsible for the *æthelingas*, and wanted to make sure they appreciated all of the benefits of battle. “Such a sweet young maid. I’ll bet her cunny tastes like honey. Make that into one of your songs.”

Rægenhere laughed. “That one would win the girls more than stories of battles, I’d wager.”

Ecgric glanced over at Eorwald, but Eorwald had nothing to contribute, having long-since disappeared under a blanket with the pretty serving girl Ecgric had hand-picked for him. At least one of them was making the most of his time.

“Go on, then!” Ecgric gave Rægenhere’s arse a nudge with his foot to try to push him off the bench. “Go and claim your treasure! Let us know if she blushes when you pull your prick out,”

Rægenhere gave him a withering look, but not long later he had disappeared with another pretty maid to a quiet place. Ecgric smiled in satisfaction.

Ecgric turned to Sigebryht, who always seemed adamantly opposed to enjoying himself, even after victory. “And you?” Ecgric slurred from inside of his horn cup, “How are you finding the spoils?”

“Well, if you mean the spears and rings, then very well,” Sigebryht said dully. “Although I’m fairly certain that’s not what you mean.”

Ecgric chuckled. “You know my tastes run toward softer things.” He glanced over to a large-breasted woman in expensive clothes with a rosebud for a mouth and a languid curve to her hips. He gave half a smile at her. She raised an eyebrow, returning it.

"I thought you'd given that up now you were supposed to be finding a wife."

"Wife hunting is thirsty work, and I've got to wet my beard sometimes," said Ecgric. "And with your standing royal order to not go near your sweet sister …”

"Leave my sister out of this,” Sigebryht warned, “Just stay away from her.”

“At your command,” Ecgric mocked. He knew he would get hard if he thought of her much more; if anyone’s cunny deserved to be immortalized in song, it was hers.

But Sunniva was not here, and the woman across the hall was looking more and more appetizing.

Sigebryht did not seem cross, only weary. "Wouldn't you prefer to save your seed for a – a cleaner sort of person? Someone who hasn't had pennyroyal with every meal since she was twelve?"

The woman did have a sort of looseness about her, and not just in the way that rich women always did. She may have been a whore, but if she wore such fine clothes and such a mountain of jewels, she must be exceptional at her job.

Ecgric speared a bit of meat on the end of his knife and examined it. "She's experienced," he said. "I'd rather have someone who knows her way around a cock than some pretty little maid who blushes when she sees it." He chewed for a moment, grinning, "And she looks like she knows her way around a cock."

"I think we've established that," said Sigebryht with a twinge of distaste. "She's probably had half of the men from here to the Humber."

"Don't exaggerate."

"I didn't think that was an exaggeration."

Ecgric took a deep draught of his beer and wiped his mouth with the back of his hand. "Well, I had better go and travel the well-trodden road before I am too drunk to walk. Have a drink for me tonight in your cold, lonely bed, my friend."

Chapter Five

Seledreorig

Dispossessed

rops from the smoke hole in the roof plunked into a bucket as the house was steadily deluged. Eadyth wondered vaguely if she ought to check that the main assembly hall had not been flooded, but she was comfortable in the small room and reluctant to leave her seat by the fire. Occasionally, the rhythm was punctured by the sound of thunder from outside, and the dripping mingled with the whisper of the thread sliding through her fingers. Eadyth stitched a patch on a pair of breeches and listened as Sunniva sang to herself, a tune that kept time with her movements as she flung her drop spindle and wrapped the shaft with the newly formed yarn.

"Do you hear that?" Sunniva cut her song off short, and Eadyth looked up.

"I think they're back!" Sunniva set her distaff and spindle down and ran to fling open the door.

The rain fell in sheets onto the yard and the paths outside, and Eadyth waited for the men to make their way up the steps. She held her breath as they entered, accounting for her sons and her husband, and even Ricbert and Ecgric, who were leading the horses away. Satisfied that they had all returned safely, she was able to breathe again.

Rædwald tried to kiss her, but she held him off. "Go and dry yourself. You look like a beached walrus," she laughed, "and you three as well," she nodded to her sons. She followed Rædwald into their sleeping room, and helped him to shrug out of his sodden clothes.

As she hung them to dry, he draped a blanket around his shoulders and sat on the edge of their bed, shivering slightly.

"Come and warm me, my love," he said, "I'm chilled to the bone." Eadyth sat on her husband's lap, and he wrapped the blanket around them both.

"Did you settle everything in Grantabricge?" she asked. His bare skin was chilly against hers, even though there were layers of wool between them.

Rædwald looked as if he had developed a sudden headache. "A stupid bloody mess, that was," he said, and when he had seen the look of concern on her face added, "We took care of it, don't worry. I'll explain it all when I've had a drink in me."

She nodded and did not press the matter. "Thank you for coming back to me," she said, "And for bringing my sons back to me safely."

"I promised you I would, didn't I?"

"You know I worry."

Rædwald paused for a moment, "I've missed you," he said, and rested his head on her shoulder. "It was hard not to have you there."

"Then let me go with you next time," she stroked his beard, "you know that men always fight more bravely if they know their woman is close by, and you've always taken me with you before. I know how to use a shield," she said it in jest, but a crease appeared between his eyebrows.

"And I never want you to have to use it," he said, and then paused. "I did miss you though, truly. I missed your smile and your voice, and I missed your body," he kissed her, sliding a hand underneath her skirt. She felt a flush creep over her chest and up to her cheeks as he moved it higher. His kisses became more urgent; his hands roamed her body under the dress. She stroked his damp hair, thanking the gods, as she always did, that she still had him.

The storm was still whistling outside, but they were warm and comfortable as they sat in the hall next to the hearth. Sunniva sat between Eadyth's knees spinning while Eadyth combed out her daughter's long hair. Rædwald told them the story of Bældæg, the son of Woden, who was killed by a lowly shaft of mistletoe; he could not, however, remember most of the tale and Sunniva had to remind him, eventually taking up the story herself. Sige and Eorwald played at merels while Rægen heckled them both for their poor moves. She lived for these moments, and lost herself in the sound of the quiet pattering of rain and the crack of the fire and the laughter of her children.

Sunniva finished the story, and was silent for a moment before she asked her father, "Will you tell us what happened in Grantabricge? This lot won't say a word!" She looked reproachfully her brothers.

Rædwald's jaw clenched. "It was nonsense, really. The whole thing started because that *swines scitte* Athelfrith thinks his nephew Edwin is hiding out in our lands, and he sent a smattering of *wycingas* to track him down."

"I thought Edwin was Athelfrith's brother, not his nephew?" Sige asked.

"How in Thunor's name am I supposed to remember?" Rædwald said, taking another draught of his ale. "It was some relation or another. Anyway, there were thirty or so men; much more than I would have expected to track down one lost *ætheling*."

"They were ready to surrender," Sige put in, "But some stupid prick decided to be a hero and try to attack the *cyning* when his back was turned."

Rædwald nodded. "No doubt he wished for renown, but it put his whole company in danger. It was all needlessly bloody, but we couldn't accept that sort of insult. At least your boy got to prove himself." He raised his cup to Eorwald, who grinned. "Eorwald did us all proud and took him down. He's a good fighter."

"He should be," Eadyth beamed at her youngest son, and then turned back to Rædwald. "So what became of the Northumbrians?"

"Father sent one back to tell Athelfrith to stop poking his nose where it doesn't belong," said Rægen, "and the rest are captives of Cynhelm. Father let him do with them as he would, provided that he didn't send any back North."

"Were any *thegns*?" Eadyth asked, "You could have gotten a ransom for them at least."

"Wouldn't be worth the trouble," said Rædwald, "The less I have to do with Athelfrith, the better. Cynhelm can ransom them if he wishes, or sell them for slaves in Francland. He'll need the gold to rebuild Grantabricge more than I'll need it, in any case."

"And Edwin?"

"This was the first I had heard of him in ten years," Rædwald said, shrugging. "I knew that he was driven out of Deira after Athelfrith took the crown and united the two kingdoms, but I had heard he was dead. He was half a boy, if I remember. If he's alive he must be round about Sige's age, or just a little older."

"Obviously he's not dead if Athelfrith's looking for him," Sunniva said. "But why would he be in Grantabricge?"

"That's what we wanted to know," Eorwald piped up with a note of impatience in his voice. "They told us that Edwin was dangerous, but I don't understand how a single man could pose much of a threat to someone half a hundred leagues away?"

"Any man can be dangerous if he can get enough men to follow him," Rædwald said.

Sige frowned. "Perhaps they heard that Edwin was raising an army?"

"That would explain why they needed to send a host to find him," Rægen agreed, "What do you think, Father?"

"I think Athelfrith is frightened for his hold on the North, and wants to make sure he's able to rid himself of claimants, even if that means chasing ghosts." Rædwald finished the ale in his cup and set it on the table. "Now, if we are done speculating, I am going to bed."

*****

It was too quiet without the other girls, and Sunniva shifted on her bed, eyes still wide open and staring into the fire's gently glowing corpse on the hearth.

She harrumphed into the bolster. She missed Wynne, and not just because her toes were cold. Wynne would understand. Wynne was more obsessed with boys than Sunniva would ever be, and would not make fun of her for her growing obsession.

Stop thinking of it, she scolded herself. *It's not as if you claimed him.*

She should have done. She ought to have hung a sign around his neck to tell the camp followers in Grantabricge to keep their hands off of him, or she would have something to say about it.

You're overreacting anyway, the logical voice in her head told her. *You don't know that he did anything at all.*

He liked her, didn't he?

Her thoughts wandered back to that night. Had he known how nervous she was? How little she knew? He probably thought her a stupid little girl…

But he had treated her like a woman. Her breath caught when she thought of his hands… she liked his hands. They were heavy and calloused, but somehow he found ways of using them that she had never dreamed possible.

Sunniva reached between her legs, moving her hips slowly and sighing at the thought of those hands. They were beautiful. *He* was beautiful; he was a pig-headed idiot, but he was beautiful, and he was so *big*, and…

She stopped moving, removing her hand and punching the bolster in frustration. Where was Wynne when you needed her? The girl annoyed her more than half the time, but playing with Wynne was more fun than dealing with the ache between her legs, even if their pillow-games were a pale imitation of what she really wanted.

She sat up on her bed and glared at the dying fire, hugging her knees. "*Swines scitte*," she muttered to the empty room, "Well, you fool girl, have you claimed him or not?"

The maidens' house was only steps from the Bricgweard, and she crossed the distance silently. The guard standing by the door tightened their hands on their spears, but released them in an instant when they recognized her.

"Can't sleep, my Lady?" one asked.

She smiled sweetly and whispered, "It's ever so lonely in the maidens' house with no girls around. I'll sleep with my mother tonight."

He smiled in a fatherly sort of way and pushed the door open a crack so that she could slip in without waking anyone. To the left of the door, she saw several men's shapes dimly illuminated under blankets, lying near the fire or tucked into alcoves. She could see him from here, his back turned to her but his broad shoulders and his hair recognizable even in the darkness.

To the right was a wall, broken by one door leading to where her mother and father kept their bedchamber, and another leading to the family's space. She could have gone to the right, to crawl into bed beside her mother and at least be assured of a quiet night's sleep under cozy furs. That would have been the sensible thing to do, after all, to go right.

She nearly laughed aloud at the very thought as she turned decidedly to the left.

*****

"What's the matter with you?" Eorwald asked. Rægen had kicked the fence post with an unnecessary amount of force, causing it to shift slightly in the muddy posthole.

"Do you want to have a go at swords?" Rægen asked, evading the question and half-heartedly trying to straighten the post. "I feel like hitting something."

"Even in all this mud?" Eorwald asked, "You must really want to hit something badly, if you run the risk of slipping and breaking your pretty face."

Rægen scowled at him.

"I will go with you when you've told me why you seem to want to break the fence and let the horses out," Eorwald said, adjusting the post and shooting an apologetic look at Gamol, who was watching them with a look of disgust.

Rægen drew in an angry breath and lowered his voice. "Do you remember that day just after the harvest feast when Father judged a case about a girl being raped by a *thegn*?"

Eorwald said nothing, but waited for his brother to continue.

"I saw her this morning, fetching water. I thought she must be ready to have her baby, but her belly was flat and she looked like she'd been crying." Rægen crossed his arms and leaned against the stable wall.

"Did you speak to her?"

"I tried. I only said good morning to her and she looked as if I had slapped her. So I asked her what was wrong, but she only said that she had fallen ill and lost the babe she was carrying, but she said that she was well otherwise."

Eorwald frowned. "Fallen ill, I'm sure."

"Should we tell Father?" Rægen asked.

"I think so," Eorwald said after considering it for a moment. "Father should know about this. He'll know what to do. Besides, Steorra has the right to divorce her husband if he's beating her, and he should owe her *wergild* for the loss of her child."

"You heard those old men in council, though," said Rægen

with a flame in his eyes, "they wouldn't side with her even if they had witnessed the beatings themselves. They say it was her fault because she got pregnant by a man other than her husband, and they would say that it was her husband's right to beat her for cuckolding him."

Rædwald was sitting to his day-meal, and listened to Rægen's story without comment. Only after he spat out a final plum stone, did he look at his sons in turn.

"You seem prudent in your suspicions," he said with aggravating ambiguity.

Eorwald waited, shared a confused look with Rægen, and looked back at his father.

"And?" Rægen asked.

"I don't know what you expect me to do about it," Rædwald said, and upon seeing the look in their faces, added, "Steorra has to bring a complaint to me. She has to charge her husband with beating her without cause, otherwise I can't do anything."

"You saw how she acted around him," Rægen said, "She's terrified! How would she be able to get up the courage to accuse him if she is too afraid to speak in front of him?"

Rædwald threw up his hands in frustrated concession. "I cannot change the laws of the land. When she charges her husband, then I will judge accordingly. Before that, I cannot help her."

"You're the one who told her husband that he was at liberty to discipline her for cuckolding him!" Eorwald said indignantly.

"And if it wasn't him, then that *swines scitte* Ceadda attacked her for accusing him of rape!" Rægen finished.

"What are you going to do about it, then?" Father asked Rægen. His tone was strange; it was almost as if he was asking what Rægen would do during a battle, a hypothetical test of his ruling abilities.

Rægen seemed to be caught off-guard about this for a moment, though he recovered quickly enough. "I want to remove Steorra from the reach of her husband and of Ceadda."

"And how will you go about that?" Rædwald had his eyebrows raised in a genial sort of way which Eorwald found confusing and irritating.

"Well, she can't divorce him if she's afraid to even admit he's been abusing her, and nothing we say will change that."

"I think Ceadda is the bigger problem here," said Eorwald. "Steorra's husband looks as if he could be blown over by a gust of wind."

"And Ceadda definitely came off worse in the ruling," Rægen agreed. "He was furious to have to pay that much silver; I can easily see him taking out his vengeance on the poor girl."

"What poor girl?" Sunniva had appeared out of nowhere, looking rather flushed as if she had been running. She gave the king a kiss and sat next to him, helping herself to a plum.

"Never you mind," Eorwald said sharply.

"Excuse me," Sunniva said, "Who made you the warden of information?"

Rægen gave them both a hard look and Eorwald closed his mouth. He was not in the mood for his sister's brazen opinions.

"I demand that you tell me," said Sunniva, glaring at all three of them in turn. "Is this about that farm girl? The one who Ceadda raped?"

"How would you know about that?" Eorwald asked.

Sunniva's face became uncharacteristically grave. "Because she's not the first girl in this village to have been meddled with by that sack of *swines scitte*." Father looked at her, seemingly astonished that such language could come out of his sweet daughter, but she ignored him. "He's stuck to serving girls and *ceorls* for the most part, but at the last feast he tried to make a move on Wynne." She said it with such ferocity that she might have been a wasp guarding her nest.

"What did Wynne do?" Rægen asked, clearly amused.

"She slapped him for his presumption, and when he threatened to tell her father that she was trying to seduce him, she put her knee in his balls," Sunniva said with satisfaction, sucking the flesh from her plum stone and spitting it out before becoming grave once more, "But Wynne is an *ealdorman's* daughter, and she knows that the law is on her side. I'll warrant Steorra thinks that she will be in even more trouble if she comes forward. Her husband could throw her from his house, or worse."

Father leaned back in his seat, as though he were taking in a mildly interesting bit of entertainment.

"That still doesn't change anything," said Rægen angrily. "There's no proof that Ceadda has done anything wrong, unless the women he's attacked come forward. Until then, he's just going to continue what he's always done."

"We could find a reason to send him away," said Eorwald, "send him as an envoy to Cantwareburh or Witunceastre, to keep him out of the way."

"So that he can harass Seaxisc and Eotisc women instead?" Sunniva growled.

Rædwald raised a hand. "That would only cause more problems in any case. No, it's best to deal with him directly."

"I have an idea," Sunniva said, getting to her feet, "I'll take care of Steorra. It's important to get her out of danger, and to let her know that she is safe. After that, you lot can deal with that *swines scitte* Ceadda."

The three men looked at one another and then at Sunniva, bemused.

"Just leave it to me," Sunniva said brightly, and left the hall at a trot.

Rædwald raised an eyebrow. "I think we'd better do as she says."

*****

It might have stopped pouring, but the rain still fell in a drizzle that seemed to drag everyone's spirits into the mud with it. Sige paced the hall, not necessarily out of agitation but as something to keep his body occupied. He hated to sit still, even for a little while, and hated it even more when he had to do it indoors.

Rægen, Ecgric, and Eorwald were dicing in the corner for scraps of silver, and Sunniva sat a little apart from them as she plied two thin strands together to make a thicker yarn. He paused for a moment, watching her as the two colors came together, dancing before she snatched up her drop spindle to wrap the yarn around the shaft.

"I remember when Mother would have to threaten you with a switching to get you to get any spinning done," Sige said.

Sunniva shrugged. "It's either this, or having to spend the day in the weaving house with all of the women and listen to Mother lecture me on marriage," she rolled her eyes.

"I had heard that she and Rædwald were planning something like that," Sige said sympathetically, "But if you were married it would mean you could have your own household…"

Sunniva's eyebrow arched, cutting him off.

"Do you not want to be married?" he asked.

She chewed her lip. "It's not that," she said slowly, "I don't really care one way or another. Drinking wine in a hall in Mercia or Cantwareburh wouldn't be much different than doing it in the Bricgweard, after all." He saw her eyes flicker upwards, not at him, but at the knot where the others were sitting together. She glanced back at Sige quickly enough that he might have imagined it.

"I have no worries about marriage," she continued. "I just don't like being used as a tool. The way Mother talks, it seems like that is the only purpose of binding yourself to some man for the rest of your life. Besides," her tone became defensive, "Why isn't she telling you to go and find yourself a woman? I don't think it's fair that their plans for grandchildren have to rest on me."

Sige snorted despite himself. "What do you think she tells me every time she has me alone?" he asked. "Why do you think there have been so many 'honored guests' who all happen to have unwed daughters?"

Sunniva giggled. "I confess I hadn't noticed, except that there are a lot of new women in the maidens' house and I don't know a single one."

"Believe me, they're not here by accident," Sige sighed.

"I should think you would be pleased to have so many pretty girls around. I don't think a night has passed in weeks that Rægen wasn't taking some girl under a blanket."

Sige cleared his throat.

"At least you have standards," Sunniva said, her eyes flicking up to Ecgric again. "Anyway, I am glad I'm not the only one she's forcing into such an arrangement."

"Well, it isn't as if it will do me much good to marry anyway," Sige said, unable to keep the bitterness from his voice.

"What's wrong?" Sunniva asked sharply.

Sige frowned. He had not wanted to bring anyone else into it, and cursed his tongue for wagging. "I had a message today. Well, it was for our mother, but it concerned me." He hated to lie, even more than to tell her, to speak it aloud.

"Sæwine has taken hold of Mother's lands in the South," he said, "He's claimed them peacefully, but he arrested her steward and set his own people there."

"How could he do that?" Sunniva said, and Sige nearly smiled to hear the indignation in her voice on his behalf.

"He found some law that stated she had been given the lands illegally," Sige picked at the flaking rim of his cup, "That her father could not have bequeathed it to a woman, and so it should revert to the *cyning* of the Eastseaxe."

"That's nonsense!" Sunniva pounded her fist on the table. "Since when is it the law that a woman cannot inherit?"

"The laws of the Eastseaxe state that a woman can only inherit property in order to hold it in trust for a male heir or a husband," Sige said wearily. He had asked the messenger to repeat the speech several times before he could completely understand. "As she was not even married until after her father had been dead a year, it meant that the lands have belonged to the *cyning* since our grandfather's death."

"Why is Sæwine waiting until now to claim it, then?" She asked, "Is he short on gold or something?"

"I don't know, Sunni," he said, sighing. "All I know now is that the life I had planned is no longer an option, and I must make do."

"But that land is Mother's property," Sunniva said, "It's yours, in all but name. You are meant to have it, not Sæwine!"

"That's not what the law says," Sige said.

"My father will help you," she said confidently, "I'll wager he will enjoy any excuse to snap Sæwine's neck."

"I don't want him involved," Sige said firmly. He had told the same thing to his mother upon hearing the news, though he was sure that neither woman would listen to him. "Rædwald is not responsible for Eastseaxe business, and I would not risk his peace with Sæwine just to secure my own comfort."

Sunniva sucked in a breath to ready a response, but Sige shook his head. "Leave it, Sunni, please. There's nothing you can do about it."

She blew out the retort but her eyes flashed dangerously, as if she took it as a challenge, but then her shoulders rounded once more as if she had been deflated.

"It will all be well in the end," he said, trying to smile, "I'm not giving up. I just have to wait."

She squinted at him as if she knew he was lying. "Well, at least it gives you an excuse to put off marrying," she said archly.

*****

Eadyth always slept better with Rædwald snoring rhythmically beside her, but she still found herself caught in strange dreams, in which Sunniva declared she would raise an army against Sæwine of the Eastseaxe, and declared that she would personally fight in shield wall with her brothers. Her panic in the dream reached its peak as Ricbert had brought the girl back dead…

Eadyth almost cried out when she saw Ricbert standing in the doorway, the rush light in his hand illuminating his gaunt face. Eadyth had to pinch herself a couple of times before she realized she was no longer dreaming.

"What is it?" she asked Ricbert as she touched Rædwald's back to wake him.

"I am sorry to wake you, but the *cyning* is needed outside. It is urgent." Ricbert said.

Rædwald snored loudly, oblivious, and Eadyth smacked him gently on the back, "Wake up, you old fool," she said, and Rædwald snorted out of sleep.

Eadyth stood and pulled a cloak around her shoulders, and Rædwald got blearily to his feet. "It can't wait until morning?"

"I'm afraid not. You'll understand when you see."

Grumbling, Rædwald crossed the hall to the large oak doors, which were standing partway open. A puddle of water was forming on the threshold as the rain entered the hall. The two of them walked onto the topmost step, to find Ricbert standing at the bottom, accompanied by four men whom Eadyth had never seen before. Ricbert's face seemed to register a queer mixture of amusement and mild distaste.

"You got me out of bed for four damp Wæliscmen?" Rædwald asked, making no attempt to hide his annoyance.

"Tell them who you are," Ricbert demanded of the kneeling man in the center. He was younger than the others, no more than thirty years, but something about him spoke of lordship.

"We are only travelers from Mercia," he said; his voice was deep and rhythmic but with no trace of a Wælisc accent. "We are lost, and came to beg for shelter and safety for a night or two."

Rædwald looked at them shrewdly, and then at Ricbert, who shook his head slightly. "If you were merely travelers," Rædwald asked them, "Why didn't you stop at one of the farmsteads along the way? Surely anyone would have offered you a bed or a dry barn to sleep in. It's not as if you could not pay them," he gestured toward the half-concealed rings around the man's wrists and the weather-stained but expensive clothing. "Why travel a dozen leagues out of the way to come here? Who are you?"

The kneeling man held Rædwald's gaze for a long time, as if deciding something.

"I think you know, Rædwald Cyning," the man said.

Rædwald studied him, taking in the rain-slicked black hair and weather beaten clothing of the soaked man, and then turned to Eadyth with a mirthless laugh. "Wife," he said, "I believe we have the pleasure of meeting Edwin, the lost *ætheling* of Deira."

Eadyth's eyes narrowed, but she said nothing. A slight wave of panic caught her; if this was Edwin, then Athelfrith's men had been telling the truth when they justified sacking Grantabricge. Rædwald had been so sure that Edwin was dead, and yet here he was, kneeling in the mud before them, his breeches soaked to the thigh and caked in mud and a Celtic-looking ring around his neck. She thought it was appropriate; his haggard face looked rather more like some Briton slave than an exiled prince.

"Why did you come here?" Rædwald asked coolly, "Why would you come to me, of all people? The Engla have never been friendly to your folk. Why would you think I would help you now?"

"You may not have been friendly to my father," the man said in a carefully measured voice, as if it had been rehearsed, "But I have heard you are a just lord, and loyal to those who serve you. I am *seledreorig*; I have no lord and no lands and no home, and I wish to offer you my friendship and my loyalty in exchange for a place in your hall as one of your retainers. I will swear on the sword in my hand and by my honor as a warrior that I will serve you most loyally."

Rædwald frowned, waving the premature oaths away, and looked at the three *thegns* who accompanied the black-haired Northman. "And must I give these men a place as well?"

"No," Edwin said, "These men are sworn to Cearl of Mercia, though they owed a debt of gratitude to me. They were only bound to bring me here safely and in secret, and they will return to Cearl when their errand is complete."

Eadyth grimaced. She disliked the idea of any foreigner sneaking into her lands, let alone Mercian swords.

"You must realize what that would mean, taking you into my service. You want me to challenge Athelfrith by openly supporting you." Rædwald's face was stony. "We would never be able to withstand him, if he came to seek his vengeance, not with the might of Deira and Bernicia behind him. I have to think of my own people first."

The man's shoulders slumped, his head bowed. "I understand," he said quietly.

"I am sorry. I cannot invite the wrath of the Northumbrians on my people for the sake of one exiled *ætheling.*"

Eadyth let out a silent sigh of relief, though it was cut short.

"But," Rædwald continued, considering the kneeling man, "I would not be in danger if a nameless man of the North Folk appeared at my hall, wishing to become one of my *thegns*. I would give him a place at my board and welcome his service, and give him every honor I would normally give to one of his station. Provided, of course, that no one was aware of his true identity."

Eadyth shifted, but Rædwald did not notice. This man had already been driven from Deira, then from the far western land of the Wæleas, and then through Mercia, dogged relentlessly by Northumbrian swords. Surely he had been disguised then as well, and yet Athelfrith's men had found him. What would stop them from coming here, to take their quarry and destroy those who had harbored him?

The *ætheling* stood and offered his thanks to the king, and Rædwald ushered him inside and ordered a servant to find food and bedding for Edwin and his companions in the hall. Eadyth took her husband by the arm once the visitors had been settled, waiting until they were back in their sleeping quarters before turning to face him.

"Please, think about what you're doing," she whispered, "We will gain nothing by helping him. You know that." She tried to hide her uneasiness, but she was well aware of how quickly she breathed and how she shifted from one foot to another.

He turned and whispered back, "I have a duty to protect those in my lands, and those who seek sanctuary in my hall. He swears no one knows he is here except for his loyal men."

"Men talk. And besides, they are not his; they are sworn to Cearl of Mercia. You know Cearl hates you after you took Cynhelm away from him." She frowned. "It would be best not to trust anyone you don't know."

"What do you want me to do?" he asked her, his voice tinged with anger, "I'm not going to turn him away; he's done nothing to offend or harm me or my family."

"Except to exist as a contending heir to Deira," Eadyth reminded him, "Athelfrith wouldn't send assassins to kill him if he was not a threat, and those *wycingas* will kill our people if we try stand in their way. Don't deny it; you have seen it happen already. You know what violence has been done based solely on a rumor of this man."

"I'm not going to discuss this with you, Eadyth," Rædwald said, "I have made my decision. We will keep quiet on his identity. No one needs to know who he is, and therefore we will be in no danger. I will not deny him a few nights of safety."

"And what if he wants you to lead an army against Athelfrith?" Eadyth pressed on, "What if he expects you to fight his battles and win back his crown? As you're feeling so generous –"

"Enough, woman!" Rædwald rounded on her. "Do not presume to tell me what to do, I am your *cyning*!"

"If you raise your hand against me, I will cut it off," she warned him coldly, and glared as she waited for him to release his tightening fist before softening her voice, "You may be my *cyning*, but I am your wife. You have always listened to my advice before, and I have never led you astray."

Rædwald chewed his lip before replying, "I will allow him to stay, for the time being," he held up a hand to stop the angry response Eadyth had perched on her lips, "But if it becomes clear that danger follows him, I will look to the safety of my own people first."

Eadyth scowled, but could not find a suitable argument. She had to believe that he would be as good as his word.

Chapter Six

Scinncræft Freona

Women's Magic

Boast all you want, but I don't believe any of you," Sunniva said loudly from her perch by the fence. "I'll bet Ælfheah here could run faster than all of you." She indicated the six-year old whose hair she was braiding. "Couldn't you, my love?"

The girl giggled. "I could beat all of you!" she agreed, making a face at all of the men. "You're all so slow!"

Sige knew that Sunniva had been working on the girl; he remembered her as being such a well-mannered child, before Sunniva had taken her under her wing.

Ælfheah squealed as Rægen picked her up, tickling her. "Is that a challenge, *mædencild*?" he said, and the little girl shrieked in laughter, kicking her legs. He set her on her feet.

"We shall see who is the fastest." He lined himself up against the fence, and waited for the little girl to join him. "Touch the tree, and the first one back wins. Go!"

Ælfheah sprinted ahead, Rægen following at a trot. She returned to the fence first, and everyone cheered her victory.

"Beaten by a little girl!" Sige said, "I am glad you're only my half-brother."

Rægen shook his head. "You are too fast for me, little one." He told Ælfheah.

"You two race now!" Ælfheah squealed, indicating Eorwald and Rægen.

"You've worn me out," Rægen said. "I think Sunni should race Eorwald, the biggest against the smallest, particularly since she's the one who doesn't believe our boasts."

Sunniva narrowed her eyes, accepting the challenge. "Eorwald is afraid I'll beat him," she said to Ælfheah when Eorwald did not step forward. "You don't know this, but I tackled a deer once as it ran away from me. I was in the woods and ever so hungry, and I had no bow or spear, and I caught it with my bare hands!" she made a fierce face and the small girl's eyes widened. Sunniva laughed and tucked the ends of her dress through her belt to free her legs. "I understand fully why he would be afraid to challenge me. Isn't that right, Eorwald?" she giggled, "scared that you'll follow in Rægen's footsteps and lose to a girl?"

"You all should race!" Ælfheah said, "All of you!"

"And I'll give a round beating to all of my brothers." Sunniva said, now poking Sige in the chest and hopping from one foot to the other. "And Edwin too, come along," she motioned the Northman, who had been watching in enjoyment from the edge of the paddock.

They had all lined up against the fence. "To the tree and back then?" Sunniva said, still dancing on her toes. Sige could not help but laugh at her energy.

"That's much too short," Eorwald said, "Around the pig shed, down to the river, around the outside of the hall, and back here."

"That's at least a mile!" Sunniva said grumpily,

Sige smiled at her. "Well then, I guess I'll win, won't I?"

"Quit your chatter, the lot of you," Edwin said with a grin, "just go!" He took off, but only got a pace or two before the others bolted after him. Sunniva and Rægen had gone off at a sprint, blazing ahead past the tree and down toward the river. Eorwald was next, then Edwin, and then Sige. Sige kept up a steady pace, and soon overtook Sunniva and Rægen, who were panting and had slowed to labored jogs.

"Keep up, little ones," Sige waved at them as he passed, and he heard an angry curse come from Sunniva.

He looked over his shoulder as he passed the pig shed, and followed the path as it curved down toward the brook. Eorwald was just ahead of him, keeping pace with Edwin. Sige shoved between the two of them, laughing. The air was wet and heavy and warm, but it filled his lungs with joy as he blazed past them, up the hill and around the Bricgweard.

He had nearly reached the paddock and turned around to see where the others had gone, and a flash of brown hair pushed past him and sprinted down to the yard.

"Oho!" Sunniva shouted back at him, dancing in place again as Sige crossed into the yard behind her.

"Beaten by a girl!" she taunted Sige, "twice!" she poked her finger at Rægen. "You boys had better train harder, or else –" she squealed and tried to punch him as Rægen put his arm around her neck.

"Look, I've caught a loudmouthed fox," he said.

"That's an ugly looking fox," Eorwald examined Sunniva when he had trotted up beside them, "but we can skin it anyway."

Sunniva squirmed out of Rægen's grasp and spun out of the way. She fixed her hair and skirts with dignity. "Tease me all you want, it doesn't make you faster," she told Eorwald.

"Try to keep that pace over ten leagues with armor and a shield," Eorwald said. "I'd beat you then."

"Your boasts are like flies, my sweet brother," she said. "Buzzing all around and easily squashed."

"He's right, though," Sige told her, "It's all well and good to be quick, but strength is more important in the shield wall." He looked at Eorwald, "And you would lose at that too."

Eorwald scowled. "Shall we have another contest, then?"

By the time they had finished, Sigebryht was bruised and exhausted, but as merry as he had ever been. Insisting on another contest, Eorwald had challenged him to grappling, then to sword play and another sprinting race, and each had taken their turn. Sige had won the spear-throwing, and had beaten Edwin at the sword, but the blunted sword-shaped bruise on his upper arm attested to his loss against Eorwald. Sunniva had watched, shouting taunts and cheers and heckling them as they practiced their war games, later accompanied by a gaggle of girls.

The girls seemed to be particularly fond of watching Edwin, a departure from their usual objectification of Rægenhere. He could not entirely blame them; Edwin was something new, something exotic, and though he did not seem to have the easy grace for which Rægen was famous, he was strikingly handsome. The girls seemed quite keen to remind Edwin of that fact, and Sige felt a twinge of annoyance with them for no reason.

Sige was watching Rægen shooting arrows at the straw-filled sack as he caught his breath after the last contest, and Edwin sat down next to him, handing him a skin of water. Sige heard the girls behind him commenting loudly on Edwin's body, but Edwin seemed to ignore them.

"You have some admirers," Sige said, taking a draught from the skin. Edwin shrugged indifferently.

Sige saw Sunniva talking to Ecgric, who had just arrived and was stabling his horse. Sige began to grind his teeth, but said nothing.

"Is there something on your mind?" Edwin asked.

Sige sighed. "Just contemplating murdering Ecgric," he said, and then laughed at the look on Edwin's face. "I'm kidding. I don't like him flirting with my sister, that's all. But she likes him, so I can't do much about it. Do you have sisters?"

Edwin's face darkened. "I had a sister. Acha."

"How did she die?" Sige asked gravely.

Edwin snorted. "She didn't die. She married Athelfrith, the whore's son who took my kingdom and forced me into exile." Edwin seemed to notice the confusion on Sige's face, and explained, "When Athelfrith became the king of Bernicia, my father wanted to secure an alliance. It was logical, after Athelfrith crushed the Gæls at Dál Riata." He picked at a blade of grass with a rather unnecessary amount of force. "I was half a boy, and didn't care, really, until the night my father died; one of his friends came to me while I slept and told me of Athelfrith's plan to kill me. Acha is older than I am, and Athelfrith knew that he would have a right to Deira through her if I was out of the way. So I ran. That was more than ten years ago, now," he tossed the shredded grass away, "and he's been hunting me ever since."

Sige wondered how a king with two kingdoms' worth of men could not track down a single man, but he refrained from asking. "Where did you go?"

"Gwynnedd, for a while," he said, "The Wæleas aren't all that bad, you know. It was quiet there, and they treated me well enough, but I seemed to earn the ire of the *rhiau*, the king's son, after… well, he decided that he did not like me anymore, and I was asked, very kindly, to leave."

"But you would have passed through Mercia to get here, how did you cross it without being noticed?"

Edwin grinned shiftily at this. "By selling myself to Cearl's daughter Cwenburg," he said. "I married the woman, and Cearl let me stay in Mercia until he became sick of lying to Athelfrith about my whereabouts. When he heard of the attack at Grantabricge and Cynhelm's swearing his allegiance to Rædwald, he was furious." His voice changed from amusement to anger. "He didn't have any way to get rid of me, though, so I think he might have actually been glad when Cwenburg died this past winter. He hates me, and when I was no longer tied to him by marriage, I found myself being escorted out of his lands by some of his lackeys. I suppose I'm lucky that he didn't finish me off then."

"Did you have any children on her?" Sige asked, unsure as to why he cared.

Edwin shook his head, "I didn't touch her," he said, and looked for a moment as if he were making up his mind about something. He seemed to decide against whatever he was thinking, however, and his mouth curved into a bitter sort of grin. "She was a bit of a cow, to be honest. I… well, I just wasn't interested. I did my duty on our wedding night, but nothing came of it." He seemed disgusted at the thought. She must have been a particularly awful woman to elicit that response.

Edwin shrugged, "And so you can understand why I am not entirely trusting of your honored father," he said, "Despite his hospitality, I have learned that I can never stay in one place for too long."

"Rædwald is not my father," Sige blurted, "He married my mother when I was six. My father was Sigeweald of the Eastseaxe."

"I can't say that I've heard of him, but I haven't heard of most of you southerners," Edwin grinned, "I suppose we are both exiles, in a way."

The air had become colder and the sun started to set behind the stable. Sige stood and held out a hand to pull Edwin to his feet. "I can't speak for Cearl or for the Wæleas, but I have known Rædwald for nearly twenty years, and I know that he is a good man, and loyal to his word. If he tells you that you will be safe here, you can believe him."

Edwin sighed. "I shall have to take your word for it."

*****

Ealdham was big enough to be a town, but without an official market it was technically just a large village on the edge of the Fens. Even so, local farmers and artisans usually traded their wares with one another, quietly going about their business as if it were the only settlement in the known world. The surrounding land was almost completely flat but for a pathetically small bit of raised ground on which the village stood. A ditch, partially filled by the eroding of the years, surrounded the palisaded village with a causeway crossing it at the front gate. The fortifications had been established a generation before, though they had never been needed, and Gieva hoped that the wall and ditch would remain unused for at least one more fighting season.

Father and Ælfhelm had taken the two horses when they had left a few weeks before, and so Gieva and her mother had strapped a few necessities onto the back of the fat dappled pony. The pony was used to roaming freely and rarely had a burden to carry, so she was moody and continually tried to scrape off her load as they passed the stable's walls and took a last look at their home.

"We'll be back soon," Gieva had said, though she did not know if her mother actually had heard her.

The village was within easy riding distance from their farm, and even walking at their fairly slow pace they found the gates just before sunset on the day they had left home. Gieva had walked in persistent fear, first that there might be danger upon the road, and then fear that her mother might get confused again and slow them down. Gieva sang songs as she walked, more to allay her own fears than anything, and when they had reached the village hall of Ealdham and saw Ælfhelm waiting there, she felt as if a weight had been physically lifted from her shoulders.

It had been a fortnight since their arrival, and she had not seen Ælfhelm in days. He was responsible for sending word to the neighboring farms of the imminent danger of attack, and something stirred deep in Gieva's guts every time she watched him ride away, sure it would be the last time.

He returned one day as a sluggish rain drove everyone indoors, and Gieva hugged him even though his wet cloak soaked her sleeves.

"I've had news of your father and Cynhelm," Ælfhelm said, taking a hot cup of broth from Gieva with thanks. He looked like he might topple over where he sat. He was hardly one-and-twenty, only a couple of years older than Gieva herself, but he looked old and haggard; his yellow hair lank and his face grim. His clothes looked slept-in, and surely he had spent at least one night under a bush, though Gieva could imagine that he had not slept in days.

"Are they still at Grantabricge?" Gieva asked eagerly. She had learned of their victory and Cynhelm's swearing allegiance to Rædwald of the Engla a few weeks before, though she had heard nothing since and was desperate for news.

"Cynhelm left there several days ago, with your father and a small host," Ælfhelm said, "He and his *thegns* learned of some unrest to the east of here, near the Wood."

"I thought you'd defeated the Northmen at Grantabricge?" Gieva asked uncertainly.

"We did, but there were only thirty or forty of them there. There was a rumor that there was another force headed this way."

"I don't understand why Northumbrians would even want to come here," Gieva said, "Unless they like salt or eels, that is."

Ælfhelm considered. "They seem to be running on revenge more than greed at this point, I think. Their force was completely decimated but for a single man they sent back to Athelfrith with a warning not to try this again. I'll wager that whatever force Cynhelm is chasing is meant to be retaliatory."

"Is this feud with Cynhelm really so important?" Gieva was picking at the bits of straw in her thread, so anxiously that she ended up tearing out too many fibers and felt the wool snap. She sniffed irritably and twisted the frayed ends together, setting down the spindle until she could have better control of her hands.

"I don't think it's a feud with Cynhelm, really. The Northmen had some nonsense story about tracking a lost contender to the Deiran throne, but if any of its true I'll eat a fish hook. He's probably just trying to excuse his dabbling his fingers where they don't belong."

She watched him for a moment. He was usually so cocky, so proud and brave; but now he just looked tired and uncertain.

"Do you know what they might plan?" Gieva asked.

Ælfhelm shook his head wearily. "All I know is that Athelfrith wants to harm my people, and I will do what I can to stop that happening. The *ealdormen* and *cyningas* can justify their wars; I just fight in them."

Gieva sat with him in silence, she fiddling again with her spindle; he staring blankly at the wood of the table. Gieva patted his hand before saying, "Go and rest, Ælfhelm. You'll be no protection to us if you're dead on your feet." She kissed his cheek and he obeyed, finding a quiet corner of the hall and leaving her with Mother.

"Who is that boy?" mother asked her, when Gieva set to spinning with her, "He's very handsome."

Gieva took a steadying breath. "You know him, Mother. He's your sister's son, Ælfhelm. You saw him at the last harvest, don't you remember?"

"Oh yes, of course, how silly of me," Mother said vaguely, "He's grown very tall."

A trickle of women and children from neighboring farms came as the days drew on, and they all claimed areas of the hall for their own. Gyrwisc and Englisc women sat together in relative harmony and sewed clothes, spun wool, chased their children, and chatted about the small doings of their families. If it were not for the gnawing apprehension in the pit of her stomach, Gieva might have thought they had simply gathered there for a festival.

Ælfhelm and the other fighting men who had remained in the village joined them in the hall at night; some men spent the nights in the arms of their wives or lovers, others stood outside the hall watching for movement on the still, flat landscape. No one drank much; there was little enough ale to go around, and the pleasantness of the evenings eventually dissolved into quiet, sober worry.

She had settled into a rhythm here; as the daughter of the local *thegn* and the close kinswoman of the *huscarl*, Gieva had a sort of prestige among the women that she neither expected nor wanted; they kept bringing small complaints to her as if she were responsible for settling them. She did her best, though she knew her desire for peace above all else did not make her a forceful leader. Usually she just hoped that both parties would realize that their friendship was more important, and forget their arguments.

She was trying and failing to settle one of these petty squabbles when a scream rent the air. She ran to the large square yard near the entrance of the hall, seeing a crowd of people with a sweating horse in the center. Wails were coming from somewhere amid the crowd, and Gieva saw one of the older women hunched over a man's fallen body.

"What's happened?" She asked no one in particular.

"It's Fridswith's son," said one of the other women, "He is an errand rider for Cynhelm."

Gieva's stomach turned to lead. She glanced around, looking for Ælfhelm, but could not see him. "Everyone," she raised her voice above the murmuring of the crowd, "You all know what this means. We have to get inside, quickly."

Several people obeyed, but Fridswith was still sprawled over the bloodied body of her son, whose throat had been slashed, blood caked down his chest and a terrified look still in his glassy eyes. He still had ropes around his arms where he had been bound to the horse, sent back as a warning to the people of Ealdham.

When Fridswith only wailed and threw herself back over her son's corpse, Gieva looked at two men who had been standing by on guard duty. "Take his body away, somewhere safe, until we can bury him." She turned back to Fridswith. "Please, there's nothing we can do, we have to get inside!"

Fridswith eventually relented and Gieva motioned for another woman to take her into the hall. The men had begun to assemble their weapons, the women frantically gathering belongings from outside. Gieva took the horse's reins and led it just outside the gates. She unharnessed the beast and smacked its rear so hard that it nearly kicked her before it galloped into the west.

"What did you do that for?" she heard Ælfhelm's voice behind her.

"If there are horses in the village when those men come, they will know we are here. They will kill them or take them for their own use. It's harder to steal a horse if it is running over a field than if it's corralled in a village." She paused, frowning at him. "They may be horses, but they are Gyrwisc horses, not Northumbrian," she said with grim finality.

He walked with her to the door of the hall, but did not enter. "Will you fight them?" she asked her cousin.

"We have no choice, if they come," Ælfhelm said. "Go inside and bar the door. Put out the fire. With luck, they'll think no one is here, and the will leave without a fight."

"We can help," she said wildly, "I can help you fight." She knew that it was a mad idea; she could hold a shield and knew how to defend herself if needed, but she knew nothing of battle and would have been more of a hindrance than a help, if she were allowed to fight.

"Help the women," Ælfhelm said gently. "They're frightened. Help them to be brave."

Gieva nodded, and threw her arms around his neck. "May all the gods protect you, my dear one. Fight bravely and die well, if die you must." She said the words haltingly, and they sounded insincere. She did not want him to die, but she could not plant the seeds of fear in him, so she prayed to every god she could think of, and she shut the door behind her.

And then they waited.

*****

Sunniva pulled her spindle from her belt, and began to pull some fibers from the distaff, twisting them between her fingers before flinging the drop spindle to set the twist. She sat with her legs crossed, her arms held aloft as the fluffy band of wool twisted itself into a fine thread. She watched Rægenhere and Ecgric as they shot arrows from short bows at the wooden wall that bordered the yard. A full-sized figure of a man had been daubed onto an old bolster, and most of their arrows had clustered together around the neck, chest and groin.

"Why do you always aim for the prick?" Ecgric asked Rægen.

"Because it would be the last place you'd want to be hit, and yet it's always the least protected," Rægen said. He pulled the bowstring back and loosed, and another arrow ended up in the painted crotch of the target.

"It wouldn't matter much if you got hit there," Ecgric said, and his own arrow hit the neck of the target. "You never use yours."

Sunniva chuckled under her breath at their conversation, and found that her thread had become lumpy and uneven as she had become distracted watching Ecgric.

"If I began to relate half of my conquests, you'd be an old man by the time I'd finished," said Rægen. "I just don't like to prattle on about it like you do."

"I am able to please women; I'm not going to be ashamed of that fact." Ecgric gave half a glance in Sunniva's direction.

"Like that girl you had in Grantabricge, what was her name?" Rægen smirked, knocking another arrow.

"Widsith," Ecgric said. He had a reminiscent look on his face which Sunniva did not like at all. He must have thought she could not hear his conversation, otherwise he would not be boasting about other women. Or perhaps he simply did not care.

"That's right," Rægen drew the bowstring and loosed. The arrow stuck in the wall, a foot away from the target. "Damn," he said, "Now you got me thinking of her. I don't think I saw you for two days after that night."

"Well, I was tired," Ecgric said, loosing his own arrow with a smirk as big as Rægen's.

"I won't be able to concentrate now. Too bad she's so far away, eh? You must be missing those perfect tits and that sweet little mouth of hers." He grinned at Ecgric, who chuckled appreciatively in answer.

Sunniva saw Ecgric glance at her again, but she did not meet his eyes. She tried to act as if she had not heard their conversation, but her fingers trembled around the wool, and when Ecgric's eyes had left her she had gathered her distaff and spindle and left the two men to their archery. She stomped into the weaving house, and threw them against the wall in her fury. The room was mercifully empty, and she felt tears sting her eyes. She cursed her own stupidity; of course he had been with other women, it was stupid to assume that just because she had opened her legs for him that he would not continue in his old habits.

It had meant far more to her than it had to him, clearly. Perhaps she ought not to have lied about being a maiden. She had wanted to seem mature, worldly; she had wanted him so badly that she had not cared if he would take it seriously when he went to bed with her. She had not had a maidenhead to break; she assumed that it had been lost on her own fingers during her youthful explorations, but perhaps if he knew how much it had meant to her, he might not have been so quick to move on to the next one as soon as Sunniva was unavailable.

She had not asked him if he had wandered while in Grantabricge. He had welcomed her under his blankets with such enthusiasm that she had been sure of his faithfulness. No man who had just eaten a feast would have been that hungry, after all.

Sunniva kicked the ground as she walked. She wanted to find this Widsith, with her perfect tits and sweet little mouth and knock all of her teeth out.

Don't be stupid, a voice said in the back of her mind, *that girl is not your enemy.* Sunniva knew that she had most likely been a whore, or some stupid *ceorl* who thought Ecgric might whisk her away to a better life.

"Pig-headed, lying sack of –" Sunniva muttered to herself, but cut off her mutterings with a hissing breath through her teeth.

She may have been a fool, but he was a liar. And liars had to be punished.

Sunniva always appreciated company, but she had never been so thankful for visitors to the Bricgweard. It was not a large gathering, but there were enough people that Sunniva decided to dress carefully for the occasion. She opted for a dress which hugged her curves and pressed her breasts together so that they looked bigger than they actually were, wearing a shift that hung lazily under the dress so that the faintest breeze might slip it down over her shoulder. She would blame the heat, of course. It was a very warm night, after all.

As she glanced in the polished bronze mirror, she grinned. Her parents would be appalled at her choices in clothing, but Sunniva did not dress for them. She looked in the mirror much longer than strictly necessary.

Godes hæmað min ears, she thought, *if I keep on preening like this, I might as well strap on a sword and call myself a warrior. Gods know only some fool man could be this vain...*

Still, she gave herself a smile. She loved the way she looked. She twisted the ends of her hair so that they coiled into a thick ringlet, shaking her head to let the curls flow over her naked shoulders. Ecgric liked her hair. He liked when she wrapped a curl around her finger, or when she slung it over one shoulder, leaving the other shoulder bare for him to explore.

The thought of it made Sunniva's breath catch for a moment, but she recovered herself. She hated what the thought of him did to her, and wondered if she would be able to carry out her plan if she couldn't control herself.

Sunniva positioned herself across the table from Ecgric and next to a *thegn* named Ealdwine. Ecgric greeted her, and she was pleased to see that he looked rather apprehensive, like a dog who knew he had done something wrong and was waiting for a kick. She nodded coolly in acknowledgement, though before he could say anything she turned to Ealdwine.

"You come from Blythburh, isn't that right?" she asked him. He was rather good-looking, she found. His hair was the color of hay, and his beard was so pale that it seemed to disappear when he turned his head just the right way, but he had a pretty face and nice legs, and gave her the same look most men did when she turned her charm on them.

Ealdwine nodded, "Yes, that's right. My father is the *ealdorman* of Blythburh."

"I've heard that your father owns a few ships," Sunniva felt Ecgric's eyes on her, but she ignored him. "I've always wanted to sail in some great ship. I've only ever been in little boats before, and only down the river. I should like to visit the sea someday." She brushed her hair over one shoulder, and took a sip of mead as the poor man began to tell her about living on the sea and how much more convenient it was when one wanted to travel, and about how rich they were getting from trade with the Franca, or some such boring talk. He was rather sweet, and she might have had some fun with him once, but she was more interested in the matter at hand.

Sunniva reached for some bread, and stretched out her leg under the table. She knew she had found her mark when Ecgric shifted slightly. She half-listened to Ealdwine, so that she could respond at just the right moments or giggle when appropriate, but the other half of her mind was more intensely occupied. She turned her smirk into a sweet smile at Ealdwine when Ecgric grabbed her foot and pushed it away. She moved it back again.

She saw Ecgric trying to make conversation with Eorwald, but he kept glancing at her. She had gotten some honey on her finger, and she put it in her mouth, drawing it out slowly, sliding it across her lip. She was aware that Ealdwine had stopped talking and was intently watching her, so she leaned toward the *ealdorman's* son and asked him to tell her more about himself.

When the meal had finished, most everyone migrated to the benches and cushions near the hearth, and Sunniva stood as if to join them. She caught Ecgric's eye and mouthed, "Weaving house." She extracted herself from the attentions of Ealdwine, who was now quite drunk and kept making motions as if to kiss her, and before he could approach her again she slipped out of the hall.

Sunniva shook out her hands to stop them trembling, and took a deep breath as she entered the deserted weaving house. Ecgric was at her heels and followed her inside.

Without a word, and with rather more force than she intended, she pushed him into one of the low stools, his back against the wall. She bent at the waist and kissed him ferociously, lifting her skirts and sitting across his lap. He was already hard and ready for her and she had to shake the lust from her mind.

"This is a pleasant surprise," he said as he slid his hand up her leg. "I had thought you might be cross with me."

"Shut up," Sunniva said, pulling his breeches halfway down his legs. He was attempting to pull her into his lap again when she pulled away and knelt in front of him. She did not see his face when she bent her head down, but heard the deep rumble of a groan above her. She had no idea what she was doing; she had never done this sort of thing before, but he seemed to enjoy it immensely, and she became strangely excited as she did it.

Stop it, you idiot, she scolded herself.

She ran her tongue along it a last time, as she had licked the honey from her finger before. She straddled him again, his time lifting her skirt and guiding him inside of her. Only when she had begun to slowly move her hips did she speak.

"Did she fuck you like this?" she said, trying to keep the pleasure out of her voice. He opened his mouth to retort, but she made a fist around his hair and pulled his head back, clamping her mouth on his to stop his words. She moved a little faster now, and sucked the skin at his neck so hard it left a dark bruise and elicited another low sound from deep in his throat.

"You don't understand," he tried to say, but she put a finger to his lips.

"Think about what you want, Ecgric," she said very quietly in his ear, "You can have this any time you want," she squeezed her legs together and was quite satisfied at the look on his face as she did so, "but you must be mine, and mine alone. I will not share you." She knew he was on the edge, and she abruptly stopped moving. She forced herself to stand, even though every part of her wanted to stay and ride him until they both found oblivion, but she stepped back and let her skirt fall back around her ankles.

"But if you would prefer a string of whores," she said sweetly, "You're a grown man, and you can make that decision for yourself. Good night."

She knew his mouth was still hanging open as she closed the door behind her, and her own mouth twisted into a grin of triumph. If that wasn't as good as a sign around his neck, she didn't know what was.

*****

Rædwald was waiting for him in the Bricgweard, sharing a meal with Eadyth. The doors were flung wide to tempt a breeze into the humid great hall, to no avail. The dogs at the king's feet lay panting forlornly, as if complaining wordlessly about the warmth.

The king motioned for Ecgric to come and sit down to join them, pushing a cup toward him. Ecgric took it with thanks, and helped himself to bread and smoked fish, before Rædwald spoke.

"When were you last in Gipeswic?" the king asked.

"About a fortnight ago," Ecgric said, scratching one of the dogs' ears as the beast put its head in his lap, "for market day. It was the biggest I've seen yet. You'd be pleased."

"Good, good," Rædwald said. "All local vendors, I assume?"

"All but one. There was a cloth vendor from Francland, though he came by way of Cantwareburh. I think he was associated with Heahcwene Bercta's men. I do remember seeing him when I was in the South, now I think on it."

"They're still here?" Eadyth asked, "I thought all those Franca went home as soon as the *heahcwene* died." She said it with a note of distaste in her voice.

Ecgric shrugged, and the dog nudged his hand to resume its stroking. "Perhaps Ethelbert wanted to keep those foreign trading connections. You know as well as anyone that the Franca are useful, if a bit flamboyant."

Rædwald nodded appreciatively. "I hope you made sure that they paid their dues," he said, "How much did you make off of them?"

"They paid in silver," Ecgric said, "a pound of it. I gave most to Ceolwine in order to improve the village hall, though. The locals didn't appreciate having their Folkmoot under a leaking roof, for some reason."

"For someone who hates administrative duties, you seem to be quite adept at managing them," Eadyth said, grinning. "I think I want to go and see the progress you've made, on the next market day."

"I'd be glad to make the preparations," Ecgric said, without much enthusiasm. The dog gave him up as a bad job and flopped back onto the ground. "Will your entire household be coming?"

"Just us," Eadyth said.

"We ought to feast the *thegns* while we are there," Rædwald mused, "how have you found them, Ecgric?"

Ecgric sighed. The *thegns* and landowners near Gipeswic had been an endless source of bother for him, but as their *hlaford* it was his lot to have to deal with their nonsense. "They don't appreciate the tariffs on the docks," he said, "They think that since they have used the Gipeswic port for so long, they shouldn't suddenly be forced to pay a tax to use it."

"They need to pay tax so that there will be a dock for them to use in the first place," Rædwald said irritably. "How can we make improvements with nothing to fund them?"

"It's not as if they don't have the gold," Eadyth said, "What do they expect us to do?"

"They think that we ought not to give so much to the poor," Ecgric said, feeling a headache coming on, "that diverting the funds we have toward the market would bring in more wealth to Gipeswic, which would benefit the poor in the end."

"That's idiotic," Eadyth said.

"I won't punish people who have had ill luck by taking away the little help we can offer them," Rædwald said. "If traders don't like the port tax, they can take their goods overland and save a *scylling.*"

Ecgric's headache was starting to take hold. "That's what I told them," he said. "I shouldn't worry too much. They'll grumble, but they'd still rather use the river than try to take their goods in a wagon."

A serving woman had come to clear away the remains of their meal, which Ecgric had abandoned. He took his leave from Rædwald in order to send out a messenger to Gipeswic to ready the village hall for the king's arrival. Once he had dispatched the messenger, he went back to the training yard. The whole business had left him with a throbbing behind his right eye, and he needed to hit something.

The whole thing left him in a sour mood, and even after he had sparred with Eorwald and with Edwin, the newcomer from Deira, for an hour, it did not relieve his annoyance. He did not care about the stupid market in Gipeswic. He wanted to do something useful. He wanted a real fight. He wanted the intoxicating feeling of impending battle. He wanted to bathe in treasure after a successful raid, with a horn of ale in one hand and a woman in the other. But instead, he got to negotiate taxes and tell off petty *thegns* for being spineless turds.

As he put away his practice sword and armor, teasing Eorwald about his tactics, he noticed Sunniva holding court over a knot of girls at the other end of the training yard, so effortlessly seductive that he wanted to hit something all over again.

It was beginning to get out of hand.

Ecgric had promised himself, when she left him sitting half-naked and open-mouthed in the weaving house, that he would not give her the satisfaction of knowing that she had won. She had heard Rægenhere mentioning that whore from Grantabricge, he was sure, but he would not let her think that she could control him this way. She was just a spoiled, manipulative little girl, and he would not give into her tantrums.

Sunniva had ignored him almost completely over the next few days, but he found himself watching her talking to her stupid friends or sitting outside spinning, or flirting with the assorted *thegns* and *ceorls* who frequented the Bricgweard. She began to invade his thoughts so frequently that he kept finding himself walking aimlessly and forgetting what he was supposed to be doing. He had forgotten how cold his bed could be without her sneaking in during the night to hide under his blankets.

Ecgric very nearly punched the wall.

The red-haired girl named Freida was in the middle of a long and drawn-out flirtation, and he found himself glancing at Sunniva the entire time. The latter gave a minuscule shrug of her shoulders as she had done that night, as if to say, "It's your decision." It was only a few moments before the red-haired girl left, looking dejected.

He walked back to the Bricgweard, hearing footsteps behind him. Sunniva swayed casually a couple of paces to his rear, staring at him with one eyebrow raised and an insolent smirk on her lips. He tried to shake her off, walking around the back and between two outbuildings.

"Go away," he said, but when she did not leave, he rounded on her. "This isn't a game, Sunniva. I am not your plaything, and I won't let you manipulate me like you do everyone else."

Her face registered no change, and the way she smirked at him made him unsure whether to take her under a blanket, or smother her with one.

"I guess I have my answer then," she said, "That's a pity." She looked him up and down appraisingly with a smirk, and then sighed. "Well, it's been fun. Enjoy your whores."

She started to walk away, but he felt such a surge of anger and raw lust that he spun her around, catching her by the throat and pushing her against the wall of the Bricgweard. She did not seem frightened that he might hurt her; rather there was a fire in her eyes that dared him to try.

She had won. They both knew it. He moved his hand away and replaced it with his mouth on the hollow of her collarbone. Lifting her easily and pushing her against the wall, he found the sweet place between her legs and she slid down with a sigh. She bit his lip and her fingers wound through his hair, pulling as he pushed into her, again and again, her legs tightening around his torso. He felt her soft cunny slide around him over and over, breathed in her scent like honey and sweat and sex and the earth itself.

"Swear to me you won't fuck other girls anymore," she said into his ear as her sex clenched and tightened around him. "Swear to me that you're mine, and mine alone."

"I swear," he panted, "*Godes hæmað min ears*, I swear it."

He did not let her down right away, but kept her pressed

against the wall, panting into the sweet-smelling hollow of her neck. She kissed him as her feet found the ground once more, as sweetly and as innocently as a maiden even as he felt the marks of her fingernails on his shoulders and her wetness clinging to him.

They heard movement from the other side of the hall, and he set her down quickly, and she rearranged her skirts and disappeared. Ecgric leaned a hand against the wall as if he had been having a piss, when Rægenhere rounded the corner.

"There you are," he said, as Ecgric laced his breeches. "Your father was looking for you." After a moment, he added, "You look like you've just run a mile."

Ecgric cleared his throat to give him time to think up a lie. "I have. Never challenge Sigebryht to a race," he said, "You'll never win." It seemed to work, as Rægenhere chuckled.

Ecgric hardly thought that "well, I was just fucking your sister," would have been an appropriate response.

*****

We are getting close, I think," Sige whispered, following the trail of blood droplets through the wood, "he came through here, see where his antler broke that branch?"

The wood was dense and shady, and thick with gnats and flies. They had tracked the hart for an hour now, and the blood seemed to be fresher the longer they followed it. It was slowing down.

Edwin was grinning, excitement etched on his face as he padded across the mossy ground. He seemed to find amusement in any activity, from sword play to hunting to drinking, seemingly ecstatic at the mere fact that he was alive. The grin was infectious.

Sige was startled as he heard a twig snap off to his left. Both men gingerly stepped in that direction, certain that they would hear the deep call of the stag as it died. They pushed deeper into the wood, and heard movement again. Sige raised his spear, prepared to give the deer a final blow to end its life.

Another crack of a twig came from behind him this time, and they looked at one another, open-mouthed, as they heard an angry squeal.

"*Godes hæmað min ears*," Sige said, "That's a big one."

The boar had seen them, and let out another angry yell before it charged toward them. Sige's spear caught in the flesh of the boar's back as it charged past him in a whirl of tusks and teeth and bristling black hair.

Sige was pulled three feet by his spear hand, which refused to let go of the spear wedged between the monster's shoulder blades. The beast rounded on him and charged again, thrusting its long snout at Sige, who had fallen to the ground. As the boar's angry yellow tusk ripped across Sige's leg, the man-sized monster squealed again, an arrow sticking out from its side. Sige got to his feet in the moment that the boar was distracted, and wrenched his spear tip from the beast's flesh. Edwin loosed another arrow, at closer range, which stuck in the boar's flank just above the first.

Sige ran at the boar, which was now rounding on Edwin, and threw a stone at its hind end. Confused, it turned again and resumed its charge toward Sige. This time, he was ready. He crouched, and as the boar raged towards him he knocked the tusks aside and felt his spear squelch through the boar's throat. The speed of the beast's attack caused the head of the spear to protrude from its back, and the giant pig squealed again, blood gushing out of its long snout.

Sige stabbed the beast through the heart with his seax, and with a final twitch it fell still. He walked to where Edwin had been knocked to the ground.

Edwin took Sige's hand and rose to his feet. "Well done." He clapped Sige on the arm, but did not let go immediately. "And thanks, I think that thing would have ripped my guts out if you hadn't been here."

"Same to you," Sige said. He felt uncomfortably aware of how close they stood to one another. He stepped away and bent over the dead pig, and shoved the spear forward through its back.

"We'd better call someone to help us with this," he told Edwin, who removed a horn from the loop at his belt and gave it three long blasts.

Sige cleaned the spear on his breeches, which now bore a large gash. The boar's long yellow tusk had glanced against his skin, which was darkening to a bruise.

"That thing nearly took your prick off," Edwin said, examining the bruise, which stretched in a long arc across Sige's thigh.

"Or worse," Sige said. He had seen a man stabbed there once during a battle; the warrior had bled to death in moments when the blade had barely nicked the inside of his leg. Sige shuddered, realizing how close he could have been to that same outcome.

Sige straightened as they heard footsteps approaching loudly from the direction they had come. Rægen and Rædwald entered the clearing with as much crashing and stomping as an army.

"What've you got?" Rægen asked, spotting the dead boar, "Woden's teats, you didn't even have a boar spear!" he looked at Edwin and Sige in surprise, who were both sweating and still slightly out of breath. "What did you do, bore it to death?" He laughed rather madly at his terrible pun, and Sige only gave him a weak smile in return.

The men carried the pig back to their camp. Rædwald had offered his congratulations and Rægen asked for a blow-by-blow account. Sige listened more than he talked, as Edwin recounted what had happened. He felt uncomfortable as Edwin made it out to be much more exciting than it actually was, Sige the obvious hero of the story.

"It wasn't as great as all that," he put in sheepishly, but Edwin and Rægen ignored him.

The wood became thinner, and they eventually started to hear the sounds of camp. A grizzled, middle-aged serving man was helping to string up a deer by its neck. A tall woman, wearing the dark green tunic and trousers of a man, stuck her seax in the deer's belly and slid the knife downward, standing back as a torrent of blood and entrails fell from the dead animal.

"How did you beat us back here?" Rædwald asked, as he came forward to greet his queen.

Eadyth wiped her hands on her tunic and kissed him. "I am a much more efficient hunter than you are." She greeted her sons and Edwin with a grin, "But it seems your blundering did not scare off all the game." She nodded toward the dead pig being carried by the two servants. "Which of you took that one down?"

Edwin pointed at Sige, and Eadyth nodded approvingly.

"Well, it tried to take us down, in truth," Sige said.

Rædwald was looking appreciatively at the deer's neck and saw an arrow's broken shaft protruding from it. "What a shot!" he said, "I'm glad you were able to catch up with it after I left."

"No thanks to that horn," she said, eyeing the horn hanging from Edwin's belt, "I had it exhausted and the damned thing bolted as soon as we heard the noise. But I caught up with him eventually. He was a good running partner." Mother patted the beast's flank, almost as if she were apologizing to it. Mother had always taught them that they should be respectful of the creatures they killed, and though she loved the hunt she always seemed rather sad when she dealt the final blow. All animals were put on this earth by the gods, she had always said, and though people may hunt them for nourishment it did not make the beast's life any less meaningful.

The dark beer flowed freely that evening, and Eadyth had prepared the deer's liver with mushrooms for them to eat along with the greasy boar shank. Sige rather missed Eorwald, who was always a good drinking partner, but Eorwald was just as loud and blundering as his father and took little pleasure in hunting. Sige assumed that if Eorwald had come, they might not have had anything to eat that night. Even so, the company was pleasant, and they laughed and sang until the sun sank below the trees.

"Boar, beer, and a bride," said Rædwald, wrapping his arm around his wife's shoulder. "That's all we really want, you know. The right to eat good food and drink strong drink, and fuck our women. Isn't that right, my love?"

Eadyth nodded and nestled into Rædwald's arm. "I believe you've caught the basics," she yawned. "Well, my *cyning*, you've had your beer and your boar, let's go and take care of that last one now."

Sige and Rægen shared a disgusted but amused look as Eadyth and Rædwald retired to the largest tent. The three men sat around the fire, talking and singing loud, boisterous songs long after nightfall.

"Your turn, Sige," Rægen said, his voice thick with drink.

"Give me a minute, let me think," Sige searched his memory for a riddle that he hadn't played a thousand times before. "Ah, I know one: I saw a tree with bright branches stand high in a grove. The tree was happy, the growing wood. Water and earth fed it well, until wise with time it met with a change: it was deeply hurt, dumb with bonds, covered with wounds, but adorned in front with dark ornaments. Now it clears the way for a treacherous foe through the might of its head. By storm they plunder the hoard together."

Both Rægen and Edwin were silent for a good while. Sige had forgotten some of the words but he was certain they would get it right away. "You'd better say something soon," he warned, "or else you've got to drink."

"Uh…" Rægen looked into the depths of his cup as if for an answer. "A tree?"

"The tree is in the riddle, idiot," Sige said. "Drink."

Rægen drained his cup and refilled it.

Edwin was muttering the riddle back to himself with his eyes closed. "I think it's either an arrow, but that doesn't seem right, an arrow isn't made from a whole tree… or, maybe… a battering ram?"

Sige raised his cup in congratulations. "That's the one."

"That's not fair, he had two guesses in one go," Rægen protested, finishing another cup of the strong dark beer. He may have had a mind for songs, but could never remember the answers to riddles, and it always worked out to his detriment. He filled and drained the cup again and got shakily to his feet. "Well, I do believe I have muddled my wits, and I'll leave you two clever folk to riddle your riddles while I dream my… my dreamy dreams."

"Up for another?" Sige asked Edwin when Rægen had left.

"You'll have to come up with some better riddles," Edwin said, stretching his long legs out in front of him, "I've got a powerful thirst."

"I've just gone," Sige said, more than a little drunk himself. Edwin had definitely come out on top in the riddle-game, which always became progressively more ludicrous as it went on and its participants became more and more muddled. He reached for the pitcher and topped off both of their cups, sitting next to Edwin and leaning against the fallen tree.

"I'll have to think for a while," Edwin grinned. "Take another turn. Let me catch you up on drinks."

Sige thought again. The game would be easier with Edwin; all of Sige's riddles would be new to him. Edwin was staring into the fire, his arms and legs crossed, shadows dancing across his broken nose and dark scruff of a beard, and it took a long time before Sige tore his eyes away to look into the fire as well.

"I am the part of a bird which is not in the sky. I swim in the sea, and yet remain dry." Sige was rather proud of this riddle; it was one of his own devising, though he knew it was painfully easy. However, after a moment of silence Edwin took a long draught of his beer and smiled in his surrender.

"You didn't even try!" Sige said, punching his shoulder.

Edwin shrugged with a look which rather reminded Sige of Sunniva when she was toying with some poor *thegn's* son. He felt a lurch in the bottom of his stomach as Edwin shifted his position, now within a hand's breadth of him. Sige rubbed his chin nervously, and felt heat radiating from his cheeks. *Too much beer,* he thought dully.

"Well, have you got a riddle for me, or not?" he asked Edwin, his voice much harsher than he had meant it to be.

Edwin seemed to think for a moment. "Yes. I think I know a good one." He took another long draught, the slight smirk still on his lips.

Sige looked hastily away, back into the red and gold flames. He felt his head spinning. *Too much beer,* he thought again, *I've just had too much to drink, and so has he. That's why he is sitting so close, that's why I keep staring. That's why I'm so hard, that always happens when I drink, I just drank too much. It's not... no, that's ridiculous.* He reasoned with himself. He felt Edwin's eyes on him, but refused to meet them with his own.

It was a few moments before he realized that Edwin had leaned toward him, his mouth a bare inch from Sige's ear. Sige swallowed with difficulty.

"I want to tell of a thing I know," he began the riddling words, "Splendidly it hangs by a man's thigh, under the master's cloak. In front is a hole. It is stiff and hard; it has a goodly place..."

He wondered if Edwin could hear his heart thumping wildly in his chest.

"...When the young man lifts his garment over his knee," Edwin said, still in a gravelly whisper. He lifted the hem of Sige's tunic and found the gash that the boar's tusk had left in his breeches.

"...He wishes to visit with the head of what hangs..." Sige felt Edwin's stubble brush his neck, "...The familiar hole he had often filled with its equal length."

A key, Sige thought stupidly, remembering the answer, *it's a key, of course it is. It's a trick, that's the point of the riddle. It's a key, not a –*

Before he could finish his own thought, he had pushed Edwin away and had gotten to his feet. *A key*, he thought. *It's a key.* The drink made him so lightheaded he thought he might fall over.

"No," Sige said, rubbing his beard again, nervously, "You're drunk. Stop it."

Edwin had stood and had caught up with Sige as he tried to walk away. "Where are you going?"

"Away from you!" Sige shot back in a carrying whisper, his head swimming and his breath coming in quick sharp bursts, "What is wrong with you? Why would you..." he fumbled for words as he tried to pass Edwin, who blocked his path. "It's not right, it's – it's unnatural. Just, just let me pass; I want to go to bed."

"Unnatural, is it?" Edwin said coldly.

"It is!" Sige was having trouble keeping his voice to a whisper.

"But every time you try to fuck a woman you end up thinking about it." Edwin said, and Sige felt a surge of something not quite like lust and not quite like hatred.

Sige had a retort ready, but it was lost. "You can't know –"

"You think I don't know how this feels?" Edwin's whisper cracked, "I've tried so many times to stamp it out, to burn it out of me, but it's still there. Every time I see you, I want to claw out my eyes, because then, maybe, it'll stop me wanting you."

Edwin's words punched him in the guts; he knew those feelings as if they were his own. He hated Edwin, he hated himself, he hated his body and his mind for responding the way it did to Edwin's hands as he pulled him closer. He hated the way his mouth opened for Edwin's tongue and the way he was fumbling at the toggles of his tent and pushing Edwin inside.

And he hated the fact that it did not feel unnatural at all.

Chapter Seven

Farað mid Hreading

Go Forth with Haste

hey waited.

Ælfhelm and the others had stood beyond the palisade, shields and swords and spears at the ready in a line. Ælfhelm glanced over his shoulder at Gieva, nodding for her to close the door. She did not want to. She wanted to reach out to them, to make the ten remaining men come back inside with them, to hide and wait for the invaders to pass. Ælfhelm gave her a stern look, and Gieva shut the door.

They waited.

Mother was humming quietly to herself and spinning in the corner, and as the sounds grew louder outside Gieva crouched down at her mother's knees.

"Mother," she said, "Do you remember why we are here?"

"Of course I do," Mother did not stop her spinning.

"Tell me, Mother. Tell me why we are here."

Mother's brow creased for a moment, and she set down her spindle. She opened her mouth to speak, then thought for a moment, then opened it again. "Because bad things are coming," she said, and she sounded so much like a child that it frightened Gieva to her bones.

"Mother, listen to me," Gieva said, but her mother's eyes were unfocused and she seemed to be looking through Gieva. Gieva had to bite her tongue to keep herself from crying as she turned her mother's face to her own. "Mother, you have to listen to me, very carefully. If the bad men come," she had to swallow the lump in her throat, "if the bad men come, you need to be very small and hide here in this corner. Can you do that? I don't know what will happen, but if you are feeling frightened, please just hide in this corner and you will be safe. Do you understand?"

Mother's eyes flashed for a moment, with a look which reflected the terror that Gieva herself felt, but the flash disappeared as the older woman nodded and smiled. "Of course, my love," she said, patting Gieva on the cheek and picking up her spindle again.

Gieva scrubbed her hands across her eyes.

They waited.

There were shouts coming from outside now. Several of the women were crying, and nearly all the children were as well. The shouts were growing distant, and Gieva knew that the men were pushing out of the village boundaries.

They waited.

And they waited.

The piece of wood which bolted the doors snapped as a man entered the hall, and Gieva's heart sank as she realized that it was all over. The man carried a shield with unfamiliar colors, and when he spoke his voice was as hard as his scarred face. "Your men are dead," he told them, "I am Ulfric, and we have taken this village and all its lands in the name of Athelfrith, Cyning of Deira and Bernicia." The man was twice the size of her father, Gieva realized, as he was silhouetted against the light coming from the door. She looked past him out into the yard, where she saw the yellow hair of Ælfhelm surrounded by unfamiliar faces. She stood involuntarily as Ælfhelm disappeared into the crowd, and the big man named Ulfric grabbed her arm.

"Where do you think you are going?" he barked, but he did not wait for an answer before addressing the women huddled around him. "You will all stay in here until we figure out what to do with you."

"Please," she said, "Please, don't hurt him." Her voice was barely a squeak, and the man followed her gaze out to Ælfhelm.

The man laughed with his fellows, and repeated her words in a mocking jeer before his voice became cold. "He fought against us, even after we offered reasonable terms. He will be a lesson to you all. Do as we say, and none of you will be harmed. Now sit down."

Gieva obeyed, still looking out of the door.

They waited.

A few hours passed, and Ulfric came back with twenty or so grim-faced warriors, carrying their swords and shields, covered in the blood of those men who had stood in defense of the village.

Gieva glanced out of the door again to try and see what was happening, but the sky had grown dark. Ulfric and his men had brought in torches and hung them in the brackets, and the shifting light made their faces look almost bestial.

"You," he pointed at Gieva, "What food have you got here?"

Gieva swallowed. "Just – just bread and – and some salt fish," she said, her mouth suddenly very dry. They were running low as it was, and she did not want to tell him of the dried meat and extra loaves that they had tucked away for when the stores ran out.

"Get us something to eat. And beer."

Gieva shook her head. "There's no beer, but there is water in the well that's good to drink." He seemed amused by the way she trembled as she spoke.

"Go and draw some water, then," he commanded, and set some of the other women to fetching food for him and his men. Gieva took a pail from next to the door and left the hall. She dared not go anywhere else but the well, but out of the corner of her eye she saw a figure standing upright next to a post in the center of the empty town square.

"Ælfhelm," she squeaked. She looked around, and saw one of the Northumbrians standing with his back to her, pacing lazily near the gate. She took a few steps closer to Ælfhelm. His face was bruised, half his yellow hair matted against his head with blood. He was breathing, but a string of rope was wrapped around his neck, binding him to the post. He fell forward slightly but the rope caught him by the throat. He gasped for breath, leaning against the post again, coughing, and opened his eyes.

When he saw her his mouth moved, but he had no voice. She was frozen, terrified to go any closer. A shout came from inside the hall and Gieva hurried to the well and dropped the pail down into its depths, retrieving the cold, clear water. As she returned to the hall, she saw Ælfhelm coughing again, the rope digging into his flesh.

Without thinking, she rushed forward, scooping water from the pail with her hand and bringing it to his lips, and again, and again, while the Northumbrian guard had his back turned. Ælfhelm sucked the water out of her hand greedily, and Gieva kicked a stone under his feet to stand on, in order to relieve the pressure against his neck.

"I'll get you out of here," she told him, as the Northumbrian turned back toward them and she rushed back to the hall.

When she stepped back inside, she heard a loud scuffling coming from the far end of the hall, though so many people were jostling about that she could not see what was happening. She wedged her way through the circle of people to find them standing around Ulfric, who was holding a woman by the hair as he forced her to the ground. Gieva knew the woman by sight, though she did not know her name. Ulfric wrenched her hair and her eyes blazed as she tried to lash out at him. The other men had stood as well, their drawn swords keeping the rest of the women from interfering.

"I told you," said Ulfric in a terrifyingly calm voice, twisting the woman's hair so that she fell on her back, "that you would be punished if you tried to fight us. Did I not tell you that?" He jerked her head so sharply that she cried out. "Did I not tell you?" he asked again, only a touch of anger in his cold voice.

The girl's eyes streamed, and she only glared at him.

"And yet you try to attack me," Ulfric said. "I tried to give you the chance. I wanted to take this hall peaceably. I have no joy in harming women. I gave you the chance, and you fought anyway."

The fire in the girl's eyes turned to terror as he lifted her by the hair, showing her like a trophy to the assembled women. "Take it as a warning," he shouted at the women.

"Mother!" a small boy of no more than six years cried, his short arms reaching out as a little girl pulled him back, shushing him in a panicked voice. The woman began to scream her children's names, but she was silenced by a blow to her jaw.

Gieva stood rooted amid the crowd of women, frozen in shock as Ulfric's dagger flashed. He forced the blade upward, slicing through the wool of the woman's dress; two other men ripped the fabric from her body, revealing the long trail of blood that Ulfric's knife had left on her back.

They held her down to the ground as Ulfric unbuckled his belt. Gieva wished that she could run away, or that she could rush forward to help the screaming, pleading woman, but she was rooted in place. Her mouth was dry, her stomach was lead, and she could not look away.

The woman had stopped screaming as the fifth man took her. By the tenth, she had stopped crying; her nose pouring blood and her mouth hanging open as she stared with blank eyes at the feet of the rigid women surrounding her. Gieva offered a silent prayer of thanks that the poor woman was unconscious as Ulfric stepped forward once more, lifting his spear.

Gieva did not sleep. She wondered if she would ever sleep again. Perhaps there would not be time. The Northumbrians might kill her before exhaustion would overtake her. Even if she could close her eyes, she dreaded what she would see. She was too frightened to even ask the woman's name. She had watched her die, watched her raped and beaten as her children screamed, and Gieva could not even ask her name.

No one spoke. No one slept. No one dared.

She huddled next to her mother, who might have been made of stone. Gieva held her hand and silently wept, but Mother could not comfort her now. She was far away. Gieva wished desperately that she could follow, that she could escape the fear as her mother did, by ceasing to see it.

She thought of Ælfhelm, slowly strangling just outside the door as exhaustion overtook him. She thought of the nameless woman's eyes staring into nothingness. It made her sick to know she could do nothing, but it was worse to know that she might have done something and simply had not, because she was too weak and scared.

Gieva wept into her mother's shoulder. She was a coward. She was a frightened, weak little girl, and she could not fight monsters.

*****

Sige rose before the sun and left the sleeping men to their rest in the hall. Everything was still hazy, the edges of the buildings blurred in the dim light before the dawn. He did not remember the dream which had startled him into wakefulness, but he went forward into the morning with a strong urge to speak with the gods. There was something calming about the *weoh*, the sacred grove, at any time, but during the early morning the veil between the worlds seemed thinner and he thought perhaps the gods might be able to hear him more clearly.

The pillars representing the gods stood forlornly in the grey morning, the remnants of previous sacrifices scattered by animals across the ground. The statues were man-high and as wide as tree trunks with the faces of the gods carved into them. Thunor's pillar was the easiest to recognize, as his hammer had been shaped of iron and inlaid in the wood, etched with sunwheels and runes of sexual potency and power. Tiw One-Hand was to his right, along with the images of Eostre and Frea beyond him. Someone, probably a woman wishing for a healthy child, had left a basket of fruits at the feet of Frea, while the flower garlands which normally festooned the statue of Eostre had dried and blown away in the summer breezes. The goddess would not mind. She would provide more flowers, after all.

Sige looked at each of them in turn. He spent a particularly long time looking at Tiw's column, naming each of the runes and thanking the God of Battle for his protection, both for himself and for his brothers.

He came last to the statue of Woden the All-Father. It was larger than the others by a head, and while the face had been carved from the wood just like the others, there was an egg-sized pale stone which served to represent the eye he had sacrificed in order to bring the knowledge of poetry to the world. He took a step closer to the statue. The base, like the others, was carved with runes. Sige shivered. The eye of Woden seemed to be watching him, and even though he knew it was only a statue, he quailed.

You should not tamper in this magic, it seemed to tell him. *It is too great for you.*

Sige's mind jumped to Edwin, and the excuses he had made to justify their night together. After all, if the All-Father practiced the same sort of magic. Why shouldn't they? It seemed to Sige that he understood something more of the world after he had been with Edwin. He knew that there was something mystical about it, and he wanted more, but he was afraid to chase it. These runes reached into the very fabric of the world, and could destroy it if left in the wrong hands.

But perhaps his hands weren't the wrong hands. Perhaps the reason he had never felt complete was because he was meant to be a part of it. It felt far more wholesome and natural to have Edwin beside him than it had ever done to lie to himself. Was dangerous honesty better than a lie?

As if summoned by the strange magic of Sige's thoughts, Edwin appeared beside him. He said nothing, but offered a sacrifice at the foot of the statue of Woden and stepped back to stand level with Sige.

Sige felt a compulsion to run away, but an equally strong pull toward Edwin. He therefore stood stock-still, his mind blank and yet swimming with the man beside him.

"You've been avoiding me," Edwin said casually, as if remarking on the weather.

Sige did not know what to say to this and still battled with the urge to run. "I've just been busy," he said lamely. "The *cyning* thinks there might be more attacks near the borders with Mercia, so he's been preparing to call the *fyrd* if need be, and I've been..." He trailed off, realizing that Edwin was not listening. Edwin was eyeing him sidelong, a smirk on his lips.

"Don't look at me like that," Sige said.

"I like looking at you."

He felt a lurch in his stomach, a kind of blissful fluttering that made him want to run, but not in panic. It was the urge to run on firm sand and let the pleasure fill his lungs and his limbs to bursting. He finally turned to look at Edwin properly. "I rather like looking at you too," he said stupidly.

The back of his hand brushed Edwin's, and he felt another lurch at the contact. He felt like his mind was being ripped apart by two horses going opposite directions, and he was deciding which one to follow.

"It's dangerous," he said finally.

"I understand," said Edwin, smiling in a way that looked like a grimace. "This isn't a path a man walks openly." He began to turn to walk away, but before he could get far Sige grabbed his wrist and pulled him back. Edwin's face split into a grin as Sige kissed him. The feeling of placid rightness with the world replaced the lurch in his stomach. The words of the gods filled his mind as he felt the pieces slide into place. It was dangerous, indeed.

"No," Sige said, brushing the hair from Edwin's forehead, "We'd better run."

*****

Eorwald came upon Sunniva as he walked back to the Bricgweard, tired and sore from helping Wulbeorn with the shearing, and wincing as he touched the hoof-shaped bruise in the middle of his chest.

"Well, it's taken care of," she said brightly, walking beside him.

"What's taken care of?"

"Steorra. I've taken care of her. She needn't go back to dirty old husband, and I think it will stop Ceadda meddling with her as well."

"How did you manage that?" Eorwald was intrigued, though annoyed that she had found a solution to the problem that had weighed on his mind.

"Steorra was terrified to press charges upon her husband or on Ceadda, because her position did not allow her much freedom under the law. She only married him because she was born a slave and this was her way into freedom, but as he's a *gebur* it's not that much of a difference is it?"

"I still don't understand…"

"I've paid her husband to divorce her," Sunniva said casually.

Eorwald glared at her, bemused. "But that will mean that she might have to sell herself back into slavery! How is that handling the problem?"

Sunniva rolled her eyes as if he was very dim. "Steorra works for me now. I've had a house built for her, and I am paying her two *scyllingas* a month to make my dresses and to do some other odd jobs for me."

He was amazed, and he did not bother hiding it. It was a brilliant stroke; Sunniva had single-handedly freed the poor girl from an abusive marriage and had given her all the rights of a property-owner, along with a sizeable income.

"And what of Ceadda?" Eorwald asked, seeing a hitch in the plan. "He's tried to go after your Wynne, what's going to stop him going after your servant?"

"If that sack of *swines scitte* wants to go anywhere near my friends or my servants, he will have to go through me," said Sunniva in a hard voice, and added with a small smirk, "and Ceadda knows that going through me will also mean going through my extremely protective father, the *cyning*. Problem solved."

She certainly had a point, Eorwald thought as they walked back to the Bricgweard together. He was still very impressed and only mildly annoyed at Sunniva's cleverness when they had entered the king's house. He settled himself at the board between Sige and Rægen as they sat to their day-meal and asked, "Where is Father?"

"There was another messenger from Grantabricge," Rægen said. "I'd think they'd be finished by now; the messenger arrived an hour ago."

"Athelfrith again?" Eorwald asked. They all glanced at Edwin, who had turned very white. "Do you think he knows Edwin is here?"

"I don't see how he could know," Edwin said uncertainly.

Eorwald frowned. He knew that all it would take would be an overly merry tongue before word got to Athelfrith that Edwin was being harbored in Wuffingham. Silence fell, and everyone looked at their uneaten food.

"We don't know anything yet," Sunniva reasoned, "It could be nothing. You all ought to wait until you know what's going on before you start turning on one another." She gave them all as stern a glance as any their mother could have given them.

It was only a few moments before Rædwald and Eadyth joined them, both looking grave. Father held up a hand to stay the questions that they all had at the ready. "Let me have a moment of peace," he said, easing into his chair like a man twice his age.

They all waited in silence while he speared a salted eel on the end of his knife, but he set it down again with a look at their faces. "Cynhelm has been attacked again," he said. "His wife and son are still missing, and there are more reports of burned farms north of Grantabricge now. They think it was Athelfrith's men. As if there could be any doubt."

Everyone was staring at the king, quiet enough to hear mice scratching in the walls.

"There's nothing for it," Rædwald said after a long pause, "I've sent Ricbert to start calling the *fyrd*. We are going to have to deal with these *wycingas*, these mercenaries, and send a message to Athelfrith. Apparently the first one went unheeded. We leave as soon as preparations can be made. I want everyone assembled in Grantabricge within three days."

"Is that enough time?" Rægen asked, "The local fighters might be called quickly, but how many men could make it there within three days?"

"As many as possible," Rædwald said. "We don't know how many men Athelfrith has sent slinking into our lands, but we will meet them with whatever force we can muster. The *fyrd* will come when they come, and hopefully sooner rather than later."

"Who will remain here?" Eadyth asked, "There is still much to do, and we can't leave the Bricgweard undefended."

"I will take thought for that before we go," Rædwald said, "We might be out of the way here, but there is always the chance that someone might cause problems while our larger force is absent, so I'll have to leave some men to guard Wuffingham and the bridges."

Most of the preparations had been made ready by the following morning. Before the sun had risen completely, Rædwald had called his family together, as well as Ecgric and Edwin, and a few other *thegns*, to make arrangements for his absence.

Ecgric looked excited, clearly ready to see some action; the duties of *ealdorman* and steward clearly had not agreed with him. Sunniva bounced along in his wake, and Eorwald could be certain that they had spent the night together, the way both kept grinning.

Eorwald had few thoughts to spare for his annoyance that Ecgric had ignored their demands that he stay away from Sunniva, however. Sigebryht and Edwin followed after them, though they both looked uneasy and muttered to one another in low voices.

"Well, I've decided," Rædwald said wearily, "My *cwene* refuses to stay behind," he sent a slightly annoyed look at Eadyth, "and so I will be leaving Sunniva to maintain the Bricgweard in our place while we are away."

Sunniva's mouth dropped open, her eyes darting between Father, Ecgric, Mother, and the ground. He thought he heard her mutter, "*Godes hæmað min ears...*" before the king continued.

"There is little chance that the Bricgweard will be attacked during our absence," Rædwald went on, "but I want to leave a few fighters behind in order to protect it. Will any of you volunteer?"

The assembled *thegns* shifted uncomfortably, and a few stepped forward after a long moment. Eorwald knew what they were all thinking, and that was of the shame that would come from having to sit at home while the rest of the men would have the opportunity of battle.

Rædwald nodded curtly in thanks, turning to face Ecgric. "I'm leaving you behind as well, as my steward. You will command the guard here, and advise Sunniva as she requires it of you. I expect everything to be run as usual in my absence," he finished, to Sunniva, "I believe you will be able to deal with whatever small matters might arise."

The excited grin slid off of Ecgric's face, to be replaced by a cold, angry frown. "Dryhten, please," he said in an undertone, apparently trying to keep his voice level, "Haven't I served you faithfully? Am I not one of your best fighters?"

"That is precisely why I am leaving you behind," Rædwald said, "I want someone I can trust to protect my home and my daughter, and someone who knows the affairs of the kingdom so that I don't come home to riots. Am I mistaken in my trust in you?" the tone of his voice left no room for a question.

Ecgric clenched his jaw. "I will do as you ask, Dryhten." he said, bitterness dripping from each word. It would have been amusing if the anger had been coming from any other man, but keeping Ecgric home while a battle was going on was about as good an idea as caging a wolf in a wicker basket. Ecgric left when dismissed, followed closely by Sunniva, both in varying states of bemusement.

"The rest of you," Rædwald said, "Be ready to leave at dawn tomorrow." The rest of the *thegns* and servants turned to continue their preparations, but Eorwald hung back.

"Is it wise to take Edwin with us?" Eorwald asked quietly, when the others had gone.

Eadyth stood close by to listen, her forehead wrinkled with worry.

"There is always a chance that Athelfrith is trying to draw Edwin out," Rædwald conceded, "but if Edwin remains here, the Bricgweard will be in danger of attack, and I will not risk that."

"But Athelfrith does not even know that Edwin is here," said Eadyth in an exasperated tone as if she had already asked this.

"It is still too big of a gamble," Rædwald said, shaking his head. "No, if we are going to draw Athelfrith's eye, I want it where my larger force is."

Eorwald frowned. "Even if Edwin isn't here, it won't stop them from attacking us here while the bulk of our force is drawn away."

"What do you think I am keeping Ecgric here for?" Rædwald asked impatiently, "The Bricgweard won't be defenseless. If Athelfrith wants to send anyone to attack Wuffingham, or any other village or town this side of the Stour, they will run into us first. Besides, it's not just about Edwin anymore. Athelfrith hates me, especially after the fiasco at Grantabricge. He wants revenge and land more than he wants Edwin, I'll wager."

"And what about Sunniva?" Eorwald could not restrain the question. It seemed a very poor choice of ruler, just a girl with no experience in the running of a kingdom. Rædwald and Eadyth looked at one another, as if they had already debated this same question.

"It is better to leave the kingdom in the hands of one of the Wuffingas line," Rædwald said wearily, as if he had spoken these words ten times already, "and I can't spare you or your brother, especially as we'll be losing Ecgric. Sunniva is resourceful and she will be well advised, and the people love her. I don't think it will be a problem, and I trust Ecgric to mind his manners while he is here with her."

Eadyth said nothing, even though she raised an eyebrow. The king gave her a warning look, and Eorwald took it as his signal to take his leave.

*****

Glancing around to make sure he was alone, Sige ducked into the thicket. Moments passed, and his heart sank at the idea that Edwin might not be able to get away.

Then, with a jolt, he heard dead leaves crunch and the familiar face appeared through the trees. Within the space of a heartbeat he had found Edwin's mouth with his own, devouring him like a starving man at a feast. He delighted in the feel of Edwin's flesh against his, as they threw their cloaks onto the leaf-strewn ground.

No blankets, no furs, no fire, just the crackle of leaves underneath them and the sound of their breathing becoming quicker and heavier as the moments passed.

There was something exhilarating about it, but gut-wrenchingly terrifying at the same time. His heart pounded a painful rhythm against his chest, then he drowned in a wave of contentment when they touched.

"We have to stop this," Sige said as he found Edwin's collarbone with his mouth. "Someone is going to find out sooner or later and…"

"We're quite alone," Edwin said. "Besides, you invited me here. The blame is entirely on you." He reached down and slipped his hand under Sige's tunic, loosening the laces of his breeches.

Sige tried to think of a reason not to do so even as he pulled at Edwin's tunic. "Eventually I'm not going to be able to control myself around you," he said, "and then everyone will know."

Edwin started a slow trail down Sige's chest with his mouth, and Sige wound his fingers through Edwin's dark hair as he felt the pressure growing with Edwin's expert attentions. "Maybe I'll beat you to it," Edwin said when he came up for breath, "I'll swear before gods and men that I love you, and then we won't have to sneak into abandoned houses or into the wilderness every time."

Sige dropped to his knees, his eyes now level with Edwin's. "You've never said that before."

"What?"

"You said that you love me."

"Yes," he said, as if it were obvious. "Of course I do."

Sige realized he was frowning, even though he felt as if his heart might burst from his chest.

Edwin made his way down Sige's back, his hands and mouth wandering so that Sige felt as if his skin was on fire. He felt the scrape of Edwin's teeth on his shoulder, and nearly collapsed as a groan of indescribable pleasure escaped him. Edwin's arm snaked around his waist, his hand expertly moving and twisting so that Sige thought he would shatter at any moment. Edwin pulled Sige back against him more insistently as his breathing became ragged and as Sige turned to kiss him he felt Edwin's body tense.

Sige did not let Edwin catch his breath before he had pushed him onto his back. Sige nearly lost himself as Edwin's low groan resounded in his ear as their bodies came together again; he buried his face against Edwin's chest and felt the pressure rising, building through his chest and down his legs and even to his fingertips. He wanted it, he needed it more than he needed food or water or even breath, and yet he did not want it to stop. It was the pain that came when he ran a long way, when he thought he would have to stop, to throw up his hands in frustration, and then –

He clamped his mouth over Edwin's, biting his lip as he felt his own body convulse.

Their hands twined together, and Sige put his head on Edwin's chest and heard his heart thumping as fast as his own. The scent of him was intoxicating, and he felt as drunk as he had been the first time. This was how it was supposed to feel. Nothing forced; nothing painful; nothing awkward, just… right.

Edwin propped himself on an elbow as Sige fell back onto the cloak. He pushed his fingers through Sige's sweat-soaked hair, and his green eyes glinted in the dappled half-light. Sige felt his heart slow as he released himself to Edwin's kiss.

"How did you know?" Sige asked after a long while in unspoiled silence. He had propped himself up as well, so as to look at Edwin properly.

"I didn't know, not really," he said, "I merely hoped. You have no idea how much I wanted you, wanted you to be… like me. I was happy to be your friend but the more time I spent with you the more I could not help myself."

Sige did know how that felt, how uneasy he had been within his own skin for so many years. "But you did know," he said.

Edwin shook his head, "I don't think I have ever fought a battle that required so much courage," he said, "but the drink made me reckless, and I risked everything for the chance to be with you." He bit his lip, half-grinning. "My gamble paid off, I think."

Sige nodded, and raked his fingers through Edwin's rough beard. He swallowed, and felt his brows creasing.

"What's wrong?" Edwin asked.

"I'm worried," Sige said, shaking his head and lifting himself from the ground.

"I told you," Edwin said, doing the laces of his breeches, "No one knows. No one saw either of us come here."

"No, it's not that," Sige said, "I mean, we are marching into a battle. Or at least, I hope we are. I don't like not knowing what I'm walking into."

Edwin took a deep breath. "It will be fine," he said after a while, "I mean, we might end up fighting, but that's a good thing. I'll be happy to feel like I'm doing something useful."

"I don't think you should fight, if it comes to it," Sige said flatly, cutting him off.

"Fuck you," Edwin laughed. "I won't let you have all the fun."

"I'm serious. If you go, Athelfrith will know that Rædwald's taken you in."

"He already knows where I am," said Edwin, "That's why he's up in the Fens."

Sige shook his head. "He doesn't know anything. He suspects. He's trying to draw you out."

Edwin glared at him. "What would you do in my place? If I told you that I don't want you to fight just because you might get hurt? I am not some helpless maiden, Sige, and neither are you. If we must die, then we will do it right and feast with the gods when we are done."

Chapter Eight

Micel Wæl Geslean

To Do Great Slaughter

Lisse rushed to Leik's side as the boy began to wail. Leik had tried to scavenge a spare bit of bread which had rolled into the rushes, and got the back of the Northumbrian's hand across his face for his trouble.

"Keep those fucking rug-rats away from me," the Northumbrian said, now raising his hand against Lisse, who was shouting at him for striking her brother. Gieva had rushed forward and had pushed the two children behind her. Leik was crying, and Lisse tried to comfort her brother as Gieva turned to look at the Northumbrian.

"And quit your moaning," The man said to the little boy, looking past Gieva as if she were not there, "or I'll use my sword next, you little bastard."

"He's just hungry!" Gieva said angrily as Leik began to cry again. "He only wanted some bread!"

Gieva got the man's hand across her face this time, but she turned away from the Northumbrian to shepherd the two children away. She heard Ulfric's deep voice telling the man something, but she did not listen. She was afraid that if she turned to face the man again, she would end up with a blade through her ribs, and then no one would be able to take care of Leik and Lisse.

She touched a hand to her cheek. It did not hurt that much, but she felt tear sting her eyes at the injustice. Lisse kept trying to turn back, as if to fight the guard. Gieva envied her nerve, and hated the fact that an eight-year-old girl was more courageous than a woman of twice as many years.

"Hush," Gieva said, as she steered Leik and Lisse by their shoulders back into the corner. Leik was still crying, and Lisse scowled. Gieva dug in her bag and found a pouch of small, salty dry fish. She looked in the corners of the bag for anything else, but there was nothing left. She handed the children the pouch, and they devoured all that was left inside. Leik held out his small, pudgy hand to Gieva, offering her one of the fishes.

"You eat it, my darling," she said. The boy's face had begun to bruise where the Northumbrian had struck him. The poor thing had only wanted to eat the crust of bread that had been discarded. She wanted to strike the Northumbrian, to let him know how it felt to starve, to be beaten, to watch his friends raped and murdered; but she looked at the ground instead.

Leik climbed into her lap and Gieva kissed his bruised cheek. He did not talk. She had never actually heard the boy speak, except for the single word he had yelled while the Northumbrians were raping his mother. She shuddered at the memory, hoping that he could not see the image as clearly as she could.

She had not been allowed to fetch water again, after one of the guards had caught her trying to sneak a few mouthfuls of water to Ælfhelm the last time. She had nearly retched at the sight of him, pale and bloodied, sitting with his back against the post with a rope still tied around his neck. His eye was puffy and blackened, and a trickle of blood dripped from the bloody scrap of tissue where his ear had been. Her back still ached where the guard had kicked her, but the pain in her body was nothing compared to the agony of waiting.

A couple of the women had offered themselves up to warm the Northumbrians' beds in exchange for extra food for themselves or for their children, and Gieva was beginning to consider doing the same as she tried to stop Leik's whimpering. Even Lisse, the tough, fiery little thing, was sitting quietly in the corner with Gieva's mother, tears staining her cheeks. Mother was still far away, staring blankly at the wall and not responding to her name.

Gieva tried very hard not to cry, but she did anyway.

Why couldn't they just leave? Surely there was nothing holding them here. Why couldn't they just take the share of treasures tucked away in the houses and get out? There was no food, no ale; no reason to stay. Why wouldn't they leave?

Gieva could hear quiet grunting from the corner as one of the Northmen was paid for his generosity. The woman sat up when he had finished, her hair tangled and her eyes glazed. The Northumbrian surely gave her some drink for her services. Maybe it would be easier that way? Maybe if she could drink enough, she might be able to let them…

Their crying had stopped, though the little ones still whimpered in their sleep.

It grew very quiet as Gieva watched the men grope their bed-warmers and fall asleep as well. Gieva heard her own stomach growling, and she drank some water to shut it up. She leaned against the wall, one hand on Lisse's back as she dreamed. Gieva felt her eyelids grow heavy, and she hoped that the sound of a man's screams were coming from her imagination, and not from outside.

Gieva bit back her tears as she soothed Lisse, who was stirring fretfully. She heard the sound again, and it ripped at her heart. The man who had shoved her the day before walked into the hall, looking grumpy. He seized the jug of ale and drank straight from it, wiping his mouth with the back of his hand and finding a place to sleep.

The screaming had stopped. She looked at the two sleeping children beside her, heard the growl of their empty bellies as they dreamed. She remembered the way the woman's body had fallen still as the Northumbrians took her. She cringed at the thought of Ælfhelm, battered and exhausted and slowly dying.

A voice in her mind laughed harshly as she scraped for an idea. It was the voice of Ulfric, harsh and guttural and filled with hate as he reminded her that she was defeated. She could simply give in, take a few scraps of bread for the children if she swallowed her pride and let them do as they wanted. Ulfric's voice was clear. She was just a girl. She was little, she was frightened, and she was weak.

"No," she whispered, so quietly that even she could not hear. She was indeed frightened, so frightened that tears spilled down her cheeks unchecked. If she died, she would die fighting, not starving on her back while foul men took what did not belong to them. It had to end.

Snores filled the darkened hall, though she was sure that none of them came from any of the women. Gieva held her breath and picked her way gingerly over the sleeping bodies. It was almost pitch-dark, but she found her way to the board without waking anyone. They had not thought to take the women's belt knives, so short and useless against warriors. She thanked the gods, for an instant that they thought so little of her.

How easy it would be to put the finger-length blade in the big man's neck! She twitched toward him, but paused, and continued toward the door. With another series of painfully slow, breathless steps, she groped her way back to the side-door and slipped outside into the darkness.

They had forced Ælfhelm to stand again, and he was shaking from cold and exhaustion, his eyes closed and his teeth gritted. She realized with a wave of nausea why he must have been screaming; in the dim light of the moon she could see the dark outlines of long, straight burns against the pale skin of his chest. He opened his eyes as she touched his face with a shaking hand. They widened in shock at the sight of her, turning quickly to fear.

"Go," he croaked.

"I'm going to get you out of here," she told him. "Quickly, before they wake up."

Ælfhelm shook his head. "No," he said, his voice constricted. "They'll kill you. Or worse."

"I don't care," Gieva lied. "I'm getting you out of here."

"I don't think my legs will work."

"I'll carry you," she growled.

He shook his head again. "I'm dying, Gieva. If you love me, you'll put that knife in my heart while I am still brave."

"I can't," she said, the knife nearly falling from her fingers. She circled behind the post and began to saw at the ropes binding his wrists. "I'm going to get you out of here."

"Please help me, Gieva." His knees bent and she heard him struggle for breath as she tried to lift him up again.

She heard voices; she felt the wave of panic overtaking her.

Gieva reached up to cut the rope tied around his neck, but hesitated as she saw the pain in his face as he slid down once more. "Please," his mouth moved, but she heard no voice.

In a quick motion, barely realizing what she was doing, she slid the knife across his throat beneath the rope. His eyes closed as his blood covered her hand, and she felt a scream rise in her chest before she stifled it. She only had a moment to register what she had done before a large hand grabbed her wrist.

"Get back in the hall," she saw fury in Ulfric's eyes as he began to squeeze, "and do not," she felt the bones grind together, "disobey me again," she felt a crack, and fell to her knees. He released her, and she sobbed, holding her broken arm to her body, covered in the blood of her kinsman.

*****

Rægen's attempts at starting a song to distract them from their trudging did little to lighten the mood. Sige tried and failed to stretch the ache out of his neck, which had come courtesy of the previous night's rest on what he could only assume was a hidden boulder under his bedroll.

Edwin walked beside him, the only one who did not seem to be hunched double with boredom. His nearly ever-present smile brightened his green eyes, and Sige caught himself glancing over to look at him, occasionally catching his eye and making his guts writhe. The way Edwin looked at him, he dearly hoped they would camp somewhere with a good, dense thicket.

"Do you smell that?" Edwin's voice was harsh after the silence of their march.

"Must be a farm," Sige said, "They burn peat here, as there's not much wood. It stinks something awful, doesn't it?"

"I don't think that's peat," Edwin said, and Rægen seemed to notice it as well. "No, that's wood smoke. Look!" He pointed westward, and Sige saw the plumes of smoke rising from behind the edge of the wood.

"That's too big for a campfire," Rægen said, always one to state the obvious, "and I don't think there are any farms off that way. Do you reckon we should go and have a look?"

They all looked round at Rædwald, who was a few paces behind and leading his horse. "Go on, then. You four," he indicated Sige, Edwin, Rægen and Eorwald, "and Leofric and Hengest as well. Just go and have a look, and come straight back to report. Straight back," he gave a hard look at Eorwald, "we will water the horses down at that stream, and meet you there."

They gathered together some light gear and set off westward toward the edge of the wood. After the dull trudging of the past two days, it felt good to run, the tall grass whipping his ankles and the shield slapping his back with every step.

They crossed the field to the forest almost silently, and regrouped just inside the stand of trees, listening. The sound of the column had long-since disappeared in the mile or so that they had run, and they heard nothing but the squeak of insects and the barest sound of a rustle through the trees. Rægen led the way, skirting the wood just inside the trees. The smell of the smoke became stronger by the step, mingled with another scent that Sige could not quite place, until they reached the clearing.

Several large mounds were smoldering in the clearing where the wood retreated, the remains of funeral pyres. Stumps and hacked branches surrounded the pyres; they had clearly used up all the dead wood and undergrowth and had hacked off living branches to provide fuel to burn the honored dead. The flames were still raging, licking at the half-burned bodies within, sending up sticky black smoke from the wet, green wood.

Spears were stuck in the ground near the pyres, surmounted with the helms of the men being burned.

"Those are Bernician shields," Edwin said quietly, indicating the painted shields leaning against the pikes.

The wind shifted as they walked closer to the burning mounds. Sige covered his mouth and nose with his hand, looking beyond the pyres. Another mound, unburned, stood a furlong away at the other edge of the clearing, and they made their way towards it. Fifteen or so men, clearly warriors by their build and dress, though stripped of all arms and armor; all had been piled in a heap, mounded with flies and crows so thick that it looked like a giant, writhing black mass. A few shattered Gyrwisc and Englisc shields lay scattered on the field nearby, and Sigebryht was certain that these were the bodies of Cynhelm's men, unburied, unburned, and left to rot.

"They couldn't have buried them?" Eorwald said, not looking at the bodies, as Sige retreated back toward the burning pyres where the smell of the smoke was stronger than that of the rotting carrion.

Rædwald had always burned or buried the corpses of those he had vanquished in battle. If men fought bravely, they deserved to be sent off properly, no matter their allegiance. That was how things worked. It was disgusting, unnatural, to leave the bodies of defeated warriors to rot in the sun like this, and Sige had to hold his breath to keep his stomach from hurling up the meager meal he had eaten on the road.

"I don't see anyone around," Sige said, "but someone is bound to be close by to collect the bones when the fire burns out." The scent of the dead men came again with a shift in the breeze and he tried not to gag.

Edwin shifted beside him, and Sige knew that he felt just as uneasy about how the northerners had left their dead enemies, in the very same glade where the Northumbrians' own warriors' pyres blazed in glory. It was an added insult, a final blow.

Edwin swallowed before saying, "They are probably in those woods somewhere, but they cannot be far."

The men all looked at one another for a moment, as if deciding if they ought to trace the northerners' steps, but Hengest pointed over Sige's shoulder.

They all spun round to see the back of some young man disappearing into the wood at a run. They looked at Rægen, who nodded once, before setting off at a silent run after the man. Only a short way beyond the trees, and Sige could hear the unmistakable sounds of men's panicked voices.

"Shields," Rægen said, slinging his own off his back and drawing his sword. They all did likewise, and Sige felt the satisfying scrape of his sword, Hryðlig, against the leather of its scabbard. They crept the last few feet into another clearing.

Rægen opened his mouth to speak to them, but in a flash of blades the Northumbrians surged forward. There was no time to form a shield wall or to do anything but react. Someone smashed into Sige's shield, and he pushed the wood upward to hack at the exposed knees of his attacker. The man went down and Sige jumped over him, finding Edwin a few paces away. Edwin had put the edge of his sword in one man's neck, but he was clutching his side and grimacing.

"I'm fine," Edwin said, waving Sige's concern away. The others had made short work of the Northumbrians, though they had been outnumbered. The one who had run off from the clearing was lying on the ground, barely twitching, and the man Sige had taken down was clutching his ruined knee. The rest were dead.

They had clearly stumbled upon a camp in the small clearing; a cook pot sat next to the fire and bedrolls were scattered throughout. No more than five or six men had made camp here, by the number of bedrolls.

A few yards away, tied to either side of a tree by their wrists, were two prisoners. One was slumped forward, held up only by the pulling of his shoulders against his bonds, and the other leaned back, pale as death but breathing slowly.

Sige and Edwin made their way to the tied men and cut the rope that bound their wrists together. The slumped man fell face-forward, clearly dead, and the pale man's shoulders creaked audibly when his bonds were cut.

"Who are you?" the pale man said, and his voice was cracked. He was naked from the waist up, and a long gash from collarbone to nipple was festering. Sige could see the white of his ribs through the maggots which had latched to the infected flesh. He was old, though still hale and grim as a warrior.

"We are Rædwald's men," Edwin said, "What has happened here?"

"Battle," the man croaked. "the northerners—" he sucked in a painful breath, the red skin on his chest stretching painfully, "Northerners were at the fight at Grantabricge." He closed his eyes, He opened them again and continued. "Fifteen *thegns* and as many *fyrdmen*. Three days ago. All dead …all …all but me." He leaned against the tree, his voice spent.

"These can't be the only Northumbrians, if so many Gyrwa and Engla were slaughtered," Sige said, "Where are the rest? Did you hear them say anything?"

"They went to… Ealdham," he did not open his eyes, "My wife and daughter… are there… please help them…" he gave a shuddering breath with each word, "I thought … they'd be safe… find them."

Sige nodded and the man took a deep, labored breath.

"I wish I could have died well," he said, his eyes still closed and his voice becoming fainter. "I've failed you, Dryhten," he looked back at the dead man.

They watched as his head drooped, and a few moments passed before his breathing stilled.

"Godes hæmað min ears," Rægen said as they arrived to move the dead men into more dignified positions. "It's Cynhelm."

Hengest kicked the ground, and Leofric cursed under his breath.

"Who is that man?" Rægen asked, "I recognize him. Do you know him?"

Sige shrugged. "He is a *thegn* of Cynhelm, though I don't know his name." he swallowed roughly. "He said the Northmen came from the fight at Grantabricge, and the rest of their force went to Ealdham."

"Where is that?" Edwin asked, trying to pretend that he had not been clutching his side.

"North of here," Rægen said, "It's not even a town, just a little village."

"Someone should go and warn them that the Northumbrians are headed that way." Eorwald said.

"They might have made it already," Edwin said, "Those men have been dead at least a few days."

"They might have needed time to lick their wounds if they have just fought a battle," said Sige. "And even a little village would be a good place to do so. If there are women and children there, we have to help them."

"We'll go," Rægen said, and Eorwald nodded in agreement.

"The cyning said –" Edwin began, but everyone gave him a look so sharp that he shut his mouth with a snap.

"You ought not to go alone," Sige said, ignoring Edwin, "Hengest and Leofric, you should go as well. Edwin and I will get back to the column and tell the *cyning* what has happened. You're more likely to run into a fight than we are. We'll send reinforcements to Ealdham behind you."

The four others filled their waterskins and took a few bites of the Northumbrians' hastily abandoned food to give them speed on their swift march, and set off northward out of the clearing.

"There's no need to look so put-out," Sige told Edwin.

"No one is put-out," Edwin said, "But I could have gone with them."

"I think we had both best tell the *cyning* and gather some reinforcements," Sige invented, "And we have to deal with that." He gestured at the single remaining Northman, whose slashed leg was pouring blood as he tried to get to his feet.

Sige approached the man, though Edwin grabbed his arm as if to stop him. Sige ignored it. "You can't walk, and I won't carry you," he told the Northumbrian.

The man grimaced. “Let me die well,” he said, “If you leave me here I’ll die anyway. Let me go with a sword in my hand.”

Edwin gave him a disgusted look. “After your men left a dozen good warriors to rot with no burial or pyre? Why should we give you the honor of a noble death?” He turned away from the man, whispering to Sige, “Let the wolves have him.”

Sige wanted to walk away, but instead kicked a dropped sword to the man. “On your feet.”

The man got to one foot with a cry of pain, balancing with the point of his sword in the dirt. He limped forward, his ruined knee gaping and gushing. He lunged a few times, unsteadily but with all the force and fury a man could offer when half of his blood pooled at his feet.

Sige smacked the blade away with his own, and then with a smooth motion, he buried Hryðlig to the hilt in the man’s chest.

“He didn’t deserve a good death,” Edwin said with distaste, when the man’s shattered leg stopped twitching.

“Many people don’t get what they deserve,” Sige said, wiping Hryðlig on an abandoned bedroll and sliding it back into its sheath.

*****

“What do you reckon we should do?” Eorwald asked, “go and talk to them, or do you think we ought to wait for reinforcements?”

Rægen’s face was set and he shook his head. “I don’t know,” he said slowly, “I don’t think there are more than twenty men at the most, but there could be more in the hall.”

“I say we go and talk to them,” Leofric suggested, “Might only be a few, and we can pretend we’ve got a whole host waiting if they don’t want to cooperate.”

“They would kill us, host or no,” said Eorwald bitterly. He did not trust the Northumbrians to offer any protection to messengers, not after he had seen what they had done to their defeated foes.

Their debate was unneeded, however, when they heard the sounds of men running up behind them; he spotted Sige and Edwin, and a handful of others probably sent by the *cyning* when the other two had brought back the news. Eorwald and the others met them at the bottom of the knoll, just out of sight of the village behind a narrow copse of trees.

"Right," Sige said when he had caught his breath, "What's the plan?"

Everyone looked at Rægen expectantly, who seemed rather surprised to be suddenly in command of half an army. "They've just fought a battle," Rægen said slowly, "So I imagine they're not at their full strength, whatever their numbers. There might be a dozen, or there might be half a hundred men stowed away in those buildings. There's no way to tell unless we go and see for ourselves."

"How do we know they're not going to just kill us the moment we try to approach?" Sige asked. "They must've heard us coming, and they'll have had time to prepare."

"I'll go and talk to them," Edwin said.

"No, you won't," said Rægen, "I will. You may follow me if you wish, but I will speak to them." His tone did not allow for argument.

There were several men outside the gate when they approached, some were dressed for war, but the one who stepped forward to greet them looked as if he had just woken up. He stood inside the gates, with no sword or shield or spear, his arms crossed and looking rather amused. Eorwald realized, with a surge of hatred as he looked at the grim face, that this was Ulfric, the same Northumbrian who had been sent back to the North after the battle at Grantabricge.

"What do you want?" he shouted without preamble.

"We are taking this village back," Rægen shouted, "You are in Englisc lands, and we will give you one hour to surrender Ealdham and go home, or you will all be slain."

Ulfric barked a laugh. "We do not surrender. We will burn the village to the ground before we yield it up."

Rægen's face was hard. "You should know by now that there is nothing for Northumbrian scum in Englisc lands but death."

A man had appeared next to Ulfric and was holding a torch, which illuminated his gaunt face in the failing sun. He had stepped backward toward the village hall, walking back and forth and holding the torch aloft threateningly.

"We will burn it down," the man said, "One more step and it will burn!"

Ulfric did not take his eyes from Rægen as the smaller man paced even quicker behind him. A few other men appeared at his shoulder, carrying bucklers and axes and swords, ready for the fight.

They all stood in silence for a long moment, glaring at one another, as the Engla slid into position, shields locked over one another's.

"Very well then," Rægen said, and the Engla warriors pushed forward.

The two guards went down almost immediately when they passed, and a handful of other men with weapons appeared and formed a crude shield wall. The torch-bearing man disappeared, but in the scuffle no one knew or cared what had happened to him.

The shield wall broke, the men scattering. Rægen and Leofric followed after, while Eorwald and the others made quick work of the Northumbrian warriors in the square before darting after them.

It was disappointing, the way the two-dozen Northumbrians scattered into the village. Eorwald and his companions had to chase them down piecemeal, knocking them down one by one until the Northumbrians surrendered or were killed.

After two men had found their deaths on the edge of Wear-gbana, and after Eorwald had received a nasty gash across his cheek from a seax, he led two captives out the western gate to meet the others outside the village. They found Rægen and Leofric standing over Ulfric. The big Northumbrian had clearly been pushed face-forward onto the ground. His face was grazed with pieces of gravel imbedded in his skin, and Rægen's seax was at his throat. The smaller man was lying dead a few paces away, and the other prisoners were pushed to kneeling positions with their hands on their heads.

"Why are you here?" Rægen hissed at the man.

Ulfric sneered, and spat on the ground at Rægen's feet.

"Where are the women?" Rægen asked, his voice level but his face full of anger, "There were women and children in this village, and men guarding it. Where are they?"

"Those were hardly men guarding this village," Ulfric said, "Greybeards and boys, all of them. They're dead; as well they should be after trying to fight us."

"And now your men are all dead for it as well," Eorwald

said, and then turning to Rægen, added, "They've burned the warriors' bodies, at least. I smelled the pyre. But I think the women must be hiding somewhere."

Ulfric laughed. "We lit no pyre for those fools. They are rotting in the sun yonder." He jerked his chin westward, "And those women and their whelps are still in the hall."

Eorwald frowned. If there was no pyre, then something was burning. Perhaps even captured, Ulfric had made good on his promise.

Eorwald shared a glance with Rægen, who understood immediately. Looking back at toward the center of the village, they saw a massive plume of smoke illuminated by the blood-red glow of flames.

"You lot, watch them," Rægen told Leofric, and he and Eorwald ran along the edge of the fence and back through the gate.

The thatched roof had caught almost immediately, and half of the building was nearly collapsing under its own weight as the fire leapt to the adjacent buildings. The main door had been barricaded with heavy logs to prevent anyone getting out and interfering in the battle, and all of them were now on fire.

"Do you hear that?" Eorwald heard screaming through the roar of the flames, and his insides turned to lead. "There are still people in the hall!"

They ran toward the back of the building, where they knew there should be another door. Indeed, this one was barricaded with heavy logs and bits of furniture, but none had caught fire yet. Eorwald realized dimly that there should have been more people standing around the hall, watching it burn; but the yard was empty.

Together they pulled the ballast away, and were able to open the door when a roaring crash and a rush of burning wind knocked them backwards. The front half of the hall had collapsed, throwing ash and smoking embers into the air. They heard more screams from inside, and had to push aside a flaming timber before they were able to enter the hall.

The flames illuminated the faces of two small children and a young woman who seemed to be shielding them with her body. The boy wailed and clutched the sleeve of the girl, who was lying unconscious on the floor. Eorwald tucked each of the children under an arm and pushed out of the hall as the boy screamed and the girl flopped listlessly in his arms.

The young woman was in Rægen's arms a moment later, and two more times they returned from the hall, but on Eorwald's fifth try Rægen yanked Eorwald away from the door by the back of his shirt. Eorwald whipped around in anger at his brother, but in the space of a heartbeat he heard the sickening sound of wood creaking and a roar of flame, and the two of them were knocked backwards a second time. Eorwald shouted in anger, coughing from the smoke and ash that filled his lungs. "There were still people in there!" he bellowed. If the door had not been blocked; if only they could have gotten in there sooner…

The color of the world went from dull brown to a vivid, bloody shade of red, and Eorwald left Rægen kneeling beside the bodies. He strode purposefully out the gate, to where the prisoners were being held by their remaining company.

Without a word, without a thought, Eorwald whipped Weargbana from her sheath and shoved the point through Ulfric's teeth and out the back of his skull. In another swift motion, he had removed the blade and sliced through the neck of another of the prisoners. The man jerked violently as his head flopped sideways, hanging by a strap of flesh.

He felt several pairs of arms grab his own, wrenching his sword away. He knew he was shouting something, but his mind had disconnected from his body.

After a moment of struggle, he fell limp and the color of the world returned to normal. He was shaking. Rægen was looking at him with a mixture of fury and complete bewilderment, and he saw the bodies of the two prisoners still twitching on the ground around him.

"What is wrong with you?" Rægen shouted at him.

"They – they killed them –" Eorwald gasped, wrenching himself out of the restraining hands. His throat felt raw from breathing in the smoke, or was it from his shouting?

"Those men were prisoners!" Rægen said, "They'd surrendered!"

"They locked them in," Eorwald growled, "They locked them in, and burned them!"

Rægen said nothing, but Eorwald felt disgusted with himself. Unbidden, he saw the faces of those women and children whom he had seen moments before the hall collapsed; it made him feel nauseated and furious all over again.

"Come on," Rægen said, and they left the company and the remaining prisoners, "We've got work to do."

There were five figures in the yard, all covered in dirt and ash: a woman of about twenty years, an old crone who was small and light as a bird, and three children. Rægen had bent over the younger woman, who was stirring feebly, her eyelids fluttering. Eorwald checked the older woman, and found she had no heartbeat. One of the children was motionless and only breathed weakly, though her brother shook her with all his little strength. Eorwald pushed a waterskin into the boy's hand to calm his racking cough. He knelt to see to the youngest child, a girl of no more than three, but stopped before he touched her as he saw the burned blood on the side of her head and her wide, staring eyes. He shut them for her, his hands shaking.

Sigebryht had long-since taken the remaining prisoners away, and after a long while the hall had begun to smolder.

Everyone seemed to skirt around Eorwald, who walked to the other end of the yard. A man hung by a rope around his neck, tied to a pole in the center of the square, his knees buckled and his face a sickening shade of purple. He had probably stood like this for days, Eorwald realized, seeing the short length of the rope that would have prevented the man from even relaxing his back without strangling to death. It was a cruel, slow way to die, but Eorwald realized that the man's throat had been cut. *Some mercy, at least,* Eorwald shuddered, and took out his knife to cut the bonds holding the man to the post as Rægen came to help him.

Neither of them spoke for a long time, but Eorwald was so distressed by the way that his brother looked at him, that he had to break the silence. "I didn't mean to..." Eorwald tried to say, "I didn't think..."

"No," Rægen said, "you didn't think. That was a stupid, stupid thing to have done." His face was twisted and furious; Eorwald could understand the anger, but the disappointment in Rægen's face made Eorwald have to look away.

"I am sorry," he said lamely. "But you saw what they did! What if we had come a moment later? I had to avenge them!"

Rægen finally lost control of himself. "Killing unarmed prisoners is not the way to seek your vengeance, Eorwald! You know better than that. You *are* better than that."

Eorwald wished that Rægen would just stripe his hide and have done. Anything would be better than the look of disappointment he now wore.

The column had arrived on the outskirts of the village a few hours later. Rædwald climbed down from his horse and handed the reins to a servant, helping Eadyth down from her own mount. Rægenhere immediately told them what had happened, carefully omitting Eorwald's actions. Eorwald stood several paces back, not meeting anyone's eyes.

"Are you hurt?" Eadyth asked, examining the blood from the gash on Eorwald's cheek.

"It's nothing, just a flesh wound." He said expressionlessly.

"I'm going to have to sew it shut or it will never heal properly, but we will have to wait until the pavilion is set up and I can get my things."

Rægen came to them a few moments later. "Mother, there are some people who were hurt in the fire; they are sick from the smoke. I've given them water, but I don't know what to do for them." Eorwald noticed that Rægen looked away from him pointedly as he spoke and it made Eorwald feel disgusted with himself all over again.

Eadyth departed and Eorwald stood and limped to meet his father, who was directing the establishment of the camp. The tents and pavilions were being erected like a tiny village some distance from the eastern edge of Ealdham, and Eorwald felt useless and jittery as he watched.

"Not the outcome I would have preferred," Rædwald said, looking at the still-smoldering buildings and chewing the inside of his mouth as he sent several men to take care of the bodies. "Disgusting savages, the lot of them."

Eorwald wordlessly nodded, worried that Rægen had said something about what he had done, but if Rædwald knew about it he did not say anything.

"What about the men killed near the wood?" Eorwald asked, "The Northumbrians left them all to rot." Eorwald pulled a bundle off of the wagon and walked with his father as they carried the packs to the camping site.

"I've sent some men to bury the bodies of Cynhelm's men, but to send Cynhelm's body back to Grantabricge. He and his wife and son can be buried there."

"So you've found them?" Eorwald knew that they had been missing since their farm near Grantabricge had been attacked, but everyone had hoped the *ealdorman's* family had survived at least.

Rædwald was frowning, his beard bristling. "In one of the farms along the road. The house was burned, but their bodies were there. The boy was hanging from a tree near the house."

Eorwald took a deep breath to keep the world from turning red again in his anger. "And Cynhelm's wife?"

Rædwald clenched his jaw. "She was not far away, naked and bound and left for dead. The boy has been dead for days, but she must have only died last night or early this morning."

Eorwald punched the side of the wagon. "*Weargas,*" he said through clenched teeth, "I swear by the spear of Woden that I will make them pay for their actions."

The king raised his eyes to Eorwald's face and looked at him as if to say, *don't pretend you haven't already seen to that.*

Chapter Nine
Bearn Wulfa
Children of the Wolf

gentle but soaking rain was coming down outside, and Sunniva snuggled deeper into the furs of the bed. She knew it was some time in the early morning, but she would not stir for hours if she could help it. Normally she would have been woken by her mother, who always seemed to rise at the break of day, and Sunniva grinned to herself as she stretched and rolled onto her side, rejoicing in the laziness of the morning.

Ecgric had arms folded under his head as he lay on his stomach, and she watched him sleep for a while in mild interest. She liked the way his skin felt under her fingers as she dragged them over the broad lines of his shoulders. He rolled onto his back, and she nestled herself inside his arm. She let her fingers continue their wandering over his chest and his stomach, and she could see his body responding to her touch even as he slept.

"Wake up," she whispered, and let her lips linger in the space just below his ear.

He shook his head. "I'm having a good dream."

Sunniva grinned and flipped her leg over his hips. Only when she had eased herself down did he open his eyes, running his hands up her waist. She closed her eyes and delighted in the feel of him. Hours passed, and the rain continued, and they dozed and kissed and talked and made love again and again, until Sunniva was as exhausted and content as she had never remembered feeling before. Only when her stomach made a loud growl, sometime around noon, did she finally rise and pull a dress over her head.

"Is this what it would be like to be married to you?" Ecgric asked, "Because I'm beginning to see the benefit."

"I'd make a terrible wife," she said, slipping on shoes.

"You don't need to be a good wife," he said, laughing, "You're rich. You can pay people to weave and sew and spin for you, and we can spend all our time making sons."

Sunniva smacked him playfully in the chest with the back of her hand, and he caught her by the wrist, pulling her close to kiss her.

"You know I'm right," he said, still holding her close to himself, brushing her hair back from her shoulder.

"Oh, come now, Ealdorman. You have to know by now that I only intend for you to be my bed-slave." She put her arms around his neck like a slave's collar, and as he kissed her again she knew it would be even longer before they would eat.

"Why wasn't this dealt with in the Folkmoot?" Sunniva sat in her father's high seat, one leg tucked under her and the other dangling so that her toes brushed the raised platform on which the chair rested. "It seems a simple matter of property damage to me."

"This en't summat you can deal with in the Folkmoot," the *ceorl* grumbled. He had a leather cap out of which straggly wisps of bone-white hair were peeking, and eyes were sunken deep into his skull of a face. "Them foreigners, they won't be answering to the Folkmoot."

Sunniva frowned. "Do you mean the priests?"

"Aye, they'd be the ones," the *ceorl* said, "The dark folk, the ones what brought that god nailed on a tree," he spat on the floor "blood magic, that is; don't never trust a man what does blood magic...."

"The shrine was on your land?" Sunniva interrupted him.

"Leofric's land, my lady," he said, "he is with the *cyning* now, elsewise I would've gone to him first, but the fire spread to my house and burned it to the ground. It's only lucky my wife and girl were not there, thank the gods."

Sunniva's head began to ache. "Do you know where the Christians are now?" she asked.

He shook his head. "They wore those great black cloaks so I couldn't see their faces, and I en't as fast as I was once, else I would've tried to catch 'em. I heard 'em though, shouting about how this was the lord's work or some such nonsense." He spat again.

She considered a moment, "they said they were doing the lord's work? I can't imagine that my father or Leofric would command such a thing."

"I don't think they meant an actual lord," Ecgric said. He had remained silent until now, looming nearby as Sunniva met with farmers and *ceorls* and performed all the duties her parents normally did. "The Christians call their god 'lord,'" he said, "and it makes for a bit of confusion."

"Begging your pardon, my lady," the *ceorl* continued, "Y'ought to punish them for this. It weren't no problem when they were just roaming about saying their piece, but this..."

"I've heard of a few fanatics running up and down the Stour, nailing crosses to Sacred Oaks, pulling down shrines to Woden, and the like. They were caught by one of the *thegns*, but his wife's a Christian and she persuaded him to let them go without punishment." Ecgric said, scowling.

Sunniva rubbed her eyes, little stars appearing in her vision. "Where are your wife and daughter now?" she asked the *ceorl*.

"A kinsman of mine is letting us stay with him and his family in Wuffingham."

Sunniva looked pleadingly at Ecgric to give her some guidance, but he merely shrugged. She had only watched her father arbitrate disputes a handful of times, and in those cases it was usually straightforward. Hear the case, deliberate with the council, and then decide on *wergild* or a flogging or hanging, depending on what the situation may warrant. What happened, then, when the crime was committed by foreign priests in lands owned by one of the king's men?

"I don't think I can make a judgment for you yet," she said, hopelessly, "I would need to speak with the one being accused, and he is not here."

She heard the *ceorl* mutter something about "little girl" under his breath, and she glared at him, raising her voice to something she hoped was commanding. "We will give you a few men to repair your house, and materials as well," she said with dignity, "When the *cyning* returns, you may bring your case before him. I suggest you track down your missing defendant before then. See Gamol and he will provide you with what you need. You may go."

"I feel like an idiot," she said to Ecgric when the men had gone.

"It's difficult," Ecgric said, "I think even the *cyning* would have his doubts."

"Who let those priests go without punishment?" she asked in frustration.

"I think it was Ælle," said Ecgric. "Would you like me to send for him?

"Don't bother," Sunniva said, waving a hand, "Father can deal with them." She grumbled a bit more under her breath. "It's so vexing. Why should these men be given special treatment? They're foreigners; they should not have rights beyond those of a slave. Not even visiting royalty are allowed to flout the law like this."

Ecgric shrugged. "They have a power over the common folk. The Christians give them hope at a better life, and they grasp at the idea. I think you know as well as anyone that it is unwise to raise the wrath of the people who put food on our table."

Sunniva chewed her lip. "You think I did the right thing then?"

"I don't think you could have done anything else."

Sunniva hated being unsure of herself, and hated even more the fact that she was asking Ecgric for his advice. "I wish I were more like my mother," she said, "No one would dare call her a stupid little girl."

"Your mother has also been a mistress of a household since she was younger than you," Ecgric was laughing. "I'm sure she had plenty of people call her a stupid little girl in her time."

She supposed he was right, but somehow had trouble fully believing it. Mother would have stabbed a man in the eye for such comments, not sat apologetically before an old freedman and offered him labor and supplies in exchange for his insults. Furthermore, she would have cut off a man's balls for looking at her the way Ecgric was looking at Sunniva now.

"What?" she asked, narrowing her eyes at him as he took a step closer.

"I think that was the last of them," he said, smiling that half-smirk that made his eyebrow rise. "We seem to be alone."

"No," she said, grinning now as well, "now is not the time, nor the place."

"For what?" He asked innocently, "I merely observed that the hall is empty. You've dealt with everything that needed attention, and you are free to do whatever you wish for the remainder of the day."

"I don't need your permission," she snapped.

"As you say my lady." He was standing very close to her; she could smell the sweat and dust on him. A moment passed as she glared at him, and he smiled amusedly back at her.

"Get out of the way." She tried to get to her feet, to push past him, "I want to find Paulinus."

"Have you decided to accept him and be baptized then?" Ecgric mocked, still blocking her departure.

"I want to tell him to keep his dogs in line," she said crossly, "I won't have the gods taking out their vengeance on us just because some stupid priests don't know how to control themselves. They might not be his, but he can still spread the word through his followers."

"Are you sure you wouldn't rather put it off until tomorrow?" Ecgric asked, "Gods know the priest will still be here, you can talk to him then." He was leaning over her, one hand on each arm of the chair. She felt a flush rise in her chest and creep up her neck as his lips brushed her collarbone.

"Not here," she breathed.

"How about here?" she felt the scratch of his beard on her cheek as he kissed the hollow under her ear. She let him linger for a moment before she pushed him away. "How will I be able to prove that I am not some stupid girl playing at being a *cwene*, if you keep distracting me? Don't you have some work to do?"

"Oh, the work of the steward is never really done, is it?" Ecgric said, "But what is life without some distraction?" He knelt in front of the seat, as if he were receiving a gift from the king, and pulled her to the edge.

He had put his hand underneath her skirt and it was halfway up her thigh when she saw the slightly hunched silhouette of Gamol standing in the doorway, and she kicked Ecgric away. He swept back from her in a fluid motion, as if he had been doing nothing more than retrieving a fallen trinket.

"What is it?" she snapped at Gamol, who looked unreasonably flustered.

"Please, my lady, you're needed outside," he stammered, "there's been an incident." He flitted back out of the hall and

Sunniva heard shouting. When she looked into the yard, she found two men holding the old farmer by his skinny arms, as the ancient man tried with all his little strength to throttle Paulinus.

"You have no quarrel with me," Paulinus was saying, holding up his hands, "I only do the work of the Lord."

"That's exactly what you said before, when you went and burned down my house, you dirty great *wearg*!" the *ceorl* had a maddened look in his eyes; Paulinus, only confusion.

"Stop this!" Sunniva shouted, walking between the two men, and turning to the farmer. "I told you that you would have justice for your burned home, or are the *cyning*'s words not good enough for you?"

"You're not the *cyning*," the *ceorl* spat.

Sunniva stiffened, raising her eyebrows. She felt immense satisfaction at the cowering look that appeared on the old *ceorl*'s face when he realized what he had said. He stammered something, but she cut him off.

"I speak with the *cyning's* voice when he is gone from this hall, and I say that your family shall have justice for what happened to your property. I suggest you leave here before I have you flogged for attacking an unarmed man in the *cyning's* hall." Her voice was cool and firm, even though her hands were shaking with fury.

"It may not have been him, but it were his folk!" the *ceorl* said, "Them foreign devils and their blood magic, y'ought to send them away, not me!"

"The only devils here are those of anger and greed," Sunniva heard Paulinus say from behind her, and she resisted the urge to roll her eyes.

"Go home," Sunniva told the *ceorl*, who shot a spiteful look at Paulinus and then at Sunniva herself, and departed.

"Are you injured?" Sunniva asked the priest, who shook his head mournfully.

"Only my pride, perhaps," he said, "But I daresay I have enough of that particular vice that I could stand to lose some."

"He had no right to attack you, and I apologize," Sunniva said.

"He was angry," Paulinus said, "It seems a few of my wayward brothers have a hard time controlling themselves when the spirit moves them."

"The spirit seems to be moving them quite frequently, of late," Sunniva said. "You are their elder, and you were supposed to keep them in line. The *cyning* will not tolerate violence in the name of your god, and nor will I."

"I do apologize, noble lady," Paulinus lowered his eyes, but his tone was condescending, as if the acts of violence perpetrated by his fellows were simply a small annoyance not worthy of much thought. "I try to encourage them to use peaceful discourse to spread the message of Jesus Christ, but sometimes that lesson needs to be re-learned by even the best of men."

"They will be punished," Sunniva said, "they have committed violent crimes against our gods and our folk, and it cannot be tolerated. You know these men, clearly, and you know what they did. I charge you to bring them to the *cyning* upon his return so that he can see that justice is carried out. I want you to swear on your Christ that you will do this."

Paulinus hesitated, "It is a grievous sin to swear by the Lord's name in vain."

"Are you the type of man to swear vain oaths?" Sunniva shot back, "I expect you to see that justice is done, or you will face the wrath of the *cyning* and the gods. Do you swear?"

Paulinus sighed, gave her a look that was simultaneously condescending, exasperated, and lecherous, and then nodded. He touched the cross hanging around his neck and said, "I swear it, then, in the name of Jesus Christ Almighty."

Sunniva nodded with finality, turning her back on the black-robed man.

"I don't think even the cyning could have improved on that," Ecgric said. "I didn't think it was possible to frighten sense into a Christian."

"Well," said Sunniva, smirking, "They wanted one of the Wuffingas line in charge. What sort of wolf would I be, if they thought I had no teeth?"

*****

Gieva knew that she was dead. She had died next to the small back door of the village hall as she hammered it with her fists, as the children cried next to her, as she felt her nails break against the wood as she tried to pry it open, as she inhaled the ash and smoke and coughed it out again.

The mighty crossbeam had fallen, wreathed in flame, between her and the remaining women, who were screaming and shoving their weight against the front doors. The smoldering thatch drifted to the floor, catching on her dress even as she tried to beat out the embers with her shattered hand. Leik and Lisse had stopped crying, and Gieva had slid down the wall, watching the flames creep nearer.

Her wrist had hurt so terribly when Ulfric had crushed it in his strong fist, but this was worse, having her lungs burn her from within as she waited for her eyes to close for the last time. She wished she had someone to release her from it, as she had done for Ælfhelm. At least then it would not hurt as much as being burned alive.

Death did not feel the way she thought it would, when it finally came. She thought it would be like floating, drifting into some sort of afterlife, but it did not feel that way at all. It felt like she was being dragged, crying and gasping, and light hit her eyes and made her cry out in pain, but her throat was raw and the cry turned into a racking cough that brought the taste of blood to her mouth. She saw someone's face above her own, hovering for a moment as she sucked in great gasps of air, and then it was gone and she heard the sound of crashing and yelling and running, as the world around her faded.

The first thing she felt was the texture of wool under her fingers. Was she weaving? The afterlife was supposed to be similar to the waking world, and she assumed she must be performing her normal tasks. It was thick, utilitarian wool, but still soft; the type she would have used to make a blanket. She rubbed her fingertips across the weave, the only thing she knew in that moment.

The second thing she felt was a sharp pain shooting up her wrist as she moved her hand, but when she cried out the sound grated out of her raw lungs, and she began to cough. Then, the third thing she felt was a hand lifting her head, and the rim of a cup being put to her lips. She drank without opening her eyes, recognizing the soothing taste of willow bark and sage and honey as the liquid calmed her coughing.

Gieva opened her eyes to find a figure kneeling next to her. She blinked several times, before the figure came into better focus. The woman had an angular, intimidating face surrounded by thick dark hair tied with a kerchief, but her silver eyes were kind and Gieva felt her body relax slightly.

"I wondered when you would be coming back to us," the woman said, brushing Gieva's hair out of her face.

Gieva's eyes adjusted and she realized that she was lying on something soft, underneath a shelter of white sailcloth. "Am I dead?" she tried to ask, but her voice caught and came out in a hoarse growl.

The woman smiled at her. "No, you're not dead, but you came very close. What is your name?"

She had to think for a moment before she could remember her own name. "Gieva."

"My name is Eadyth," the woman said. "You're safe now. You breathed in a lot of smoke, so it will hurt for a while to breathe and talk. You're in the camp of Rædwald Cyning of the Engla."

Gieva sighed in relief at the sound of that name. "Does that mean the Northumbrians have gone?" she asked, despite the grating in her lungs.

"For now, we hope," Eadyth told her. "You needn't worry about that now. You're safe here, and you need to rest, but first I need to tend to your arm." She pulled out a small knife from her belt and carefully cut the sleeve of Gieva's dress, which was still stained with Ælfhelm's blood, though Eadyth did not question her about it. When the fabric came away, her skin was deep blue and her wrist twice its normal size. Eadyth cleaned the dried blood away and splinted Gieva's arm with a piece of wood, wrapping it from fingers to elbow with a length of cloth.

The sharp pains which had been searing through Gieva's arm turned into a dull ache as Eadyth helped her strip off the filthy torn dress in which Gieva had almost died, and Gieva awkwardly stuck her splinted hand into the sleeve of a fresh tunic. It was a man's garment to be sure; her legs stuck out oddly in front of her and the fabric billowed around her body, but it was clean and soft. She could not care much, at the moment.

Gieva had settled back onto the bed when she noticed the ashy and blood-stained boots of a man standing outside the mouth of the tent, their owner's face just out of the line of her vision.

"What is it?" Eadyth was looking up at the man.

He came nearer and knelt down beside Eadyth to speak to her. "Father wants to speak with you," he told Eadyth, but his eyes fell on Gieva.

"Very well," Eadyth sighed, making sure Gieva's arm was securely bound. "Gieva, this is my son, Rægenhere," she told her, and the man smiled at her. He had a wound across his eyebrow and was covered in soot and blood, but his expression was so full of concern that Gieva could not help but to give him a weak smile in return. She would have guessed that he was Eadyth's son without her explanation; he had the same dark hair and silver eyes and the same powerful build, like some sort of animal built for running. Even that concerned smile seemed to drive away the clouds. He was terribly beautiful, she registered dully; she was far too exhausted to fully appreciate it.

Eadyth took her leave, but the man called Rægenhere remained kneeling beside Gieva. "How are you feeling?" he asked her. His voice was gentle; it had a deep, musical quality and she wanted him to keep talking.

"I was certain that I had died." She examined his face for a moment, and realized that she knew him. "It was you, you took me out of –" her voice constricted as she began to cough, and he lifted her head to give her more of the willow bark medicine Eadyth had left behind.

She winced as she swallowed, opening her eyes again and feeling her skin redden where his hand touched her cheek.

"I owe you my life," she said faintly.

He shook his head. "You owe me nothing." She saw a flicker of a smile cross his face, but it disappeared so quickly she might have imagined it.

She felt the willow bark taking effect, and her throat and lungs relaxed as he sat on his heels and watched her in a sort of awed silence, and Gieva might have felt uncomfortable if he had been anyone else, but there was something disarming in his expression.

"Who are your kin, Gieva? Are you Englisc?"

Gieva shook her head. "Gyrwa," she said, "But my father is a *thegn* of Ealdorman Cynhelm, who is loyal to Rædwald Cyning."

"I knew Cynhelm," Rægenhere said, "It was terrible to lose such a great man." She did not ask how this person knew Cynhelm; she assumed most warriors knew one another, and this man was clearly a warrior.

"Who is your father?" he asked.

"Godrinc, Godwine's Son."

"He fought with Cynhelm?" he asked, though his tone did not make it a question.

Gieva nodded, and Rægenhere gave her a sorrowful look which did not need explaining. Gieva felt tears sting her eyes before she realized why they were there. She had known when the Northumbrians arrived at the village that Father was almost certainly dead, but the look Rægenhere gave her confirmed her suspicions and it wounded her all over again.

"Was anyone able to find my mother? I was separated from her in the hall when the roof started to fall down, but then I passed out and I could not find her again." She cleared her throat, panic causing the words to spill out. "Her name is Mæga. She's got yellow hair like me, and she's rather thin, and she sometimes does not know where she is, so I must find her…" her voice failed when Rægenhere looked at the ground instead of at her, and she knew.

It was her fault, all her fault. She had told her mother to stay as quiet and small as she could if she was frightened, and her mother had most likely been crushed when the hall had collapsed. Gieva swallowed as Rægenhere spoke.

"We only were able to pull you and a few others out of the hall before it collapsed; you were all unconscious, and two did not make it."

"What about all the others?"

"The few women in the hall could not get out before the roof collapsed. I am sorry." He looked at the ground.

Gieva felt sick as the realization slowly came to her. "Few women?" she asked.

"Yes," he said miserably, "At least three. I may have seen a fourth, but we could not get to them."

"The rest ran out?" she asked, grabbing at the last shred of hope she could think of, "They ran out, surely? When you unblocked the doors, they ran out?"

"No," he said gently, as if she had simply misheard, "I've told you, the last three could not get out."

She closed her eyes, feeling tears streaking her cheeks and falling into her hair. "Not three," she whispered. "Thirty."

*****

Eadyth found Rægenhere sitting next to Gieva, just outside the opening of the tent. The Gyrwisc woman's face was streaked with the tracks of tears, though she was sleeping now. It would take days, maybe weeks, before the tears would stop completely, Eadyth knew.

Eadyth smiled faintly at the way Rægen looked at the sleeping woman. Gieva's uninjured hand lay on the coverlet, and Rægen's was inching towards it, as if he had a mind to hold it in his. He pulled his hand back and simply watched her, heedless of his mother standing behind him.

"Let me look at your eye," she said, kneeling beside him. There was a gash through his eyebrow, courtesy of a nearly missed enemy blade. It had bled freely, as head wounds often did, but it was not deep. She handed him a damp cloth and it came off black with soot and dried blood when he wiped his face with it. The soot may have been gone, but his expression was still grim.

"Are you in pain?" she asked.

Rægen shook his head and looked back at Gieva, who was stirring feebly as if caught in a dream.

"She just needs to rest. And so do you." Eadyth said gently.

Rægen tore his eyes from Gieva and back to Eadyth, his face filled with distress. "Do you know how many people we pulled out of that hall?"

Eadyth shook her head.

"Five." He said. She noticed the way his eyes kept moving back to Gieva's sleeping face. "Gieva told me that there were thirty women and children hiding there when the Northumbrians came. We found eight. We saved three. All but three died screaming because we couldn't reach them in time."

"That's not your fault," Eadyth said, gripping his shoulder, "No one would have thought the Northumbrians could have acted so cowardly. You did everything you could."

"I went back to the village," Rægen said, ignoring her. "I went to see if Leofric was able to track down any survivors who might have run out of the hall."

"And?"

"And he showed me where they were putting the bodies," he said. "Burned corpses should never be that little."

Eadyth closed her eyes for a moment as she absorbed what he said. She could not find adequate words, and shook her head.

"I never would have noticed if Eorwald hadn't heard them, if he hadn't smelled the smoke and realized something was wrong. What if he hadn't noticed? They all would have died. I did nothing." He was still covered in soot and blood despite his effort to clean it off, his dark hair was matted and his jaw clenched.

"There's nothing I can tell you that will undo what has happened today, but three people are alive tonight because of you, who would have died otherwise. That should count for something." Rægen looked pointedly at the ground, but Eadyth lifted his chin so that their eyes met. "You fought bravely and you did what you could to save the lives of the innocent. I would never ask more of you." She studied him for a moment, and added, "I would tell you to go and rest, but I know you won't listen, so I'll ask you to stay here and watch over Gieva for me. I daresay she's been through enough today, and she might appreciate a friendly face when she wakes."

He nodded stiffly, and she saw his hard eyes soften slightly as she left him to his charge.

Rædwald had thrown the prisoners into a guarded paddock, but one of their number was being forced angrily toward the pavilion by Ricbert as Eadyth passed. She followed Ricbert and his captive and found her husband sitting on his high seat at one end of the pavilion, looking wrathful and kingly as his eyes fell on the Northumbrian. He caught her eye as she slipped inside and shook his head very slightly, so she did not say anything.

"Tell me," Rædwald said to the captive man, "Did Athelfrith receive my message?"

The man scowled. His greasy brown hair was shot with grey, and he wore dull silver rings in his beard. "I am not aware of my *cyning* receiving any message," he said impatiently.

"I seem to remember sending another Northman back to Athelfrith several weeks ago," he said, his voice bitingly cold, "Do you remember what I told him, Ricbert?"

Ricbert raised an eyebrow. "I believe you said that you would give the Blood Eagle to the next of his men that you found in your land, Dryhten," he said.

"That's right," Rædwald nodded with a bark of a mirthless

laugh, "Now, you see how that puts me in a bit of an awkward position, because here I am, not even a full moon's turn past, and I hear that Athelfrith's people are in my lands again, doing precisely the thing I had warned him about. Perhaps Athelfrith did not believe my words? Perhaps I ought to show him that I will not tolerate his disrespect?"

"It was not me, my lord, I promise, it was an accident! I was not a part of the army, I came as a messenger and met them on the road, and –"

"I won't have it said that I don't keep my word," Rædwald interrupted him again, "So you will need to give me an excellent reason to not to personally rip your lungs out."

"I am an emissary!" the man was shocked.

"You are a prisoner of war," Rædwald told him, "if you had been an emissary you would not have brought half a hundred warriors with you to burn my folk in their beds. You would have finished your errand and gone home."

The emissary glowered. "And what sort of reception would I have gotten? Would you shove a sword in my mouth? That son of yours seems to think that's how to treat foreigners, anyway. I can see I should expect no honor from the swine of the Fens." He spat on the ground at Rædwald's feet. Rædwald ignored the slight, but stared venomously at the man.

"You fail to convince me of your worthiness as an errand boy," said Rædwald, "But I will not keep you from saying your piece. Speak, man."

The man swallowed, his eyes darting around the room to the hostile eyes boring into him. "I bring a message from Athelfrith of Northumbraland. He wishes to learn the whereabouts of the traitor named Edwin. Your cooperation is the least you can offer after you massacred our warriors at Grantabricge."

"You know, it is amusing that Athelfrith feels the need to beg for assistance, and then calls it a massacre when his men attack my allies and are defeated fairly." Rædwald said with a glance at Ricbert. If Ricbert found it amusing, he did not show it. "I still haven't heard anything that makes me want to spare your life."

"Athelfrith wishes to bring you terms, if you would let me speak," the emissary spat, but immediately covered his insolence with a harsh courtesy, "noble *cyning*, I beg you to hear the terms that Athelfrith offers. It would be to our mutual benefit."

Rædwald raised an eyebrow, and the man took it as an invitation to speak. "Athelfrith wishes to make an alliance with the great kingdom of the Engla. He offers you the support of his considerable army and his eternal friendship, if you would help him in this matter. Return the turncoat Edwin to him immediately and remove yourselves from these northern lands which belong to him by rights, and he will forget your past disagreements and offer you his friendship and support in your…" he paused delicately, "your future endeavors."

Rædwald considered this for a moment. "It seems as though I'm on the losing end of this deal," he said, "Your *dryhten* offers me his eternal gratitude, you say? And yet I am out a valuable hostage and have yet to avenge my own people, who, I might add, were not trained warriors but women and children." He spat the last sentence out like poison. "How would I benefit from such an arrangement?"

"Athelfrith would be a valuable ally both in war and in peace," said the messenger, "and only a fool would deny his assistance. Only a fool would give up the chance to end the wars which have resulted in the deaths of so many innocent people,"

"Innocent people who you Northumbrian *weargas* murdered in the first place!" Eadyth shouted before she was able to stop herself, and Rædwald shot a silencing look at her. She glared at the man, whose gaze returned to the king, ignoring her.

"But perhaps the offer could be sweetened if my lord offered to help you claim the lands south of the River Humber for the Engla people?"

Rædwald frowned, and something like triumph appeared on the emissary's face. "That is impossible," Rædwald said.

"They said taking Dál Riata would be impossible as well," the emissary said, and everyone in the room shuffled nervously. Athelfrith's victory over the Gaels was indeed famous, and proved his prowess on the battlefield. After a pause for effect, the man continued. "You are of course at liberty to decide if you wish to make Athelfrith your ally, or your enemy. I hope I may return to my *cyning* with your answer as soon as you have one." He bowed low.

"There is nothing to think about," Eadyth told him. Rædwald had excused himself from the company of the men to think things over, but Eadyth had followed after him at an angry trot. "You offered Edwin your protection, and this man wants you to sell him for a few empty promises?"

Rædwald chewed his lip and said nothing.

"You're not considering it, are you?" she felt a furious heat rise in her chest. "After what they did? You want to make an alliance with him?"

"You don't understand," he said after a while, "Athelfrith is one of the most powerful men in the world. I don't want to make him my enemy."

"He is already your enemy!" Eadyth said, "You must have a very short memory, husband."

"It would be imprudent not to take this opportunity," Rædwald mused. "We could put a stop to all of this bloodshed. It would stop him harassing our lands, and what happened in Ealdham might never happen again…"

Eadyth could not believe her ears. "You think that sucking Athelfrith's prick will really end his violence against our people?" she asked him, "And you would turn over a man you swore to protect, in the name of his empty promises? A man who has become as good as a son to you? How could you even consider it?"

He would not meet her eyes.

"I never thought I would see it," she spat, "the great Rædwald of the Wuffingas, a fucking coward. Are the laws of the gods not enough for you? Are the rules of hospitality and sanctuary worth nothing?"

"You were the one who said I should turn him away," Rædwald stormed, "You were the one who thought it would only bring misfortune, and now you want to protect him, at the expense of your own family?" His eyes burned with white-hot fury as they had done the night when Edwin had arrived at the Bricgweard. "I should have sent him away. I should have turned him over then, and it would never have come to this."

Eadyth barked a sarcastic laugh. "He would have done it anyway. Athelfrith wants to rule, don't you see? Edwin is just an excuse to invade our lands and murder our people."

He took a deep, steadying breath. "You know we don't have the strength to counter Athelfrith, not with all of the North united behind him."

"And you think giving him Edwin's head will stop him? You think murdering a guest in your own hall, dishonoring yourself and all of your kin, will stop Athelfrith taking whatever he wants?"

"If it is a choice between his life and the lives of all your sons, and all the people of this land, which would you choose?" his fists were clenching and releasing as he spoke. "I told you that if the choice came between him and the Engla, I would always choose my own people. If yielding to Athelfrith on this one matter could secure my people from harm –"

"You are their *cyning*!" Eadyth shouted, "YOU protect them from harm. Do you think we train our sons to bend the knee to every jumped up *ealdorman* who wants more than he deserves? No, Rædwald Cyning, We teach our sons how to fight. We teach them to stand proudly in the face of danger, to yield to no one!"

"Sometimes you have to know when you are beaten," he said, "you give up a battle to win the war."

"For almost twenty years I have seen the most powerful warrior I have ever met abandon the ways of his fathers in the name of protecting his people. You have been bowing your whole life, to your father, to Ethelbert, to his *swines scitte* of a god, and for what? Are your people any better off for it? Were those women and their children any safer for it?"

Rædwald broke his angry glower. "Would you have Athelfrith take my head instead?" he asked her, his mouth a hard line behind his beard. "Is the life of that man so important?"

"Athelfrith will only have your head if you kneel before him," Eadyth said. "And if you betray a man you have sworn to protect in the name of meaningless promises, after what Athelfrith's men did today, I will hand your head to him myself."

He looked as if he might strike her, and she readied herself for a blow, but it never came. Instead, he looked back toward the pavilion and called to Ricbert.

"Go and find Edwin," he said, his voice dripping with fury.

*****

The cowshed had been vacated by its occupants when the Northumbrians had arrived, and Sige leaned against the wall and watched Edwin pace, chewing a fingernail. There was little room to maneuver as it had become a sort of makeshift armory, and Edwin kept knocking over the spears leaning against the wall. The wound on his side had been tended by Eadyth, but he moved gingerly and winced as he bent to pick up the fallen weapons.

"I knew this would happen eventually," Edwin said, waving away Sige's concern. "Every single time I start to think I've finished with him, he finds me again."

"Rædwald won't turn you over," Sige tried to reassure him. "I've told you, he is as good as his word. If he wanted to turn you over to Athelfrith he would have done already."

Edwin shook his head. "I have been toying with Fate for too long," he said, "Athelfrith hates me, and he won't stop until he's put my head on a spike. I should have died a hundred times by now. Maybe it's time I stop this game and let him have me."

Sige grabbed him by the shoulders. "Stop," he said dangerously, "Never talk like that again. You're alive for a reason, and I won't let you submit so easily."

"Didn't you see what they did today? Didn't you see that hall burning? Have you forgotten how small those bodies were that we pulled from the rubble? Are those men and women and children that we've just buried worth a single man?" Edwin's face was contorted and desperate as he looked into Sige's eyes. Only a few months ago Sige would have known the answer, but now he was unsure. He deflected instead, "So raise an army, there are still people who are loyal to you. Call them to you, and defeat Athelfrith and reclaim your crown."

"It's not as easy as that. There are few enough men who would readily defy Athelfrith, and they are all still in the north. Any messenger I send would be killed, and if I went myself... I might as well just walk straight into Athelfrith's hall and have done with it."

"Rædwald will help you. After all of this, he hates Athelfrith more than ever. And I will help you, if Rædwald will not."

"Rædwald has done enough," Edwin said, "I've told you, I won't have any more of his people dying needlessly for me."

"That's his decision," Sige clenched his jaw. "And the decision of those who fight for him." He drew closer to Edwin, whose hands were shaking slightly. He took them in his own and they grew still. "Rædwald won't do it just for you. His own people have been affected by Athelfrith, and he is not a man to take that sort of insult lightly."

"You'd be surprised what some men will put up with for the sake of power," Edwin said bitterly. "I was tied to Cearl by marriage, and he still felt it would be easier to dispose of me when I merely became an inconvenience. If Cearl had been offered lordship of all of his rivals' kingdoms, how long do you think I would have kept my head then?"

"They are not the same."

"They are both *cyningas*. Given my history, I have a bit of a hard time trusting that sort completely."

"Rædwald may be tempted," he admitted, "He has wanted control of his enemies' territories for as long as I can remember," he frowned, shaking the thought from his mind, and his voice sounded far too confident as he said, "but I think he will make the right decision in the end. Why are you laughing?"

Edwin shook his head, "Because I am afraid that I will die very soon, and not in the way I might have hoped. I have to laugh or I might scream."

"If you die tonight, you'd best tell Hel that I am on my way," Sige said fiercely, catching Edwin up in his arms, his voice muffled against his shoulder, "and tell her to prepare her just punishments for me as a slayer of king and kin, because if Rædwald decides to hand you over he'll get my sword in his eye before he has a chance to regret his choice. And stop laughing!"

"I'm not even dead yet and you're already plotting your revenge?" Edwin said, raking his fingers through Sige's hair as he pulled away. He held Sige at arm's length and looked at him as if he would never do so again. "You're a fearless, reckless, stubborn ass, and I love you for it."

They heard footsteps outside the armory, and Edwin turned to the door, straight-backed and grim. When Ricbert entered, his face was set in a hard line that made Sige uneasy. Years of knowing Ricbert had taught him that the old man would never betray any information he intended to keep to himself, and it did nothing to help his nerves.

Sige felt his guts writhing as he watched the one he loved more than anyone else walk out the door and toward his almost certain death.

The king sat in the high seat in the pavilion, which was small and dirty and cramped with a mass of Englisc warriors. Sige tried to catch his mother's eye to ask silently what was about to happen, but the queen stared down at the gold rings clustered on her wrists. She could have been sleeping, or praying, though her hands were clenched.

The crowd was silent when they entered, and Edwin's head was raised defiantly as he led the way through the mass of people. A Northumbrian stood near the high seat, unchained and looking complacent. Sige stood within an arm's reach of the northerner, his cloak concealing the tight grip he had on the hilt of his seax. He was already planning the moves he would make if Rædwald called for Edwin's death: first stab the northerner, then it was only two paces to the king's seat – the king wore no armor and he could finish it quickly – and then he would have a running start out the back of the pavilion. He might not get away, but it would be enough time to distract everyone. Time for Edwin to run.

He glanced at Edwin, who shook his head minutely, pleadingly, as if he could see into Sige's mind.

"Well," Rædwald called to the northerner, and he took a step forward. "Tell the assembly the terms that Athelfrith Cyning has offered me regarding the exchange of Edwin of Deira, so that they can know why I make my decision."

It was an odd choice of words, and did nothing to ease the leaden weight that had fallen into Sige's stomach.

"Yes, of course," the northerner gave a little spasm of a bow, and then addressed the company at large. "My noble *dryhten* Athelfrith, rightful ruler of the kingdoms of Deira, Bernicia, Lindsey and the Isles–"

"Get to the point," Rædwald warned.

The Northumbrian shot an irritated glance at the king, but continued. "Athelfrith Cyning has long wished for the return of Edwin, formerly of Deira, to be judged according to the laws of our land, for his suspected crimes." Sige saw Edwin's eyes narrow at this, as the Northumbrian pressed on. "Athelfrith offers his friendship and his gratitude and future support to Rædwald Cyning of the Engla, for his help in this matter."

"Now tell my men what else your *cyning* offers me in exchange for this favor," Rædwald had a glint in his eye, though if it was from greed or anger Sige could not be sure. "Tell my assembled warriors and the women and children of the Fens about Athelfrith's offer of all the lands below the Humber in exchange for his wayward *ætheling*."

"It is as you say, noble *cyning*," said the messenger, visibly flustered, "In exchange for Edwin; my *cyning* offers his support in claiming the kingdoms of the Eota, the Hwicce, Mercia, and the Eastseaxe for the Englisc people. You would be the *heahcyning* of all lands below the Humber in all but name, in exchange for this small favor, subject only to Athelfrith himself. However, if you do not wish to aid him, you will be counted as one of his enemies, and Athelfrith's enemies do not long outlive their offences against him."

Sige watched the rise and fall of Edwin's breath, wondering how many he had left.

"I see we are of one mind," said Rædwald, and Sige's grip tightened around his weapon's hilt. "I will not deny that I desire lands beyond my own borders, and I would be pleased to have a powerful ally who could aid me." His face was unreadable as he continued, "I am well aware of Athelfrith's prodigious skill in battle, and he is not a man I would ever want as my enemy." He paused, and there was an ear-splitting silence. "But anyone who would suggest that I break laws of featly, of justice, of hospitality and of honor, a friend who expects me to ignore the repeated rape and slaughter of my people for the sake of conquest and meaningless promises is a false friend and no friend of mine." The glint in Rædwald's eyes had turned into fire, and the grin on the Northumbrian's face slid off in a heartbeat.

"Get out of my sight," Rædwald spat, "and tell your *cyning* that the next time he thinks he can bribe me after slaughtering my folk, he had best come in person. His yellow guts will make a fine meal for my hounds."

The Northumbrian turned white, and cowered under the glare from the king. "Yes, I – I will tell him," he stammered, backing out of the hall.

"Let him go," Rædwald called as one of the *thegns* tried to stop the Northumbrian from passing. "We do not harm messengers."

Sige stepped toward Edwin, but Rædwald got there first. "You are safe here as my ally and my friend," the king told Edwin in a carrying voice, and pulled him into an embrace. Sige could barely hear the king as he added in Edwin's ear, "I have started a war for you, boy. Do not make me regret it."

*****

The days stretched as languidly as Sunniva did, tossing her spindle aside and reaching over to stroke Ecgric's arm. He was mending something and humming to himself, though the hum might have been a growl.

They had learned from a messenger that the king and his entourage had met with a few skirmishes near a small town she had never heard of, but she had heard nothing since. Sunniva knew that Ecgric was itching to join them. He hated the steward's duties, and envied his father, who was, as usual, at the right hand of the king. He was restless, she could tell; no matter how much the two of them enjoyed their freedom while everyone was away, it was like watching an animal trying to claw his way out of a pen.

"I want you to teach me to fight," Sunniva said, and Ecgric looked up from his mending, startled.

"You know how to use a shield, don't you? Isn't that enough for a woman?" He laughed as she scowled at him. He had learned the hard way not to tell her what she, as a woman, was capable of doing, and she would not let him forget those lessons in a hurry.

"What do you want to learn?" he asked before she could give him a tongue lashing, "It's easy enough to throw a javelin, I suppose, or –"

"I want to learn everything," she said, laughing. "Javelin and bow and axe and spear, but I think the sword ought to be first."

Ecgric seemed rather amused at this, but nodded. "It's not just a matter of waving a sword about," he said, "Your sword is not your primary weapon. You have to use your shield and your legs just as much as a blade. In truth I do most of my fighting with an axe. It does more damage."

"That seems to suit you," Sunniva said with a laugh, "But there's something rather more heroic about fighting with a sword." She felt giddy at the idea, and thought of herself garbed as a man and fighting alongside her brothers in a shield wall, like some warrior queen of old.

She met Ecgric in the yard, having changed into a man's tunic that reached to her knees. Ecgric helped her to find a shield and blunted practice sword. She felt rather foolish and very small compared to Ecgric. Her legs were sticking out the bottom of the tunic like pale spindles and the sword and shield were heavy in her hands.

Ecgric looked at her for a moment with amusement, which made her scowl. He took weapons of his own before saying, "There are two sorts of fighting that you usually do in a battle," he said, picking up a shield and spear. "The first is in the shield wall, when your main weapons are your shield, obviously, and your spear or an axe," he stood next to her and braced his shield against hers to demonstrate, resting the untipped ash spear on the rim. "This way, you can brace against the other shields and break the enemy's wall, or make a sort of turtle's shell to protect against arrows or javelins, like this," he bent on one knee and she did likewise, holding the shields at an angle.

Sunniva nodded. She had seen him practicing something similar with her brothers, so the concept was not entirely foreign. "What do you do when the shield wall is broken?" she asked, standing again.

Ecgric moved to face her. "That is when things become dangerous, and you have to choose your weapon according to your opponent," he said. "It also takes the most training, because you have to be ready for anything, you can't just rely on the shield wall to protect you."

"I'm ready," she said, mimicking his stance. She was turned at an angle, with the shield held in front of her in her left hand. The look of amusement crossed his face again, and Sunniva lunged at him, smacking him in the thigh with the flat of her blade. He took a step back, the amusement turning quickly to annoyance.

"Well done," he said, "but when we're practicing, it's best to make a noise before you strike. These swords may not have a blade but they can do some damage if improperly used. It's just common courtesy when you spar with someone." He pushed her shield up with the tip of his sword. "Hold it up. Always protect your neck and chest. You haven't got a heart in your knees."

Sunniva lifted the shield, surprised at how hard it was to hold it up for an extended period.

"I'm going to attack you," he said, "and you will try to fend me off with the shield. Don't use the sword just yet, just defend yourself for now and practice using the sword as additional protection. Offensive strikes are useless if your guts are spilling onto the ground." He stepped forward, and Sunniva was ready. He cried out each time he lunged, and Sunniva deflected the blade again and again. She had learned to use the shield from her mother, as most girls did for the defense of their homes, though it was different with a heavy sword in one hand. She wanted to be on the offensive, however, and after the fifth successful deflection she pushed against Ecgric's shield with her own, shouting before aiming the flat of the blade at his shoulder.

Her arms began to feel tired almost immediately from the weight of the weapons. They practiced for quite a while, Sunniva dancing with the shield and Ecgric aiming rather lazy blows at her. She was learning quickly, but by the end of it she felt as if her arms had melted.

"It's not fair," she said, "you're much taller than I am and I can hardly reach you."

Ecgric shrugged. "You have to get inside my reach. Try thrusting the shield upward to knock the blade out of the way, and go for the knees. If I'm fighting with a sword it's hard to get at you if you're too close."

She tried again, this time ducking below his sword strike, thrusting the shield over her head and pretending to slice the back of Ecgric's ankle with her blade.

"Good," Ecgric said. "It's also a good move if you have a bearded axe, because then you can hook the enemy's knee with less effort. I think that if you were dropped in a battle right now, you might be able to do a fair amount of damage."

"How many did I kill?" Sunniva asked excitedly, and then scowled when Ecgric laughed.

"If they die from infection in the next few months," he said, "then two, perhaps. None of those blows would have been lethal."

"How are you supposed to kill a man if you can only reach his legs and arms?" Sunniva asked crossly, "Men can still rape and kill if they have a stab wound in the leg."

"Which is why I always use an axe," Ecgric said. "It does more damage with fewer strikes."

"If I have an axe, I could just cut his head off. But I like swords better." Sunniva looked at the practice blade, secretly thinking of what she might name her own sword if she were ever able to fight.

"You don't need to behead a man to kill him. Besides, killing a man is hard. You don't realize how hard until you have to do it. Taking him down is usually enough. Just get him out of the way, remove the threat, and move onto the next one." Ecgric had taken Sunniva's sword and shield from her, setting them inside the shed with the rest of the equipment.

"What do you mean; it's hard to kill a man?" Sunniva said. "Because they have so much armor on?"

Ecgric frowned at her. "No, not that. I mean, it does things to you. Even if the man is happy to go to the gods, even if he dies well, you still are there when the lights leave his eyes. You still hear the sound of his body hitting the ground. Even when you have the blood-joy, even when you have to kill them, those are things that stay with you."

Sunniva cocked her head slightly. She knew that Ecgric loved battle more than anything in the world, and was famous for his ferocity on the field. It was strange and rather endearing, to think that he had such a measure of compassion in him. She took his arm as they walked back to the Bricgweard, eager to change the subject.

"Maybe next time you won't treat me so gingerly," she said, as they entered the king's house. She immediately unbuckled the belt around her short tunic and stripped it off, preparing to change into a normal dress instead. A short garment might make it easier to run or jump, but she felt awkward and ungainly and preferred her own clothes.

"Let's wait until you can actually lift the sword without getting tired," Ecgric said, "And I will help you learn to use it properly." He grinned as he looked at her now-naked body, and reached around her to knead the muscles of her shoulders and upper arms. "You're going to be sore in the morning," he said.

Sunniva shrugged. "I'm usually sore after a night with you. That does feel good, though." He squeezed her shoulders once more and his hand moved to her breast, but she smacked it away, grinning.

"What made you want to learn to fight, anyway?" Ecgric asked, flopping onto the bed and putting his hands behind his head as he watched her un-braid her hair.

Sunniva had asked for his help primarily for his benefit, so that he could have something to keep himself occupied while he remained, bored and useless in Wuffingham, while the others were off fighting. She decided it was not the appropriate tack to tell him this, however, and said, "Just a lark, really. But you might not always be around to protect me, so I'd better learn to fight for myself." She lay next to him, snuggling into the comfortable and familiar place under his arm.

"I'm not going anywhere," he said, stroking her cheek. He was doing this a lot in the past few days, becoming quiet and saying things about love which made Sunniva profoundly uncomfortable, though she could not figure out exactly why it should bother her. She twirled the end of his hair between her fingers, anxious to find a change of subject. "Your hair is almost as long as mine," she said, "Doesn't it get in the way? I know mine does."

Ecgric shrugged. "I've never had a problem. I always tie it back anyway."

"Paulinus told me a story about someone who had power in his hair," she said, "But the names were all so strange I couldn't remember it. I think when it was cut he died or something. Rather funny considering the way he shaves his own hair."

Ecgric scoffed at the mention of Paulinus. "All of his stories are nonsense anyway," he said.

"Aren't all stories nonsense?" she asked, "I mean, I've never seen a giant or a dragon, have you? Maybe people from his land think our stories are nonsense and that enchanted hair and a maiden mother are normal for them?"

"I'd rather hear stories about the real gods," Ecgric said. "Tell me a story, Sunniva. Give me some good dreams after my hard work, for I am tired." He said it in a superbly dramatic sort of way that made Sunniva smile.

"You haven't done anything to be tired!" She said, but he gave her a pleading look and she relented. "You're like a little child sometimes," she said, and looked at the edge of the Tiw rune peeking out from the neck of his tunic. She traced it with her forefinger.

"I'll tell you a story about Tiw One-Hand. Back before even the Romans lived in these lands, when stinking bogs covered all the country, there was a giant, horrible wolf. The Fennwulf was so great that he could devour even the tallest warriors in one swallow, and the people lived in fear of him, even though he was still in his youth and had not even come to his full strength. The gods were afraid that he would continue to grow and would eventually be able to devour the gods themselves. The All-Father said that the Fennwulf must be bound, but no one could make a chain strong enough to hold him.

"Eventually they called upon the great dwarf smiths, who were able to make a magical ribbon, which would be able to bind the Fennwulf forever. They wrought into it six rare things: the sound of a cat's feet, the beard of a woman, the roots of a mountain, the nerves of a bear, the breath of a fish and the spit of a bird."

"So that's why those things no longer exist," Ecgric said, touching Sunniva's chin with his thumb. "No beard for you, I'm afraid, it's all gone into the forging of the Fennwulf's chain."

Sunniva laughed, and continued her story. "The gods tried to bind the Fennwulf by force, but he was too quick and too strong for them. They decided to play to his vanity. The gods therefore claimed that they merely wished to test their great chain and that only one as strong as the great Fennwulf could ever break it. They would bind him, and then take the chain off again if he was unable to break through. But he was the cleverest of wolves, and suspected that they might be trying to trick him.

"So the Fennwulf said to Woden the All-Father, 'I am not as blind as you, Old Man, though I know I can beat you. I will let you test your great chain on me, but I require a hostage. Place your hand in my mouth before I am bound; if you are true to your word and will indeed remove my bonds, I will allow you to remain unscathed. If you have lied to me, I will have your hand as wergild for my bondage."

Sunniva smiled at the look on Ecgric's face. Even grown men loved the bravery of Tiw, and he listened to her, stroking her hair absently as she spoke. "Now Woden knew that the Fennwulf had found them out. He was on the point of abandoning the plan, when the god Tiw, Lord of all warriors, stepped forward.

"'I will take your place as hostage,' he said to Woden, and the Fennwulf was glad, for Tiw was the greatest warrior and the wolf would be pleased to cripple him and thus rid himself of an enemy. And Tiw placed his sword hand in the mouth of the Fennwulf as the dwarves wound the chain about the beast. The wolf tried to break the bonds, but they were made of magic and would never break until the world was ended.

"'It seems your dwarf friends have a great magic indeed,' said the Fennwulf, 'for I cannot break these bonds. Your test is complete, now the time has come to release me, or else I shall close my jaws and the great warrior Tiw will never be able to fight again with sword or spear.'

"And Tiw looked into the eyes of the beast, and the Fennwulf knew in that moment that he would not be freed, and in his anger he closed his massive jaws –" Sunniva clapped her hands together loudly, "and tore the mighty hand of Tiw from his wrist, just as Tiw knew he would. For Tiw was brave and knew that his sacrifice would save the lives of many, though he would not be able to fight as he once did. And he became Tiw One-Hand, and the great warriors look to him for courage in battle, when they fear the end is near."

"I've always liked that one."

"You would," Sunniva said. "Do you pray to Tiw before a battle?"

Ecgric nodded. "And to Woden and to Thunor, and to all the nameless gods that time has forgotten."

"But you're not afraid of dying," Sunniva said, "so why do you bother praying?"

"Everyone is afraid of dying, to a certain extent. I'd be more afraid to be injured and to die slowly in agony than to have a quick, painless death in honor while fighting. But if it's my Fate to rot, then I ask the gods for strength to endure it."

Sunniva had to agree. She had seen the results of a failed death, and she did not wish that on anyone, let alone someone so eager to chase glory. She hated the idea of him languishing with an infected wound for days before succumbing to it. Unconsciously, she put her hand in his. She did not like the idea of him dying, and she hoped that he would not do it for a very long time.

*****

Rægen had not left the girl's side in days, and Eorwald was growing impatient. She was by no means ugly; she had sad, greenish-brown eyes and a softly curving body that any man would find attractive, but so ordinary that Eorwald would not have been able to find her in a line of one. He had known Rægen to have pursued and won much better looking women in the past with far less zeal. He had not much time to think on it, though, before he was interrupted by the voice of his mother.

"How is your cheek?" she asked briskly, kneeling on the ground next to him and examining the line of stitches along his jaw.

"Still there," he said dully as she slathered some spicy smelling ointment on the cut.

"You'll have a very fierce scar after this," she said fondly, getting to her feet. She added, almost as an afterthought, "Your father wishes to speak with you."

Eorwald frowned. "He's angry, isn't he?"

Eadyth was silent for a moment, closing the pot of medicine and replacing it in the pocket of her apron. "Yes," she said slowly, "but not at you, not really."

"I wouldn't have killed them; I just lost control…" Eorwald began, but Eadyth cut him off.

"He is not angry, but he will be if you don't hurry," she said blandly.

Eorwald found his father sitting next to the fire at the mouth of the pavilion, mending a leather jerkin with a thick strand of sinew and a heavy bone needle. "Come and sit with me," he called to Eorwald, but did not look up from his work. He bound up the last stitch and knotted it, then melted the end with a red-hot knife to keep it from pulling out. Rædwald tossed the jerkin aside and looked at Eorwald intently.

"We will be leaving in two days," Rædwald said. "I need to leave a small company to make sure Athelfrith doesn't send any more of his creatures to harass the Fens, and I had thought to put you in command of them." He seemed to be weighing his words carefully.

"Yes, of course, I'll be honored to…" Eorwald said, pleased at the absence of reprimand, but his face fell when he saw the grim look his father gave him.

"I said that I *had* thought to leave you here," he said, "That was before I found out what you did in the village." He paused, and Eorwald began to prepare his defense in his mind during the long silence. "It was not necessary. They would have had their justice, after they had been brought to the leader of the victorious army. Once they had surrendered, you had no right to kill them. Not like that."

Eorwald looked into the flames between himself and his father. "You didn't see what they had done," he said quietly, "They wanted a fight, and so we gave them one."

"I thought I had taught you to be a leader, not a butcher."

"And what kind of justice would they have been given?" asked Eorwald angrily, "What sort of *wergild* would have been just compensation for raping and torturing women and children, for trapping them in a burning building? You weren't there, you didn't see what – what they did," the heat evaporated from his voice as the images crept into the edges of his thoughts, and he blinked to push them away. "I don't even remember doing it; I was so angry that I just acted without thinking."

It was a long time before Rædwald spoke again. "I am not happy with what you did," he said, "it was unbecoming of an *ætheling*. Even when a man commits a brutal crime he should be given the chance to atone for it and die well. You did not give them that chance."

"They did not deserve that chance," Eorwald said through gritted teeth, "They deserved to go screaming into the afterlife and feel the same pain they inflicted on those women."

"I would be lying if I said I did not agree with you," Rædwald confided, "Even after seeing the sorts of things that I have seen it is impossible not to be affected by something like that."

Eorwald crossed his arms to stop his hands from shaking, but Rædwald seemed to have noticed. "Fury is a great thing," Rædwald said, "When tempered with judgment. You are going to lead men one day, Eorwald, perhaps even as their *cyning*. If you cannot control your fear and your rage, then fear and rage will own you."

"I'm not afraid," Eorwald said angrily.

"You are either lying, or you are an idiot." Rædwald said, "But you are also young, and I want to give you the chance to learn from your actions. I will let you remain here in defense of the Fens," he said, "but under the command of Ricbert. I do not think you are ready for command yourself."

Eorwald tried to hide his annoyance, lest his father change his mind, and accepted. It would be better than going home to Wuffingham; at least if he remained in the Fens there would be a chance of proving himself worthy of his father's trust.

"What of Rægen?"

"He will return to Wuffingham with me." Rædwald said. "I trust you don't envy him?"

Eorwald shrugged. "I had thought that you would have wanted him to learn more of command." He could not entirely hide the sarcasm in his voice, and Rædwald noticed.

"Rægenhere has already proven himself to be a capable leader in battle," Father said with the slightest stress on Rægen's name, "and he must now learn to rule a land at peace." Father returned to his mending and Eorwald knew that he was being dismissed.

He left the pavilion in a sour mood, and kicked the root of a tree as he passed, though he missed and swore at the pain in his toes as they caught the edge and his foot twisted.

"That bloody tree," he heard Rægen's voice from behind him, "Always picking fights with people. I've tripped over it half a dozen times already."

Eorwald scowled. "What do you want?"

"I am in search of something to eat," Rægen said, ignoring Eorwald's tone, "Come with me. You can explain why you're in such a bad temper."

"I'm not in a bad temper."

"Of course not," Rægen said, "You just need a cup of sweet milk and a pat on your head before you have a lie-down."

Eorwald scowled, but he followed his brother anyway.

When they had procured some bread and a jug of ale, and after his temper had cooled somewhat, Eorwald explained what their father had told him, though Rægen did not display the amount of indignation that he would have wanted to see.

"I shouldn't want to be left on my own to command yet; I don't know what you're so upset about." Rægen reasoned, "Ricbert's a great warrior and an even better leader; you should be pleased to be learning from him."

"That's not it," Eorwald said, leaving out his twinge of frustration that Rægen had already proven himself as a forceful battle commander and fit to rule a kingdom, "Father doesn't trust me. He thinks I acted too hastily in the village."

Rægen frowned and did not look at Eorwald. "He is not wrong."

Eorwald's temper flared again. "After the things your woman told you, after seeing all that they had done; I thought you'd be on my side at least!"

Rægen did not answer immediately. "To tell you the truth, it frightened me." He hesitated, as if gauging Eorwald's silence. "I was angry too, and I would have had no greater pleasure than to see them punished, but that was brutal, what you did. I thought you had gone mad."

Eorwald had wondered the same thing. He did not remember doing it; he only remembered the dead children they had pulled from the burned hall and then his furious march toward the prisoners and then the blood and brains on his sword; perhaps he was indeed losing his mind.

"I acted as I saw fit," he lied, "but my idea of justice just didn't seem to agree with that of our father."

Rægen pursed his lips, but did not pursue the issue. He filled their cups from the jug and dug into his pouch for some dried meat, which they both chewed for a while in silence. Eorwald was deeply immersed in his own thoughts when Rægen suddenly stood to greet his yellow-haired distraction, who was passing by.

Eorwald raised an eyebrow at the smitten look his brother gave the woman. She seemed to light up at the sight of him, and Rægen went forward to take the woman's splinted hand gently in his, perhaps asking her how it was feeling. They talked for a moment, though quietly enough that Eorwald could not hear.

Eorwald realized the look of revulsion that must have appeared on his own face, and hastily rearranged his expression to one of indifference when she smiled at him. He lifted a hand in greeting, though he did not bother rising from his seat between the tree roots. Eventually Rægen returned and plopped back down, and Gieva wandered off.

"What?" Rægen asked, a grin still plastered on his face.

Eorwald could not help but laugh. "You are besotted," he said, "and I have absolutely no idea why."

Rægen looked at him as if he were debating throwing a punch for insulting his lady. "So what if I am," he said, "Why shouldn't I be? Gieva is the finest woman I have ever known. She's beautiful, she's kind, and she's clever…" He stared in the direction she had disappeared, as if waiting for her to return.

"She's not that beautiful," Eorwald said. "She looks like every other Fen girl around here, and the Gyrwa aren't known for their looks."

Rægen shook his head, as if trying to explain something very simple to someone who was quite dim-witted. "It's not just a matter of looks," he said, "She's been through so much, and she's had to be so brave to do so, and yet none of it has hardened her. And she's clever and sweet, and have you seen the way she moves? She's so graceful and gentle and … and beautiful." He finished with a sigh.

"She has got nice tits," Eorwald conceded. "Have you two…"

Rægen shook his head. "In time, maybe," he said, "I'll wait." A deeply contented look appeared on his face which made Eorwald feel as if he were intruding on something indecent.

"Well, I don't see the appeal," Eorwald said, and ripped off another bite of dried meat, "but I won't judge your decisions. Of course I know a fair few girls at home who will be devastated at the loss of their handsome singer to a Fen girl."

Rægen smiled, still looking dazedly to the place where Gieva had just been. "They'll find others."

Chapter Ten

Eftsiđ

The Return Journey

cgric was struggling to stifle a yawn as another petitioner came to speak to Sunniva, and he passed the time by pacing to the edge of the hall and peering out into the sunshine. It was a beautiful day and he wished he could be out doing something useful, but he did not want to miss the chance to get Sunniva alone when she had finished playing queen.

A line of pale dots caught his eye, emerging from the wood beyond the fields. He squinted, ignoring the woman asking the princess for assistance in replacing a broken wagon, and saw the short train of figures making its slow way across the bridge.

Sunniva had dismissed the woman and came to stand with him in the doorway, leaning against it languidly and looking at him with only vague curiosity.

"Were you expecting anyone, my lady?" he asked quietly. Ecgric was tense; perhaps it was his desire to see some action, but Ecgric did not take for granted that unexpected visitors would be friendly.

Sunniva shook her head and her face darkened suspiciously. "Take a few men down to meet them." She had adopted her queenly voice. He nodded assent and beckoned to the two guards to follow him down the lane toward the approaching visitors.

He marked two men on horseback, accompanied by a third and fourth in a horse-drawn wagon. The wagon was piled with gear, covered in a sheet of sailcloth.

"Wes ðu hal!" The foremost horseman shouted when they

were half a furlong away. He was holding up his hand in a gesture of greeting, and Ecgric's hand relaxed slightly on his sword hilt, though he did not let go.

"And you," Ecgric said. "What business brings you to the Bricgweard?" He did not have much time for pleasantries, until he could establish whether or not the visitors meant any harm.

"I come to meet the great *cyning* Rædwald of the Engla! I wish to do him honors and bring him gifts to forge a new friendship. May I have an audience with him?" The man was absurdly cheerful, and though he spoke excellent Englisc his voice was flavored with some accent that Ecgric could not place. "We paid our dues at the wood bridge yonder, and I was told that we would be able to have an audience before the high seat."

Ecgric considered him a moment. He thought he recognized him, but he could not be certain. "You may follow me, and I will take you to the great hall," he said. He preferred not to tell strangers that the king and three quarters of the army were not at home, though the man would find out soon enough.

They arrived at the Bricgweard, where Sunniva was sitting in the high seat and speaking animatedly with one of the older *thegns*. When Ecgric entered, she perked up immediately to see what he had learned.

"My lady, there is a man to see you, his name is – oh, just go in." Ecgric did not like the look in the man's eyes when they alit on the princess. Sunniva looked beautiful as always, her hair falling in a lazy plait over one shoulder as she cocked her head slightly to one side in polite interest. The visitor rushed forward, leaving his associates behind near the doorway.

"And who might you be?" Sunniva asked. She was gracious, but wary.

"My fair *vrouwe*," the man said, inclining his head in deference, "I am called Godomar, son of Grimbald of Heldergem."

"Oh, you're Frankisc!" Sunniva said delightedly, her wariness shelved for the moment.

"What is that you called her?" Ecgric asked. He worried that it might be some foreign slight.

"*Vrouwe*?" Godomar asked, taking the interruption in stride, "Oh, but it only is a show of respect in my language for the daughter of a *cyning*, or a woman of noble birth."

Ecgric scowled, and Sunniva seemed to notice the tension and piped up, "I met a Frankisc man not long ago in Gipeswic;

he sold me some lovely silk."

"Indeed, beautiful *vrouwe*, I know of whom you speak. It is because of him that I am here now; I was told of the generosity and greatness of the royal family of the Engla and I wished to make the acquaintance of Rædwald Cyning."

"I speak for my father," Sunniva said tactfully.

"Of course you do," Godomar nodded his head respectfully. "You have the bearing of royalty."

Sunniva seemed pleasurably flustered, and the man took it as a sign to continue. "Perhaps I should explain," He said, "I was, until recently, a member of the entourage of Heahcwene Bercta, until her death several years ago. Since then I have wanted to establish new trading ports throughout the lands of the Engla and the Seaxe, as I believe such trading would benefit both of our peoples."

Sunniva nodded for the man to go on, and he did.

"My associate informed me that he had personally met the *cwene* of the Engla and her daughter, and that they were both generous and lovely, and I knew that I had to meet a man who was so fortunate as to have such women in his family."

"So you sell cloth as well?" Sunniva asked.

Godomar nodded. "My land is known for its fine textiles, and though I do not sell them myself, I do oversee several trade operations. I am a – oh, I forget this word in Englisc – I am a *graf*, which is a man who has lands and leads wars and speaks with the king…"

"An *ealdorman*?" Sunniva prompted.

"Yes, fair *vrouwe*!" he said, "Anyway, that is why I have come to see your father, but I hope you will accept my gifts of friendship on his behalf." He motioned for his companion to come forward. The man was carrying a hefty casket, and Godomar opened it in front of Sunniva. Ecgric circled around to the side of Sunniva's chair to see what had made her eyes open wide in delight. There was a fair mound of gold, in ingots and in rings, and some folded pieces of silk.

"This is very generous indeed!" Sunniva said. Though she kept a queenly sort of voice, Ecgric could hear the hint of a girlish squeal which wanted to escape. Sunniva loved pretty things, and this chest was heaped with them.

"This is merely a token," Godomar said. "A gesture of good faith and friendship from the Franca to the Engla. Please accept it with my compliments."

Sunniva was grinning. "I accept them gladly, sir. Please stay in our hall and let us return your friendship." She rose from the chair and gave an instruction to Gamol to procure food and drink for the Franca and the other *thegns* who were milling about the hall. Sunniva walked out the door, and Ecgric followed behind her.

"Is that a good idea?" Ecgric asked. "You don't know these people."

"Don't be rude," Sunniva said quietly, but in a voice that did not allow for argument. "They are guests, and I will do the same thing my father would do in my place, which is give them food and a place to sleep for a few nights. Do you have some objection to hospitality?"

Ecgric shook his head. He had no real reason to distrust Godomar, save the lascivious way in which he had looked at Sunniva, but that would hardly do as an argument. "Of course not."

Though the *thegns* and their wives appreciated the change of pace, none took to the Frankisc men more thoroughly than Sunniva. It was one thing to see Sunniva offering her smiles to some hopeless *thegn*; this was different. This was real competition, and it made Ecgric want to punch the foreigner's perfectly sculpted jaw into splinters.

"Mountains!" Sunniva was saying, "I've always wanted to see real mountains."

"It is true," Godomar said. "They are some distance from my village, but we made our way through a mountain pass when we travelled to Rome. They look as if they are piercing the sky, and the tips are capped with snow, even in the summer."

Sunniva's eyes were wide. "You've been to Rome? Our Christian is from Rome. His name is Paulinus. He is out on an errand for me, otherwise I would introduce you." Sunniva's face darkened slightly, but she brightened again as she looked at the tawny-haired Frankisc man. "I should like to visit Rome someday. It sounds quite exotic."

"It is a grand city, and full of history," Godomar agreed. "And receiving the Holy Communion from the Pope himself was a great blessing indeed."

Ecgric scowled. Of course he was a Christian; most of the foreigners had accepted the false nailed god generations ago. "Is it true that Christians are not allowed to marry or have sex?" Ecgric asked Godomar. Sunniva looked at Ecgric with suspicion.

"Forgive me," Godomar said after an indecently condescending pause, "I forget that not all people in this country have accepted the Gospel. Allow me to clarify. Only priests and monks are asked to avoid the temptations of the flesh, but we laypeople are quite free to marry and love as we please." He was looking at Sunniva as he said the last part, and Sunniva blushed uncharacteristically.

"Let's have some music," she said, "Will you sing us a Frankisc song?"

Godomar lowered his eyes, "I am no great singer, fair *vrouwe*, but I will do as you wish. Do you know the story of Weyland the Smith?"

Sunniva nodded and a few other people voiced their enthusiastic approval of the choice of story. Godomar began to recite the story in his own language, which was strange and throaty but not completely sundered from Englisc. Ecgric recognized many of the words, but they seemed strangely warped as if he were randomly replacing Englisc words with Latin. The crowd seemed to be enthralled with the nearly-unintelligible tale, or at least the strange accent of his words, though Ecgric thought that Rægenhere would have been able to do a better job of it, and in a language they could all understand.

Sunniva cheered enthusiastically when he had finished, and then excused herself for a breath of air. Ecgric followed her, watching her long hair swing behind her. Strangely, the evening made him ache for her even more than usual, and his desire to touch her was winning out over his urge to break the Frankisc man's teeth.

"You didn't have to be so rude," Sunniva said conversationally as they left the hall.

"How was I being rude?" Ecgric asked innocently, "I mistrust him, that's all."

"Because he is a foreigner?"

"Because he is a stranger and I have promised your father that I would look after you," Ecgric said. "I have to be vigilant."

Sunniva pretended to examine her arms and torso for damage, and said in a mocking tone, "Well, I do believe I have survived the night with the nasty Frankisc man unscathed. Thank you for your vigilant service."

Ecgric ignored this. "He seems to like you very much."

"I am very likeable. And so is he. Everyone is having a pleasant evening with an exciting new guest. Well, everyone except for you." She looked at him and a mischievous glint appeared in her eye. "You're jealous, aren't you?" she said, and Ecgric looked away from her.

"I just didn't like the way he was looking at you, like you were a piece of meat," Ecgric said defensively, "It's disrespectful."

Sunniva laughed. "I love that you're jealous. It proves that I own you."

"You don't own me," Ecgric said, but he could not stifle a grin.

"Oh, but I do. I possess you completely, and there's nothing you can do about it." She was running her forefinger down his chest, drawing closer and fixing him with an impish stare.

Ecgric surveyed her for a moment, and then she squealed as he picked her up, carrying her as if she were a sack of flour. She giggled and pounded on his back, kicking her legs feebly as he hoisted her over his shoulder and carried her around the back of the hall.

"This proves nothing," Sunniva said, when Ecgric had set her back on her feet, "I may be little, but I still own you." She grabbed the neck of his tunic and pulled him down, and he succumbed to the feel of her lips opening and her tongue sliding into his mouth. She was right, of course. She did own him, and he did not mind in the least.

*****

"Gieva!" a high-pitched squeal met her as she walked around the perimeter of the camp. Without realizing what was happening, two flashes of brown collided with Gieva's waist, nearly knocking her to the ground. Every time she saw them, she offered a quiet prayer of thanks to Frea for protecting Leik and Lisse, and for sending the *æthelingas* to save them from the burning hall. Only the three of them had survived the horrors of

Ealdham; the two children had seen so much in their short lives, and Gieva could barely restrain her happiness that they were still with her.

"We had to find you!" Lisse said, still hugging Gieva's waist. She was crying, and Gieva's heart sank.

"What's the matter, my darling?" Gieva asked, dropping to her knees so that she could look properly at the children.

"They are taking us away!" Lisse said miserably. "They are taking us back to our home!"

Gieva cocked her head slightly at this. "Who is taking you away?"

"Our grandfather," Lisse said. "He has come to find us, and he is going to take us back to live with him. He is… he is the one who will take care of us now." She said it as if she were trying to comfort Gieva, trying to explain that it would all be well, but she was still crying.

Leik shook his head and buried it against Gieva's chest, throwing his arms around Gieva's neck now.

"But that is good," Gieva said without enthusiasm. She had been worried about the future of the two little ones ever since she had discovered that they had survived the fire, but now it came to it, she did not want to be parted from them.

"But we wanted to go with you," Lisse said, looking shiftily at the ground. "Leik can't sleep without you there."

Gieva tried not to look as sad as she felt. "I cannot take care of you, my sweet one," she said. "I have no home now. I cannot give you what you need."

"But we want you!" Lisse stomped her foot on the ground.

An older man appeared at Lisse's side. "Lisse," he said gently, "it is time for us to go."

Gieva had to fight the urge to tell him that he could not take them away, and she swallowed hard, looking into Lisse's eyes. Their grandfather retreated a few paces to let Gieva say goodbye, but now that she had to, she did not want to.

"Lisse," Gieva said, smiling despite her tears, "my brave, strong girl. You must be brave now, just as you were when those bad men came. Your grandfather will take good care of you, but Leik needs you now. You must help him to be brave."

Lisse's lip trembled as she nodded.

Gieva turned to Leik, who was playing with a lock of Gieva's hair, tears still rolling down his fat cheeks. She kissed the bruise across his face and gently disengaged his fingers, putting his hand into Lisse's.

Gieva could not stand still for a long time. The question of her future was pressing even more heavily on her now that the children had gone. Gieva had no kindly grandfather who might take her in; her only kin had been Ælfhelm and – no, she did not want to think about that now. All she knew was that she could not stay here, in this land of death and dread.

The queen was flitting from place to place, shouting orders and answering questions as she passed through the bustle of the imminent departure. Gieva shouldered her way through and finally caught up with her when Eadyth stopped at the entrance to the pavilion.

"My Cwene," Gieva panted. "Please, may I speak with you?"

Eadyth seemed annoyed at the interruption, but her expression seemed to soften when she saw Gieva. "Of course," she said, and gestured that Gieva should enter the pavilion. "And my name is Eadyth. You know that."

Gieva did of course know that, but it felt odd to be familiar with the queen, now that she knew who she was. The large pavilion was empty, the grass trampled from the constant traffic around the king. Gieva had practiced the words, but now that it came to it, she felt as timid as a mouse.

"Gieva?" Eadyth asked, impatiently but not unkindly, "come now, what do you need?"

Gieva swallowed, and the words came out in a squeak. "Take me with you." She was surprised the queen had even heard the words. She adjusted them, "Please, I want to go back to Wuffingham with you. I cannot stay in Grantabricge after you leave. I… I just can't bear it."

"My dear," Eadyth said, "your place is here, with your people. Surely you wish to stay and help them rebuild? Do you have kin near here? They could take you in until you can return to your own farm." Her words were not harsh, but Gieva felt stung by them.

Gieva's eyes filled, unbidden, with tears. "No one is left," she said, "No one. I am… I am alone." Her throat felt tight and hot as she thought of Mother trapped in the burning hall, and Father dying in glorious battle, and Ælfhelm begging her for death and Leoma crying out in the night, and knew that they would never come back to her. She wanted to run from the pavilion, but she pressed on. "I wanted to ask you if you might – if you would take me into your service. I can sew, and I can braid hair, I'm good at weaving and I can spin fine yarn very quickly, and I could do whatever you ask of me; I have nothing left here now. Please, I beg you to take me with you." She tried and failed to conceal the fact that she was crying.

Eadyth regarded her for a moment, and then pulled Gieva into her arms. "Of course, my dear girl," Eadyth stroked her hair, and Gieva felt her tears release onto the queen's shoulder, "You may come with us." She released Gieva and held her at an arm's length. "But you will never be a servant to me. You are a daughter of a long line of brave men and strong women, and you come to us as a kinswoman and a friend. If you wish to return to the Gyrwas in the future you may do so, but you will always have a seat in our hall."

Gieva had only been to Grantabricge once before, when she was a little girl and her father had sworn himself to Cynhelm. She remembered the tall wooden walls around the perimeter and the bridge over the river Granta, from which the *burh* got its name, but she had remembered it being much bigger the last time.

There was food and drink in the hall, but there was no joy in it. The king offered gifts to those of Cynhelm's men who had stayed in defense of the *burh*, and they drank to the memory of those who had died.

"The day will come when all men must die," the king said, "and hopefully as bravely as Cynhelm and his courageous warriors. *Nu sculon herigean rincas mihtig, ond munen þǣre onsægunge. Hægel.*" We should all praise these mighty warriors, and remember their legacy. Hail! He raised his horn and everyone repeated the word, "*Hægel,*" before drinking deeply. Gieva closed her eyes and drank to the memory of her father, and of Ælfhelm and the men who had died protecting them, and even of her poor mother and her little sister, and Leik and Lisse's mother, and the dozens who had died at Ealdham. They had not fought the Northumbrians in a shield wall, but they deserved praise just the same.

When the feasting was done, Gieva curled up under her blanket in one of the alcoves in the hall, but could not sleep immediately. She listened to the conversation die down to a quiet, low rumble. She watched the fire begin to die down and the torches were extinguished. The hall became quieter. Gieva felt her eyes close.

She was in the hall again. Not the large, well-built hall of Grantabricge, but the small, leaking, cramped village hall of Ealdham.

No, she thought, *no, I left this place, I can't be back here.*

It was dark, and she could hear the sounds of people snoring. But it wasn't snoring, not really. It was the sound of voices, very faint, all around her.

"I did what you told me," one of the voices said. "I stayed small, and quiet, just like you told me I should do."

Gieva looked round for the voice but could not find it.

The voice began to grow panicked. "I did what you told me to do. I'm frightened. I will hide, like you told me to do." The voice repeated over and over.

Gieva looked around frantically now, but it was too dark for her to see. She reached out to find her mother, but the other woman had made herself so small that Gieva could not seek her out in the darkness.

"Mother," she cried, "Mother, I'm coming, please hang on, I will get you out of here," she felt the tears streaming down her face and she groped in the darkness, the whispers growing louder and louder.

"Why did you get to live?" one of the voices said. It sounded like a child's voice, frightened and crying. "Why do you get to live but I had to die?"

Gieva whipped her head around, but the voice was all around her. She heard the woman screaming as the Northumbrians raped her. "Coward!" she screamed, "you coward, you should have done something! You should have fought back!"

"You murdered your own kinsman and yet you live!" shouted another voice, "you are a coward and a kinslayer!"

"Mother!" she screamed, "Mother, please help me, I am so frightened!"

"Kinslayer!" the voices were shouting, "he will never enter the Feast because you took his life! You should have died screaming, Kinslayer!"

The dark hall began to lighten with the yellow glow of a fire, and Gieva could see them now, their flesh burning and bubbling away, their voices harsh and hoarse, and she tried to scream but smoke filled her lungs. The fire began to catch on her clothes, stained with the blood of her kinsman, and licked her skin as the roar of "Kinslayer!" filled the burning hall…

Gieva kicked her blanket away, and it took her a moment to realize that it was not actually on fire. It was dark, but not the pitch-blackness that it had been; the glowing coals illuminated her skin, which was still connected to her bones, her hand still wrapped in its splint.

She realized that there was someone sitting next to her, and squinted in the darkness to determine who it was. The hand touched her cheek and wiped away the tears and sweat. "It was just a dream," Rægenhere whispered.

Gieva wanted to say something, but she sobbed instead. Rægenhere's arms were around her in an instant, and she gripped his shirt as she wept silently into his shoulder. She heard his voice, low and soft. He was singing, though she could barely hear the words, and the deep rumble of his voice held her as securely as his arms did.

There had been a light, clean summer rain that night, which tamped down the smell of smoke and dust. It only lasted a day, but it left everything cool; the air was thick with moisture and a green smell. There were explosions of flowers in patches through the wide meadow as the long column of people made their way along the road. Gieva wandered away from the column to gather some of the flowers, twining their stems together into a long chain. It was slow work with her right hand still splinted and wrapped, but her fingers were free to move and she had made so many blossom crowns as a girl that she did it almost without thinking.

She had nearly picked enough when she saw Rægenhere approaching her. She looked away from him, embarrassed. He had spent the night by her side, holding her, singing quietly in her ear, but she felt a fool. She was still so frightened and so lost, and she felt a strange twinge of guilt as she thought of how kind and beautiful he was, and how much she had loved sleeping with him beside her.

"I don't want you to be left behind," he said.

"I like the quiet." Gieva bent to pick up another flower. "There was no need to come and fetch me. I won't go far."

"What are you making?" He kept pace with her as she walked through the damp grass.

"Just a daisy chain," she said absently, twining another stem through the loop of the first. She looked around for another purple flower, but saw only a sea of yellow and green. Her annoyance plainly showed on her face, which seemed to frighten him off, as he had stopped keeping pace with her.

A moment later, however, he appeared by her side again.

"The final jewel in your crown," he said, holding out his hand to show her the purple blossom.

She prayed to all the gods that he would not see the color rise in her cheeks when her hand brushed his as she took the flower from him.

"You look like an *ælf-mæden* off to do some mischief," he said when she had placed the string of flowers on her hair.

"Didn't your mother teach you anything about the *ælfcynn*?" she said, "You ought not to come too close or I'll steal your shadow."

"You can have my shadow if you want it," he said, his fingertips tracing the line of her cheek, drawing her closer, "although I am rather attached to it." His lips brushed hers just as lightly as if it had been an accident. She jumped back as if she had been burned. He hesitated, and, seeing her surprise, he took a step back. "I am so sorry," he said, "I shouldn't have done that."

Gieva swallowed. "No, I suppose not," she said it impassively; though her heart was thudding so loudly she was sure he could hear it. It was too soon. Too soon. She ought not to feel the fluttering of happiness at his touch. Not yet. Her lips tingled where they had touched his. She felt a leaden sense of guilt at how much she liked it.

"Please forgive me," he said, "I had no right to touch you without your permission. I didn't even consider the fact that you might not be interested." He looked nervously at her face, waiting for a reaction. "I'll just go…"

"No," Gieva said more forcefully than she had meant to do. "I'd like you to stay with me."

His face lit up in a grin. She felt another little lurch of guilt, though less insistent than the first, as her own lips curved into something like a smile as well; as she slipped her hand into his.

"Do you think you'll ever come back?" Rægen asked as they walked a little apart from the column through the knee-high grass speckled with flowers.

Gieva looked back once more, and Grantabricge had disappeared. "I should," she said slowly. "I know that it would only be right for me to return here and rebuild my father's house, and try to pick up the pieces, but…" she took a deep breath, "I just can't. It hurts too much."

Rægen watched the ground as they walked, apparently unsure of what to say, but eventually he seemed to find some words. "I hate that you were put in the middle of all of this. That any of this had to happen to you."

Gieva squeezed his hand. "Wars are never just between *cyningas* or *ealdormen*, after all. Someone is always caught in the middle. This time it was simply my fate to be one of those people." She looked toward the north, where she knew her home lay beyond the horizon, and her thoughts were interrupted. "Is that a horse?" she asked.

Rægen squinted in the same direction and confirmed. There was indeed a horse trotting lazily toward the column, and when it had drawn close enough, Gieva gasped with painful recognition.

"That's Freolice!" Gieva cried, running forward. She clicked her tongue a few times, slowing to a walk as she approached the horse, Rægen following a few paces behind her. "You've found me, my old friend!" Gieva said as Freolice sniffed at her hand for a treat. Gieva lamented the fact that she had nothing to give the dear beast.

"It's my father's horse," she explained as she held out her hand for Freolice. The mare looked at Rægen, ignored him, and let Gieva stroke her dappled neck.

He had had the good sense to dart back to the column to grab a rope when he had seen the free-running horse, and Gieva took it from him and slipped it over Freolice's neck to keep her from running off again.

"Where did she come from?" Rægen asked.

"I set her loose from Ealdham the night the Northumbrians came," she said, stroking Freolice's nose absently. "I didn't want them to steal her if the battle turned sour."

"Good idea," Rægen said, letting Freolice sniff his hand and giving her a pat on the nose.

Gieva smiled, "Yes, I thought it was rather clever. Ælfhelm thought it was a bad idea, but I figured she was better free than a prisoner." She stopped and felt a lump develop in her throat.

"Who is Ælfhelm?" Rægen asked.

Gieva's smile disappeared and she considered how much of the story she thought she ought to tell him, but remembered how he had been there for her in the dark when she was frightened, remembered his voice surrounding her and keeping the nightmares at bay, and she decided it would not do to lie.

"He was my cousin," she said, looking down. She could almost see the stains of his blood on her broken hand.

"What happened?" Rægen asked quietly. They were well enough away from the column that no one could hear, but she was still afraid to say it aloud. She licked her lips, bending her fingers painfully within the splint.

"I let him go," Gieva said finally. "They wanted him alive. They were torturing him, mutilating him, and he was dying. So I helped him. That's why the big one broke my hand. He was angry. But Ælfhelm was no longer their prisoner, and that's what matters. Even if it makes me a kinslayer." She choked out the last word, hearing it screeched again in her ears. She was afraid that he would be disgusted with her, but she fixed him with a hard stare all the same. The nightmares might tell her differently, but in the light of day she knew that she had done the right thing, and she wanted Rægen to know it as well.

"You sent him to the gods," he said quietly. "You came to comfort the dying and take him home. You are no kinslayer. You are one of the *Wælcyrigena*, the choosers of the slain." He brushed a wisp of hair back from her face. "If I should be so lucky that you could find me on the battlefield and take me to Woden's halls, I would never fear death."

She wondered if he would kiss her then, and part of her rather hoped that he might. But the larger, miserable part of her wanted only to let him hold her while she imagined that his words were true.

She glanced back over her shoulder at the wide expanse of fenlands. It was over. She could take their memories with her. Her mother and father, who always loved her; her sweet little sister; her brave, handsome cousin. She would never forget them, but they did not have to haunt her. As Rægen took her good hand in his, they led the foundling horse back to the column and Gieva left the ghosts behind her.

*****

Sunniva's appetite for food and drink and good conversation seemed to have doubled while the Frankisc men were with them, and even the dismal weather did not have its usual effect on her mood. It was dull and damp, but so far only had threatened rain.

Godomar had lured her to the fireside where he was teaching her a new dicing game from the East, and she felt a little flutter in her stomach every time he called her "beautiful *vrouwe*," or when he would casually touch her arm while they were speaking together.

She glanced over to Ecgric, and the giddy flutter was replaced by an ache somewhat lower in her belly. She remarked to herself how different the two were. One, bright and handsome and rich as pure gold; the other, hard, lustful, and powerful as iron. How strange that she could like both of them for such different reasons, and yet why shouldn't she be able to have both?

When Godomar gave her yet another gift, this time a pair of pretty little silver brooches, Ecgric looked as if he could have ripped a log in half with his bare hands. She would have liked to see that, frankly, but she was more interested in the presents.

Ecgric was toying moodily with the big silver ring he always wore, refilling his horn cup with ale at regular intervals and seeming to grow increasingly agitated as Sunniva flirted with Godomar. She noticed that Ecgric refused to touch the strong red wine that Godomar had brought to share with them, preferring their own boring, dark brown beer.

The wine was stronger than mead or ale, and it rose to her head after only two cups. She'd never tasted anything like it before. She was not entirely sure if she enjoyed the tart flavor, but she liked the way it loosened both her tongue and her legs. She realized that she was glancing over at Ecgric more and more, even as she talked with Godomar.

Godomar left to speak with some of his own men for a time, and Ecgric took his vacated seat. For once he did not seem to be glowering. On the contrary, the way Ecgric was looking at her made her want to take him behind the hall and let him ruin her.

"It's rather hot in here," she said, "I'm going to go outside for a moment."

She left the hall and waited in the shadows for him to follow her. He caught up with her a moment later, and they walked around the outside of the Bricgweard. She stumbled slightly; the wine rising to her head and making her dizzy.

"I think the Frankisc man is trying to get you drunk," he said, half-jokingly. "You shouldn't spend too much time with his sort. Foreigners and Christians. You can't trust them."

Sunniva stopped in her tracks and glared at him, incredulous. "And you should not presume to tell me with whom I may associate. I have opened my hall to a friend in the spirit of hospitality, and you have moaned the entire time for no reason, except that he reminds you that you are not the only man in my life. I should not have to justify being gracious."

"It's a little more than graciousness," Ecgric said. "It seems as though you like him." He said it as if it was a jest, but he seemed genuinely concerned.

"Yes. I do like him. He is clever, and tells excellent stories, and he's well-travelled and good-looking and brings me lots of presents. So yes, I do like him." Sunniva's arms were crossed. She normally enjoyed seeing him in a jealous rage because it almost always led to a night of furious passion between them, but the charm was quickly wearing off and she was beginning to become quite annoyed.

He was frowning and she heard a twinge of anger in his voice though he tried to keep a reasonable tone. "You said that you would not share me, and yet you seem to be opleased to give your favors to other men. How is that fair? Perhaps you ought to creep into his bedtonight, instead of mine."

Sunniva stopped walking, turned to Ecgric and slapped him as hard as she could. "Are you some insipid washerwoman now, to be playing these games?" she asked venomously.

"I might ask you the same thing!" he said, looking as if he wanted to throttle her, but he balled his hands into fists.

"Go fuck your whores then," she spat, "maybe then I'll be able to show simple courtesy to a man without you pissing yourself with jealousy!"

They glared at one another for a long time, and she hated how much she ached to have him, raw and powerful as he was in that moment. She steeled herself against it and did not break eye contact.

His eyes seemed to soften and he attempted to touch her arm, but she became stiff and pulled away, wrenching her hand out of his grip.

"Sunniva, please," he reached for her again but she glowered at him.

"Do not touch me," she said through gritted teeth. "I am your lady and you will not touch me without my permission. Now get away from me." She said each word as if she were shooting an arrow into him. The look on his face was satisfyingly pitiful but furious at the same time, and he turned away. She kept glaring at him, trying to keep her hands from shaking by balling them into fists at her side.

Pig-headed man, she thought grumpily as she returned to the hall. He followed not long after, though she ignored him. The few times Ecgric caught her eye they stared at one another venomously, and she looked back to the bright, well-built figure of Godomar. Her cup seemed to refill itself, and she found herself moving closer and closer to the Frankisc *graf*.

"Tell me about Rome," she said to Godomar. She was twirling a lock of hair around her finger but she realized that for once she was not doing it in order to make Ecgric jealous. Indeed, she was becoming rather giddy from the drink and the way Godomar was watching her. They had moved to a more comfortable area of the hall to play a game of merels, though neither of them had taken a turn in quite a while.

"Well," Godomar shifted so that he was very close to her now, "Think of the biggest town you have ever visited, and then push all of those people into a space the size of Wuffingham village, and you've got the idea. It's terribly crowded."

"I like crowds," Sunniva said, "And they have great tall buildings there, don't they?"

Godomar considered a moment. "There are still a number of large buildings made of stone," he said, "Though some have crumbled or were destroyed in fires over the years. Most of the churches still stand, however, and they are tall and richly painted and sculpted. I think you'd enjoy seeing them."

"I'll bet they're beautiful," Sunniva slurred, leaning forward.

"The beauty of Rome is a rush light compared to your brilliance, fair *vrouwe*," Godomar said, and Sunniva realized that she was blushing.

"It is good to see you smile," he said, "You seemed rather upset earlier, after the fight with your husband."

Sunniva stopped smiling immediately. "What?" she blurted.

"I am sorry, I did not wish to interfere, but I heard some heated voices and I just wished to make sure that you were well," he said.

Sunniva opened her mouth with realization and closed it again. "Oh, that," she said. "It was nothing. And he is not," she put a deep stress on the word 'not,' "my husband."

Godomar looked politely interested. "Oh, pardon me. I only assumed that he was because you spend a good deal of time together."

"No, no," she said lightly, waving a hand. She realized that Ecgric was watching her, and was sure that he could hear what she was saying. "He is my bodyguard," she said. "No more than that."

Ecgric stood and left the hall, his face a blank mask, but she knew what he was thinking. She shifted even closer to Godomar and sipped her wine.

"Oh that is good news," he said quietly, and she felt another giddy flutter as he moved one of his pieces to capture hers. He was close enough that he could have kissed her, and she half-closed her eyes in anticipation, but he pulled back when he had made his move. She blinked and licked her lips once, nervously.

"Would you take me to Rome, the next time you go there?" Sunniva vaguely registered her voice slurring. "I should very much like to travel." She drained the cup and felt the heat rise into her cheeks again.

Again she felt a sensation in her stomach as if it had been plucked out by a swooping eagle, as he brushed one of her curls back over her shoulder. "It would be my very great pleasure," he said, and he refilled her cup.

Sunniva woke with a throbbing headache and her mouth tasting like bile. She did not remember precisely how she had gotten to her bed. She lifted herself onto an elbow, judging by the light in the room that it was morning. She staggered to the basin and splashed water on her face, swearing loudly when it dribbled down between her breasts. Well, she had had the presence of mind to undress, at the very least. She thought for a moment. She remembered someone carrying her to bed. She felt a flush of embarrassment at the idea that it might have been Godomar. She had been much too drunk last night, she knew. How much had she actually had?

Godes hæmađ min ears, what must he think of me?

Sunniva had not much time to think on it, however, when the door creaked open.

"What do you want?" she asked Ecgric. Her eyes had not yet adjusted to the glare from outdoors and she could not read his expression. He entered the room. She wished he would leave it again.

"I wanted to check on you," he said. His tone was flat.

Sunniva scowled. "I am quite well, thank you." She chewed each word and spat it at him. "I was very well cared for last night." She had a desire to make him angry, and by reminding him that Godomar had been the last one to see her awake the previous night, she knew this would hit the mark.

"Yes," Ecgric said, "By me."

Sunniva opened her mouth once or twice but she had no words.

"You were unwell," he said. His voice was still level and it made her want to hit him. "I helped you to your bed so that you would not make a further fool of yourself."

Sunniva wanted to shout several well-chosen curses at him, but her head was still cloudy. She satisfied herself with a snort of derision.

"Well, it was my duty as your bodyguard." He said the last word very slowly and she finally heard some anger in his voice.

"Oh, just stop it!" she shouted at him. "You aren't a Christian, so stop being such a martyr." She was satisfied to see, now that her eyes had adjusted to the light, that he was angry as well.

"Did you fuck him?" He asked. His voice was now contorted with suppressed rage.

"Go to the woods," she very nearly screamed at him. "Now."

"What?" he paused, nonplussed. He was tensed, ready for an argument, but his eyes were narrowed in nothing but confusion.

"We are going to fight."

Ecgric barked a laugh despite himself. "What are you talking about?"

Sunniva pushed him out the door and followed after, still half-naked. It was early, much earlier than she had thought. It was also quite cold, she realized, and she ran back inside to put on shoes and a proper tunic.

"Woods," she spluttered as she emerged again, wanting to slap the baffled half-smile off of his face, "Go. Now. I don't want anyone to see this except for you and me."

She watched him walk confusedly in the direction of the wood, and she yelled at him, "Get a sword, you *swines scitte*." He detoured toward the practice yard to retrieve a blunted practice sword and a shield.

Sunniva followed him, seizing weapons of her own and walking briskly and intently and staring straight ahead as she went, until they had reached the woody area near the Bricgweard.

He looked back at her for only an instant before her sword flashed, catching him off guard. He essentially abandoned his sword arm as she doled out furious hacks against him. He shouted in alarm when she smacked the dull sword hard against the outside of his knee, realizing that she was not simply playing a game. She slashed at him and shoved her shield into his, pushing him deeper into the wood.

"What is wrong with you?" he shouted at her.

"I – am – angry –" she said, smacking at him with each word, and paused for half a moment to say, "I am tired of you trying to tell me what I can and cannot do!" he parried each of her sword blows with his shield and began to slide into a legitimate warrior stance. "Obviously my words mean nothing to you, so I need to teach you a – lesson!" she shoved her body weight against his shield and swore when she could do little to shift him.

He got a few blows in but they were ineffectual, either because she was too furious to feel pain, or because he did not actually want to hurt her. She hoped for the latter. She wanted him to underestimate her. She had been practicing. He had taught her how to fight, and now she would show him what would happen when he tried to control her.

"Well I --" he whacked her once on the shoulder, "am tired of your games!" He ducked as she slung a furious strike at his head.

"No more games," she said. "We fight. I win, and you mind your own fucking—" she hit him in the flank, "—business!"

She ducked below his shield and hooked her foot around the back of his knee, and he had stumbled backward a pace or two, before she ducked out again and heaved her shield against him so the he fell over. He swore loudly as he made to get to his feet, but she had already put the dull point of her sword to his neck.

"Submit," she ordered.

He said nothing and she kicked his shield out of his hand, straddling his chest so that he could not move.

"Submit." She pressed the dull point just slightly harder.

They stared at one another for a long time and she felt the rise and fall of his chest under her. She could feel his pulse through the dull iron. He held up his hands in surrender, bewildered.

Sunniva threw away her sword and, still straddling him, forced him to sit upright, clamping her mouth on his as his free shield hand found her breast. It hurt slightly when he squeezed it and she pulled away, slapping him across the face. The same angry fire that sometimes glinted in his eyes did so once again and he roughly pushed her off of him, pinning one of her arms above her head by the wrist.

She bit his lip and dug the nails of her free hand into his shoulder. A forceful groan of pleasure erupted from her mouth as he found her cunt with his fingers. She was wet and full of incomprehensible rage and lust as she growled "I hate you," in his ear, and she opened her legs for his fingers as he pushed two of them inside of her.

"Likewise," he growled, and she groaned again as he moved his fingers and caused her to writhe beneath him. She lifted her leg and in one push had him on his back again. She yanked at his breeches and found what she wanted. It was hard and strong and angry as he was, and she cried out as she impaled herself on it.

Sunniva lay on the ground panting when she had finished with him. She was still half-drunk from rage and alcohol and sex, her heart hammering and her body still convulsing in spasms of pleasure. Ecgric lay a few feet away, quite as still as if she had killed him. She wondered for a moment if she had done, until he sat up. He was grinning that stupid grin that she hated and loved at the same time, and she wanted to punch him all over again.

Her blood cooled and her muscles unclenched, and she sat up as well. Her throat was raw from screaming at him and her head was throbbing. Ecgric got to his feet and held out a hand to help her up. She glared at him as she got to her feet without his assistance and said, "This isn't over."

"I certainly hope for a rematch," he said, and they gathered their weapons and went back to the Bricgweard together.

Somehow the physical manifestation of her anger against Ecgric helped to calm her more than talking ever did. She was exhausted and her ears were ringing, but she did not feel the need to box his ears anymore. Beating him with a dull sword was infinitely more satisfying.

She had no few twigs and leaves stuck in her hair, and it took her a rather long time to comb through it all. The wine from the night before, coupled with the exertion of beating the pulp out of Ecgric had begun to creep up on her by the time she had finished. Her head was splitting, but when she tried to drink some weak beer to banish her headache it only made her queasy.

When the door opened, Sunniva glared at the entrant in annoyance. "I am still cross with you, Ecgric," she said when she saw who it was. "Why don't you go away and do something useful?"

Ecgric entered the room unbidden, and Sunniva put down her comb to scowl at him.

"Sunniva," he said, dropping to one knee in order to put their eyes at a level, "I am sorry that I did not act graciously toward your guest. It was unbefitting of someone in my position. More than that, I am sorry I made you angry. You know that was not my intent."

Sunniva raised her eyebrow skeptically. "Is this all you needed? All I had to do was to hit some sense into you with a blunt instrument so you could learn some common decency?"

Ecgric gave a sigh that seemed drenched in weariness. "I am trying to tell you that I acted poorly, so do you accept or not?"

Sunniva still looked at him quizzically, but picked a piece of twig out of his hair. "You need to stop being so jealous," she said. "If I wanted to sleep with other men then I would have done already. There's a reason you share my bed, you know."

Ecgric nodded sheepishly and Sunniva was still perplexed. It was so out of character for him to apologize for anything, that she wondered what ulterior motive he may have had.

"Does this mean you will stop being so rude to my guests?" she asked, pulling her fingers through his tangled mess of hair.

"If it means I can go back to the whores," he said, but she knew that he was jesting as he found her lips with his own.

She poked him in the chest. "You are such a pig!" she said, giggling as he kissed the side of her neck.

He shrugged noncommittally and she allowed him to explore for a moment, before he stopped suddenly. "Do you hear that?" Ecgric said, looking over his shoulder at the still-open door.

Sunniva perked up as well, hearing the sounds of movement from outside. She walked to the door, tying her hair back in a braid, and saw several *thegns* milling about and speaking excitedly.

"What's going on?" Sunniva asked loudly to no one in particular.

She heard a shouted answer, and turned to Ecgric.

"You ought to tidy yourself up a bit," she told him, "you wouldn't want to greet the *cyning* looking like you've just been out in the woods fucking his only daughter."

*****

Rædwald sat and talked with the Frankisc man for half the evening about trading and ships and all those things in which Eadyth took little interest. She settled herself with watching the people in the hall; many of their men who had gone north were being given food and drink and gifts for their service, and the noise in the hall steadily grew as they showed off their new wealth.

Rægen and Gieva were closeted together, and Eadyth was pleased at how happy they both looked. Gieva would always have the burden of grief behind her eyes, but they both seemed to glow when they were together and she was pleased for them to have found one another. Sige and Edwin were laughing over a game of dice, and Sunniva was looking at Ecgric in an entirely indecent manner that made Eadyth want to box the man's ears.

She felt a pang at the absence of Eorwald, though. He would be well enough with Ricbert, but it calmed her when all of her children were under a single roof.

The hall became quiet once more as people began to curl up under blankets for the night. She saw Sunniva depart for bed, but she knew that she would be back at some point in the night to visit Ecgric. *Just as long as she doesn't get a bastard in her...* Eadyth thought resignedly, and bade everyone goodnight.

"You seem to have made a valuable friend," Eadyth said to Rædwald when they had retired to their chamber. She pulled the heavy golden ornaments from her ears and placed them in their bowl, and began to work on unwinding her hair.

"Godomar has some interesting insights into our trading practices," Rædwald said, "He and his family have been dealing in cloth for generations, and he's grown so rich off of it that he has become an *ealdorman*, or whatever the Frankisc equivalent is. *Graf*, I think he said. It's fascinating to be able to speak to someone who actually trades instead of *thegns* who only think they know what they are doing."

Eadyth let him prattle on about Godomar for some time before growing weary of it. She ran her fingers through her now-unbound hair and said, "If you keep talking like this, I might just have to stab him in a jealous rage."

Rædwald ceased his exaltations and smiled at her. "It's always good to have allies," he said with a shrug, and changed the subject. "Are you pleased to be home?"

Eadyth nodded, taking off her dress and hanging it on the hook by the door. "It's nice to see that nothing's burned down while we were away."

"I don't know about that," Rædwald said, suddenly cross. "Sunniva's had her hands full." He sat down on the bed and Eadyth climbed behind him, rubbing away the knots in his shoulders.

"Let's save it for the morning, shall we?" she said, moving his hair and kissing his shoulder. She loved that they were still broad and strong and curtained by the silver and gold hair that had been whipped about by the breeze into a tangled mess. She combed her fingers through it and put her arms around him. "I think we have some other things we ought to take care of tonight."

When morning arrived, Eadyth rather wished that she had let Rædwald tell her what had been going on, because she was not prepared to hear what the Christians had started doing to occupy their time.

Paulinus the Priest was the first to meet with the king the following morning. Sunniva sat next to Rædwald in Eadyth's normal seat in order to explain the actions and decisions she had made whilst they had been gone, and so Eadyth stood nearby with Ecgric. There were two more priests with Paulinus, both looking thoroughly unhappy to be there. One was very young, no more than nineteen or twenty years, flushed and fiery-eyed with red hair; the other was perhaps ten years older than Paulinus and had the same self-righteous composure that Eadyth found so annoying in Christians.

Sunniva was saying something to Rædwald that Eadyth could not hear, but she saw Rædwald's face grow steadily darker.

"Tell me what happened near Leofric's farm," Rædwald asked the younger priest, who suddenly looked frightened. The older priest began to say something, but Rædwald cut him off. "I am not asking you," he said, and turned back to the younger. "Tell me, boy."

The priest looked rather annoyed at not being addressed as "Father," as all of the other Christians called him, but licked his lips and began, "I believe there was a fire. A serving man's house was burned."

"Yes," said Sunniva, "and tell the *cyning* what caused that house to be burned?" She was gripping the arm of her chair anxiously.

"It was an accident," the young priest said with a touch of panic in his voice, "the fire was not meant to spread."

"There never should have been a fire in the first place!" Sunniva said loudly, shooting a look at her father which clearly was meant to say, *you see what I've had to deal with?*

"It was collateral damage in the ongoing work of the Lord," said the older priest, and Sunniva moved forward as if she might slap him. Eadyth rather wished she would, but Sunniva seemed to regain her composure and sat back in her chair.

"And what was this 'work of the Lord?'" Rædwald asked, putting a calming hand on Sunniva's arm. "You," he pointed to the younger priest once more.

The young one licked his lips and looked around, glancing over his shoulder at Paulinus and then back to look at Rædwald's knees. "We were cleansing the countryside of demons," he said quietly.

"Demons?" Rædwald asked conversationally.

The boy nodded. "By…" he looked around again, "by burning their altars."

Rægen and Sige had been standing at the edge of the platform chatting quietly and not paying attention, but Sige perked up like a hound on a scent when he heard the young priest say what they had done.

Eadyth's hands balled into fists and there was a ripple of agitation through everyone in the hall; even those who had accepted this nailed god knew that damaging a shrine to Woden or Eostre or any of the real gods would result in cataclysmic bad luck, even if the damage had been accidental. Purposeful destruction, now, that was something foreign and sickening that no one seemed to be able to wrap their minds around.

The elder priest piped up, "the altar to the Witch of Hell was burned to cleanse the lands of the corrupting influence!"

"You burned a sacred altar to Eostre!" Sunniva said in such a queenly voice that Eadyth had to admire her. "Have you no shame? No sense of decency or honor?"

"What do pagans know of honor?" the elder priest said venomously, but Paulinus put a hand on his shoulder to shut him up. Eadyth stepped forward, glaring at the man and touching the handle of the seax at her hip.

"Enough of this," Rædwald said with a warning look at Eadyth. "You two have desecrated a shrine, and that is detestable in itself. But the fire spread, and burned the home of an upstanding *ceorl* in the employ of one of my retainers. You will pay for the repair of both the house and the altar, and you will each give an additional *scylling* to the *ceorl* for the destruction of his property."

The terrified young priest seemed to relax that the price was only in silver. A good deal of silver to be sure, but far less than the cost of his life. The older priest looked insolently at Rædwald, but Paulinus stepped forward.

"I thank you for your swift justice, my *cyning*," Paulinus said in his usual greasy way, "I offer my sincerest apologies for the poor judgment of my fellows. Sometimes they can take themselves rather too seriously, you see, and—"

"You were supposed to be minding them," Rædwald said. "When you came here, you promised that none of your men would do anything except preach. Did you lie?"

"No, not at all," stammered Paulinus, "It simply got out of hand."

"I ought to have the lot of you hanged as vandals," said Rædwald.

"Please, *cyning*," said Paulinus, "You were baptized, you accepted Jesus Christ into your heart, and surely he is telling you that we mean only to do his work." His voice was so calm and reasonable that Eadyth wanted to cut out his tongue.

Rædwald was glowering, every eye in the hall fixed upon him. Eventually he looked up at Paulinus and said, "Your men will be confined to your house. You alone may go to perform mass, but your men are to stay away from the village. I will not have you bringing your bad luck among my people."

Paulinus looked as if he might object to this, but decided against it. "It will be as you ask, *cyning*," he said, and ushered his men out of the hall, the young one still looking terrified and the older looking as haughty and entitled as ever to have wriggled out of punishment.

The hall erupted with conversation almost immediately, and Sige and Rægen came toward the high seat to discuss what had just happened. Rægen seemed confused and agitated, and Sige was white with rage. Rædwald held up his hand before any of them had a chance to speak.

"It gets them out of the way," he said in answer to their unasked questions. "I won't kill men who are under the protection of the *heahcyning*. This is the only way." He said it quietly, and the look he gave them all silenced any further protests.

"Bloody, miserable, foul –" Eadyth heard Sigebryht muttering as he stumped out of the hall toward the practice yard. She saw him wrench open the storage shed and yank out a dull iron practice sword and a lump of charcoal that was usually used to draw targets for shooting practice. He scraped a large cross on the lumpy straw-filled dummy, and with a fury Eadyth had only ever seen in Eorwald, Sige swung the sword. The straw that had been the dummy's guts spilled as his sword sliced through the rough sack holding them in. He hacked again and the head came clean off, and again so that the sword stuck into the wood pike holding the whole thing up.

"Sunniva should have gotten rid of them," Sige muttered mutinously, wrenching the sword's blade out of the wood and dropping it to the ground. "We knew this would happen eventually. What does Rædwald think he is playing at?"

Eadyth sighed, shaking her head slowly. "You know that those priests are under Ethelbert's protection."

"And that gives them the right to burn altars? To desecrate shrines? Rædwald knows that they will just do it again, and yet he did not even punish them!"

Eadyth knew those thoughts as her own, but the reasonable portion of her mind had to take over now. "Your step-father was right. He knows that they deserved to be punished properly, but they are under the protection of Ethelbert and killing them would serve no good purpose. You don't understand how Christians' minds work, Sige. They aren't deterred by punishment. They thrive on it. They want to die for the sake of their god so that others will take up the mantle and continue their work."

"So if we ignore them then they'll stop?" Sige asked sarcastically. The tone was like nothing she had ever heard from him before, and it took her off her guard for a moment.

"I don't think anything will stop them," said Eadyth, looking into the East.

Chapter Eleven

Onsængunga and Bletsunga

Blessings and Sacrifices

Sige had promised, when the king decided to side with Edwin rather than turning him over to Athelfrith, that he would thank the gods properly upon his return to Wuffingham. Now, after learning what the priests had done to the shrine of Eostre on Leofric's land, he knew it would only be right to go to the *weoh* now.

He had nothing to offer the gods, he realized as he reached the hollow, and he was on the point of turning back to find something suitable for an offering when he heard the sounds of voices from the clearing. He could not see what was happening through the fog, but he heard the sound of a hammer or an axe striking wood and quickened his pace. When he entered the clearing he saw the carved pillars which represented the gods, and the silhouette of the massive Sacred Oak which protected them all, shrouded in mist. He heard the sound of a hammer again, and as he passed through the fog he saw two figures moving about.

"Wes hal," he called in a tentative greeting to the worshippers, who were robed in heavy, hooded cloaks, but they did not seem to hear him, nor did they seem to be praying. One was holding something that looked like an axe. He drew it back, and swung it in full force against the side of the Sacred Oak.

Fury and disbelief boiled in Sige at the sight of it, and he closed the remaining distance between himself and the two figures in several long strides. "What are you doing?" he shouted. One of the figures put his hands up and tried to stop Sige from touching the one welding the axe as he swung it again, burying it deeply into the side of the Oak.

"Stop this!" Sige yelled, slamming his body weight into the first man and knocking him to the ground.

"There are devils here," the axe-man said, drawing his weapon back again, but Sige grabbed the handle and wrenched it from his hands, "Devils, who have corrupted your king and made him forsake the ways of the Lord!"

Sige glared at the man, kicking the fallen one's hand aside as he reached for the other.

"You dare to interfere with God's work?" the older man said, his eyes blazing and a bubble of spittle forming at the edge of his mouth. "This is a shrine to devils and demons and draws the wrath of God! We must cleanse these people of their sins and their false idols so that the light of Christ can shine through!"

Sige stared, open-mouthed and sickeningly dumbfounded at them, and then back at the Oak. It was still solid and massive, but the Christian's axe had left deep wounds in its skin and sap stuck to the blade of the axe like blood.

"May all the gods strike you dead and the wolves feast on your guts, you miserable cowards," he said, stepping toward the axe-man.

"Your false gods will do no such thing," the elder Christian said, wedging himself between Sige and the axe-wielder. "If they were real, then they would have done something already! The one True God protects us from your devils, which are no more than wood to be hewn under our axes!"

Sige followed the Christians' eyes around the semicircle of pillars, each depicting one of the gods. He had not noticed before, having been so focused on the Christian's desecration of the Oak, but as he looked around at them he felt his stomach drop like lead.

The pillars to Eostre and Frea had been stripped of their finery, and Frea's pillar had been ripped from the earth itself. Thunor's iron hammer had been taken out of the wood and had been used to smash the front of the statue to Tiw. But the worst was the desecration of the statue to the All-Father. The stone which had been his eye had been pried out and was half-trodden into the dirt, and there were cut-marks across the carven face, leaving it unrecognizable. The sacred runes had been hacked with the axe so that they were unreadable, and Sige felt a surge of panic that the protective spells that would be broken if no one was able to read them.

"Those are your heathen gods," the old priest said, as the younger priest tried to wrench the axe out of Sige's hands. Sigebryht pushed the weedy youth away and continued to stare around in disbelief, his palms sweating gainst the shaft of the axe.

The old priest's face twisted into a grin. "Nothing but splintered wood and demonic magic. Kneel and we will bless you in the name of the Father— "

Sige swung and the Christian did not finish. There was a strange look of euphoria on the man's face as the axe dug itself into the shaved skull.

A puddle of piss appeared between the younger Christian's feet. "Please, do not hurt me!" he wailed pitifully. "I beg mercy!"

Sige almost gave it to him, but when he glanced back at the maimed statues of his gods he shoved the young priest against the Sacred Oak, his hand around the man's throat.

"Mercy?" he growled, "Mercy? I hope for your sake that your god is real so that he might save you from the vengeance I will bring on you." He squeezed tighter and the man's face began to purple as he spluttered and scratched at Sige's wrist to no avail.

"Sigebryht!" he heard a voice and looked over his shoulder as the Christian's legs began to jerk. "Stop! What are you doing?" Eadyth was running and just before the Christian's corrupted spirit left his body, Sige's hand was prized away from his neck.

The Christian began to splutter and cough, and Sige tried to throttle him again but Eadyth pulled him back. "Stop, Sige, Stop! What's going on?"

"Look!" Sige choked, indicating the statues. Eadyth turned slowly and her face fell. She covered her mouth with her hands, eyes wide in shock. She looked down at the two Christians, one whose blood splattered on the ground next to the bloody axe and the other, whose legs were twitching slightly as his eyes stared into nothingness.

"I'm going to rip his fucking –"Sige shouted at his mother, but Eadyth caught him as he lunged forward again.

"Stop, you can't do this here!" Eadyth looked as if she might be sick as she pulled him away from the Christians. "Sigebryht," she said in a measured but shaking voice, "You have spilled blood in a holy place. Do not make it worse."

Half an hour later, Paulinus was kneeling in the rushes before the high seat. "Please, *cyning* –" Paulinus sniveled before Rædwald, who wore a look of extreme disgust. "Please, just let me give my companions the proper death-rites!"

Sigebryht looked in disgust at the greasy little man who knelt in front of his step-father. The flame-eyed axe-wielder's blood still stained the hem of Eadyth's gown; she had wasted no time in making good on her promise to the youth.

No one in the hall seemed to pity Paulinus, after they had found out what his companions had done to the *weoh*, unless it was to feel a shred of sickened pity for the way a grown man could scrape and beg for his life.

"You and your men lost that privilege when you defiled the *weoh*." Rædwald was almost as angry as he had been when he had spoken to the Northumbrian messenger outside Ealdham. "I told you to keep your men under control and they violated our holy place. There can be no forgiveness. Your priests will be given no burial and their souls will wander in torment until the end of the world."

The priest crossed himself. "Please," his voice was shaking as he wept, "Remember your promises, *cyning*! Remember the day you accepted Jesus –"

"I have no use for your nailed god," Rædwald growled. "And I have no use for those who serve him. Get out of my lands and never show your face here again."

Eadyth followed Paulinus out of the hall, with a look of such fury in her eyes that Sige followed her. When the priest had reached the palisade at the outer edge of the village, Eadyth had caught up to him. He grunted as she kicked the knees out from under him.

Paulinus said something, but Sige could not hear. He could, however, feel the anger radiating from his mother as she stepped behind the priest and wrenched his chin upwards, touching her seax to his throat. Sige had tensed as the Christian nearly shit himself with terror.

"Let me go, please, I beg you!" he sniveled. "I am under the protection of the *cyning*!"

"Oh, grow some balls, you worthless turd," Eadyth snarled. "I will not dirty my blade with blood as unclean as yours. I do not think my husband's words were clear enough."

"I am leaving, I am leaving! I promise!"

"You will not speak of this to anyone. You will tell no one how your priest was killed."

"Yes, my Cwene*!* I promise!"

"You will tell your companions, all of you vermin who perpetrate violence in the name of your god that they will not try to spread their disease here."

"But my Cwene," Paulinus whined, "it is our duty…"

Eadyth cut him off. "I swear by all the gods that if I ever see you or any of your creatures again, you will earn the same death as your worthless excuse for a god."

The priest nodded feverishly, the blade of the seax leaving a thin, shallow line on his neck.

"Start running," Eadyth whispered, "and pray that I don't decide to follow you."

Sige realized that he was gawping at his mother, but he hastily rearranged his face as she turned back to him. The priest's black robe had long-since flapped out of sight, but Eadyth's fury was still palpable.

"Why did you tell him not to say anything?" Sige asked stupidly, when he had regained his composure.

"You know that they will use the priests' deaths as a rallying point. We must not give them the opportunity to think that they have any more martyrs on their hands. They are butchers and liars, not saints."

Sige nodded, still perplexed.

"And you should say nothing either." Eadyth said. The fire behind her eyes seemed to cool slightly. "I don't want any of his creatures coming after you."

"Why would they –" he asked, but Eadyth shook her head.

"I told you, we will not speak of it. They are dead. That is the end of it."

Sige nodded, unsure. "What do we do now?" he asked.

Eadyth frowned. "We rebuild."

Edwin had returned from his examination of the *weoh* a little while later, looking bewildered. "They've moved the bodies," he told Sige, "and they are beginning to repair the statues. Wuduwine is going to start work on a new statue for Woden, but he says he can repair the damage to the others."

Sige grimaced. “I know that these are only statues, but the sight of them vandalized and violated like that; it was as if those Christians were defiling everything that we are, everything that makes us human.” He had not realized how much it had shaken him until he had calmed down from the initial shock.

Edwin sighed. “No one expects something like that. I would have thought that everyone was civilized in the face of foreign beliefs. The Wælisc are Christians but they were still welcoming of my gods, even though they did not believe in them. I had thought that all Christians would act the same way. If Christ is so powerful, why would he care if he was worshipped or not?”

Sige did not respond. He was still too stunned after seeing something that had once been so permanent, such an intrinsic part of his life, reduced to a desecrated mass of splintered wood. After a while, he asked, “Where did they put the priests’ bodies?”

Edwin pursed his lips. “I don’t know. Somewhere out of sight of the gods.”

“I think I should bury them,” Sige said.

Edwin looked bewildered. “Why?”

Sige did not really know why. He had personally cursed the priests’ foul spirits to torment after the way they had defiled the holy place, but somehow he felt uneasy about leaving any man to rot. “It feels like bad luck to leave them for the carrion birds. I worry that I might be cursed as well.”

“Why on earth would you be cursed?”

“I’ve spilled blood in a sacred place where all men should be at peace. No weapons should ever be drawn that space, and the Christian priests are never meant to see bloodshed.”

“Are you afraid their god might find you?”

“It’s not funny, Edwin. They knew that our gods would do nothing to protect the altars. They knew that Thunor would not strike them dead with a lightning bolt for trying to cut down the Oak. That’s why they had no problem doing it.”

“But their god did not protect the priest from being killed,” Edwin said reasonably. “You were acting on behalf of the real gods for destroying the one who dishonored them.

“They felt they were acting rightly. That old priest was not even afraid to die; he looked like he had just died in glory on the battlefield.” Sige sighed. “I know that I’ve done wrong. I should not have killed them there. I should have waited, brought them to Rædwald, or at least have taken him outside of the *weoh*. I feel like I have to make up for my crime."

"I think Woden will understand if we leave them to rot," Edwin said, and Sige was annoyed at the sound of a jest in his voice.

"You don't know what Woden thinks," Sige said, and in his heart he added, *because the All-Father is now just a splintered piece of wood.*

*****

The king had given Gieva all of the rings and wealth which he would have given her father for his bravery, but she did not want any of it. She had no use for gold or weapons, and they only reminded her of the family that she had lost. At Eadyth's suggestion, Gieva had used some of the unwanted wealth to build a house on the land the king had given her, only about a quarter of a mile from the Bricgweard. It was sturdy, it was simple, and it was hers. She planted vegetables and herbs, she visited with Eadyth, she spun and wove blankets and hangings for the walls, and even made cheese from the bad-tempered nanny goat. It was not exactly the same as rebuilding her life, but perhaps it was good enough to be getting on with.

Rægen came as often as he could; he was frequently away on errands with the king and as such she did not see him nearly as often as she wished to. Even so, she would nearly run to him when his beaming face would appear at her door, and they would walk together and talk for hours. Slowly, gradually, she felt her shattered life beginning to mend itself. She was not happy exactly; it would perhaps be a long time until she could feel properly happy again, and she still felt guilty whenever she kissed Rægen or when she would laugh and she would have the swooping feeling of joy in her stomach.

One afternoon, Eadyth made her way down to Gieva's house with a basket of food and a jug of ale to share. She had been teaching Gieva some of the properties of herbs and how to tend wounds and the like, and Gieva soaked in the information. Mother had tried to teach her these things, things any woman ought to know for the care of a family, but more often than not

Mother would become confused and the lesson would remain untaught. She only felt a twinge of guilt that she was finally learning things that she ought to have learned as a child. The lessons were far too important to leave room for guilt.

They ate and talked as they always did, and decided to walk down toward the edge of the wood in the hopes of collecting some of the summer fruits that grew near to the stream. Eadyth's mood seemed to match the dull, grey sky as it threatened rain.

"Is there something troubling you?" Gieva asked when they had reached the stream.

Eadyth sighed. "There is always something troubling me," she said, "it is one of the great joys of being responsible for a lot of people. That business with the Christians..." Eadyth trailed off with a growl of irritation.

Gieva clenched her jaw. It was a terrible thing to have happened, and she had nearly wept when she had seen the desecrated *weoh* and the spilled blood of the foreign priests. "What type of god would condone that?" She asked for what felt like the thousandth time, "it's just awful."

Eadyth shook her head wearily. "A god who is taking over the world," she said, her voice uncharacteristically quiet. She began picking through some of the plums that had fallen to the ground, tossing the rotten fruits away and adding a few of the better examples to her collection. "The Christians are hard enough to deal with, but with everything that's been happening in the North, and trying to establish the trading port at Gipeswic, it's all been a nightmare."

The basket slipped from Gieva's fingers and the fruits scattered across the grass. She'd taken off the splint on her arm, but she was stiff and clumsy as she tried to pick up the fallen plums. "I do not envy your responsibility," she said. "It must be very difficult to be a *cwene*."

Eadyth nodded. "I haven't felt so lost since I first came here, when I married the *cyning*. I felt like an outsider. I felt like a stupid child, and I just wanted to run into the woods and live like a wild thing for the rest of my life. I was buried under a mountain of fear and responsibility, and I didn't know how to get out from under it." She smiled, as if at some long-lost memory, "but I had to remember something my father told me when I was young. When there is a job to be done, you just have to do it, piece by piece. So I just had to start digging away at the mountain a little at a time. Eventually it levelled out and I found my stride, but it was hard going."

"I must remember that," Gieva said.

"Yes, fathers tend to give good advice. At least mine always did. I am sure mothers do as well, though I never really knew mine."

"My father did as well," Gieva said sadly, "and my mother," she paused for an instant, swallowing, "she did her best."

"As do you," said Eadyth, putting her hand on Gieva's shoulder. They gathered up their baskets and headed back toward the village. "You are doing so well, despite everything that's happened," Eadyth said. "I am quite proud of your resilience."

"I don't know about that," said Gieva, shrugging, "I've just had a lot of bad things happen to me, and I have had to either adapt to them, or die of despair. In truth I sometimes wonder if the latter wouldn't be easier. I still cry at night. I still feel like it's my fault that they all died, and I wish I could bring them back, just so that I could tell them how sorry I am." She swallowed again, as a hot lump had formed in her throat. "And aside from you and Rægen and Sunniva, everyone seems to want me to get back to the Fens where I belong."

"Girls can be cruel sometimes," Eadyth said.

Gieva became angry at the thought of the taunts and snide remarks she had received since her arrival. "Do you think they don't like me because I am not Englisc? Some people in the north don't like the Gyrwas, but I didn't think the differences were that great..."

Eadyth laughed. "Oh, my sweet girl," she said, "You must give us more credit than that."

"I didn't mean to offend…" Gieva said, but Eadyth stopped her with a smile.

"You misunderstand," Eadyth said, "I don't think the young ladies of Wuffingham dislike you because you are Gyrwa. It is much simpler, and much stupider than that." She was grinning now. "They envy you."

Now she was quite confused, and Eadyth laughed.

"I'm proud that I have a son who is kind and brave and beautiful," Eadyth said, "And I am pleased that he likes you, because you are also kind and brave and beautiful, and you two clearly care about one another. Those girls, however, are not pleased, and they are envious, because each one of them had thought that Rægen would sing them pretty songs and look at them the way he looks at you."

Gieva bit her lip, still unsure.

"Pay no mind to them," Eadyth said briskly, "Those girls are just that; girls. They will gossip and bicker and then they will find men just as silly as they are and they will slowly begin to grow up."

It was not exactly comforting, and not so easy to ignore the snide remarks when you were stuck indoors doing activities which left tongues free to wag, but Gieva knew that Eadyth was right. Besides, Gieva knew the way he looked at her, and the thought of that look was enough to weather any storm of words from petty young women. She hefted the basket higher on her arm, her lips twitching into a smile.

They were halfway back to her house when Gieva saw two men hurrying toward them. Gieva knew Rægen's long, slightly lazy gait almost immediately, and then recognized the broad, strong man she usually saw with Sunniva, whose name she did not remember.

"My Cwene," the broad man said when he drew near, "you're needed in the Bricgweard."

Eadyth frowned. "Can't it wait?"

"The *cyning* asked to see you immediately. He's had a messenger from the *heahcyning* and he wishes to speak with you."

"Thank you, Ecgric. I'll come with you." She handed her basket to Rægen. "Take these back to Gieva's house for me, won't you?" she said, and Rægen lagged behind with Gieva while Eadyth and Ecgric hurried back toward the Bricgweard.

"Don't you need to go back with them?" Gieva asked Rægen when Ecgric and Eadyth had departed.

"I can think of a host of other things that I'd rather be doing," Rægen said with that same grin that always made the world seem to light up. "Besides, I've already heard the message. There is going to be a *cyningesmot* soon, and father is to go to Cantwareburh in a fortnight. I expect Ethelbert wants to draw up a new law code and wants the input of his supporters." His smile made her want to collapse.

The dull grey sky had begun to spit a few drops of rain. "Do you know the *heahcyning* well?" Gieva asked.

"I have met him a few times," Rægen shrugged. "The last time was a few years ago, Ethelbert and his family had come to visit my father at the old hall near the Wood Bridge. Father was quite ashamed of the old thing, so he made sure to double the workers on the Bricgweard so that he'd never have to entertain in such squalor again." he smiled reminiscently, "Anyway, Ethelbert was rather fat and slow even then, and very fond of his drink, but sharp as a needle and as wise a *cyning* as anyone could wish. He would not have become *heahcyning* if he wasn't a man people looked up to."

"I hope that everything goes well, if the *cyningas* are to meet," Gieva said, "I know there has been some tension between your father and Cearl after Grantabricge."

"I shouldn't worry about that," said Rægen. "Ethelbert is the one keeping all of the other *cyningas* in line. It's the same with *ealdormen*, really; they fight and squabble amongst themselves, but in the end their loyalty is to their lord. So my father might dislike Sæwine of the Eastseaxe or Cearl of Mercia, but as they all look to Ethelbert as their leader, they will not openly war against one another."

"That is one good thing, at least," Gieva said, grinding her teeth. She hated the idea of war, having tasted it so bitterly in the past few months. He seemed to notice her agitation and turned the conversation to happier subjects, as they skirted the fields full of thickly growing green wheat and freshly-shorn grazing sheep.

They were still a long way away from Gieva's house when it started to rain in earnest. They were both soaked to the skin within moments, half-running and laughing as they were splattered with fat drops of rain, many of the plums tumbling out of their baskets. She gave it up as a bad job and slowed to a walk, and Rægen turned back to keep pace with her. She glanced at Rægen as he walked beside her, and was rather amused to find that he was staring intently at the way her soaking dress clung to her body, but he looked at her face as soon as she caught him.

"You are perfectly welcome to look," she said quietly, grinning, "I haven't got anything any other woman doesn't have."

"No, you have far more," He stopped walking and took her face in his hands, and kissed her. He could do it a thousand times, Gieva thought, and every time she would feel as if she'd been struck by lightning. Rain water rolled down his cheeks and she tasted it on his lips, and she pulled him closer, almost frantically. *How strange,* she thought dully, he had kissed her many times now, and she had loved every single one, but the shock and pain had still been too sharp in her memory and the guilt kept her from doing anything more.

Gieva had been surprised, and pleased, that Rægen had never pushed her into anything that made her uncomfortable. It made her feel safe to know that he would wait for her, and she had been more than content with stolen kisses and evenings snuggled into his arm by the fire.

It was almost like a lightning bolt through her chest as her body responded to his kiss, his touch, his body. She realized she was shivering, but did not want him to stop kissing her. She pushed up on her toes to keep him close to her, but he pulled away, slightly breathless.

"You're trembling," he said. She nodded vaguely and tried to kiss him again, but he took her hand. They abandoned the plums and ran back to Gieva's house.

She pushed open the door with shaking hands, and when they were both inside she turned to face him. Without speaking, she gave him a hard look and pulled his tunic over his head. She hung it on the line near the fire, and he came up behind her, putting his arms around her waist and unclasped the brooches that held her sodden dress closed. She felt almost weak when she felt his lips on the side of her neck. She still faced away from him as she lifted the underdress over her head, still shivering; his hands were still cold, and her nipples puckered when he touched them, but she liked the way it felt; his cold hands and the warmth of the fire alternating on her skin sent bolts through her body again. The fluttering in her belly was gone, replaced by a dull ache somewhat lower down. She felt paralyzed where she stood, letting him draw his fingertips down her waist until she turned around to face him again.

"You are so beautiful," he said, first looking at her naked body and then at her face, which she knew would be bright pink. She rather wanted to say the same to him as he grinned at her and the dim room seemed to become bright, but instead of speaking, she put her trembling hand to his waist, pulling the strings.

She was not an idiot; she knew what happened between men and women and what parts went where, but she felt strangely uneducated as they stood naked and facing one another.

"I've never done this before," she said.

"You do want to?" He asked hesitantly.

She nodded vigorously, pulling him close once more.

They leapt underneath the blankets on her bed, both still slightly damp and shivering, and she kissed him more eagerly than she had ever done before. It was mad and wonderful and strange to have him naked in her bed, his hands and his mouth finding places which Gieva never thought could give her such pleasure, and when she finally guided him inside of her there was no pain, no tearing, no blood; only a perfect happiness Gieva had thought she would never find again.

Rægen watched her as his breathing slowed. "By all the gods," he said, "By the sun and moon and stars and earth, I love you." His voice was muffled somewhat as he kissed her with every word, stroking her hair away from her face.

Gieva's open mouth curved into the biggest smile she had felt in weeks, months, even. "That's a mighty oath to swear," she said, "it's not just because I let you into my bed, is it?"

Rægen kissed her forehead, her cheeks, and her lips. "I've loved you since long before now," he cupped her cheek in his hand and grinned, "Though I can't say I'm not delighted you've let me into your bed."

She swallowed, finding tears in her eyes. "And I love you," her voice was suddenly hoarse, but she did not try to say anything more. His eyes were so bright and his grin so huge that all she could do was to kiss him.

"Do you want to be my wife?" he asked, resuming his stroking of her cheek, but suddenly looking uncertain.

The question caught her off guard. Her immediate thought was yes, of course she did, but her voice had left her. She opened her mouth but she could not answer him immediately.

"It's too fast," she managed to get out, and he was immediately crestfallen. She brushed her fingers through his still-damp hair. "I do want to be your wife," she said, "I love you, Rægen. I love you and I want to marry you, but I can't yet. I am still broken, and I need more time to mend." She bit her lip, knowing she might begin to cry again.

"Then I'll wait," he said, tucking a stray curl behind her ear and kissing her forehead. "A week, a month, a hundred years; as long as you need."

Gieva closed her eyes, nestling into his arms, and could feel the pain and the fear eroding away. It may not disappear completely, but he would wait for her, with her, until it was small enough that it did not cast its shadow over them. And that was why she loved him.

*****

Sunniva was sure that it was impossible for anyone not to like Gieva, but she had to give the rough side of her tongue to more than one girl who would make snide comments behind Gieva's back. Even Wynne had earned a smack from Sunniva after saying something about the "Gyrwa Fen-snake." Wynne had not spoken to Sunniva in days for that, which made Sunniva even more cross. She knew why Wynne was upset and jealous, but it was unfair. Rægen had never wanted Wynne, and she should not be so put out that he had found someone else, someone who made him so happy. More than that, Gieva should not be punished for Wynne's unrequited love.

Gieva would perhaps never be considered breathtakingly beautiful, but she had a gentle sort of sad loveliness which drew Sunniva's eyes, and she enjoyed the grace with which Gieva moved. Sunniva had always relied upon her own beauty to mask her inherent clumsiness and impatience, but Gieva seemed to have the grace of a warm wind at the beginning of summer, soft and patient and temperate and comforting. Even the way she spoke was gentle. It was no wonder that Rægen was utterly smitten by her.

Gieva noticed that Sunniva had been watching her sew a design onto the neckline of her new dress, and smiled. "Will you join me, my lady?" she asked.

"Don't call me 'my lady'," Sunniva said for the thousandth time. "We are friends. You should call me by my name."

Gieva nodded. "Habit. My apologies."

"I wish I had the patience for that sort of design," Sunniva said, examining the cloth in Gieva's hands. It was an elaborate pattern of interlaced birds in blue thread on the deep red background, the heads of which ended at the center were the neckline drew together. The majority of the design had been completed, but small marks had been made with charcoal to indicate the overall arrangement.

"It does take a great deal of patience," Gieva said. "I think I've been working on this side for a week. I hope I can finish it by the next feast."

"Speaking of which," Sunniva said brightly, fishing in the pouch at her waist for the reason she had come, and pulled out a small bundle wrapped in white cloth. "I have a present for you."

Gieva's face lit with pleasure and confusion as she accepted the bundle, and Sunniva watched as she uncovered the matching gold brooches within.

"I thought they would work well with the style of dress you're making." she indicated how the two clasps could be worn to fasten the coat-dress together.

Gieva grinned broadly and kissed Sunniva in thanks. "They're beautiful!" she said, "What have I done to deserve such pretty toys?"

Sunniva looked at her knowingly. "Call it a wedding present."

Gieva looked pensive and did not say anything, so Sunniva spoke instead.

"You know he's going to ask you," she said. "If he hasn't asked already, that is."

Gieva blushed, and the effect was somewhat enchanting as she tried to hide her grin behind the golden curl that had fallen in front of her eyes.

"Has he?" Sunniva's eyes widened conspiratorially.

Gieva lowered her glance back to the brooches. Sunniva gave her the same look she usually reserved for the most titillating gossip. "I see. You naughty girl." She laughed at the shocked expression on Gieva's face. "There's no need to turn so red, my love. There's nothing wrong with playing a bit before you've said the words. Gods know I won't judge you for having a lover, even if you do plan to make an honest man out of him."

Gieva rolled her eyes. "Well, yes, I know that," she said, "And the truth is, he did ask me to marry him, just before he went with the *cyning* to Cantwareburh." She sighed. "But I told him that I wasn't ready."

"Rægen didn't take advantage of you, did he?" Sunniva was suddenly angry. If Gieva wasn't ready, then Rægen had no right to expect anything of her. She was sure that she had taught her brother better.

"No, it's not that!" Gieva said, and drew in a long breath before she spoke again. Her voice was a strange mixture of happiness and sadness that made it almost musical to hear. "Everything in my life has moved so quickly, rather like I'm in a fast-moving river and I'm just trying to find a rock to grab hold of so that I'm not swept away." She was opening and closing the pin on one of the brooches, not looking at Sunniva.

Sunniva was pleased that she would not have to beat her brother roundly for disrespecting his lover, but she saw the sadness in Gieva's eyes and reached out to put her arm around her shoulders. "I can't imagine what it must be like," Sunniva said, "to have gone through all of that. But I understand not being ready. I'm not ready either."

"To marry Ecgric, you mean?"

That was not what she meant, and it confused her for a moment. "No," she said slowly, trying to collect her thoughts, "No, I can't marry Ecgric."

"Why not?"

Sunniva did not know how to answer. In truth, she did not want to marry Ecgric. She did not want to marry anyone, really. She liked him, certainly. She liked the way his body fit with her own and she liked feeling the heavy raw power of his arms and his mouth on hers and the way he would sometimes lose himself and pull her hair or pin her arms down as he made love to her. She even liked the playful easy way in which they could talk for hours and make fun of the *thegns* and fling pieces of food at Sige when he was being too solemn. She liked that he challenged her; made her think. Ecgric was a lover, not a husband. There was a reason that she made him spill his seed on her belly. There was a reason she had always changed the subject when he hinted at the idea of marriage. Besides, if her parents planned to use her as leverage in an alliance, then she could not be attached. It was just too complicated.

"It just can't happen," Sunniva said eventually.

"Have your parents made you a match already?" Gieva asked understandingly. "I had a friend whose parents arranged a match for her with a man from the village. She had a lover already, and she wanted to marry him, but in the end she wedded the man her parents chose."

"Yes, that's what will happen to me eventually, I expect." Sunniva sighed, trying to smile. "We women don't get much say in the matter. Did your friend like the man at least?"

Gieva shrugged. "She was happy enough, I suppose. She was with child within half a year, at least, and she would never have been forced to marry a man she didn't like. But I imagine she was sad to lose the one she really loved."

"Even if I had the choice, I don't know that I would take Ecgric instead of some *ætheling*," Sunniva said, as if in response to Gieva's unasked question. "I don't know if I would marry anyone at all." She felt the same wild defiance she always felt when someone told her what to do, and the ideas of the exotic came dancing into her mind. "I want an adventure," she said in her fancy. "I want something exciting and dangerous to happen so that I don't feel so useless waiting for other people to decide my life for me."

"What would you do on your adventure?" Gieva asked indulgently, picking at one of her stitches.

Sunniva remembered the ideas which had been put into her head by Godomar when he had visited, and thought of all the adventures she might have if she had not been born to be political currency. "I'd go south, where it's hot even in the winter and there are giant monsters and people with skin like jet. I'd go east where the priests all come from and see what their gods look like. I'd go north to see the white bears that live on ice and then I'd go west and chase the sun."

Gieva laughed, "You'll give Rægen some competition in poetry if you continue like that."

"Perhaps I'll learn new songs and challenge him," Sunniva laughed as well, "I'll go back to the old country where the songs came from. I'll fight in a shield wall and drink and fuck like a warrior, and I'd be a *cwene* or an *ealdorman* in my own right and no man's consort."

"Do you really want to fight in a battle?" Gieva asked. "It sounds terrifying."

"I don't know," Sunniva said, "But that's the point, isn't it? I want the option. I don't like people telling me what to do. If someone says that I cannot be a warrior, then that is all I want to do. If someone says I can't take a lover or travel the world, then I can think of little else until I've done it."

Gieva laughed, "Defiance suits you."

"But not you?"

Gieva said, "I don't think I have it in me to be defiant anymore, if I ever did. I don't crave adventure or glory or danger. I've had enough. You may not want to be a wife and mother and live a quiet life, but I do."

"Somehow," Sunniva said, "that seems to suit you as well." She slumped slightly, "But you are independent and you can do as you wish, even if it's to live a quiet life."

"Would you really rather trade places with me?" Gieva did not say it accusingly, but Sunniva felt guilty all the same.

"I only mean you get to have a choice in what your future holds."

"And you don't?"

"There's a point when my wishes end and I have to think about the good of my family and of my people, and so I don't really have a choice in the end, do I?"

"Perhaps not," Gieva said.

It was dark when Sunniva left Gieva's house, but the moon was high and bright and she could see her way back to the Bricgweard easily. She was looking up at the moon and wondering if she could chase it in a ship when it set, when she stumbled on a stone and fell face-forward into the dirt.

Cursing herself, she stood and brushed the dirt from her hands and knees, hearing the echo of her voice bounce from the stables across the yard, but the echo sounded strange, deeper than her own voice. And there were two of them.

Instead of calling out, she followed the sound of the voices. The horses were at pasture but the sounds were coming from the stable, and she glanced around the side to find something so peculiar that made her forget completely about her discussion with Gieva. Two men were locked together in an embrace so passionate that it made her nights with Ecgric look like clumsy children playing at kissing.

Sunniva's mouth dropped open, and she took a step back. That was supposed to be women's magic. She knew men sometimes had sex with other men when there were no women about, on a campaign or at sea, perhaps, but such a practice was strange and unnatural and prohibited to all but the gods, as it was a source of profound and dangerous power. Such a thing was supposed to be an affront to the very laws of nature, because it could never result in a family, but the two men touched one another in such a way that she knew that this was more than lust or convenience; it was love. Profound, fervent, abiding and passionate love. The very kind she was afraid of feeling for the man she had taken as her lover. How strange it was.

She watched in mild curiosity for a moment, the couple completely unaware of her, when the darker-haired of the two shifted his head, and she tried to stifle a shocked snigger when she realized that it was Edwin. The giggle was stifled for her, however, when she realized the man with whom Edwin was sharing his intimate moment was her brother Sigebryht.

I guess I'm not the only one who doesn't get a choice, she thought, as she slowly and silently left them to their business.

*****

There was something inherently alarming about the Fens, though the slight danger was overshadowed by the sweeping sense of boredom which resulted from being stuck in them. Eorwald considered, as he burned a bit of the sinking peat for warmth and looked out over the wide, flat expanses of the land, how dull it would be to die in these bogs. Not fighting in a battle or even as an old man, but by accidentally falling in drunk one night, never to be seen again. He knew it happened; several accounts circulated of finding blackened bodies in the marshy areas where the locals harvested their peat; perfectly preserved but quite obviously dead. It did not help his mood to dwell on the reeking fens, but the lack of other activities made it inevitable that his mind would end up sinking down into the brown water.

There was nothing redeeming about the village of Ealdham now, any more than there was in the fetid marshlands that surrounded it. The few comforts that the village might have offered at one point were lost in the fire that had killed almost the entire population.

Eorwald was moodily flinging bits of grass into the small camp fire, waiting for it to burn down to coals for cooking. Eorwald hated cooking for himself; he wished that the communal oven in the village had survived the ransacking; then at least he might buy some proper bread off one of the remaining Ealdham residents who had wandered in after the battle to rebuild their village.

Ricbert had made no sound as he approached, and Eorwald jumped as the older man sat down next to him. "We should leave this place," he said.

Eorwald perked up at the idea. "But the *cyning* told us to remain here and keep a look out for more Northumbrians…" he said cautiously, not wishing to interrupt Ricbert's steady thoughts.

"There's nothing here for us anymore, and it's not a strategic point for protecting anything or for readying for a strike," Ricbert said. "What do you think we should do?"

Eorwald hesitated. He did not want to immediately jump at the idea of leaving this grim place, but at the same time he did not want to miss the chance to do so. "Do you think we might make a better base somewhere else?"

"I already know what I plan to do," Ricbert said, "I'm asking what you think the best course of action might be."

Eorwald appreciated Ricbert's steady method of teaching rather than the impatient, harsh lessons usually taught by the king. Ricbert was offering him a chance to make decisions, to try his strength. "I would go to Grantabricge," Eorwald said after some thought, "it is much better fortified."

"And a repeated target for Athelfrith's men," Ricbert said. "It is well guarded, true, but not a strategically advantageous point to set up a watch on the North."

"Elge?" Eorwald tried again, thinking of the wide island deep in the fenlands.

"How would we get all of our men out to the island without someone taking notice? There are bound to be spies lurking about and they would notice a small fleet of boats going out to Elge repeatedly."

"Mæduwic, then," Eorwald said, growing frustrated. He thought that Grantabricge would be the best solution, but Ricbert seemed to be putting him down at every turn. Perhaps a sarcastic answer would stop Ricbert's condescension. Surprisingly, though, Ricbert cocked his head in consideration.

"That might work," he said, "It's not far from here, and fortified but not well-manned. I believe you may have hit upon a good idea." If Eorwald had thought Ricbert capable of sarcasm, he might have thought that Ricbert was simply being ironic.

Eorwald did not entirely understand the strategic value in an obscure market down, but it would be better fortified than their village of tents. "There are enough people there to support the army," Eorwald suggested hopefully.

Ricbert considered a bit longer, and gave something approaching a smile. "Mæduwic it is."

"Wait," Eorwald said as Ricbert stood to leave, "What was your idea?"

Ricbert raised an eyebrow in something even closer to a smile, and left Eorwald to his fire.

While Ealdham had been inhabited by burned ghosts and surrounded by salty wetlands, Mæduwic was full of living, breathing people and set amid wide meadows which swept up to meet it from a clear, fast-moving stream nearby. He liked being able to sleep the town hall and having someone else to cook his food for him. Ricbert seemed in a better mood as well, though his exterior was as grim and forbidding as ever.

Leofric and Hengest had remained with them, and they too seemed pleased to have found themselves in a better situation than camping on the outskirts of a dead village. Leofric missed his wife and child back in the south, but he was cheerful enough despite all that and knew plenty of riddles and songs to keep them entertained. Hengest, even with his ruddy and pockmarked face, had a knack for plucking beautiful girls out of thin air; a skill which Eorwald appreciated immensely, though the women seemed to be well eager to make friends with them. Eorwald loved it when a soft body and a pretty face appeared at his side with little to no effort on his behalf.

Tonight was a particularly pleasant occasion; there had been a skirmish a few miles north of Mæduwic along the river, in which Eorwald had led his small company to victory over a group of angry warriors from Lindsey. There had been no deaths on either side, merely a lot of posturing and a few injuries, but the Lindsey warriors had surrendered without terms almost immediately. They had been *wycingas*, mercenaries, in the employ of Athelfrith and had not been keen on dying for the sake of a king who was not their own, so Eorwald had taken their weapons and any gold they happened to carry, and let them go on their way.

As an indulgence, a particularly fine mutton stew and several barrels of strong beer had been waiting for them upon their return to the town hall, and Eorwald and his companions ate and drank while women seemed to find their way under the men's arms before the men realized what had happened.

"You're so fierce," tonight's woman said in a fluid voice. She had her arm around Eorwald as soon as he had sat down, her hand sliding over the stubble of his hair, "Tell me about the battle, won't you?"

"Sixty men, all fierce and horrible as *weargas*," Hengest contributed, "and they had snuck up on us from the darkness of the woods, and it was a bloody battle but the *ætheling* rallied us and we were able to strike down our foes…"

The woman's eyes opened wide but Eorwald looked away somewhat ashamedly. The only blood had occurred from stupid mistakes and injuries and the only *weargas* that they had seen were the ones painted on several shields; but that was what boasts were for, making everything sound much grander than it really was.

"How brave," she cooed in Eorwald's ear.

He liked her scent, something like the smell of fruits cooking in honey over a camp fire. He put an arm around her waist and drew her closer. "Tell me your name," he said.

"Rian," she said.

"You're Wælisc, aren't you?" Eorwald asked. He had not met very many Britons, and the few whom he had known had been angry, dark-haired men. The only dark thing about Rian was the mass of freckles on her nose and cheeks which made her look almost tanned, but they were framed by the vivid red hair that curled around her face.

"I suppose I am," Rian said, her voice lilting slightly but without the strong accent that other Wælisc people usually had. Her lips were hardly an inch from his ear, and within a moment they were tracing a line across his jawbone. Eorwald hesitated, and the few words he had were swallowed up by the sudden appearance of her hand on his leg, moving slowly upwards.

"Do you want me to stay with you tonight?" she whispered. "No one likes to sleep alone." She leaned against his arm and the top toggle of her dress came undone, baring a shoulder that was nearly as freckled as her face.

"I'd like that very much," Eorwald said, pulling her closer.

He returned to his meal with Rian sitting beside him, though he was caught off-guard by the way she was looking at him; not at him, in truth, but at the food he brought to his mouth.

"Have you eaten?" he asked, pulling a half-torn loaf toward them and broke a piece off for her. "Please, share with me."

"I haven't eaten," she said in that lilting, breathy voice, "I thank you, my *ætheling.*"

She sopped up some of the mutton broth and ate the bread as if she had been denied food for weeks. Eorwald watched her for a moment, puzzled, but when she had finished she resumed her attentions to his neck, and he forgot to think about anything except how quickly he could get her under a blanket.

There was too much merrymaking for him to want to go to bed yet, in any case. He drank and sang with his companions, kissed Rian and listened to stories. Some men had gotten to their feet as a raucous song was sung, dancing – no, staggering about in a circle, really – until they nearly collapsed.

It was a long time before he finally decided he had had enough, and found his bedroll near the fire. Rian slipped in beside him. She kissed him as she reached beneath the blanket and found him already hard, her tongue sliding against his and her dress opening. Eorwald slipped his hand under the neck of her dress and found one of her breasts, small and freckled with a pointed nipple that hardened under his fingers. She was skinny, but in the stretched sort of way that usually meant someone had been hungry for a very long time, but he could hardly bring himself to notice that.

In a practiced move, she lifted her skirt and opened her legs. He pulled the blanket over the two of them, brushing a hair away from her eyes. She had beautiful eyes, he noticed, bright blue and fringed with soft lashes that caught the light of the dying fire. They closed and a smile touched her lips as he pushed deeper.

They heard a couple from across the hall begin to grunt with lovemaking, and Rian giggled. She had a rather pretty smile, Eorwald thought. She sighed and pulled him closer to her as he thrust into her, again and again until he felt the pressure grow to a head. He had just enough wits to pull away from her at the last moment, but nearly collapsed onto her.

Rian adjusted her dress and lay next to him, and Eorwald put his arm around her. Girls liked that sort of thing, after all. He liked the scent of her hair and the warmth of her skinny body, and he soon fell asleep.

Not long later, however, he felt her stirring next to him and he immediately sprang awake. Rian was sitting up, and put a hand on his chest to calm him.

"What's wrong?" he whispered. It was still quite dark and everyone was still asleep.

"Nothing's wrong," Rian whispered back, "But I wasn't sure how much you wanted tonight."

This was a puzzling thing for her to say, but he stroked her arm. "I'll bet I could go again if you wanted to," he said.

He couldn't see her face in the darkness, but knew she was smiling when she said "if you like, but it will cost you more."

Eorwald froze, and was profoundly thankful that she couldn't see his face clearly, for he knew he must have turned scarlet. He had been so stupid. Rian was a whore. He had thought, for one blissful but completely idiotic moment, that she had simply been a local girl who liked him, but of course, she was expecting to be paid at the end of the night. He wrestled with himself for a moment, weighing the benefits of her company with the embarrassment of having to solicit a prostitute. *Well,* he thought, *everyone's seen me with her, and they must know what we were up to, so the damage is done.*

Rian was waiting for an answer. "Stay tonight," Eorwald said firmly, "We can take care of everything in the morning."

"As you wish," she said cheerfully, still in a whisper, and curling up next to him under the blanket. If this was the blessing he received for a sacrifice of a few coins and a bit of pride, it was well worth it. After all, he had plenty of gold.

Chapter Twelve

Fela Endas

Many Endings

"It is so strange to me," Edwin said, glancing up at Rægen and Gieva as they sat at the high table sharing a look which only newlyweds could contrive, "how some people end up together. Your brother could have any girl in the country, and he chooses her. I just don't see it."

"Well, you wouldn't, would you?" Sige said playfully, "I know your tastes and they don't seem to run toward that type of girl."

"No indeed," Edwin said. "I prefer someone taller and a little more robust." He drank deeply, finishing the cup rather quickly and reddening beneath his dark beard. "Also, I prefer someone with a prick," he whispered in Sige's ear, and Sige snorted into his cup.

Edwin winked, looking back at the high table. He seemed deep in thought for a moment but eventually said, "I don't know many people who decided on their own to get married, besides *ceorls*, maybe. I barely knew Cwenburg before our marriage."

Sige always forgot that Edwin had been married to the daughter of Cearl of Mercia. It made him jealous to think of Edwin making love with a woman, though it eased his mind to know that there had never been any real affection between them. "We can't help who we love," Sige said quietly. "And it's not as if Gieva isn't a good match. She owns her father's lands in the Fens now, and all the wealth that came from his salt operations, so she is a *thegn* in all but name now."

"As if Rægenhere cares about that," Edwin laughed, "Well, if any people were well-suited to spend their lives together, it is those two." He raised his cup and shouted, "Blessings on the couple!" and the majority of the people sitting nearby drunkenly repeated his toast. Gieva grinned and nodded in thanks, and Rægen lifted his own cup and replied, "We are already blessed with such wonderful friends!" and everyone shouted in approval and drank heartily. It was the seventh or eighth time someone had shouted a drunken blessing at them, and Sige knew that Rægen and Gieva probably wished to leave the feast and finish their wedding night properly.

Sige watched the people in the hall becoming more raucous as the night progressed, the music growing steadily louder and the guests dancing and singing and shouting more blessings at Rægen and Gieva. There hadn't been such a feast since the opening of the Bricgweard, and every person in attendance had drunk and eaten enough to support a family of *ceorls* for a month. Gieva and Rægen drank from the same gold-fitted horn, filled with the spiced mead that would continue to flow for a full moon's turn, to keep up their strength while they worked on making a baby. For all anyone knew, they might have already succeeded. It was no secret that they had spent every night of the past month together; perhaps the flush on her cheeks was not simply from dancing.

"Look how happy they are. They are allowed to love each other." Sige held out his cup for a serving woman to refill it.

Edwin gave him a small smile, the flirtatious kind that made Sige want to kiss him. "What a sight that would be, if we might marry the ones we loved. Imagine the wedding night."

"I already am," Sige said. He was drunk, and he ought not to be saying such things, but the thought of it set his heart racing.

"It is time for the bride and groom to go to bed!" Ecgric slurred loudly, standing as several other people stood as well. Rægen and Gieva were grinning broadly as they were rather roughly pushed out of their seats and toward the door. Gieva looked mildly terrified, but she laughed despite her apparent uneasiness. Sige and Edwin followed close behind, shouting drunken advice and blessings for a quick conception. A few people were making bets on how long it would be before she was pregnant, but Sunniva yelled at them and they stopped their gambling.

Everyone crowded around the door to Gieva's house. She was ceremonially given the key by Eadyth, and Gieva opened the door and Rægen picked her up, carrying her over the threshold. The doorway was a portal, of Gieva's transition from foundling maiden to established wife. Sige was happy for her, and happy for his brother, who was beaming and staring at Gieva as if she were more radiant than the sun itself.

Eadyth and Sunniva and at least five other women went in, and with great pomp and no few giggles, they tucked Gieva into her bed, fully clothed. Rægen sat next to her and removed the crown of flowers from her hair, and tossed them at the crowd, who shouted raucously as they scrambled for the good luck charm. Sige was secretly thankful that it was no longer the custom to watch the wedded couple consummate their marriage; the ceremonial deflowering was sufficient. The crowd cheered and made its way back to the hall, leaving Rægen and Gieva to enjoy one another.

"Well, our dear *ætheling* is no longer a maiden," Ecgric said as he passed them. Sige and Edwin chuckled appreciatively, but Edwin tugged on Sige's arm to get him to hang back after Ecgric had passed. The crowd had left them behind, and without another word Edwin walked silently in the opposite direction, back towards the granary on the boundaries of the Bricgweard. It was one of their usual hiding places; the sacks of grain and flour created alcoves that were excellent for sneaking into, provided no one came collecting any grain or beer. The memories of their stolen moments together, coupled with the drink, made Sige dizzy and he took Edwin's hand as they walked, and they shared a glance which caused him to pick up speed. When they had reached the granary, Edwin pushed him roughly against the inside wall and kissed him as fiercely as he had done the first time. His skin was cool and his muscles tensed, and Sige wanted to feel every inch of him.

For a long time afterward they lay on their cloaks, spent and panting. Sige had pulled on his breeches and Edwin stood, pulling him into a kiss that made Sige want him all over again. He ran his hands through Edwin's hair, felt the strong muscles of his back, and breathed the scent of the two of them that clung to his skin. He was on the point of pushing Edwin back to the ground to have him again, but a noise made his blood freeze.

The door had scraped open, and the *ceorl* standing in the doorway gasped when he saw them. Sige and Edwin were still locked in an embrace, and three men stood frozen, staring at one another, the *ceorl*'s face illuminated by the greasy orange glow of the rush light.

Edwin wasted no time. He rushed forward, and pinned the *ceorl* to the wall by this neck. The rush light had dropped to the floor, but the fat spilled and continued to burn sluggishly at Edwin's feet. The *ceorl* looked terrified as Edwin spoke something in his ear, and nodded frantically as Edwin dropped him. The *ceorl* ran from the storehouse, tripping over the threshold as he went.

Edwin turned around and pressed the heels of his hands into his eyes as Sige quickly laced up his breeches and threw his cloak around his shoulders.

"*Godes hæmað min ears*," Edwin said quietly, not moving his hands.

Sige was trying not to think of it and pretended to be particularly interested in his belt buckle.

"We can't keep doing this," Edwin said.

Sige tried to smile but it seemed to come off more as a grimace. "One of us always says that, and yet we keep doing it. It was close. We should have been more careful, but we were both drunk. We'll be more cautious next time."

"What if I don't want there to be a next time?" Edwin said acidly.

"You don't mean that."

Edwin made some kind of indistinguishable sound in his throat. "No, not really." He made the sound again. "This is dangerous, Sige."

"I've told you, we'll just be more careful –"

"No. I mean, this is really, really dangerous. If he says anything… I think I've frightened him well enough, but you could never be sure. *Godes hæmað min ears*, what if he says something?"

"He won't say anything." Sige tried to sound confident but he failed miserably.

"You know what happens to men like us," Edwin choked, "we can justify it all we want, but they won't see things the way we do." He gestured vaguely towards the Bricgweard.

Sige did know, and tried to drive the idea from his head, of a man being beaten and hanged. Sige had no words to say and watched Edwin's darkened face.

"I think of that every time," Edwin said. "I try to ignore it, and I try to tell myself that you can just be my secret and that I will stop, that there won't be a next time, but I just can't. I can't stay away from you. It's only gotten worse. The more we are together, the more I think about it, and yet I can't stop." There was a note of hysteria in his voice now, and he swore under his breath again.

Sige wanted to say, "Then don't stop," but he could not find his voice. He swallowed a few times. Finally, he found some words. "I'm not afraid of dying," he said.

"Nor am I," Edwin said, "And if it is my fate to be mutilated and killed for this, then I will accept it and go as bravely as I can." He took a breath as if to keep his voice from shaking, but failed at it. "But I can't see that happen to you. Even if you were brave and did it for me, I would die in fire and pain a thousand times rather than see that happen to you."

They threw their arms around one another and the dizzying euphoria that Sige had felt only moments before had turned into a physical, tangible pain somewhere in his stomach. He knew that there could be no torment worse than seeing Edwin maimed and humiliated simply for loving the wrong person. He did not want to let go of Edwin, who was hugging him so tightly that they might have been a single piece of stone, trying to be ripped apart by howling wind. He had a thousand words buzzing in his head that he tried to sort into language, but in the end only three made their way out.

*****

Eadyth found her husband in the hall, poking at the hearth fire with a stick. "I see the messenger's gone."

Rædwald sighed and put a log on the fire, stabbing into place with his stick. "Every time I think we've got things sorted, another bloody problem comes along."

"Rægen told me that it was not good news," she said, though she knew the reason her husband was so cross; she waited for him to get around to it in his own time.

"The *heahcyning* is dead," he grunted after a few moments in irritated silence.

Eadyth nodded. "How did it happen?"

"In his sleep, apparently," Rædwald said. "No one really

knows. He was well enough when we saw him at the *cyningesmot*, but his woman woke up one morning to find him dead. Bit of a nasty shock for her, I'd imagine."

Eadyth looked into the fire as it caught the new log and grew to a blaze that illuminated her husband's face. She hoped that it was simply the light of the fire which made the lines around his eyes look so deep.

"What will happen now?" she asked.

"I'll have to go south again," Rædwald said, and seeing Eadyth's puzzlement added, "He was traveling to Mercia and had stopped somewhere just past Lundenburh, and that's where he died. His body will be taken back to Cantwareburh at some point but there is to be a moot following his funeral in Lundenburh."

"But you've only just gotten back!" Eadyth said. "Why would you have another moot so soon after the *heahcyning*'s death?"

"It's exactly when we need to have another moot," Rædwald said. "Tensions were high at the last one; Cearl of Mercia decided not to bother showing up, and you know as well as anyone what a royal twat Sæwine is..." he seemed to see the look of annoyance on Eadyth's face at the mention of her old enemy and changed his tone. "It will be a chance for the *cyningas* to meet and solidify our alliances. Either that, or declare war on one another."

"That's not funny." Eadyth glowered, and Rædwald put a hand on her shoulder.

"You worry too much, my love," Rædwald said. "The death of the *heahcyning* won't change anything. We all respected Ethelbert too much to start any wars during his funeral." He did not seem entirely certain of this, but his smile was reassuring.

She settled next to him and they both sat in silence for a long while. Eadyth felt a pang of worry. They had had twenty-odd years of peace and plenty with Ethelbert as the high king. What they needed was another leader, another *heahcyning* to whom the kings could swear allegiance. She nuzzled against Rædwald's chest, and had a glimmering of an idea.

"What if you were to take Ethelbert's place?" Eadyth asked.

"Hmm?" Rædwald was absently stroking Eadyth's arm and not paying attention.

"You could be the new *heahcyning*."

Rædwald stopped stroking her arm and looked at her face. "Don't be daft, woman."

"I'm not!" Eadyth said, "Think about it. Athelfrith essentially holds all the lands north of the Humber now. He has an enormous force, and we have too few of our own men to fight him. We've seen that."

"What does that have to do with –"

"Just listen," Eadyth said, her heart beginning to beat faster. "If you could unite the southern kingdoms, show them what a threat Athelfrith is, and they could fight with us against him."

"The others won't send their men to fight my battles," Rædwald said. "Mercia is the only other kingdom affected by Athelfrith, but Cearl will be the most likely to turn on me. Why would the Hwicce or the Eota or anyone else care? They'd be happy to see me destroyed and take my lands when Athelfrith is done with me."

"That's why you have to strike first, and put the idea into their heads that they need a leader so that they can fight the greater enemy. Show them all that Athelfrith needs to be stopped. Make them want to fight him."

"I don't understand what you think will happen if I did."

Eadyth grunted her annoyance. "Set yourself up as their leader. Make alliances on your own terms. Win their allegiance, and use them to crush Athelfrith. Think of what you could do against his rabble with a thousand southern warriors."

Rædwald was biting the inside of his mouth in thought. "I don't have anything to offer them. Think what you would do in their places, if a rival king asked you to send your own men to fight a war that you had nothing to do with. They won't accept. An alliance, perhaps, but once it came down to it you know they would find some reason not to fulfil their promises."

They both collapsed into thoughtful silence once more, but were distracted by their daughter entering the hall. She was smiling sweetly as ever, and sat down near them. "What's wrong?" she asked, "has someone died?"

"Heahcyning Ethelbert of the Eota," Rædwald said.

Sunniva's smile faded. "Oh." She blushed and pulled out her distaff, her cheeks flushing pink and her mouth tightening as if to hold back any further rudeness.

"Sunni," Rædwald said slowly, as if he were trying to assemble a thought out of logs, "Do you remember the story of

Friðosibb?"

Sunniva looked up from her spinning and nodded, and Eadyth understood the idea that Rædwald was trying to build.

"She was a princess in the old country," Sunniva said, her fingers still busy with the spindle. "Her brothers and her father were killed in a blood-feud with a neighboring tribe, and she became their *cwene* and swore revenge on the ones who killed them. But then Frea came to her in a dream and told her that it if she sent men to fight them, they would all be killed and her line would end forever, so she sought peace by marrying–" Sunniva's mouth opened into a perfectly round "oh" of realization. "I see what this is."

"With the *heahcyning* dead the alliances are so unstable that…" Rædwald began, but Sunniva cut him off.

"I'll do it," she said, "If you want to arrange a match for me, so that you can make an alliance, I'll do it."

Eadyth, who had been ready for an argument, was taken aback. "What's brought this on?" Eadyth asked, unable to hide the note of suspicion in her voice.

Sunniva licked her lips and glanced out the door. "I just –" she took a breath as if steadying herself for something. "I just know that I need to grow up and do what's expected of me."

Eadyth felt a surge of affection for her daughter and the sacrifices she was willing to make, and pleased that her words had actually gotten through to Sunniva. Eadyth turned back to her husband, a sudden wave of an idea hitting her. "What if Sunniva were to go with you to Lundenburh? You can gauge the political climate, see who might be interested in an alliance, and that way Sunni can have some say in the matter if you want to make a marriage for her." Eadyth knew what it was to marry someone she barely knew; she had done it twice, and only one of the matches had ended happily. She turned back to Sunniva. "We won't force you to marry anyone you don't like," she said. "You are very brave to do this."

"No, I'm not," said Sunniva, "I want to keep my family safe when I cannot fight to defend them. I don't get the pleasure of being brave. I just have to do my duty."

*****

Ecgric drained the last of his beer from the skin, and swore loudly when he found that it was leaking. He threw the skin to the side of the road and mopped up the spilled beer from his tunic with the hem of his cloak, but the horse was agitated at the sound of the skin flopping into the grass, and danced sideways. The small annoyance led him to kick the horse's flank in frustration and it shot forward, bucking its back legs rather half-heartedly. Ecgric bellowed a loud oath when he had gotten the damnable thing under control, and wrapped his cloak around himself, glowering at the leaden sky.

He tried to think of things that were warm, like the sweating beast below him, or some hot mulled mead, or the heat in his muscles when he was fighting, or the lithe figure of Sunniva riding him; even in the cold and the damp, he could still get hard thinking of her. He closed his eyes to see the image more clearly in his mind, imagined the feel of her small breasts, which fit so perfectly into his hands; thought of the way she might bite her lower lip and the whimper she would let out when he teased her cunny with his fingers…

The images carried him almost to the edge of the wood, where he turned slightly southeast over the bridge across the stream which flowed into Wuffingham's manufacturing area. He could see the mill close by, and a few other buildings downstream, which all needed a steady supply of fresh water to fuel their tanning and milling and wool processing activities. He crossed the Wood Bridge and found the Bricgweard looming above the surrounding village, and suddenly felt exhausted and eager to find a fire and a drink.

The sun had set by the time he reached the Bricgweard and handed his horse's reins to a serving man. He was still aroused from thinking of Sunniva, and he had to stand outside the door for some time before his blood had cooled sufficiently to enter the hall.

The main hall was empty, but he went directly to the king's house where he found the royal family all lounging around the hearth, the remains of their day meal being retrieved by serving women. Rædwald stood up as soon as he saw Ecgric enter, and came to greet him.

"How did it go?" he asked, calling for some hot mead to be brought for Ecgric. "How many southern men should we expect?"

"Two hundreds from the South Folk," Ecgric said. "And twenty or so of those are *gedriht* and *huscarls*, as you know. The rest are farmers and the like, but I'm sure that they will have their men in fighting shape by the time they see any battles." It was not a lie, but not necessarily the truth. He was disappointed at the sluggish way some of the *thegns* had promised to fight for their king; it was unbecoming. The majority of them were eager to follow their *dryhten* into battle; Rædwald was a superb commander and a generous lord, after all. It was the handful of cowards that set Ecgric's teeth on edge. The *cyning* needn't know about those now, though.

Ecgric had seen Sunniva out of the corner of his eye, dicing with Sigebryht and Edwin; she was reclining slightly on a cushion and he could see the curve of her hips under her dress, and it made him forget how to count.

"When will you leave for Lundenburh?" Ecgric asked, wrenching his eyes away from her and back to the king.

"Two days hence," Rædwald said. "Sooner, if possible, but I mean to take a large retinue with me."

"Do you wish me to be in that retinue?" Ecgric asked tentatively. He rather hoped that there would not be a repeat of the previous excursion, during which he was forced to remain behind.

Rædwald shook his head. "I need you to continue to raise the *fyrd*, especially Eni's men," he paused at the look on Ecgric's face. "Oh come now, don't look so disappointed. You know as well as I that there won't be any fighting in Lundenburh. You should gather all the men you can and meet your father in the Fens. They've moved camp to Mæduwic, which should be able to support anyone you might take with you. There have been rumors that Athelfrith might be mounting an attack, so the more men we can assemble to head him off, the better."

"And who will remain here?" Ecgric asked, somewhat relieved.

"I will go with the *cyning* to set them as far as Mældune," said Eadyth, "and then I will return here with several *thegns* to watch over the Bricgweard. Sunniva will go in my place, and Rægenhere will go as well."

Ecgric finished his beer, nodding his acknowledgement. "It seems we have our work cut out for us, then."

Rædwald shrugged noncommittally. "I hope that enough of our folk might be able to speak with the southerners and persuade them that Athelfrith is dangerous. Even so, we should be prepared for some resistance and ready our own forces. How soon can you be ready to go north?"

Ecgric considered for a moment, trying not to become distracted by the way Sunniva had just smiled at him. "If you need me to, I can leave as soon as a new horse can be saddled," he said reluctantly.

Rædwald shook his head. "No need to set off at once. Stay tonight, at least. I'll have Gamol get everything ready for your departure tomorrow."

"Thank you, Dryhten," Ecgric said gloomily. He disliked the idea of only getting to spend a single night in the Bricgweard before having to spend another week in the saddle, but as he glanced back at Sunniva he decided to make the most of his limited time with her.

He finished eating and casually wandered over to where Sunniva and her brother were dicing. It was different from the normal game, where the player would bet, and then the highest number rolled would win. This was a lying game of Sunniva's own invention, and Ecgric had grown rather fond of it, despite losing his silver ring to her several weeks before. It flashed heavily on her finger as she counted out her winnings. They were playing with a mixture of *peningas* and hacksilver, and Sunniva's pile was substantially larger.

"It's not my fault that you're a terrible liar," she was saying to Sigebryht, and winked at Ecgric when he sat down beside her to watch.

Sigebryht scowled at her, and Edwin laughed. "Lying isn't a virtue, Sunniva," Sigebryht said.

"Nonsense." Sunniva said, "Lying is the finest thing a person can do, if he's good at it. Anyhow, it's not lying. It's merely boasting, and anyone will tell you that boasting is an art form in itself."

"She's got you there," Edwin said, and Ecgric chuckled.

Sigebryht smiled indulgently at his sister. They both pushed an equal amount of silver in to the center of the board, and picked up the antler dice in their respective cups. Edwin counted, and on "three!" they both slammed their cups down, trapping the dice within. Each peeked at the number they had rolled, and then they would bet based on who they thought had the higher roll. If a player was particularly good at lying, he could win the game by tricking his opponent into thinking he had a high number. A player could quit at any moment, but if one of them decided to show the dice, the highest roll would get the money. It was quite clever, really, and Ecgric loved the battle of wills which it incited, though he knew that the painfully honest Sigebryht was not as skilled a liar as Sunniva.

Sigebryht glared at Sunniva for a long while, and she sat with a sweet, complacent smile on her face. "Well, what do you bid?" She asked innocently.

Sigebryht pushed a few scraps of silver into the pile in the center, and Sunniva did the same. Then she added a few more, and back and forth they went for some time. Ecgric had seen both player's dice when they lifted their cups; Sunniva had rolled a four and Sigebryht a five, and so Sigebryht would win if either of them called to show their numbers. However, Sunniva was the best liar that Ecgric knew, and Sigebryht seemed to think that she would have him beaten. Before he had risked too many of his coins, he resigned, and all three men groaned when they lifted the cups and Sunniva scraped the pile of silver toward her, grinning.

"That's it," Sigebryht said, "I'm going to bed before you leave me a beggar."

"Oh my poor Sige, I would never have that," Sunniva said, picking up a couple of the *peningas* and pushing them into his hand, "Go and buy yourself something pretty, won't you?"

Edwin was doubled up in laughter, while Sigebryht rolled his eyes and tousled her hair as if to remind her that she was still his little sister, before leaving them. Edwin followed and the two had left Ecgric and Sunniva alone for the moment.

"He's just angry that I won, because he is as transparent as weak beer." Sunniva said, scooping her winnings into the little pouch she carried on her belt.

"Well it's not really fair, is it? I mean, you made up the game, so of course you're going to win."

Sunniva shook her head. "No, I didn't make it up. The Frankisc man, Godomar, taught me while he was here."

Ecgric's smile vanished, as it always did when she talked about the damned foreigner. She had been quite taken with him, and it still rankled even though the stinking prick had gone back to wherever he had come from. Even something as simple as instruction on a new game made Ecgric want to track him down and beat him bloody.

"I've missed you," Sunniva said quietly, glancing him up and down appraisingly, a hungry look on her face. Ecgric struggled to change the subject while he still felt that the king's eyes were on him.

"Where is Rægenhere?" he asked stupidly.

Sunniva chuckled. "He's just gotten married, where do you think he is?" she jerked her head at the alcove at the far end of the house, nearest to the door, where Rægenhere was sitting huddled under a blanket with his woman and giving her a thoroughly slavish look.

"At least *we* try to be discreet," she said, rolling her eyes.

They talked for a while, and after some time the king and queen departed for bed. Gieva and Rægenhere had gone as well, back to their own house; meanwhile Sigebryht had left to relieve himself outside and Edwin was already asleep.

"We're alone," Ecgric said quietly, putting his hand on Sunniva's knee and stroking it so that the hem of her dress rose slightly, revealing the white skin of her legs.

"Not here," she said, glancing at Edwin, who was snoring by the fire. Instead, she took Ecgric's hand and they went quietly out the door, to the space between the two houses where he had fucked her half a hundred times. The very memory made him hard again, and knowing what lay underneath her cloak and her dress tempted him to push her against the wall; so he did.

He kissed her, and she tasted like the spiced mead she had been drinking. It was much colder now and she shivered slightly as she hungrily opened her mouth for his tongue; she was taut as a bowstring under his wandering hands but he did not want to simply have her against the wall as they often did; he wanted to savor her after so many days apart.

"The maidens' house will be empty," she said, reading his thoughts. They crashed through the door when they found their way to the deserted house; she kissed him as if he were her only source of air, her hands already working to pull away his cloak and tunic. He threw their cloaks on the bed and pushed her down onto them; since the women were gone, only a couple of bare straw mattresses remained in the cold room. It did not matter; his blood was boiling and he very nearly ripped her dress in his eagerness to see her naked body.

Sunniva pushed him away. "Light a fire, won't you?" she asked, her teeth chattering. Ecgric swore to himself, and fumbled in the dark to find kindling and strike his flint to light it. Within a few moments he had a small fire going, and warmed his hands for a moment before turning back to Sunniva. With a groan, he found that she had taken off her dress, and was leaning on one elbow facing him. He stared longingly at her, loving the way her skin turned golden in the light of the fire and the way her nipples were standing hard in the cool air, peeking through the locks of hair that fell around her shoulders, her legs crossed so that he could just barely see the tuft of dark hair between them. It was as if the daydream which had kept him occupied on his journey had become real.

"You don't know what you do to me," he said, kneeling next to her and brushing his fingertips along her side.

"I know precisely what I do to you, which is why I do it," she said as she flipped her hair back to reveal her collarbone, where his lips rested almost immediately. He worked his way down, as he had done in his daydream, taking her nipples one by one in his mouth and sucking them, flicking them with his tongue and he heard the desire in her breath. As lightly as he could, he traced a line with his lips down past her navel to the cushion of dark hair, and took in her scent as she opened her legs for him. Just as in his imagination, she whimpered when he teased her, first with his mouth and then with his fingers, and then with both at once, and she was grabbing his hair as he rejoiced in the taste of her. She nearly crushed his head between her legs as she let out a soft, shuddering sigh, and for a moment he decided that he would be quite pleased to die this way, but she relaxed slightly and released him. Her sex was still tensing and releasing as he entered her, and he had to force himself not to finish too quickly. A low, guttural moan came from both of them as he moved. He sped up, and the sound of her voice and the feel of her body were almost too much for him.

"Pull out," she panted urgently.

He fully intended to spill his seed outside of her body as he usually did, but before he could her muscles tightened again and she moaned, and the sensation of it caused him to unexpectedly release as well. It felt so much better like this, for both of them, but he knew he ought to have taken the usual precaution.

Even with the fire, the room was cold and he pulled his cloak over the two of them.

"You ought to have pulled out," she said, looking only mildly annoyed as she lay on her stomach.

He kissed the tip of her shoulder and drew slow circles on her back with his fingertips and said, "I couldn't help it." Her skin was so soft under his fingers that he continued to stroke her back, pulling his fingers through her hair. She stretched and sighed contentedly, reminding Ecgric of some sort of lanky cat basking in a patch of sun. He half-expected to hear her purring.

"I guess we'll just have to hope that you didn't get me pregnant," she said after some time, "or you'll have to marry me to protect my honor."

"So be it," Ecgric said quickly. "I'll marry you even if you aren't with child." He tried to pull her close to kiss her, but she stiffened and he looked at her, puzzled.

"I was teasing," she said. She rolled onto her side, a foot away from him.

"I wasn't," Ecgric said, trying to close the gap to hold her again, "I want to marry you. I want to have you all the time, in our own house in our own bed, and see you every morning." It was not simply because he knew girls liked to hear that sort of thing; he did want to marry her. "Do you want to be my wife?" He asked, certain that she would smile and accept him.

Instead, she sat up, moving even further from him, her expression unreadable but for a deep crease appearing between her eyebrows. "Ecgric, you know why I'm going to Lundenburh with my father," she said. It was not a question.

"You are going to Lundenburh to pay your respects to the dead *heahcyning*," he said coldly.

Sunniva glared at him, as if he were being thick. "You know the real reason I am going. They don't need me at the *cyningesmot*; we both know that. Father wants me to meet some of the *cyningas*, so that he can make a marriage and an alliance with one of them. Don't pretend you don't know that."

Ecgric said nothing, but he could see that Sunniva was getting annoyed with him.

"Pout all you wish, it won't change anything. I told my father that I would at least talk to people. I don't know if anything will come of it, but you know why I can't be attached."

"I'm not pouting," Ecgric said, "And if you don't intend to marry some stranger, why don't you just stay here and marry me?"

"You don't want to marry me," Sunniva said shiftily, "I'd be a terrible wife. Let's leave that particular punishment to some old *cyning*, eh?"

"I do want to marry you!" Ecgric said, painfully aware of the petulance in his tone. He wanted to grab her, to shake her shoulders, to make her realize that he loved her, but he refrained. She didn't like to be touched when she was angry; he had learned that much from their many arguments. "I thought that you might feel the same way, but I guess I was wrong."

"Don't you dare," Sunniva said, "don't you dare make this my fault." She was standing up now, her naked body taut with irritation. "You knew what this was. You knew that this," she indicated the space between them, "could never end happily."

"Why not?" Ecgric asked. "You are a free woman, and I am a free man, and we can marry whomever we choose. Why shouldn't we be able to be happy together?"

"Because I don't get a choice, don't you understand?" she shrieked. Her face was scrunched up in anger and he could see tears in her eyes. She wrenched on the linen shift so hard that the stitching at the shoulder tore open slightly.

Ecgric shook his head. "And so you would sell yourself for the sake of an alliance? For a few extra men on the battlefield or a trading agreement?"

"I would let a thousand men use me as their whore if it meant that I could protect my people, if it meant that I could do something to bring my family and my kingdom honor."

"But you'd be unhappy."

Sunniva said, "How can you know what would make me happy? In your mind, I shouldn't marry someone who could give us wealth or warriors, but I should stay here and be your sweet little wife? You would see the world burn so that you could keep me for your own? What about what I want?"

"I thought you wanted me," he said. He wanted to beat himself bloody for the resentment he could still hear in his own voice, but he could not stop.

"Don't you think this is hard enough for me?" She did not wait for him to respond. "I know my lot. The gods decided to grace me with a cunt and no other weapons. If I must marry, if that is the price for your life, or the life of my brothers or my father or mother or any one of my kin, then I will gladly give up my freedom and my happiness to protect you. All of you. That does not make me a whore. It means I've grown up, and you should as well."

Ecgric frowned. He hated being wrong, and he hated feeling like a sulky child while a girl ten years his junior lectured him about duty and honor. She was glaring at him, and in her fury and passion he knew that she was the only woman he would ever want to be with. He had to know. "Do you love me?" he asked.

Sunniva looked away from him as she pulled her cloak over her shoulders. She bit her lower lip and it seemed to tremble, though it could have merely been a trick of the firelight. She looked back at him but did not meet his eyes as she said, "No. It was just a game. And now it is over."

Chapter Thirteen
Merehengestas
Ships

Eadyth wanted nothing more than to curl up in her own bed and sleep, but she knew nothing could be done about it. She felt strangely exhausted despite not having done much that day; sitting astride a slowly ambling horse did not require a considerable amount of effort. Even so, she found it a struggle to keep herself upright. She had agreed to accompany the king and his entourage as far as Mældune before returning home with Gieva, but as the second night on the road approached, she decided that this was a bad idea.

"What's the matter?" Rædwald asked, pulling his horse beside her.

Eadyth sighed. "I am just feeling a little ill today. It's probably the weather." It was cool and the leaves had begun to turn yellow and fall to the ground, crunching as they passed through the woody area southwest of Gipeswic.

Rædwald reached over and patted her leg in a comforting sort of way, and she gave him an insincere smile as she wrapped herself more tightly in her cloak. A trifling cold would not be enough to slow her. She would weather the aches and sniffles in silence.

They were not fortunate enough to find a friendly and loyal *thegn* to open his house to them, and that night Eadyth piled herself with cloaks and blankets and shivered next to her husband in bed until his natural oven-like heat finally reached her bones.

"Are you well?" Gieva asked her the next morning. "You are very pale. You ought to drink something warm before we set off again." Gieva always seemed to feel personally responsible when anyone was unhappy, and Eadyth let her push a cup of warmed elderberry wine into her hands before the camp was packed up again.

"It's nothing," Eadyth said, when Sunniva asked her how she was feeling, a mile or so down the road. "Really, you all ought not to worry about me."

"You just look awfully pale," Rægen said, a little while later.

"Would you like to ride double with me?" Rædwald asked, after they had stopped to rest and water the horses.

"Enough!" Eadyth groaned, "I am quite well, and if you all don't stop pestering me I shall turn this entire column around and go straight home!"

"Mother, Mother!" Sunniva was saying, her voice faint and hazy. Eadyth could not seem to get her eyes to focus on her daughter's face.

"I'm fine," she was trying to say, but her mouth was not working properly.

"Mother, you fell off your horse!" Sunniva said, panic in her voice.

"Don't be ridiculous," Eadyth said, but upon raising herself on an elbow and looking around at several people's ankles, she realized that she had, in fact, fallen off of her horse.

"You fainted," Rædwald said, hugging her and speaking quietly into her ear. "Dytta, you aren't well. Stop trying to be a hero and let us take care of you."

Eadyth glared at him for a moment, and promptly turned away and vomited onto the ground. She reluctantly nodded for Rædwald to help her to her feet.

The camp was set immediately in a large flat meadow, and Gieva and Sunniva wrapped her in half a hundred blankets and stoked a fire in the center of the pavilion while Eadyth watched in grumpy silence. It was pointless to set up the camp. There were hours left of daylight and they were losing too much time by delaying; but Rædwald had ignored her protests. She felt dizzy and exhausted, and annoyed that they were wasting wood in the middle of a pleasant day. Even when it was chilly, she never bothered to have a fire inside the pavilion, even though it was equipped to function as a hall. She had known too many winters when food and fuel were scarce, and she had always been reluctant to waste either. However, at present she was far too tired to say anything.

Eadyth may have been annoyed at the stop, but she secretly appreciated the fact that she did not have to sit shivering atop a horse that day. She felt spectacularly hungry as well, but every time she tried to eat a piece of bread or to drink a cup of weak beer she simply threw it back up. She slept fitfully, kicking off the blankets and then trying to readjust them when her sweat-soaked skin became cold again.

She dreamed of the mounds across the river on the South Tún, where her husband's ancestors were buried. She had only been there a handful of times and avoided the place when she could, but in her dream she was compelled to go there, certain that he would know what she was looking for once she found it. She saw a black boar at the edge of the wood, which glared at her fiercely before wandering back into the shadow of the trees. That was not what she was looking for. Eadyth moved forward, but nearly tripped over two massive ginger cats which wore harnesses like carthorses. There was some significance to them, Eadyth thought, but like the purpose of her quest, she could not see it.

The barrows looked different, she realized. There had been about ten of them, all man-high but nondescript with grass growing in a lush green carpet. The cats rushed forward, and she was surprised to see two additional mounds, one with the stubble of grass dusting it, and the other one much larger, newly dug and bare of vegetation. There were imprints of hundreds of feet near the newly dug barrow, and the cats sniffed the tracks eagerly.

A sudden sadness fell on Eadyth as she looked at the two new mounds, because she knew to whom they must belong. She suddenly wanted to sleep, or perhaps to cry, but she knew that she was supposed to be looking for something important and should press onward.

Suddenly the cats jumped, hissing with their hackles raised at the mound of earth. Something was causing the earth to shift, and Eadyth felt a wave of panic. Barrows were full of treasure, she knew, and where there was treasure there would of course be a dragon.

Eadyth needed to run away, knowing that the great worm would appear within moments, but she was rooted to her place. She heard a voice, almost like a whisper but dripping with venom, coming from the mound, and she could not move.

"I will take them," it said.

Eadyth could not speak.

"I will take them all, every treasure you own…" the voice hissed.

Of course it would, she thought stupidly, it was a dragon. Dragons take treasure and hoard it for their own uses. No matter. She had plenty of treasure and little use for it.

"I will take them and watch them die," it said. "I will cut them and burn them and watch them starve, and I will laugh as they scream…" There was a gurgling sound beneath the hill, the sickening semblance of laughter, and then the gut-wrenching sound of a child crying. Eadyth instinctively ran forward in order to find the child, to protect it from the dragon. She ran around the hill, looking frantically, but the mound was empty and bare and she found herself back in the spot where she had started, the child's voice growing louder all around her.

"I will devour them," the worm said, "just as I devoured the ones who died inside of you, and just as I will devour you after you hear them crying in their shame …" the hiss froze her blood and burned her skin, and she felt the darkness appearing on the edges of her vision as the mound moved again, the dark soil churning and cracking. "You will drown in the river of your tears as I destroy them all. You will choke on the ashes of their burning bodies." She saw the mound split apart and the prow of a ship appear from within the soil. The timbers were rotten and the metal was rusted, and her nostrils filled with the smell of rotting flesh as the ship pulled forward. The worm's hiss turned into a scream of fury as the ship emerged, and Eadyth saw its black shape curled in the crater left by the boat's massive hull. The world was growing steadily darker, her vision becoming hazy at the edges. The cats scattered toward the wood where she had seen the boar, and the ship seemed to follow, then turned its prow and began to head toward the river and, ultimately, the sea.

Eadyth resigned herself to the fact that she would be eaten by the dragon, which was drawing steadily closer to her, slithering its massive dark body out of the mound, blood pouring from its eyes and filling the crater. The blackness began to swirl around her.

There were some voices that Eadyth could not recognize, and the smell of burning sage. Surely it was her flesh burning; the dragon had wrapped its body around her and she had felt its fetid breath on her skin as her hair burned and her skin bubbled and sloughed away, and she heard the terrified screams of her children calling for her.

Then there was a flash of light and a swirl of feathers, and the vague voices became louder, calling to her. There was a crash of thunder like a massive hammer striking an anvil, and the cats bounded forward, this time pulling a two-wheeled chariot. A woman rode in the chariot, holding a spear, her blue eyes and her red hair blazing as she pounded forward, driving the spear into the dragon's flesh. Eadyth felt the worm squeeze and felt her body break in the beast's death throes, and the last image she saw was her mother's face framed in wild red hair.

"Dytta."

Eadyth's eyes snapped open and she felt the brush of a hand on her forehead. She was soaked in sweat, or perhaps blood, she could not be sure. She was having trouble breathing, as if the dragon were still crushing her.

Rædwald was squeezing her hand, stroking her forehead with something soft and damp, and wiping away her tears, for she was crying.

"You were dreaming," Rædwald was saying, but Eadyth was more intently focused on determining if she was alive or not. His hands cupped her face and he stroked her damp cheeks with his thumbs. She felt her muscles relax and her breathing slow. She touched his face and smiled weakly at the look of concern.

"I don't think I'll make it," Eadyth said slowly, but before she could finish her thought she felt a wave of nausea and leaned over the side of the bed, feeling her empty stomach spasm as she tried to rid her body of the poisonous dream.

Rædwald gripped her arm. "Don't say that, Dytta. You'll survive this, there's no need to despair!"

Eadyth wiped her mouth and could not help but laugh at his concern. "You silly old ass," she said, "You know it would take more than a trifling illness to take me down. I was trying to say that I don't think I'll be able to go as far as Mældune after all. I had better just head home."

Rædwald looked concernedly at her. "Is it a good idea to travel in this state?"

"If I must be ill, I'd rather do it in my own house," Eadyth said weakly, leaning back on the bed. She took Rædwald's hand. "It's only a couple of days' journey back. I'll be fine."

He was skeptical. "Let me send one of the wagons back with you. You can ride in it and Gieva can take care of you. I'll send Rægenhere back as well."

"There's no need for that," Eadyth said. "Rægenhere needs to go with you! He is your heir and he should be by your side at the *cyningesmot*."

"He is my heir, and he will go where he is needed," Rædwald said. He had donned his kingly voice, and Eadyth knew she did not have the energy to argue with him. She also knew that Rægen would cheerfully agree to anything, and so he would be of no help in persuading the king otherwise.

*****

Lundenwic was easily four times the size of Gipeswic, and had grown up as the trading center for the fortress of Lundenburh. It was easy to understand the appeal. The Thames was massively wide here and could only be crossed by ferry, and dozens of cargo ships lined the docks as they passed.

The stink of fish and horse mingled with the sweet, yeasty scent of the communal oven as they passed; small children ran barefoot chasing one another with sticks as their mothers scolded them for getting underfoot. Dozens of people had set up trestle tables, and the shouts of the traders drowned any apprehensive thoughts Sunniva might have had. Instead, she was filled to the brim with excitement, basking in the glow of the frenetic activity that now surrounded her.

"Is it market day?" she asked her father, who was surveying the activity imperiously from atop his horse. "It is so crowded!"

"No, this is just what it's always like here," Father said, grinning. "There's always a shipment going in or out, and people are always willing to buy. It's often cheaper to buy on market day, but if you need a bit of metal or some cloth, it's convenient to have it available." He surveyed the people excitedly. "I hope to make Gipeswic as busy as this, someday."

Sunniva thought that this was a stretch; Gipeswic was a fine market town and under her father's guidance it had blossomed into a bustling trading station, but she knew that it would never be as convenient or as popular as Lundenwic. She gave her father an indulgent smile nonetheless. "I'm sure it will be even better," she said.

The commotion of Lundenwic nearly made her forget how unhappy she had been during the journey, but as soon as they left the lively trading center it came back to her in full force. She toyed with one of her rings as she rode alongside Edwin and Sige in sullen silence. It was the massive silver one she had won from Ecgric during a drunken dice game, before everything was spoiled. She did not know why she wore it; it was much too big for her finger and it only served to remind her of him. She found herself fiddling with it every time she thought of him, and it made her angry. She kept thinking of that night; about how selfish Ecgric was and how cross she had been when she had stormed out on him.

Sunniva had known that once her blood cooled she would be able to speak to him again and they could return to normal. She had entered the king's bedroom at the back of the hall silently and slipped into bed beside her mother. She silently cried into Eadyth's shoulder and Eadyth stroked her hair without question until Sunniva fell asleep, and Sunniva steeled herself to face Ecgric the next morning.

But Ecgric had gone, before the sun had even risen. No one had been awake yet except for Father, who had seen him off, and if Ecgric had mentioned anything to Rædwald, the king did not speak of it to her. Sunniva waited until she was alone to scream a curse at Ecgric, hoping that he was not too far to hear her.

They left the trading port of Lundenwic and headed inland somewhat toward the *burh* and the old town. The ruined Roman city nearby had been abandoned for a hundred years, but people were slowly starting to rediscover its uses and several rich families had set up residences in the countryside nearby. Each was within easy walking distance of the *burh* in case of attack, and their farms were lush and beginning to grow a deep golden color, signaling the coming harvest.

"It's very well-fortified," Sige explained, indicating the high palisaded walls of the *burh*, "Because these lands are so hotly contested. The Thames is so useful for trade that the kingdoms are always fighting for it."

"So who holds it now?" Sunniva asked.

"Sæwine of the Eastseaxe" said Rædwald, "Although in truth no one really controls this area. There are several *ealdormen* who own land and farms here and serve the various *cyningas* as the fancy takes them, but in essence this area is autonomous."

"This is probably a good thing," piped up Edwin, "because it means that this is about the closest thing to neutral territory as we could hope for."

Sunniva considered for a moment. "That's why mother didn't want to come down to Lundenburh, isn't it?" she asked her father, "She hates Sæwine because he took her lands when she married you."

Rædwald nodded grimly, and Sunniva could hear Sige grinding his teeth.

Edwin looked at the pair of them confusedly. "How did he manage that?" Edwin asked. "I could not imagine the *cwene* allowing anyone to seize her property.

Sunniva looked at Sige, who only stared at his clenched fists around his reins. He did not speak, so Sunniva explained.

"When my grandfather died Mother inherited his lands. When Sige's father was killed in battle, Sæwine tried to marry my mother before his pyre had even burned to ash. She refused him, and he decided to use a different route to taking control of her lands. He found an outdated law that allowed the property to pass to him, rather than to Eadyth's son."

"She is still the owner of those lands, and they should pass to Sige upon Eadyth's death. That is, they would have done if Sæwine hadn't interfered." Father said.

"But instead," said Sige, "They will now revert to the *cyning* of the Eastseaxe upon my mother's death, because of the Eastseaxe law that says that a woman cannot inherit property without a male heir."

"But she did have a male heir!" Edwin said hotly.

"Not at the time," Father shook his head. "When Eadyth's father died, Sige was not yet born. Eadyth holds those lands only in name now, as a steward. Sæwine claims that he did it as a courtesy out of love for Eadyth, to allow her to keep the rents from the land, less a small tax to him."

"And the role of steward is not hereditary," said Sige. He had bitterness in his voice that Sunniva had rarely heard before.

He had always been the odd man out, and it pained her to know that he would have to be, in essence, no more than Father's retainer for the rest of his life, when he should have been an *ealdorman* in his own right. It rankled as much now as it had done when he first told her. She thought bitterly that her father should have made Sige the *ealdorman* of Gipeswic rather than Ecgric, but thinking of Ecgric only served to make her more grumpy.

"Why are you staying in Sæwine's hall, then, if you hate him so much?" Sunniva asked, pushing Ecgric out of her mind.

"Peace is more important," said Sige. "Sometimes we have to swallow our pride and put up with a lot of disappointment in order to protect the ones we care about." He looked hard at her, but it was as if he was looking past her. "I'm sure you know that better than anyone."

Sunniva sighed as she glared at the imposing wooden palisade of Lundenburh and what would await her inside. "Indeed I do."

The town's mead hall was just as enormous as the rest of the *burh*, slightly bigger than the Bricgweard and just as grand, though much older. Sunniva was on the point of wondering if father had gotten all of his ideas from Lundenburh and the surrounding villages, but was interrupted by her father introducing her to the king of the Eastseaxe.

"My daughter, Sunniva," father was saying, and she immediately put on the sweet smile she used for speaking with important people.

"You are just as beautiful as your mother," Sæwine said. "It is a shame that she could not be here. I've known her for years and I was looking forward to seeing her."

"I am sure the *cwene* regrets not being able to come," Sunniva said, "She felt it best to remain at home to oversee the opening of the market at Gipeswic. Now that the harvest is nearly at hand everyone will be terribly busy." She had rehearsed this, and she knew her father was pleased that she had not given any of the true reasons that Eadyth had not come back to the land of the Eastseaxe.

Sunniva made idle chat with the king of the Eastseaxe for a few moments, and knew almost immediately why someone could hate him. He seemed to think very highly of himself, and told her very loudly and very frequently that he was a Christian, and how had spearheaded the building of a new church near the Thames dedicated to some saint or other. Sunniva found it difficult to keep the smile on her face, but she did anyway, trying to forget the fact that this was the man who had stolen her brother's birthright. Somehow, she made it through her conversation with Sæwine and eventually managed to extract herself to speak someone who would not set her teeth on edge.

That night there was to be a feast, and Sunniva was bursting with excitement for a change of company and the diversions that only a large feast could provide.

It would be hours yet until she would need to prepare, so she and Sige and Edwin decided to go into Lundenwic to visit the vendors. They passed several extremely pleasurable hours walking up and down the ribbon of road that bordered the river, soaking in the frenetic atmosphere and the rowdy calls of traders and fishermen and their foul-mouthed wives.

Sunniva stopped at one of the docks to examine one of the largest ships she had ever seen. It could have held at least sixty oarsmen, and the prow and steering board were heavily decorated with carvings of sea dragons that seemed to undulate as it bobbed heavily in the ebb of the river. She was examining the size of the ship when she heard a voice behind her which made her heart skip.

"My beautiful *vrouwe*!" the voice said, and she turned to find the Frankisc man Godomar approaching her as she stood rooted to the dock. She grinned stupidly at him and saw Sige and Edwin sniggering at her over Godomar's shoulder.

"I see you are impressed with my ship," he said.

"This is yours?" Sunniva asked, wide-eyed. "Yes, it's beautiful. Did you come here from Francland in it?" she had rather forgotten how to form coherent sentences.

"Indeed I did," said Godomar, "but tell me, what brings you to Lundenwic? I had not hoped to see your fair face again."

"My father is here for the *heahcyning*'s funeral."

"Ah, yes," he said, "I am here for that unhappy reason as well. I had meant to be off by now, but as the *heahcyning* had been so gracious to me and to my kin, I felt it only right to remain behind to pay my respects."

He was terribly handsome, and Sunniva rather lost track of his words as she lost herself in the cut of his clothing and his tawny mane of hair. He was taller than any Frankisc man she had ever seen, and his legs made her nearly swoon, particularly in the lazy way he stood. She fidgeted with her ring as she watched Godomar's mouth moving. She knew now how Wynne had felt about Rægen, but she did not much mind feeling like a silly girl as Godomar held out his arm for her to escort her back to the guest houses.

Sunniva had brought her casket of jewelry and several dresses to choose from, but she found it extremely difficult to pick the right one. She was giddy for the feast, despite the solemn reason for which it was being held. She was taking so long that the serving girl who had been sent to help her dress started to make harrumphing noises, and Sunniva picked the blue dress with gold embroidery, and had the girl braid her hair into an elaborate confection of plaits and gold rings. She slipped gold and silver bangles on her arms and hung swathes of glass beads from her neck, which had been gifts from Godomar himself, and went to join the party.

Sunniva looked around for Godomar at the feast, but she did not see him. She turned her ring around her finger, unhappy that he was not there to take her mind off of the ring's former owner. She had wanted to see Godomar, to have him compliment her and call her "beautiful *vrouwe,*" but it seemed that tonight she would be disappointed. She had been certain that so high a lord would have been invited.

Her mind was taken away from the handsome Frankisc man, however, as she was caught in a whirlwind of introductions, and she smiled prettily and chatted with everyone. Sunniva sipped some mead to wet her throat after so much talking, and two women appeared at her elbow.

The first was a large-breasted, pale, shy-looking girl a few years older than Sunniva, who wore so many ornaments that she looked as if she had been dipped into molten gold. The second was somewhat older and much more imposing and queenly, with hair the color of a raven's wing and a tall, slight figure that might have been carved from glass.

"You're Eadyth's daughter, aren't you?" the dark-haired one asked. She had a surprisingly low voice for a woman, slow and melodic.

Sunniva was rather taken aback at the lack of formality from the woman, but she took it in stride. "My name is Sunniva, Rædwald's daughter of the Engla," she said.

"Ethelburh, daughter of Ethelbert of the Eota," she replied. "This is my father's wife, Leasið." The younger girl nodded in distracted acknowledgement of the introduction.

Sunniva opened her mouth once or twice, realized that she had nothing to say, and smiled. "I am pleased to meet you both. I was worried that there would be no young women to talk to here in Lundenburh." Indeed, Leasið was hardly older than Sunniva herself, maybe twenty years at the most, and Ethelburh might have been Sige's age. Apart from the two of them and a smattering of serving women, everyone in the hall were twice their age.

"Few enough of us, I'm afraid," said Ethelburh, shrugging as if it did not make much of a difference to her.

Sunniva turned to Leasið. "I am very sorry to hear of your husband's death, my lady," she said.

Leasið seemed distracted looking over to where Edwin and Sige were speaking to another young man. "Oh, that," she said, "yes, it was rather awful," she said in a dreamy sort of voice, "But the *heahcyning* will rest well now, at least."

Ethelburh gave her stepmother a disapproving look and caught the eye of the man with Edwin and Sige. Sunniva asked, "Is that your brother?"

"My twin," she said lazily. "Eadbald Cyning of the Eota. I am surprised you haven't met him already." She called imperiously to her brother, "Eadbald, come here."

Eadbald made his way through the crowd followed by Edwin and Sige. Introductions were made. Eadbald was a handsome man, a stouter, bearded version of Ethelburh, with the same long face and dark hair. They spoke genially for a few moments, talking about all those stupid things one discussed with strangers. Unusually for Sunniva, she listened and watched more than she spoke. Ethelburh took immediate control of the conversation, and through her manner was rather abrupt Sunniva decided in only a moment that she liked the other woman. The same could not be said of her brother, however. He greeted Sunniva pleasantly enough, but his conversation was lacking and he seemed constantly distracted. His eyes frequently darted to Leasið, and Sunniva recognized the expressions that passed between them as the same as those she so often had shared with Ecgric. She cursed herself for thinking of him again.

Sunniva saw that Sige had left them, but Edwin remained and talked to Ethelburh for some time. Feeling slightly overwhelmed, she excused herself and found Sige sitting alone, drinking moodily and watching the knot of people Sunniva had just left.

"That family's not half-strange," Sunniva said, glancing in the same direction as she sat beside him.

Sige raised his eyebrows as if to keep himself above the gossip, but failed. "You do hear stories," he said. "Ecgric's full of them. I mean, he lived here for almost ten years. I know that he used to fool around with Leasið while she was still the *heahcyning*'s mistress, though it seems her stepson has taken a fancy as well…" he trailed off, and Sunniva realized the expression which had appeared on her face. She hastily tried to rearrange it.

"I didn't mean to upset you," Sige said, abashed.

Sunniva scoffed. "I am well aware of Ecgric's exploits."

"I know you were fond of him."

She found it harder to scoff at this. "Yes, I suppose," she said lamely, "You know that he is good company. Anyway, what's done is done and there's no use talking about it."

They both collapsed into moody silence for a moment. "You look awfully cross tonight," Sunniva said, "is something wrong?"

Sige looked around at the assembled *cyningas* and *ealdormen* and their women. "I don't like this. The very air seems tense."

"It's almost as if everyone is on the brink of war with one another!" Sunniva said.

"That's not funny," said Sige reprovingly, "You ought not to joke about that."

"I wasn't joking," said Sunniva. She gave a theatrical sigh. "I suppose it's up to me to make a match with one of these men and end all this fighting, eh?"

"Now that we are here, I am beginning to think that is more important than ever."

*****

Gieva glanced at Rægen, who was riding next to the cart. Gieva was pleased that he had come home with them. He trotted along cheerfully beside them, his voice comfortingly low as he sang a song to keep their spirits high. If he was unhappy that he was not going to Lundenburh with the others, he did not show it.

The journey back to Wuffingham was much swifter than the journey south, but the cart ride was bumpy and Gieva worried for Eadyth. A bed had been prepared for the queen in the back of one of the gear wagons, and Gieva sat beside her on a pile of baggage to keep an eye on her. The queen was shivering, but she kicked her blankets away as if they were coiling snakes every time Gieva tried to bundle her up again.

"I wish we were at home," Gieva said miserably to Rægen, who was pacing nervously as the horses were watered and they all took a few bites of food. "None of the herbs I need are in season, and I didn't think to bring any of my stores. Spells can only do so much; without proper herbs I don't know what more I can do for her."

"What should we do?" Rægen asked.

"She needs proper medicine," Gieva said despondently, "We have to get home as soon as possible. Otherwise, I do not know what might happen."

"It's another day's walk at least."

"Then we had better start moving as soon as may be." Gieva said, looking back at Eadyth's pale face.

They had walked for another few hours into the darkness, until it became too dangerous to take horses over the nearly-invisible road. Gieva curled up next to Rægen under their cloaks to get a few hours of sleep before setting off again. She had barely closed her eyes when he was shaking her to wake up in the cold light of dawn.

A few hours after they had started walking again, one of the guardsmen fell forward into the leaf-strewn road. He had been walking behind the wagon, one of a dozen men sent back to Wuffingham to guard the queen. Gieva told the cart-driver to stop, and jumped down from the wagon to see to him. A man of about thirty, broad-chested and usually ruddy-skinned, he was as pale as Eadyth and burning with fever. Rægen helped to lift him onto the cart and gave Gieva a pained look.

"They'll be fine," Gieva lied, "We just have to get home."

Gieva was exhausted and close to tears by the time they finally crossed the bridge into Wuffingham. It was with a massive sigh of relief that Gieva entered her house and found the full pouch of feverfew, and another one half-full of yarrow. Rægen led the cart up to the hall and Gieva gathered her things, rushing up to the hall and starting a fire to prepare her medicines.

By the time darkness fell, two more of their men had developed fevers and were lying near the fire with the others. Rægen was sitting with his mother, anxiously holding her hand and watching Gieva as she worked.

Gieva went to sit next to him, feeling Eadyth's forehead with the back of her hand. "She's still burning," Gieva said miserably. She shook Eadyth's shoulder gently. "Eadyth, wake up and drink this."

Eadyth grudgingly opened her eyes and looked around confusedly for a moment before she realized where she was. "When did we get back?" she asked in a croaking voice.

"A few hours ago. Drink this medicine." Gieva helped to tip the hot liquid into Eadyth's mouth, and she winced at the bitterness.

"Well, you've made it right," she said. "Thank you for taking care of me, my dear."

Gieva squeezed Eadyth's hand in acknowledgement, and went to check on the others in her care. Some women had come to assist in caring for the sick and Gieva was glad for their assistance. Unfortunately, within a few hours many of her helpers had developed fevers, as did the young children they had brought with them. The hall was filled with the sounds of retching and children crying, and Gieva started to stumble as she made her way between the bodies lying on the floor of the hall.

It was well past midnight when Rægen pulled her away from the sick folk. "You must rest," he said, "my sweet one, you're hardly going to help anyone if you fall ill yourself."

She protested loudly, and a few of the other women turned to look at them.

"Go and rest, my lady," said one of her helpers, who looked rather tired herself, "We can manage here for a few hours."

Her voice was so calm and soothing that Gieva grudgingly relented.

"I'm still sleeping in the hall," she said to the girl, "wake me if anything changes, or if you need any help." Rægen led her to one of the alcoves and lay down beside her, covering them both with a soft woolen blanket. It was beyond bliss to lie down, though she felt guilty about leaving the helpers to take care of everyone. Rægen was asleep within moments, and Gieva lay quite still in his arms, listening to the slow rhythm of his heart as she slipped into dreamless slumber.

Gieva woke up before the sun had really risen, feeling very hot and stifled by the blanket and the blazing fire coming from the center of the hall. She had thought that Rægen was trying to shake her to get her to wake up, but when she turned to face him her heart sank to find that he was pale and shivering, and his skin burned like fire.

"No, not you too," she said miserably, stroking his burning cheek. He looked apologetically at her, as if he had done her a personal injury, and she brushed his damp hair away from his face. She helped him up so that he could sleep closer to the fire, and only reluctantly did she leave his side in order to check on the others. Tying her hair back and rolling up her sleeves, she made her way to each of the sick people in turn. Two of the serving women had fallen ill during the night, one being the sweet girl who had insisted that Gieva go to rest. The hall was filled with the smell of vomit and shit and smoke, and it made her queasy. Gieva was overwhelmed and exhausted and close to tears, but she flitted between the sickbeds and spoke comforting words of healing over the people as they piled into the hall one by one. The *godeswif*, a white-haired, tough looking woman, arrived to assist them, and put her hand on Gieva's shoulder.

"You've already done my work for me," she said kindly. "If I had come sooner, it would not have made a difference, except to be an extra set of hands. You are a skilled healer."

Gieva wanted to smile, but her mouth only trembled. Not skilled enough, she thought as she brushed sweat-soaked hair from her sleeping husband's face.

That night, while Gieva watched the life slip from the girl who had been her helper, she heard the sobs of a woman sitting nearby. The woman had been cradling a small boy, no more than a year old, stroking his red hair and kissing his cheeks. The poor child had been dead for hours now, but his mother rocked him as if he were sleeping.

"What did you call him?" Gieva asked gently.

The woman shook her head. "We hadn't given him a name yet," she said, looking at the baby's pale face. "He wasn't old enough to have a proper name. We just called him Little Brother." She began to weep harder now, and Gieva could not think of anything to say that might help her. It would be useless to remind her that many children died before reaching a year, or that she should be grateful that she still had other children who were healthy. Nothing would get through, however. She touched the woman's back, offered a quiet prayer to the mother of the Earth to take the child into her keeping. The woman continued to rock and sing to him as Gieva turned her attention to Rægen.

He was leaning over the side of his bed, and his body heaved but nothing came out. He eventually fell back, his breathing labored. Gieva stroked his face, calling him back into wakefulness. She did not move from her place at his side, and she stopped feeling guilty as the others began to rise from their sick beds.

The next morning many of the others had clearly recovered from their illnesses. The crowd in the hall had begun to clear, but Rægen still lay burning, his chest rising and falling in harsh bursts, his eyes fluttering behind his eyelids as he groaned Gieva's name.

"I'm here," she said, beginning to cry from exhaustion and grief. "You have to come back to me, my love. You don't die like this; it is far too ordinary for you, my *ætheling*. You will not die today."

She did not move for the rest of the night, and only when she felt a gentle but trembling hand stroke her face did she realize that she had fallen asleep with her head on Rægen's chest. She grasped his hand, kissed it, and sat up, looking dazedly into his eyes.

"You've come back to me," she said, her mind muddled with exhaustion and relief.

"Of course I have," he said, his voice was hoarse and weak, but he was smiling. "You called to me. I would not disobey your command."

*****

Ethelbert's body had been sealed, unburned, in a wooden coffin and placed in honor on a handsome ship which would make its way down the Thames and down the coast back to Cantwareburh.

"It's strange that they didn't burn his body," Sige mused.

"Christians don't cremate their dead," said Edwin distractedly. "Even when they are far from home, they would rather cart a corpse around than participate in a pagan practice."

Sige frowned. He had no problem with burying the dead, but if a man had died a hundred leagues from home as the *heahcyning* had done, it was customary to burn the body and transport only the bones. He did not like this Christian tradition of carting a moldering corpse across the country; but then, he did not approve of most Christian traditions.

Sige glared at the priests as they threw drops of water and made their hand gestures at the box, trying to fight the urge to slide a sword into one of them. He was still angry about the incident at the *weoh*, and every time he saw a Christian, he felt the nearly unconquerable urge to draw his blade and vent his frustrations.

Edwin was standing next to him and, perhaps in response to Sige's teeth grinding, stood just close enough to him that their arms barely touched. Sige could not help feeling a sense of calm as he focused on the bare patch of skin which connected the two of them. He wished he could take Edwin's hand or kiss him, but fought that urge as well. It had been weeks since they had last been together, and Sige did not know how much longer he could last. It was no strange thing for them to spend time together, dicing or drinking or talking for hours, but he knew that there was a line between the love of friendship and the love that they were not allowed to show to the world. He wondered if it would be easier if he did not spend any time with Edwin, but pushed the thought away immediately. The forced playacting of friendship was far better than not having Edwin in his life at all.

After the funeral, the kings retreated into the hall to speak together again. Sige had no idea what was going on, and did not intend to press Rædwald for the information. If the king wished to share his thoughts, he would do so in his own time.

Indeed, that evening before retiring the king came to him, looking grim. He did not speak immediately, but Sige noticed the deep lines around his stepfather's eyes as he sat down.

"This isn't going as well as I thought it would," Rædwald said.

Sige frowned. "I am sorry to hear that. I take it that the *cyningas* are unwilling to consider an alliance?"

"They might have done, once," Rædwald said enigmatically, "but with one thing and another..." he rubbed his eyes wearily. "Sæwine was furious when he learned that we killed their priests."

"I'm the one who killed them," Sige said bitterly, "Don't take the blame for my actions."

Rædwald coughed dryly. "I am responsible for your actions as your step-father and as your *dryhten*. Sæwine wants a *wergild* for the priests."

"What does Sæwine have to do with any of this?" Sige asked, dumbfounded. "The priests weren't Sæwine's men, so why should he care?"

"He says that the *wergild* should be a token of penance for your crimes, and that he would use it to finance his new church to repair the slight you have inflicted against God." Rædwald looked as if he would be quite pleased to rip Sæwine in half, but he took a breath to steady himself. "The prick wants a hundred pounds of gold for it, which is of course ridiculous. An *ealdorman* isn't even worth that much, let alone some foreign priest." He rolled his eyes. "It doesn't matter. He's not getting it. I have told him that you were punished in accordance with our laws and that that should be enough. "

"But I wasn't punished," Sige said, glancing shiftily at the king.

"I won't punish you for killing those men. We both know that it was wrong, but the gods will dole out their justice for spilling blood in their defense." Sige waited for the 'but' and it soon came. "But I think that it might be prudent to lie low for some time."

"What do you mean?" he asked. His mouth went dry and he felt his heart begin to beat faster.

"There are too many people who want your guts right now," said Rædwald, "Sæwine in particular, but also Ethelbert's son Eadbald. He isn't a Christian but he has enough friends who are, and he does not wish to upset them."

Sige was stung with the injustice of it, but nodded resignedly. "What should I do?"

Rædwald sighed. "That remains to be seen."

"Are you going to send me away?" he realized how much of a child he sounded, but could not help himself. He had lived with a constant, nagging fear since his childhood that the king would one day send him away from the hall and he would be left *seledreorig*.

"I don't wish to send you away," said Rædwald, perhaps understanding the fear. "I will continue to speak to the other *cyningas*, and in the meantime I want you to stay out of their way. Do not anger anyone or give them cause to harm you. It's bad enough that you are so close with Edwin."

Sige stiffened. "What about it?"

"Surely you've noticed," Rædwald said, "that to these men, Edwin is more valuable than any alliance. I'm not the only one who has been offered favors in exchange for Edwin's head."

They both glanced at Edwin, who was amusing a small knot of people some distance away. Sige began to grind his teeth again. He wanted to rush to Edwin, to throw his body in front of an enemy spear for him. No one would take Edwin without going through Sige. He had made that promise the night that they had arrived in Ealdham, and he would not break it now.

"I should not have brought him here," Rædwald said at length. "I had thought that he might be able to persuade some of them, but I realize now that it was a bad idea. I'll wager half of them have only refrained from killing him out of respect for the *heahcyning*. No one wants to start a war during a funeral."

"It wouldn't be the first time," said Sige. "How do we know if can trust any of these people?"

"We can't," said Rædwald simply. "You trust the men who fight beside you in a shield wall. I have never fought beside these men, only against them. I will make peace with them for the sake of defeating a greater foe, but I will never trust them. A man cannot show his loyalty while his sword is sheathed."

"I don't understand," Sige said. His mind had wandered, creating a barrier around Edwin, as if his willing Edwin to remain safe would protect him.

"I mean that once a man draws his sword, you know where his loyalties truly lie. If he will not draw it at your side, then he might as well be pointing it at your heart."

It sounded very grim to Sige, but Rædwald gave a half-hearted smile and said, "You are a good man, Sigebryht. You're an honest and loyal man, and that is why you have no mind for politics."

Sige swelled with pride at this, but the gnawing worry came back. "I suppose it's even more vital now that we find Sunniva a match, isn't it?" He tried to say as light-heartedly as possible though he felt as weary as if he had been in a battle.

"Sæwine has been quite keen on her," Rædwald said. "He's been hinting at a marriage pact for days now."

Sige glared at him. "You can't be serious."

Rædwald laughed mirthlessly. "I'm not interested in your mother tearing my balls off. But Sunniva knows what a prick he is. You know her, once she decides she doesn't like someone, there's no shifting her."

"What about the others?" Sigebryht felt somewhat guilty using his little sister as bait, but he knew that Rædwald's charm was not going to be the thing to win the lords of the land to their side.

"Plenty of men want her, but they don't want the baggage that comes along with her," Rædwald said bitterly. "They would be happy to have a pretty young wife, but they are less keen on the idea of fighting a war for her father."

"Perhaps you should broaden your scope," said Sige, "she doesn't have to marry a *cyning* or an *ætheling*; what about a wealthy *ealdorman*? What about someone who is rich and could benefit you by giving you wealth or trading opportunities?"

"Trade and wealth are not my priorities at the moment," said Rædwald. "I need an army."

Sige sat in thought for a moment, looking at Sunniva, seeing the torchlight reflected on the strings of beads and gold trinkets which the wealthy and powerful Frankisc man had given her. She had been terribly keen on the foreign *ealdorman,* he remembered, the man who was so rich and handsome and powerful in his own land…

Then, as a lightning bolt of realization struck him, Sige said, "why not both?"

Chapter Fourteen

Modgeþanc

Plans

The weeks of steady meals and easy living had made a marked improvement upon Rian. She was still skinny and flat-chested, but she no longer looked drawn and wasted as she had done when he had first met her. She seemed more cheerful as well; she had always been friendly, but now there was a genuine light in her eyes which made Eorwald much more confident in his choice to keep her with him.

Eorwald knew that his men were talking about him, but he did not care. He liked Rian. She had spent every night with him since the first, and he did not see how the gold – not to mention the food and drink and lodging – that he gave her were any different from what he might have given any other girl. They were just presents to him; a ring or a couple of *peningas*, and she was happy to spend her nights with him. He liked to believe that she enjoyed it.

It was damp and cold the night Eorwald told Rian that he loved her. Or, rather, he blurted it at her without thinking, as her limbs draped over him, both of them covered with a blanket as they listened to someone play the harp very poorly. Her hand had made its way into his trousers and he was so overwhelmed with the sensation that he forgot himself.

She gave him a half-smile, but in his slightly-drunken state he could not be sure if she pitied him, or if she might have been deciding on her own feelings.

"I want you to come and live with me when I go back to Wuffingham," he continued. "I want you to be a free woman and I will make sure you have a house and a livelihood and that you won't have to... well, you know... anymore."

Rian removed her hand from between Eorwald's legs and touched his cheek, the sad smile still on her lips. "You are so good to me," she said. "I really don't deserve it, but I am grateful."

"So will you?" Eorwald asked.

Rian shook her head. "I could have a fine house and a farm and a dozen sheep of my own, but that is not the life I know. I can't spin or sew or make cheese or brew beer, and any children I might try to bear would end up half-wild; I have never learned how to do anything else, apart from what I do now."

This was surprising. "Didn't your mother ever teach you..." he said, but stopped at the look on her face.

"My mother died when I was a baby," she said, "and I lived in my uncle's house until he started letting his friends pay to put their hands up my skirt," she said in a matter-of-fact tone, "Eventually I decided I might as well keep the money for myself and I ran away, and I've been doing this ever since. I don't know anything else."

"But you could have a much better life," Eorwald said.

Rian still had the sad look, but it was not sadness at her own plight, but rather pity, as if she thought him a misguided idealist. "What would you do?" she asked, "Take me back to Wuffingham and make me your wife? Your servant? Or would you continue to give me pretty trinkets to wear on my wrists while I keep your bed warm?"

"You're too good a woman to continue like this," Eorwald pleaded.

Rian smiled. "You wouldn't tell a shepherd to stop raising sheep because it's dirty work, but you want me to give up my livelihood simply because it's not the type of work you think is dignified?"

"But..." Eorwald began stupidly, but Rian cut him off.

"I will stay as long as you're here to keep me, but you must realize that this is all that we will ever be able to have together." She looked him in the eye and he saw some sadness as if a remnant of the innocence she had lost was showing through, or perhaps it was his own reflected in her eyes.

He decided to be happy with his situation, despite the twinge of embarrassment he felt every so often. He weathered the comments from Hengest – as if the other man could judge anyone, with a whore on each arm every other evening! He focused on honing his war-craft by day and enjoying Rian's company by night. It might not have been perfect, but it could have been worse.

A few days later he found Ricbert in, if possible, an even surlier mood than usual. He had been speaking with a messenger who was looking tired and haggard, and after he had sent the messenger to get some food and rest, he spoke to Eorwald.

"The *heahcyning* is dead," he said without preamble. "Nearly three weeks ago, now."

Eorwald did not attempt to hide his surprise. "How did he die?"

"In his sleep, but no one knows how exactly."

"Well, he was rather old," Eorwald said, shrugging. "Does anyone think he was done in?"

"I don't think so. He was a good man," Ricbert said. Eorwald did not speak, but let Ricbert continue in his own time. "I might not have agreed with his decision to ally himself with foreigners, and I was angry at his despicable desertion of the gods, but he was a great leader despite all that. I don't think anyone designed to murder him, but now that he's dead, I worry that the kingdoms will fall into chaos again."

"I wouldn't mind a bit of fighting," Eorwald said.

Ricbert shook his head. "You like skirmishes and quick, bloody battles; not the sort of things we had to deal with before you were born. We are stretched thinly enough fighting Athelfrith; what will happen when the peace is broken with Mercia or the Eota? You remember what happened at Ealdham. Think of that happening tenfold, in every village; that is what will happen if we go to war with our neighbors once more."

"They wouldn't do anything," Eorwald said, trying not to think of what had happened at Ealdham. "Ethelbert wasn't the only reason we made peace. My father–"

"Your father is a subject of the *heahcyning*, the same as the others. Every kingdom is now going to fight for supremacy without someone to control them." Ricbert grimaced, which was as good as any other man rubbing his eyes in weariness. "I do not know what might happen, but I know your father and I know his type. *Cyningas* don't want to rule little kingdoms. They will squabble for power and Athelfrith will have to do nothing more than to stretch out his hand to take everything while our backs are turned on one another."

Eorwald was frowning deeply. "So what do we do?"

Ricbert looked him in the eye. "You tell me."

"Athelfrith is the bigger threat," Eorwald said after a few moments of consideration, "And the men we have here are in a good position to hold him off, but we need more warriors to stand a chance against him. Even with every fighting man in the country, though, we have no idea where Athelfrith might make a stand."

"He seems pleased enough to harass our fenlands," Ricbert said, not really as a question, but he stroked his beard just the same.

"But he might think that Mercia is a sweeter prize in the end," Eorwald said. He thought for a moment, "Let me take a few men and we can scout out the Fens. If there are Northumbrian camps, it might point to an invasion. Athelfrith surely knows of Ethelbert's death by now, and he might think that this is a good time to strike."

"That makes sense," Ricbert said, rubbing his chin. "Athelfrith would want to scout these lands in order to plan an attack; if we can get an idea of their movements, we might have an advantage."

Eorwald grinned. "I'll wager that they're trying to make their way to Elge," he said. "It's what I would do. It's easy to defend and strategically located for an attack on our lands. That's why I wanted to go there after we left Ealdham."

Ricbert nodded. "Then that is where we should look first. Ask for a few volunteers, no more than three or four. They will need stealth and secrecy more than they'll need force."

Eorwald paused at the word 'they.'

"I had thought that I would lead the scouting mission," he said, failing to hide his frustration.

"Your place is here," Ricbert said. "You are their *dryhten*."

"We both know that I'm not the *dryhten*," Eorwald said, annoyed at the pretense. "I am under your command here."

"But you are an *ætheling*, and this is a risk you should not take. We will send someone else to scout. It is too dangerous for you to go."

Eorwald stared him down. "So you will send my men out to fight and die in my place while I sit here and do nothing? I won't have it. I will never back down from a fight, or put my friends in danger without offering to fight beside them," he said, "you're the one who taught me that."

They glared at one another for a long while. "You'll go anyway, won't you?" Ricbert asked resignedly.

Eorwald gave him a sly look. "Try to stop me."

Eorwald felt a manic sort of joy at the idea of doing something other than drinking and dicing and playing at swords. He could not tolerate idleness easily, and the fact that he had been resigned to a life of it grated on his nerves, despite the distraction Rian offered. He had not noticed how little he had worked while encamped in Mæduwic, but now he felt slow and doughy as they began to make their way out of the town and toward the wood.

There were five of them: Leofric and Hengest had their usual places by his side, as well as a youth named Eastmund and a *thegn* from Mæduwic called Frodrun. They went on foot but led a light and speedy pony behind them to carry the little baggage they brought, all fleet of foot and eager for a job to do.

They marched northeast from Mæduwic and camped on the borders of a small stand of trees not far from the Roman road. They lit no fires and slept under bushes, as they knew that they were nearing Elge and did not wish to be seen. Eorwald drew the first watch and sat huddled beneath his cloak, wishing he knew as many songs as Rægen did, in order to keep his mind from wandering into sleep. He woke Leofric after four hours of bored silence, and dreamed of Rian as soon as he rested his head on his rolled-up cloak.

They continued on the next day in a line toward the sweeping marshland which they knew concealed the isle of Elge. They did not have any means of crossing the water to get to the island, but they were certain that once they got close enough, they would be able to determine if there were men encamped there.

The stink of the fetid water and the slight sucking sound of the stream nearby made Eorwald think of the slimy monsters which must live within. Before he could think too much on it, however, Eastmund caught his attention. A barely-visible plume of smoke was emanating from somewhere in the trees a league or so away to the west, in the opposite direction of the Isle of

Elge, wafting up from the wood at the other end of the meadow.

"Bloody idiots, making a fire," Eorwald said.

"Not idiots," Frodrun said, "They probably don't expect anyone to be watching them. No one ever comes here, except occasionally to hunt in the woods or to fish the streams. It's dangerous to come out here if you don't know the way, so they probably think that no one will bother them."

"I was sure that they would have gone to Elge," said Leofric, who turned to Eorwald, "Do you reckon we should go and investigate?"

Eorwald did not wish to leave their course, but he wanted to know who might be setting up a camp in an otherwise uninhabited stretch of fetid marshland.

Ricbert knew that they were going to travel up to Elge; if they did not return, he would be able to follow their trail in order to find them. If they left the path now, Ricbert would not know. They would be on their own.

"Dryhten?" Hengest prodded, when Eorwald was silent.

"Elge is another day's journey," Eorwald said, considering. "We'll go and investigate, and continue the journey if we find nothing." He turned to Eastmund. "Tie up the pony inside those trees, and then follow us, but not too closely. Keep us within sight, but stay out of sight yourself. If something goes wrong, get back to Mæduwic as quickly as you can to tell Ricbert."

Eastmund's face fell. Eorwald knew he had been hoping to tag along in case of a fight, but he would be disappointed. "You knew when I brought you that this would be your duty. Are you incapable of doing your duty?" He sounded very much like his father the king when he said it, and it gave him a strange sense of pleasure.

"Yes," Eastmund said resignedly.

Eorwald nodded in acknowledgement. "Very well. Listen for us, and pay attention. If we are not back before dark, go back to Mæduwic. If you hear sounds of a fight, go back to Mæduwic. If you see anyone besides us, go back to–"

"Yes, I understand," Eastmund said moodily.

Eorwald and the others gathered some light gear from the horse's packs. They all brought swords and seaxes, and Frodrun slung a bow on his back. Frodrun could shoot a squirrel's eye in the dark, but Eorwald prayed that he would not need to bend his bow that day.

"There and back again," Eorwald said as they set off, leaving a glowering Eastmund behind them. "We stay silent, and we get back here safely. We don't need to start a fight we can't win outright."

They reached the edge of the wood and began to pick through the trees and underbrush silently, finding the open area where there seemed to be a well-established but temporary residence. Northumbrians. His suspicions were confirmed; the few shields and banners that Eorwald could see matched those they had seen at the Wildwood near Ealdham. He had to push the idea of angry slaughter from his mind. "There and back again," he told himself quietly. "Don't start a fight you can't win."

A large pavilion stood some way away, surrounded by tents and the crushed grass that went along with a prolonged stay in a single area. Men were cooking and drinking, practicing fighting with wooden swords and spears, cursing and laughing and carousing with a few camp followers. It looked so ordinary that Eorwald forgot for a moment that these were their enemies.

"How many?" Leofric asked in a whisper.

"At least fifty," Hengest said with a touch of worry.

"Look!" Leofric pointed to a lean-to building with open sides in which a massive store of arms was housed. "And I thought they would only send a scouting mission. *Godes hæmað min ears…*"

Eorwald had to suppress the panic rising in his chest at the number of men gathered here. He looked around at some of the spears stuck in the ground, propping up shields that bore the unmistakable sigils; those he had only ever seen on Northumbrian shields, ready for war.

Even this small encampment outnumbered the garrison at Mæduwic, and if his assumption had been correct and this was merely an auxiliary force in advance of a proper army, then the small force of the Englisc would be pitifully outmatched. He sent up a silent prayer that reinforcements would get to Mæduwic before Athelfrith ordered anyone to attack it.

He knew, however, that the gods did not simply grant wishes; he would have to do what he could to cripple the Northumbrians so that they would not be able to attack at all.

"I have an idea," he said, ignoring his own advice to stay hidden, and he ordered the others to remain behind. They whispered protests, but he ignored them.

There were too many men nearby for them not to notice someone wandering into their camp, so Eorwald adopted a profound coolness which he prayed would keep him unnoticed. He wore no identifying clothes or weapons besides Weargbana and his seax, and he covered them with his cloak and drew the hood over his face as if he were merely warding off the early autumn breeze. He could almost hear his companions holding their breaths as he strode confidently into the Northumbrian camp and sat down in front of a camp fire, staring moodily into its depths. There were few people here, and he had so far gone unnoticed. He allowed himself a breath, looking around.

"How long until we march?" one of the men asked irritably.

"No idea," his companion said. They were a few paces away at a small fire of their own, ignoring Eorwald completely.

The first man groaned, "He didn't say anything about a strike? Now would be the time. Rædwald's people are scattered and unprepared, we might as well attack."

"They may be unprepared, but they are in a town," said the other. "We haven't got resources for a siege."

"We haven't got resources to sit on our arses all day, either," said the first. "*Godes hæmað min ears*, what does he plan to do?"

"Do you think Hwitegos tells me anything?" the other voice said. "Gods, what I wouldn't give for a whore and a drink. I'd settle for something sour and stale, as long as it's wet."

"The whore, or the beer?" the first chuckled.

"Colred, get your lazy arse back to the pavilion," a third voice came, and Eorwald glanced up to see another man pounding his way toward them. "All of you!" He shouted so that Eorwald could hear as well, and Eorwald raised a hand as if in acknowledgement, hiding his burning face.

The two grumbling men made their way toward the pavilion, as Eorwald leaned forward as if to bury the coals of the camp fire in ashes so they would not burn out. He poked a long stick into the center of the coals until the flames began to catch on the end. He resisted the urge to look over his shoulder at the place where he knew his were hidden, and instead rose carefully to his feet and brought the burning brand with him. He crossed back to the outside of the ring of tents and toward the wooden structure housing the weaponry, kicking a pile of dead leaves and bracken toward the back. He cursed their foresight to put the armory so close to the pavilion, where the men had gathered. Enough were making their way toward the pavilion that he went unnoticed, though his heart was pounding.

Eorwald nodded in acknowledgement of one of them, and breathed again when the man walked past without comment. His hands were shaking as he thrust the brand into the pile of dead leaves at the rear of the structure, holding his breath again as he waited for them to catch. He saw a wisp of smoke and the beginnings of a flame.

He allowed himself a triumphant grin as the flame began to grow and start to blacken the wood of the lean-to and the racks on which the weapons were leaning. He backed away slowly, speeding only when he entered the edge of the trees and bursting into a sprint when he no longer saw the tents behind him.

He did not stop to explain when he found his companions, but motioned for them to follow him at a run through the tangled undergrowth.

They stopped, panting and sweating once they had run far enough from the camp to assure their safety.

"What in the name of Thunor's prick was that about?" Leofric asked breathlessly. His answer came soon after with the sounds of muffled shouts coming from the direction of the camp and a strong smell of smoke. Eorwald grinned, his blood surging.

"They can't attack us if they have no weapons," he said manically. Of course it wasn't entirely true; most true warriors would have their own kit and could fight just the same, and of course a small fire would not completely destroy iron-tipped spears, but they would have to re-fit them, and that would take time.

He paused for only an instant, realizing that he might have made a huge mistake, but did not allow himself to dwell on it. No, it was done, whatever happened. It might buy the Engla time.

Or it might just warn the Northumbrians that we are still out there, ready to be attacked, he thought.

"Brilliant," Hengest said, his excitement mirroring Eorwald's own. They walked swiftly back in the direction of Eastmund and the horse, picking their way through the darkening woods. It was nearly nightfall, but they would make it to the edge of the wood long before it became dark. It was idiotic, what he had done. He should have left well enough alone. He could have been captured or worse and he was still tense.

They continued through the woods, and Eorwald was so focused on getting back to Eastmund and the pony that he did not immediately notice a shocking, searing pain in the back of his leg just below the knee. He winced as if it had been a bee sting, but it caused him to miss a step and lurch forward.

As he struggled to his feet and looked down, he saw the bloody point of an arrow sticking awkwardly out the side of his calf, the feathered, unbloodied shaft sticking stupidly in the air behind him. It had clipped the edge of the muscle and was hanging by a thin band of skin, but he roared in anger and pain. He glanced behind to see a troupe of warriors running at top speed behind them, and heard the cries of his companions ahead.

"Go!" he shouted, and Frodrun sprinted ahead without a second glance but Hengest and Leofric lagged. "Go!" Eorwald shouted again, and Leofric turned back to Hengest and shouted the same thing. Hengest reluctantly turned and ran the same direction as Frodrun while Leofric returned to Eorwald. The shouts of the attackers came louder and Eorwald hear the thrum of a bowstring as another arrow flew past him into Frodrun's back. Eorwald tried to run again but tripped, snapping the arrow's shaft as he landed. He shouted in pain and yanked the bloody point to pull the rest of the shaft out, hearing Leofric's yell and the sound of metal clashing. He rolled over to draw Weargbana, but realized that the straps had come loose and his sword was lying several feet away near Leofric.

"Stop!" he shouted at the men who had been turning to attack Leofric and Hengest, and they were momentarily distracted. "We are hunters!" he cried, grimacing through the pain in his leg. "Stop, please!"

The Northumbrians were nonplussed and lowered their weapons momentarily, and Eorwald pressed his luck. "We meant no harm, only to catch some rabbits or a deer to feed our families!" He doubted that the Northumbrians would care, but they seemed to believe him. "Please don't hurt us!" He hated the sound of those words leaving his lips, but the look on Leofric's face made him continue.

"Just hunting," Leofric gasped, and Hengest nodded in agreement. There were twelve or so of the Northumbrians and only three of them. A fight today would do no good; they would all be killed if they struggled, and someone would need to warn the others. Someone had to get back to Mæduwic.

"Bring them back to camp," one of the men said. Eorwald shot a glance at Leofric as the three of them were roughly pushed forward. He hoped that Leofric understood the message that he could not say aloud.

Eorwald tripped, on purpose this time, and Hengest bent to pick him back up. With a voice that Eorwald could barely hear himself, he told Hengest, "Run."

Hengest nodded imperceptibly and the two of them were pushed roughly to their feet. Eorwald glanced at Leofric again, and with a shout Leofric kicked one of the Northumbrian's feet out from under him. The Northumbrian's fist collided with Leofric's face and Eorwald rushed forward, bowling them all over into a writhing, angry pile of kicking legs and flailing arms. Eorwald saw Hengest dart off without a glance before any of the Northumbrians noticed, and Eorwald continued to push and kick until he knew Hengest was gone. His leg screamed in protest as he fell to the ground again, and then he felt an elbow in his back.

"I'll have your guts for that," one of them said.

"Just bring them back to camp," said the Northumbrian who was clearly in charge. "Hwitegos will deal with them."

The two were shunted in front of the large pavilion where a tall, warlike man was standing next to a camp fire. Hwitegos was clearly a nickname but also, clearly, an apt one. He was young, but his hair and beard and eyebrows looked almost white; his skin was so pale that the blood showed through the translucent skin, making his eyelids look red against the icy blue of his eyes.

"Hunters?" he asked when one of the thugs had told him the situation. He surveyed Eorwald and Leofric for a moment. "I don't like liars," he said. "You are no hunters. You don't hunt deer with a sword and a seax, and you don't need leather and iron to do so either."

Eorwald stared him down; his face set in a grimace of pain which he hoped looked intimidating. He could feel the blood seeping into the wool of his trousers and wondered how long it would be before he lost enough blood to pass out.

"Who are you?" Hwitegos asked. It was unnerving, his casual tone partnered with the cold blankness of his face.

Eorwald said nothing, and Leofric followed his example.

"You are clearly warriors, and as we are attempting to rid this land of Engla, I can only assume that you are Engla yourselves and serve the traitorous coward Rædwald."

They still said nothing.

"Why so quiet?" Hwitegos asked. "I don't plan on harming you yet. Although it appears someone already has done…" he glanced at Eorwald's leg, the torn cloth of his trousers soaked with blood. "Perhaps we should deal with that before we discuss anything else."

Eorwald tried not to scream. He tried very, very hard not to scream, but he screamed anyway as the red-hot iron grated through the flesh of his leg. He nearly passed out from the pain of it, but instead spent an agonizing, entirely conscious eternity screaming as the knife moved into the arrow wound.

"If you were to tell me something that I might like to hear, I will be able to finish sooner," Hwitegos said. Eorwald clenched his jaw so hard he thought his teeth might break, but said nothing as he waited for it to be over. He had seen wounds staunched with hot iron many times, but normally it was a quick necessity and he had never realized how much it would hurt. The heat would seal the blood and prevent infection, but the pain was almost unbearable. He would rather be stabbed or beaten bloody or anything else before being burned. He had thought for one stupid moment that Hwitegos might have been doing him a kindness by tending his wound, until he felt the iron searing its way through his skin and flesh and realized that the Northumbrian was merely using a convenient form of torture.

There was only so much flesh that Hwitegos could burn, however, and eventually he removed the red-hot iron from Eorwald's skin.

"Warrior indeed," Hwitegos said with a note of admiration in his voice. "I would not have thought that the Engla were brave."

Eorwald's head dropped down to his chest, and he was panting and sweating as if he had just run ten leagues.

"I am planning to kill you at some point, and I don't want you dying of an infection beforehand," he said with a hint of a shrug.

"Do it then," Eorwald spat. "Just kill me now."

Hwitegos shook his head. "I don't think so. I have a feeling, and correct me if I am wrong, that you two could be quite valuable to me, once we've had a chance to talk."

"You're wrong," Eorwald growled.

Hwitegos smiled. "I've told you, I don't like liars." He called to one of his men, after putting away the now-cooled knife, "I think these two are well enough to stand up, now."

*****

Gieva could not make it over the threshold in time, and cursed herself as she emptied the contents of her stomach into the straw rushes on the packed earth floor. She was sweating as another wave of nausea struck her and she felt her belly cramp. She did not dare to move for a few moments, but felt a gentle hand brush her hair away from her face as the sickness passed.

When she looked up, Rægen was pushing a drinking bowl full of water into her hands. She sipped it slowly. Rægen took the bowl when she had finished, and helped her to her feet. She was rather shaky, and the smell of her sick on the floor made her want to retch again.

At the look of disgust on her face, Rægen scraped the soiled rushes into a pile and dropped them onto the dying fire. It flared and stank somewhat, but the smell dissipated quickly. Gieva tore a leaf of mint from the drying rack and chewed it to rid her mouth of the sour taste, drinking a few more sips of water.

Rægen asked, "How do you feel?"

Surprisingly, she felt much better than she had done only moments previously. "It's nothing," she said. "I've probably just eaten something that didn't agree with me." It had come upon her suddenly just as she was falling asleep, though there was no accounting for it. She watched the soiled rushes turn to ash as the room became dim again.

Rægen had put his arm around her to lead her back to bed. "You've caught it too, my heart, I am sure of it. There is still a foul wind in this village, but I had hoped that it would have passed you by. My sweet Gieva." He spoke in an unrelenting stream and touched her brow. She did not feel feverish; she had been dizzy and nauseated to be sure, but felt relieved now. It had been more than a week since the last few people in her care had risen from their beds, after all. She was certain that the foul wind which had touched the village had long-since passed them by.

"I am sure it was just something I ate," Gieva said. "There's no need to fuss over me." He ignored her, and fussed and fretted over her until she had put a finger to his lips to stop him talking. "I'm fine," she said, and he kissed her forehead as she nestled herself in his arms.

As she lay in the darkness, he pulled her closer to him and she held his hand as it rested between her hips, just below her navel. Suddenly, a thought came to her which gave her pause and made her heart flutter. What if it was not just a normal bout of queasiness?

Maybe, she answered herself, and glanced through the darkness at Rægen's now-sleeping face, and her heart leapt again. It was as if she were trying to gently say no to someone by giving them a glimmer of hope. *It's not impossible*.

Though she rested quietly, sleep eluded Gieva for the rest of the night and she rose at the first cock-crow, wrapping a cloak around her bare shoulders rather than bothering to relight the fire. She softened a piece of yesterday's bread in a cup of ale and ate it, hoping that getting a bit of food in her belly would stop it from hurting. The idea she had had the previous night came unbidden to her mind, and she entertained it for a moment before brushing it away. She did not want to let her hopes rise. Not yet.

Rægen began to wake as Gieva sipped the rest of the weak beer, and she watched him for a while, his eyes still half-closed with sleep and his hair mashed against his head on one side. She felt a surge of affection for him as he looked around blearily for her, and she went back to the bed to sit beside him.

"Are you feeling better?" he asked.

"Much better," Gieva said, trying and failing to smooth his hair down. "It was nothing, really." She kissed his forehead and got to her feet to mend the fire, but he caught her by the hand and pulled her into his arms.

"I don't think I'll ever be used to this," he said, brushing a curl away from her forehead and letting his fingers trace the line of her cheek, "I keep wondering if you're real. It's like some kind of dream."

"It's a good dream, isn't it?"

Rægen nodded, grinning. He kissed her, sliding his hand along her waist and playfully squeezing her breast. She winced slightly when he did so, and he looked apologetically at her.

"It's nothing," she said. "Sometimes they hurt before I get my blood, that's all." She smiled and kissed him again, moving his hand back up and giving him a wry smile. Her heart began to pound at the feel of his body next to hers, but the fluttering did not depart.

Maybe, she thought, *maybe.*

Eventually they had to get up, though she did so with great reluctance. It was washing day, sunny and breezy for the first time in weeks, and Gieva knew that everyone would take full advantage of the fine weather to give everything a good cleaning. It seemed that every house had clothing fluttering on ropes or lying to dry on bushes or fence posts, and after she had laid her own clothes and blankets to dry in the sun, she made her way up to the queen's chamber.

About once a month, the queen ordered the massive bathing tub brought to her bedroom and filled with scalding hot water to wash in. It was something Gieva had never experienced before coming to Wuffingham. Of course she washed her hands and face regularly and would occasionally rub a bit of soap through her hair to keep away lice and fleas, but it had always been an unpleasant and chilly experience, and usually took place in an icy stream. This, however, was a luxury she had grown to love.

The queen was already sitting in the tub when Gieva entered. A young serving woman stood nearby, looking rather red in the face; Gieva knew that Steorra and several others had likely carried at least a dozen buckets full of scalding water to fill the large half-barrel shaped container. Eadyth looked profoundly content; her hair was slicked back and she was picking dirt from under her fingernails.

"I see that you've become accustomed to our little ritual, have you?" Eadyth said, squeezing the water from her hair as she stood up. "I thought that after the events of the last few weeks, we ought to have a proper wash."

Gieva helped her to step carefully out of the tub and Eadyth pulled a tunic over her head while Gieva stripped off her own dress. "Wait," Eadyth said, grabbing her arm before Gieva could step forward into the bath. Gieva felt slightly uncomfortable as the queen looked her body up and down with a raised eyebrow. The look turned into a slight smile and she released Gieva's arm, helping her to step into the water. It had cooled slightly, but it felt so wonderful that Gieva dunked her head beneath the surface immediately and felt as warm and content as she had ever been, despite the peculiar look Eadyth had just given her.

When she surfaced, Eadyth was watching her, the same strange look on her face. The serving woman had come forward to comb out her wet hair, and Eadyth looked as if she might laugh.

"Gieva," Eadyth said conversationally, "are you feeling quite well?"

Gieva did not speak at once. "Did Rægen say something?"

Eadyth smiled. "He mentioned that you felt ill last night, but I think we both know that it was not something you ate, and you are clearly not as ill as you might be if you had caught the same sickness that everyone else had."

Their eyes met for a moment, and Gieva felt that she could be candid. "How did you know?"

Eadyth laughed. "I've been pregnant six times," she said, "I know what it looks like. Your cheeks have had the prettiest little blush on them for a week, not to mention the fact that your breasts are enormous and you look as if you are about to vomit. When was the last time you bled?"

Gieva thought about it for a moment. It usually came just before the full moon but she could not remember getting her blood in a long time; she had not paid attention lately, as she had been so preoccupied. "Nearly two moons' turns now," she said quietly, finally letting herself hope. She felt a grin cross her face as she thought about it, and she touched her abdomen covertly beneath the surface of the water. She had not dared to hope, but perhaps she could, now.

They were all terribly busy over the next several days: Gieva worked in the garden to tend her medicinal herbs, which had been much depleted during the pestilence of the past weeks. Meanwhile, Rægen was taking care of the duties normally performed by the king, and he was proving to be an excellent ruler.

She missed him, but she knew that it was for the best. She slept with him in the great hall rather than in their house so that he could entertain his father's *thegns* properly, and she was almost grateful that he was unable to spend much time with her; she kept needing to rush away to empty her stomach into a bush, and she was glad that these bouts usually happened after he had gone on some errand.

She did not know when she might tell Rægen. She was bursting to tell everyone, now that she realized that she was not imagining it, but he would be the first to know. On the other hand, she knew very well that being with child did not necessarily mean that she would stay with child. Her mother had miscarried three children, and two had died within a year; even Eadyth had lost two babes when they had come too early.

Gieva panicked at the thought. What if she told him, and then she miscarried as well? She hated the idea of making him sad, for a moment she considered keeping it all a secret until she was too big to hide it anymore. The sweet fool would probably be oblivious to her pregnancy until she put a squalling child in his arms.

She wandered into the hall as several *thegns* were leaving, and Rægen looked pensive as he sat in the high seat. He seemed taller, broader; more kingly as he assumed the role he was born to fill. It gave her a strange twinge of excitement to think that he would one day rule them all as a generous and capable *cyning*.

Rægen's pensive gaze was broken as she approached him, and he immediately grinned when he saw her, rising and taking her in his arms.

"I'm not interrupting, am I?" she asked. She wondered if he would be able to feel her belly through her dress; she knew that it would not grow big for a long time, but even now she felt like it was beginning to stick out.

"Of course not," he said, "but you would be a welcome distraction even if you were. How may I serve you, my love?" he asked with an air of mock solemnity.

Gieva giggled at him. "I just wanted to see your face," she said. "It's so fine today. Would you like to go for a walk?"

Rægen shrugged. "That sounds much more enjoyable than anything I had planned to do today," he said, and took her hand.

They left the Bricgweard and headed down toward the stream that skirted the wood, where the plum trees grew. Rægen seemed to breathe deeply, taking long draughts of the air. "I can't think of anything that could be better than a beautiful day with a beautiful woman," he said, squeezing her hand gently and grinning at her.

Gieva stopped short and turned to face him, unable to resist. The moment was too perfect. She took his hand and put it on the space below her navel. "I can think of something."

He looked at her for a long moment, puzzled, and she almost laughed aloud as his eyes widened. He opened his mouth a few times, but no words came out. Instead, he dropped to his knees in front of her and hugged her waist, and she blinked away tears. When he stood again, he cupped her face in his hands and kissed her as lightly as he had done the very first time.

"I don't think I've been this happy since you agreed to marry me," he said, his face alight.

Gieva realized that she was crying. "And I don't think anything has ever made me as happy as seeing your face right now."

*****

Sunniva was flushed and tired from walking around the crowded streets of Lundenwic and her purse was considerably lighter. She walked arm in arm with Sige, with Edwin following close behind them, but both men seemed agitated.

"Stop pulling my arm, Sige," she said, "Both of you, calm down. You're acting like there's an *ælf* coming to steal your shadows."

Edwin and Sige shared a glance that seemed to contain hours of speech, but they did not share any of it with Sunniva.

"I wish you all would stop leaving me out of everything," Sunniva said grumpily. "I hate being kept in the dark when there is intrigue happening within my own family!"

Sige patted her arm in a reassuring, brotherly sort of way which Sunniva found incredibly condescending.

"We are supposed to be having a pleasant time. Don't worry about it now."

"It's hardly a pleasant time if you two keep looking about like a knife-man is going to jump out and stab you," Sunniva said. "If there is a knife-man he isn't likely to strike in broad daylight in a crowded market, so you might as well relax."

"She's right," Edwin said quietly, but he was still tense, his face drawn.

"Of course I am," said Sunniva. "Now, I want some cloth for a new dress, and you two need to help me pick something."

She really only had a passing interest in the cloth for sewing purposes; in truth she was eager to see if Godomar would be in the area, overseeing the trade of his imported fabrics. A new ship had come into the port and this end of the high street was full of frenetic activity as bolts of brightly colored silks and wool and linen made their way off of it and into the hands of greedy buyers.

Sunniva ran her fingers over some of the silks, groaning in longing delight at the deep blood-red shot with flecks of gold thread. "If I wore that in a mead hall, I'd look like I was on fire!" she said. "I have to have some," she said, despite the protests from Sige that such material would hardly be practical or cheap. "It's not as if I am going to go and till the fields in it;" Sunniva said, "Why shouldn't I have a pretty new dress?"

"You would look absolutely radiant in that cloth." Sunniva heard Godomar's voice. "Of course, you look radiant in almost anything." He kissed her hand and she felt her cheeks turn scarlet while Edwin rolled his eyes.

"You see?" Sunniva said to Sige, "Godomar says it would be pretty, and he knows more about cloth than you two ever will."

Sige sighed and nodded to the vendor that they would take the cloth. "You are so spoiled," he said to Sunniva, and she grinned as he reached into his pouch for some silver.

"Odgar," Godomar said as the vendor started to haggle with Sige over a price, "This is a gift for my fair *vrouwe*. You and I will discuss gold later."

"Yes, *graf*," the vendor bowed, taking away the fabric to be transported back to the *burh*. Sunniva squealed with delight and thanked him profusely.

"It is a trifle," he said. "I would not see such a fine cloth on anyone else. Only you could do it justice." He held out his arm for her, and she took it happily.

They walked together, with Sige and Edwin tailing her. She rather wished that they would leave her alone, but she knew that they would not. Godomar's conversation was pleasant as always, but there was something odd in his expression.

"Is there something troubling you?" Sunniva asked.

Godomar's mouth twitched in annoyance and he shook his tawny head. "The new silks were not the only thing which came on the ship," he said. "I have learned that there have been raids and revolts on my lands while I have been away, and my brother Walaric begs for my return to drive out the invaders."

Sunniva frowned. "That's terrible," She said. "I imagine you're eager to go home and set everything right." He looked sidelong at Sunniva and she had to keep herself from giggling stupidly. She fiddled with her ring and tried to rearrange her face into a look of concern.

"It is troublesome," he said. "They'll have been fighting for weeks by now, but most of my army are untrained farmers and stable-boys who have never held weapons before. To make matters worse, there was a foul pestilence a year ago which killed half of my remaining fighting men." His voice was dark and bitter.

Sunniva opened her mouth to say something, but she was lost in his words as he said, "The northerners are hardly better-trained than any of my own men, but if I could get the edge over them and crush them, then I would be in great debt to whoever helped me."

"Yes, that is troublesome," she said. "I wish I could do something to help."

"Your mere presence is a gift in itself," he said, and she thought her knees might give out when he brushed a stray hair from her face. "There, that's better," he said, tucking the hair back into place. He sighed. "It is a shame, really, to leave this land and its treasures, never to return." He said the last word as his eyes met hers, and she was quite sure that if he were not holding her arm, she would fall over.

"Why won't you come back?" she asked abruptly. "Surely you know that you are welcome here, at least in my father's lands."

"Ah, my fair *vrouwe*," he shook his head, "It is not so simple, I am afraid. If I have no trade here, I can hardly justify the cost to cross the sea. It is a tragedy, for I think that I shall never find a treasure so fine in my own lands."

Sunniva swallowed with difficulty, her mind working feverishly. "Trade in Gipeswic," she squeaked. "My father wants to build the trading port, and there are enough rich men and women that they will pay handsomely for materials as fine as yours. I promise the journey would not be wasted, if you returned after you've settled things in your own country."

He considered her for a moment, and she wondered fleetingly if her tongue had gone away without her. She heard Sige cough from behind her and she scowled over her shoulder at him, expecting him to give her a look as to shut her up, but his eyes widened and he nodded for her to continue.

"That would be a great boon," Godomar said slowly, "but not many of these *cyningas* are willing to make an alliance with a foreign lord; they are too busy fighting amongst themselves."

"I wouldn't say that," Sunniva said.

"*Wes hal*, Father," Sunniva said, interrupting his conversation with Oswy, one of Sigebryht's men who had come down from Wuffingham with them. She was giddy with excitement, though she did not explain any of her ideas to the men. If her mother had taught her anything, it was that carefully sowed seeds always grew the deepest roots.

Rædwald excused himself from his friend and smiled affectionately at her. "Well, my sweet, how much of my gold did you spend today?"

Sunniva grinned. "Oh, I made some very valuable purchases today. Will you come with me, so that I might show you?"

Rædwald smiled indulgently. "As you wish," he said, and followed her out of the hall to where Godomar and Sigebryht and Edwin were waiting.

"Graf Godomar," Father said genially. "I had not thought to see you again on these shores!"

"I had not planned to remain, noble Cyning," said Godomar, inclining his head slightly as a show of respect. "As I was just telling your fair daughter here," he indicated Sunniva, who felt herself blushing as he smiled at her, "I had stayed to pay my respects to the *heahcyning*, but now I receive word that my lands are being attacked."

"I know that struggle," said Father. He looked at Sunniva confusedly for a moment, but Sunniva waited for Godomar to continue in his own time.

"My noble *cyning*," said Godomar after a pause, "I have learned that your goal in coming to Lundenburh was not simply to pay your respects to Heahcyning Ethelbert. I believe you are looking to make an alliance in order to deal with the threat to your kingdom, is that right?" Godomar asked.

Rædwald looked shrewdly at him, seemingly impressed that Godomar knew so much. "Indeed, that was part of my purpose when coming to Lundenburh," he said. "We are being overrun by the Northumbrians and I had hoped to gain some reinforcements to my side."

"I understand the problems of having northerners repeatedly attacking your lands," Godomar said bitterly, "as I frequently deal with the same problems. I believe that you and I might be able to assist one another."

Sunniva grinned as she saw comprehension dawn on her father's face.

"What is it that you would ask of me?" Rædwald said.

"I know that you wish to build up the market town of Gipeswic and make it into an important trading center. I believe that I can make that dream a possibility."

Sunniva was grinning now as she saw the look of greed on her father's face.

"That is tempting," Rædwald said. "Foreign goods always draw customers, after all." Sunniva saw a flash in his eyes, and she tried to stop herself grinning stupidly.

"I think it would be to our mutual benefit," Godomar said. "My noble *cyning*, think of the wealth that we might build! Think of how much your town would grow and thrive under such an alliance! If my friends know that their efforts are not wasted in sailing to your land, I am sure they will follow my example and bring even more rich and exotic goods to sell to you. Think of how grateful your fighting men would be to serve such a wealthy and generous lord!"

"You will bring all of your trade to this country through Gipeswic," he confirmed, "You will no longer trade directly in Lundenwic. You must trade with my people only, so that they may pay the appropriate tariffs to send the goods further inland."

Godomar nodded once and said, "I believe that is a reasonable request. Much simpler, my noble Cyning."

Sunniva was grinning, almost bursting with excitement. Her plan was working. Perhaps if Godomar traded exclusively in Gipeswic, she might be able to see him more often.

"So we are in agreement?" Rædwald asked.

"I will swear on holy relics," said Godomar.

Rædwald's eyebrows creased. "I have no use for relics," he said. "Superstitions are not legally binding."

"Well," said Godomar with a hint of aspersion, "I would ask one more boon of you as a part of our new friendship, which would provide a personal bond between us as well." He looked at Sunniva. "I wish to take your daughter as my wife. I have long intended to marry, and I am certain that she would be an ornament to my hall in Heldergem."

If it had been anyone else, Sunniva might have slapped someone for not consulting her on the matter of her own marriage before it was proposed, but she was so astonished and pleased by the idea that she did not have time to be annoyed.

"That is up to her," Father said, looking carefully at Sunniva.

Sunniva twisted her ring, driving the thought of its previous owner from her mind. "Yes," she spluttered.

"Very well," said Godomar, giving her a look that made her knees weak, "I think we have some arrangements to make."

*****

This hall was no different than any other. It was crowded and stank of piss and vomit from those who had overindulged in drink and food, and the sounds of drunken laughter filled the fetid air. In a larger hall like the Bricgweard this never bothered Ecgric, but in the close quarters of Eni's house, it was overwhelming.

One hard fact was that Eni was vital in protecting the North. The other hard fact was that he was extremely uncooperative in doing so. Although he was technically an *ealdorman* and sworn to Rædwald, for all intents and purposes Eni was the king of the North Folk while Rædwald ruled the South. The horn of land on which their kingdom rested was a large place after all, surrounded by coastline, and there were simply too many people for a single king to be able to keep track of them all. Ecgric had known that the division of power had always rankled Eni's sensibilities; Eni was the elder of the two, but their father had decided that Rædwald would be the best fit to rule, and Eni had taken the slight personally. Rædwald had warned Ecgric of this, but Eni's animosity toward the king was so clear that Ecgric would have figured it out on his own. He tried to avoid speaking about the king if he could help it, but as he was there on the king's mission, it was rather difficult to leave his name out of the conversation completely.

After the fifth or sixth attempt at talk, with only grunted responses on Eni's behalf, Ecgric gave it up as a bad job and decided to change his tack toward speaking to Eni's wife, Ælfgifu. According to all reports, she was a genial, clever woman; perhaps she might have some control over her husband's decisions.

"The *cwene* asked me to send her regards," Ecgric said as he took a long draught of beer, but Ælfgifu tapped him on the shoulder and shook her head.

"I have to see your lips move when you talk," she said, touching her ear, "otherwise I can't hear you." Her voice was rather loud and strangled, but not unkind.

Ecgric paused, trying to sort through what she had just said, as she watched him with a gentle smile. A bolt of realization shot through him and he felt his ears turn red, but Ælfgifu had the grace to ignore it. He had not realized that she was deaf; he had seen her speaking to her husband and her sons earlier with no difficulty. He had to admire the way she overcame the handicap with such self-assurance.

He repeated his question, slower this time.

Ælfgifu grinned more broadly at the mention of the queen. "Eadyth is such a dear woman," she said. "I miss her terribly. I used to go and visit her fairly often, but..." she trailed off, rolling her eyes at her husband, who had occupied himself with his beer. "How is she? How are her children?"

Ecgric did not want to talk about Eadyth's children. The anger and shame was still fresh in his mind, and talking about Sunniva would only bring it to the surface again. He thought for a moment of telling her that Rægenhere had gotten married, but he knew that Eni was the one person in the world who hated Rægenhere, as his sole competition to the throne of the Engla. He thought about mentioning Eorwald, who had stayed in the Fens to defend against repeated attacks from Athelfrith, but again, he was sure that it would only serve to annoy Eni. "They are very well," he said at last, and Ælfgifu smiled complacently.

"And how is your father?" she asked.

Again, Ecgric was caught off-guard. "I wasn't aware you knew my father," he said.

Ælfgifu grinned, and the light from the fire glinted in her eyes so that the fine lines around them smoothed and the silver streaks in her dark hair appeared golden. The mischievous look she gave him reminded Ecgric of Sunniva, but in an instant the look was gone. “Another old friend,” she said.

Ecgric shrugged. “He is as he ever was,” he said, remembering to speak slowly. “I mean to meet him in Mæduwic once I have collected the *fyrd*.”

Ælfgifu pursed her lips, seemingly deep in thought, but her face brightened as four men approached them. “Ah, have you had the chance to meet my sons?”

Ecgric shook his head, and she indicated each of them by name. “Ænna, Æthelhere, Æthelwold and Æthelric.” Ecgric tried to match names to faces, but they all looked so much alike that he gave it up. The men were all young and stout, with the same golden hair and blue eyes of the Wuffingas. Two of the men, he could not begin to determine which was which, had well-dressed women in tow. The women were both quite pretty: one with dark auburn hair and the other fair as flax, and in a former life he might have taken full advantage of the look the lighter one was giving him; but when he considered it, all he could think of was Sunniva. *I must be growing up*, he thought dismally as the flaxen-haired woman looked away dejectedly.

He noticed that the men spoke with rather exaggerated hand movements when speaking with their mother, and he wondered if they had some kind of gestural language to aid her in understanding. Ælfgifu was skilled at reading lips and could perhaps hear some of the sounds they made, but she seemed to communicate much easier with her sons than with anyone else.

“Ecgric has come from your uncle the *cyning*,” Ælfgifu explained to her sons, “there seems to be a spot of bother with the *cyning* of the Northumbrians, and Rædwald is raising the *fyrd* to fight him.”

The two younger men lit up in excitement. The other two seemed mildly interested but skeptical.

“Is he really planning an attack?” one of the younger brothers asked excitedly.

Ecgric nodded. “He intends to avenge the slaughter of the women and children at Ealdham and for the repeated sacking of Grantabricge,” he said, and the two younger brothers looked at one another with the glint that only green boys eager for battle seemed to possess.

"And a bloody lot of good it'll do him," Eni said irritably, skewering a bite of meat on the end of his knife. "Trying to fight a war in the middle of the harvest? I ask you…" He rolled his eyes.

"Athelfrith is growing bolder," said Ecgric, "He will attack whether it is harvest or the dead of winter. He obviously does not care for the rules of war; otherwise he would not have attacked a village of unarmed women and children." He was growing tired of Eni's sarcastic remarks and decided to put a stop to them.

"And how am I to make any difference?" Eni asked, his voice growing hot and his face becoming very red. "I have few enough men as it is, and now my blasted brother wants to take forces away from my lands and send them to die in the North?"

Ecgric glared at him incredulously. "Your lands? You may rule the North, but you are still an *ealdorman*, the same as me. Rædwald is your *dryhten*. You are sworn to him both as his brother and as his retainer, and it is your duty to protect the lands of the Wuffingas." He tried to keep his voice cool and logical, but he was tired of the laziness and complacency of this man, and he simply wanted it to be over.

Eni glared at him, and Ecgric glared back. One of the younger sons piped up, "I want to fight! We ought to go to the aid of our uncle!" and his brother joined in the sentiment.

"I would be pleased to take you with me," Ecgric told the boy, not breaking his eye contact with Eni. "If your honored father approves, that is." He tried to keep the acid in his tone to a minimum, but failed.

Eni scowled at him. "I don't see why I should approve of you taking my sons to be slaughtered,"

"We want to go!" said the other son. "Please, Father, it is only right to fight alongside our kinsman and avenge the slaughter of our people!"

There was a scuffle of words between the brothers, supplemented by Ecgric and Eni, but they were cut short when the harsh voice of Ælfgifu rose above them.

"Cynhelm was your friend and ally, whatever your opinions are about the *cyning*," she said slowly, "You would let his death pass without being avenged?" She did not say it accusingly, but Eni looked ashamed. Eni took another draught, breaking the staring match. He glanced at his wife, who seemed to give a minuscule nod, and he slammed his cup on the table as he made a frustrated noise in his throat. "What does the *cyning* ask, then?"

It took a long while to explain what the king needed, and Eni was not an attentive listener. Fortunately, the two younger brothers were keen to see battle and were excitedly taking in the details of the war with Athelfrith. Æthelhere and Æthelwold were so close in age and in looks that they might have been twins, and at fifteen and sixteen years they were eager to see their first battles. Ecgric wondered why Eni had not sent them on raids or skirmishes to test their strength by now, but after speaking with Eni for a few hours he realized that Eni was not terribly keen on doing anything useful unless it benefitted him directly.

When the sun rose again, they had negotiated the number of troops to be sent, along with Eni's responsibility for keeping control of the coasts. There were plenty of ways for Northumbrians to get into the Wash, but only a few places where they might get close enough to land that they could pose a threat. Eni agreed to post troops at these strategic locations, along with several ships to patrol the coastlines.

As they mounted their horses, Ælfgifu appeared at Ecgric's side.

"Please take care of my sons," she said. "And take care of yourself as well."

"Of course, my lady," said Ecgric, "The *cyning* will not let them get too close to danger, I promise. It will be a good experience, and I will teach them all I know."

"Then I needn't worry," she said, grinning. She looked back at her husband, who was standing in sullen silence at the door of the hall. "I am sorry that my husband has been so uncooperative in all of this."

Ecgric did not really know what to say to this, but decided that politeness was the best route. "I am pleased that he has seen the importance of stopping Athelfrith."

"In truth I do not know that he has," said Ælfgifu slowly, "But he won't go back on his word. Now, off you get, before you waste the whole day." She kissed her two youngest sons before they mounted their horses. "Fight bravely, and if you must die, do it with a sword in your hand," she told each of them, "I expect plenty of stories when you return," she added with a wink, and they nodded in that grim but excited way that only young men on the eve of their first battle could manage.

Æthelhere and Æthelwold were fairly decent company, despite their inexperience. Ecgric found the ride much more tolerable with lively, bawdy companions, and they made their rounds through the villages of the North Folk in good spirits. It seemed that many of the fighting men had been preparing for their arrival; the *huscarls* had made their way through the villages and informed every man and strong boy to gather their weapons and prepare to march west.

"Listen to me," Ecgric said as he examined each new batch of men, "your *cyning* needs strong arms and stronger hearts to fight for him. These lands – your lands – are under attack. Athelfrith has killed too many of our people. He has burned too many of our villages. You must fight for your land and for your *cyning*!"

A few of the younger men always shouted in agreement when he made this speech, while their elders usually frowned or nodded or looked blankly at him.

"Do you know what Athelfrith's men did to Cynhelm's people?" Ecgric asked, "His monstrous *weargas* locked women and their crying children inside of their own village hall, and do you know what they did?" He paused, looking hard at each man. "They ones they did not rape and murder, they locked inside before they set it on fire! They burned them, just as they will burn your women and your children. Would you sit by and let that happen?" He raised his voice in challenge, gesturing to the women waiting nearby to see their husbands off. "You," he pointed at a sour looking middle-aged man, "are you going to sit by and wait, shivering in fear while your grandchildren have to watch their mother raped and murdered by a band of Northumbrian *weargas?*" The man shot a glance at a young woman in the crowd, and shook his head furiously.

"I will fight for my *cyning*!" he shouted.

"What say you all?" Ecgric asked the group of men at large, and they all shouted their agreement, shaking their spears and pounding their shields.

"Drink with me, my brothers!" Ecgric said, and several *ceorls* passed around cups, some of horn and some of wood or clay, and filled each with a splash of mead. "Drink with me, and swear your oaths." He held his cup aloft and bade them to repeat his words. "I swear before this company that I shall fight to the death for my *cyning*." They repeated, half-mumbling, and he shouted the words at them, "If my *dryhten* shall die, I shall take his place and fight as he would have fought." Their voices became louder. "If any man here sees me taken with weak heart and run away, he shall remind me of this pledge made here before my kin." Ecgric gave a stern look at each man, and then drank from his own cup. The warmth of the mead spread through his limbs and he felt a surge of energy that only impending battle could bring him. "You all have sworn, and you all must take courage. You may live and you may die, but you are brothers in the eyes of the gods and I know that you will all fight bravely, and if you die, you will die well." The men all drank and their women took away the cups. Some were crying, others giving their men hard looks and words of encouragement. Ecgric gave them a few moments to say their goodbyes, and led the men away to join with the rest of the column.

He repeated the action in every small village along the old Roman road, gathering five men in one village, ten in another, only one or two in the next. Even with so few fighting men, the column slowly multiplied as they skirted the Fens and made their way toward Mæduwic.

Ecgric was painfully aware that quantity was the not the same as quality, especially when it came to fighting men. He might have had a formidable host, if any of them could actually hold a weapon properly. If Ecgric thought that Æthelhere and Æthelwold were young, it was nothing compared to the majority of the fighters now following them. Most had barely seen fifteen winters; lanky, bare-faced boys with axes that they could barely lift. When they stopped to camp, Ecgric set his *gedriht*, the expert, battle-hardened warriors, to training the boys and the unskilled men in combat. Despite their efforts, he began to grow nervous that they might run into a fight before they arrived at Mæduwic. If they did, half his men would be slaughtered before they could gasp in surprise at an onslaught.

"You have to overlap them!" he shouted at two of the idiots, wrenching their shields closer together as they tried to form a shield wall. "Your shield is the only thing protecting your brother. If the brunt of the force is here," he pushed on one of the shields, "it will spread the force through the shield wall instead of hurting the one it hits. If you do not protect the man to either side of you, then you will not be protected either!"

As soon as he was satisfied with their practice, he would give them leave to eat some of their meager rations and huddle under their cloaks for a few hours' sleep. In reality, it meant many long nights practicing by firelight and forcing the younger, weaker men to lift their shields and swords repeatedly to build up their strength. Sunniva had been a better student than these boys. He tried not to think of her, tried to push his mind to training his men.

They were still frustratingly slow to learn, but Ecgric had to remind himself that they would not bear the brunt of the force in any case. The *fyrd* was there to add to the numbers in the army, to intimidate the opposing forces. The *gedriht* – the battle-hardened, veteran warriors – would be the ones who did most of the fighting, while the *fyrdmen* would probably stay behind their shield wall, praying to Tiw and hoping they would not piss themselves as they waited for it all to be over. He did not grudge them their fear. Farmers and stable boys and shepherds had no taste for battle; each had given his word that he would not run away, and that would have to be enough.

On the fifth day, they came upon a small village protected by a wooden fence and a ditch, but when they drew closer they found that the entire village was empty of both man and beast. The village hall, which should have been just up the lane from the gate, was burned to the ground along with several of the adjacent buildings.

"We shouldn't be here," said Æthelwold, "This village is cursed."

"Don't be stupid," said Ecgric.

"There are no birds," said one of the *fyrdmen*. "No birds nor beasts nor any living thing. It's not natural, none of it. We ought not to be here."

Ecgric had never been a superstitious man, but even he felt a wave of unease at the sight of the dead town. He led them in a wide arc around the palisades, and heard the muttering of the men as he did so. There was no one to collect for the *fyrd*, and no point in staying. They were barely a full day's ride from

Mæduwic now in any case; perhaps the inhabitants of this area had gone there.

When they made their way out of the village, however, they discovered what had happened to the local men. At least thirty mounds had been dug in the meadow nearby, and further beyond were the remains of an abandoned camp site. He heard more muttering from the men, and knew that the fibers of their resolve beginning to break.

"Listen!" Ecgric said, catching the attention of his men. "Look at what those Northumbrian dogs have done to this village! Look at the havoc they have wrought, and what they will continue to do! If any of you doubt your courage, remember these barrows. Remember all the women and children who burned in this village, and the brave men who were slaughtered while trying to defend their homes. Think of them and you will find your strength." A roar of approval came from the men, and Ecgric knew that the shreds of their resolve were slowly knitting back together. He only hoped that it would hold until the battle was joined.

Chapter Fifteen

Oferfangen

Taken

odomar seemed to be pleased with his future bride, and Sunniva basked in his attentions. He had given her chests upon chests of wedding presents, gold rings and expensive cloth, and had spared no expense. It was a matter of haste, as he was anxious to get back home and settle affairs in his own country, but Godomar had not wished to leave without sealing the bargain between himself and Rædwald. Sigebryht did not begrudge him this, but he had not thought to be forced away so soon.

Sunniva seemed as excited as if she were actually being married that day. Godomar insisted that though the betrothal might happen in Lundenwic, that the wedding itself must take place in Heldergem, to be sanctioned by the priest, or bishop, or some other person Sige did not care about. Sunniva did not seem to care, either way. For her, it was as good as two weddings. She drank and spoke with everyone despite hardly knowing anyone present; it was one of her great gifts to put everyone at their ease and to command the love of anyone she met. Sige wished that he could be happier for his sister. She would be excited for her adventure, he knew. She had always dreamed of leaving the small, dull village of Wuffingham, and she was getting her chance. He wished he could share her joy to be going as well.

Sigebryht thought of how happy Rægen and Gieva had been during their wedding feast, and felt a twinge of regret that Sunniva would not be able to experience the same joy, surrounded by family and friends and people she had known from childhood.

Even now, those present looked like they could chew rocks; as if they might pull a knife on Godomar at any moment. Sige supposed he could not entirely blame them. Many of them, or at least their sons, had been suitors for Sunniva at one point or another, and even though they had not wished to seal the bargain with Rædwald, he knew that they must still feel slighted. It seemed to be a truth universally acknowledged that any bad alliance with one of your own was vastly superior to the best arrangement with a foreigner.

"I am sorry to be losing you," said Rædwald with only the hint of a drunken slur in his voice, "but I think this ended up better than I could have planned."

"You are certain that you won't need every man you can get?" Sige asked. He wanted an excuse not to have to go, but he did not wish to seem cowardly.

"I daresay we'll manage without you and Oswy and the others, though I will miss your sword by my side," Rædwald said fondly, "Ecgric will have collected Eni's men by now; hopefully they're up to scratch. I am glad that you'll be there to keep an eye on Sunniva."

"Two eyes, as always," said Sige. He glanced at his sister, who was grinning at the man she would soon have for her own.

"I'll look for you to return as soon as the seas are clear," Rædwald said. "I expect this uproar with the Christians will have died down by then, and Sunniva ought to be settled."

Sige shrugged. "I won't leave her until she is settled, but I will return as soon as I am able."

"She'll make friends soon enough," said Rædwald, "You know her."

Sige tried to smile at this, but he was sure it looked more of a grimace. "What do you make of this?" Sige gestured to the men in the hall, all seeming to stare daggers at Godomar and at Rædwald himself.

Rædwald's mouth tightened momentarily, but he shook his head. "They have no right to be offended. They refused my offers of an alliance, and I decided to make it with someone who understands the benefits of a friendship."

Sige hoped he imagined the slight note of unease in Rædwald's voice. He nodded gravely, and the king was pulled away to speak with someone else, leaving Sige in thoughtful silence.

Sige did not wish for the night to end, despite the tense atmosphere. The more he thought about it, the more Sunniva's public betrothal to the Frankisc *graf* seemed a bad idea; though it was far too late to do anything about it. It had been as good as a slap to the face of the kings and *ealdormen*, and all looked just as sour as if she had slapped them indeed.

He shamelessly stared at Edwin; tried to take in the last precious hours that he would still have with him, trying to distract himself from his unease by staring at the man he loved.

"When do you leave?" Edwin asked conversationally, but he failed to keep his tone light as he sat down next to Sige.

"Tomorrow. It'll take a day or so to get out to the sea from the river, and we will sail as soon as possible."

"And then you'll be in Francland." Sige heard a slight crack in Edwin's voice.

"It won't be for long." He too was unable to keep his voice from breaking. He wished Edwin did not sound so melancholy. The other man always seemed to make even the direst situations bearable, and if Edwin was unhappy…

"But you won't be here," Edwin said. "You'll be a world away, fighting someone else's battles on a strange shore."

Sige sighed, "I don't have a choice."

"I know that," said Edwin, "And I know that it's for the best. Sunniva needs you, and I'd sleep better knowing that some Christian wasn't planning to rip your guts out."

"I'd sleep better with you beside me," Sige whispered, and clenched his jaw as Edwin looked away.

"Don't make this harder," Edwin said; his voice suddenly very hoarse.

Neither man spoke for a long time. Sige was mired in thought, aching to touch Edwin, to hold his hand or to kiss him or to brush his fingers through Edwin's dark hair. It hurt to look at him, but he let the pain seep into his bones.

Ethelburh glided toward them like a black swan out of nowhere. She smiled at them, but neither returned it.

"You don't have to look so glum," she said, glancing at each in turn, "It's supposed to be a happy occasion."

Edwin clenched his teeth and turned on his heel and left without another word. Sige forced himself not to stare after him as he walked away, though Ethelburh watched him with her eyebrows raised.

"Well, someone seems to be in a temper," she said with a sniff.

Sige tried to think of a reason to leave as well, but Ethelburh gave him a piercing look that rooted him in place.

"It's not really a merry night for anyone, is it?" Ethelburh sighed.

"Of course it is," Sige said with little enthusiasm. "It's supposed to be, anyway."

Ethelburh rolled her eyes. "This is a farce," she said. "It's a disaster waiting to happen, and I saw it coming a mile off. I have been telling my brother for months that he ought to make an alliance with your step-father," Ethelburh said. "I don't like the Franca, and I don't think any of our folk should have anything to do with them."

"But your mother was Frankisc," Sige said confusedly.

"Which is exactly why I know what sort of people they are," she said, as if she were explaining something very simple to someone very dim. "I told Eadbald that he needed to stop thinking with his prick and just marry Sunniva, but he is an idiot. He would see Athelfrith take all of the lands below the Humber just so that he could have his fun." She shot an irritable glance in the direction of her twin, who was speaking with Leasið, and heaved a theatrical sigh. "And this whole business has caused a lot of frustration which could have been avoided." She gave him a strange, almost pitying look. "I do apologize for the sadness it's caused you."

"Well, I have to admit I would rather not have to go to Francland," he said shiftily. "Too many Franca, you know."

"I feel there is more to this story than you are letting on," she said, far too knowingly for his comfort.

"It doesn't matter," said Sige, and knew that his shiftiness would only fan the flames of the rumors. "I'm going."

She arched an eyebrow, but simply nodded in acknowledgement. They stood in an awkward silence for a moment, and she gave him the same strange piercing look she had done before. "Well, you had best make the most of your last night on these shores."

Sige raised his cup. "I'm trying," he said.

She looked at him carefully, and glanced over to one of her women, who was trying and failing to flirt with Edwin. The woman gave an almost-imperceptible nod before turning back to

Edwin, who was looking so glum he might have had a rain cloud over his head. "I am tired," Ethelburh said. "Would you be so kind as to walk me back to my house?"

Sigebryht whole-heartedly wished he could think of a reason why he shouldn't, but Ethelburh glared at him. "I wish to go to bed and I insist that you escort me back to my house. I will not walk alone."

He was still frowning slightly despite trying to put on a pleasant expression as he walked with the Eotisc princess. He worried for one insane moment that she might be luring him to her house for an unseemly reason, and his fears were heightened when she asked him to go inside with her.

"I am not trying to seduce you," she said wearily, guessing his thoughts. "I have something for you that I did not want to give to you in the hall."

The sky was still tinged pink in the west, but the house was completely dark inside. Sigebryht ducked inside the doorway and his torchlight lit the room. It was spacious and comfortable, richly decorated with hangings on the walls, and big enough for a family of ten.

"I've always kept my own house here," she explained in an off-handed sort of way, "We come to Lundenburh so frequently that I grew tired of sleeping in the hall. This way, my women and I are able to have some peace. You never know what sort of men will come to Lundenburh."

"Mmm," Sigebryht said noncommittally.

"It affords a good deal of privacy."

Sigebryht was far too unhappy to care much about what she had to say. He liked her, but even Ethelburh's conversation could not shake him from his misery. He was still worried that she would expect more of him, something that he could not give her.

"I should be getting back to the hall, my lady," he said, not looking at her.

"No, you shouldn't," Ethelburh had a very forcible way of speaking without raising her voice, which made him stay put. "Not yet."

He waited awkwardly for a few moments, wondering if she would try to engage him in conversation again, and was on the point of walking out in spite of her command, when he heard the door open behind them. The woman Sige had seen before gave

Ethelburh a sly smile and slinked into the room, followed closely by a thoroughly bewildered Edwin.

"As I told you before, it affords a great deal of privacy." Ethelburh said, sharing only the barest smile with her companion.

Edwin had his mouth open in a rather comical way, but closed it again as Ethelburh made her way towards the door. "What are you doing?" Edwin asked.

"I believe that it is a little crowded in here. I think my ladies and I shall sleep in the hall tonight, after all." The smile which had before had seemed forced and insincere now finally reached her eyes.

Sige dared himself a shred of bewildered hope, but Edwin still looked skeptical.

"Why are you doing this?" Sige asked quietly, when Edwin seemed too stunned to ask.

Ethelburh smiled again, but it was sad and tired. "You two might be the only honest men I have met here, and yet you have to hide in the shadows. Don't say anything," she said wearily, holding up a hand to stay Edwin's question. "It is enough that I know. I can see the way you two look at each other."

As if to prove a point, Edwin was looking at the floor, while Sige stared at the hem of Ethelburh's dress.

Ethelburh gave a sigh drenched in weariness and waited until both met her eyes again. "You deserve to say goodbye. I promise that no one will disturb you, but I would recommend that you return to the hall before daybreak."

She and her serving woman left the house before Sige and Edwin could close their mouths from the shock.

"It's a trick, I am sure of it," said Edwin, once the sound of footsteps had disappeared.

The same nagging feeling struck Sige as well, but the look in Ethelburh's eyes as she had left made him sure that she was telling the truth, and that no one would find them out. "We don't have to," he said quietly. "We can go back to the hall now, if you want."

Edwin looked at him miserably. "You know what I want. But the risk is too high."

"The risk has always been high," Sige said. "But the risk of never seeing you again is much higher."

Edwin watched him for a moment, and without another word, kissed him. This was not the frantic, passionate kiss that they so often shared in secret; it was long, slow, and gut-wrenching. They both lay down on the soft, bed, outfitted for royalty with thick pelts and soft blankets. A few days ago, Sige would have pounced on Edwin, would have torn his clothes off and have taken full advantage of their solitude. Now, though, they simply lay in each other's arms, drenched in the silence.

"Do you remember the last wedding we saw?" Edwin asked abruptly after a long stretch of silence, "That was a night to remember."

Sige nodded. Indeed, he did remember that night. He remembered the way he had felt, how drunk he had been on Edwin's flesh, how naturally their bodies came together, how blissfully happy and loved he had felt; and how it had been shattered in an instant by someone minding his own business, pounded into the dirt by the very idea that someone might discover their love. Even now, a dagger of that same fear touched his heart, and he knew that Edwin felt the same way.

"I thought I would never get to be with you again," Sige said at length.

"And yet here we are."

"I think we owe our lady of the Eota a large debt for her kindness." Sige said, grinning.

"I'll give her half of Deira, once it's mine again, and a mountain of gold. You can contribute some of that Frankisc cloth. I'm sure that would be enough to show her our gratitude."

Sige laughed, for the first time in what felt like weeks. "I hope you don't go trying to conquer Northumbraland until I get home. Tell Athelfrith he can sit and stew in the North until I come back from Francland."

Edwin pulled him closer, and they were silent, simply holding one another and trying to stretch out the moments that were passing too swiftly away. Sige felt the same lump in his throat at the thought that this would not happen again, after tonight.

"I don't want you to go." Edwin said hoarsely in his ear.

Sige swallowed the lump but his voice was cracked. "You know why…"

"Of course I do, but it can still make me sad," Edwin brushed his fingers through Sige's hair. "I've finally found you, and you're being ripped away from me. It's not fair."

Sige looked at him for a long time, trying through the darkness to etch in his memory every part of Edwin's face: his broken nose, the black scruff of his beard, the lazy way his hair flopped over his green eyes; every part of the person he loved.

"Do you ever wish you were… well, like everyone else?" he asked Edwin.

Edwin answered immediately. "No. It might be harder to walk this path, but I wouldn't change anything. The stolen moments are worth a lifetime of feeling out of place."

Sige kissed his brow. It was true. He knew nothing would ever be as beautiful, or as painful, as loving Edwin. It stabbed him like a dagger in his heart, but as long as it hurt, he would be able to keep Edwin with him.

"Will you wait?"

"Of course I will, as long as you promise to come back."

"What if I don't come back?" Sige asked.

"Then I will meet you at the Feast."

*****

It had been two nights, and Eorwald pushed all his remaining strength into standing upright. His injured leg was next to useless, and he had to lean to one side to keep his balance. He had a sickening memory of the man at Ealdham who had been tied to a pole like this, and he wondered how long the warrior lasted before his legs gave out and he strangled to death.

Still, he stood firm. He would not die like this, gasping for breath at the hands of Northumbrian *weargas*. He straightened his good leg, gritting though the pain in the bad one, and kept his mouth firmly closed.

"How's your leg?" Leofric said from behind him when there was no one around to hear them. It was beginning to get dark and the Northumbrians had started to eat their day meal, leaving Eorwald and Leofric alone for the moment.

"Well, it feels rather like I've had a hot knife shoved through it," Eorwald said. "I'll be fine," he added to make up for his harsh tone. "Are you all right?"

"Well enough," Leofric said. "I'd rather have a nice lie-down and a cup of something strong, but there we are."

"Stop talking!" a voice came from near the fire, and Eorwald and Leofric were silent.

"So, what's the plan?" Leofric asked when the Northumbrians had decided to ignore them again.

Eorwald cringed at the heartiness of Leofric's voice. "I – I don't have a plan." He grimaced as he shifted his weight slightly. "Leofric, I'm sorry I've gotten us into this mess. We should have gone straight back, but I was trying to act the hero, and now I've ruined–" He stopped short when he heard the sound of footsteps behind him and heard Leofric's grunt as someone punched him in the stomach.

"I said shut your mouths!" the man's voice said, and Eorwald heard Leofric splutter as he doubled up from the force of the blow, the rope around his neck pulling tight. Eorwald cried out in protest and tried to kick at the man with his injured leg, but the man simply grabbed it over the arrow wound and squeezed hard enough to make Eorwald grunt.

Eorwald's leg dropped and the guard returned to his meal. The Northumbrians were growing rowdier, drinking and laughing as the evening progressed. The smell of meat and flat bread made Eorwald's stomach ache almost as much as his leg did. He tried to think of something, anything that he might do to get them out, but he became distracted when the guard and a few of his friends began to pelt them with their gnawed bones and other bits of food. A clay cup cracked Eorwald in the side of the head, startling the dogs which had come to scavenge the projectiles, and Eorwald felt warm blood trickling down the side of his face. The men continued with their game for some time, until a shout put a stop to it.

"Bring him," said Hwitegos's cold voice. His voice came from the pavilion, though Eorwald could not see. Some hands untied the bonds holding the pair of them together, but a harsh voice said in Eorwald's ear, "Sit down. And if you try to run, your next bonds will be a noose."

Eorwald slid down the pole, and the hands re-tied the rope around his neck and the other around his wrists. His wound touched the dusty ground, but he could not shift his position without choking. He gritted his teeth, feeling the absence of Leofric behind him.

He could hear shouts coming from the pavilion, but the word "No!" had only just left his mouth before a boot caught him hard in the chest, knocking the wind out of him.

"You'll get your turn, *swines scitte,*" the man told him.

Surely enough, an hour later – perhaps longer; Eorwald could no longer reckon time – Leofric was half-dragged back to the post, sitting but bound just as tightly as Eorwald had been. The men wrenched Eorwald to his feet, shoving him roughly into the pavilion.

"Well," said Hwitegos lazily, "You might as well get on with it and tell me why you're here."

Eorwald had no intention of speaking, and stared dully over the man's shoulder.

A rat-faced man was pacing behind the pale one, brandishing a long stick that might have been a spear once, but with no point and cut down to the length of the man's arm. The rat-faced man disappeared from Eorwald's line of sight, but Eorwald did not care. He glared at the pale man, his mouth tightly closed.

The stick met his shoulders once and he jumped at the shock of it, but he did not cry out. His throat was raw and he was sure that even if he had done, no noise would have emerged.

"What is your reason for being here?"

"Nothing," Eorwald grunted; the stick made an audible crack as it collided with his lower back this time.

"What are you called?"

"Nothing." His shoulders again. He was pleased that he had still not cried out in pain, though he felt the aching bruises beginning to form.

The rat-faced man had circled around again, and Eorwald met his eyes. They were just as beady and rat-like as the rest of him. Another sharp blow; this time to the side of his head. He fell sideways, his bound hands unable to catch himself. He grunted as he fell onto the ground, his breath leaving him as another strike met his ribs.

"That will do," Hwitegos said tonelessly. "You and I shall speak more later," he said to Eorwald, and turned his back. Eorwald was shoved roughly to his feet, though he could barely walk on his infected leg, and fell against the pole as they tied him up again. At least he was sitting this time.

The bruises did not throb much after a while, and sitting with his back against the hard pole was almost as good as sleeping in a bed. He leaned his head back, letting sleep take him – kidnap him, more like. He did not know how long he would have to rest, and if he was to leave – well, he had to be on form, no matter what happened. He might as well take his chance while he still had one.

Hwitegos did not appear again the next day, but he was in the pavilion when Eorwald was shoved through the flap.

The rat-faced man sat with Hwitegos, and the latter looked up in bored coolness as Eorwald was brought to his knees in front of him. The rat-faced man jumped to his feet immediately, retrieving something Eorwald could not see.

Stripped to the waist, he bit his tongue against the sharp sting of the willow switch. After a while it began to feel like a single massive welt over the bruises from the day before; the rat-faced man did not spend long letting the sting of the old lash fade before striking a new. He remembered vaguely the switchings he sometimes got as a boy when he had done something stupid with Rægen; Mother used to make them cut their own switch, their fingers already stinging as they sawed through the thin willow branches. A sharp snap and a gasp, and it would be done, and they would be off to find some other minor transgression to commit.

He smiled ruefully at the memory. Well, he had disobeyed, after all. Perhaps he deserved a switching for his stupidity?

"Nothing," Eorwald grunted as Hwitegos asked him again what his name was, and where he had come from, and why he was there. It became easier to chant after each bite of the switch against his back.

"I'm growing weary of this," said Hwitegos, and Eorwald chuckled. He got another hard snap across his back, and felt a tiny trickle of something wet and hot roll over the welts.

It hurt quite a bit more to sit against the post that night.

Two more days and nights passed and Eorwald realized that he was dreaming, but he preferred the dream to waking and he refused to open his eyes. In his dream, he had somehow found himself at home, dozing happily in his bower with Rian at his side. He kept his eyes firmly shut as he pursued the dream, kissing her, watching the light touch the midnight-blue eyes. As she climbed on top of him and he slowly regained consciousness, he could practically hear her moaning.

Eorwald felt the dull cramp in his back from sitting half-upright for so long, and his dream slowly slipped away, though he could still hear Rian in his mind. She had told him that she would await his return, but it had been overa week, now. Would she miss him? Would she simply move on to the next place when he was no longer there to keep her?

The burns on the backs of his legs were still stinging, over the switch marks and the bruises. He shifted slightly to let the burn on his back leave the hard wood of the post, though the air touching it made him want to scream again.

He did not know when they had brought Leofric back, but Eorwald felt him move on the other side of the post.

"Leofric," Eorwald whispered, "Leofric, are you awake?"

"Mmm," Leofric's voice came from behind him.

"I have an idea," Eorwald said.

"Well, that makes one of us," said Leofric.

"You sound terrible."

Leofric seemed to sigh. "Yes, they rather seem to enjoy tormenting us, eh? It's getting tiresome, really, but it's not surprising."

"Why?" Eorwald asked stupidly. "Why do they take you so often?" He winced at the welts and bruises from the beatings and lashings that happened at least once a day, but they had taken Leofric twice as often and for at least three times as long each time.

"Because I'm not worth anything to them," Leofric said. "Frankly, I'm surprised they haven't just finished the job by now."

Eorwald felt his guts lurch at this. "But – you're a hostage, same as me, why do they keep beating up on you?"

"But I am no *ætheling*," said Leofric. Eorwald knew he did not want to say anything more, in case of an eavesdropper, so he did not push the subject.

"What's your idea?" Leofric asked, his voice still bewilderingly cheerful.

"You know how they take us round to the cesspit every so often? Well, I can distract them and you could –" Eorwald began, but Leofric cut him off, his voice rising slightly.

"No. I won't leave you."

"You have to," Eorwald whispered, more frantically now, "you have a family… you need to make it through this. I'm useless on this leg, but you have a chance to get away."

"So I can go home and tell my son how I abandoned my *dryhten* in an enemy camp to be tortured or worse?" Leofric said, his voice rising. "No. We leave together, or we do not leave at all."

Eorwald was on the point of arguing, when he heard footsteps once more and a loud, angry voice shouting, "How many times do I have to tell you lot to shut up?" one of the large, lumbering guards approached and smacked Leofric across the side of the head.

"You've been quite enough trouble, you *swines scitte*," the man said as Leofric's kick made contact with his shin. "Since you two can't seem to stop chatting, I believe I will have to separate you." Eorwald felt the man fumbling with the ropes behind him, and saw the man put his boot in Leofric's back to get him to walk while Leofric shouted an angry curse.

"Maybe we ought to take your tongue for speaking to us this way," the man said with a sickening sneer. "You don't seem to want to tell us anything important anyhow."

Eorwald shouted something incoherent as the man pushed Leofric away. Eorwald could not see where they went, but it was not far; he heard men jeering and craned his neck round to try to see what was going on, but they had gone out of Eorwald's line of sight.

His insides turned to water as he heard the strangled scream of agony that came from beyond his sight, and then heard laughter, accompanied by the sound of a scuffle and mocking jeers.

"This one just doesn't learn, does he?" said one of the men. "Do we need to teach you another lesson?"

"I wouldn't mind some target practice," some man answered. Eorwald heard incomprehensible shouts and more scuffling. He wrenched his head around once more as he heard the thrum of a bowstring and a muttered curse from the supposed archer.

"Just the legs; keep him alive," said the other, as if he were coaching a child. "We can work on the other one next."

Eorwald struggled at his bonds, writhing and twisting and feeling a stab of pain in his leg and in his back as he fought against the ropes. Without thinking, he bellowed, "Dryhten!"

The laughter stopped and Eorwald used the moment to bellow again, "Stop! Don't hurt him! He is the *ætheling*! He is Rædwald's son!"

Chapter Sixteen

Styrunga

Movements

Godomar was pacing up and down the docks, making huffing sounds every few moments and stopping his hand as if he wanted to chew a fingernail. Sunniva sat nearby on a chest, fiddling with Ecgric's ring. She did not want to stop wearing it, even though she had put that part of her life behind her. She twisted the silver around her finger, feeling anxious and rather nauseated as she shivered in the cool breeze wafting from the water.

"It's just one delay after another!" Godomar muttered, still pacing. Sunniva did not know what to do to comfort him; he was still an unknown quantity to her in many ways, and she was never entirely sure how she was supposed to act around him. The frustration of their delay had caused him to dispense with his usually gentile manner, but she could forgive him for that. She was eager to be off as well, and they were already two days behind schedule. Much longer, and the sea would be too dangerous to sail.

Sunniva rose to her feet and strode over, putting a hand on his arm. "Do you know how long it will take to repair the ship?" she asked in her calmest and sweetest voice.

Godomar shot an angry look at her. "Who knows," he snapped. "I am certain that there is some mischief that is keeping me on this God-forsaken island."

Sunniva ignored the slight. "Don't fret, my dear," she said. "All will be well."

"Just one bloody nuisance after another," he said, as if he had not heard her.

Sunniva did not know what to say, and frowned as he began pacing again. He was not nearly so handsome when he was cross, she noticed. His face creased into lines of worry and frustration, and as he walked away from her his shoulders slumped so that he looked like a cripple. Thinking it best to leave him to it, she wandered back toward Sige and the ten other Englisc men who had been sent to accompany them.

"Do you know when we'll be underway again?" asked Sigebryht, who was examining a torn seam in his leather jerkin, appraising it to see if it would be worth mending.

Sunniva shook her head. She felt rather restless, though she could not determine exactly why. It was as if something slimy was writhing around in her guts, and she felt as if she might be sick.

Sunniva pulled her distaff from her bundle, and began to spin. She wondered if the sheep in Francland had similar wool, or if it would feel different in her hands. She ought learn to spin flax – she had never liked it, as it was hard to draw it evenly and always broke, but she supposed fine women in Francland would use more linen than wool.

"What are you doing?" Godomar's voice interrupted her thoughts, and she drew her brows together in annoyance, despite the mundane quality of her musings.

"Just spinning," she said, holding up the distaff and spindle as evidence, curious why he did not seem to understand. "I supposed, since we would not be off for a while, that –"

"My treasure," Godomar said, taking her elbow in a gentle but irresistible way and making her stand, so that her distaff fell from her arm onto the ground, "Do not sit on a stone thus. I do not want people to think that my future wife must spin wool like some…" he swallowed in distaste, and then shook his head. "There is no need to spin, my jewel. If you need cloth, you need only ask."

She glanced at Sige, whose eyes were fixed on his jerkin and bone needle, though he was making no motions except with his eyebrows. She might have been a child being scolded for stealing honey cakes, and she felt her cheeks burn.

"I am not used to having idle hands," she said, "I must have something to do."

He laughed aloud, pulling her arm again so that she walked beside him. "My treasure, you needn't *do* anything. You are my wife now, and in my land – your new land, my little jewel – you are only expected to enjoy life, to sit by my side and sparkle like the gem you are. You will have a dozen servants to tend to your duties for you. If you would like something to do, come with me and you may meet our host."

He spoke quickly as he whisked her away, and she did not even have a chance to put her spinning away properly. She knew it would take hours to pick all of the dirt and pine needles out of the wool that was now lying on the ground in an untwined mess.

But why should she be annoyed? She always hated spinning, ever since her mother handed her a spindle at the age of five and told her to fill the shaft or she'd get a switching. Mother had always insisted that even royal women had to make sure their business was seen to; even queens could not lie about in idleness all day. Sunniva had always sniffed at this, but it had still been a fact of life. She ought to be pleased that she would no longer have to do the tedious chore. Godomar was so considerate, though perhaps he did not understand.

Her hands empty now, she let Godomar put her wrist in the crook of his arm as he led her toward the village hall. She still felt strange little twinges in her belly when she looked at him, radiant and golden as he was. He patted her arm and she had to stop herself from giggling.

"Two more days," Godomar muttered as they walked. "I had hoped to be gone by the full moon, and here it is waning and I have still not gone!" He sighed hugely, and patted her arm. "But do not worry yourself about that, my little treasure. I am sure we will be well treated tonight, and I will personally see that you receive every comfort."

He had been as good as his word, when they were invited into the hall. There was no private room in this hall, but there was an alcove drawn with a thick woolen hanging where the lord slept, at the end of the building. The lord had insisted that Sunniva take the bed, though Godomar took this as a matter of fact. He was always looking out for her comfort.

The village hall was cramped and musty, despite the comfortable bed, and Godomar was still somewhat peevish as they ate the day-meal and the people in the hall retired to games and songs. Godomar left her to speak with some of his men, insisting that she go and rest. Sunniva did not wish to make him cross when he already had the ship to worry about, and so tucked herself into the blankets and twisted her ring as she stared up at the ceiling.

She did not draw the curtain, though; she was not very tired, having done little except smile and sparkle, as Godomar had requested. Her face was tired from the grinning, but it was hardly different from anything she did in her father's house. She smiled and chatted and looked pretty even before she had met Godomar – the only difference was that now he would kiss her fingers and called her his "beautiful treasure," as his blue eyes sparkled under a mane of thick tawny hair.

Sunniva was bored, and she contented herself with watching the people in the hall, illuminated with the greasy torchlight. There were several small knots of people talking and drinking together, welcoming the women who had made their way into the hall. The women – whores, to be certain – immediately attached themselves to various men, slinking into quiet corners of the hall to earn their *peningas*. One couple found their way into a corner near where Sunniva sat curled under her blanket, paying her no notice whatsoever. The man was strongly built and had a dark beard that rather reminded Sunniva of someone she wished to forget, and she twirled her ring around her finger in rapt silence as she watched the man taking his whore from behind, half-obscured in shadow. She realized how quickly she was breathing, how her stomach tightened and how she could not look away.

The man finished with his woman and went to re-join the company, and Godomar appeared at Sunniva's side, still looking cross. She put on a gentle smile, but he did not return it. "It is only for a few days," she reminded him. "Once the ship is repaired I am sure that we will have an excellent journey."

"How would you know that?" he asked snappishly.

Sunniva narrowed her eyes, but knew that it was simply his bad mood talking. "Because the weather is fine and there is a good wind. The men tell me that means there will be little need for rowing and we will make good time crossing the sea."

"Why don't you leave the navigation to the men? You ought not to worry about such things." He said it gently, touching her face as he did so, and she was pacified. He was under a great deal of strain, after all.

"It pains me to see you unhappy," she said in her sweetest voice. She looked coyly at him through her eyelashes, giving him a slight smile as she brushed his arm with her fingertips.

He looked at her appraisingly as she gave him the same look she usually gave Ecgric when her legs were feeling loose. The same look that usually made Ecgric's eyes turn to fire and made her blood hot. She wanted to feel that way about this man, the man she would marry.

She moved her hand to his leg, stroking his knee. He just needed a release, surely; that must be why he was so cross. He had done nothing more but kiss her chastely on the mouth to seal their betrothal; in his land it was apparently not appropriate to do anything more until the marriage could be consummated. Even that kiss, so gentle and innocent, set her aching. No one would know if they went under a blanket, just this once.

"Is there anything I might do?" she asked, sliding her hand up his leg. She jumped back when he flicked her hand away. It was not hard, but it startled her.

He took her by the wrist, his fingers only delicately brushing her skin. "I will lie with you when we might do it in private, when you are my wife," he dropped his voice so that only she could hear. "And I will not put on a show for these men."

Sunniva's cheeks burned. "Of course," she said. "Forgive me."

"You don't know any better, my treasure," Godomar said, brushing her cheek with his thumb, "But you will learn."

*****

The jar was smashed into a hundred tiny pieces, but Eadyth glared at Rædwald when he tried to pick them up. "Leave it," she said icily. "Just get out."

"Will you please just listen to me?"

"No."

"You were the one who wanted to find Sunniva a husband…"

"I said get out!" Eadyth shrieked, reaching for another projectile to hurl at her husband. He caught her by the wrist so that she could not throw the half-empty cup of ale. The liquid poured pitifully to the floor, and Eadyth dropped the cup.

"Let go of me," she hissed.

"Not until you hear me out."

"I don't want to." She lowered her eyes from his, feigning surrender. He released her wrist and she shoved him away. "My children," she said, "you've sent away my children, Rædwald."

"You know why I did," he said, his voice infuriatingly measured and calm, "Godomar did not wish to delay his departure, and I needed to seal the alliance. My only choice was to arrange the marriage before he left."

"I don't want to hear your excuses!" Eadyth said, "I don't care about your alliances. You went behind my back and married off my only daughter without even consulting me!"

"You're overreacting," said Rædwald, trying to sound soothing but only making Eadyth even more furious, "Sunniva is going to be well-cared for, and she will be very happy with Godomar. He is the best match we could have made for her."

"But you didn't have to send Sige too," Eadyth said miserably, ignoring the logic. "You've always wanted him gone, and now you've taken your chance."

It was now his turn to look angry. "That is a lie and you know it," he said, "I have loved Sigebryht as my own son for twenty years. If I wanted to send him away, I would have done." The fire cooled in his voice. "The Christians were calling for his blood, and this was a way of protecting him. You have to see that." He held out his arms to Eadyth as if to hug her, but she took a step away from him.

He was in the right, Eadyth knew, and it infuriated her. "I am never going to see them again, Rædwald. Do you understand that? I will never see my children again, and it is your fault."

"It's not forever!" Rædwald pleaded, "Sigebryht will be back in the spring, and I am sure that Sunniva will travel back with Godomar when he has business in Gipeswic." He reached out to touch Eadyth's cheek, but she slapped his hand away.

"Just go," she said. Finally, he seemed defeated. He trudged out of the room without another word, and Eadyth bent to retrieve the pieces of the shattered jar.

Eadyth sat in the hall that night with her spouse, but she excused herself with a headache after a few interminable hours of pretending she was not filled to the brim with white-hot fury.

She had been lying in the dark for an hour now; staring into the dim shadows cast by the light from the hall, but did not turn over when she heard his footsteps approaching the bed.

"We will have to leave soon," Rædwald said hesitantly, as if he was not sure if she was still awake. "Eni has sent word that Ecgric's come to collect his men in the North. They'll all be at Mæduwic by now. There's no point in delaying any longer."

Eadyth made a noncommittal noise to indicate that she had heard.

"Dytta," he said, and she felt his weight on the bed behind her, "Let's not leave it like this."

She turned over, annoyed by the use of the name and incredulous at the idea that he would go without her. "Leave it?" She snapped, "What are you talking about?"

"When I go to the North," he said.

"What do you mean, 'I?' I am coming with you."

"I just thought that –"

"Just because you went behind my back, it does not mean that I do not still have a job to do. If there is battle then I must be there to tend the wounded and prepare the dead. I must be there for the two of my children I still have left." She said the last part with such venom that he looked as if she had actually bitten him.

"Dytta," he began again.

"No," Eadyth said. "You do not get to call me that."

He climbed into bed, but she wished that he would leave it again. She heard him snoring behind her and she was torn between the desire to hit him and to put her arms around him. Her stupid, thoughtless, brilliant, brave and infuriating husband had acted in the best interest of her family, securing an honorable and lucrative match for her daughter; protecting her son from angry Christians who were out for his blood after killing of one of their priests. She hated that he was right, and she hated the fact that she could not admit it to him. She rolled back over to face him, finding his sleeping face only a hand's breadth from her own, his hand outstretched as if he had been trying to touch her. Her heart had turned to ice after what he had done, and she closed her eyes to keep it from shattering.

No one was happy to be heading north again, and it was with a wind at their grim faces that they set off. There was no possible way to move that many people and that much gear at speed, and their progress was maddeningly slow. No one seemed to know exactly what might be at the end of the long grey road, and the unease was almost palpable. The young men bounced about in excitement for their first battles, eager for war and the promise of glory. She wondered if it made it worse, to see how excited they were to go out and die.

She clenched her fists, released them, and kept walking.

Eadyth watched Rægenhere walking some distance ahead of her, holding his wife's hand. Gieva's hair shone gold in the few rays of sun which were brave enough to peek through the clouds, and her cheeks were flushed from the combined effect of the exercise and her pregnancy. Rægen looked at Gieva as if she might have been made of pure sunshine as they grinned and talked together in quiet voices. Eadyth enjoyed a moment of happiness for the pair of them, and it distracted her from her own gloom.

She saw Edwin out of the corner of her eye, and felt a pang of regret for him. Edwin was always cheerful and joked almost as much as Rægen, but she had not seen him smile since his return from Lundenburh. She knew he missed Sigebryht; the two had formed a bond almost instantly after Edwin had come to the Bricgweard. She knew that Sige had always felt like the odd-man-out, and he had surely found a kindred spirit in Edwin. Brothers in arms were as close as blood, after all, and she knew that they would both be quite desolate without one another.

She clenched her fists, released them, and kept walking.

She looked back at Rægen; thought of Eorwald. At least if something happened to them, she would know. At least if it came to a fight, she would know that she had been there to make sure that they fought bravely and died well, if that was to be their fate.

Sige might even now be fighting in some battle on a foreign shore. Sunniva might already be pregnant with the man's baby – what sort of man was he? Would he be a good match for her? Sige would look after her, she knew, but Sunniva was so unpredictable – what if Godomar did not make good on his promises? How was anyone supposed to know what a Frankisc man thought was honorable? Why had Rædwald –

She clenched her fists, released them, and kept walking.

Why had Rædwald been so quick to ally himself with this man? She knew nothing about Godomar, except the fact that he had charmed his way into Rædwald's greedy affections. She had only met him when he came to the Bricgweard. How was she supposed to know if he would be a good husband for her daughter? How was she supposed to know if he would treat Sige and his men with honor while they were his guests? What if their ship capsized? What if they were beset by *wycingas* as soon as they made landfall? What if –

She clenched her fists, released them, and kept walking.

She knew that Sige was in danger here. She knew that from the moment she saw the blood on his hands in the *weoh*. These Christians would be out for him, ready to take their vengeance for their fallen brothers. Their disease was spreading, quicker now as more and more people latched on to the infected teat. And Rædwald had let her daughter marry one of them? Would her children forsake the ways of their fathers now that they were in a new land? Sige would not. Sige was so stupefyingly devoted to the gods that he would never accept the useless god of the Christians. Sunniva was agreeable to anything, but Sige would set her straight. Gods, how she wished she could just tell them –

"Eadyth?" Gieva's voice interrupted Eadyth's thoughts. Eadyth felt her warm hand around hers, though her own was still clenched tightly.

"I'm fine," Eadyth snapped, but shook her head as if waking from a bad dream. "I'm sorry, Gieva."

"Don't be sorry, Gieva smiled, squeezing Eadyth's hand when it had finally unclenched. "Would you like to talk?"

Eadyth wondered, if she opened the floodgate of her thoughts, if there would be simply too many to come out. "I want to stop thinking," she said, nearly kicking the ground in irritation. "It's like a hive of bees in my head."

"Are you worried?" Gieva asked.

"Of course I am," said Eadyth, "I am in a constant state of worry, every moment of every waking hour, and again during my dreams. I wonder if I shall ever have a thought again which is not a panicked premonition of what might happen to my children."

Gieva nodded. "Isn't that just part of being a mother?" she asked, though her tone sounded as if she were looking for reassurance. Eadyth looked at her questioningly, and she went on. "I keep having these thoughts, as if my mind is forcing any possible scenario at me, one by one, no matter how absurd it might sound."

"Like what?" Eadyth asked, diverted.

"They are so stupid!" Gieva said in as close to an irritated voice as Eadyth ever heard her use. "I mean, some make sense, like if something were to happen to –" she licked her lips, looking at Rægen's back with a wince, "But most are absolutely ludicrous! I woke up thinking of what would happen if I put the baby down while I was trying to milk the goat, and had all of these thoughts about the goat stepping on the baby, or the baby somehow climbing into the bucket and drowning, or eating some herb that was actually nightshade…" She glanced at Eadyth, "I'm just being foolish, right?"

Eadyth laughed, and it felt strange to feel a smile stretch her tight mouth. She patted Gieva's hand. "Of course it's foolish," she said, "It's what motherhood does to our minds. I'll bet you've already worked out what you might say to someone who complains that your baby is crying too loudly in the hall, haven't you?"

Gieva looked ashamed. "Nothing that I would ever say aloud," she muttered. "And when I'm not fretting about something ridiculous, I'm crying my eyes out over something even more ridiculous."

"When I was pregnant with Eorwald," Eadyth grinned, "I burst into tears one day when I decided how badly the clouds must feel, because people always cursed at them for darkening their day."

Gieva exploded into giggles at this. "I started crying because I trod on my cat's tail, but later that night she brought me a dead mouse and I wept because she was so kind, even when I had wronged her."

"We are ridiculous beings, my dear," said Eadyth, still laughing. "And I could tell you a hundred times that everything will be well, and you will still not believe me."

Gieva smiled. "I know you wouldn't believe me, either, if I told you the same thing."

Eadyth looked at her sidelong, and Gieva gave her a knowing look. Eadyth squeezed her hand, and they kept walking.

*****

At least the shooting had stopped.

"He is the *ætheling*," said Eorwald again, "If you hurt him, you will lose any ransom you might have gotten for him!" They seemed to be communing with one another in low voices, but Eorwald could not hear them. He slid up the stake to which he was tied, feeling splinters dig into his arms, but he could at least see over the tents where they were using Leofric for target practice. "You've already cut out his tongue; don't make it worse! If you send him home, we both know that Rædwald will pay handsomely for him. What will your *dryhten* say if you lose out on such wealth?"

One of the men, a watery-eyed middle-aged fool, appeared in front of Eorwald. "What do you know of it?"

"He is my commander," said Eorwald. "The one you've been using for target practice, he's Rædwald's son. But I know just as much as he does. Leave him alone, and I'll give you what you want. He told me not to say anything, but I can't watch you hurt him anymore."

Another of the men appeared, and then a third, all looking at one another with varying degrees of panic or skepticism. "I say we just kill them both now," one man said, "Save a whole lot of trouble, won't it?"

"And you'll miss out on everything I have to tell you," said Eorwald. He said it all in a single breath, as if forcing it out might help it sting less.

"We know where his forces are, you stupid bastard," the watery-eyed man smacked him on the side of the head. "How do you think we'll ransom him if we don't know where his father is, eh?"

"You lot really are idiots, aren't you?" Eorwald mocked, "Do you think that the *cyning* hasn't been planning an attack on Northumbraland for months? Ever since you filthy *weargas* attacked our women and burned them alive at Ealdham? If my timing is right, they will already be at your front gates. It's just too bad I won't personally be able to see your *swines scitte cyning*'s head on a pike."

The Northumbrians looked at one another, a silent conversation of worry occurring between them. "Tell us what you know."

Eorwald shook his head defiantly and got a fist in his stomach.

"Tell us!"

"I want to see Hwitegos."

They looked at one another again, and disappeared without another word. Eorwald looked over to where they had tied Leofric, but he was gone. He prayed that Leofric had not said anything, and he prayed even harder that no one had decided to finish the job.

An eternity passed. He felt nauseated, but he knew that it was only partially due to his worry for Leofric. The wound in his leg oozed something foul-smelling and sickly. The skin surrounding the burned hole was vivid red and he could feel the heat rising from it into his blood. He knew that the arrow had been touched with something poisonous; it was only a matter of time before it ended him.

He clenched his teeth against the wave of nausea which washed over him, and it passed. A moment later, after feeling the cold touch of a knife on his wrists, his bonds were cut and Hwitegos appeared in front of him.

"What do you know?" Hwitegos asked. If Eorwald had not known better, he would have thought Hwitegos might have been worried.

Eorwald looked away pointedly. "I know a lot of things," he said, "I know, for one thing, that your men have done serious injury to the one man you would have wanted to keep whole."

"You're lying," said Hwitegos, but he seemed uncertain.

"You won't know now, will you?" said Eorwald. "It's not as if he can really speak for himself, is it?" He stretched his newly unbound arms, feeling the stabs of sensation returning to them. "Fortunately, there is still someone who knows a thing or two about Rædwald's movements, who might be able to help you."

"What would you know about it?"

"Why do you think I was traveling in the company of the *ætheling*?" Eorwald asked, enjoying how flustered his condescension made Hwitegos. "I am his servant. His right hand."

"And you would betray him?"

Eorwald frowned. "I am his man. I would not betray him. I want him to be safe. If anything, I betray him by letting you know who he is. I want you to ransom him back to Rædwald Cyning and keep me in his place."

"But you would betray your *cyning*?"

Eorwald sighed. "I don't want to, but Rædwald has never cared for me the way his son has, and though I do it with a heavy heart, I must think first of the life of my *dryhten*." He focused on the pain in his leg and let it register on his face. None of it was a lie, exactly, but he tried to keep any hint of falsehood from his face. "He is of no further use to you. Keep me. I'll tell you everything."

Hwitegos left him without pressing him for more information, and Eorwald saw no one for the rest of the day. When it was growing dark, he knew that one of the guards would come to take him to the cesspit as he did every day. He was still bound, but in exchange for the information about the supposed *ætheling*, he was given a bare patch of earth and a cloak to sleep under, rather than being forced to sit with his back against the stake in the center of the yard. He still had the nearly unconquerable urge to run every time he was forced to his feet, but the burning in his leg reminded him that he would not get far before another arrow found him. The burning in his heart reminded him that he would not leave Leofric, even if he tried.

"Where have you taken my *dryhten*?" Eorwald asked. The rat-faced man kicked him in the ribs and told him to shut up. He asked again. And again, he got a boot in his flank.

He was rudely awakened by the white head of Hwitegos looming over him, sometime later.

"I want to know where Rædwald's men are." Hwitegos said.

"Have you ransomed my *dryhten* back yet?" Eorwald asked.

Hwitegos looked at him shrewdly. "The time is not right for that yet."

Eorwald sighed and lay back on the hard earth of his makeshift bed. "Then the time is not right for me to tell you how far my *cyning*'s forces have gotten."

Hwitegos glared at him. "We seem to have a problem, then. I am having a rather hard time believing anything you say, so why would I give up my most valuable hostage on your word? Anyhow, we would have had a messenger by now that Rædwald's forces had gotten past us."

"Messengers can be killed or captured," Eorwald shrugged. "And you have a considerable force here, so it is a shame that you are not able to defend your *cyning* right now. Who knows, he might already be dead." He received a hard punch in the guts for that and it knocked the wind out of him, but it was worth it to see the panic on Hwitegos's face.

"You're lying."

"Only one way to find out, isn't there?" Eorwald said. "Release the *ætheling*, and I will tell you where Athelfrith's men are being slaughtered. Perhaps you might get there in time to reclaim his body. Or what's left of it."

Hwitegos looked down at Eorwald's leg. He shoved his finger into the blackened, pus-filled hole. Eorwald clenched his jaw in pain, not taking his eyes away from the pale man.

"It seems that this wound has begun to fester," Hwitegos said in his quiet, drawling voice as he twisted his finger, "Of course, I would not feel badly if you should die. You have been rather a large thorn in my side. Part of me wants to put a dagger in your guts and have done with you."

"Do it, then," said Eorwald through his gritted teeth, "But you've already made a mute of the only other man here who can tell you anything, so you ought to weigh your choices carefully. I'm going to die soon anyway, so you might as well get what you can out of it." That was not a lie either. He could feel the heat from the wound rising through his leg, and as the cold sweat began to bead on his brow he knew that he could not have much time left.

Eorwald watched as Hwitegos studied him, perhaps examining to see how long he might last, or if he ought to use torture, or if ransoming the supposed *ætheling* was worth all this trouble.

"We are taking him tomorrow, at first light." said Hwitegos, "now tell me."

"Let me see him, please," said Eorwald.

"You're awfully demanding for someone in your position."

Eorwald said nothing, but Hwitegos's cold eyes seemed to soften. "I understand the love of a man for his *dryhten*," he said at last. "Even a turncloak has some dignity, it seems. I will allow it. You can look your *ætheling* in the eye to explain why you've decided to betray your *cyning*."

Leofric had at least been stowed inside of a tent, bare and cold, but sheltered from the wind. He sat with his bound arms around his knees, looking terrified and exhausted. Eorwald knelt in front of him, feeling the burning in his leg as the wound rested on the dirt.

"Please forgive me, Dryhten," Eorwald said, putting a large stress on the last word as he felt Hwitegos's eyes on him, "I have to tell them, to spare your life. I am sorry." Leofric's eyes were wide in confusion and horror, his mouth caked with dried blood. He opened it to speak, and Eorwald saw, through some of Leofric's broken teeth, the ragged, burned wound where his tongue should have been. Eorwald looked back into Leofric's wide eyes, steeling himself. "You will be ransomed back to the *cyning*, your father," he said, trying to give Leofric a hundred words in a single look. "Please forgive me. I did it for you," and then he added in a whisper, "for your son."

"You must not harm him any further," Eorwald said acidly to Hwitegos. "And you must return his sword. The one you found, the one with the claw-shaped pommel." He felt a twinge of regret that he would be letting Weargbana go, but it would be better needed where it was going. "Gods know you've damaged him badly enough that the *cyning* won't recognize him without it."

Hwitegos looked from Eorwald to Leofric several times before speaking. "As you wish. Now tell me what I want to hear."

"Your word. I want your word that you will not harm him before you return him to the *cyning*."

"You have it." Hwitegos said.

Eorwald turned to Hwitegos but did not look into the cold, pale eyes. "Go northwest of here, past Lincoln, where the Roman road crosses the River Idle. That is where Rædwald has sent his force. That is where he will make his stand."

*****

The trailing fingers of the Wash reached out as if to collect them, drawing them forward. The woods began to disappear, to be replaced by wide, sweeping meadows, then spongy, damp peat bogs; and then, she knew, would be the marshy wetlands that seeped into the great bay of the Wash and out to the Sea. They were skirting the meadows entirely, staying well west of the treacherous bogs and sticking to the Old Roman road and the smaller paths which branched off of it as they made their way northeast from Grantabricge.

She did not miss the burh much; it might have offered a few more of the creature comforts any person would enjoy, but she felt just as happy sleeping under the stretch of canvas as she would have done anywhere else.

The third day of marching drew to a close, and they found themselves in a meadow bordering the salt marsh. The turf was firm underfoot, but there was a sharp, caustic smell in the air, which Rægen seemed to dislike but which filled Gieva with a strange sense of longing.

"There's a saltpan nearby," she explained, at the questioning look he gave her as she breathed in the familiar scent. "My father traded in salt, so that's how I remember the smell. They build canals to bring in seawater and let the water dry in shallow pools and pans to leave only the minerals. I'll bet that flat area is where the salt is being made." She pointed ahead to where there was a small pool at the edge of the meadow, with a few ramshackle buildings nearby. Rægen nodded briefly at her explanation, and she trailed off, frowning.

"What's wrong?" she asked.

Rægen sighed, his eyebrows creased. "I am sorry," he said wearily. "I did not mean to be cross with you. I'm just anxious."

"I didn't think you were being cross," she said gently. "What are you anxious for? The battle?"

Rægen shook his head, tossing his saddlebag onto the ground outside their tent. "No, a battle would be a welcome change. I hate waiting. I hate the uncertainty. I wish we knew where the fight would be."

"You don't know that there will be a fight," Gieva said reasonably, "Or if there is, it might not be right away. Do you think your father might negotiate terms with Athelfrith?"

"The *cyning* is done with negotiating," said Rægen. "He might have done once, before we went to Ealdham, before we saw what Athelfrith's men liked to do for fun." his voice was as bitter as Gieva had ever heard it, and she knew his anger as her own. "I don't want to negotiate," he said firmly, "I want to crush them once and for all, to pay him back for Cynhelm and your family and all the innocent people of the Fens he decided to slaughter."

Gieva took his hand, and he stroked it with his thumb, looking down at their intertwined fingers and then at her face.

"How are you feeling?" he asked.

She shrugged, not wanting to look at his silver eyes lest she start crying again. She had just cause to want to cry, but lately it seemed as if anything could release the flood.

"Gieva, my heart," he said, "You are so beautifully serene, but I wish you would tell me if you are unhappy. You don't need to hide your feelings from me."

She finally looked up at him, and felt her lip tremble. His face was so filled with concern that she knew the flood would come whether she wished it or not.

Gieva licked her lips a few times before speaking. "We passed my father's farm this morning."

His face fell. "Why didn't you say anything?" It was not accusatory; quite the contrary, it was understanding and gentle and it made her cry even harder than she would have done if he had indeed been cross with her. She ducked into the shelter, sitting cross-legged on the furs as he pulled her into his arms.

She hiccupped for a few moments into his shirt as he stroked her hair. "I didn't want to think of it."

Rægen nodded, kissing her brow and hugging her. "I will go with you, if you wish to go back."

"No," she said slowly, "I want to remember my home as it was. I think it would hurt too much to go there."

"Of course."

She grimaced, not sure how to put the rest into words. She only found herself crying harder, panic building in her chest as she felt her hands trembling against his arms.

"Gieva, what is it?" he asked worriedly, "Please, please, my love, tell me what's wrong?"

She could not draw breath for a long time; she felt as if her chest would catch fire, as if her eyes would burst from crying.

"Rægen, I don't want to go back to Ealdham," she sobbed, "I know we must pass through to reach Mæduwic, but…" the rest was drowned in her tears, but he only pulled her closer and let the mountain of her fear crumble into his arms.

"We will not pass through Ealdham," he said firmly.

She swallowed and wiped her eyes, hiccupping again as he took both her hands in his.

"I'm being silly," she sniffed, clearing her throat to rid it of the hoarseness. "You have enough to worry about without me going to pieces."

"You're not being silly," he said with as close to anger as she had ever heard him use with her before. "Gieva, you are allowed to be sad. You're allowed to be angry and afraid and worried. What's more, you don't need permission!"

She did not know what to say, and instead looked at her hands, folded around his.

"If I could choose, I would make it so that you never had cause to weep," He said, "But memories are sharper than swords sometimes, and you are not silly for feeling your wounds."

Gieva felt the edge of her mouth quirk upwards. "You are always such a poet, even when the subject of your verse is a mess," she sniffed. "Thank you for helping me to be strong."

Rægen's face was hard, his silver eyes boring into hers. "You are already strong, Gieva. You are brave and strong and beautiful and clever and you are the most wonderful person I have ever known, and you don't need me to tell you that."

"Sometimes it helps," she said, and he returned her smile so that her heart fluttered and the dark fear seemed to shatter.

Gieva knew that he would not think less of her for worrying, but she did not think that it would do any good to constantly remind him of the fact.

She knew what she had gotten herself into; if she wanted to know her husband would be safe, she would have married a farmer. She would not have fallen in love with an *ætheling*, a warrior. Even so, she looked over her shoulder at the column of people following them. Though many were indeed trained warriors, a great number of them were farmers or shepherds or grey-bearded old men trudging behind them, uncertain if they would ever see their own families again. The days on the road seemed to weigh on their shoulders, and she could feel the weight of fear pressing on her as well. Even a farmer had to fight sometimes, and a simple life was no guarantee of peace. She had learned that the hard way.

They saved the horses and walked together, and she could not help but smile at him every time he squeezed her hand. He had been right; she did not need him to tell her her worth, but knowing how much he loved her made the fear and worry and exhaustion easier to bear.

Still, Gieva felt tired; she had not slept well the night before, having been woken up four or five times by vivid, strange dreams.

For four nights now, she had dreamed that the baby came prematurely and that Eadyth had insisted that the half-formed infant take up his duties as king. Gieva always protested, but the babe was taken from her arms just before she woke in a panic.

She was sick of these stupid dreams, waking in a panic every other night because she had some ominous vision of everything awful that could possibly happen. Even Eadyth's assurance that it was nothing out of the ordinary could not calm her. At least she had Rægen, who would stroke her back without opening his own eyes, his hair sticking up wildly where it had rested on his arm, and she was comforted.

Rægen would be king for a long time before their child would, she reminded herself, and the baby was not coming for another four months at least.

She was feeling the effects of a poor night's rest as she tried to keep up with Rægen's long strides.

Though she tried not to make a fuss, he clearly noticed when she began to take shorter steps and lag behind.

"You're not walking anymore today," Rægen said firmly, and he took the reins of a fat brown pony from his serving man.

"I'm fine," Gieva protested, "I'm not some helpless little –"

"You're exhausted, and you are carrying my baby, and you are getting on this pony," he commanded, but Gieva laughed at him. He was not very good at being stern, but she obliged him and let him boost her onto the pony's back. The beast was small but hardy, and Gieva leaned against one of the bags of gear which had been strapped to its back. As the sun reached its zenith and moved slowly westward, she suggested that she was quite well enough to walk again, but had a small sense of satisfaction when Rægen gripped the reins tighter and shook his head. Her feet really did hurt.

It was nearly nightfall when they arrived outside of Mæduwic, a small town set amid a wide, sweeping meadow near a swift stream. It was a beautiful place, but the trampling feet and shouts of men detracted somewhat from the tranquil scene. The king and queen went to the hall to speak with Ricbert and Ecgric, who had come to greet them, while Gieva and Rægen went to prepare their camping site.

Rægen, as the captain of one of the companies, was constantly moving between his men on the road, laughing and singing and talking with them to keep their spirits high. Gieva smiled as she watched him, but seeing the way his breeches hugged his legs or the dimple in his cheek when he smiled made her anxious to get him alone as soon as possible.

The tents were set up an hour before nightfall, and Gieva got her wish as she dropped her bag on the ground outside of the tent.

"I didn't see Eorwald when we arrived," Gieva said distractedly, pulling the tent flap back and tying it to the thick wooden stake to keep it open.

"I'm sure he's around here somewhere," said Rægen. He's probably brooding about how dull it is here."

Gieva removed her cloak and flattened her dress over her front. Before she was able to duck into the shelter, Rægen hugged her from behind. He touched the swell between her hips and said, "You're starting to show."

"I feel like a cow," she replied, putting her hands on top of his and cradling the bump.

"You are beautiful," he said, kissing her cheek before they both ducked into the tent.

Gieva watched Rægen as he pulled off the dusty tunic he'd worn on the road. She enjoyed watching him as he made certain that his kit was in order, and she suddenly felt ravenous, but not just for food. Without a word she took the clothes away and kissed him. Rægen responded in kind, pushing her back down onto the furs and almost immediately finding her breast through the neck of her dress.

He seemed enthralled with how large they had gotten. Her nipples had grown dark and seemed to be constantly hard, and so sensitive that the barest touch of his fingers or his lips set her aching for him. She felt like her nerves were on fire, and when she slid down onto him she let out a loud moan of pleasure, and he ran his hands along her hips and touched her breasts and she rode him until she felt her body spasm. This seemed to inflame him even more; she was usually quiet and reserved when they made love, but the sound of her jubilation excited him and by the time he finished, they both were exhausted and pleased beyond measure.

She still wanted more, but they were both spent and she contented herself by lying beside him and trying to comb through the tangles of his hair with her fingers. His hair was not long, just brushing his shoulders, but a cowlick on the side of his head always made him look somewhat disheveled even when he had actually combed it through. It was endearing to her, and strangely amusing to think that the man who would one day be king had wild hair that stuck up on the side. No one remembered little details like that, when the men were immortalized in song. No one boasted in triumph that their king had messy hair, or that when he smiled he had a dimple in his cheek that made her knees buckle, or that he hated eggs, or that he was ticklish under his left ear. She did not care, though. Those things were for her to remember, for her to keep safe if the worst should happen. She would hold that, just as lovingly as he held her now.

He surely was not this way all the time. It was common enough for a man to be tender with his wife and his children in private, but he must be hard as iron on the battlefield or when dealing with his rivals. King Rædwald was stern and hard, but she knew from the way Eadyth talked about him that he was gentle with her and listened to her advice. Gieva had never seen Rægen fight, with the exception of watching him play at battle with his friends, and he had always approached that with the same playful energy he took to most things. She wondered if he lost that when he fought real men with real swords and real blood.

Rægen was dozing, his arm draped around Gieva's waist and a supremely contented look on his face. Gieva rolled over and kissed his forehead and he opened his eyes immediately, as though he had not actually been sleeping. "Is it time to eat yet?"

Gieva giggled and kissed him, on the lips this time, and suddenly felt a strange lurch in her belly. Her eyes widened, and Rægen's mirrored hers in worry.

"What's wrong?" he asked; his hand immediately going to the barely-visible bump on her abdomen.

"He moved!" Gieva squealed, and waited silently for it to happen again, but it was still. She knew that he would not be able to feel it, but to her it felt as if her belly had turned completely over and then back again.

"It's good to know he's still in there," she said, more to herself than to him. Her heart was beating fast, but slowed as she did not feel the fluttering again.

"Why do you say he?" Rægen asked, "Can you tell if it's a boy or a girl?" He seemed in earnest, and she laughed at how little men seemed to know of pregnancy.

"Of course not," she said, "but everyone hopes for boys, so we always assume it's a boy until it comes out and proves us wrong."

"It could be a girl," Rægen said, as though trying to start an argument, "I wouldn't mind a sweet little *mædencild* to give me kisses and sing me songs. And she'd look like you, so she'd be the prettiest girl anyone had ever seen." He seemed to contemplate this for a moment and added, "Of course, then I'd be outnumbered by women-folk..."

Gieva rolled her eyes, but still enjoyed his flattery and his jests. "I just want a child, that's all," she said quietly, "I don't care if it's a boy or a girl. We will have plenty of both, so no one needs to feel outnumbered."

"Well, I look forward to providing this one with lots of brothers and sisters, then," he said, and she giggled as he pounced on her once more.

Chapter Seventeen

Menn Ne Næfre Scierað

Let No Man Tear Asunder

"Put an arrow through my eye before I let them do that to me won't you?" Oswy said to Sigebryht.

"She agreed to it." Sige shrugged, "She thinks it would be a sign of trust and understanding. And Godomar was insistent."

"He ought not to have forced her into it."

"Manipulated, more like," said Sige. "Godomar does not force anyone into anything." Sige felt uneasy about Sunniva's decision to be baptized before her marriage to Godomar, and even a little disappointed with her. She had always been far too frivolous when it came to the gods. She placed her offerings and said the words as she was expected to do, but she had always approached it with the same genial indifference she did with most chores.

He could not really blame her, though. Godomar had been furious as they disembarked on this strange Frankisc shore, raving about his god cursing their voyage. A sudden storm had come from the north, heaving the ship and soaking them all to the skin and giving them all a good fright. No one had been lost, and the storm was over almost as quickly as it had begun, but Godomar was in a rage as Sunniva spent the remainder of the journey leaning over the gunwale.

Sige had joked with a green and shaky Sunniva about Thunor being cross about something, and Godomar had shot them both a furious look.

"That storm was not the work of some pagan superstition," he had muttered angrily, "it was almighty God taking out his vengeance upon me for bringing a pagan woman to be my wife."

"Please," Sunniva said gently, still rather pale and sick-looking, "It was just a storm." She touched his arm but he jerked it away.

"I do not think that storm was mere chance. The seas should still be clear at this time of the year. I am sure that God is sending me a message that I must not marry a pagan."

Sige frowned, but said nothing.

"Is that what this is about?" Sunniva asked understandingly, "that is no matter. I can become a Christian if you wish."

Godomar brightened immediately, as if he had been waiting for this response. "I think that would be wise. There are no noble women here who are pagans. It would make the people uneasy if their lady did not share their faith." The slick tone of his voice was slowly returning. "Yes, my treasure, I think it would be best."

And so only days later Sige and his men stood on the edge of a frigid river, somewhat separated from Godomar's family and retainers. Sunniva had a sour look on her face as if she might be sick, and he could see her shivering as she stood in the waist-deep water.

The priest, a man just shy of his middle years with pale reddish-gold hair and a build like a warrior, gave her a gentle smile as he said some prayers in Latin. She flinched away when he moved to rub something on her forehead, and Sige rankled as some of Godomar's household laughed at her.

Sunniva shrieked as the priest bodily pushed her into the water, and Sige tightened his hand on his sword hilt. Before he could do more than think of moving forward, however, the priest had lifted her up and said some more words as she spluttered and dashed water from her eyes.

There was a response from the crowd, as if it had been rehearsed, and though Sunniva seemed to echo the people, Sige kept his lips firmly shut. Sunniva shivered, looking like a drowned rat as one of the women stepped forward with a thick, rabbit-fur lined cloak and wrapped it around Sunniva's shoulders as she waded out of the river, and the assembled company cheered, returning toward the village.

Godomar's hall was no different from any other back home, except perhaps in its opulence. Godomar was rich enough to have a massive hall with a separate bed chamber for himself and his bride, as well as separate sleeping quarters for the *huscarls* – or whatever they called them here – and important guests. Sige and his men slept in the main hall, which suited him well enough. The Frankisc men were suspicious of Sige and his companions, and even though he could understand little of their language, their whispered sneers transcended tongues.

Sunniva disappeared into the bedchamber for the next several hours with some of her serving women. The Franca milled around the hall, talking and greeting those men who had returned with Godomar. Sige could not understand half of what was said, though he was sure at least part of their words concerned him.

He heard the word "*vrouwe*," which he knew to be the Frankisc word for "lady;" he heard Godomar's name several times and even his own name, though the looks on their faces were impassive. He watched as some people spoke to one another genially, and then when one of them turned his back the others stared daggers and whispered behind their hands.

"Overwhelming, isn't it?" Oswy asked.

Sige raised his eyebrows but did not say anything.

"When does the feast start?"

"When Godomar has finished preening, I expect," Sige muttered. "I imagine Sunniva has been ready for hours."

"It will be interesting to see what a Frankisc wedding looks like. You hear stories, but I suppose nothing is like seeing it for yourself."

"A Christian wedding," Sige corrected, though the thought made him want to spit. He did not like the idea of a god of death being invoked to bless a marriage.

"No swords, then?" Oswy asked.

Sige shook his head. "Rædwald gave me one for her, but I doubt they exchange swords here. I think they just make new swords for sons, rather than the mother holding it in trust for him." He unconsciously touched Hryðlig, hanging at his belt. It had been his father's sword; his father had given it to his mother at their wedding, and she had passed it to Sige before his first time fighting in a shield wall. The sword Mother had given to Sigeweald in defense of their family was now buried with him. If the Franca did not exchange swords, what would Sunniva give her son before his first battle? What would Godomar protect his family with? It was a practical exchange of gifts. It was a pact to be sealed. That was the way things were supposed to work.

Someone, perhaps a kinsman of Godomar, raised his voice above the low murmuring in the hall. He said something in an ostentatious tone, and the crowd slowly began to file out of the hall. Sige shrugged at Oswy's questioningly raised eyebrow, and they followed.

"You," a woman tapped Sige's elbow as he made his way outside. She was no higher than his shoulder, but she glared imperiously at him. "You come bride get, now," she said, waving him to follow her. Sige gestured for Oswy to go with the throng, and Sige followed the short woman to Sunniva's bedchamber.

Sunniva still looked queasy, but at least she was dry now. She seemed to be wearing every scrap of jewelry she owned atop her crimson dress. Her hair was braided, but it was covered by a long silk veil which was bound with a fillet studded with gems. She very nearly shone, though her face was blank and pale.

"You're supposed to escort me," she said. "You lead me to the church and give my hand away to Godomar."

Sige nodded, watching as the women fluttered around Sunniva. The latter looked blankly at something far away.

"What's wrong?" he asked, ducking to see her eyes under the veil.

Sunniva shook her head, smiling and seeming to come back to herself. "Just nerves. I don't really know what to expect. Godomar explained a little to me, though. I'll tell you what to do."

Sige led his sister by the arm out of the hall, while the women followed behind in a procession toward the chapel, about a hundred paces away. Everyone was clustered around the mouth of the stone building, watching them approach; Godomar was standing at their head next to a man Sige recognized as the priest who had baptized Sunniva; Godomar watched Sunniva as if she were a particularly fine horse being brought for his inspection. Sige reflexively tightened his arm around Sunniva's, and she squeezed it, glancing up at him and smiling reassuringly.

The priest spoke words to the crowd, though in Latin rather than Frankisc. The people watched respectfully, though Sige was half-certain that none of the people present would understand the words any better than he did.

"You put my hand in Godomar's," Sunniva whispered to Sige, and he did as she told him. The priest led the couple into the chapel, and the assembled folk followed after them.

Sige was pushed to the side of the small stone building, though he could still see Sunniva and Godomar kneeling at a rail in front of the ornate gold cross. She had her head bowed, her hands folded in the same way as Godomar. The priest appeared with a gold cup, touching Godomar's forehead before giving him a piece of bread, saying more words in Latin, and then offering Godomar the cup. Sige could see Sunniva watching the *graf*, and she copied his movements as the priest turned to her and repeated the sequence.

More Latin, and the priest nodded to Godomar, who lifted his bride to her feet. She moved stiffly – surely her knees must be aching – and Godomar took her hands in his. As Sige had expected, they had no call for swords. No gifts were exchanged at all, though Godomar and Sunniva both responded with something affirmative-sounding when the priest put a question to them. It sounded vaguely like a marriage vow, though he could just as well have been asking their opinion on honey cakes.

Godomar kissed Sunniva on the mouth before the people in the chapel began to cheer, and the ceremony was over. Godomar looked as if he had just received a grand gift and wished to show it off, while Sunniva was blushing so furiously her cheeks threatened to blend with her scarlet dress.

The priest led the pair of them out of the chapel again and into the square, where they filed back toward the hall. Sige felt a squirming in his guts when Godomar enteredl first, leading Sunniva by the hand. He caught Oswy's eye at the way they had entered their home as a married couple.

"It's just the way they do things here," Sige said, more to reassure himself than for Oswy's sake. "They don't know that it's bad luck. I'm sure it doesn't mean anything."

There was the usual exhchange of gifts and pleasantries before any food or drink was offered, and it took Sige a long time to make his way to his sister. She sat beside her husband at the high table, looking pleasurably flustered as she glanced over at her new husband. Sige had never wondered what Sunniva saw in the man; he was excessively handsome and had the most refined manners of anyone Sige had ever known. She had the same look on her face that her silly friends often got when looking at Rægen, though on Sunniva the expression was strangely off-putting.

Godomar meanwhile looked at her as if she were one of the jewels at her throat, glancing around the hall as if to make sure no eye strayed from the beauty of his new bride.

Sige pushed through the mass of people, waiting his turn to speak to Sunniva. He withdrew the trinket from his belt pouch; heavy iron the size of his palm and beaten into the shape of a hammer. There were sun-wheels and runes carved into the metal; images in miniature of Thunor's iron hammer in the *weoh* at home. He was not sure what made him lower his voice when he reached her seat, but he decided that he did not want Godomar to hear.

"I know that Christians do not think it is important," Sige said, placing the hammer in Sunniva's lap. She smiled as she looked down, putting her hands carefully over the hammer and pressing it to her belly.

"Our mother, and her mother before her, carried one like this," he said quietly, "To give your children strength. I had it made in Lundenwic before we left. It's not the prettiest thing, but I think it must work; Mother did have you, after all."

Sunniva beamed, tears springing into her eyes as she pressed it to her. "Thank you, Sige," she said, tucking the amulet surreptitiously into the ornately decorated purse at her belt before it coul draw Godomar's attention.

A feast of staggering proportions was offered once the pomp and ceremony had been completed, and Sige and his men were able to forget their unease for a while as they ate and drank together. A hall was a hall, in the end. Wine was wine, and meat tasted good no matter where they were sitting.

Sige hoped for another chance to speak to Sunniva, and as he had finished laughing at a jest of Oswy's he turned to find her beaming at them.

"I hope you are enjoying yourselves," she told them. All of these men had known her from the time she was small, and they all looked at her almost as their own sister. They nodded and thanked her and her husband, and she sat with Sige for a while.

"Does it feel different, being a Christian?" Sige asked.

Sunniva shrugged. "Not really. The baptism was a little… strange."

"You looked like you were about to murder that priest for getting you wet."

"It was just cold," Sunniva laughed, "Convenient, though, as I needed a bath anyway." She seemed to notice his look of unease.

"Don't tell Mother," she said.

Sige had to laugh at that. "If you wish."

She grinned, but her smile faded quickly and she still looked as if she might be sick.

"Are you feeling quite well?" Sige asked.

"Of course I am," Sunniva hesitated just long enough for him to know that she was lying. "I'm just tired. It's been a busy day."

They were interrupted by her husband, who took her away by the arm in order to meet someone. Sige watched from a distance, still feeling uneasy. She did not look well. She had bags under her eyes and her face was sallow and yet her cheeks were flushed as with fever. Surely a dunk in a cold river could not make her ill so quickly.

A man appeared at Godomar's side, so similar to the *graf* in looks that Sige was sure he was a kinsman; greyer of face and hair and somewhat shorter, though more heavily muscled than Godomar.

"Right little ray of sunshine, that one is," said Oswy, who was looking at the scowling newcomer. "Who is he?"

"It must be Godomar's brother," Sige said, "Walaric. Sunniva told me that even though Godomar is the *ealdorman*, he doesn't command his own forces, instead his brother commands the army so Godomar can see to matters of state. Sunniva said Walaric is the justice as well, though I am not sure what that entails."

"Well, I suppose he looks like a commander," Oswy conceded, "But I'd follow that man into battle about as quickly as I would a hedgehog." The other men barked in laughter and Sige raised an eyebrow.

"You don't like him?" Oswy asked.

"I don't like any of this," said Sige, and drained his cup.

There was little enough to do here; Sigebryht felt out of place and useless as he and his men practiced swordplay and awaited instruction from Godomar – or his brother, in reality. There was supposed to be an imminent threat to Godomar's lands, and yet Godomar seemed to be more interested in parading his pretty new wife around to visit his *thegns* than to do anything useful. Mustering troops would take weeks, and Sigebryht knew almost nothing about Godomar's plans for the future. All he could do was to keep his men honed and battle-ready, and wait.

Sunniva seemed to have been consistently shut away or carted along with Godomar, and the moments that Sige spent with his sister were few and far between. She seemed to be growing more and more pale and tired-looking, but after the fourth or fifth deflection of his questions, Sige stopped asking. She did not smile much anymore, and he missed it. She had always been so clever, always making him laugh. He missed her. He missed his home. He missed Edwin. He channeled his anger and frustration into training his men, but it did nothing to relieve the throbbing pain that Edwin's absence had left in him, or the unease that came from watching his little sister paraded about like some exotic treasure.

The priest who had baptized Sunniva made an appearance at the edge of the practice yard one morning, and seemed enthralled with Sige's men, who were pummeling one another with dulled weapons.

Sige watched his men for a while, trying to ignore the spectator, but the priest stood too close not to acknowledge his presence.

"It is fascinating, isn't it?" said the priest, surprisingly in Englisc. "The interplay of body and weapon. It is an art, isn't it?"

Sige nodded, surprised out of his indifference. "I don't often meet priests who enjoy the world of battle," he said, "and it is even more seldom that I meet one who speaks my language here in this land."

The priest smiled, and looked almost ashamed with himself. "The art of battle has always interested me. As for the language, I have made it my work to study all manner of tongues, so that I might better serve the Lord. My name is Mathias."

"I'm called Sigebryht. I am honored to meet you, Father."

"I have noticed that you and your men seem to be having some difficulty in learning our language. I imagine this is causing you some distress?"

Sigebryht nodded. "It certainly doesn't help matters."

"Might I offer my service as a tutor? I have already agreed to instruct Vrouwe Sunniva in the language, and it would be no trouble to include you in our lessons."

Sige grinned for the first time in what felt like years. "I would like that very much," he said. It would give him a chance to talk to his sister, as well as to receive vital tutelage in the language. It was not simply a matter of understanding the gossip; communication was vital in a battle, and one misunderstood word could mean the difference between life and death.

"Tell me, Sigebryht," said Mathias, "I know that the *vrouwe* was not a member of our faith upon her arrival here in Heldergem. Might I be correct in assuming that you and your men prefer to pray to the old gods?"

Sige tensed, knowing where the conversation was headed. "Does it matter?"

"Not really," Mathias said. "As much as I would wish that all of God's children could be brought into the fold, I know that many still cling to the beliefs of their fathers."

Sige could not help but smile. He had met with a great deal of hostility regarding religion ever since he had arrived in Francland. He was unable to make sacrifices to any of the gods as there were no temples or Sacred Oaks, and he felt as if the eyes of everyone in Heldergem were watching him, waiting for a misstep.

"Might I offer a suggestion?" asked Mathias. When Sige nodded, he said, "If you require a place to pray, there is a fine grove of trees not far from here where some of the peasants still worship in the old way, in secret. If you leave by the north gate, it is only a mile or so along the river. I don't know how they practice in Engla-land, but if you wish to retreat quietly out into the grove on occasion, it will not be hard to find."

"Why are you telling me this?"

Mathias glanced at the men practicing their swordplay, and then back to Sige. He seemed to scrutinize him for a moment, and then smiled. "I know what a comfort it is to have a degree of normality when things are strange. It is my duty to lessen the suffering of those around me, and you are clearly suffering."

He could not deny this. "I thank you," he said, and added without thinking, "I have nothing against your Christ."

"That is good to know, Sigebryht," Mathias said.

"I only mean to say," Sige was flustered, and his mouth was running away without him. "That he is probably a good god, for you. But he is not my god."

Mathias nodded. "I understand. I hope that you might come to know him in time, but until then, you know where the grove is. I will see you soon for your lessons."

*****

She was naked, covered only to the waist with a blanket, as calloused fingers brushed between her breasts. She did not open her eyes, but let the fingers continue their wandering, joined after a moment by the scratch of a beard against her belly. She felt her lips curving into a satisfied smile, surrendering to the touch.

Sunniva let the rough hands explore her body, inside and out, until she thought she would die from waiting. She reached between her legs to run her fingers through his hair, which she knew would be the color of rusted iron…

Sunniva's eyes snapped open.

The man beside her stirred slightly, his back rising and falling as he lay on his stomach. She leaned on an elbow, looking at the golden hair and the strong muscles of his back. He really was staggeringly beautiful.

Sunniva stared at him, clearing her mind of the images of a moment before. Godomar's hands were gentle and soft. Why would she ever have preferred the rough callouses and the scratching beard and the waving coarse hair that she tangled her fingers in as he—

She shook her head this time, but licked her lips all the same. She could feel the slickness between her legs and she knew that it was not all her husband's doing. The dream had sent her blood racing, and she forced herself to look at the handsome man lying beside her.

It was not his fault that she had been so hesitant. He did not know that she liked to be touched, to be teased a bit before. It was not his fault that it had hurt. How was he to know that Sunniva wanted to find release as surely as he had done, when he had groaned and rolled off of her? She could have told him what she wanted, but she simply did not.

In truth, she had been so distracted that she had not thought to ask him to keep touching her. He had looked down between them, an edge of concern creasing his eyebrows.

"I thought you would have bled." He might have been frowning, but she could not tell for certain.

She shrugged, wondering why it made a difference. Her blood always came on the full moon; was this some Christian superstition?

"It is not my time," she said, trying to pull him closer. She wanted more of those kisses, so sweet and warm, but he pulled away from her.

"I was assured you were a maiden."

"I am," she had the lie ready, though she still could not understand why it mattered. For some reason, she felt it better to pretend that those nights with Ecgric had never happened – those nights when she would arch her back in ecstasy as he made love to her again and again – no, those were better left unremembered, if not for her own sake, then for Godomar's peace of mind.

"That is to say," she looked up coyly through her eyelashes at him, "I was, until tonight."

He smiled at her, stroking her cheek.

"I am sorry," she continued, "that I had no maidenhead to break. It happened while I was riding." It was not entirely a lie this time.

"My little treasure," he said, "Think nothing of it. Plenty of women do not bleed the first time. I am told that it does not hurt so much, once you get used to it."

"You are very kind," she said sweetly. She took the hand that he was using to stroke her cheek and bit her bottom lip as she tried to lead it down where she really wanted it, but he only smiled at her and lay down on his back, putting his hands behind his head.

It was not his fault. He did not know.

Sunniva watched him sleeping now, wondering if he might rouse himself and have her again. She reached out a hand, stroking his back.

"What is it?" he asked suddenly.

Sunniva kissed him, drawing a finger down his chest. "I only wondered," she began, but he took hold of her wandering hand.

"Not now," he said, "I am tired."

"That is unfortunate," she said, biting her lower lip and moving her hand again, "Because I am wide awake..."

His fingers were firmer around hers. "You do not want to seem overexcited. It is unbecoming."

She froze, drawing her hand back. "I did not think –"

"Do not worry, my little treasure. I am more than satisfied. Please think nothing of it." He kissed her, and she melted into his embrace. They would have a lifetime to get to know one another. It would not always be this way. The awkwardness would fade over time. She was happy if he was happy.

Sunniva settled into his arms, and he brushed her hair away from her face before she heard the heavy sounds of his breathing as he fell asleep. He really was so very kind to her.

*****

Eadyth was certain that if she gripped the arm of her chair any harder, it might turn to dust in her hand. She wanted to scream, but she sat silently with her teeth tightly clenched as Ricbert told her what had happened. Rædwald looked as if he might throw something.

"When was this?" Eadyth asked.

"Twenty days, now," said Ricbert. "Eastmund was shot in the back and barely made it home. He did not know what had happened; only that the others never made it back to meet him. The boy was delirious with fever and he died before he could tell us precisely where they had been. We haven't found the others, dead or alive."

Eadyth shuddered and tried not to think of the possibilities. Either her son, together with his companions, had been killed and left to rot somewhere out in the wilderness, or they were the captives of Northumbrian *weargas*. Either option was repulsive to her. "Surely you've sent someone else to look for them?"

Ricbert rarely showed emotion, but now he looked aggrieved. "We've found no sign of the Northumbrians' c//amp, or of Eorwald or his men."

Rædwald had stood up and looked as if he might murder Ricbert where he stood. "You were supposed to take care of him!" Rædwald shouted, "He was under your protection, and now he is gone!"

Ricbert did not say anything, and had the good sense to look rightly ashamed.

"I trusted you," Rædwald said, more quietly now but with anger she had rarely heard in his voice.

"Stop this," Eadyth said, feeling more exhausted than she had done in years, and putting her hand on Rædwald's arm so that he would not bodily injure Ricbert. "Eorwald acted as we would have expected him to act. He did not want his friends to go into danger without him. I know two men who would have done the same thing."

Rædwald shot a furious glance at Ricbert, but snorted as if to agree with Eadyth. "You seem awfully calm about this," he told her.

"On the contrary," Eadyth said, "I have half a mind to run screaming from this hall right now. But I also know that we can't do anything without a plan."

"Do you know which way they were headed?" asked Rædwald.

"Northwest of here, that's all I know," said Ricbert. "They were just going to walk straight along the river. I imagine the Northumbrian camp is close by the river, but we cannot know how far. None of the other men have been able to find it."

"Very well," said Rædwald, still looking angrily at his oldest friend, "Get Ecgric and tell him to gather some men together. We will –" he suddenly stopped, and looked out the door to the hall, where a young man had stumbled in.

"Dryhten!" the man panted, "Please, you must come quickly! There are men coming from the North, about a mile away. They say that they have the *ætheling*!"

Eadyth was stiff with anxiety as they mounted their horses and set off. Surely enough, barely a mile north of Mæduwic there was a line of several mounted men, as well as a full shield wall, waiting for them. A white-haired man kicked his horse forward, raising his hand in greeting to Rædwald.

"*Wes ðu hal!*" said the white-haired man. He was smiling genially, but his tone was like ice. "I command the army here. I assume you are the great Rædwald Cyning of the Engla. I've heard a great deal about you!"

Rædwald might have been made of stone as he sat atop his horse. "Who are you?" He stared at the Northumbrian, waiting for him to speak again.

"I am called Hwitegos," said the man, "At least, you may call me that."

A stupid name for a commander, Eadyth thought dully, but she could see now that he was not an old man at all despite the nearly white hair. His icy grin, his freezing eyes, and his straight-backed coldness nearly set her teeth chattering.

Rædwald simply glared ahead, and Hwitegos seemed to take the hint that the king was in no mood to bandy words.

"I will not bore you with pleasantries, noble *cyning.* I believe we have something of yours," he paused theatrically, looking over his shoulder at the line of mounted men standing a short distance behind him. The one in the center had his head covered in a sack, and his arms were bound in front of him and he was hunched as if he might topple from his horse at any moment.. Eadyth's stomach turned over as she realized who it must be.

"We happened upon some vagrants who claimed to be hunting in the woods near our encampment," explained Hwitegos, as casually as if he had been commenting on the weather, "Of course, we knew this was not true; after a bit of prodding we came to find that one of the spies we captured was none other than the Englisc *cyning's* son!" Hwitegos gave a mirthless laugh that chilled Eadyth's heart. "Naturally, we knew that we could not simply kill him as we had done the others, so we decided to see if the great Rædwald of the Wuffingas would like to strike a bargain for the life of his son."

"Why have they covered his face?" Rægenhere asked Eadyth. His voice had a note of panic, as if he worried that they had done some irreparable harm to his brother.

"I expect that they didn't want him to see the way they had come, or he'd tell us where their camp was," Eadyth invented wildly as Hwitegos continued his story. She felt the same sinking feeling that she knew Rægen was experiencing.

"Enough of your prattle," Rædwald shouted at Hwitegos. "You will surrender the *ætheling* to me now, or your men will be slaughtered and your heads put on pikes as a warning to the rest of your kind."

Hwitegos tutted. "That is a rather rude thing to say, and hardly good form for a hostage negotiation. I think you are forgetting that your son is in our power, and your ill-mannered words might mean the end of his life."

"How do I even know that it is the *ætheling*?" Rædwald asked. "You could have anyone there. Show me his face."

Hwitegos shook his head, smiled and brought forth a sword belt. "It would do little good to show you his face," the white man said, "I am sorry, but my men can be a little… overzealous. I think this will do as identification." The seax sheath was empty, but the sword still remained in its scabbard, the leather of the belt wrapped around it. The sight of the claw-shaped pommel caused Rægen to gasp, though Eadyth shot a terrified look back at him to shut him up.

I see you recognize the blade," Hwitegos said. "In any case, your son told us what we needed to know. Not that he can tell us much now; we did end up having to loosen his tongue." Some of the men chuckled at this, and Eadyth's blood froze.

"What do you want?" Rædwald asked through gritted teeth. He had never been able to remain calm where his children were concerned, and Eadyth silently willed him to keep his temper lest they harm Eorwald.

"Oh, great *cyning*," said Hwitegos, "I am only a servant of my *dryhten* Athelfrith, and I cannot make demands. Although I think we both know what he wants. If you were to stop this game, this posturing, he would be very grateful. We all know that your cause is doomed;" he added in a soft voice, "Why make this harder than it needs to be?"

"These are Englisc lands," said Rædwald, "Athelfrith will never rule here."

"That remains to be seen, but we are getting ahead of ourselves. I think for now perhaps you might think the life of your son is worth a token. We will take Mæduwic off of your hands, and you may have the *ætheling* back."

"You're out of your mind," said Rædwald.

"A silly little market town in exchange for the future ruler of the Engla?" Hwitegos raised an eyebrow, "forgive me, but it seems that I am not the one who is out of my mind."

Eadyth looked across at the figure she knew was her son. She wished she could see his face, that he could see her and know that everything would be well. But as she watched him, she saw him shake his sack-covered head as if to tell them not to accept the terms. She pulled her horse beside that of her husband and gave him a meaningful look.

"Your son will die," said Hwitegos, "are you sure you want that to happen?"

"Father, please," someone said, but it was not Eorwald's voice. It was Rægen. "You can't let them kill him!"

Eadyth silenced him with a sharp look and then caught her husband's eye. It nearly wrenched her heart out of her chest to tell him, "If our son dies, it will be as a brave *ætheling* who did his duty in defense of his home, and he would never allow us to accept such terms." She saw him swallow hard; heard Rægen's horse stepping anxiously behind them.

"I will not negotiate with you or your kind," Rædwald said, "Leave these lands or there will be war."

Hwitegos shrugged. "Have it your own way, then." He turned his horse, trotting the few paces back to the prisoner. He removed Weargbana and cast the sword belt aside, and drove the point into his captive's chest.

Eadyth did not remember falling from her horse, but she hit the ground running as a scream was torn from her lungs and into the wind. She heard, rather than saw, the body fall from its horse and hit the ground; she heard Rægen screaming Eorwald's name, and heard the hooves of horses thunder away as ten or so of her own men on horseback followed at a gallop after them.

Eadyth fell to his side as she heard the hooves and footsteps of people behind her. Blood had started to appear on the wool of his shirt, his chest moving feebly around the sword blade buried in his ribs. She could barely grip the sack as she pulled it off of his head.

Another shriek of mingled horror, grief and indescribable relief left her. It was not Eorwald.

She realized that Rægen was beside her, and with a swift motion he had cut the bonds around Leofric's wrists. Rægen placed the seax in Leofric's hand, and Eadyth could not be sure whose hands were shaking harder. Leofric's eyes were sliding in and out of focus, his mouth bubbling with blood as he mouthed the words "my boy, my boy."

"I'll tell your son how brave his father was," said Rægen, clasping the dying man's hand. Eadyth could not speak, and watched Leofric shake his head and mouth more words. He was grabbing the section of Weargbana's blade which was sticking out of his chest, the sharp edge cutting his hand. He spoke again, and though his speech was strangled and hoarse, she could understand the single word.

"Eorwald?" she breathed, and Leofric nodded.

"Is he alive?" asked Rægen frantically.

Leofric gave a tiny nod and Eadyth let out an involuntary cry.

Leofric's body shook as Rægen held his hand around the handle of the seax. Even though he had been murdered by a coward, he would die with a sword in his hand. Eadyth prayed that one of the *Wælcyrigena* would find him and see him safely to Woden's hall, as she vowed retribution on the foul *wearg* who had sent him there.

Rægen met Eadyth's eyes, his mouth a furious line and his hand clenched around Leofric's. He dropped his eyes down to those of his dead companion, which he closed. "Go happily to the Feast," he said; his face a mask of confusion and horror and grim determination as he carefully removed his brother's sword from his friend's chest.

*****

Mathias's suggestion turned out to be fruitful, and Sige was grateful for the opportunity to escape the frenzied activity of the great hall and disappear into the grove. There were no statues or altars, but there was a clear spring into which people would deposit offerings, usually of glass beads or trinkets if they could afford them, or small wooden carvings or food if they could not. He never saw anyone there, which suited him well enough. Most of the locals had taken the nailed god, and though he was sure that many still followed the old ways in secret, none would wish to receive the ire of their lord by making offerings to the "pagan devils," as the Christians so often called them.

Sige had not seen is sister in days, as she had been visiting one of Godomar's retainers with her husband. She returned only that morning, looking as if she wanted a month's worth of sleep.

He invited her to go to the grove with him, and was prepared to pull rank as her elder brother if she would not go. She was far too tired-looking, far too subdued; it was not like her at all. A few moments of solitude in the presence of natural stillness would help to ease whatever anxiety she must be feeling, surely.

He had not expected her to agree, and he was pleased as she walked with him in silence along the leaf-littered path. There was a perfect stillness in this place; the autumn sun was still bright and forced its way through the leaves of the ancient trees, creating patterns on the mossy ground. Eventually the lane opened to a meadow, ringed by tall, ghostly grey beech trees with an ash at the far end. No breeze ruffled the surface of the water, and Sunniva stood as hard and still as the deep pool.

Only after she had stood for a long while, looking into the clear depths of the spring, did she say, “Thank you for bringing me here, Sige.”

Sige watched her shrewdly for a moment. “Why won’t you tell me what’s wrong?”

“Nothing is wrong,” Sunniva said.

“You’re lying.”

She glared at him, but a slight smile played across her lips and her normal brisk tone hinted at returning. “Where is this attentiveness when you lose to me at dice?”

“There’s a big difference between lying to other people, and lying to yourself,” he said. “I can tell that you are unhappy.”

Sunniva swallowed. “I think it’s just taking a while to get into a rhythm here. I had thought that my marriage to Godomar would be… I think we are still getting used to one another. He is so very kind to me, so attentive…” She said lamely.

Sige could hear the wealth of information that she was leaving unsaid. “It is hard to be so far from home, so far from the people we care about,” He said unhelpfully.

"Well, I'm glad you're here," Sunniva said, "I think I'd be quite lost if I were alone." He put an arm around her and she sniffed and half-smiled. "It's hard, isn't it? Having to wonder if you'll ever see him again? Unsure if you haven’t made a terrible mistake?”

“You miss Ecgric, don’t you?” he asked, trying to ignore the way she had said it and the knowing look she was giving him.

“No,” she said quietly, as if trying to convince herself of the fact. “I don’t know. I miss how we were. It was like a game then, and I think I miss that. But I did care about him, and I wish Ecgric could know that. I left things so badly with him, and I don’t want him to think I did this out of spite, but I know that’s the way he will take it.”

Sige did not know what to tell her that could possibly make anything better, so he simply listened as she let the floodgates open.

"He asked me if I loved him," she said. "The night before he left to collect the *fyrd*. We had a row, and I was so angry with him, so I told him that I did not."

"But you lied," Sige finished for her.

Sunniva nodded and chewed her lip. "I did love him. Maybe I still do. I don't know anymore. I thought that I knew what I wanted." She looked down at her hands, and Sige noticed her twisting a large silver ring around her finger. "At least you got to say goodbye," she said miserably. "At least you left Edwin knowing that you loved him."

Sige's insides turned to ice.

Sunniva gave him a watery smile and rolled her eyes. "Oh come now, don't look so appalled. I don't care what you get up to at night. Anyway, who would I tell? It's not as if I have any friends here. Every one of these Frankisc cows seems to hate me."

"I know the feeling," Sige said bitterly. "Sometimes I wonder if we didn't make a huge mistake coming here at all. I came here to help fight Godomar's enemies, and yet it seems enemies surround us even in his hall. We should never have gotten involved with foreigners."

"You know it was for the best," she said, but she was clearly uncertain herself. "It will all be well in the end, you'll see. You'll be able to go home soon."

"I won't leave you until I know you are settled," Sige said at the despondent look she gave him. She wiped her eyes on her sleeve and composed herself before they turned and began to walk back toward the great hall.

They had left the wood and were not far from the village's palisades, when a loud voice caused Sunniva to jump.

"Where have you been?" shouted Godomar from half a furlong away, storming toward them in a rage.

"We've just been for a walk," Sunniva said brightly. "It was such a lovely day that –"

"I expect you to be at my side to welcome our guests," Godomar said in a measured voice when he drew closer, "and when my friends asked after my fair wife, I could not find her. You have embarrassed me. What was I supposed to say? That my bride was prancing around in the wilderness with some strange man?"

"I was with my brother, not some strange man" she said, "There was no need to –"

"I don't care," said Godomar flatly. "I have told you that I do not want you leaving the village without my knowledge." He shot a venomous look at Sige as if Sige was some sort of *ælf*, stealing Sunniva away to do some magic upon her.

The two men glared at one another, Sunniva put her hand on Sige's arm with a look that seemed to say, *it's not worth the fight.*

"Of course," she said, and Sige watched as his spirited, defiant sister walked meekly back to the village with her husband.

*****

Hwitegos had taken almost the entire army on his errand after they had moved camp for the second time. He was sure they had not gone far, but they had covered his eyes and ears each time they threw him onto the wagon, and he could not have told East from West in the dim forest even if he had tried.

Eorwald wanted to believe that the pale man would keep his word and would ransom Leofric back to the king, but a nagging feeling was eating away at his stomach and made him queasy. He was certain that Hwitegos knew more than he was letting on. He was cruel and dangerous, but he was clever. Hwitegos would always look several steps ahead, adjusting the circumstances so that they would always be in his favor. Eorwald had laid the false trail, but how soon before Hwitegos realized it? If Hwitegos discovered Eorwald's lies before Leofric was safe… he did not want to think of it.

He would have to get away from the Northumbrians as well, but that was a much harder feat to accomplish. There were hardly any men still at the camp, but even so, Eorwald was weakened by the infection slowly creeping from the arrow wound. He could barely stand, let alone fight his way out of the camp.

"Get up," a harsh voice said. Eorwald assumed that his usual guard had gone away with Hwitegos. At least the kick in Eorwald's back was the same as always.

Eorwald did not get up. He remained lying on his back, half-covered in the cloak and fully covered in a layer of sweat. He had shivered through the night, slipping into half-remembered fever dreams filled with blood and sickness. He fought to wake from them, but when he did, he realized the living world was little better.

"I said, get up!" The man shouted, and Eorwald got shakily to his feet. It was unseasonably cold, and he felt the bite of a chill wind even as heat rose from the wound on his leg. He was able to reach the cesspit, but the guard jumped back in disgust as Eorwald fell to his knees and the meagre contents of his stomach found their way out.

"Ugh," said the guard, "Just... just hurry it up."

Eorwald got to his feet and the guard shoved him back to the camp once more, where he found the cloak and lay shivering beneath it. He dimly registered his surprise that the guard had neglected to re-bind his hands, and Eorwald was careful to keep his back to the man lest he remember that the prisoner was still unbound. The guard settled with a grunt not far away, huffing and puffing irritably about such a charge.

A few hours passed in slow, shuddering silence, Eorwald heard voices behind him.

"Bloody waste of time, this is," said the guard. "Bastard's half-dead. Puked all over my shoes and all. Might as well just cut his throat and have done."

"Hwitegos wants 'im alive," said the other, "In case the negotiations go ill."

"I ought to stick him again for fouling up my boots," the first man grumbled.

"Ah, just leave 'im," said the second man, "come on into the warm. Looks like rain tonight, and you'll want something hot and wet, eh?" He chuckled at his little joke, and Eorwald was sure he was making some rude gesture. "A few more lasses arrived last night. Thank the gods for giving us whores," he said with relish.

Eorwald tried not to groan, lest he draw attention to his unbound hands. He lost his thoughts in the memory of Rian's blue eyes, her thin arms draped around him, her smile...

He realized with a jolt that he was alone. For the first time, he was alone and unbound. Was he really that close to death, that they did not bother keeping their guard on him? He hesitantly peeked over his shoulder to where the guard might have sat, but the tree stump was vacated. He saw the glow of firelight beyond several tents. The tents would be empty, he knew, their occupants going south with Hwitegos and the supposed *ætheling*.

He knew that it was mad, that it would never work, that he was too sick to get far before they slit his throat. He was going to die anyway. At least this way it would be quick.

He waited as the sky began to grow dim and the laughter of the men grew louder. Carefully, as if he might have been a shadow, he got to his feet. He remained stooped behind the eye-line of the tents. It was almost too easy, he realized; a clear shot into the wood. The drizzle of the past few days would mean that the leaves would be wet and soft, and though he would be more likely to leave footprints, he would be able to run silently over the spongy ground.

He hurried forward, still crouching and gritting his teeth at the hot pain in his leg.

There was movement not far away to his right, and Eorwald froze. He felt dizzy and his heart pounded as he backed away several paces back into the line of tents, before realizing how close we was to the two guards who had left him earlier.

"Won't matter much in any case," one of the men was saying. "I'm rather hoping the negotiations go sour and then Hwitegos will let us have some fun with 'em. It'll be good sport, eh? Maybe a bit more target practice? I feel it's my solemn duty to finally make the brute squeak."

"We was having good target practice before," grumbled another of the guards. "I'd rather get rid of both of 'em. That big one, 'e's been nothing but a nuisance. I'd not mind putting a couple more holes in 'im."

"Ah, he ain't got long anyhow," said the other. "If he weren't such a pain in my arse, I'd put 'im out of his misery. Colred got 'im with one o'his arrows, and you know them arrows is tainted. Nasty way to die, but I'm happy to let 'im go slow."

"D'ya reckon Hwitegos will kill the *ætheling* if the Englisc *cyning* don't want 'im?"

"Bound to. Bastard's useless now."

"What do you think we'll get for 'im?" the thinner voice asked.

One of them made a disparaging noise. “We’d be lucky to get a *scylling*. The Fen-scum’ve got no honor, no family loyalty. Besides, Rædwald won’t want ‘im after what we done to ‘im. D’ya hear ‘im try to talk?” he laughed, and made a grotesque sound of someone gurgling and attempting to speak.

As it had done at Ealdham, the color of the world seemed to go from dull brown to vivid, blood red. Eorwald forgot the pain and the sickness; it was as if the world had slowed to a stop as he stepped into the ring of light from the fire and found the guard’s head in his hands. He twisted and the guard’s neck snapped like a dry twig. The other barely had time to shout in alarm and draw his sword before Eorwald wrenched it out of his hand and buried it in the guard’s guts. He clamped his hand over the guard’s mouth and watched as the lights left his eyes.

Retrieving the blood-soaked blade and still feeling the cold sense of purpose mingling with the heat of the poison coming from his leg, he found a second, larger group of men carousing with their camp followers not far away. They stood in alarm, their wenches sliding from their laps, and came at him with blades drawn. In a slow, calculated dance, he felt their lives end on his stolen sword. They rushed him and he held them off, while the women shrieked and huddled together in fear.

Eorwald dimly registered the dead men lying in the pool of blood at his feet, and walked past the knot of frightened women, all of whom stared at him as if he were death itself.

He turned, seeing the half-illuminated camp turn slowly back to brown, dimly registering the blood of fifteen men spattering his face and hands, terrified women cowering together and knowing he could end them all where they stood.

He ran.

His leg stabbed with pain with every step, but he ran. The leaves muffled his footfalls, and he breathed in the cold air as if it were strong drink. He did not stop. He could not stop. If he stopped, they would find him. He had killed every man who had crossed his path in that camp, but there could have been more. They would see the bodies; see the lake of blood he had created. They would find him. They would burn him and beat him and shoot him with more poisoned arrows. He would not give them the chance.

The poison began to reach his heart, but he ran as if each step would pump it out again. He gasped as he suddenly fell forward into the muddy water of a stream, the icy flow cooling his burning leg and energizing him, washing the blood from his hands. He sucked in mouthfuls of the water, and walked in the shallow bank downstream.

The moon was veiled by clouds, a gentle drizzle falling into the stream. He began to shiver, but kept walking. His leg ached and burned even in the icy water, and his feet began to grow numb as they sucked through the mud of the stream bed. But still he walked, as quickly as he possibly could, making his way down the muddy river.

The stream bed eventually became too deep, and he left it to walk through the tall grass of the meadow. And then he fell to his knees, shaking and numb with cold, and crawled, until the veil of clouds drew away from the moon. He had reached the shelter of another stand of trees, and with the last ounce of strength he possessed; he dragged himself into a tangle of thorn bushes. He did not know if the thicket would offer enough shelter. He did not care. He did not feel the wound anymore. He did not feel the pain in his back or the scratch of the thorns against his skin. All he could feel was the poison, and he let it consume his body like fire.

Chapter Eighteen
Broðru
Brothers

Gieva did not know Leofric well, but she knew from Rægen's accounts that he was a good man, and fiercely loyal to the *æthelingas*. He had been strong, young and hale with an entire life yet to live, with a wife and a young son who would still need him.

It was only once she had cleaned his battered body that she found how badly he had been tormented. It wasn't just the fact that they had broken his jaw and cut out his tongue; his torso was covered in bruises and burns and welts; his eye was blackened, and she found the broken head of an arrow embedded in his thigh, as if someone had simply yanked out the shaft rather than removing the point properly with a knife.

"I can't believe this," she said, choking back tears. "What could he have done to deserve such a death?"

Rægen's face was twisted with anger, but he said nothing. He stood by while Eadyth and Gieva prepared Leofric's body. She cleaned the sword wound as best she could, while Eadyth found clean clothes for him. Eadyth was agitated and seemed to be on the verge of tears at every moment, and Gieva was not surprised. As the queen dressed the dead man, Gieva put her hand on Eadyth's arm.

"It could have been Eorwald," Eadyth said with a ragged voice, "and I am selfish because I am glad that it was not." She touched Leofric's cold face. "And now his child will grow up without a father, and my son may even now be even worse off than this."

"We'll find him," said Rægen, "we are going to find Eorwald. I am going to kill Hwitegos and avenge Leofric, even if I die in the attempt." His voice was strangled with grief and worry.

"Not if I beat you to it," Eadyth said coarsely. "But you don't know that you will find him. He could be dead by now. You heard what that foul Northumbrian said!" Eadyth's voice became frantic in a way that Gieva had never heard before, "He said that they killed the rest of them."

"Leofric said he was alive," said Rægen, "and I will believe that until I am handed Eorwald's body and proven wrong."

Gieva tried not to think of what might have happened to Eorwald, whether he was alive or dead. If they had thought that Leofric was the *ætheling* and had tortured him thus, what could they do to someone they thought of little importance? She shook her head. "He is still alive, I am sure of it," she said at last. "He might have even escaped. We cannot despair."

Rægen shoved his way out of the shelter without another word, and Gieva heard the sound of a pile of firewood being knocked over. She had never seen him so angry, but she decided to let him settle his nerves for a while before going after him. Together, she and Eadyth replaced Leofric's torn clothes and combed his matted hair, and Eadyth said some words of protection for his family.

Gieva emerged from the shelter and sought out Rægen. He was not far away, pacing and biting the inside of his mouth as he always seemed to do when he was distressed.

"He was a good man, and very brave," she said quietly, reaching out to him. "You know you will meet him at the Feast someday."

"I am afraid," he said, as if coming out of a dream, "I am afraid that I've lost my brother, when I should have been here to protect him."

Gieva looked up at him, touching his face and seeing the anguish in his eyes. "This was not your fault, and you know it," she said. "Eorwald was – is – a brave and resilient man, and he will come back to us. I won't let you despair. You will find your brother, and the two of you will fight together again, and avenge the coward who killed your friend."

They both peered past the camp's borders toward the North. After the parley several of Rædwald's men had bolted after the Northumbrians, and six or seven Northmen had not been able to outrun the vengeful Englisc warriors. The heads had been mounted on spikes some distance beyond the camp as a warning to Hwitegos and his kind. The sight of them unnerved Gieva, and she turned her eyes back to Rægen.

"We are going to go north," Rægen said. "The longer we wait, the further Hwitegos will have gotten. I am going to find my brother."

Gieva took a slow breath and nodded. She looked into the grim, furious face that she loved so well and said, "You will find him. You will bring him home."

She knew he would not be back that night, but she kept glancing toward the North as if she might see him riding victoriously back across the river with Eorwald laughing at his side. Eventually it became too dark to see anything, and she retreated to her tent.

She could not sleep alone, and as soon as she saw the sky begin to lighten she pulled a mantle around her shoulders and sat outside. The sun rose higher and higher, and Gieva became more and more restless. She tried spinning, but the thread ended up lumpy and uneven from her lack of concentration, breaking when she tried to twist it too much. She set it aside and walked around the camp for some time, watching the men in restless activity, all waiting for their lords to return. They loved Rægen as much as she did, and she knew they would have gone with him if he had asked, but the party would need to be small to be effective.

She wondered if they might have found Eorwald or his companions by now. Surely they had at least found something, but what if they met with danger on the road? Would there be a fight? She did not want to think about the fact that Rægen was not outfitted for a real battle. Again she found herself at their tent, and set to spinning again, breaking the thread and throwing it aside in frustration. Again she walked around the camp, repeating the cycle until the sun had begun to fall once more.

Just after nightfall, she heard hooves. She dropped her distaff and ran toward the sound, counting the shapes of horses in the dim light of the torches and camp fires. One of the horses bore a rider with a large, person-shaped bundle draped behind him.

"No," said Gieva weakly, covering her mouth, as she noticed the size and shape of the bundle slumped over the horse's back. Rægen jumped down from his own mount, looking grave.

"It's not him," he said hoarsely, not looking at her.

Gieva watched as Rægen's companions took the body from the horse. She could not see the man's face, as he had been wrapped tightly in a cloak.

"Hengest," Rægen said as the men placed the shrouded body on the ground.

Gieva looked from Rægen to the cloak-covered dead man and back again. Rægen was frightening to look at, his normally kind and beautiful face clenched in twisted rage, every muscle in his body taut. She put her arms around him and he squeezed her so tightly she could not draw breath for a moment. She did not care. She held him just as tightly, trying to absorb some of his pain, to lessen his burden.

He finally released her and looked down at the body. "He died fighting. I know that, at least. His wounds tell his story." Rægen put his face in his hands, and ran his fingers through his hair with a long, low groan of frustration. "I don't know where he is, Gieva. I was sure that if we could find their camp, he would be there."

"You found their camp?"

"What was left of it," he said. "There had been a fight. We found at least fifteen bodies – no, none of ours –" he said at the look on her face, "but there was no living person to speak of. We couldn't go on; the light was beginning to fail and we couldn't risk them coming on us in the dark, so we had to leave the trail." He looked at her almost apologetically, as if he needed to explain himself. "We found Hengest's body not far away." He closed his eyes as if driving out a horrid thought.

Gieva glanced back at the cloak-covered body, but tore her eyes away almost immediately. Something was wrong about it, but she could not stand to learn what it was. She did not know what to tell him, and settled herself by putting her arms around him again.

"I've abandoned him," he said, his voice muffled by her shoulder, "I should have been here instead, but I wasn't. I should have protected him, and now he has surely been tortured and torn apart, I know it."

Gieva swallowed the thought, as if it would stop that eventuality from happening. She could not let him despair, though despair began to creep into the edges of her thoughts. "All we can do now is to give the proper respects to Leofric and Hengest. They deserve no less."

Leofric and Hengest would not be buried here, in this place where they had been mutilated and slaughtered. A large, single pyre was built the following day in the field south of Mæduwic, and Gieva watched as the two dead men were laid upon it. She began to cry when she saw Hengest's body, and what the Northumbrian attackers and the decay of time had done to it; she could not look long before she had to tear her eyes away. She wished they could have kept the cloak over him, but she knew that even in death he deserved to see the sky clearly. Gieva was startled when she heard Rægen's voice rend the air, rising above the cracking flames.

Swelces siblingas sceada ofslægen
Sculon singan freondes, sorigende on sele.
Hwæt! Đa fyrdrincas caflice hie farað
Astealdon on ærende wyrd ærest ða onfinde
Đara agristlicra wundena, hiera willum cweðað lastword.
We munon ðara mihtena, mihtig gemynda.
Đa banselas biernað ond beorhtnys us ablænde
Gastas gægniað afre, hwæðre we greotað.
Æfre abiðan in gemynd swa swa æðele ðegnas ær.

Beloved kinsmen, slain by criminals,
Their friends shall sing, sorrowfully in the hall.
Lo! Those warriors, when bravely they went forth
On errand, fate first found them.
Their terrible wounds will speak of their legacy.
We remember their strength, mighty in our memory.
The bodies burn, and blind us with their brightness;
Their spirits will have joy forever,
Though we here grieve.
Ever shall they live in our memories,
As noble *thegns* of old.

When they finally left the pyre, the moon was high and the air was cold and still. While the others returned to the village hall to drink the memory of Hengest and Leofric, Gieva and Rægen walked around the perimeter of the camp toward the lane that led to the Eastern Gate of Mæduwic. She did not ask why; it was clear that for Rægen, the grief was too near for him to make any more songs that night. She took his hand as they walked in silence, hearing the rustle of animals in the dry grass beyond the camp's boundaries. It was eerily quiet on this side of the village's palisade; a bare stretch of fence spread out on one side, abutted by the wide meadow that was now illuminated by the waning moon.

Something rustled in the distance, and Gieva stopped short, listening hard.

"What?" he asked, alarm in his voice.

Gieva held up a hand for him to be silent, and looked ahead to the source of the disturbance. As she trained her eye on the figure through the darkness, it fell face-forward into the waist-high grass. Without thinking she lifted her skirts and ran toward the crater in the grass left by the falling body.

She reached the figure and dropped to her knees beside him. Even in the darkness, the wide shoulders and shaved hair were unmistakable. His legs were caked to the thigh with mud, his shirt filthy and sodden. She pushed his shoulder to roll him over, and pressed her ear to his chest. As she found the heartbeat, she heard him groan. She looked up as Rægen arrived, dropping to his knees in shock.

"And where in the name of Thunor's almighty prick have you been?" Rægen asked his brother, his voice ragged with anger and relief.

Eorwald said nothing, but he groaned again.

"He's burning up," Gieva said when she touched the side of Eorwald's face. His beard and hair were caked in mud, and even in the darkness she could see blood on him. "Can you walk, Eorwald?" she asked him, "we must get inside."

Eorwald nodded, and Rægen helped him to stand on his shaking legs. He limped heavily, favoring his left leg, but Rægen held him upright. "Come along, brother," Rægen said, "I've got you."

*****

Everything was wrong.

Sige watched in frustration as Walaric tried to shout half-hearted encouragement and threats and mocking jeers in turn as the army became steadily more agitated. Sige was no great speaker, but his own men protected their brothers, forming a short but impenetrable line and readying themselves for the fight. The Franca were cohesive in small family groups perhaps, or a few friends together, but nothing even close to what he was used to. They were almost useless as a unit, and Sige could not help but feel panic growing in his own belly at the sight of the other men fidgeting and shooting nervous glances at one another.

Walaric had insisted on breaking up the force into three, and all three shield walls might have been separate armies for the cohesion they showed. A single shield wall was more effective, or perhaps two with the rear being made of archers or spear throwers who could come forward to broaden the wall if needed, and a few men in reserve at the back of the lines to stop anyone who made it through the wall. Sige chewed his lip. The *graf* and his brother had all but begged for Sige's assistance in training their men, but now the efforts would almost certainly be for naught. Walaric would not listen to any of Sige's advice on tactics, and Godomar amicably went along with his brother.

The *huscarls* – or whatever they called themselves here – stood in the center, Walaric and his men to the south, and Sige's men to the north. In a large, well-trained army this might be a decent tactic; the three groups could act as separate forces and surround the enemy. But these were not Mercian or Northumbrian warriors. The Franca had an entirely different way of fighting, and it almost frightened him how little control the commanders had over their troops.

The rabble that they had collected to fight were scattered throughout the better-trained professional warriors; men holding pitchforks were standing shitless between heavily-armored warriors with axes and swords. Sige felt a twinge of pity for the poor men, crossing themselves and looking up at the sky to their god, knowing that they would be the first to die when the swords sang.

"Fight bravely, and if it is your fate that you should die, then die in honor," Sige told his men. "Remember the oaths you have taken to protect your brothers. If one of your brothers should be taken by fear, remind him of his own promises and hold to your own." He paused, watching the apprehension on their faces. "We've all got wives and lovers waiting for us back home," he said with a grin, "Let's make sure to bring home lots of treasure, or we'll never hear the end of it."

A hearty laugh rippled through the men, and some of the frightened locals chuckled as well. Sige knew that these Frankisc men would leave them as soon as first blood was drawn, but they were not his priority. His men, his proud, hard Englisc fighters, had followed him willingly into this strange land. He would make sure that they got home.

He heard Godomar's voice over the breeze, and looked ahead to see a solid wall of warriors rising to meet them. They were too far away for him to see their faces, but even from a distance he could see their cohesion. They were a unit, a single force, not three bands of rabble fighting against their will.

"We will defeat them!" said one man from behind Sige, one of the middle-aged veterans who had been assigned to Sige's command. "We will defeat these devils! We will defeat the Seax-people!"

Sige's thoughts came to a jarring halt as the men cheered, and he looked back at the man who had spoken. "Seax-people?" he asked, and the man looked rather surprised to be addressed directly.

"Yes," said the man, "The people of the Seax, the devils who want to take these lands from my Graf Godomar, who rules us by the grace of God! We will give no ground to these savages and pagans!"

Sige caught Oswy's eye, who looked as perplexed as Sige felt. He did not like the fact that Godomar's invaders had the same name as Sige's own people; it was surely a change in the tongue. He seemed to recall that the words for stone and for seax were very similar in Frankisc, and tried to move the idea from his mind. These could not be those people his ancestors left in the old country generations ago. These were the enemy, not his kin.

They marched forward, and he could hear the shouts of the enemy line. They were chanting, banging their weapons on their shields and stepping in unison until they were less than a furlong away.

"They haven't even got proper weapons!" whispered Oswy. Sige squinted and saw the points of the Seax people's spears, sharpened and fire-hardened, but with no metal points. They might do some damage, but they would only do it once before breaking. Only a few held swords or perhaps a round shield; the others carried heavy foresters' axes and hammers, but all carried seaxes no longer than a man's forearm.

They watched for the signal from Walaric, and Sige called to his men to pull into a tighter line. His guts squirmed as they marched forward. It was an idiotic idea to charge first, but he had no choice. He began to build speed, his brothers keeping a solid line beside him, the rabble in back.

"Turn around," he muttered in an unrelenting stream, wishing that the enemy could hear. "Just go. You will all die. Fools, turn around while you have the chance."

But they did not turn around. His head pounded as their lines crashed, pushing against one another, and the smell of blood and shit and cracking iron immediately met his nostrils. He fought defensively, surprised at the fury of the enemy as they smashed shields, crying out words that sounded abhorrently familiar.

"Seaxe!" they shouted. "Take heart! The gods are on our side!"

His shield dropped and a fire-hardened wood point dug into the gap between his leather scale armor and his shoulder, breaking off half a foot of splintered wood as Sige knocked the owner to the ground with his shield. The man wore a hammer pendant around his neck, where a Christian might wear a cross, and Sige thought of the hammer which had been wrenched from the statue of Thunor in the *weoh*; of the one he had given to his little sister on her wedding day.

He had to shake his head. A distraction now would mean death.

"Flank them!" cried Sige, and his men followed him around the perimeter of the melee. They regrouped; all ten of Sige's company still fighting fit but wary. "No Englisc man dies today," he said. They cheered the words, and the enemy encircled them. They fought through the circle. Sige's shoulder throbbed, but he dared not take out the stake digging its way deeper into it; it would not be worth the loss of blood in the middle of the battle.

He wished that these Ealdseaxe, these Old Seaxe men, would go back to their farms and bed their wives in peace. He tried not to kill them; he tried to knock them down or disable them, but not to kill them, but they were ferocious. Though the fighters did not seem to be trained warriors, they were as hard as nails and as bloodthirsty as wolves. He wondered if he was losing his mind when he heard the shrieks of women, but as two of them took down one of Godomar's men, he realized that he was not imagining it. The two women sprinted away toward the main Frankisc force, and he did not see them again.

He saw Godomar cutting down the smallest boys and the oldest men, ducking and dodging the hammer-blows of the enemy warriors. He watched as Walaric hewed the bodies of dead men even as they lay at his feet, seeing the manic flame in his eyes. So it passed, and Sigebryht warded off fierce blows from the Ealdseaxe, striking only when necessary and keeping an eye on his men. They were all there, all fighting, but in the same defensive manner as Sigebryht. "No one dies," he muttered, stepping back over the bodies.

Sige thought that he might have been imagining it when the heard the word "Retreat!" shouted throughout the fray. He sighed in relief, finally sure that the Seax-people had decided that it was not worth the slaughter. He waited for them to pull back, and regrouped with his men. But the Seax-people did not stop their onslaught. They pushed forward, and Sige realized that it was not they who had called the retreat.

It was Godomar. He was running away.

With a sense of deep revulsion, Sige and his men turned and ran toward the regrouping Frankisc host. Retreat? How could they retreat? What cowardice was this?

A cry of victory went up from the Ealdseaxe, painfully close and familiar. "*Numende sige!* We have victory! Praise Thor! Praise Tyr! Praise Odin! Praise the gods of victory!"

Everything was wrong.

*****

Ecgric helped to hold Eorwald down as Gieva cleaned his wounds. An arrow had passed just beneath the skin in the muscle below Eorwald's knee, and someone had clumsily cauterized the wound with a hot knife at least a fortnight previously, but not well enough to prevent infection from taking hold and spreading through his body. Gieva had taken the tools away from Eadyth, whose hands were shaking. Ecgric soon understood why the queen was unable to do the job. Gieva would have to slice away the burned tissue, and Eadyth looked as if she would faint when she heard Eorwald's scream of pain as the red-hot brand touched his skin.

"Nearly done, nearly done Eorwald, you have to be still, please, I'm nearly finished but you have to lie still," Gieva said soothingly. She looked as if she was about to cry, but her hands were steady and she worked quickly. Ecgric had always thought that Gieva would probably feel a lifetime's remorse for swatting a fly, but even he wished he could cover his ears. Eorwald roared in pain, but he did not move his leg, allowing Gieva to work quickly with Eadyth watching, ashen-faced, behind her. Within a few moments, she had finished and was wrapping the wound tightly with clean bandages.

Eorwald had been lying quietly for a long while now, forcibly being given a draught of hot mead and herbs by Eadyth. Everyone's eyes were upon him, and yet he looked as if he might be better pleased to leave the hall screaming.

It was not fear, that look that Ecgric could see in Eorwald's eyes. Eorwald was far above such small matters. Fear was for farm boys who pissed themselves before a battle, for people whose imaginations showed them visions of horrors to come. This was different. It was the hunted, empty gaze of a man who had lived those horrors, who was still living them.

They all sat in tense silence for a long time, and the sound of Eorwald's voice seemed to cut through the silence like a knife. "I'm not dead, am I?"

He looked around at them as Eadyth shook her head, and Eorwald closed his eyes in something like disappointment.

It was a long time before he spoke again. His voice was cold and harsh after the silence, and it rasped as if he had not touched a drop of water in a month.

"Where is Leofric?" he asked tonelessly.

"How are you feeling?" Eadyth asked, touching his face and looking grave.

Eorwald stared blankly up at her. "Answer me, Mother. I want to know what happened."

Eadyth glanced at the king, who gave her a minuscule nod.

She looked away pointedly as Rædwald explained what had happened at the meeting with Hwitegos.

Eorwald's face fell, but it was more bitterly resigned than truly sad, though he did not seem upset at the idea that they would sacrifice him to save the village. Perhaps he wished they would do so now.

"I thought it would save him," he said. "I was sure that if they thought he was the *ætheling,* then they would stop hurting him."

"You don't have to say anything now," Eadyth said, "You should rest."

"No," said Eorwald firmly, but in the same deadened voice. "You have to know what happened."

He began to tell them everything in a long, unbroken monotone. He explained his idea to learn what he could by sneaking into their camp, his burning their gear, and his escape from the camp. Eorwald them told how he had been shot in the leg and Leofric and Hengest had stayed behind while Frodrun was killed, and they were all captured. The monotone was broken when he began to explain how they had distracted the guards long enough for Hengest to get away, and no one met his eyes.

"We found his body a league north of here," Rægenhere said at the look of question on his brother's face. "It must have taken an entire army to bring him down."

Eorwald clenched his jaw and the same look of deadened guilt and exhaustion came back into his face. Ecgric was grateful that Rægenhere did not tell Eorwald the state in which they had found Hengest's body in the wood. Let Eorwald think that he had been brought down fighting a host of Northumbrians. It was not a lie. He had died fighting, and it had surely taken at least three men to bring him down at last, but Eorwald didn't need to know the rest. The truth would break him.

"They were torturing Leofric," Eorwald said. "After they caught us, he was fighting to get out, fighting against the guards, and they beat him for it. They cut …" he swallowed, flinching, "They cut out his tongue because he was trying to talk to me, trying to make a plan to escape. They were going to kill him. So I told them that he was Rædwald's son. I thought that if I could get them to realize his worth, then they would just ransom him back to Father. Even if they killed him, they would stop torturing him, and that had to be enough. I said that I would tell them secrets if they sent him back home."

Rædwald tensed. "You didn't tell them…" he began, but Eorwald cut him off.

"I just made up stories," Eorwald said. "I told him that you had amassed an army of Mercian and Seaxe warriors and that you had an auxiliary host already marching on Athelfrith." He seemed to grow frantic, as if he needed them to understand, "I just kept talking, just kept making up lies that they believed. Hwitegos believed me." Eorwald looked down at his hands, which were balled into fists in his lap. "I thought it was done, that they would send him home and that they would come back to kill me. But it didn't matter. I knew that the point they put in my leg was poisoned. I knew that I was going to die anyway."

Gieva looked, as she always did when someone was in pain, as if it had caused her a great personal wrong. She reached out hesitantly to touch him or comfort him, but thought better of it. She settled herself by clutching her long golden braid, her eyes darting between the men.

"But you got away," Rægenhere said, "you escaped."

"I resolved that if I was to die, I would do it as a free man and not as a prisoner," Eorwald said. "They thought that I was too sick to go anywhere, and that's how I managed to get out. There were so few of the guards left, that they decided I wasn't worth watching. I killed some of them…" he hesitated, as if deciding how much more he wanted to say, "And I managed to get away from their camp. I walked in the riverbed until I couldn't go on…" he looked apologetically at Rædwald, as if he was ashamed that he had not been able to run the entire journey back to Mæduwic. "I hid in a thicket until I heard horses. Then – I thought I was dreaming – I heard Rægen's voice."

"You should have called out!" Rægenhere said, almost angrily. "We could have gotten you back home sooner!"

"I thought I was dying," Eorwald said simply in the same deadened voice as before. By the look of him, he might have been. "I thought it was a dream brought on by the fever, but I followed the sound anyway. I was so cold and I could barely walk, but I followed the trail and crossed the river, and then I thought I died." He looked unhappy that it had not been true.

"You're safe now," Eadyth said thickly.

Eorwald did not seem to agree with her.

A few days passed before Eorwald forced his way out of bed, despite the combined efforts of Gieva and Eadyth to keep him there. Ecgric did not interfere, but he did not help either. He felt sickened that the sight of Eorwald made him recoil. He ought to speak to the other man, but something about the look in Eorwald's eyes took away any words.

Ecgric saw his father leaving the hall, and Ricbert had a look of profound concentration on his grim face.

"Want to fight about it?" he asked, half-jokingly. Ricbert nodded silently and led the way to a cleared area outside the palisades where men liked to practice.

He always forgot that his father was an old man when he had a sword in his hand. Ricbert was as quick and agile as he would have been in his youth, and was still the strongest man Ecgric had ever known. Each of his hits was like a hammer stroke, and Ecgric felt slow and weak against him.

"Your body is a weapon," Ricbert said between hits, "you've let yours get dull."

"It's rather hard to stay honed when you are training a bunch of field-hands and blacksmiths," Ecgric said.

"Then you had better work harder before we leave."

Ecgric ducked and deflected a blow at his head with his shield, touching the point of his sword to Ricbert's chest. "We are finally going, then?"

"Eorwald's given us a good deal of information about Athelfrith's movements. He's laid a false trail for the Northumbrians, and no doubt his captors have sent word to the North. They think that we have another army traveling into Northumbraland as we speak. The *cyning* wants to meet Athelfrith in the North where Eorwald said the forces would be."

"Is it a good idea to try to fight Athelfrith in his own territory?" Ecgric asked, failing to deflect a blow to his ribs in his distraction.

"At this point, I don't think it matters. Eorwald thinks they will be near the River Idle, where he told them Rædwald and his men were waiting. We can meet them there, and finish this once and for all."

"We've been saying that for months," said Ecgric, adjusting his grip. "Do you think we will ever really end it?"

"My *dryhten* is going to war, and I will fight for him," said Ricbert simply. "If it means that Athelfrith will stop attacking our lands, so much the better. If not, we will fight again."

They whacked at one another some more in silence, each preoccupied with his own thoughts. Ecgric saw the queen walking near the hall, looking grim. "The *cwene* must be relieved," Ecgric said, "We all are, but after all that happened with Leofric, she must be happy to have her son back."

Ricbert sighed. "It's a relief for all of us, and Eorwald has been an immense help to figure out what the Northumbrians are up to. I wish the knowledge had not cost so much."

"Well, it will be a great boon to have him fighting for us when the time comes. We can use all the men we can get." Ecgric thought irritably about the woefully undermanned army. "Speaking of which, I haven't seen Sigebryht lately. He is coming, isn't he?"

"Sigebryht is with Sunniva," Ricbert said, "I thought you knew that."

"Ah," said Ecgric. "I'll bet that's a disappointment for him. I hated being stuck in Wuffingham while everyone was finding good action up in the Fens." He twisted and landed a blow on his father's leg.

"I'm sure he'll find some good fights over in Francland," Ricbert said, and Ecgric winced again as his father smacked his arm with the sword.

"I thought you said he was with Sunniva?"

Ricbert halted, as if unsure if Ecgric was jesting. "He is. Rædwald sent him over when Sunniva married that Frankisc man."

Ecgric realized that his shield arm had dropped to his side and he lifted it again, knocking Ricbert's blow aside. He backed a step away, and Ricbert explained, almost apologetically, "They made the match while the *cyning* was in Lundenburh. Her new husband offered Rædwald a mountain of gold and a trading agreement for her. He is an *ealdorman* in Francland. Sigebryht went to command a small force to aid the man in his wars… I forget the man's name."

"Godomar," Ecgric said. "His name is Godomar." He turned his back on his father without another word, and stormed away through the encampment and toward the Mæduwic village hall. He half-wanted to hit the king for selling Sunniva to the foreigner, but it left him in an instant. She had made the choice. She had decided what she wanted, and it was not him.

*****

Everyone was looking at him, and he hated them for it. They all were watching him as if he was something breakable, as if he might shatter at any moment. It did not matter that they were right.

Mother fussed over him, but he knew that nothing he could say would deter her. Gieva had done so as well, but he had snapped at her and she slunk away looking like a kicked puppy and did not try to hover again. He felt a twinge of regret for her; she had meant no harm, but she still annoyed him. She was too pure, too perfect, to infuriatingly gentle and patient, even after everything she had been through. Somehow it made Eorwald feel even worse for being so angry about his own lot.

He still felt sick and weak from the infection, but it was passing. The pain in his leg was dissipating as the wound closed, aided by the poultices and expert care that he resented so heartily. The infected blood was slowly being replaced by poisonous thoughts. He had learned what they had done to Leofric when he had been brought for ransom. At first, he had felt a deep pang of remorse for his friend, but the sadness had quickly turned to loathing for those who had done it. Eorwald sat uselessly in his sickbed, unable to run or to practice fighting or to prepare for their journey north.

He watched the fire, imagining the torments he would unleash on Hwitegos when he found him. He would burn him, he would take red-hot knives and slowly carve his pale flesh; he would listen in satisfaction as Hwitegos cried for mercy, as Eorwald would cut out his guts and burn them while the pale eyes stared in horror. He would rip out his tongue and feed it to the hounds. He would kill them all, one by one, every man who had ever had a part in it, slowly and painfully as they screamed for mercy.

His mind was so deeply immersed in the thought of revenge that he did not immediately notice the person sitting beside him.

"Father thinks you should stay here when we go north," Rægen said, and Eorwald felt a renewed surge of rage. He turned his head slowly in disbelief. Rægen was staring into the fire as well, as if he were afraid to look at him.

"You might at least grow a pair of balls and look me in the eye when you tell me to take the path of cowardice."

Rægen finally turned, glaring at him. "I never said anything of the sort."

"You think that just because I am injured, I ought to stay here and wait while you get yourself killed. I can fight, and I will fight. I will not be brought down by something as stupid as this." He pointed to his bandaged leg.

"I don't want you brought down by anything, you idiot!" Rægen bellowed. He almost never shouted, and it startled Eorwald into silence. He was angry, angrier than Eorwald had ever seen him, but after a moment his face softened and he sighed. "But I would never ask you to walk the path of cowardice." He reached next to him and brought forth a sword in its scabbard, wrapped in its belt.

Eorwald stared at his sword, but did not reach out for it.

"You should take it." Rægen said.

"That is bad luck," said Eorwald. "That blade killed Leofric."

"And it will avenge him." Rægen held out the sword and Eorwald took it. He removed Weargbana from its scabbard, and hefted it. It had been cleaned and sharpened and shone as brightly as it had done when it was new, but the knowledge that blood of his friend stained the blade made it weigh heavy in his hand.

"You will have your vengeance," Rægen said, "but don't let your hatred eat you before then."

"I think it already has," said Eorwald. Rægen looked him in the eye at last, and Eorwald saw something there that was not quite fear and not quite sadness and not quite pity. It was the look Rægen had given him after the battle at Ealdham, and it wounded him to the core.

Rægen took a breath and looked away, and they were silent for a long time. Both looked into the fire, listening to the sounds of people talking and preparing for their departure throughout the hall. Eorwald looked down at his sword, and slid it back into its sheath. "The next time I draw this, it will be at your side."

"Our swords will sing together that day," said Rægen, and for the first time in weeks, Eorwald smiled.

He knew that they were still watching him as they made their way north. He bit through the pain in his leg, taking each step as naturally as he could. He knew that his father was scrutinizing him, watching for weakness, waiting to tell him that he would have to stay behind while his brother fought without him. Eorwald would not give him that opportunity. Each step sent a surge of poisonous resentment through his body as he created arguments as to why he would be able to hold his own.

He saw the happiness in Rægen's face as he walked with his wife. Gieva's face was flushed and Rægen kept putting his hand on her growing belly, grinning stupidly. He wished he could be happy for Rægen, but seeing the two of them made Eorwald miss Rian. He hated her, but he missed her. He knew that he could never have hoped for that sort of affection from the whore, but he had dared to dream, and his dreams had been dashed when he found her gone after his return. He had loved her. He had wanted to give her a good life, and she had left the moment his back was turned to find someone who would continue to pay her. She did not care that she was giving herself to his enemies. She did not care about him. No one did.

He had been a fool. He imagined her laughing at him behind his back after he had told her that he loved her. He wanted to see her again, to feel her legs wrapped around him, to hear her say that she wanted him... he wanted to look into her blue eyes and watch the light leave them as he squeezed the life out of her... to hear her arm rings jingle as she jerked and twitched... the rings he had given her...

He had to shake his head. No, he would never hurt a woman, especially one he had loved. No betrayal would ever bring him to that. The very idea of it made him physically sick. Something on the edges of his mind was beginning to crack, and he blinked his eyes against the pain growing behind them.

The sun was bright and flickered through the leaves that sheltered them from the west, but the dull points of light were like daggers in his eyes. He shielded them with one hand, staring at the dappled ground. He could see the shapes of men in the points of light, could see jeering faces and cold eyes and the biting glare of swords, and he hated them.

Don't let your hatred eat you, Rægen had said, but Eorwald could not see a way to escape the anger and the hatred, no more than he could escape an infection. It was in his blood, and would not stop until the blood ceased pumping.

He jumped as an arrow brought down a man several paces ahead of Rægen, and unslung his shield from his back without thinking, the poison in his blood turning to fire as alarm swept the column.

"Shields!" he heard his father's voice, and without thinking he dived forward, pulling Gieva behind one of the gear carts and joining the others to form a double-levelled wall of shields around the women who had crouched beside Gieva. More arrows stuck in the shields; one or two more of the warriors fell. The long column of gear wagons and *fyrdmen* clumped together almost immediately, the shield wall forming in opposition to the invisible attackers in the woods.

"Come out here and fight us, you miserable cowards!" Eorwald shouted at the empty wood as he looked through the minuscule gap in the interlocked shields. He could see movement between the trees, but it might just as easily have been the rays of the sun filtering through the leaves.

Another arrow hit Eorwald's shield, barely a hand's breadth from the gap through which he was peering. "Careful!" Rægen said, but Eorwald ignored him. He was crouched and had no room to draw Weargbana, so he carefully removed his seax.

He heard some of the women cry out as a few arrows stuck in the gear wagons, and then there was silence. Deadly, horrible silence. Then there was a shout from within the wood, and something hit his shield.

He did not know where they had come from, but the force of the enemy hit their shield wall like a hammer stroke. They had not had time to see them coming, no chance to see what they looked like or who they were, but the enemy knew what they were doing. They had been waiting, watching for the column.

"The dark-haired one!" he heard someone cry, "Get him alive!"

Eorwald looked frantically at Rægen as they said this, but the enemy did not seem interested in the future king of the Engla. Instead, a surge of men began to round on Edwin, who fought off their attacks even as they were redoubled. Eorwald dropped his shield and drew Weargbana, feeling a surge of power from the two weapons as he hacked his way through the pitiful enemy line and felt spines and ribs and brains split on the edges of his blades. He felt the icy bite of a knife-edge on his upper arm, but somehow the flow of his blood felt more perfect and bracing than a draught of cold water. It cooled the poison, and his mind was as clear as the sky above as they made swift work of the attackers.

It only took a few moments, and the men who had come for Edwin lay dead around them. Ten or so of their own men had been killed, mostly the poor fools who had been dragged from their harvest to fight a war they never wanted in the first place. A couple of the enemy warriors were still writhing and twitching in their death throes, and Eorwald panted as he watched his father lean down to speak to one of them.

"More Northumbrians?" Rægen asked when the man had given a final jerk and fallen still.

Rædwald looked up, a terrible mixture of fear and anger and hatred etched on his face. "Mercian," he said, "They were trying to get hold of Edwin to take him to Athelfrith."

"This has to end," said Eorwald. His fist clenched around Weargbana's hilt, which was slippery with blood. He stood defiantly in front of his father, giving him a hard look as he passed. He did not need to ask the question, for Rædwald answered it with a nod. Eorwald had proven himself. The wet heat of his blood leaving his shoulder throbbed, taking some of the poison with it.

*****

The men had returned home in the early hours of the morning, exhausted as if they had marched through the night. Sunniva pasted on a gentle smile in order to welcome her husband home, but it slid from her face when they drew near. Godomar spared the barest look in her direction and ambled past on his tall horse before she could say anything. She could ask him for news later. He would be exhausted now, and she decided that it would be best to wait.

She turned back and found Sigebryht leading his full company of Englisc men. She threw her arms around his neck, thanking the gods that he was not hurt. "I'm so glad you are safe," she said, embracing each of the men in turn. "Come inside, and tell me about the battle."

Sige's face darkened and he exchanged a glance with Oswy. "Best not to speak of it here," he said quietly.

"What are you talking about?" Sunniva asked.

Sige looked around at the men returning to the hall and to their own houses in the village. "Just make sure there is plenty to drink," he said. "I think that these men will need it."

Even after a few cups of strong, bitter red wine, Sige was reluctant to say anything. Sunniva tried to make conversation with her husband, to welcome him home after his labors, but she might as well have been speaking to his battle-axe for the reception she got. She felt uneasy, nauseated, as she twirled her ring around her finger and anxiously waited for someone to tell her something.

At last, Sunniva got Sige alone and was able to pry it out of him.

"I am not letting you pass until you tell me what's happened," she said imperiously, crossing her arms and barricading him in a corner with a stare of daggers.

Sige blew out a long breath, glancing around as if to make sure that no one was listening. "We've lost, Sunni."

Sunniva's jaw dropped and she eyed him skeptically as she closed it again. "No, you couldn't have done. There were too many men returning, surely you did not lose."

"We… we were forced to retreat." Sige said it as if each word was poison.

"We do not retreat," she said, as if that would change the facts.

"I did as I was commanded," Sige said in a leaden voice, glancing over to Godomar. "I would not speak of it, if I were you. We must pretend that this never happened."

She was furious. How could her husband, a strong, capable warrior, retreat from a battle? She had known stories of men who had seen their armies were decimated and yet fought singly against a hundred men rather than lose their honor. That was what was supposed to happen, not this. It was cowardice. It disgusted her, and she planned to get the answer.

"I will not pretend anything," Sunniva said. "I want to know the reason."

Sige's eyes pleaded with her. "Just let it go, Sunni. We've suffered a setback, and we will fight again another day. You'll only serve to anger him, and no one needs that just now."

"Very well," she said, with absolutely no intention of letting it go.

Sunniva was edgy while she sat in silence in the hall, turning her silver ring around her finger. She was too agitated to stay in the stifling hall much longer, and withdrew to the bed chamber as soon as she could. She hated most everything about this hall, but the private room was a luxury and she retreated gladly to it now. No one would miss her, anyway.

Godomar was quiet when he entered the bedchamber a while later, and he was still quiet when Sunniva offered him a cup of hot wine and hung up his clothes for him. She just had to play it carefully, and she would find out what happened. After all, she wanted news of the battle, and as her husband, he would surely confide in her.

"I am pleased that you've come home safely," she said, returning to him and kneeling in front of his chair. He glanced at her, though in the light it almost looked like a glare of contempt. She was sure that she imagined it.

"Might I help to relieve your tension?" she smiled, looking up through her eyelashes at him and sliding her hand slowly up his leg. She was rather disgusted with him, but she missed the touch of a man. He would never match the lovemaking skills of Ecgric, but she knew that it would improve eventually. She knew that the stress of the impending battle had not helped, nor had his tendency to drink before bed; but he had been away from her for long enough that she knew he must be aching for a woman's touch.

"Would you give it a rest?" Godomar said irritably. "I am tired. I don't have the energy to slake your lust right now."

Sunniva's eyes narrowed at him. "That was unkind," she said. "I understand that you are frustrated about being defeated, but that is no reason…"

She was startled as she felt a sting on the side of her face, and she could not speak. She touched the burning cheek, her mouth opened in surprise. He had slapped her.

"You will not speak of it," Godomar said. Sunniva was still shocked past words. His blue eyes were like daggers stabbing into hers, and for the first time in her life, she was afraid of a man. When his voice and expression softened, it did not assuage her fear.

"I am sorry that you've caused me to discipline you," said Godomar, "but you must learn to hold your tongue. Things are different here. You will understand that eventually."

He did not spend the night with her, but she woke to find him waiting at the door holding a small wooden casket. She frowned at him and turned away, but he sat down on the bed beside her and handed her the casket.

"Open it," he said. His voice was as gentle and soothing as it had been the first time she met him.

She slid the catch and opened the little box to find a glint of gold. It was a crucifix, rather like the one he always wore, but smaller and set with blood-red jewels. It was very pretty, but she still frowned at him.

"A fair jewel to adorn my fair jewel," he said gently, touching her cheek. She felt it burn from the previous night, and she wanted to slap his hand away.

When she did not respond, he looked at her sadly. "I regret what happened last night. I did not wish to hurt you."

"Then you shouldn't have done it," she said. Her voice was too quiet, and she swallowed, looking away from him.

"We must put it behind us," he said, lifting the jewel out of its casket and lifting the gold chain over her head. It rested heavily on her chest. He touched his fingers to the underside of her chin so that she looked at him, and she saw again the golden prince who had come to Wuffingham a lifetime ago.

"I will not strike you again," he said, "I promise. It was unbecoming and I regret having to do it, but I give you my word that I will never raise a hand against you again."

She swallowed, and was sure she could see the remorse in his eyes. "It is beautiful," she said. Her voice was still too quiet.

"Just as you are, my treasure," he said, kissing her cheek gently. "Smile now," he said, "you are much more beautiful when you smile."

In the days that followed, Godomar seemed to have atoned for his actions. He was charming and gentle with her, and she was able to forgive him for striking her. Perhaps she had been wrong to pester him. She supposed all of this was to be expected of the Franca; they did not have the same regard for women as the Engla did. He had promised that he would not raise a hand to her again, and she must believe him.

Sige was sitting beside her, his elbows on his knees as he looked at the fire. He had always been solemn, but what little humor he sometimes exuded seemed to have been sucked out of him. Was it the defeat, or something more?

He did not seem to want to be disturbed from his thoughts, and Sunniva did not bother pressing him. She turned to the woman sitting beside her, a round-faced, smiling girl whose hair and neck were covered by a wide veil.

Hilde was one of the women affiliated with the church, a sort of female monk called a nun, but she had been a companion to Sunniva since she had come to Heldergem. Hilde rather reminded Sunniva of a baby-minder or a wet nurse; the other girl was at least a year or two her junior, but she could flutter and fret just as much as a grandmother. Sunniva wondered what sort of role a woman might play in a church that forbade women from being priests. Hilde called herself a "novice," whatever that meant, and though she was allowed to spend her days as a companion to Sunniva, she spent her nights in a large house connected to the church and was often absent doing business on behalf of the priest.

"Hilde, would you like to play at dice?" Sunniva asked. She had never tried her luck against the girl; perhaps she would be less open than she seemed.

A cat trotted past Sunniva's ankles, winding its way around and settling itself on one of her feet, its tail peeking out from under her skirt.

Hilde smiled, but shook her head. "I do not gamble," she said, "although I would not mind a game of merels if you are agreeable."

Sunniva had never much liked the game; Sige was better at it and always captured her pieces in only a few moves, and the only times she ever won had been against Eorwald or Wynne. Neither had much of a mind for strategy. Well, perhaps Wynne did, but only when it came to boys.

Sunniva sighed, though Hilde was so engrossed in the game that she did not seem to notice. Sunniva missed Wynne. Hilde was a pleasant enough companion, but based on everything Sunniva knew about Christians, Hilde would not be the sort of friend that Sunniva had left behind in Wuffingham. She and Wynne had been bed-friends since they were old enough to walk, sharing every secret and every triumph, every silly story and every tear. Sleeping alongside her husband ought to have been enough, but there was something much more comforting about snuggling a girl after hours of talk, than letting a man press against you after a rather unsatisfying few minutes beneath the blankets.

Sige excused himself after a while, and the two women sat on the bench closest to the hearth, taking turns moving their black and brown game pieces. Hilde was a far better player than Sunniva; she took her time as she looked placidly at the board, blinking quickly as she planned her next move. Sunniva knew that she was too impatient when it came to the strategy, and usually moved to catch Hilde's piece without realizing that two of her own would be taken in the next move. Three or four defeats later, Sunniva suggested a game of knucklebones instead.

The cat had made another appearance, slinking grumpily into Sunniva's lap. It had an ugly, mottled brown coat and half its ear had been chewed off in kitten fights, but it purred when she scratched its head.

She remembered playing knucklebones with Wynne in the yard at the Bricgweard. She remembered watching Ecgric sparring with her brothers, remembered the way she had cornered Ecgric and had taken him for her own, just as surely as Hilde had cornered one of Sunniva's black pieces…

"Hilde," Sunniva said, "Have you ever loved a man before?"

Hilde raised her eyes to Sunniva's, and her cheeks blossomed red.

"I don't mean to offend," Sunniva said suddenly, but Hilde only shook her head.

"I've been with the church for a long time," she said, though Sunniva noticed that Hilde did not meet her eyes.

"I know you live in that house next to the church," Sunniva said, "Are there other women there?"

Hilde nodded. "There are more in the monastery to the north of here. My sisters and I are only here as support for Father Mathias, to help with the running of the chapel."

"And to teach me how to be a good Christian woman," Sunniva grinned, and Hilde smiled back. It was strange to have her here; not quite an equal, but not a servant. The Franca had strange customs indeed.

Sunniva absently scratched the loudly purring cat as Hilde tossed the knucklebone, scrambling to catch up the white bones on the table before the thrown one fell. Sunniva giggled as she watched the otherwise placid woman bite her lip as she tried to catch the bone, but it tumbled out of her hand.

Without warning, Sunniva ran to the hearth, and with a loud, angry heave, her stomach emptied itself into the ashes. The cat streaked off once more, glaring reproachfully from under one of the benches.

"Oh no," said Hilde, "Are you well, Vrouwe?" She put a hand on Sunniva's back, and Sunniva looked up at her, wincing slightly as her stomach roiled.

"I'm fine," she muttered. "I think I might go and lie down for a bit, though."

"May I get you anything?" Hilde fluttered, chivvying Sunniva toward her bed chamber.

Sunniva smiled weakly. "Just some quiet solitude is all I need. I will see you tomorrow."

Closing the door behind her, Sunniva slid down the wood panel, closing her eyes. It was not possible to deny it anymore.

She lifted her skirt and reached below as she had done every day for weeks, praying to see a spot of blood on her fingertips to ensure that it was not true. She leaned against the door, propping her elbows on her knees. It had been nearly four months since she had last bled.

She had been married to Godomar for one.

Chapter Nineteen

Bearn Forlætende

Lost Boys

incoln's palisades had disappeared in the drizzle and haze before they had gone more than a mile. Lincoln was a convenient place to lodge and fortunately neither friendly to Athelfrith nor to his allies, and they were able to regroup and recover from the surprise battle along the road. It was unnerving the way people seemed so keen to give up their lives for the sake of a bounty; that for the modest sum of gold offered by Athelfrith for Edwin's head, they would willingly walk into open slaughter.

Eadyth understood the bonds which tied a king to his retainers, and she knew that a good *thegn* would do anything in the service of his lord; but these men were completely unconnected with Athelfrith. Why would they take up arms for a king who meant to destroy them?

Rædwald spurred his horse to keep pace with hers. "What is on your mind, my love?"

Eadyth kicked her own horse to leave him behind. She still felt a perverse need to punish him, to make him know that she was still angry with him even after all that had happened in Mæduwic. It rather reminded her of something Sunniva might have done to one of her suitors. She had descended to the mind games and punishments of a seventeen-year-old girl, and it disgusted her. Even so, she could not let Rædwald know that she had forgiven him. Not yet.

They marched forward, sending out small groups of men to scout the area for enemy activity. Eorwald had told them about his lies to Hwitegos; that there might be an attack at the town of

Lincoln, and Rædwald was sure that they would find Hwitegos's men before they arrived at the River Idle. They were disappointed to find that the Northumbrians had been seen heading straight northwest without stopping, three days previously.

And so they marched northwest, passing gently sloping fields of golden wheat and barley and skirting lines of yellowing trees, all damp and drooping. There was nothing right about their journey. It was too late in the year; too close to harvest; the weather too bleak. Even if battle went well with few deaths, there would be too few men going home to their farms, and the harvest would suffer. If there were injuries, they would be more likely to succumb to infection and illness because of the cold and the damp; it was impossible to keep that many wounded men warm and comfortable inside pavilions and lean-to shelters. Even now, they were starting to run low on provisions; in this country there were few enough friendly landowners who could provide supplementary food and their own stores were becoming much smaller by the day. There were a significant number of men in the *fyrd*, enough to create a decent army once they had been trained up, but they needed to eat. At least there was plenty of salt. Her father had once told her that if a man had a decent amount of salt, he would not complain of the thin pottage and no meat. She prayed that this old wisdom would hold true.

Rædwald had appeared at Eadyth's side again, and this time she had no room to shoot ahead of him. He took the opportunity to speak to her. "The scouts we sent up north to the river have returned. They say that there is a force massing along the west bank."

Eadyth did not look at him, but nodded in acknowledgement. "What river is that?"

"The Idle," Rædwald said. "It's about ten leagues northwest of here. We will make camp on the southeast side and hopefully join battle in a few days."

Eadyth's stomach lurched somewhat at the idea, but she nodded stoically. "Very well. The River Idle, then."

The road grew muddy in the slow drizzle, and they could not continue further that day. They set camp in a clearing with double the normal guard stationed around it, though there was not a farm or village for miles around.

She paced the pavilion as Rædwald and a handful of his captains met over the trestle table, though she did not meet any of their eyes.

"They know we are coming, and they've taken the better position," said Rædwald, shaking his head. "We'll have no choice but to meet them on this side of the river. There's no way to cross but the ford for twenty miles in either direction, and they'll be sure to have captured it."

"What if we doubled back?" Ecgric suggested, "We cross near Lincoln, and catch them from behind…" his voice failed as Eadyth saw Ricbert's head shaking.

"They'll have thought of that," Ricbert said, "Delay would only mean a drain on what little resources we have."

"Tell me about the terrain," Rædwald asked the scout.

"The camp is next to the ford, and they will most likely cross it to reach the meadow on the east side if we meet them in battle. The river is bordered by thickets, no more than a furlong wide, but thick enough to hide in."

"Would they expect us to cross and meet them?" Rædwald mused.

"I do not think so, Dryhten," said the scout, "there is no space between the river and the Northumbrian camp, and the land is steep on their side."

"They're drawing us in," said Ecgric.

Someone made a noise of agreement, and Rægen said, "If Athelfrith has set himself up to draw us into the plain so obviously, he cannot expect us to do so. He would want us to try to attack from the West."

Eorwald, who towered over the other men, shook his head. "Hwitegos is with them, and he will have planned every single detail. He knows we will wait for him. He will have guessed at this very conversation, and he will have planned for it."

It was the most Eadyth had heard Eorwald speak since he had returned from the Northumbrians' captivity, but the hollow sound of his voice made her flinch.

Rædwald made a noise of frustration. "I don't care if he's expected it. We will meet him in battle on the plain on the east side of the river." He paused for a moment, and said, "No, Ricbert, I won't play games. I'm sick of this posturing. It's time to end it."

"Dryhten," Ecgric said slowly, "You know as well as anyone that we haven't the force to counter Athelfrith. Not head on."

Rædwald was breathing in that heavy way that he always did when he was thinking hard. "I have faith in my men," he said firmly.

"No," Eadyth said, barging between Rædwald and Ricbert as the men stood in stoic silence. "You will not walk into this knowing that you will be slaughtered. You do not fight a battle you know you are going to lose. It is almost as dishonorable as running away from it."

"Eadyth," Rædwald said warningly, but she glared around the circle.

"You will think of a plan, and you will do it before we take another step forward." She was frowning at him now, warning him. "I cannot burn your bones if there are no men left to haul the wood, Rædwald Cyning."

They returned to their talk, though she knew that there would be no more of this nonsense about blazing into an open battle against twice their number of enemy warriors. She left them to their tactics and pushed out of the pavilion.

She wanted to beat Rædwald bloody, but she also wanted to kiss him and stroke his hair, and then box his ears for his stupidity. Rædwald may not have liked the dance of deceit, but that did not mean that he could not follow the steps as well as any man. That was not the man she had married, had loved for twenty years. How dare he take her sons on a suicide mission? How dare he fall short of his potential? He had too much left to do, to waste it all on the easy path.

Eadyth kicked the ground as she paced outside of the pavilion now, the glow of the torchlight spilling out in daggers through the openings. The drizzling cold rain and mud froze her to her bones, but she did not want to go inside.

She was planning what she would say to Rædwald if he decided to go through with his fool plan, when a shout from the edge of the camp shook her out of her thoughts. There were several men running toward the sound, and the noises of a scuffle.

A moment later the guards had two men in tow, men in light leathers and soft shoes, with seaxes and belt knives at their hips and little else.

"Scouts!" one of the guards said, as he pushed his captive forward.

"Name yourselves," Rædwald barked at the two men, who had been forced to their knees in front of him. One was no older than Eni's sons, and the elder was in his middle years and had a rat-like face under rat-like brown hair. They had been chosen for their wiry swiftness, perhaps, but they had not been swift enough. Both men simply looked up at Rædwald, with varying degrees of panic.

Eadyth glanced at her husband, and then at her sons. Rægen's face registered the same surprise as everyone else's, but she was so startled by the look in Eorwald's eyes that she nearly had to take a step back. He looked like a wolf straining at a chain to rip the elder man's throat out, his eyes blazing and his fists clenched.

"I will not ask you again," Rædwald said, "name yourselves and name the one you serve."

The younger man shot a glance at his companion, who had opened his mouth, but the elder shut it again. Both looked up in a sort of terrified defiance.

He turned to Ricbert, lowering his voice. "I do not have time to wait. I need them to talk. Do what you have to do."

"I'll take care of it, Father," Eorwald said, stepping forward, though some invisible leash still seemed to be holding him back.

"No," Rædwald said, and Eadyth saw a flash of something like fear in his eyes for an instant as he looked at his son. "I need you to come with me. We have more to talk about."

*****

Sunniva felt strangely calm when she looked at the leather-bound stacks of thin sheepskin that were the pride of the church. Father Mathias had two of them, and the most elaborately decorated one was more beautiful than anything Sunniva had ever seen. He told her that it was their holy book, the one he would hold up during mass and read from in the strange stony Latin language. She did not care to read the words, but she stared at the symbols in wonder. They looked rather like runes, and though she could not understand what they were meant to say, she liked to look at the red and brown ink interplaying across the thin, stiff vellum, curving around brightly colored figures of men and beasts.

Father Mathias would not let her touch the leaves, but he turned them for her so that she could see the other pages. Some had figures of people, drinking from cups or praying. One page had the image of an old man reading a book, which was very similar to the one she looked at now. The figure sat within an arch, topped with the image of a winged bull. The fanciful picture drew her eye and she longed to know the stories contained in the small panels on either side of the man.

"That is an image of the evangelist Saint Luke," Father Mathias told her. "He was the one who wrote the life of Jesus Christ that is contained in the other pages. You see the small images on the side?" he pointed out the small figures standing in the column spaces, "these are scenes from the life of Jesus. When he healed a man of dropsy, when he taught his disciples while standing in the boat…" he indicated one panel, and then another, working through to explain what each one was.

"Does the book say what the stories are?" Sunniva asked. She still felt silly speaking in Frankisc, and her questions always sounded childish.

"Indeed they do," Mathias said, "Though we like to have pictures to accompany the words, so that those people who do not know Latin can know the stories as well as monks and priests."

Sunniva studied the image. There was a hole in the vellum where the sheep had been blemished, but the hole had been decorated with a pretty design to make it look like a sun. She was amazed at how much the book must have cost; each leaf had to be cut from the skin of a sheep, and scraped and dried until it was thin and stiff as dry oak leaves, and then decorated by up to ten monks with symbols and pictures. The fact that the church owned two books with jeweled and carved covers made her wonder why the priest always wore such old and patchy clothes.

"Your church must be very rich to have treasures like these," she said as Father Mathias put the book away on a shelf in the heavy locked cabinet where the other books were held.

"Indeed, your noble husband is a generous donor to the church and gives us many gifts," he said. Sunniva shifted uneasily at the mention of Godomar, and Father Mathias put a hand on her arm. "Though I understand that even the best of men can occasionally lose their tempers," he said gently.

Sunniva reflexively pulled her veil over the side of her face. There was no mark, but she felt her cheeks burning at the memory.

"Sometimes God must test our resolve," Father Mathias said enigmatically. "Would you like to hear a story, My Vrouwe?"

Sunniva shrugged. She always liked to hear new stories; they took her mind off of the world around her. Sometimes Hilde would tell her stories from their country. Some were similar to tales she would have told by the fireside with her brothers, and some had the pious tinge of the Christian church about them. She preferred to sit with Sige of an evening, telling stories about Tiw and Woden and Thunor, and their deeds. They always seemed to give her courage when she was feeling lonely or frightened. She doubted that Father Mathias had such tales, though.

"Is it a story from that book?" she asked.

"No, those are the Holy Gospels," he said. "This is a story from long before the time of Christ. There was a man named Job, who lived in the Holy Land a long time ago…" he began, and Sunniva had to stifle a snicker at the stupid name.

Without noticing, Father Mathias went on. "Job was a wonderful man, and was very righteous and honored God with many sacrifices, and for that he was blessed with healthy livestock and many strong sons and daughters. God spoke with the Accuser Satan,"

"Who is Satan?" Sunniva asked.

"He is the deceiver, the opposite of God. He tempts and tricks people into thwarting God's will." He explained, which was not really an explanation at all, but he continued after she did not ask any further questions. "And so, God spoke with Satan, boasting of his devoted follower. Satan told God that Job was fickle; that he only praised and sacrificed to God because he knew he would continue to receive gifts.

"So God let Satan take all of the blessings away from Job, and left the old man broken, destitute and sick, and still Job praised and sacrificed what little he had to the Lord."

Sunniva raised an eyebrow at the story, but said nothing. This god was obviously not fulfilling his part of the bargain if he offered no blessings for sacrifice.

"His friends suggested that perhaps God was punishing him for a past sin, but Job knew that he was blameless; he began to become upset. After all, a just God would not treat him so harshly, to come against them with such force. He began to lose hope, and asked of God why he was being treated so cruelly.

"So God came to Job in the form of a whirlwind and said, 'you were not there when I created the foundations of the Earth; therefore how can you possibly question my judgment?' and Job was humbled; he knew that he was a small creature compared to Almighty God, and confessed the error of his ways, for God knows all, and sees all, and is all-powerful. No one can see all ends, and therefore we must take what He gives us in His divine knowledge."

Father Mathias patted Sunniva's arm in a fatherly sort of way, and she was far more comforted by the kindness behind his effort than by the effort itself. "Do you understand, my child?" he asked.

Sunniva nodded, not wishing to offend him. The entire story was the most ludicrous thing she had ever heard. The gods – the real gods – might have their quarrels, but they would never act cruelly to a person who had always served them faithfully. Any god who was so vindictive could hardly be all-powerful.

The annoyance in her heart died as Father Mathias looked at her expectantly, and she nodded. "You are great comfort, Father, truly."

Sunniva was reluctant to return to her quarters, as she assumed that Godomar would be there. She did not want to speak to him now. He had surely felt great remorse for his lapse, but even so she did not want to see him. Or rather, she did not want him to see her.

Sunniva touched the swell of her abdomen under her dress. She hated her body now, as she had never done before. She hated the fact that her hips stuck out like knives around the distended stomach. She hated how weak she had grown, how frail, how thin. She had always been slight of figure, but she had been strong and healthy and beautiful. She had loved her body. She had loved the soft curves of her breasts and hips, loved the way she could run faster than all of her brothers, loved the fire that built in her muscles when she held a sword. It was like thinking of a friend that she had lost, and she missed that friend terribly.

The only thing she liked about her body now were the angry red marks which had appeared on the sides of her swollen stomach. They looked like claw marks where the skin had stretched and broken around the small bump, perhaps the closest thing she would ever have to battle scars. She had never wanted the tiny thing growing inside of her, but even so, she loved it, like she loved the marks it left on her body. She wondered if it would look like Ecgric. He was hard and fierce, but he had been beautiful in his own way; to her, at least. Perhaps her child would be fierce and beautiful too.

Sunniva twisted her ring as she thought of Ecgric. That fool man, he had been so invested in his own pleasure that he did not take the precaution to spill his seed on her belly. Now that seed was growing. He was a part of her now, more than he had ever been before, and she hated him for the strings he had tied to her.

He has no strings tied to you, fool girl, a voice in the back of her head told her. *You could have gone to the godeswif the moment you realized your blood hadn't come. You let this happen, just as much as he did.*

Sunniva stamped her foot on the ground, as if having a heated argument with an invisible opponent. He may have been clever when it came to strategy, and he may have been witty and made her laugh on more than one occasion. It was true, also, that he made her think, and had taught her what he knew without a concern that she was a woman. She had to give him that.

He was still a fool man, and nothing would convince her otherwise.

"They could talk of little else but how beautiful my wife was," Godomar said with pleasure. He removed the heavy wool coat; a tawny thatch of hair peeked through the open neck of his tunic. Sunniva wondered that the sight could still make her melt, even as she froze under his gaze.

She had smiled and chatted with his retainers and their women while the men hunted, – she could not remember their names, as she had met so many of them in the past weeks – but no one had really listened to her anyway. The men laughed about game and the women tittered about nothing, and Sunniva pasted a smile on her face and said very little. She was as eager for gossip as any girl could be, but even she could not stand the insipid conversation for more than a few moments. As long as she was there to sparkle like his little gem, no one would care that she had been fervently wishing to be anywhere else.

"I was pleased that you were the one to bring the stag down," Sunniva said. "You must be a formidable hunter."

Godomar smiled indulgently at her, and touched his lips to hers, holding her to him for a moment before eyeing her up and down with a slight smirk on his beautiful face. "My beautiful little jewel," he purred, "Take off your dress, my treasure. I want to admire your beauty properly."

Sunniva did not move. "I… I do not feel well. I may have caught a chill. I am sorry, my dear husband, but –"

"Take off your dress," he said again firmly, though his slick tone did not change. She lifted the hem over her head, trembling despite the warmth of the fire. It was not in her nature to be ashamed of her body; there was nothing wrong with it, nothing sinful or unnatural, but under his gaze she felt as if she were some damaged, evil thing. She tried to suck in her stomach and covered it with her arms nonchalantly so that he would not see, but his gaze fell to the space between her hips. A flash of emotion came into his face, but only for a bare instant, before he returned to smiling at her.

He came closer, and Sunniva was unsure if he would hit her, or kiss her. He lifted a hand and she flinched away, but he touched her upper arm, stroking it, caressing it.

"If I had known that you were a whore, I'd never have married you," he said in that gentle tone. His fingers tightened around her arm; not hard, but she could not pull away.

"Whore?" she raised her eyebrows, "I am no whore. Why would you say such a thing?" she tried to sound innocently shocked, her breath coming out in a whimper.

"You are with child." He looked over her naked body, a look of disgust crossing his beautiful face for only an instant as he stroked her arm.

"I am your wife," Sunniva said, trying to sound as indignant as possible while swallowing her nerves, "you ought to be pleased that I am carrying your child, that I became pregnant so quickly. I only wanted to wait until I knew for certain before I told you…"

"Yet another thing you've kept from me," Godomar murmured. "You are adept at lying. You told me that you were a maiden when I married you, and yet you never bled on our wedding night. And now you are pregnant – pretty far along, too. What else have you been keeping from me, my treasure?"

The gentle tone was more terrifying than the words, and she swallowed hard. "I was a maiden when I married you," Sunniva said, "I lost my maidenhead while riding a few years ago, like plenty of other girls. I told you that." She realized she had lapsed back into Englisc, but she was too nervous to care. She had to ensure that he thought it was his child, and she could not do so in a foreign tongue.

"You probably lost it to the horse itself, you lying cunt," he purred in Frankisc, brushing the backs of his fingers along her collarbone, the other hand still tight around her wrist. "And you are not in your den of wolves and whores, so you will speak our language."

"I've done nothing wrong," she whispered as his thumb and fingers straddled her throat. It was so gentle, so loving, as he drew them upward, tilting her head back. She swallowed again, putting more effort into not screaming than she had ever done before. His fingers traced the line of her neck upward until she felt his thumb brush her lips.

"Please," she mouthed. His right hand was still tracing her cheek and her lips, but his left had a tight grip around her wrist, "Please don't hurt me."

To her surprise, he released her arm. "My treasure," he said, "My little jewel, my sweet little flower," he put both hands on her waist, pulling her close to him and kissing her gently on the lips. "I promised that I would not raise a hand against you."

She was shaking, frozen in place as he looked at her apprais-ingly.

"You will wait here," he said.

Sunniva nodded, bending down to pick up her shift.

"No," he said, "Just as you are."

He left the room, and Sunniva heard some noise from the hall as if a dozen people were leaving hastily. She dared not move, dared not even breathe, and she began to feel lightheaded. She licked her lips, swallowed, and licked her lips again. They tasted of him. They tasted of the honeyed words and the gentle sound of his voice.

She had her eyes closed as she heard the door open once more, and they flew open. Godomar had returned, but he was not alone.

Sunniva covered her cunny with one hand, her breasts with her free arm. Godomar approached her, looking at her as if she had just done something foolish and unnecessary. He moved her hands away, as she looked over his shoulder at Walaric.

The *graf's* brother had a face that could have carved rock, but a light in his eye revealed his pleasure at seeing her clad only in her hair.

"What is he doing here?" Sunniva whispered.

"He is my justice," Godomar said, and for a moment he sounded as if he regretted it. "I will not beat my wife, but when one of my subjects flouts my commands, that person must be punished. I cannot break the laws of my land, but I will do you the kindness of not making it public."

She took a step backwards, but Walaric had her by the wrists and wrapped a leather cord around them, looping the center around the carved wooden bedpost before she could even think to run.

"I've done nothing wrong!" She tried to yell, but her voice came out in a shrill squeak. "Please, I've done nothing –"

The leather strap hit her hard on the back of her thigh, causing her to jump and twist away, before a second blow landed on the side of her other leg.

"Stop!" she cried, "I've done nothing wrong!"

"Keep her quiet," Godomar said lazily, "I don't want people knowing that my wife is so ill-behaved that I have to discipline her."

Sunniva felt a wad of fabric being shoved into her mouth, and she almost gagged on it before another blow made her let out a muffled scream. Walaric brought the strap down again, but the edge of the leather dug into her flank this time. She dropped to her knees, but the rope pulled her arms almost out of their sockets as she fell. Rough hands lifted her again, and she took the moment of respite to spit out the wad of material.

"You will die screaming, you foul *wearg*!" she cried, "You son of a whore! You –"

Walaric's fist collided with her stomach, and she lost any breath she might have used for a curse. She tried to suck in another breath, but another made contact and she bent double, despite the ropes digging at her wrists and pulling her shoulders. She felt his knee in her stomach as she tried to straighten, and the leather strap found her back again.

"That's enough," Godomar said levelly, after she had felt the leather bite her five or six more times.

Sunniva panted as the bond was released, and her arms swung back painfully to their rightful places. She fell onto her back, edging away as Godomar approached the edge of the bed. Her chest and stomach were burning, her back and legs screaming. She felt something cramping deep in her guts, writhing and twisting as if he were still hitting her.

"I will send for you if you are needed again," said Godomar, and Walaric ambled out of the room.

Godomar bent to lift Sunniva's chin. She was crying openly now, tears streaking down her face and neck into her hair. He shook his head sadly, brushing his thumb across her lips once more.

"My little treasure," he said, stroking her cheek, dragging the fingers of one hand down her neck while he reached to his waist with the other.

"Please," she sobbed, "Please, just leave me alone."

"I have forgiven you for your fornication," he cooed, brushing her tear-sodden hair away from her face. "I will not appreciate it if you decide to disobey me again." He put a hand between her knees, wrenching her legs apart so carefully, so gently, so lovingly. "Come, my treasure. Let us put it behind us. Show me the smile that I love so much."

*****

Eorwald went over the plan in his mind a dozen times, even as he lay on his bedroll and stared at the canvas of his tent. He had not bothered to climb under the blanket; he could feel the damp cold seeping down to his skin, but he did not care about it.

They had talked for hours, discussing how to meet Athelfrith in battle. It was too easy; too simple. There had to be a trick, a way of complicating the plan. Athelfrith might have been the type to instigate a respectable, open battle, but if he had Hwitegos as one of his captains…

Eorwald blew out a harsh breath. He did not plan to forget that pale man in a hurry, though he wished the roiling panic in his guts would subside. Eorwald had been no different in Hwitegos's hands than the two men they had captured, bound and tortured for information. Eorwald knew how hard it had been to keep his mouth shut while men beat him and burned him, and these men were stalwart. No information was forthcoming, it seemed, and they were running out of time.

No, they were not the same, he realized. Ricbert did not like torturing anyone, and did it only out of necessity. The scouts knew what they were getting into. Any enemy found within a camp would be captured and put to the question. Even Eorwald had known that, before they had taken him and his companions. If they would just say something that Rædwald could use, Rædwald would be merciful.

No, Eorwald told himself, *I don't want him to be merciful. Not to that rat-faced piece of filth...* Eorwald clenched his fists again, ready to punch the nearest thing that moved. He was so close. So very close, and he could do nothing. The sound of bowstrings shattered his memory, the laughter of men and the jeering shouts pounded their way back into his head…

Eorwald was sitting up and was halfway out of the tent before he realized what he was doing, but he did not stop. He knew Ricbert had gone to bed by now; even the muffled voices from the next tent of Rægen and his woman had ceased. Eorwald crouched and retrieved his kit bag, removing three identical items.

The enemy scouts had been tied kneeling against empty weapon racks a short distance away from the camp, surrounded by a few guardsmen holding their spears and facing away from the prisoners in a circle. The younger man was no one Eorwald recognized, but he was not important. The two looked tired and the rat-faced one slumped against his bonds, but Eorwald knew that they had not said anything worth hearing. Not yet, anyway.

The guards did not pay any attention to him, but merely ducked their heads in acknowledgement of his presence and let him get on with his business. It was the great benefit of being an *ætheling*; that everyone always thought he was on an important errand for the king, even when he had been all but forbidden from doing exactly what he was planning.

"You may leave for now," Eorwald said, "I will call if you are needed."

The men glanced at one another, but they did not argue. They stood in a group some distance away, while Eorwald was left alone with the prisoners.

The rat-faced man only looked up when Eorwald had crouched in front of the rack. Eorwald shot a glance at the younger man, which he hoped looked threatening enough to keep him quiet. He turned back to the other, his hands shaking with suppressed rage.

"What is your master planning?" Eorwald asked coolly.

The man shook his rat-like head, his lips pressed tightly shut. Eorwald looked at the younger man, whose face was bloodless.

"Did your companion tell you how good a shot he is?" Eorwald asked the ashen man, "Because he's had a great deal of practice."

Eorwald picked up one of the three identical items he had brought with him. He put a fingertip on the arrow's point, twisting it in contemplation. "I'm surprised they didn't make you an archer," he lifted the arrow, bringing it down so hard on the kneeling rat-like man's thigh that it slid straight through to his calf, and stuck in the dirt below. The man's scream did not get far before Eorwald had his fingers around his neck, stifling any sound.

"You remember me," Eorwald growled, his mouth a hand's breadth from the man's ear. "But more importantly, I remember you. I remember the sort of games you like to play. I remember," he dropped his voice to the slightest hissing whisper as he took another arrow from the ground, "everything."

The man's pointed face was purpling as Eorwald felt the vocal cords scrape together, as he felt the blood pressing past his fingers with increasing difficulty.

"I'm not a good shot, unfortunately," said Eorwald, "And I don't like games." He pressed the arrow into the man's gut, in the arc where his ribs met. He wanted to savor the moment, the sweetness of his revenge, but the man's body had already stopped twitching by the time the arrow's bloody point found the wood of the weapon rack.

Eorwald let go, and the man's head dropped to his chest. He turned to the younger again.

"Is there anything you'd like to tell me?" Eorwald asked, reaching for the other arrow.

The king was not asleep when Eorwald flung open the flap of the pavilion. He sat on a stool, his fingers tented in thought, staring into the flame of a single rushlight on the table. He lifted his eyes when Eorwald entered, though he did not move.

"There are two forces," Eorwald said breathlessly, not waiting for Rædwald to speak. "Athelfrith is leading you into a trap."

*****

Sige and his men returned to the hall just before nightfall, when it had grown too dark for any more swordplay. He was exhausted, but he laughed at Oswy's joke and sat down with his men to join them in a cup of bitter red wine. He glanced around the hall for sight of his sister, but he only saw Godomar and his men sharing in some private conversation. Godomar had just said something which made them all laugh appreciatively, though he only leaned back complacently in his chair.

It had been bad enough that the men had retreated from a fight, had scampered back in cowardice from the Seax-people. Sige could feel disgusted at their cowardice, but it was the look on Sunniva's face the morning after they had returned that had set his teeth on edge. She may have denied anything had happened, but the tears in the corners of her eyes betrayed her lie.

Godomar was dozing in his chair now, his cup half-slipping from his hand as his men chatted together in their drunkenness. Sige made for Sunniva's bedchamber silently; he had every right to visit her, but he knew the *graf* would demand answers of him that he simply did not want to give.

The door scraped against the stone floor, and the room was dim within. A foul stench found his nose as he stepped through. It smelled like a battlefield, like blood, metallic and cloying. It took him a moment to find Sunniva in the dimness.

She had a blanket twisted around her bare legs, stained with something far too easily recognizable. She lay on her side, panting and clutching her stomach,

"Sige," she whispered, before she grimaced and something seemed to deepen the stain on the blanket.

"Sunni," he rushed forward, kneeling beside her, gripping her shoulder.

"I can't breathe, Sige, I can't breathe," she gave a short gasp and began to cry, pulling at the fabric of the blanket as if it were a strangling snake. She took a few shuddering gulps of air, and her face twisted in pain. Sige began to panic as he watched her writhing feebly as she yanked the blanket away; she had become so thin that he could see her ribs, dark purple bruises spread across her skin and below that, a small but distinct protrusion between her bony hips.

Sunniva gave another quavering sob and Sige saw another gush of clotted blood flow onto the bed. She clutched his arm as he tried to comfort her, and he shouted for help. He kissed the top of her head as he hugged her, more and more tightly as her grip grew steadily weaker.

"Sunni," he said, patting her face as her eyes slid out of focus again, "Sunniva, stay with me. You have to stay awake. Stay awake." He shouted again, and with a sigh of indescribable relief he saw Oswy appear at the door. Oswy gawked blankly for a moment, looking first at Sunniva, half-naked and bleeding, and then at Sige in horror.

"Get help! A *godeswif*, a woman, anyone!" Sige shouted at him, and he ran out the door. "Sunniva!" Sige said frantically, trying to shake Sunniva awake. She was losing so much blood, her face deathly pale and her body trembling. "I've got you, please stay with me, Sunni," he said as her body tensed again, longer this time, and she let out a low groan. He glanced down, and his heart sank when he saw what had emerged. She was crying, but the sound was growing fainter as Sige shook her to stay awake, stroking her hair and calling her name.

A pair of women rushed into the room, and though they tried to shoo Sige away he would not let go of Sunniva. She was trembling, and another feeble spasm took her and more blood gushed out. Sunniva kept trying to look down, but Sige held her so that she would not be able to see her dead child lying between her legs. He felt tears in his eyes as he held his little sister, willing her to stay alive as the women took the half-formed baby away. The bleeding had not stopped, and Sige saw her eyelids flutter as she slid in and out of consciousness.

"I've got you, Sunni," he said, "I've got you." He called her name over and over, shaking her, patting her face, but she became limp and white in his arms, and he knew that it was only moments before she would be gone.

*****

They were half a league away from the lazy, sludgy river known as the Idle, and Eadyth watched the sky as the smoke from the enemy camp rose beyond the line of trees to the northwest. It was densely green, with stands of trees growing in a line like a shield wall, and a broad, sloping moor which she was certain would be drenched in blood in only a few days' time. It might have been beautiful, but at present she could find little joy in anything.

They used the remainder of that day and the next to make ready; swords and axes were sharpened, spears fitted with iron points, arrows fletched, mail and leather armor repaired. It was tense work, though they kept their spirits light with songs and stories. Eadyth listened to Rægen recite a few verses while she made sure all of her medicinal supplies were in order, and Gieva tore strips of cloth for bandages.

"Go on, give us another one," Gieva pleaded with Rægen.

"I think I want to hear a song from Eorwald," Rægen said as Eorwald entered the pavilion. "I'll bet he's got some good stories now."

Eorwald did not meet anyone's eyes. "I haven't learned any new songs, and you know I'm rubbish at making them up," he said. His voice was still hollow and leaden as it had been since he had come back, but he gave Eadyth a very small shadow of a smile as he turned to her. "Mother, will you mend this for me?" he asked, holding out a wool tunic.

"I ought to be sewing you up," Eadyth said, studying her son's face. He seemed to blink much more frequently now, but she thought perhaps that might be expected. He had experienced things in the past few weeks which grey-bearded men had not seen in their entire lives. As such, she felt that she was at perfect liberty to treat him gently.

"I am fine," he lied, touching his injured shoulder. "It was just a little cut. Not worth stitching."

Eadyth examined the torn tunic. "Of course. I'll do it right now. Would you like to sit with us?"

Eorwald looked around at Rægen and Gieva and seemed to be having some sort of internal battle. "I don't want to intrude," he said hesitantly.

"Don't be ridiculous," Rægen said. "Gieva was just about to tell me a riddle. Let's see how slow you are to figure it out."

Gieva opened her mouth in mock surprise. "I'll thank you not to volunteer me, sir," she said. Eorwald sat down next to his brother, and Gieva gave him a kind smile which he did not return.

"Very well, I think I know a good one." Gieva was looking out into the camp through the opening of the pavilion, and said, "I was in there where I saw something, a thing of wood, wound a striving thing, the moving beam —it received battle wounds, deep injuries; spears caused the hurts of this thing; and the wood was fast bound cunningly. One of its feet was stable, fixed; the other worked busily, played in the air, sometimes near the ground."

"A loom?" Rægen suggested after a moment's thought, and Gieva smiled and nodded.

"That was hardly original," Eorwald muttered. "Women only seem to care about weaving. Of course she'd think about something boring."

Gieva's smile faded.

"That was unkind, Eorwald," said Rægen sternly with an apologetic look at Gieva.

Eorwald did not look ashamed with himself. "I'd better go," he said, and left the pavilion without retrieving his tunic from Eadyth.

"I am sorry, my love," Rægen said to Gieva, but Gieva shook her head.

"He's not himself lately," she said sadly, "It's not his fault."

"It was still uncalled for," said Rægen. "He might have had a rough time of it, but he has no right to disrespect you. I'll speak with him."

The two women watched Rægen disappear after his brother.

"He is right," Eadyth said, "Eorwald knows better. I am sorry."

Gieva looked out of the opening after the two men. "He is still hurting," she said gently. "I don't think even he knows how badly."

That night was to be a *symbel*, as there always was before an important battle. Eadyth slid gold rings on her arms and braided her hair, trying to let her mind become blank.

Gieva was dressed simply and the small swell of her belly could be seen under her dress. The two of them would bear the cups for the *symbel* along with some of the other women who had come with them into the North, and they would offer their prayers as the men drank and boasted and promised to protect one another and to fight bravely.

The men were all standing and watching Eadyth as she filled Rædwald's giant aurochs horn with mead. It was incredibly heavy, fitted with gold on the rim and holding enough mead to get ten men stinking drunk. Her arms shook slightly as she held it aloft.

"Great warriors and dear friends," she said, "I bless this drink that it will give you strength and courage for the battles ahead. May it help you to remember your oaths and your holy bonds in the eyes of the gods. *Wes ðu hal. Feoht modiglice ond forðfer wel, gif eowere wyrd is þæt.*" Hail! Fight bravely and die well, if that is your Fate.

She drank a mouthful of the mead and listened to the shout of "Hail!" from the men. Eadyth turned to her husband. "*Wes ðu hal, Rædwald, cyning Engelcynna. Feoht modiglice ond forðfer wel, gif þin wyrd is þæt.*" She looked in his eyes for half of a heartbeat, but looked away as he put the horn to his lips.

She offered the horn next to her sons, kissing each on the forehead and offering prayers to all the gods for their safe return; and then to Ecgric, and then Ricbert and the other *ealdormen*. She slowly made her way to each man present in the pavilion, giving them her blessing and praising their bravery. She felt hollow inside, but she did not show it. She would not show it.

Rægen brought out his harp and Eadyth caught the end of one of his songs as she passed near him. Gieva was standing not far away, listening with tears in her eyes. Eadyth stopped and listened as well as she heard the hope of glory flowing from her son. He sang of the bonds of brotherhood; he sang the song of crashing iron; he sang of the *Wælcyrigena*, the choosers of the slain who would guide the valiant dead to the halls of the gods. The men sat listening in silence, drinking deeply. When Rægen stopped, they erupted in cheers and boasts, ready to make their vows to fight together in the face of overwhelming odds.

Eadyth glanced over at Eorwald. He talked merrily with his friends, but his smiles were short and forced and he kept looking around warily as if someone might jump out at him from behind a curtain. Eadyth felt a fresh wave of anger when she thought of what the foul Northumbrian *weargas* had done to her son. He was well enough physically now; the wound in his leg had begun to heal and he was as strong and fit as ever. Eorwald was fearless, even to a fault, and to see him cowed was worse than his wounds.

She remembered when he was small and had disappeared from her side one day. She had looked all over for him, becoming sick with worry, only to find that he had climbed the thatch of the old hall and was looking through the smoke hole at the very top, speaking with one of those invisible companions all children invented. She had called to him, trying to keep her voice level and calm so as not to frighten him and make him fall, and he cheerfully bade farewell to his invisible friend and scooted down the roof and into her arms. But now, her fearless son was sitting with his friends, safe as could be, and he looked as if he were being chased by wolves.

She felt stifled by the number of people in the pavilion and retreated, her duties complete. She was exhausted, weary beyond the reach of sleep, and she needed to be alone. When she finally entered her tent, she punched the furs of her bed with such force that her knuckles cracked.

She blamed Rædwald for everything that had happened to their son, but she knew that she was wrong to do so. She wanted a reason to be angry with him, but it was growing harder to find one. He had not sent Sunniva and Sigebryht away on a whim, after all. He had left Eorwald in capable hands with Ricbert, and Eorwald had volunteered to scout. What had happened after that was the work of fate. But they were her children, and when her children were in danger, the rational side of her mind was immediately silenced and taken over by the fierce protectiveness of a wild animal.

Her rage ebbed as she poured some ale and sat cross-legged on the bed, watching the candle flicker. She thought of the night before she had sent Rædwald off to battle for the first time, when they had first met at the court of Ethelbert. He had been begging her to marry him for weeks, and she kept putting him off. It was fun to flirt with him and entice him with her wealth and her wit and her beauty. But only a few weeks later she had learned that they would be leaving for war. The night before they were to leave, there was a *symbel* very much like this one. The men had cloistered themselves in the hall, drinking and boasting and offering prayers to Tiw and Woden and Thunor for their blessings and strength, and they had fallen asleep with the heat of the glorious battles to come fresh in their blood.

When they had gone to sleep, Eadyth had crept into the hall and found Rædwald sleeping with his back against the wall, his then-golden hair shimmering slightly in the light of the fire. She had picked her way silently around the sleeping men. She had woken him with a kiss, sitting astride his legs. He opened his eyes and had looked at her with something like amazement as she guided his hands beneath her dress, kissing him deeply and wishing it to last forever. Even after he had filled her with his seed, she had held him close to her, winding him in whatever spells she could think of to keep him safe when he went to fight.

"I'll marry you when you come back," she had whispered. He had indeed come back, draped in victory and the wealth of battle well-fought. Rægenhere had been conceived that night, and she was certain that the spells of the *symbel* had found their way into her unborn son and made him such an exceptional warrior. Rædwald had fought plenty of other battles after plenty of other nights spent in the *symbel*, and she had always been there by his side, to kiss him and make love with him and soothe away his fears. Until tonight.

Eadyth came back to herself when a breeze made her candle flicker. This was the first time they would not spend the night before a battle in each other's arms. She felt disgusted that she still had not managed to make it up with him, and swallowed the hot tears forming a lump in her throat.

As if he had heard her thoughts, Rædwald appeared at the opening of the tent as Eadyth stood up to leave it. He was clearly not sober, but stood straight and tall. Eadyth sighed and felt her body and her heart soften at the grim, almost sad look on his face as he held out his arms.

"I need you," he said.

Eadyth went to him and let him put his arms around her.

"I am sorry," he said into her hair, "I am sorry for everything. I know that you must hate me now, but I want you to know that I never meant for any of this to happen." His voice was quiet and his speech slightly slurred, but she knew that it was not the drink that made him talk like this. She led him to the bed and let him hold her, feeling the ice of her heart start to melt.

"I could never hate you," she told him. It was the truth.

Rædwald was quiet for some time, and his expression pained her more than if he had wept. "I think I am going to die in this battle," he said.

Eadyth remained expressionless, but she felt a fist clench around her heart. "You are not afraid to die," it was not a question. She knew that of him. He chased death just as surely as any man, staying alive only so that he could go on fighting another day and win even more glory.

Rædwald continued. "I am old. I can't react the way I used to. It's probably time for me to find the end. I've buried too many of my friends, friends who have died gloriously while I remained behind." He drew in a deep breath. "I'm frightened, Dytta. I want to die bravely but don't know if I'll be able to find my courage if I don't have you on my side."

Eadyth's frozen heart broke at the use of that name, and she knew how hard it was for him to say the words. She took his face in her hands and looked into his eyes, the stormy grey-blue eyes that she loved so well. His face was lined and drawn and he had more silver than gold in his hair and his beard, but he was still the same brave, strong, beautiful warrior she had made love with on that night so many years before.

She put her arms around him. "I will always be on your side."

Chapter Twenty

Hildbilla Hleodor

The Song of Swords

Dew made the canvas of the tent sag, giving the air a heavy, musty smell. Gieva lay on her side on the low pallet and piled the blankets over her legs, but she was sure that no sleep would come. The furs were thick and the tent's fabric kept out the wind, but she still shivered. She tucked her feet into her dress, pulling the blankets around her head to ward off the chill.

There was nothing to do now but to wait. She dared not reenter the pavilion now – the *symbel* was as sacred as any ritual in the world, and the men needed to be together now. They needed to form these bonds, to make their promises to protect and honor one another.

Her eyes opened as a fluttering, icy breeze filtered into the tent. She did not remember falling asleep. It was still dark and she heard the gentle, mournful sound of an owl in the distance as the sailcloth rustled and the flap closed.

She did not need light to see who it was, when Rægen lay down beside her. She pulled the blanket around him, letting his warmth flood through her. She felt his lips on hers; she thought she might weep with the sweetness of it. He tasted of mead; his skin smelled of clean sweat and wood smoke and something that made her ache to have him closer.

He kissed her as if he could not breathe without it, but his hands were patient and cool against her skin. She sighed as their bodies joined. He moved as if he had all of the time in the world, as if he had to make the moment last forever. His body did not leave hers, though she would not have let him go even if he had tried. She gave herself to him again and again, feeling the connection, wrapping him in her love and her protection and praying it would be enough.

She brushed her fingers through his hair as he laid his head on her stomach, cradling the mound. She heard the low rumble of his voice as he sang, and smiled though she could barely hear the quiet words. She let the sound wash over her like water. There was nothing else; no impending battle, no worry for the future. There was nothing but him and the tiny life inside of her, nothing beyond the canvas walls of her world.

"Gieva?" Rægen's voice rent the stillness.

"Yes?"

He paused, as if slowly drafting the words out before he spun them together. "Would you think less of me, if I told you I was worried for tomorrow?"

She shifted so that she could look into his face, though it was only a dim silhouette. "Of course not," she said firmly, "Though I would wish to know what makes you worry. I've never known you to fear battle." She carefully omitted her own crippling fear.

"It is not the battle I fear," he said, "The song of swords gives me life. I would never back away from it."

"Then what do you fear?"

"That when the battle is won or lost, when the *Wælcyrigena* have come and gone," he paused, swallowing, "That I will look around me and everyone I fought with, everyone I loved, will be corpses at my feet. That I will have to smell their bodies burn; that I will have to tell their widows how bravely they fought. That I would have to explain the reason I was unable to protect them; the reason I was unwilling to follow them."

Gieva kissed his forehead. "My heart, why would I think less of you for that?" Gieva asked, brushing her hand through his hair again. "There is a pain like no other, to know that you are alone, the last of your kin and your friends. There is no greater desolation than that. I would never think less of you for fearing it."

Rægen sighed, and Gieva felt his hands cupping her cheeks, and his lips against hers. She was sure she tasted tears on his lips, though if they were his or her own, she could not tell.

He slept in her arms, and she did not stir until she heard the murmur of voices and dull clang of gathered weapons from outside the tent.

"It is time," Gieva said gently, kissing his brow. The gray light of dawn was nearing, the world cold and still outside the expanse of sailcloth.

Rægen sat up as if he had not slept at all, looking into the distance with a firm set to his face, though a smile quirked the edges of his mouth as he dressed. Gieva waited for him outside the tent, her breath making clouds as she wrapped the fur-lined cloak around her shoulders.

He was smiling as though to himself, his face lighting the morning before the sun had even lifted its head.

He bent to open his gear chest, but Gieva forestalled him. She wordlessly opened it herself, lifting first a padded wool coat from its depths. He shrugged into it, and she felt his eyes upon her as she tied it closed, letting her hand linger just long enough to feel his heart racing.

He slid the mail hauberk over his head as if it had been the lightest wool, and she fastened thick leather bracers around his forearms, taking his hand and kissing it. Every piece was a prayer, every ring of his mail a spell of protection.

The belt held a loop for an axe, and a short stamped leather sheath for his seax, but his scabbard hung empty at his hip. Gieva lifted Wælcyrige from her own chest before he could say anything, its blade protected by a wolf's pelt, drawing it from its wrappings. It shone in the dim light of morning as she kissed the pommel. She offered it to him, and his hands closed around hers.

"This is yours now," he said, though he was smiling. He had given it to her on their wedding day to hold in keeping for their first son.

"I think that you two deserve one more fight together," Gieva said. "You've never lost a battle while you've carried this sword. Take it, and give our child a fitting legacy." The warm weight of his hands kept hers from shaking.

He nodded slowly, taking Wælcyrige and gliding it into the scabbard. She fixed her eyes on his face, trying to smile confidently.

Rægen raised a hand to her cheek, brushing his thumb to smooth away a tear she did not even know had fallen. "You are carved upon my heart, my dearest one," he said.

She let his words fill her; consume her; as she rose on her toes to kiss him. She felt a pang as they touched and another when they parted. Gieva had to swallow whatever tears might have tried to escape, and she smiled up at him, letting the pride of the moment replace any fears. She took a deep breath before speaking the words.

"Beloved," she said, "Go forth with joy this day. Fight bravely, and if it is your Fate to die, die honorably with a sword in your hand so that you may feast with the gods."

Gieva watched as he walked away, toward the throng of men, *his* men, who cheered as he approached. They would gather with the other companies soon enough, but they offered their love to none other than their *ætheling* at this moment. He embraced his brother, whose face was hungry, eager for the coming storm. He grinned at several men, who were just as excited-looking as he was; he put a hand on the shoulders of some with an encouraging word; nodded gravely at others in silence as they fell into place behind him. She heard the voices of the men, rising in a rhythmic clamor as they marched past, led by their *dryhten* to meet their fate.

Wilt þu hieran, hilderinc? Wilt þu folgian, hilderinc?
Wilt þu hieran hildbilla hleodor?

Will you hear, soldier? Will you follow, soldier?
Will you hear the song of swords?

Rægen's voice rose above the others, and Gieva felt a stab of joy and worry and grief and love at the sound as it passed away from her.

Þa hilderinc, eftsið hwælwæg him hwearf
To freadryhten for he, hwær freondas
Selesecg socon scieldas, his sweord sungen.
Swolfor ond searogim – sundorgiefe in sele,
Rest onfor oarsele for. On breost guðbill
Beornes ellen begeaten mid þon byrnsweorde.
Fæs ode witu wæpna þeah weop he mid guðwæter;
Banhus breotende , breatm beadwe.
Wifmenn Wodnes him gereahton – Wælcyrigan –
Hleodor hildbilla on hræfna hie het þider.

That soldier returned; the whale-road took him
To the lord of the free ones, back where his friends,
Shield-shakers and spear-*thegns*, would sing of his sword.
Rings he received, special gifts in that mead-hall,
And rest for his body. On his breast rested his sword,
His men found courage by that flashing weapon.
Bites of weapons were cleansed, though with blood he wept,
His bone-house broken by the battle dance.
Wælcyrigan found him, Woden's women,
Guided by the raven's call and the song of swords.

The sound faded as they marched on.

Wilt þu hieran, hilderinc? Wilt þu folgian, hilderinc?
Wilt þu hieran hildbilla hleodor?

"Wilt þu hwierfe, hilderinc?" Gieva whispered, "Will you return, when the song of swords is over?"

*****

Eorwald roared in exhilaration when he saw Ecgric's crested helm appear behind the crouched shield-wall, and the look of panic on the Northumbrian faces as they were cut down from behind, some splintering away to deal with the auxiliary force, some looking around in panic at their commander for a signal. For a moment, he was not cross about not leading the charge to flank the second band of Northumbrians. Seeing his plan in action was so exhilarating that he screamed in joy.

Eorwald looked over at Rægen, who wore the most excited grin he had ever seen, eager to rejoin the fight now that the ruse had been thwarted. Eorwald could not help but smile as well, the frenzy building in him as they re-formed the shield wall.

They did not have long to regroup before the main host of Northumbrians surged forward once more, trying avoid the swords and spears of the warriors behind them while running directly into the swords and spears of the Southern shield wall. They had broken. The mad idea had worked; the Northumbrians were in chaos as they tried now to form three separate lines.

The king raised his sword and cried, "*Engelcynn!*" and the men answered with their own shouts as they stabbed and kicked and hacked their way through the enemy line. The Northumbrians gave little ground; many of the men who had splintered away from the main host had returned to it, forming a circle around their *dryhten*.

Athelfrith wore a spectacular helm that blazed in the weak sun, burnished and faced with a mail neck-guard; easy to see amid the dull iron of his fellows and unmistakable as their king. Eorwald saw Edwin to his right, hopping over bodies and furiously hacking at everyone who stood between himself and the Northumbrian king. Eorwald could not help but admire the man's passion for slaughter.

He pushed through the onslaught, fending off blows and strikes as if they were flies. He felt the excitement, the white-hot blood-joy pounding through his heart as he bellowed oaths and battle cries at the top of his lungs. It was like being washed clean again, to feel his blood pounding in the fire of battle. He wanted it to last forever.

Suddenly, with a wave of poisonous fury that guided his blade into a Northumbrian skull, Eorwald saw a flash of pale white skin and blue eyes rimmed in red.

Eorwald lunged forward and almost froze at the same time. He felt a tangible need for his blade to find Hwitegos's heart as the pale man withdrew his sword from an Englisc ribcage.

They were so close, but it seemed an eternity to cross the distance. Closer, closer; he could see the cold glint in the pale man's eyes; closer; his white mouth had curved into a grin; closer…

A dull pain erupted in Eorwald's shoulder over the half-healed cut as a blade glanced against his mail, and he turned for only a heartbeat to fend off his attacker. A wave of Northumbrians had returned from fighting Ecgric's men, and Eorwald saw men closing in around his father.

Rædwald's axe glinted, sending arcs of blood over the attacking men's heads. The Englisc warriors behind him expanded and retracted like the breath of a living body as they pushed against the renewed Northumbrian onslaught. Eorwald glanced back to where Hwitegos had stood. He was gone. Eorwald bellowed a curse as he tore his eyes away, his feet pounding over blood-soaked earth to hew his way back to his father.

He cried out and several scattered Englisc warriors appeared at his side, and together they drove a stake through the Northumbrians. Rædwald's men spilled out of the wound in the Northumbrian shield wall, circling them.

A spear neared his face, the red-brown tip coming ever closer, when he lifted his shield at the last moment to knock it out of the way. His own spear dove underneath the iron-bound wood, burying itself in a warrior's groin as he ploughed through him with his shield. He wrenched the spear free, and kicked the Northumbrian in the chin as he tried to grab hold of his ankle, and felt the bone crunch under his foot.

He rushed forward to a pair of men grappling; the Northumbrian had pushed the Englisc fighter to the ground and was trying to rip the shield away from between them. Eorwald dropped his spear and pulled out his sword, slicing the man's thigh from behind. The Northumbrian turned and hacked at Eorwald's torso as he fell, but the layers of iron rings and boiled leather turned the blade away. Eorwald's sword found the man's throat in a heartbeat and he pushed off again, to find Hwitegos and finish what he had started.

*****

The shouts of confusion and fury were more beautiful to Ecgric's ears than the finest poetry. His force was small, but expertly manned and perfectly arrayed as to break through a shield wall. Ecgric was at the center, finally knowing he was where he belonged, his blood boiling and the shouts of his brothers coming from behind him. His sword sat placidly on his hip as he held Liðwreca, his heavy bearded axe, in one hand, and his shield in the other.

While most of Athelfrith's men were focused on defending themselves from the arrows and javelins of Rædwald's main host, Ecgric and Ricbert led two small companies of *gedriht* around the edges to break the lines of the second force that had been sent to catch Rædwald off his guard from behind. Athelfrith's lines curved back in on themselves in the shape of a disorganized and grotesque smile, while Ecgric led his men forward in a single line.

I must remember to buy Eorwald a whore for each day of the year, when we are done with this, Ecgric thought, beaming at the perfection of the attack. The *ætheling* had gotten more information from those scouts in an hour than anyone else had gotten in six, and despite the rather brutal tactics he knew that no one was complaining of the information. Without the knowledge of the second Northumbrian force – well, Ecgric did not need to think of that now.

The Northumbrians gathered themselves as Ecgric's company curved around them, and they broke off in precisely the way he had thought they would. It was so seamless he might have wept, but instead he grinned manically and shouted, "Now!"

He saw the men to his right and left lag a pace or two as their line turned into a point with Ecgric at the center. His shield overlapped those behind him, and all of them knew that each shield would protect the next. With a shout of "*Onðringa*!" they charged forward, and the wedge sliced into the spindly protective arm of the enemy shield wall. There was a crash of iron on wood and the satisfying sound of more iron carving into flesh and leather as they pushed as a single unit, breaking through the line.

More confused shouts erupted as Ecgric hooked his bearded axe around the top of a Northumbrian shield, yanking down and then driving the iron binding of his own shield into the man's jaw. It knocked him off balance and Ecgric hooked the bottom edge of Liðwreca around the man's neck and jerked. The man's neck snapped and he fell to the ground.

Ecgric looked up to see his father give a perfunctory nod of approval, and saw that the second Boar's Snout formation had done its job well. The *fyrdmen* had found their courage, and were fighting just as savagely as the *gedriht*. There were now three separate groups of warriors: two clusters had been dismembered from the main host by the flanking Boar's Snout formations, and the main host, now engaged with Rædwald's *gedriht* led by the king and his two sons, and another band was led by Edwin. Several of the Northumbrians had returned to the main host to protect their king, but many remained to fight against Ecgric, their eyes bright with the promise of glory. With furious sweeps of Ecgric's battle axe, however, those lights were very soon extinguished.

Edwin had charged forward, fiercely protecting the king. Ecgric was nearly deafened by the shouts and the sounds of colliding shields, but heard his father's command above the din, not to let any more of the severed Northumbrians re-join the main host. Ecgric and his men formed a line to separate the stragglers, forcing them to back away from the host and toward the river. The water was slow-moving and thick with churning soil, and even though a few might cross, most would be trapped in the sticky quagmire of the muddy banks.

The stragglers formed a shield wall again, and though they were drastically outnumbered even by this scanty host, the enemy were confused and disorganized by the unusual tactics of Rædwald's auxiliaries. Again Ecgric shouted "*Onðringa*!" and they clashed shields once more.

He scanned for his comrades in his peripheral vision, and had a moment of panic when he saw more Northumbrian than Englisc shields. In his moment of distraction, another blow struck him, this time dully in the back as if someone had rammed a shield boss against his spine. He fell forward, twisting to hack at whoever had slammed into him, and felt his axe catch someone's flesh as he felt the shield catch the ground. He fell onto the shield before he could let go of the handle and his arm was wrenched sideways, and with a strange sucking he felt his left shoulder being ripped from its socket. For a half of a heartbeat he was sure that his arm had been torn off, but it was still at his side, limp and slightly lower than it should have been. He released the shield and tried to grip his Seaxe, but squeezing the hilt shot a bolt of pain up his arm that made him bellow several of his favorite curses.

Well, that changes things, he thought, clasping Liðwreca in his good hand and adopting a different position. His left arm hung uselessly at his side, unable to grasp a shield or another weapon, and he was extremely vulnerable. He watched as one of his men was set upon by two Northumbrians, who hacked him to the ground with axe and cudgel. Ecgric slung the back of the axe into the first man's temple, and then kicked the club-carrying man to the ground, his bearded axe finding the man's ribcage an easy feast.

Ecgric only had half a heartbeat's length to mourn his friend before he saw two more Northumbrians running toward the river. One tripped, falling face-forward into the shallow water, and the other kept running, wading and sucking his way through the river and across to the other side. The retreating warrior had abandoned his weapons as they weighed him down, but the mud seemed to suck at his feet as he trudged, and he sank deeper and deeper into the water before Ecgric's thrown spear caught him between the shoulder blades.

The one who had tripped was trying to get to his feet, but Ecgric put the point of his sword to his neck before he could move. His face was beardless and completely covered in black mud and presumably shit, and the little expression that Ecgric could see was terrified.

"Submit and I won't harm you," he said to the boy, but the boy merely spat a mouthful of mud at him and swung his arm wildly, the edge of his seax glancing against Ecgric's calf. Ecgric cursed and kicked him in the head so hard that it knocked him out. His head lolled sideways and Ecgric left him to drown or survive as the gods saw fit, but gave him a sound kick in the back before he limped away.

They had defeated the auxiliary group, but Ecgric felt another surge of pain in his shoulder and in his guts as he realized how few of them were still standing. Only eight or so remained on their feet, most sporting injuries similar to Ecgric's or worse. They rounded the surviving Northumbrians into a group and Ecgric left a few men to guard them while the rest went back to join the main host.

It was quiet now, but it was far too quiet for the aftermath of a battle, and it made him uneasy. Ecgric rushed back through the trees to where the main hosts had faced one another. With a lurch of horror he saw the bloodiest battlefield he had ever looked upon in all his years of fighting.

Battle had always been Ecgric's true love. He relished the rush of clashing shields and the way his blood boiled waiting for a fight, and he knew that if it was his fate to die he would go happily to the gods with his sword in his hand. He knew many of these men would feel the same way, and even though he knew that they died honorably, he felt sickened by the scene before him. Black crows circled the skies above them already, waiting for their chance at the feast. These were not the wise ravens of Woden, the messengers and guardians; these were the carrion crows, the ones who delighted in battle even more than the warriors whose flesh they would soon consume.

*****

The pale man had disappeared, and Eorwald pounded through the mass of fighting men for a trace of him, his hand clenching around Weargbana's hilt and his blood boiling. The blade needed blood, and only the icy blood of the white Northumbrian would satisfy him.

"To the *ætheling*!" a cry went up from Eorwald's right, as a cluster of men ran toward the stand of trees. Rægen's men, he realized, and without sparing another thought for Hwitegos, he surged forward after them. His shield and sword split a path through the remaining Northumbrians, as he felt panic rising as he looked for his brother.

At last he saw him, cutting down one, then another, then another of the enemy, but he was slowly becoming overwhelmed. Eorwald wiped the blood from his eyes as he pushed through the group of warriors converging on his brother.

"Well, good to see you again, Little Brother," Rægen shouted, kicking a Northumbrian in the chest.

"Having fun?" Eorwald yelled back, over the din of crashing metal and shouting men. Another, and another, and another fell and Rægen's men pushed off to find more Northumbrians to kill once they were sure that their *dryhten* was safe.

Rægen glanced around, satisfied that they had escaped the Northumbrians near them, and allowed himself a breath. "How many have you gotten?"

Eorwald shrugged, shaking some of the blood from his blade. "Gods know. Six, seven maybe? I've wounded enough others. How about you?"

Rægen moved to one of the Northumbrian bodies near him and plucked the spear from the man's guts, checking that it was intact and hefting it to check the balance. "A nice round number for a nice round baby boy," he said. "At least ten for me."

"It doesn't count if they're all green little farm boys," Eorwald said, his heart still pounding. "We'll call it eight."

"Nine and you've got a bargain," Rægen said, laughing. He looked around the roots of the trees at the bodies, scanning for an intact shield to replace his own broken one.

Eorwald scanned the clearing, his senses as tight as his limbs. "Let's get back to –"

Rægen was running forward, his eyes blazing. "Get down!" he shouted, and Eorwald ducked just in time for something to bounce sharply against the top of his helm. He saw the spear quiver in the dirt as he spun round, facing the attacker. Rægen had already lunged at the spear-thrower, and the pair toppled to the ground. Rægen rolled over the other, landing in the low-lying branches of a yew tree.

A blow struck Eorwald between the shoulder blades, and he spun round to find another man brandishing a heavy hammer in one hand, with a seax in the other. Eorwald ducked a second blow, as the hulking warrior staggered a pace and rounded for another attack.

Eorwald took the momentum of the man's next swing to duck under his reach and drive his sword into the hammer-wielder's bowels, thrusting up hard. He pulled away, taking a step back and turning to see Rægen. Rægen grinned and took a step to close the distance between them. The spear-wielder sprang to his feet, darting in front of Rægen as he moved forward. Rægen was laughing as he drove the point of Wælcyrige through the man's chest. The smile still did not leave his face as the felled man swung wide; the blade of the man's seax drove its way through the side of Rægen's neck. As the man fell sideways, the seax ripped forward in a torrent of blood, as horror was ripped from Eorwald's lungs in a scream he could barely hear.

Eorwald's vision shattered as the hammer slammed into his temple, the force of the blow throwing his helm off of his head. Eorwald swung, and his sword found the man's chest. He left it there, spinning around to find his brother through the blinding stars.

Eorwald lurched forward, sharp points of light stabbing his vision as he brought Rægen into focus. Rægen's eyes narrowed in confusion, but the grin was still on his lips. He stared at Eorwald blankly for half a heartbeat, before falling with a sickeningly mundane thud into the roots of the yew tree.

Eorwald stumbled to his side and hopelessly pressed his hand to Rægen's neck. He felt the slow glug of his blood as it poured through his fingers and heard the sucking sound of air that would not reach his brother's lungs.

"I've got you," Eorwald choked as Rægen gripped Eorwald's arm. Eorwald's hand shook violently as he removed it from Rægen's neck to hold his brother's hand tighter around the handle of Wælcyrige. Rægen's eyes slid out of focus as a final gush of blood poured from his laboring heart into the roots of the yew tree.

As the light left his brother's eyes, the stars in his own eyes turned to bloody fire. Eorwald stood and turned back to the giant man, grabbing the hammer that was now just out if its owner's reach. The big warrior lay clutching his belly, dying slowly but moving to stand again even with Eorwald's sword in his guts. Eorwald slammed the hammer into the man's helmet-less skull, wrenching the sword away as the big man fell to the ground. His shield gone, he pulled his seax from his sword belt as two more Northmen came upon him. He felt his heart beat at twice the normal speed, but the upward thrust to the first man's belly felt slow and calculated. He removed the blade from the first warrior and in a cold, vicious sweep brought it down through the leather cap and bone protection of another's brain. Viscera clung to the blade, flying off in arcs as he furiously hacked at the on-comers, all intent on defiling his brother's corpse. Through the pounding of his ears he heard shouts.

"Edwin! Edwin is dead! Over there, by the tree!"

Eorwald paced around his brother like a beast. Fools. They would cut off Rægen's head and carry it before Athelfrith like a trophy before they realized that it was not Edwin at all. He tightened his grip on his dual weapons, his mind sliding into the perfect stillness that preceded other men's deaths.

Six more Northmen lay on the ground now, and within a minute two more had joined them. He leapt from the backs of two heaped corpses to drive Weargbana into the neck of yet another. He glanced around, seeing no new attackers but waiting to spring at the first sign of movement.

His heart slowed gradually and his senses smoothed as no one came. His head throbbed where the hammer-man had hit him, and he could feel something trickling out of his ear and down his jaw.

Eorwald staggered a few paces, and then fell to his knees. His vision was hazy; the world was spinning around him, and he vomited violently on to the ground, his head stabbing with pain as the trickle of blood slithered onto his neck.

He glanced back at Rægen, undisturbed in the lake of blood near the tree's roots. Eorwald stood unsteadily, ready to spring again as a figure approached.

The blood red of his vision faded to blues and greens and browns as he realized the relaxed way in which the figure drew nearer. He squinted, wiping the blood and sweat from his eyes, and saw his father walking toward him, his helm tucked under his arm and his blood-soaked axe in one hand.

Rædwald looked at the ground around Eorwald, who stood panting and covered in blood and brain and mud and sick. His eyebrows were raised in mild surprise and approval. "I see you've been busy," Rædwald said, as if Eorwald had merely hit a fine blow against a sparring partner in the practice yard. He had not noticed the final body lying beyond the mountain of dead Northumbrians.

Eorwald was having trouble focusing on his father's face, but breathed deeply to steady himself. He swallowed, prepared to tell his father what had happened, when another figure approached them, slighter and clutching his side, his helm gone and his hair a mess.

"By the gods," said Edwin, putting a bloodied hand over his mouth. His gaze had fallen to the final body.

It took Father a moment to register what Edwin was looking at, but he followed Edwin's gaze and let out a bone-shattering roar of grief and anger, pushing Eorwald aside and falling to his knees beside Rægen's body. He did not move for a long time, but his shoulders shook. Eorwald was having a hard time remaining upright, his head throbbing and blood flowing steadily down his ear and onto his neck.

They heard a shout, and the sounds of renewed battle coming from beyond the patch of trees. The clanging metal sounded fuzzy and dull, as if Eorwald had a thick blanket wrapped around his head. Edwin took off at a sprint toward the trees, but when Eorwald made to follow him, Rædwald shouted at him to stay.

"Get him back to the camp," he said, his voice thick and hoarse and his eyes blazing with a fury Eorwald had never seen before. "Before anything happens."

"But—"

"Do as I say, Eorwald," Rædwald said, retrieving his battle-axe and saying, as he followed Edwin into the trees to join in the recommencing battle, "It is over."

Chapter Twenty-One

Wælcyrigena

Choosers of the Slain

ain started to fall so lightly that it barely touched the ground, but the hem of Gieva's dress was sodden as she strode through the grass. She hefted her basket into the crook of her elbow, shifting her grip on the water pail as the handle became more slippery with the falling rain.

A boy of about fifteen years was lying unconscious underneath a shield as she passed; Gieva wondered if one of his companions had covered him to save him further injury after he'd fallen. She tried not to think of the fact that the companion would probably never see the fruit of his labor. The boy stirred as she gently lifted his head.

"There, now," she said gently, letting him drink from the water dipper. "It's over, brave *hilderinc*." The boy seemed pleased that she had addressed him as a warrior, but as he looked around his beardless face fell. He looked at her questioningly, but she had no answers for him.

"Can you walk?" she asked.

The boy got to his feet.

"You need to help me," Gieva said. She had plenty of helpers, mostly *ceorls* who had not seen much of the action, but this boy needed to something to do. "What is your name?"

"Wagi," he said. His voice still had the lightness of youth.

"Follow me," Gieva said. The boy obeyed.

As she made her way down toward the river, she saw a man leaning over the body of a fallen comrade, and she approached at a trot to offer her aid.

When she drew near she realized that the kneeling man was in fact Ecgric; he had no helm and his hair was disheveled and matted with blood in places, but he did not seem to be injured. The man on the ground was wearing a helm and stirring feebly, but Gieva could not see his face. Gieva touched Ecgric's shoulder, and he jumped, and then winced at the sudden movement.

"It's you," he said, relieved. He was reaching down to the injured man with his right hand, his left hanging lifelessly at his side.

Gieva examined Ecgric's shoulder without touching it. Even through his jerkin and mail shirt she could see an extra lump just below his shoulder. She said, "It's dislocated, but I can fix it."

"Help him first," Ecgric said. She wondered what had happened to him to put him in such pain; surely such a man as Ecgric would barely flinch at a dislocated shoulder.

She pushed the other warrior's helm up and frowned when she saw that it was Ricbert. He was breathing, but it was shallow and irregular and his eyes were closed. He had sustained several injuries to his neck and arms but they were not deep; Gieva focused instead on the massive gash in his left thigh, which was gushing blood even as Ecgric pressed his good hand to the wound to staunch the bleeding. Something, a battle-axe, most likely, had driven itself through the knee-length shirt of mail and down to the bone, taking the metal with it. Even soaked in blood, she could see the pieces of rings embedded in his flesh, and it was very likely they had been driven into the bone as well.

"I'll need to fix your arm first," Gieva said to Ecgric, waving away his protest, "because you have to help me to take him up. Bite this." She handed him a smooth piece of wood from her tool basket. "This might hurt."

Ecgric nodded, and followed her directions as she put him into position. He lay on his back, and Gieva took his wrist, putting her foot in his armpit. "Ready?"

He bit down on the wooden block and shouted a muffled curse as she pulled, firmly but smoothly, and Gieva felt his shoulder snick into its proper place. He spat out the wood and flexed his arm, nodding grimly that he could move it properly now.

"It's going to hurt much more in a little while, but at least you can use it. I need your help. The cloak."

Ecgric handed the torn cloak to her and she ripped off a long strip. She wrapped Ricbert's leg it as tightly as she could, fearing that it might hurt him, but he did not seem to care or even notice.

"Wagi," Gieva said, and the boy appeared at her elbow like a summoned dog. "You two must get him back to the camp. Eadyth will know what to do; just hurry."

Ecgric pulled his father's arm around his shoulders and Wagi did the same, and they dragged Ricbert up the sloping lawn towards the camp.

Gieva looked around, seeing a knot of people emerging from a thicket of yew and ash trees. Several men had created a rough stretcher out of a cloak and two tree branches for one of their fallen companions, and made their way up the hill. She began following them in hopes of offering them her assistance, but she jumped as a hand grabbed a hold of her ankle.

"*Wælcyrige*," a voice said, "You've come to take me to the Feast?" It was a Northumbrian, but one of very high rank; he wore a bright helm and burnished mail shirt, though there was a wide gap in the rings. He had one hand over his stomach, in a vain attempt to keep his entrails from spilling out. He was unsuccessful, and she tried not to look at the way his body seemed to split down the middle. His shield was splintered a few feet away and he clutched his short, heavily decorated seax in one hand; his sword was shattered into three or four pieces a distance away, gold glinting from the pommel.

"Soon," she said, "You'll be there soon." Her voice shook as she watched him writhing, as if he was trying to run away from the pain of dying. His eyes were unfocused, and there was a thin trickle of blood dribbling from his mouth into his dark, grey-streaked beard.

"Will – will you help me?" he asked, and he sounded almost childish, his voice quavering, and she suddenly remembered another man begging her for the same favor a lifetime ago.

She knelt next to the dying man as she had done for too many others that day, and watched him gasping and writhing pitifully on the ground. "Please," he said, "Let me go to Woden's hall with my brothers. I cannot..." the slick redness of his belly quivered slightly, as he drew painful breaths, "I need help."

The last words came in a whisper, his eyes shut tightly as if it might block out the pain. He was so frightened, even though he was tall and strong, even though she knew he had probably dreamed of this day as long as he'd held a sword. She knew that he deserved to die well without fear. If she helped him, he would still feast with the gods all the sooner, but if she didn't, he would die in agony and perhaps lose what courage he still had. She left his seax in his hand and she took instead the broken head of a spear from the ground nearby. It was not hard to see where the point needed to go.

"Die well, brave *hilderinc*" she said, leaning into the shaft and pushed the spear's point through his ribcage, feeling it slide into the thumping muscle that would soon be stilled, "and go happily to the Feast. May you find rest in Woden's halls."

He let out a shuddering groan as he met her eyes, and thanked her wordlessly as he died. She closed the man's hand tighter around the grip of his seax. She was no messenger of Woden, but perhaps she had made it easier for one to find him. Her hands were shaking furiously as she stood and retrieved the water bucket, and she had to take several unsteady breaths before moving on.

Gieva knew that she could not retreat yet, that she must continue helping those who needed her. Another smattering of *ceorls* had appeared to assist her, and she was able to gather her wits enough to direct their efforts, even with her stomach churning and her head spinning. Hours passed, and she began to only find those men who did not need her help anymore.

She was exhausted beyond anything she had ever felt; even the sleepless, fearful nights in the captivity of the Northumbrians had not left her so weary. All she wanted to do was to curl up in her bed with Rægen at her side, talking and dozing and listening to him singing to their unborn child. She checked each man for a heartbeat, tended those who could be saved; comforted those who could not. The thought gave her hope: she had to help another person, just one more, and then another, and a few more after that.

The hard part was almost over.

*****

Many of the men who returned first did not need her care, whether because they had not been hurt, or because they were beyond healing. Eadyth offered ale and water to the uninjured *fyrdmen* as they brought their fellows back in a steady, sickening river. She knew many of them by sight, if not by name, but she knew far too many by name. She knew their families and could almost hear their wives and mothers crying from their distant farms and halls. She did not ask the boys the course of the battle. She would know soon enough. Her worry would do them no good when the knowledge might paralyze her.

She was wiping her hands on a towel, standing to gather her wits for a moment when three men hobbled into the camp. She instantly recognized the man on the right as Ecgric, who was pale as snow and helping a young *ceorl* to support a slumped third figure between them. Eadyth let out a small "oh" of grief when the figure lifted his iron-grey head to meet her eyes.

"In here," she said without thinking, pointing into the open-sided shelter to the low trestle table.

Ricbert was breathing, but each movement of his chest seemed labored. The leather and rings which armed him had turned a significant number of blows, but he had been struck by several long blades around his shoulders and even by a glancing blow to his neck. There was a blood-soaked fragment of wool wrapping his upper thigh, bound in haste on the field. She could see the pain in Ecgric's face as he looked at his father, and he seemed to think that grinding his teeth together would help to alleviate it somehow.

"Steorra," she called, and the girl appeared at her elbow a moment later. She was wide-eyed and shocked at the sight of Ricbert, but she remained silent and set to helping Eadyth unfasten Ricbert's armor. The older man groaned as they shifted him, though Eadyth tried to move him as little as possible.

"You ought to have been more careful, you old fool," she said, brushing his hair back from his forehead. His skin was cold and wet with sweat and other people's blood, but he opened his eyes and looked at her, smiling slightly.

"Apologies, my Cwene," he said sarcastically with a wince, "It is over. We've won."

Eadyth gave him a tired smile, though she could not feel relieved at the words. She groaned when she saw the massive purple bruises blossoming on Ricbert's chest. "You've broken some ribs," she said, "Anything else I should know about?"

Ricbert shook his head slightly. Eadyth cursed him good-naturedly a few times as she examined his leg. She carefully cut the knot with her short knife; the wound had begun to clot in the short time it had taken Ecgric to return to the camp with him, but when she pulled the bandage away it opened again, blood soaking his leg and pouring onto the table. She staunched the wound with a clean rag, examining it as closely as she could without causing it to bleed again. Some of the iron rings from his mail shirt had come loose and had followed the axe blade into his thigh, and when she moved the rag for a moment, she saw the mangled flesh glint with scraps of iron rings all the way down to the bone.

"Ecgric," she said, trying to wake him from the daze in which he had sunk, "There is strong mead in that pitcher. Bring it to me." He did, and she lifted Ricbert's head. "Ricbert, drink as much as you possibly can right now."

Ecgric helped to tip the mead into Ricbert's mouth as Ricbert shakily leaned on an elbow. He took several long draughts, then a breath which made him wince, and then a few more, downing most of the jug's contents and finally lying back on the table with a low groan. Eadyth waited a few moments to let the drink do its work, numbing the senses so that she could help him without causing him too much pain.

"I have to take these rings out, and sew your skin up," she said, and Ricbert gave her a wan smile. "Bite this," she said, giving him a strap of thick leather. "I thought you were old enough I wouldn't have to do this anymore!" Eadyth said, trying to smile but only grimacing as Ricbert's eyelids seemed to grow heavy.

Ecgric came forward and let his father grasp his good hand.

Eadyth uttered a prayer to Woden for his help to steady her hands which she could not keep from shaking. Her voice was drowned by a low cry from Ricbert when she began to cut away the mangled skin of the wound. She needed a clean surface to stitch together, and needed to remove the metal fragments as well, so she was forced to put her fingers into the gash and pull them out one by one. Ricbert's fingers whitened around those of his son as he twisted in pain. She tried to ignore the screams of her oldest friend, but it wounded her to think that the man she thought was made of iron could be made of fragile flesh like this.

Ecgric had to pin his father's arms down so that he would be still, but after a few moments Ricbert passed out.

There was a pile of blood-sodden rags on the ground next to her, and she knew that it would most likely double in size by the time she had finished. She worked quickly, taking the costly silk thread from around a dowel and threading it through a sharp curved bone needle. It was no different than sewing a piece of fabric, she had to remind herself. Steorra helped to hold the two sides of the gash together and Eadyth locked the stitches in place, pulling firmly but carefully, the strong silk thread gradually knitting the skin together. She finished and tied it off, wiping away the remaining blood and smearing on a concoction of honey and herbs, binding his leg as tightly as she dared from groin to knee in a long linen bandage.

Ricbert returned to consciousness a few moments after she had tied off the bandage, looking rather ashamed with himself. Ecgric was ashen; he looked at Eadyth with something like mingled thanks and pleading, but Eadyth could not offer him any comfort. She kissed Ricbert's brow, touched Ecgric's shoulder, and left. She could not pause, even for them.

Eadyth dunked her hands into a bucket of water to wash away the blood, but it had already stained the sleeves of her tunic up to the elbow. She did not much care that she had ruined the garment, but it was damp and cold from sweat and blood and she shivered. The sky half-heartedly spit a few drops of rain, but not nearly enough to wash away the blood of the morning. It had been a gruesome battle, far worse than any Eadyth had ever seen. She was used to sewing wounds and preparing the dead for burial or for the pyre, but the number of dead was beyond her count. Grizzly injuries piled into the camp, and a constant stream of bodies followed. With a great army came great casualties, she realized, and she could never have hoped that everyone would survive the battle.

She did not have time to spare for herself. She shook out her hands, drawing in a deep breath as she wiped them on a towel before moving on.

As Eadyth finished tending yet another wounded man, she heard thudding and panting as a boy of thirteen or so sprinted into the camp and nearly ran into her. He tripped over his own feet and fell, sprawling, in front of her.

"The *cyning*!" he cried as he lifted himself off of the ground. "The *cyning* is dead!"

Eadyth felt her knees nearly give out as her heart stopped. No, no, he could not be dead, the boy was lying. Rædwald was not dead. She swallowed, and her voice was gravelly as she said, "What happened?"

"The false *cyning* of the Northumbrians was killed in the battle, and we have won, my Cwene!" The grin on his face changed to shock when she slapped him hard across his face.

"You nearly made my heart stop, you little *swines scitte*," she had to stop herself shrieking at him, and took a breath, "Next time perhaps lead with the name of the enemy, not that your *cyning* is dead," she added in a low mutter, "Stupid boy."

"Yes, my Cwene" the boy said tentatively, rubbing the side of his face where she had smacked him. "I am sorry, my Cwene, what I mean to say is that Athelfrith has been killed, and our great Rædwald Cyning is victorious!"

She nodded, grinding her teeth. "He is returning now?" she asked.

"Yes, my Cwene," he said, flinching slightly as if she might hit him again, "He is returning, but there is word that the *ætheling* Edwin has been killed along with Athelfrith."

Eadyth shook her head. *All of this work, all of this fighting, and the stupid boy got himself killed anyway.* "Go and have a cup of something warm before you leave again," she told the boy gently, "I thank you for the news." He bobbed his head a few times as he backed away from her, still rubbing his cheek.

Eadyth paced the mouth of the pavilion as she waited for the stream of people to return, following the king. She could see his standard being carried behind him, but the procession may have been going backwards for all the haste it made. She looked into the empty pavilion for a moment, trying to keep tears of exhaustion from stinging her eyes.

"Dytta," she heard a voice behind her.

She rushed forward and threw her arms around Rædwald's neck. "You've come back to me. Oh thank the gods, you've come back."

He hugged her for a moment, but gently disengaged her arms. "Come with me," he said, not looking her in the eye.

She followed him past a few tents to a clearing, and looked down on the ground to where a dark-haired man lay on a cloak. Edwin, she knew; he was dead after all. But Edwin did not have hair like that; Edwin's hair was short, and Edwin was taller and had black hair, not brown; Edwin was standing in front of her, looking down at the figure lying on the cloak...

Eadyth collapsed to her knees and touched the face of her son. She wanted to cry, or to scream, or to shove a sword through her heart, but she was silent and still as stone as she knelt beside him. A ragged wound at his neck was clotted with dried blood, but the whisper of a smile was still on his lips, as if he had been laughing. She took a deep breath to stifle the cry that was building in her.

"Did he die with his sword?" She whispered, but when no one answered, she shouted it, "Did my son die with as sword in his hand?" She did not look away from his face.

"He died well," she heard Eorwald's ragged voice come from above.

Eadyth nodded and took a deep, steadying breath. She kissed Rægen's brow, the pale skin cold under her lips. "Go happily, my brave son," she told him, before rising to her feet. She looked around at the circle of men, all in various states of injury or exhaustion. She saw Eorwald standing a pace or two apart from the rest. He was trembling, though from cold or hurt or weariness she could not tell.

She closed the distance and hugged her youngest son so tightly she thought her arms might break, and he shuddered as if he would collapse at any moment. "It's over," she said in his ear. "You are hurt. Go to your tent and I'll be there in a moment."

He nodded, and she watched as he retreated into the field of tents. Rædwald seemed as if he was about to speak to her, but she silenced him with a look.

"Take the *ætheling's* body into the pavilion," she said to no one in particular. She forced her voice not to shake. When Rædwald made to follow her, she shook her head, but did not look at him. She could not look at him.

She dismissed the men when they had laid her son's body on the table in the center of the pavilion. One of the men handed her Wælcyrige, Rægen's sword. She gasped when she saw fresh blood on the edge; she had been squeezing the naked blade with her bare hand.

Eadyth set the sword carefully on the table beside him, and finally felt the scraping of a scream leave her throat. Her lungs emptied and her knees hit the hard-packed ground beneath her.

When she had no tears left to give, she felt a hand on her shoulder. She stood and flung herself into Rædwald's arms without looking or thinking. "Our boy," she said her voice barely more than a whisper. He stroked her hair, and she felt the uneven pattern of his breath and knew that their tears were the same then.

Eadyth pulled the flap of Eorwald's tent aside, letting it fall again as she ducked inside. He had placed his sword belt, rings, boiled leather armor and helm in a neat pile inside the chest, and he lay with his back to the entrance. She watched him for a moment to make sure that he was breathing; just as she had done since he was born.

"It's only me," she said when he jumped at the touch of her hand on his arm, "Sit up and drink this."

"I don't want anything," his voice was dead as he spoke to the empty expanse of canvas in front of him.

"Do as I say, Eorwald," she said, and he sat up to face her. The white of his right eye was stained a bloody red, and she could see a massive bruise forming on the side of his head where the hair was shaved; a wide trail of blood crusted down his face.

"Drink," she said, pushing the cup into his hands. "It's for the pain."

"I'm not in pain," he said, but drank anyway. He scrubbed a hand under his nose when he'd finished, and it came away streaked with blood as well.

"You're not in pain now, but you will be." She wiped away the blood from his head, from his ear, from his lip.

Eorwald winced, and the minuscule motion seemed to tax his strength. He looked like he might fall over at any moment.

She pressed the skin of the head-wound gently and was relieved to find that the bone was firm; whatever had struck him had not cracked his skull. "Thank the gods you were wearing a helm," she muttered, glancing at the dented metal on the floor nearby. "What were you hit with?"

"I don't remember," he said, blinking hard as if trying to focus on her, "I can't remember any of it, it was a blur after –" he stopped suddenly, closing his eyes and gritting his teeth. "It was so fast, so sudden, he killed the one but it was too late… I was too late…" Eorwald stopped again, shaking his head slightly as if he were trying to rid his ears of water. Eadyth wrapped her arms around him, partially to comfort his sorrow, but mostly so that she could not see his eyes, which had seen so much in so few years, wide and horrified and full of something that frightened her more than she wanted to admit.

"It's over," she said again, kissing the top of his head. "It's over. You've fought hard today, and you did all you could."

"But it's my fault," he said, "I couldn't save him, Mother."

"Eorwald," she said, taking his face between her hands and making him look her in the eye. "Tell me what happens to warriors who die fighting?"

Eorwald did not speak immediately. "Mother, this is silly," he said, his voice slurring slightly, from exhaustion or a concussion she could not be certain, "It's not the time for stories…"

Eadyth held his gaze even though it frightened her. "Tell me what happens to warriors who die fighting," she repeated.

"They are taken by the *Wælcyrigan* to the halls of the gods where they are honored guests and feel no pain or grief," he recited.

"And would Rægen wish you to feel pain on his behalf for being able to feast with the gods?" It was difficult for her to say it, as she felt so much pain herself, but she kept her voice level.

Eorwald looked at his knees, and then back into her eyes. His own were filled with tears, shining against the stain of blood.

"But he went without me."

Eadyth was sure that her heart had broken when she had seen Rægen lying on the ground, but realized with a stab of pain that it had been shattered again. "We will have a chance to grieve," she said, "But you have to rest. Lie down, now."

"You don't have to do this," he slurred as she pulled a blanket over him and hummed a quiet song, just as she did when he and his brothers and sister were small. "I'm not a child."

He was so tall, so broad and strong, and yet as small and helpless as he had been the first time she had held him.

"You are my child." She told him, stroking his cheek and kissing his brow as he closed his eyes.

A shallow blow had cut Athelfrith's hamstring and brought him low, and a blade had opened his belly, but it had been a spike driven into his heart which had caused the Northumbrian king's death. He was still gripping an ornately decorated seax, and though his bowels were hanging halfway out of his body, he looked to be at peace. Eadyth was displeased. She had wanted to watch the *wearg* die in person.

Rædwald's wolfhounds were sniffing eagerly at the gash that stretched from Athelfrith's groin to ribs. An absurd memory came to Eadyth in her husband's voice.

"Tell your *cyning* that the next time he thinks he can bribe me after slaughtering my folk; he had best come in person. His yellow guts will make a fine meal for my hounds."

But his guts were not yellow. They were red and purple and bloody, the same as any other man's. It was incredibly disappointing. For so long now, she had thought him some kind of monster, a *wearg* who was made of something other than flesh and blood and bone, but she now saw clearly that he was made of all of these boring, ordinary things.

She had half a mind to let the dogs have their way, but shooed them off as Rædwald came to her side, Edwin at his elbow.

"He's younger than I thought he would be," said Eadyth. The Northumbrian king's dark, thick hair was hidden under an ornate helm, which Eadyth kicked away. She might have thought him handsome if she did not hate him so much. Deep brown eyes stared into nothingness and his dark brown beard was caked in blood. "We ought to let the crows have him," she said. "After all of this. After every evil that he's caused. Let him rot."

"He is a *cyning*," Rædwald said quietly. Any heartiness that had once been in his voice had vanished. "He may have been my enemy, but he still died in battle. He died well, and every man who dies well deserves to be sent off properly."

"I will not waste any labor burying this *swines scitte*," Eadyth spat on the corpse. "Nor will I waste wood burning his body."

"I'll do it," Edwin said, his face the same color as that of the dead man. "I'll bury him."

"Do as you will then," Eadyth said. She left the Northumbrians, the dead and the living. She did not know why Edwin wished to take care of the body of his enemy. It reminded her in a flash of something Sigebryht might have done. She blinked away the angry tears and returned to the camp.

Eadyth might have wished to leave everything behind, to simply run home on her two legs and never see any of them again, but she forced herself not to break. She directed the able-bodied to tend the wounded, to gather wood, to begin the rebuilding. These men had done their fighting; in the days that followed, she must do hers.

The sun was beginning to set, turning the grey world a bloody red. Eadyth watched the flames catch the kindling at the bottom of the pyre, slowly touching each twig, rising until it engulfed the structure. Rædwald dropped the torch at the base, and Eadyth held his hand as they watched the flames lick upward and obscure the body of their son.

She glanced at Gieva, whose hands hung limply at her sides as she looked into the fire, her eyes deadened and devoid of tears. She had turned to stone, and the sight was more heartbreaking than if she had been weeping and tearing her hair.

Ricbert and Ecgric were there as well, despite Eadyth's instructions. Ricbert would not be kept away. He had seen Rægen brought into this world, after all. It was such a long time ago and yet not nearly long enough. Ricbert had taught her sons how to fight and had been as good as a second father to them. She wondered at his stamina to even stand upright given his injuries, as he leaned heavily on a stick and was helped along by Ecgric, whose arm was still tightly bound in a sling.

"And yet we linger," Ricbert said to Rædwald, wincing as he shifted his weight to put his hand on the king's shoulder.

"And yet we linger," Rædwald repeated Ricbert's words in a hoarse voice. His eyes were red and there were heavy bags under them, tracks of tears making lines down the soot and blood still staining his face.

Eadyth felt her own tears flowing in long, unbroken streams down her cheeks as she looked around. Too many fires were lit in this place. Too many bones would be gathered here; too many bodies buried on this stretch of land near a muddy river, so far from home. This was war. This was the magnificent, sacred thing that men dreamed of, men who would now feast with the gods while their women and their children and their fathers and mothers and brothers and sisters were left behind, forced to mend their shattered lives and pretend that it was glorious.

Moments passed, or an hour, or perhaps several years, as they stood in silence while the pyre burned. She jumped when the structure collapsed upon itself, taking Rægen's bones into the blaze with it. A cry escaped her, but it was carried away by the wind and the sound of her husband's renewed grief.

Eadyth was startled once more when Ricbert's hand suddenly left her arm. He had fallen to the ground, his face deathly pale in the firelight. She dropped to her knees and touched his face. "No, no, no," she sobbed, feeling his skin burning under her fingers.

"Get him back to the camp!" she screamed at no one, and several pairs of hands lifted Ricbert to carry him away. Eadyth looked back at the pyre, still burning painfully brightly, tore her eyes and her heart away from it.

"Torches!" she shouted, "I need light!"

Someone brought fire to the pavilion where they had set Ricbert upon the trestle table that had held her son's body only hours before. Rædwald stood out of the way, chewing his lip with wide eyes that seemed to beg her to save his oldest friend.

Ricbert's eyes were closed. His face was burning, his lips dry and cracked, his body limp. She pulled her seax from her belt and sliced through the bandage around his leg. The wound was still knitted together with the strong silk thread, and the edges were still clean with no sign of infection.

"You old fool!" She sobbed, wiping her eyes on a clean patch of her sleeve. Her hands were shaking violently and she took a step backwards, overcome with a sudden wave of panic and anguish that threatened to break her.

The pavilion flap opened and Gieva stepped in. Her face was blank, her eyes dead, but she approached without a word and put her hands around Eadyth's own, steadying them. Eadyth stared at her, pleading, apologizing that she could not help, but

Gieva had turned to Ricbert and immediately set to re-binding his leg.

"He's burning," Ecgric said as he stood near his father's head, watching Gieva work. "What's wrong with him?"

Gieva tied off the end of the bandage and put her head to Ricbert's chest. "His heart is too fast," she said in a monotone.

Rædwald had touched Eadyth's arm to guide her out of the pavilion, but she jerked away from him and remained rooted, watching Gieva's steady hands as the other woman gently moved Ricbert's clothing aside to examine his body.

"The wound hasn't broken open," Ecgric said, "He should be better now!"

Gieva shook her head. "Something is poisoning his blood." She used the seax to cut away Ricbert's tunic, revealing a thin cut along his collarbone. The skin was bright red and the scratch was filled with yellow pus that stank and stuck to the fabric of Ricbert's shirt. Eadyth winced at the sight. She had been so focused on his gaping leg in the aftermath of the battle that she had not worried about the thin slice on his chest. Now it was likely to take his life.

Gieva held her seax in the torch flame, waiting until it smoked and began to turn red at the edges. She touched the heated blade to the cut, and Eadyth flinched as she watched Ricbert's body twitch feebly as the wound smoked and the smell filled her nostrils.

Eadyth did not remember leaving the pavilion, but she found herself outside. She glanced around, disgusted with her own cowardice, and her tears began to flow afresh. She half-wanted to hear Ricbert screaming in pain, for it would tell her that he was still alive. She could not take another step; she was shaking, weeping, and she did not know what to do.

A flutter of light left the pavilion, and Eadyth turned to find Gieva outlined in the glow. Eadyth could not see her face, but her shoulders were hunched and she walked slowly out of the pavilion, as if she did not know where she was.

"Gieva," Eadyth was startled by how choked her voice sounded, but Gieva spoke before she could say anything.

"I don't know if he will live," Gieva said, her voice still quiet and toneless. "I've burned the wound. I don't know if it will be enough."

"I should have done when he first came back!" Eadyth sobbed, "It's my fault! He's going to die because of me!"

"Hush," Gieva said, taking Eadyth in her arms as if she was a child. "It is in the hands of the gods now."

Eadyth hiccoughed and Gieva released her. The girl's eyes were far away, cold and lifeless, not looking into Eadyth's. She simply stared into the distance where the fire was still burning. Eadyth wordlessly shifted aside as Gieva shuffled slowly back toward the pyre, her hands limp at her sides and slick with blood.

They had put Ricbert in the king's bed, and Eadyth, Rædwald and Ecgric had stayed by his side the entire night. Eadyth sat on the edge of the bed and touched a damp rag to Ricbert's forehead, certain that the cloth would catch fire from the heat of his skin.

"Do you remember," Eadyth asked the sleeping Ricbert quietly, while the others paced the pavilion out of earshot, "You were the one who came to tell me that my husband was dead after the battle at Wibbandun. You brought me his spear, and handed it to Sigebryht. You told him that you had a boy of your own, and that one day you would introduce them and they would be great friends." She realized that Ecgric was listening, though he did not look at her. "And you told me that I should not despair, even though I cried. You didn't know what to do to help." She felt a sob rising in her chest even as she smiled at the memory, and she wiped his brow again. "You were the only friend I had then. And now, I don't know what to do to help you." She took his hand, clammy and limp as it was, and squeezed it.

"He's the reason we met," Rædwald said hoarsely. "At Ethelbert's hall. I saw you talking to Bercta and he got fed up with me staring and not paying attention to our war-games, so he told me he'd kick me in the prick if I didn't get up and talk to you."

Eadyth choked on something that was half a sob and half a giggle. "I'd forgotten about that," she said, and they were all silent for a long while.

Ecgric shook his head. "It's not fair."

Rædwald sat down as well, putting a hand on Ecgric's uninjured shoulder but saying nothing.

"No one who has fought in that many battles should have to die like this," Ecgric said bitterly. "What kind of game is this?

Men who fight should get to go to the Feast. That is the way things work."

Eadyth took a deep breath, wishing that she could comfort him, but she felt the same way. Why was it that the bravest and the strongest were not given their rewards? "Perhaps he's not meant to go to the Feast yet."

"How can you know that?" Ecgric asked.

"I can't bear to think that someone like him could be kept from the halls of Woden unless there is a very good reason," she said, and looked back down at the prone figure in front of her. "You had better hurry up and get better," she told Ricbert crossly, "you'd just better had. You have to go on fighting, and end in glory with a sword in your hand. Not like this."

His face was blank and his eyes closed, but she felt his fingers tighten slightly around hers, as if to say, "I'll do my best."

Chapter Twenty-Two

Gemynd

Memory

he remembered fire.
She remembered searing flesh and cries of pain.
She remembered cold air and hot wind.
She remembered the smell.
She remembered bones.
She remembered ash.

Gieva felt the weight of Wælcyrige as she held it out for the king, who placed the sword in front of the shrouded bones. Eadyth was singing something, a song of mourning probably, but Gieva could not hear the words for the screaming of the wind in her ears.

Even now, as she stared into the chamber that would lock him away from her forever, her eyes stung with the tears that she could not shed.

Gieva saw Eorwald standing nearby, but he took no notice of her. She knew that part of her felt a deep sense of pity for Eorwald, for everything that he had been through in the past months, but it was difficult for her to feel anything other than a throbbing ache where her heart should have been.

She had not spoken to anyone except when absolutely necessary. She only ate when Eadyth forced her to put food in her mouth, and though she could hardly move from her bed, she did not sleep. All she wanted to do was to cry, to let the scream that had been building in her heart tear its way out of her lungs, but nothing came. Nothing but emptiness.

It had all passed slowly, like a nightmare from which she could not wake, half-remembered in a morning that never came to ease the darkness.

When she had returned to the camp after the battle, blood-soaked and exhausted, she found her way to the tent. He was not there, but she had not expected him to be. She cleaned her hands and walked toward the pavilion where she was sure to find him, probably lifting a strong cup of beer and saluting his brothers in arms who had gone joyfully to the Feast.

The thought had made her smile as she walked along the lane of trampled grass, when she stopped short. Eorwald had nearly run into her as he walked; he did not seem to see her immediately but he flinched away from her hand when she put it up to stop him knocking her over. His eyes were unfocused and he had a trail of dried blood coming from a wound above his ear, and he staggered as if drunk. He blinked once, and then again, as if trying to bring her face into focus.

"What's happened to you?" she asked kindly, gripping his shoulder, "you're hurt; please, come and sit down." She tried to lead him to a stump nearby, but he did not move.

"Gieva," he said, finally seeming to see her. Their eyes met for half of a heartbeat, in which he shook his head slightly and she felt her insides turn to lead.

"Where is he?" she breathed, though she did not hear any words Eorwald may have said.

Gieva found herself at the entrance of the pavilion without knowing how she gotten there. She entered and found herself next to the trestle table, touching the cold hand that had been warm only hours before. A fresh wave of anguish washed over her as she looked at the wound that had ended his life.

No, she thought, *how will he be able to sing now?* The blade which had silenced his voice seemed to stab her and she felt a scream building on the edges of her heart. The grief wanted to escape. It pressed against her ribs and pounded in her head, so powerfully real that she knew it would break her body as it forced its way out of her. She wished that it would. The loss burned her so keenly that the tears seemed to evaporate before they could flow from her eyes.

"Rægen, my heart," she said, touching his cheek, calling to him as if it would bring him back. She pressed her lips to his, pretending for a moment that they were still warm.

Hours passed, or perhaps only a few moments, and the ashes had blown away into the cold morning. She barely remembered watching the pyre burn; she could almost recall speaking to Eadyth and somehow finding her hands covered in blood. Somehow the sky had grown lighter; the opaque blanket of cloud too bright for her eyes. They stung with the ashes that she could not wash away.

She had gathered the bones together and put them into the casket, so that they could be taken to the land of his fathers. It was her duty, and though other women offered to help, she did not want anyone else to touch the bones. They were his, though they were not him. They were bones. He was gone.

The mourners began to dissipate, making for the boats which would take them to the other side of the river, into the world of the living. It might have been a beautiful place if she could forget the fact that each of the frost-crusted hillocks had been made because another child had been left fatherless.

She was alone now. Her hands clasped together in front of her, and she felt the swelling between her hips. She had not felt a stirring in weeks, since before the battle. She was certain that the baby must have died as well. Perhaps it was for the best, though she would not be able to weep for it.

There was nothing now. Everyone who had loved her was gone. All of her kin were dead. Her husband was dead. The child, the last thing she would ever have of him, was dead.

She could die too.

She could fall asleep and let the cold take her, and no one would know any better, because everyone was gone. She could not think of what might happen in the future. The future was ash, and though it choked her, no tears came.

Gieva did not know how she had ended up lying next to the freshly packed earth of the mound, or why she was so cold. Her eyelashes were touched with frost, and it took her a moment before she could see the figure in front of her. She did not know who it was, and she did not care. She just wanted to sleep. She would stop feeling cold soon; stop feeling empty.

Someone lifted her up, but she did not have the energy to fight it. She closed her eyes and put her arms protectively over the dead child inside of her, as the strong arms carried her away.

And it moved. Rolling, tumbling; the stirring of life within her body restarted her heart.

She remembered life.

She remembered the warmth of his arms around her.

She remembered the light of silver in his eyes.

She remembered his voice as he sang to their child as it danced with joy inside of her.

She remembered how to cry.

*****

The plum trees were bare of leaves, their branches drooping and damp. Eorwald shivered. He had forgotten to put on a cloak. Come to think of it, he had forgotten why he had come down to the river at all. He scrubbed a hand through his short hair. It was time to shave it again. His fingers brushed the place where the hammer-wielding man had struck him. It did not hurt anymore, but the thought of it made his head ache.

Why was he out here? He could not remember, and it nagged at him. He had needed to come outside for some reason, but then he had been thinking of Hwitegos, of his pale, red-rimmed eyes and his sneering grin, and he had forgotten why he had left the hall.

He realized that he was digging his fingernails into his palm and released the fist, trying not to think of the fury that was building at the thought that he had not been able to kill the pale *wearg* during the battle. He looked at his hands. They were shaking.

He turned for home.

Gieva was outside her house when he passed. She glanced at him but looked away immediately, hurrying inside. Eorwald had felt the poison surge in his blood when he had seen her with dry eyes after the battle. Rægen had been completely besotted with this woman; had prized her above anything else in the world, and everyone had thought that she loved him just as much. It had infuriated Eorwald to see that she did not shed a single tear after Rægen had died in glory on the battlefield. She had been like stone, unfeeling and cold. He had hated her for it.

At least he had done, until he found her lying against the barrow after they had buried Rægen's bones on the South Tún.

Something about her broke his poisonous heart that day. He had held her in his arms as they sat in the boat that took them back to Wuffingham, and she had soaked his shirt with her silent tears. She had not said anything then, and she had not spoken to him since that day. He did not know what good it would do in any case.

He returned to the practice yard and heard the thrum and smack of arrows hitting their mark. A swelling of nausea hit him like a wave as he remembered the sound, and he was sure that he could hear someone screaming. Eorwald ran forward, a dull ache still pounding in his head and in his calf where he had been stuck, so long ago. He reached to his hip for his sword but found only his belt knife. Panicking, he pulled it out anyway.

When he reached the practice yard, he stopped. It was only a few men shooting at the straw target next to the fence, laughing and heckling one another. They did not see him, and he walked away as quickly as he could without someone noticing.

He felt his breathing coming in quick gasps as he rounded to the back of the Bricgweard and leaned against the wall. The poison was coming back; he could feel it creeping up from the now-healed wound in his calf and slowly making its way to his heart.

A foul taste filled his mouth, of the blood and ash of battle, of the sickness of the aftermath. His lips felt numb, almost as if he had had too much to drink, though he had not touched a drop in days. Nausea flooded his stomach, and he leaned against the wall, sliding down slowly until he was sitting.

Eorwald wondered if he had fallen asleep as he sat there. He suddenly felt exhausted, disorientated, as though he had run a hundred leagues in the dark. His head ached and he realized he was lying on one side, trembling so that he could feel the gravel stabbing his arm even through his shirt.

The foul taste and the nausea did not depart. His knife was still in his shaking hand, but as he tried to slide it into its sheath he sliced the edge of his finger with the sharp blade. A small drop of blood appeared on his fingertip. It was red and warm, not black and smoking as he thought it must have been. He remembered the feeling, when he had been wounded in the fights after his captivity, how the blood seemed to help release the poison. How good it had felt.

Without thinking, he drew the tip of the knife across his thigh, slicing through the wool as easily as the flesh of his leg. He felt the same strange sweeping relief as a line of blood began to soak through the fabric.

His hands were no longer shaking as he went to the Bricgweard, entering the anteroom silently. He touched the thin line of blood on his leg as he stripped the torn trousers off, and found another pair before looking around the deserted room.

Few *thegns* had come back with them, instead returning to their own homes following the battle. No one remained in the Bricgweard except for servants and the odd *thegn* with no one to go home to, but everyone was outside or away on some errand or other.

The king and queen were away as well, though he knew that they would not speak to him now anyway. Father had wept and raged and cursed men and gods for the loss of his firstborn son, but he had not spoken more than a few words to Eorwald since.

Everyone had gone. Eorwald had no one now, no one to talk to; no one to grieve with, and he did not know what to do. Ecgric remained in the North with his injured father; half of his friends were slaughtered in the battle, and the other half had rushed home to their families as quickly as they could.

And Rægen – his companion since birth; his teacher and his best friend –

Eorwald clenched his teeth and sank into one of the alcoves, wrenching shut the woolen hanging, though he knew that no one would see him anyway. It was not shameful to weep for the loss of a brother. No one would think less of him for that, even weeks later. It was not his grief that he tried to hide, now.

He felt the stinging of the thin cut on his thigh, and drew his finger against it. The clotted blood flowed afresh as he opened it with his finger, drawing out the poison, the grief, the shame, the sickness.

It made him remember that he was not dead. He did not know if that was a good thing, but feeling the physical pain was infinitely better than the lost moments; the confusion of not knowing where he was or how he had gotten there. His knife's handle seemed to dig into his side, as if to remind him that it was there. His very blood seemed to ache to make its way out of his veins, to draw the venom with it.

It called to him, and he answered. He had no choice.

*****

Hours.

Godomar's weight had pressed down on her as he stared her in the eyes, his hands tight around her hips and his eyes boring into hers. Every thrust sent a spasm of pain through her hips and up her back; deep, throbbing, nauseating. Sunniva could not breathe, and he only pressed harder, thrust deeper whenever she tried to look away from him.

Hours before the bites of the strap stopped stinging; before the bruises where Walaric's fist had met her sides had stopped throbbing. Numbness trickled through her, but for the strand of agony in her core.

Hours before he finally spent himself. She could see a dark stain against his flesh when he finally got to his feet. She could hear him saying something about being a maiden reborn as he kissed her mouth, stroked her cheek, and covered her with a blanket.

Hours.

Hours and hours and hours beyond count seemed to beat her as she lay on the bed, her heart and her belly and her back and her legs aching and cramping so badly that she could not even gather the breath to scream. She leaned over the edge of the bed and emptied her stomach into the rushes.

Hours before the pain came to a head.

Hours before Sige found her and called to her as she felt consciousness slipping away.

Hours before that last shuddering gasp of pain.

She could still see it every time she closed her eyes. Barely larger than her hand, its eyes shut, its tiny body barely even human-looking, lying between her legs and covered in her blood.

No, not it. He. Her son.

It had taken only moments for the blows to kill him.

It had taken hours for her body let him go.

*****

"You must leave," one of the women said. She was twice as wide as a man and nearly as tall, and as stern a face as any grandmother. "She will be quite well enough without you."

"I will not leave," Sige said. He made no move to rise, though the woman was tugging at his sleeve.

The woman muttered something about obstinate fool men, but she stopped picking at his shirt and took a step back. He ignored her tapping foot behind him. At least it was not Godomar.

Godomar had only come a few times in the week since Sunniva had almost bled to death, both times accompanied by a handful of his retainers. All stood in the door solemnly while Godomar bent over Sunniva's sleeping form, and they nodded in appreciative gravity while Godomar wept and cried loud prayers to his god that she would be healed. Sige felt the bile rising at the display, and might have shoved his seax in the *graf's* retreating back if there had not been a flutter of women who had taken his place.

Sige now rolled his eyes at the woman now tutting behind him, but he took Sunniva's hand. Her skin was cool again, the fever gone but sweat still sticky on her palm.

He almost jumped when she seemed to grimace in her sleep, and her eyes fluttered open a fraction. She did jump when she saw him, a mask of fear crossing her face for an instant before her face collapsed back into smoothness. She squeezed his hand weakly, licking dry lips and wincing.

"Sige," she rasped.

"I'm here," he said. "Do you need anything?"

Her head shook slowly, and fell to face him. Her eyes were half-closed, wavering as if she could not keep them open. Sige gave a despairing look at the woman still fluttering around behind him, and she left with a few more words about obstinate men. Satisfied, Sige looked back at his sister.

"I'm here, Sunni," He repeated.

"Please don't tell Ecgric," she breathed hoarsely, "Don't tell him. I don't want..." she took a labored breath, "I don't want him to be sad. Don't tell him I lost it."

Sige took a moment to understand the words, and sighed. "Did he know it was his?"

She shook her head. "Ecgric did not even know I was pregnant. No one knew." A sudden flash of fear crossed her face as she said, "No. That is not true. Godomar knew whose it was."

Sige felt his guts solidify into lead.

Godomar knew.

How convenient that Sunniva had suddenly fallen ill. It was all very clean. Very tidy. Godomar did not like things to be messy, after all.

"Will you do something for me?" She asked, and Sige cleared his head of the furious images forming within.

"What is it?"

"Give a sacrifice on my part," she said, "I can't go myself." She frowned, and a tear leaked out of the corner of her eye. "There's a ring on the table. Use it as an offering. Make sure that..." her free hand strayed to her torso, "The gods will take care of him now."

Sige nodded sadly and kissed her forehead before leaving.

Sige stepped to the edge of the pool and touched a bit of the ice at the edge with a foot. It cracked and floated away to show the treasures beneath, illuminated for the moment by the weak ray of sun making its way into the grove. He did not know many of the prayers to Frea or to Eostre or the Mother of the Earth; he knew the words for a good harvest and chants at a wedding feast, but there was no reason for a man to learn the lore of childbirth. He hoped his words would be enough.

"Eorðe, ure modor, rec sunu sweostor min." Earth, our mother, take my sister's son into your keeping. He thought for a moment, frowning. She was no maiden, no mother, no crone. She would not ask for fertility, or for love. If Sige knew anything about her, he knew that she had never wanted that world for her own. He dropped the heavy silver ring into the half-frozen pool, watching it sink, twirling, down to the bottom. It glinted faintly in an instant of sun, but the clouds drew together and the image was gone.

"Thunor," he added, *"eoten-bana, hiere gief ellen eowerostne to þæm þæt toweard guð to winnenne."* Thunor, the slayer of giants, give her your strength to fight in her battles to come. "Give us all strength," he muttered as an afterthought.

The small pond, iced at the edges, was still as always. It was protected from the wind by the surrounding stand of trees, their bare limbs ghostly white against the dark background of the woods. There was no Sacred Oak here, but a single ash tree stood sentinel at the far end of the pond, its spear-point leaves littering the ground around it. An image flashed across his mind of the All-Father at the foot of the World Tree, trading his eye for a chance to drink from the well and bring poetry to the world. He half-expected to see a grey-cloaked man at the foot of the ash, contemplating some bit of deep wisdom.

It was the thing he needed, wisdom. If he were as wise as Woden, he might have known the proper course. He would be able to decide.

Sige heard footsteps approaching from behind, but waited for them to reach him. Only then did he turn.

"I would not have expected to see you here, Father," Sige glanced over at the priest, who stood level with him.

"God is in the trees and the water, just as he is in the churches built to his glory," said Mathias, though his tone had an edge of agitation under the calm surface.

"But you did not come here to pray," Sige said.

Mathias took a long breath. "No, Sigebryht. I came to speak to you. The *graf* has received word. Rædwald and his household were attacked on their way to battle with the Northumbrians. The king was slain, and so was the *ætheling*."

Sige swayed. "Which…" he had to swallow with difficulty, "Which *ætheling*?" It did not matter the answer. Whatever it was, he was not ready for it.

Mathias shook his head. "I cannot say. The messenger had few details, and rumor is much stronger than truth when it comes such a distance."

Sigebryht blinked hard a few times before blowing out a breath of cold air. "Does Sunniva know?"

"My Vrouwe keeps to her room," Mathias said, his eyebrows drawn together and his mouth curved in a bitter frown. "Graf Godomar says that she is in too delicate a state to have visitors."

The bones in Sige's hands nearly cracked as she clenched his fists. "I will tell her. She ought to know." He took a step forward, but Mathias put out a hand.

"Let me pass, Father," Sige said carefully, though he did not let Mathias doubt the warning in his voice.

"You cannot tell her," Mathias said.

"If her father and our brothers are dead, she has the right to know," Sige growled, "And if someone is going to tell her, I will."

Mathias gave him a level look. "Please do not do anything rash."

Sige shook his head. "What I plan to do is none of your affair. I only wish to speak to my sister."

"If you do as you plan, it will be the worse for both of you." Mathias persisted, looking him in the eye as if he could see into the pit of Sigebryht's mind. "She is safer where she is."

Sige swallowed. "I don't know what you mean by that. I only wish to tell her what has happened. There is nothing more to it."

Mathias lowered his eyes, nodding slowly. He muttered something that might have been a prayer. "When a man is watched as carefully as you are, he must tread just as carefully. A misstep taken in haste can have greater consequences than you could imagine."

"Do not talk to me in riddles," Sige said through clenched teeth. "Speak plainly, or mind your own affairs."

"Godomar watches you. He waits for a mistake. Do not make one. Do not give him cause to harm you." Mathias said sharply. "I will not make it plainer."

"What is he planning?" Sige asked. "If he plans to harm my men, or Sunniva—"

"I do not know if he plans anything. I was not told to seek you out to tell you. I am only here now because I think you have the right to know. You know his alliance is broken with the Englisc king now. If you give Godomar a reason, any reason at all, he will kill you. You have to know that."

Sige did not respond.

"You must trust me," said Mathias earnestly.

Sige nearly scoffed. He would never fully trust a Christian. There was no part of him that could do so.

"I am going to speak to my sister," he said firmly.

"Sigebryht, you must listen to me," the priest said to Sige's back, but Sige did not turn around.

"Oswy," Sige hissed at the other man, who was leaning on a fence post talking to a pretty young woman when Sige approached. Oswy took his attentions from the girl, who was twirling her hair around her finger, before his face fell at the sight of Sigebryht.

"What is it, Dryhten?" Oswy asked, moving away from the girl and lowering his voice.

"We are leaving," Sige muttered, glancing around. "Gather the men. We leave after nightfall. Take nothing that you cannot strap to your back."

Oswy frowned. "What's happened?"

Sige swallowed, unsure if he could say the words without his voice breaking. "Rædwald Cyning is dead, and perhaps his... possibly his sons are dead as well. I worry that without an alliance to stay Godomar's hand, he may decide we are of no use to him anymore."

Oswy's face registered surprise, then grief, then panic, and then grim determination, in the space of a heartbeat. He nodded, his mouth set and his arms stiff at his sides.

"Tell the others," Sige said. "But do not let anyone know what you are doing."

"What of our lady?" Oswy whispered.

"I will take care of her," Sige said. "Make for the docks after nightfall, and get on any ship leaving tonight. I will meet you there, but if I do not, you must leave before the tide. If I am not there, take whatever ship will bear you." He pushed a heavy sack of silver into Oswy's hand. "Go home, and tell whoever is in Rædwald's seat that Godomar's alliance is dead."

Oswy frowned, his eyes wide. "Sigebryht..." he said slowly, "What is going on?"

"Do as I say," Sigebryht told him. "I will explain everything to you when there is time, I promise. Just make sure you get home."

"Of course, Dryhten," Oswy nodded grimly. The girl had long-since gone, and Oswy took a deep breath before rushing away.

Sige clenched and released his fingers before making for the hall. Sunniva was strong enough, no matter what Godomar tried to say. She was tough. She was fiery, clever, stubborn, and fierce, and Sige would not let that Frankisc *wearg* beat her into the ground any more.

His heart nearly skipped as he thought of taking her home. They just had to make it to nightfall, and they could slip out and make their way to the ship. Once aboard, Godomar could do nothing to stop them. They might escape with nothing but the clothes on their backs, but that hardly mattered now. They would be safe. He just had to tell her.

The hall was quiet, though he was not surprised. Few people remained in the village during the winter, and the few who did remain were out doing errands or chores for their lord and taking advantage of the relatively mild day to work out of doors. Sigebryht strode to the door of the *graf's* bed chamber, ignoring the handful of servants going about their business.

"Sunni," he whispered, pushing open the door. He glanced at the bed, and saw only a mound of blankets and furs. She had been all but confined to her room since she had lost the baby and he had not seen her in days, since she asked him to give the sacrifice. She was probably still sleeping, still trying to recover. He knelt beside the bed, putting his hand gingerly on the mound. Something rustled behind him just outside the door, but he did not turn to see who it was. Probably one of the servants.

"Sunni," he said, pressing on the mound, "Sunniva, we have to get out of here. Tonight. We have to leave this place for good."

She did not turn over, but it did not matter. She trusted him, and she would listen, even if she did not understand. The panic grew as he heard the servants rustling about. He did not want to be overheard, even if it was by serving folk.

"Dress warmly, but do not burden yourself. We have to move fast. We –"

Chapter Twenty-Three

Breotende

Broken

ilde set to warming wine with herbs in a pot on the hearth while Sunniva looked blankly at the rushes on the floor. They intertwined and crossed one another in patterns like ravaging beasts, and she followed them with her eyes. A wolf here, a bear there; a raven with outstretched wings seemed to fly toward the door. They danced together among the dirty pieces of straw, still covered in flecks of her blood.

"Here you are," the other woman said, pressing a horn cup into Sunniva's hand. Sunniva sipped the wine, and knew in part of her mind it tasted nice, though she took no pleasure in it.

Sunniva picked up the scrap of fabric she had been embroidering, digging the bone needle in and out with about as much enthusiasm as she had taken to drink the wine. It was one pastime that Godomar thought befitted a woman of her status, though she still hated it. Her fingers had callouses from the pricks of the needle, and the cloth was puckered and ugly where she had pulled the thread too tight.

Hilde sat beside her and copied her movements, though her simple stitching was far neater. Sunniva barely looked up when she heard voices from outside, and the sounds of hooves and feet crunching on the dirt of the yard. She swallowed, put aside the mangled fabric, and got slowly to her feet.

Sunniva only spared him a glance before her husband had dismounted and came to kiss her formally on both cheeks.

"My treasure," he said, "Are you not happy to see me?"

She bit her tongue, letting her mouth twist into something she thought might resemble a smile.

He seemed satisfied, and he turned to his men. "I shall meet you all later. I have been neglecting my sweet wife."

Sunniva let Godomar lead her into their chamber, and he waited next to the closed door until she had pulled his cloak from his shoulders and hung it on its peg on the wall.

"Oh, but I have missed you," he said, lifting her chin with one finger and touching his lips to hers. She swallowed a sob as he guided her to the bed.

"No," she tried to say, but she could not even hear her own voice. A cool rush of air hit her legs as he lifted her heavy wool dress over her hips; his hands were gentle as he forced her to her back.

"I don't want to," she said, louder now.

His face grew hard as he positioned himself above her. "I've told you before, my treasure," he pressed against her and she winced, "I will not tolerate disobedience."

"Please," she said as he penetrated deeper, "They said I am not yet healed, I haven't –" the rest of the sentence was drowned in a whimper as he pulled out, and thrust back in so quickly and so hard that she felt something tear.

Godomar put his lips beside her ear as he rent her again and again. "I have already forgiven you for your fornication," he whispered, "If God has decided to punish you further then it is His will."

Sunniva's stomach roiled. A thread in her mind seemed to snap as she wound up her fist, letting it collide with the side of Godomar's face.

He blinked once, and a muscle twitched in his jaw, but he only took her by the wrists and pressed them into the bed until he had finished with her. He rose to his feet and tied the laces of his breeches, smoothing the wool of his tunic over the top.

"You will go out into the hall, where Walaric is waiting. You will summon him here, and when you return, you will be punished."

She leapt to her feet, but did not take a step. She felt her weakened muscles clenching.

Godomar surveyed her as if she were a mildly interesting bit of entertainment. "I have allowed you some indulgences, my jewel. You were upset that your foul pagan of a half-brother abandoned you, and I have been more than understanding that you cannot comprehend his cowardice," his expression became a fraction stonier, "but my patience has its limits."

"He did not abandon me," she hissed, "You've killed him!"

From the start, Godomar had pretended that nothing had happened the day Sige had disappeared. He was happy to pretend that the wooden stakes outside the west gate did not exist. He did not let her pass the west gate, after all, but she had still seen their heads. She had counted them, looked into each mangled face while Hilde had tried to pull her away; faces she had known since she was a child.

Three were missing from their number. She did not know if she ought to feel relieved that Sige was one of those three. This was foul enough; what would they do to him? What had they done already?

"Your brother fled while his men attacked us," Godomar said soothingly, "He turned his foul pagan hide the moment he was in danger, and left his men to receive their punishments while he escaped to safety."

"You're a liar!" she raised a hand and darted towards him, but he flicked it away as if it were a bothersome fly.

"My patience is wearing thin, my little flower," Godomar said. "If I must fetch Walaric myself, I will be extremely disappointed."

"Assault," said Godomar, when Walaric had closed the door behind him. "Not to mention slander and disobedience."

Walaric nodded stoically, circling behind Sunniva, taking both of her wrists in his large hands. Godomar stepped forward, unclasping the brooches that held Sunniva's apron dress on her shoulders. He carefully removed the jewels, placing them tenderly in a box, as the dress fell to the ground. The shift followed after, and he took her hands in his when it had been pulled over her head.

"Defiance is not a comely feature in a woman," Godomar said, pinning her forearms to his chest. No need for ropes or thongs. He would look her in the eyes this time.

Sunniva did not have the strength to resist Godomar's fingers encircling her forearms, and she had to put every scrap of energy into the hateful gaze at Godomar as the thin switch struck her back and her shoulders. She could almost feel the welts growing with every bite.

"That is for your insolence," he said.

Something much thicker and much harder found the backs of her legs. She made it through seven or eight blows, before her knees gave out. He still held her arms, standing casually as blow after blow dug her knees deeper into the rushes before him.

Godomar released her arms, and she dropped to the floor, her hands hitting the rushes hard as she fell.

"That is for your slander, for calling me a liar." Godomar said quietly. He looked at Walaric now. "I will let you take care of the punishment for assaulting a lord. I must return to my men."

He crouched on one knee before Sunniva, stroking her cheek. "Do nothing to harm her face, though," he said, "My little treasure is so very beautiful."

*****

"It won't make me any worse to tell me what's going on," Ricbert said, sitting up and propping himself on a cushion. "It's not as if I can just get up and start taking my vengeance."

Ecgric did not believe his father's words for an instant, but decided to tell him anyway. "The men traveling back to Eni's hall were attacked as they passed Elge," he said, stoking the dying fire.

Ricbert's brows drew even closer together. "What of Eni's sons?"

"They've returned here safely. Æthelhere was wounded, but not badly. Æthelwold is well enough, but they're both shaken. They were attacked without warning as they left their camp, and there was a bloody fight. Strays and vagrants from the battle at the Idle, I expect."

"Yes," said Ricbert, "That sometimes happens. Disinherited men tend to wander after a battle and take out their revenge on the ones who wronged them. Do you know how many there were?"

"No more than fifty, according to Æthelwold," said Ecgric, "Not enough to be called a real army, but enough to cause some damage."

"And too many to be assumed to be leaderless," said Ricbert.

Ecgric watched his pensive father for some time before saying, "Who would be leading them? Did Athelfrith leave an heir?"

"He has a son," said Ricbert, "Eanfrith, I think he is called. I don't know much about him, except that he was one of Athelfrith's captains. Buggered if I knew which one, though."

"Edwin would know," suggested Ecgric.

"Edwin is too far away for us to ask him anything," Ricbert sighed. "I think at this point, we ought to leave Northumbraland to the Northumbrians. There is a large host who swore themselves to Edwin, after all. They will deal with the wanderers who are still loyal to Athelfrith."

"What of the men who attacked Eni's sons?" Ecgric asked hotly. He did not appreciate the idea of leaving the attack unavenged. "We can't send more men as an escort, or we will be completely outmanned here."

"Perhaps we ought to leave, then?"

Ecgric scoffed, "Very well, Old Man, get up and let's go."

Ricbert gave him a hard look and moved to rise from his bed.

Ecgric immediately shook his head. "It was dangerous enough getting you back here to Mæduwic after the battle. You're not well enough to move yet, and even if you were, you cannot fight like this. You'll be too vulnerable."

"I don't care. Let them come." Ricbert said bitterly.

"Don't be stupid," Ecgric said. His brisk annoyance at his father's stubbornness was quickly returning. "We will stay here. Æthelhere and Æthelwold can wait to return home. Eni gave us his men; he didn't say when we had to return them."

"I thought I'd taught you better than that," said Ricbert. "You know that these men need to go home."

"You know I want to leave this place as much as anyone else," said Ecgric, "But I don't want you dying on the way."

"If I die, I die. You can't change fate any more than you can change the weather. You'd best get ready for the journey. It is time we left this place for good."

Ecgric felt sickened every time he glanced at his father, who was sitting in a baggage cart like a feeble old woman. It was not the way things should have been. Ricbert had seen and survived more battles than any person Ecgric knew, and yet the honorable blow which should have killed him had given him a wound which would not heal. It had been weeks since the battle, and every time his father seemed to improve, he would slip back into sickness, recovering a few days later. He kept overexerting himself, Ecgric knew. If he insisted on fighting, he would do it properly. He would heal first, and fight again another day.

Æthelwold was telling Ecgric, for what felt like the hundredth time, of how they had fought against the Northumbrian warriors who had attacked them the last time they had come this way. He gave it the usual embellishments of a battle remembered, supplemented by exclamations from his brother, and Ecgric tried to seem pleased with them. The boys were excellent fighters, despite the lack of practice offered by their father. They had fought in Rædwald's line during the battle, protected somewhat but still in the thick of things, and even now they still had the blood-joy on them.

He remembered being that age, so eager to fight and to whore his way across the country; so eager to be a man. He had fought for Ethelbert when he was no older than these boys, and just as wide-eyed and excited. Bercta had taken him into her bed for the first time that night, as the *heahcyning* lay soaked in mead and bloodlust in the hall. People thought it had been scandalous for him to have slept with the *heahcwene*, but he did not care. She was not the old crone many made her out to be. She had been beautiful, and intelligent, and had taught him how to please a woman.

As he thought of Bercta and the youthful nights he had spent in her bed, he tried to suppress the thought of Sunniva. The memory of her was beginning to drive him insane. He had thought that it was simply the touch of a woman that he had missed, but after trying and failing to have some pretty northern girl, he knew that this was not the case. It was Sunniva he wanted. It was the spoiled, stubborn, fiery woman who had gone to find adventure somewhere far away in the arms of a man Ecgric hated. She was the one he wanted, and yet she was the one he would never have.

"Someone's smitten," Æthelhere told Æthelwold in a falsely-worldly voice, and Æthelwold sighed. "I know that look."

Ecgric wheeled round, glaring at the younger men. "How would you know that look? You can't even grow a beard. What do you know of women?"

"I know that you've just admitted to thinking about one," said Æthelhere, and Æthelwold grinned.

Ecgric rolled his eyes. "Not everything is about women, you know. For your information, I was thinking about the death of the *ætheling*." It was not entirely a lie. Rægenhere's death had been a blow, and he had thought about it often. He was pleased that Rægenhere could die with honor in battle, but Ecgric had looked forward to fighting alongside him for many years to come. The younger men at least had the decency to look solemn.

They arrived in Eni's lands without incident. Ecgric was unsure whether he should be grateful or disappointed at the lack of action on their journey, but the point was rendered moot by his worry for his father. The journey had caused his fever to return, and they rushed along the old Roman road to get to Eni's house as quickly as possible.

Ælfgifu met them a mile from the hall, having received the messenger Ecgric had sent ahead. She welcomed them all, and had a bed and medicine prepared for Ricbert in a house in the village.

"You two are welcome to remain here as long as you need," Ælfgifu said in her harsh voice as she slid gracefully from her saddle, "I won't have you traveling again until your father is well."

Ecgric frowned. He had wished to be back in Wuffingham by now; they had only taken this detour because they needed to return Eni's sons home safely. The thought of a winter spent in this house while his father slowly died made him want to claw his eyes out.

Ricbert woke again the day after their arrival, though he had developed a deep, racking cough that seemed to shake his very bones. He fell into a coughing fit almost immediately after opening his eyes, but managed to choke down some water before falling back onto the bed. "I can't keep doing this," he said, and Ecgric heard the weight of exhaustion in his voice. "I don't understand why the gods keep doing this to me."

Ecgric sat by his father's side. "What are you talking about?"

Ricbert grimaced. "Every time I sleep, I keep thinking that it'll be the end. That finally, after all this time, I will be able to die. And every single time, I find myself on a bed, covered in sweat, with a half-healed axe wound which should have killed me." He was bitter, so angry and tired that it dripped from his voice. "I hate it," Ricbert said to the thatched ceiling, and began to cough again.

"Father," Ecgric said slowly after Ricbert had stopped shaking with the coughing fit, "I think the gods have decided to keep you here for a reason …"

"Don't bore me with your pious nonsense," Ricbert said, "It's clear that the gods don't give a pig's shit about me, or they'd let me join them."

Ecgric held up his hand, feeling rather lightheaded. "Let me finish." He knew if he did not say it, he never would. "I believe that you have some part yet to play in what is to come, but we can't know the course that your road will take. If you want…" he swallowed, unsure if he wanted to continue. "If you need me to help you, I will." Ecgric hated mincing words, but he could not force himself to say the words he needed to tell his father.

Ricbert's face softened to something Ecgric had rarely seen before. "My son," he said, his voice croaking. "Such a course would benefit neither of us." He started to cough again, so hard that he could not draw a proper breath for a long time. When he had finished, he ground his teeth together until he could take a breath. "Although I cannot say that the idea has not crossed my mind. It would be so much easier, wouldn't it?"

Ecgric did not say anything, but his breathing grew faster at the thought. Would he be prepared to do it, if his father asked?

"You are no kinslayer, and I would hope that I have enough integrity not to make you one."

Ecgric swallowed the lump that had suddenly grown in his throat. "Well, then, Old Man, you'd better drink that draught Ælfgifu made for you, and I'll be ready to practice swords with you as soon as you're up."

*****

The laughter in the hall was more subdued than it might have been, but it made it sound as if life might have been returning to Wuffingham, even in this deadly cold of winter. Light flooded the hall from the blazing fire and the torches, reflected in the gold and silver jewelry of its occupants.

Modraniht was the night to celebrate women, to rejoice at the imminent return of the sun after Yule, and as such the women spent the night feasting and drinking as if in a *symbel.*

Gieva had grown somewhat tired of feasting; the Yule festival had drained her physically and emotionally, and the large number of people made her feel jostled. Tonight was different, though; Gieva listened more than she talked, and drank little, but ate her fill of mutton stew and honeyed cakes and the smoked herring she seemed to crave incessantly these days. The men had departed after the *godeswif* had blessed the mothers and young women, both those who had borne children and those whose bellies were still heavy.

Gieva ate and talked alongside Eadyth and the other women, and felt content for the first time in months.

"I miss Sunniva," Gieva told Eadyth as the two of them settled together near the fire. "I wish she could be here."

"She would have complained of boredom and snuck off to sleep with Ecgric at the end of the night," Eadyth said with a grin.

"I'm sure she would have," Gieva laughed. "Oh! Feel the baby kicking!" It delighted her to feel the life inside of her, and she felt the need to share every time it happened.

Eadyth put her hand on Gieva's belly. "You have to say, '*Ic sæde! Þis is gecyðed!'* 'I say! It is stirring!' or the *godeswif* will be cross with you." She laughed. "I think she must have turned over. Feel how the kick is at the top?"

"Yes, I think that happened a few days ago. It rather hurt, but I think it's settled now. But why do you say 'she'?" Gieva asked.

"Because this is a night for women," Eadyth said, grinning. "No boys are allowed."

Gieva patted her belly and nestled against Eadyth's shoulder, listening to a little serving girl sing a song about springtime. She slipped into sleep, lulled by the girl's singing and the warmth of the fire and the women around her. She tried to enjoy herself, but a sinking feeling reminded her of how much she did not want to return to her own house the following day. Most of the women would be gone after tomorrow, and even if she were to sleep in the great hall, she would be alone. She wished she still had Rægen to sing away the cold and the dark of the midwinter; she missed his body beside her, the way his arms always found her even in the darkness. She had been so numb, so dazed during the weeks following the battle that tore him away, that she'd had no heart to feel lonely. Now, among all these women, sheltered by friendship and love, she realized how desolate she really was.

When the women emerged from the hall the following morning, they were astonished to find that the sun had appeared from behind the thick blanket of clouds, making the early morning frost glimmer on every surface. It was bitingly cold, but somehow the edge was taken away by the soft sunshine on her face.

She watched many of the women leaving Wuffingham with their families, waving goodbye to their friends and sharing in a last cup of hot mead before they went.

Rather than returning home herself, she wandered around the village, wrapped tightly in a thick cloak and fur-lined boots. Somehow it was reassuring to know that the sun still existed, even though it had been hidden for so long. She stayed outdoors almost all day, walking in a wide loop around the village, down past the half-frozen stream, even down to the Wood Bridge; in order to take in the few rays of sun that pierced the frost.

Her cheeks burning from the cold and her belly rumbling for something hot to put in it, Gieva wandered toward the now-deserted Bricgweard just as the sun had begun to set. She saw no one, and so she was startled to hear the sound of something heavy being dropped on the ground and a roar of frustration coming from the other side of the stable.

Eorwald was alone where the men liked to practice swords; the hand holding his sword was shaking, and he stared at it, transfixed. His eyes were narrowed in concentration and it seemed as if he was willing his hand to remain still.

Gieva approached him slowly, unsure of what to do. She was frightened; she saw a deep, terrifying madness behind his eyes even though he was not looking at her, but she pushed herself forward. The faint jingling of her jewelry made him look up from his shaking sword hand.

"I can't hold it," he said to no one in particular, as if trying to work out a riddle.

"You could tighten your grip," she suggested lamely. She did not know the first thing about swords, but these seemed the right sort of words to say. "Or hold it with two hands?"

He shook his head. “I can’t hold it.” He blinked hard, flinching as though an invisible hand had struck him. “I have to, I can’t lose it again. They're going to come for me, and if I can’t fight back, then they’ll be able to kill me this time, but...” He swallowed with difficulty, and she saw his arm tensing as he nearly dropped the sword again.

The fear in his voice made her stomach turn over. This wasn’t right, he was a warrior, an *ætheling*, and it was not right for his voice to sound like that. Despite her fear, she crossed the distance between them. She took the sword in her own hands and gently removed it from his grip.

“Eorwald,” she said, and he seemed surprised as she said his name. “No one is coming for you. I don't know who you think they are, but you are safe here.” She slid the shield from his hand, and placed it beside the sword on the ground.

“I'm never safe," his voice had an edge of panic, though his words slurred together, “They’ll take me and they’ll torture me again. The poison won’t leave, it’s in my blood.” He swallowed again, flinching. “I can taste it.”

Gieva’s insides felt as if they had turned to ice. “No one is coming for you,” she repeated, her own voice shaky now.

His breath quickened and his hands were shaking harder than before; he swayed as though he might collapse. She took his hand and led him to the wall, and helped him to sit against it. He was trembling so violently; he must be freezing, but he was covered in sweat. It felt indecent of her to be standing there; intrusive; ghastly.

When he hit his head against the wall the first time, she jumped. The second time, she flung herself forward. For a moment she thought he was doing it on purpose, but the third time it happened, his head lolled sideways, his eyes unfocused and blinking hard. She straddled his legs and pressed her body against him, flinging a hand behind his head. He threw back once more and she winced as her hand was smashed between him and the wood, but she did not let go.

"I'll protect you." Gieva's heart was fluttering with panic and pity; what if she wasn't strong enough to hold him? What if he pushed her off or lashed out at her, or harmed himself, or harmed her baby? She hugged him tighter, pressing his arms between their bodies and whispering in his ear, "Hush. I'll protect you. No one is coming for you. You are safe." She chanted it over and over as his panicked breaths shuddered beneath her. "You're safe."

He was still shaking, groaning in sharp gasps, and it was all she could do to keep a hold on him.

"No one is going to hurt you. You are safe." She felt his shoulders relax, but she still did not let go. "Hush." she kissed his cheek and pressed it to her own as she repeated the words in his ear. "You are safe." She stroked the stubble of his head, feeling the lump he had raised there. "Hush," she chanted. Her own heart seemed to slow as well as she repeated the words. "You are safe."

She heard his voice, but it was ragged and quiet next to her ear. She loosened her grip on him just enough that he was able to extract his arms, but they fell to his sides.

"Hush," she said, pulling back just slightly so that she could see him properly.

"Eorwald?" she said tentatively, ducking so that she could look him in the eyes despite her unease. She slicked the sweat away from his brow, his skin freezing and damp. His eyes darted from her to the ground, to her again, wide with confusion.

Gieva licked her lips, watching him before hesitantly asking, "Eorwald, what happened?"

He blinked hard once or twice, swallowed, and finally looked up.

"I don't know," he said, tears springing into his eyes. The terror behind the stormy grey-blue had faded, replaced only by confusion and sadness.

Eorwald extracted a hand and scrubbed it against his eyes. "My head," he mumbled.

"You hit it on the wall," she said, touching the lump under his shaved hair. "It's not bleeding."

He took a few long breaths, looking at nothing.

"Can you stand?" she asked. "No," she put a hand against his chest to stop him; he was still shaking even as he tried to press his hands on the ground. "Take your time."

She climbed off of his legs and crouched beside him, her hips aching as the baby rolled around in agitation. She pressed a hand to the side of her stomach and the rolling was replaced by a slow swaying.

A long time passed before Eorwald got to his feet.

"Come with me," she said, taking one of his arms. She felt an angry stab of pain in her feet as the feeling returned to them. It was only now that she realized how cold she was. The ground crunched with frost and her knees ached, and the baby was kicking her in the ribs. She picked up the sword where it lay on the ground, and carried it with her. Eorwald grasped her other hand as they walked to the Bricgweard, stroking it mindlessly with his thumb; his hands were damp and cold, but at least they were no longer shaking.

She led Eorwald not to the Bricgweard, but down the lane to her own house. She opened the door and he entered obediently, and she fumbled for a fire poker in the darkness. She was suddenly so weary it took her far too long to stir the buried coals into a flame, which she blew back to life with a few shuddering breaths. She used a splinter to light the lamp; the flame from the fat gave off a sickly orange glow.

When she finished, she looked up to see that he stood as still as stone, staring at her and at nothing all at once, blinking and shaking his head slowly. It seemed as if every muscle in his body might give out at once. Gieva carefully removed the sword belt at his waist and folded it, returning the naked sword to its sheath. She motioned for him to sit on the stool and she helped him to take off the heavy outer garments. His tunic and breeches were soaked with sweat and melted frost, and she made him remove those too, wrapping a heavy blanket around his shoulders and guiding him to the bed.

Gieva looked away from him so that he could not see the tears that sprang in her eyes when she saw the scars crossing his arms and chest. Some, on the backs of his forearms and a few crisscrossing the space above his knees, made her teeth clench. It had been weeks – months, since the battle. Those cuts were no more than a few days old.

Gieva shook her head. It did not matter when they had happened; there were too many of them. Far too many for someone with barely twenty winters to his name.

She hung the clothes next to the hearth and sat next to him on the bed, pulling the blanket tighter around him.

"You need to sleep," she whispered.

"I don't sleep," he said, his voice slurring. "Not since –" he swallowed hard, squeezing his eyes shut.

"Shh," Gieva soothed. "You are safe."

"I'm not safe," he whispered.

"Yes, you are," she said, sitting closer and putting an arm around his shoulders. "You are safe, Eorwald. You may not believe it, but it is the truth."

"I might not be attacked by a Northumbrian today," he muttered, "But I am not safe. There's poison in my blood. It's in here," he pressed his palm into his temple, grimacing as he pounded the heel of his hand into the side of his head. Gieva thrust out a hand to block it, seizing his hand in both of hers.

He raised his eyes to hers, desperate and exhausted and confused.

"You are safe," she repeated with a calm she did not feel as she glanced at the straight, shallow cuts on his forearms, on his legs. Still red, still healing. "No one will hurt you," she repeated as he put his head on her shoulder. "Not even you."

Chapter Twenty-Four

Eftarisen

To Rise Again

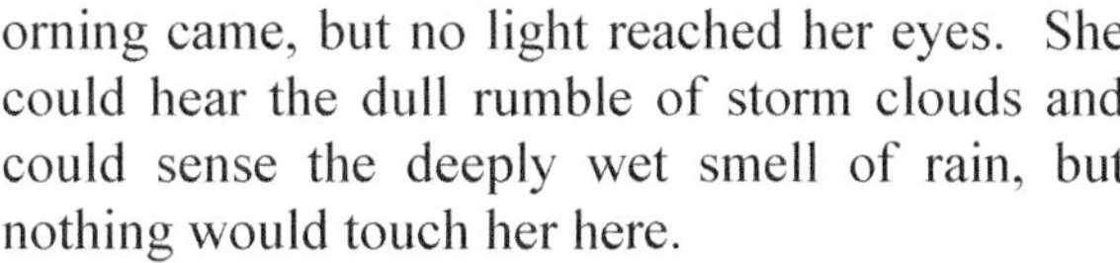

orning came, but no light reached her eyes. She could hear the dull rumble of storm clouds and could sense the deeply wet smell of rain, but nothing would touch her here.

Sunniva knew one or more of her ribs had to have broken under Walaric's boot, though perhaps the reason she could not breathe was not because of the bruises or the broken ribs or the stinging open cuts from the thin willow switch.

She shifted position, raising herself on an elbow, but fell back down again. What was the point? She could sit up; she could tidy herself, put on her clothes. She could comb her hair. She could go into the hall; she could smile and speak demure words that would please her husband. It would be hard, but she could do it.

She could lie here on the ground, letting the sharp rushes poke into her side and into the switch marks. She could stop eating, stop drinking; stop breathing. She could stay here until she died. It would be easy, and she could do it.

She could fight it. She could claw and scratch and bite and weather each tormenting blow, until he killed her. She could scream, she could curse him to a shallow grave. She could escape. It would be…

Impossible.

Sunniva knew that was impossible. She was alone, completely alone, and very, very small. She knew that everyone would be on Godomar's side. Even the kindly priest woul tell her to obey her husband; that it was her fault and that she deserved it as punishment for her many sins. Christians did not get divorced, after all. She could not accuse him of beating her; he had not raised a hand to harm her. He had been true to his word. He was not the sort to seek out whores either, when he had his little jewel to press onto her back while she cried silently and waited for it to be over. She could not pretend he had never slept with her in order to ask for an annulment of the marriage, when half the court had seen the dead baby they had all assumed was Godomar's ill-fated heir. She had no recourse, and Godomar knew it as well as she did.

No, they could not – would not – get divorced. It was not what Christians were supposed to do. They weathered the bad times and tried to make the best of their lot, assuming that they would be granted peace in the afterlife in accordance with their suffering. He would tell her that any unhappiness she suffered now would be rewarded tenfold if she was faithful.

Maybe it was better to submit. Maybe it was better just to let the current take her. It would hurt less. Perhaps after a while, it would stop hurting altogether.

She heard the door scrape open, and feet crunch on the rushes behind her. She wanted to tell him not to touch her. She wanted to fight him away, to stop him violating her again. She wanted to scream, but only tears came, squeezed from her tightly-shut eyes.

The footsteps neared her, and she let hands roll her onto her back. He would take her again, she knew. It would not hurt if she did not fight it.

"Sunniva?" a girl's voice seemed to shatter the silence. Sunniva had never heard Hilde use her right name, but somehow the sound of it pushed a sliver of life into her.

"Let me help you," Hilde said, lifting Sunniva's shoulders. The broken rib throbbed, but Sunniva barely noticed the pain.

Hilde all but lifted Sunniva to her feet. She was surprisingly strong for being only as tall as Sunniva's nose.

"I don't need your help," Sunniva said expressionlessly as Hilde guided her to the bed. She did not look at the other woman, though she did not resist her when Hilde helped her to push her arms through her shift.

Hilde ignored her, climbing behind to comb through Sunniva's tangled hair with her fingers, and weaving it into a braid.

She returned to Sunniva's side, taking her hand.

"He has no right to do this," she said, brushing one of Sunniva's tears away from her cheek.

"He has every right," Sunniva muttered. "He is my husband and my lord. He has claim to my body when he wants it, and I will give him sons. That is the way things work." Once, she might have said the words with a bite of sarcasm. Now, she was not entirely sure that she did not mean them.

Hilde frowned.

"Christ submitted to his fate. I must do so as well." The words tasted foul coming out of her mouth, but she knew the foulness came from their truth.

"You never seemed to be the type of person to submit to anything," Hilde said quietly. "It was something I admired in you."

"Defiance is not an attractive virtue in a woman," Sunniva repeated Godomar's words now, and wanted to vomit. She looked at Hilde, who was watching her with mingled anxiety and disappointment. Sunniva felt disgusted with the other woman for admiring someone so stubborn, so arrogant, so sure that she could fight forever.

"I might as well just submit. I don't know what else to do," Sunniva said.

"I cannot tell you what to do," Hilde said, her eyes falling. "I could tell you what a good Christian would say. A good Christian would say that when a man strikes you, you must offer the other cheek for him to strike as well."

"That is what a good Christian woman would do," Sunniva agreed.

Hilde's face fell into something that might have been disappointment. "It is," she repeated solemnly. She opened her mouth to say something more, but a scraping sound seemed to snap Hilde back into a genially indifferent tone.

"Vrouwe," she said, "Do you require anything else of me?"

Sunniva was unsure what had caused the change, but her question was answered as another figure entered the room.

"Leave us," Godomar said to Hilde, who ducked her head in deference before glancing back at Sunniva with disappointment and pity etched in her eyes.

Sunniva got to her feet and stepped toward her husband. She lowered her eyes from his, but let him take her hands. It was what a good Christian woman would do.

"My dearest little treasure," he said sadly, "I am truly sorry that you forced my hand. You know that I do not like having to discipline you."

She nodded slowly, still not meeting his eyes.

"I hope that it will not have to happen again," he said. "I will forgive you, if you are ready to offer me an apology."

She swallowed. "I beg your –"

He cut her off, putting a finger to her lips. "You beg?" he asked, his eyebrows rising.

She looked down, and understood. She dropped to her knees before him, taking his hand in both of hers and pressing her lips to the gold ring he wore on his forefinger. It was what a good Christian woman would do.

"I have not been a good wife to you, nor a good subject. I beg your forgiveness for my misdeeds and I –"

"That will do," he said gently, touching his fingers under her chin and lifting her to her feet. "I hope to see you in the chapel when you have dressed yourself, and you may ask forgiveness of the Lord. After that, we will put it behind us." He smiled gently at her and turned to leave, stopping for only a moment. "Wear that blue dress. It is so comely on you."

Sunniva lowered her eyes and turned to collect her dress, putting it on with fumbling fingers and tying her belt loosely as she dared, so that it would not press against the bruises. She still thought it might slip over her bony hips with the slightest movement. She pulled a veil over her hair, tying it with a woven fillet around her brows. She draped the jeweled cross over her neck, its red gems glinting like blood in the dim light. It was heavy and gaudy, but it was what a good Christian woman would wear.

She made to close the jewel casket, but paused.

Dull iron seemed to shine more brightly than the silver within, and Sunniva reached into its depths. She removed the small hammer-shaped amulet which Sige had given her so long ago, which had been a token for her mother and her grandmother before her.

A good Christian woman would not carry this.

It was raining hard now, but she did not run to the church. She walked slowly, the rain plastering the thin veil to her head, the mud caking on the bottom of her cloak.

Godomar was already there, waiting for her. He knelt at the rail facing the ornate golden cross, his hands folded and his eyes lifted to the ceiling.

Sunniva approached, and Godomar rose to his feet, crossing himself and bowing to the golden ornament which towered above him.

"I shall leave you to pray," he said, stroking her cheek. "When you return, I shall put a son in you, and we will forget what you have done."

She smiled demurely, and knelt before the altar as she heard Godomar's footsteps leave the deserted chapel. She looked at the cross, the gold etched with the figure of a man and the outer rim piled in gems. She bowed her head before it. It was what a good Christian woman would do.

A good Christian woman. That was what she had become, after all. Christ told women to bow before their misery, that there would be justice in the next life; to accept humiliation while asking for more. That was what a good Christian woman would do.

Sunniva nearly shrieked at the sudden upwelling of revulsion in herself. The girl she had been would have fought relentlessly against any man who tried to tell her what to do. She would have killed a man for raising a hand to her. Was that girl gone? Had she left that girl behind when she left her home and took a new god?

Sunniva heard a clap of thunder from the storm outside, as if it were in answer to her question.

She looked down to see the cross Godomar had given her hanging between her breasts, heavy and gaudy and sickeningly bright. She wrenched it over her head and threw it against the wall before her, and it made a loud clinking sound as the chain smacked the horrid gold cross standing on its plinth.

"Shall I turn the other cheek to him? Shall I kneel before you like a bitch to heel, so that you can crush me into the dirt?" she asked aloud to the impotent god of the Franca, but the God of Thunder answered her with a resounding boom that came from the darkening sky outside and reached into her heart.

No, daughter of kings, she heard the deep rumble of the thunder call to her, *it is better to die on your feet than to live on your knees. Rise now, brave* ætheling. *Rise now, and fight.*

*****

The procession down the old Roman road was slow, but not nearly as slow as it had been when they had made their way to Eni's hall all those months ago. Ecgric felt his spirits lift at the sight of his father, sitting astride his horse and as hale as Ecgric had ever seen him. After weeks of recovery, he had finally vanquished the infection that kept seizing him, and his wounds had healed. He might be a little stiffer now, a little slower to react, but he was alive, and Ecgric was glad.

"I was starting to think you'd keep me shut up with Eni forever," Ricbert said.

"Wouldn't that please you?" Ecgric asked genially. It was a fine day and his spirits were high that they were finally leaving the north after wintering with Eni's family.

Ricbert sighed. "I'm glad to be shot of them. There is a reason I was always Rædwald's man, and not Eni's."

"I'm sure there are some who will miss your company," Ecgric grinned. "Ælfgifu, for one."

"That's not funny," Ricbert scowled. "*I* do not meddle with the wife of my host." He gave Ecgric a stern glance which Ecgric returned with an even bigger grin.

"Ælfgifu is a very old friend. I was pleased to see her again and I am sorry that we have parted."

Ecgric raised an eyebrow, but at a glance from his father, he dropped the subject. "Well in any case, I'll be glad to be home. I've heard that there is some unrest in Mercia. Maybe the *cyning* will send a raiding party to take advantage." It had been too long since Ecgric had seen a fight; the battle at the River Idle had shaken him, certainly, but somehow he thought that a nice, healthy raid would help to set things to rights.

"The *cyning* wouldn't be able to come, even if he did send us," Ricbert said sadly, "He hasn't been able to come on a raiding party in at least ten years."

"He probably enjoys getting the spoils, though," Ecgric said in jest, but Ricbert gave him a hard look.

"He hates it, actually. Rædwald loves battle just as much as you do, perhaps even more. I think sometimes that he might have preferred to stay an *ætheling* and spend his days carting treasure back from vanquished Mercians."

"Who says he can't do that as a *cyning*?"

"In the old days, it might have been possible," Ricbert said wearily. "But the minds of *cyningas* have long turned to subtlety and politics. Rædwald might despise the games, but he has a good head for them. If the alliances were all broken, or if there had never been a *heahcyning* in the first place, perhaps we all would have carried on as we did before."

"I think I would have liked that," Ecgric said.

"I think you might not have been born if that had happened," said Ricbert. "If we had been fighting the Eota, I would not have married your mother. Fate takes strange turns."

Ecgric nodded. "I have always heard that you two were very ill-matched," Ecgric said. "That she was too rash and impulsive, and you were too stubborn and quiet, and that you never met but you started fighting like dogs."

Ricbert gave one of his rare laughs. "She was very opinionated. But that was not to say that I did not care about her. She was a good woman and a good wife, and she gave me a strong son. I was sad when she died."

"Did you love her?"

Ricbert thought about this for a moment. "I don't think I knew her well enough to love her, but I did care for her, despite our differences. That is all we can really hope out of a marriage, isn't it? Love is for the young, after all." He seemed to give Ecgric a knowing look and Ecgric shifted in his saddle.

*****

The king was visiting some of his men to the East, but the Bricgweard was still packed with people who had arrived early for the festivals of Eostre. Thegns and their families milled around, laughing and drinking; young men and women kissed and giggled with one another; children squealed and chased each other around the hearth.

Normally a bustling, jostling festival full of shouting and laughing and the smell of drink and piss might have set Eorwald on edge if he had been alone. He was certain that if Gieva had not been sitting beside him, he would have felt overwhelmed by the poison in his blood; if she was not there, he would have collapsed again. He would have another hole in his memory, a dank pit of thought filled only with the vague memory of a foul taste in his mouth and an aching exhaustion in every muscle.

It had not happened again since that night that Gieva had saved him. The half-remembered night came back to him in pieces, even after he had tried to recall what had happened.

He had felt the poison returning, quickened by his memories and his panic that he would be taken again. He could not remember what had brought it on. At first it had been memories of Rægen lying on the ground, sucking in breath, torrents of blood pouring from the gash at his throat – then it had changed; he remembered the blood that filled his vision as a storm took him, stabbing and cutting through the leather and iron and bone. The men he had killed, the men whose blood stained his hands and his sword and his heart, they came to him in sleep all the time, sleep that was drenched in blood and filth and sickness…

The gaps in his memory made him want to hit his head against a wall, as if that might shake something loose. His last fading memory had been of the foul taste of blood and iron in his mouth, and then an overwhelming weakness as he had fallen to the ground, but the rest might not have even happened for all he remembered of it.

He only remembered the end, the moment he woke from the darkness. At the edge of the pit where his memories had been, there was a light. It was not a gaudy or a shining thing; it was just *there*. He did not need to reach out for it, because it embraced him first.

"You are safe," it had said.

As the light held him – as *she* held him, he thought for a moment that it might be true. The panic and the confusion and the exhaustion floated under the surface, but they could not break through the light.

Even when he found himself sleeping in a strange bed in a strange room, he knew he was protected. He remembered watching her sleeping for a long time; she had not moved, but her eyes were closed and a crease had appeared between her eyebrows that he was sure he had never seen while she was waking.

The crease disappeared as she opened her eyes, and the corner of her mouth rose in a reassuring half-smile.

"How are you feeling?" she asked.

Eorwald swallowed. "I'm not sure," he said truthfully. "Sick, I guess." He glanced around, mostly so that he would not see the look of worry cross her face. "This is your house?"

Gieva nodded. "I hope you're not upset that I brought you here. I only wanted to help, and I thought going back to the hall might make things worse."

He shook his head fervently. "I'm not upset," he said. He felt his cheeks and his ears burning; he knew it had nothing to do with sitting on her bed in nothing but his smallclothes. "Gieva, I am sorry for what happened. I am sorry if I frightened you."

Gieva sat up properly now, and put her hand on his back. "You did not frighten me," she said, but he knew she was lying. "You do not remember what happened, do you?"

He clenched his teeth, making certain that tears would not fight their way out as he shook his head. "I am weak. I should have been able to fight it. I'm a coward and a fool and I might have hurt you, or I might have hurt…" he glanced down at her belly, round beneath her shift. He realized how quickly he was breathing, and worried that the poison might start flowing again. "You should have stayed away."

She put one hand on her belly. "You didn't hurt either of us. The baby is just fine, and so am I." She took his wrist and placed his hand on the side of the bump, and he could feel something swirling around under her skin. "See?" she asked, smiling gently.

He felt soothed by the gentle stirring under his hand. He kept it there, and she rubbed his back with her free hand.

"Thank you," he said at last, finally looking her in the eyes. "Thank you for everything. You don't know how much you've done." It was hard for him to say, and he worried what she might think of him. They had never been friendly; they had barely spoken before the battle at the Idle and not much more afterwards, but she had risked her own safety to care for him when he had been at his most vulnerable. He was wretched with shame for how he must have looked, broken and frightened and a moment away from falling upon his own sword and ending it all.

She did not say anything, but rubbed his back in acknowledgement of his words. Her hands were warm and soft and she was watching him, not with condescension, but with the caring concern she gave to all living things.

Gieva glanced over at him now, grinning. “Baby’s kicking,” she said, and put his hand on the side of her belly.

“That must feel so strange,” he said, shaking his head in wonderment.

Gieva shrugged. “A bit. Baby doesn’t move much these days; I think he must not have much room anymore.” She glanced at his horn cup, still filled with the amber-colored mead, and at the untouched bread in front of him.

“I’m just not hungry,” he said to her unasked question, as she raised her eyebrows.

“Please,” she said. It was not pleading, but not an order, either.

Eorwald tore off a piece of bread and put it in his mouth, though it could well have been a chip of wood for the pleasure he found in it.

She was eating now as well; giving him pointed glances as if she were trying to lead by example. He very nearly grinned at her attempts, and humored her by finishing the half loaf in front of him and even a few pieces of meat.

Eorwald watched her for a while as a deep, warm contentment built in his chest. He knew now why Rægen had loved her. He could see it now, how kind and graceful and brave she was, and he loved her for it.

There was nothing in him that could see her as anything but what she was, though. Even if she had not been as near as kin to him, even if she had not loved his brother with every scrap of her being, he knew that he would never want that part of her. Even more than that, he knew that she would never have given it to him anyway.

Gieva winced and put a hand on the side of her belly. It was so big now, much bigger than it had been the last time he had found another hole in his memory. She was a small woman, and her stomach seemed to take up her whole body now, but she was strong and had carried the extra weight with ease.

Eorwald watched her concernedly, but she waved a hand at him. “Just moving about,” she said when the pain had passed. “No, Eorwald, I’m fine, really.” She rolled her eyes good-naturedly and pushed him back into his seat. Instead, she put his hand on the side of her stomach where the baby was still kicking.

A few moments passed, and she seemed to settle back into her seat. "It's a little too noisy in here for me," she said. "I'd rather sleep at my house."

Eorwald got to his feet. He had begun to feel slightly ill-at-ease about the number of loud drunken people in the hall, and surely she had noticed. The men whooped and hollered as they always did when he spent his nights with Gieva, but he did not care. They could think whatever they pleased. Whatever he had with Gieva, it made them both happy, and he would gladly weather obnoxious comments for the comfort it provided them to have someone close by.

He helped Gieva to get awkwardly to her feet, and she made her way halfway across the hall before stopping. She leaned her hand against one of the support beams, her face set in a grimace.

"Are you sure you're all right?" Eorwald asked.

Gieva nodded. "Just overexcited, I think." She was still frowning, but after a moment it seemed to release.

"The baby isn't coming, is it?" He asked, terrified that she would say yes.

"No, not yet," she said, smiling when the pain had passed, "I don't think so. I think it's still too early." She waved a hand dismissively. "But the sooner I get home in my own bed, the happier I will be."

They made their way down the lane, Gieva stopping occasionally to catch her breath. She moved slowly and he did not mind waiting for her, but the small amount of exertion it took to walk down to her house seemed to tax her enormously. The moment she had entered the house, she leaned on the raised hearth and let out a low groan. Eager to help in some way, he filled a drinking bowl with water and took it to her.

"I was wrong," she said with a grimace, when she had drained the drinking bowl, "I think the baby is coming after all."

"Should I send for someone?" Eorwald took the bowl back, and found that his hands were shaking, so he set it down quickly.

Gieva breathed deeply and shook her head. "It's just starting. I just want to rest, for now. Will you just hold me?"

It was something he knew how to do, at least. She lay on her side so that he could put his arms around her, and he felt her limbs relax slowly. She dozed for a while, and then stirred when the pain came again.

"Hush, now," Eorwald said, letting her squeeze his hand as she rocked her hips and groaned under her breath. As the contraction passed, she released him and sat up.

"I need to walk," she said breathlessly.

The night passed slowly. She paced the room, then sat with her legs spread wide and leaning her elbows on her knees, then lay back down on the bed, in a cycle which seemed to repeat endlessly. He sat with her and held her hand or stroked her hair, anything that might comfort her, but every time she stood to walk around, he was certain that the baby would fall out where she stood.

When he voiced his fears, she smiled at him wearily. "It doesn't work like that," she said. "My waters haven't even broken; it won't be coming for a while." It amazed him that she seemed to know exactly what to do, despite never having had a child before, and he knew that she would tell him what she needed. He had helped horses to foal and sheep to lamb, but somehow making the comparison with Gieva seemed the wrong thing to do.

He was holding her again as she slept fitfully, waking every so often when one of the pains would come. He realized that he had fallen asleep as well when he was suddenly woken by the odd sensation that he had pissed himself, and he wondered with a stroke of panic the he might have had another of his episodes.

Looking down, he saw that Gieva's shift was soaked. It had not been him after all, and he sighed as she lifted herself into a sitting position.

"Go and get Eadyth," she said, her voice strangely calm. He was sure that if he had woken with a massive gush of water coming out of him, he would not have been quite so composed. He got up quickly, rushed out the door and up to the Bricgweard.

It was even colder now; judging by the lightening of the sky he thought it must be near dawn. He ran through the hall, nearly tripping on the sleeping bodies within and flinging himself through the door to the king's chamber.

He shook Eadyth awake, and she seemed to know what was happening before he even said anything. "Did the waters come?" Eadyth asked, getting out of bed and collecting her cloak.

Eorwald said, "Yes, just now. She's at home; I didn't know what to do, but she sent me to fetch you." He felt a strange lurch of panic; what if she had the pains again and he wasn't there? What if she fainted or fell down while he was waiting for Eadyth?

Eadyth seemed to understand his worry, and put her hand on his shoulder. "Go back down to Gieva's house. I will be along shortly. Everything is going to be fine."

He sprinted back out of the hall and down the lane. When he entered her house, Gieva was sitting on the edge of the bed with her elbows on her knees, leaning over and hissing slowly through her teeth. Her face glimmered slightly with sweat in the light of the fire, but she gave him a fleeting smile as he sat beside her.

"Eadyth is coming," he said weakly, and Gieva nodded.

"You look terrified," she said, grinning at him when her pain had passed. "I am fine, I promise – ah," she stopped and let out another low groan, and he let her grip his hand again.

"Just breathe," he told her. He realized he was holding his own breath as she squeezed his hand, and when she relaxed he did as well. She collapsed sideways into his arms, and she began to cry.

"Hush," he said unhelpfully.

"It hurts," she panted, "It hurts so much."

It made Eorwald anxious to see her in pain, and he glanced at the door repeatedly, hoping his mother would come. She knew everything about childbirth and medicines, perhaps as much as the godeswif herself; though hopefully the latter would not be needed unless something went wrong.

"Hush," he said again. "I'm here; just grab a hold of me when it comes again."

Gieva whimpered against his chest for a while, and then tensed as another contraction came, and she gripped his arm. Eadyth arrived soon after Gieva had relaxed again, and knelt next to her.

"You're doing beautifully," Eadyth said briskly as she knelt before Gieva. Eadyth moved quickly, putting a hand between Gieva's legs and feeling for something, pursing her lips until she seemed to find what she wanted. Eorwald had no idea what she was doing, but Eadyth seemed satisfied, nodding and grinning at Gieva. "Not long now," she said enigmatically.

Eorwald helped Gieva to put on a clean tunic to keep her warm, and then danced nervously at the side of the bed, positive that he was in the way. "I should leave," he said.

"No!" Gieva said, reaching for him. "Please stay with me."

Eadyth smiled. "You heard her, Eorwald. Gieva, when you feel another pain, fight the urge to push. You'll want to push, but you're not quite ready for that yet, so just try to relax and breathe until it's over."

Gieva nodded and leaned her elbows on her knees again, looking exhausted already. Eorwald wondered if she would be able to keep up her strength if it took much longer. He knelt on the floor in front of her, and she put her arms around his neck as another pain racked her body. He hugged her as she groaned into his ear. He tried to take deep breaths so that she would follow his lead. He waited for it to pass, but she did not stop pressing down on his shoulders.

"Eadyth," she cried, but did not release him, "Eadyth, I have to push, I have to…"

"Just breathe," Eadyth said, "Deep breaths, my love. Deep breaths. Wait for the next one…"

"It hurts!" Gieva cried. "I have to push, it's coming …" it seemed to come on stronger this time and lasted a long while; she relaxed slightly but immediately tensed again, emitting a long, low cry as she gritted her teeth together.

Eadyth rushed over and knelt beside Eorwald, helping to pull Gieva's hips forward so that she was squatting. "Good girl," she said, "good girl, keep going." she paused and reached under Gieva's leg to feel her sex again and glanced up quickly. "Gieva," she said quietly, "Reach down."

Gieva released Eorwald's arm with one hand and reached down between her legs, and Eorwald watched her eyes widen as she felt something that Eorwald could not see.

"Eorwald, get behind her and keep her from falling," Eadyth said.

He moved behind Gieva and put his hands on her waist, trying to whisper something soothing but feeling his voice constrict. She began to whimper in short, perfunctory gasps as Eadyth helped her, both women's hands somewhat hidden by Gieva's large belly. He looked over her shoulder in mild horror as he saw both women's hands wrapped around a frightening looking, brownish-purple protrusion. But Mother was grinning and nodding, so perhaps it was not as horrifying as it seemed. Gieva caught her breath for a few moments, leaning against Eorwald's chest, and then began to push once more, gritting her teeth but bearing down in silence.

"One more, my love, one more, the head is out, just one more big push, come now," Eadyth was saying in a soothing, unrelenting stream, and Eorwald was transfixed as he watched Gieva take a single deep breath and bear down, and a moment later silently pulled a slimy, purple bundle up to her chest. She half-collapsed into Eorwald's arms, and pulled her so that she sat on the edge of the bed, letting her lean her back against his chest.

Gieva started to shiver as if she were cold, clutching the small thing to her. Wasn't it supposed to start crying? Eorwald looked at his mother, who seemed to be holding her breath; Gieva clutched the baby to her bare chest, and a long moment passed before an angry, rattling shriek filled the room. Gieva's body seemed to relax completely back into Eorwald's arms, and she stopped shaking. Eorwald looked over her shoulder; the baby was gripping a lock of Gieva's hair as Gieva cradled it against her chest. Its eyes were closed and it was squalling already, as if the world had done it deep personal wrong in the moment it had been alive.

Eorwald looked up to see his mother crying, though she had a huge smile on her face; he had rarely seen her cry, and did not know what to do. She fluttered around for a moment, and then brought a soft woolen blanket and laid it across the baby. Eorwald stroked Gieva's hair as the baby became quiet, making small motions with its mouth; its eyes were still closed tight.

Gieva lifted the blanket and examined the child's feet and hands. Eorwald was amazed at how minuscule they were; flexing and relaxing by moments. She looked between its legs and grinned.

"It's a girl," Gieva said, and Eorwald could hear the happiness in her voice even though he could not see her face. "Look at her," she said, "Look, I've... I've just had a baby!" She seemed terrified and fascinated at the idea. She stared down at the little thing, and Eorwald heard Gieva's voice break in a delighted sob as the baby's eyes opened.

"Hello, little one," she said to the newborn, "my *lytling*. I am so happy you're finally here."

Eorwald tried to move back onto the bed so that Gieva could lie down, but Eadyth stopped him. "Not just yet," she said quietly.

Gieva was staring at the infant, kissing her head and breathing deeply through her nose as if the little thing were the most fragrant blossom. She was oblivious to everything else, but he could not blame her. It was enchanting to see.

Time passed slowly and the rope connecting mother and child had stopped pulsating, and began to grow pale. Eadyth collected two lengths of cord and gently moved the baby to tie one of the strings a finger's length away from its navel, and the other just below that. In a single swift motion, Eadyth took a sharp knife and sliced through the cord between the two knots.

"We just have to wait for the rest," Eadyth informed Gieva, but Gieva did not seem to care. She was fixated on the baby, who was rooting around like a pig digging for acorns. Gieva lifted her heavy breast to the child's mouth, a bead of yellowish liquid already forming on her nipple, and the baby took it immediately, seeming to jerk her head around to find what she wanted.

"Why are you laughing?" Eorwald asked her quietly.

"It feels strange," she said. She tickled the baby's cheek as she began to suckle. Eorwald rather enjoyed watching, feeling the wave of calm that seemed to radiate out of Gieva as the baby nursed.

"Just tickle her foot when she falls asleep," Eadyth said. Gieva did so, and the little one gave a slight jump before her mouth moved once more.

A little while later, however, Gieva became agitated again as with another pain. Eadyth moved back between her legs and began to give Gieva a few words of encouragement as Gieva began to bear down again, and a moment later Eadyth took away the afterbirth. She used damp, warm towels to clean Gieva's legs, as Gieva sighed and leaned back again, switching the baby to the other breast as if she had done it a thousand times before. She had to tap the child's feet once or twice more; she kept falling asleep, snuggled happily in Gieva's arms.

Gieva smiled vaguely as she lay on the bed, fixated on her child. Eadyth cleaned up the mess and adjusted the blanket around them. Eorwald kissed Gieva's cheek and looked down at the baby. She was ugly, but perhaps all newborns were supposed to look that way. He had never seen a baby this new before. She had an angry, puckered little face and her thick brown hair that was slicked to her head. Gieva gently rubbed it with the edge of the blanket and it stuck up wildly, particularly on one side, and he knew everyone in the room thought of the same thing. Even with the joy of the moment, even with the excitement of bringing this child into the world, the three of them keenly felt the stab of the thing that was missing.

"I wish he could see her," Gieva said; her voice barely louder than a whisper and touched with tears. "She's so beautiful."

"You both are," Eadyth said, kissing Gieva and then kissing the baby's messy brown head. Even Mother sucked in the fragrance as if it were an intoxicating draught, before rising and bustling about to clean up.

The little girl continued to suck, looking up at her mother with dull grey eyes. Gieva stared at her as if she was the most beautiful thing in the world. Eorwald had to agree with her. He felt every drop of poison in his blood drain away as he realized what perfection, what beauty, had come from all of this blood and pain. Eorwald held the two brave girls as they rested, and watched the baby's tiny red face relax into sleep.

"You ought to rest after your hard work," Eadyth said to Gieva. "I'll take her."

Gieva looked slightly disappointed as Eadyth gently removed the bundle from her arms, but she leaned against Eorwald once more.

"You must be exhausted," he said, wrapping her in his arms. Gieva had already fallen into a deep, well-deserved sleep.

*****

"You realize what this means, don't you?" asked Rædwald quietly, stroking the messy brown hair of his granddaughter as Eadyth held her. In the moment that Eadyth had been holding the baby, Gieva had fallen asleep where she sat. Eadyth felt no need to wake her. She was happy to give Gieva the chance to rest, and even happier to take the chance to hold the baby.

"Hmm?" Eadyth asked absently, making faces at the little girl in her arms.

"Eorwald is my heir now."

Eadyth had to blink out of her torpor. "Of course he is. Even if this one," she indicated the baby, "had been a boy, Eorwald would still be your heir."

Rædwald rubbed the end of his nose, not looking at her.

"Have you got another wife who I do not know about, with a few extra sons to take your place when you are dead?" Eadyth asked defensively.

Rædwald did not speak immediately, but continued clenching his teeth and stroking the baby's head absent-mindedly. "I worry about him. Something's happened since he was in the hands of the Northumbrians, and it's only gotten worse since Rægen died. Surely you've seen it."

Eadyth felt her cheeks grow hot. She had indeed seen it. It was as if something had broken in Eorwald, something which seemed to be causing more damage than his physical wounds ever had done. "It was a hard thing for him," she said, her voice shaking slightly. "He needs time."

Rædwald frowned. "Some of the men have begun to talk. They think that he's lost his nerve. How could he lead them if they don't respect him?"

"He isn't leading anyone yet," Eadyth said, dodging the question. "I will remind you that you are the *cyning*, not Eorwald, and it is likely to stay that way for a long time. You did not become *cyning* until you had thirty years on you, and Eorwald hasn't even got twenty. You have plenty of time to groom him for command."

"I should have done before," Rædwald said, shaking his head. "I had assumed that Rægen –" he broke off, swallowing. "I had assumed that this wouldn't be a problem. I should have taught them both; the gods are punishing me for favoring one of my sons over the other."

She put a hand on his arm. She had never seen a man go through such grief as Rædwald had done when they had buried their son's bones in the tomb Rædwald had been preparing for himself. "Make up for it now," she said gently. "Make him into a leader that men will be proud to follow."

Eager for a change of subject, Eadyth asked, "Have you heard from Edwin lately? Is he having any trouble with his *thegns*?"

"I had a messenger from him a week ago. He's put down a few skirmishes near the borders with Mercia just after the battle at the Idle, but nothing since then." He frowned. "I don't know what that means, but hopefully they are not part of a larger trend.

No one was going to try anything in the middle of winter, but now that the new fighting season is approaching I think there might be some stirrings of discord."

"I would think that Edwin would have gotten rid of anyone still loyal to Athelfrith's family," Eadyth said. "I'm sure there are enough men who are loyal to Edwin to take their places."

Rædwald began chewing his lip. "I don't think the dissention is coming from Northumbraland," he said. "I heard a lot of talk while I was in the West, about Mercia allying themselves with the Wæleas. Athelfrith's sons were driven west when Edwin returned home, and I worry that they might be stirring up trouble."

Eadyth blew out a slow breath through pursed lips, and they both sat in thought for some time. "None of this would have happened if Ethelbert were still alive," she said at length.

"No, I think not. But then, that was a different world. The *cyningas* once were happy to try their hands at alliance, and Ethelbert was so powerful no one questioned his lordship over us. But now we've realized that it's much harder to provide for your men when you can't go on raids, and peace is dull work. It doesn't surprise me that the Mercians and the Hwicce want some action."

"Perhaps there could be a new *heahcyning*," Eadyth suggested. "Keep everyone in line."

"Well, there was a rumor that Eadbald, Ethelbert's son, wanted to take the title for himself, not realizing that it is not something that is simply passed down the male line. No one would accept that boy as *heahcyning* anyway."

"Oh?"

"He's half a child, really, and completely useless. I met him when I was in Lundenburh. His twin sister is more of a leader than he is."

"But he has a large army. Perhaps that will persuade people?"

"Are you saying you want a chit of a boy who married his own stepmother to be your *heahcyning*?" Rædwald asked, his voice half-joking but half-angry.

She could not help but grin. "Of course not. I want *you* to be the *heahcyning*."

"Don't be ridiculous," Rædwald said, narrowing his eyes.

Eadyth raised an eyebrow at him, and he grew cross. The

baby started stirring in Eadyth's arms, trying to suck her tiny clenched fist. "Well, think about it," Eadyth said. "I believe that if anyone has the right to be the *heahcyning*, it would logically be you. You know how famous you have become for your victory at the River Idle, and you have an excellent mind for the intricacies of politics. I know you don't care for them," she added hastily, seeing the look on his face, "but you know how to rule better than all of the other *cyningas* combined."

"It's not as simple as that," Rædwald said gruffly.

"No, indeed," Eadyth said, and she could tell that Rædwald was becoming annoyed as she grinned broadly at him. "If only someone owed you a debt. Perhaps if you had helped someone to achieve a great victory, and that person was now in a position of power and could vouch for you and persuade the other *cyningas* that you ought to be their leader…"

He was glowering into the fire and Eadyth grinned once more. The seed was planted, though she had thought it was painfully obvious. Now she just had to wait for it to grow.

She stood and walked over to where Gieva was sleeping in one of the hall's alcoves.

"I'm no use to her anymore," said Eadyth, when Gieva opened her eyes, "I have nothing she wants." She handed the baby to Gieva, who grinned blearily and stretched out her arms.

"Is anything the matter?" Gieva yawned, apparently seeing the king's face as he stomped out of the hall.

Eadyth rolled her eyes. "He is just realizing he has a bit more authority than he thought he had, and he is trying to reconcile himself with that fact."

Gieva nodded. "Oh. I thought that it might have been about Eorwald." She looked sheepish.

"I thought that you were sleeping for that," Eadyth said. "I'll never believe your snores from now on." She said it genially, but Gieva frowned, and put her daughter to her breast. The baby started to suck hungrily, making little grunting noises as she did so. Gieva did not look back up; she did not seem to want Eadyth to see the dark look which had passed across her face.

"Eorwald will be fine," Eadyth said, though she could not say it with the confidence she might have been able to use once. "He is resilient. He's just been through so much that it might take a while." They were the same words she had told Rædwald, but she still had a rather hard time believing them.

Gieva was silent for a long time, and Eadyth knew that something was eating at her, something she wanted to say but could not.

"Is there something you need to tell me?" Eadyth asked.

Gieva looked at her baby rather than at Eadyth, but before she could answer, Eorwald himself came into the hall, bringing a light draft of cool air inside with him. He gave Eadyth a perfunctory nod of greeting, and sat down next to Gieva. Eadyth hoped that she imagined seeing his hands shaking.

The baby had fallen asleep again, with Gieva's nipple halfway out of her mouth, a placid and dreamy look on her face. "Do you want to hold her?" Gieva asked Eorwald, pulling her tunic closed.

Eorwald seemed reluctant, but Gieva pushed the little one into his arms before he had a chance to protest. The baby had grown immensely in the past few weeks, but even so she looked minuscule in Eorwald's hands, which were suddenly no longer trembling. Eadyth saw the faintest glimmer of a smile on her son's lips as he looked at the baby.

"That's better now, isn't it?" Gieva told Eorwald in a voice that Eadyth could barely hear, "She is safe, and so are you. You are both protected." Gieva had moved her arms as if to shelter the pair of them, one hand on Eorwald's back, the other gently touching his hands as he held the baby.

Eadyth watched them for a moment, and felt a wave of sadness and love that made her chest ache. Rædwald had been right. There was something broken in her son, something that would not be healed by herbs and draughts. Even so, even with Eorwald damaged as he was, she knew that Gieva was the only one who knew how to hold him together, and she thanked the gods that Gieva had been brought into his life.

Chapter Twenty-Five

Isene Geworht

Iron-Forged

The needle slid through the cloth with a faint whisper as the wool thread followed, and Sunniva lifted her eyes only slightly so that she could see the men. She shifted, feeling a dull cramping in her stomach and then a welling of relief.

The wise woman in the village had said it would only take a few hours to be effective; Sunniva had intended to wait until the evening, but the moment she returned home her fingers had popped open the wax seal and she had poured the mixture into her wine before she realized what she was doing. The sooner the better, she supposed.

She adjusted the thickly folded wool between her legs discreetly, bending down to pick up another skein of thread, knowing that the remedy had done its work. She glanced up at Godomar, who was lounging in his high seat with a cup of wine in his hand, and she uttered a silent prayer of thanks that whatever filthy seed the man had put in her would not take hold. She felt a smirk tweak her lips at her secret rebellion. It was a rather messy and uncomfortable solution to an even messier and more uncomfortable problem. Sunniva no longer fought him when he pushed her onto her back, but as long as there was pennyroyal and tansy to be found, he would never have that claim on her body.

Godomar pointed to the seat opposite him in invitation for his brother to sit, though Walaric remained standing, so stiffly that Sunniva thought he might have been tied to a post.

"It is too early in the year," Walaric was muttering, as if he did not want Sunniva to hear.

"Which is why no one will see it coming," Godomar said in a normal tone, uncaring if Sunniva did hear. "They work themselves into frenzy if they are prepared for a battle. This way, it will give them no time. They will be crushed before they even see the boot falling upon them."

Walaric made some more grumbling murmurs as Godomar sipped his wine. Sunniva picked apart a knot forming in the thread.

"You know that I will do as you command," said Walaric a few moments later, after a hard glance from Godomar. "I only counsel prudence."

"Your opinions are noted," Godomar said coolly, "and if I wished to heed them, I would do so. I wish to march north before Easter."

"Father Mathias will not approve of you marching to battle during the Lenten season," Walaric still did not shift position, still rigid in place.

"Father Mathias has nothing to say that I wish to hear," Godomar snapped, "And I wish never to hear that foul man's name again. Do you hear me?"

Sunniva did not see as she re-threaded her needle, but she knew that Walaric nodded stiffly.

"I shall begin the conscription, then," Walaric said, "How many do you require?"

"No," Godomar said languidly, "I have another task for you."

"I am responsible for raising the army when you require it of me," Walaric said, "And as such, I –"

"If you knew how to raise a proper army, we would not have been defeated and we would have no need to attack them now," Godomar hissed, finally seeming not to wish Sunniva to hear them. She let her features grow blank and pretended to seem particularly interested in the cloth in her hands.

Walaric was silent for a moment, and then choked, "What is it that my lord would command?"

"You have an even greater honor," Godomar's voice quickly returned to its normal brightness, "You will watch over my fair jewel while I am away."

Sunniva bit her cheek and forced her head to remain bowed over her embroidery, though she could not help but swallow hard. Her throat was dry and she gave a small cough, which she cursed silently.

Within a heartbeat Godomar had pushed a cup of wine under her nose, and she took it without looking at him.

"Would you not like that, my little treasure?" he asked, touching her chin with a finger to raise her eyes to his.

"I should be glad of the protection," Sunniva said blandly.

Godomar smiled indulgently at her, and pinched her cheek lightly, turning back to his brother with a stony face. "I will not have any harm befall my jewel. I trust you will know how to manage any mischief that may arise."

*****

Ecgric had never been overly comfortable in his house near Gipeswic, but it was nice to spend the night under a proper roof again. The property he had been given by Rædwald so long ago had been well-managed in his absence, but the whole place did have a certain air of neglect about it, and he felt overwhelmed with the amount of responsibilities he would have to deal with upon his return.

His errands in Gipeswic complete, he made his way down to the crowded docks. They always gave him a sense of satisfaction to see; he may have been reluctant to take the responsibility in the first place, but a job done well was always satisfying. There were half a dozen riverboats mooring here, and another handful bobbed in the middle of the river, waiting their turn to unload.

A ship had just come in, some river boat loaded with foul-mouthed sailors and crates of goods. They had been transferred from a sea-going vessel, and now that they were on the small barge there was hardly any room for the twenty men picking their way through the baggage. He watched them unloading their wares absently for a while, and had to look twice when he saw a final man making his way up the dock.

"Oswy?" he called to the man. He turned, and indeed it was the pale, bearded warrior who had left for Lundenburh with Sigebryht half a year before.

Oswy seemed just as startled to see Ecgric, but embraced him with a bewildered grin.

"What are you doing on a trading boat?" Ecgric asked.

Oswy's face drooped slightly. "I was catching a ride," he said shiftily. He glanced around nervously, as if someone were about to stick a knife between his ribs. .

"When did you return? I thought I would get word when Sigebryht came home, but I haven't heard anything."

Again, Oswy seemed to be debating with himself. "I came alone," he said. "Ecgric, you have to tell me, who –"

He was interrupted by one of the sailors shouting at him, "You promised payment," said a gruff looking sailor with a ruddy face and almost no neck, "Quickly now, else I'll feed your guts to the fishes."

"Of course," Oswy said wearily. Before Oswy could reach into his pouch, Ecgric flipped the sailor a *pening.* The man caught it, raised an eyebrow, nodded, and went back to unloading the ship.

"That wasn't necessary," Oswy said.

"Don't worry about it," said Ecgric. He would have been amazed if Oswy had had silver with which to pay the sailor; his clothes were torn and stained with mud and sea-spray, and he looked as if he had walked a mile through brambles. "Come and rest at my house tonight."

"Ecgric, who sits in the Bricgweard?" Oswy's eyes were flitting around the docks and back to Ecgric with such speed they seemed a blur.

"What?" Ecgric asked, nonplussed.

Oswy looked as if he might grab Ecgric's shoulders and shake him. "Who sits in the Bricgweard? Who is the *cyning*? Tell me!"

"Rædwald," Ecgric said, staring at Oswy. "Have you gone mad? It's Rædwald. He is there now."

Oswy swallowed, though he did not seem relieved by this news.

"What's happened?" Ecgric asked slowly, as Oswy put a hand to his mouth. "Oswy, tell me."

Oswy's face was ashen, his eyes wide. "I must speak with the *cyning* immediately. The Franca have betrayed us."

To Ecgric's surprise, the Wuffingham was bustling with a flurry of activity as he, Ricbert, and Oswy galloped up the road from the Wood Bridge. He kept glancing at Oswy as if the man would fall off of his horse at any moment, though he had made it the twenty miles from Gipeswic with a grim determination on his white face.

When they entered the Bricgweard, they found the king deep in talk with a man Ecgric immediately recognized as Edwin.

The winter had not been kind to Edwin, but he certainly looked more of a king than he had done when they had parted. His beard and hair were longer, though a scar cut down his cheek on one side to leave a streak of white skin amid the dark hair. He looked grave as he sat in conversation with Rædwald, but they ceased their talk and his face broke into a grin at the sight of the newcomers. Rædwald embraced Ricbert so heartily when they walked through the door, that Ecgric rather felt as if he were intruding on something indecent.

There were a few other people loitering in the hall, including Eadyth and Eorwald. The latter two greeted Ecgric and Ricbert gladly, and Eadyth's face lit up at the sight of Oswy.

"Where is Sigebryht?" Eadyth asked, looking around as if her son would pop out of the shadows.

"I must speak with you, Dryhten," Oswy said, pointedly ignoring the queen. His voice was slow and leaden, and he glanced around as if he did not want anyone to hear.

"What's happened?" Rædwald asked, ignoring the request for privacy.

"As I say, Dryhten, I must speak with you." Oswy looked around at them, clearly uneasy at his audience. "We've been betrayed," Oswy said flatly, when it was clear that no one planned to leave. "I did not realize the extent of it, until now."

"Explain," Rædwald growled.

Oswy swallowed before speaking. "We received word that you had been attacked by a Northumbrian army, and that you and your sons were all slaughtered."

Ecgric waited for a response, but none was forthcoming. Everyone stared at Oswy, who seemed to have a lot of trouble looking anyone in the eye.

"Sigebryht had been worried for some time, about Godomar's intentions," Oswy continued, "Especially after my lady miscarried. Godomar's men seemed to hate us, and I think Sigebryht was just waiting for a good enough reason to leave, and to take her with us."

"Why?" Rædwald asked, his voice cracking the silence like a whip.

"Godomar was disgraced in battle not long after we arrived," Oswy said, "and it made for tension between the Engla and the Franca. When we learned that you had been killed," He glanced up at the king, as if bewildered that the man was still standing there, "When we heard the rumor, I think Sigebryht knew that Godomar would kill us all. If you were dead, Dryhten, Godomar would have no reason to keep us alive. I came back on Sigebryht's orders," Oswy said miserably, "I gave my word, Dryhten. I promised that I would bring the message to whoever sat in the high seat of the Bricgweard, that Godomar had no intentions of fulfilling his promises."

"I daresay we can go without silks," Rædwald muttered, and his eyes shot back to Oswy. "I don't understand why Godomar would suddenly decide to kill Sigebryht. Sige never did anything to the man, did he?"

Oswy frowned even deeper than before. "The enemies who defeated Godomar were called the Seax-people. The Seaxe."

Eadyth's mouth dropped open. "Ealdseaxe," she murmured, "My kin, in the old country. Sige's kin."

Oswy nodded. "Sigebryht's heritage was never a secret, but something put it in Godomar's head that we all were spies for the Ealdseaxe; that we had orchestrated his defeat. He even started suspecting my lady Sunniva."

Ecgric clenched his jaw so tightly that he thought his teeth might shatter. Everyone looked to be in varying states of disbelief. Eorwald was stony-faced as his mother, his eyes huge; Rædwald and Ricbert looked at one another as if having a silent conversation. Edwin might well have been a corpse for all the blood left in his face.

"Sigebryht decided that if the league was broken, we would have to leave, and sooner rather than later." He grimaced, "He said he would collect my lady Sunniva, and he would meet me and the other men to take one of the ships leaving Francland for Lundenburh. He made me promise – he made me swear that I would leave on that ship," he drew in a painful-looking breath, "with or without him." His face fell, and he looked on the verge of tears. "I made it to the ship, and waited as long as I could.

Ulfgar was the only one who made it before the ship left."

"Where is Ulfgar?' someone asked, but Ecgric did not bother to see who it was.

Oswy seemed to swallow again before saying, "There was a fight, as our men tried to leave. Ulfgar was wounded, and he... it was a dirty arrow. He died on the journey."

Ecgric heard a howl of grief, from one of the people who had stopped to listen. A kinsman of Ulfgar, probably. He wished he could feel sorry for the man, but his face and his brain were frozen, his eyes fixed on Oswy.

"And the rest?" Eadyth's voice sounded about to break.

Oswy closed his eyes, and opened his mouth to speak, but Ecgric did not hear the words. He was out the door before he realized where he was going. He knew what had happened next. He did not need to hear it spoken aloud.

Ecgric knew little enough about Godomar, but he knew enough about men with power to know what had become of Sigebryht and the other Engla. An alleged spy was never treated gently. A look at the blankness in Eorwald's eyes would tell anyone that.

That foul Frankisc snake had Sunniva. Bonds of marriage did not protect spies. It was bad enough to think that she cared for the man, but if he had harmed her...

He tried to steady himself, but he shook with anger and with a roar he put his fist through the wattle-and-daub wall of one of the outbuildings. He vaguely registered the ache in his hand, but he did not care.

Nothing would satisfy him, if she had been harmed. He would kill the man with his own hands, feed the guts to wolves, and then he would find the bastard's corpse and rip it in half.

His own guts were lead as he thought of Sunniva, the woman he had loved, always full of that beautiful fire. She would fight back, if anyone hurt her. But how long could she fight, while surrounded by men who would kill her kin and her along with them?

He slid down the wall, and for the first time in years, he found himself weeping. He knew that he would never hold her again, would never hear her laugh, or see her fierce silver eyes glinting with mischief, or even fight with her as they had so often done. He had come to terms with the fact that she was gone, but somehow knowing that she was happy brought him comfort.

But she was not happy. Not if what Oswy said was true. She had miscarried – would Godomar have blamed her for losing his child? If Godomar thought that Sunniva was just another Ealdseaxisc spy… his thoughts sped as quickly as he could think them, a torrent in his mind. She was in danger. She was a captive, and if Godomar decided she was not to be trusted…

Ecgric did not look up when he saw boots in front of him. Only when the person bent down did he glare at him. Edwin was so pale he might have been dead, but his eyes burned furiously.

"What do you want?" Ecgric asked. His voice was hoarse, but he did not care.

"I want to find them," said Edwin.

Ecgric glanced up, bitterness dripping from every word. "You heard Oswy. They'll both be dead by now, along with all of their men."

Edwin glared at him. "You are giving up hope so easily?"

"There is no hope to give up," Ecgric shot back. "Why do you care? You have no debt to us. Get back to your lands and let us move on."

Edwin's hand clenched into a fist, but he released it; his face was blazing. "I won't give up. If they are still alive, I will not abandon them to fear and death in a strange land. Not while I have strength left."

"And if they are dead?" Ecgric asked blankly. He was momentarily distracted by someone else emerging from the Bricgweard, but looked back at Edwin, whose face was hard and still blazing with resolve.

"Then they will not rest on foreign shores in disgrace, but in the land of their fathers," Edwin said. "Are you with me?"

*****

Gieva tried not to grind her teeth together as she rocked the little one; she wanted to stop her ears with her hands. The visitors were polite to her and did not go near her house, but she did not like hearing their loud voices from far off as she tried to get her baby to sleep. Gieva already had a hard time sleeping with her *lytling*, her little one, waking her at all hours of the night to nurse. The baby wanted to suck almost constantly, and Gieva always had to fight back painful tears whenever her daughter latched onto the cracked and broken skin of her breasts. But after a few moments, the waves of calm would wash over her and she would stop caring how much it hurt. It was rather like giving birth; she remembered how she had cried and gripped Eorwald's arm as she pushed through the pain, but in the end the result was so blissfully perfect that she could hardly remember the hours of exhaustion and pain which had come before.

Eadyth was visiting with her, helping to tidy the house as Gieva nursed her Lytling. It was such a relief to have her; Eadyth was helpful and caring and happy to answer Gieva's numerous questions on motherhood.

"You are so much better at this than I was the first time," Eadyth said, throwing soiled rushes onto the fire and scattering new ones, "Are you sure you haven't already had some children I don't know about?"

Gieva laughed and swapped the baby to her other breast. Her little pink mouth pouted as she latched on, her fingers gripping a stray lock of hair on Gieva's shoulder. "She's just an easy baby," Gieva said. "You don't give me any trouble, do you my Lytling?" She tickled her daughter's cheek with her finger and her mouth twitched into something like a smile as she dozed and sucked contentedly.

"You're lucky then," Eadyth said. "Rægen squalled night and day for the first two months at least. I think the *cyning* wondered what he'd gotten himself into." She stroked the baby's messy brown hair. "She does look like him."

"She does," Gieva said. "Wake up, Lytling, you're not done yet." She jostled the baby slightly and she resumed her suckling.

"If you keep calling her that it'll stick," Eadyth said. "You'll give her a proper name and no one will remember it because they'll always call her 'little one.'"

Gieva shrugged. "So be it. I'll still call her Lytling even when she's grown taller than me." Lytling was asleep now, and Gieva knew that she could watch her for hours. She had grown out of looking like a misshapen root vegetable and now looked more like a baby, and was growing so quickly that she began to resemble a fat little ball of bread dough.

"You should rest for a bit," said Eadyth. "While the baby is sleeping, otherwise you'll never get a chance!"

Gieva nodded in agreement, "Thank you so much, Eadyth," she said, kissing her on the cheek. "I don't know what I would do without you."

"It is my privilege, and my right as her grandmother," said Eadyth, who bent down to kiss Lytling's untidy brown hair. "Come up to the Bricgweard tonight," she told Gieva, "Ricbert and Ecgric returned to Gipeswic a couple of days ago, and they should be arriving here today."

"What about her?" Gieva asked. She admittedly enjoyed the excuse not to go into the hall with everyone else; she would sometimes even give Lytling a little poke so that she would cry and Gieva had an excuse to bring her home. Eorwald always saw through this ruse, but he would gladly depart with her.

"Steorra can take care of her for a few hours if you don't want her in the noise," Eadyth said, perhaps guessing Gieva's thoughts. "You really ought to come. You saved Ricbert's life. He will want to thank you personally."

There was no argument for this, and she nodded reluctantly.

Lytling woke again, looking around the room with her bright silver eyes and gurgling happily. Gieva slipped her daughter into a sling so that Lytling could nurse while she walked toward Steorra's house, and by the time she had left her baby in Steorra's care, Lytling was fast asleep once more.

She was even more hesitant to go now, but she walked toward the Bricgweard. She did not find anyone she knew immediately, and she was on the point of heading back home to wait for a while when she saw Ecgric's powerful figure burst from the hall and stomp out of sight. She had not realized that he had returned already, but she did not want to go to greet him while he was in such a state.

A moment later, she saw Eorwald walking out of the hall as well, looking shaken and confused as he found himself next to a knot of men practicing at swords. He stopped short, staring at them as he clutched his forearm, and Gieva walked purposefully toward him with a deep feeling of unease. He was standing at the edge of the yard watching the other men, and every time their swords would clash he seemed to jump. His arms dropped to his sides and thin streak of blood rolled down his wrist.

Not again, she thought as she closed the gap between them. His back was to her, so she cleared her throat quietly so that he would not be startled when she touched his back. "Eorwald," she said quietly, and he jumped again despite her precaution.

"Eorwald, will you please help me with something?" She slipped her hand into his shaking one and pulled him gently away from the yard, trying to ignore the men looking at them.

"I can't," he tried to say as she hurried him away, but she squeezed his hand to stop his words.

"Hush," she said, "Come along."

He was trembling furiously by the time they entered Gieva's deserted house. She led him inside, and turned to look at his face.

"It's all happening again," he said, staggering slightly away from her. "I can't do it anymore. They are gone, they are all gone…" He pressed the heels of his hands into his eyes. She could see the cuts on his forearms, half-hidden by the sleeves of his tunic; red stained his fingertips and blackened his nails as if he had clawed his own skin.

"Is it coming?" she asked carefully. He seemed to be able to tell when one of the attacks would come, and she feared for him now. He was always so exhausted, so ashamed, so weak, after he had one, though they had seemed to stop ever since the baby was born.

Eorwald shook his head, though he was still shuddering.

"They're dead, Gieva," he said. He moved his hands and she saw that his eyes were wide and bloodshot.

"Who is dead?"

He took a few deep breaths, and then in a slow, rattling voice, he said, "Sunniva. And Sige. In Francland. It is almost certain that they've both been killed."

"No," Gieva said, "No, that cannot be true."

He did not say anything. He began to grip his forearm again, his nails digging into the skin. She pulled his hands away and held them in hers, but he yanked them away.

"Why am I still alive?" he shouted at the sky, as if it would make the gods hear him. "Sigebryht and Rægen were a hundred times better men than I am, and they are gone. And I am still here..."

Gieva took his hands in hers again, if only to keep him from beating his palms into his forehead. "Hush," she said, "you don't know anything for certain –"

"I hear them talking, you know," he said, his face suddenly dark and twisted with anger. "I know they wish I had died and Rægen had lived. Everyone wishes that. You wish it too. No one would want me for their *cyning*; no one would follow a man who cannot hold a sword, who forgets things," he paused, wincing, "a man who is broken."

"You are not broken!"

Eorwald closed his eyes. "I am. My mind is shattering. I can feel it." His voice was quiet and terribly calm, and it frightened her more than it would have done if he had shouted. "I should have died," he said. "I should have died so many times, and they all took my place. My brothers, my friends, even my little sister, and here I am, the one no one wants, the one who is here when hundreds of better men should be in my place." He dug his palms into his eyes again. He was not breathing properly. He stared at her and at nothing, every muscle in his body clenching. He put a shaking hand to his hip and put it on the handle of his seax, drawing it from its sheath.

"No!" Gieva screamed, and threw herself at him as he turned the point toward his chest. The point had pressed barely a finger's breadth through the wool of his shirt and into the space between his ribs as she knocked the blade aside with the side of her hand. She realized vaguely that it had cut her arm as she wrenched it out of his grip, but she threw it away with such force that the point stuck in the wooden door.

Eorwald looked as if he might hit her as he balled his shaking fist, but he saw the blood on her arm and dropped it. His face turned into a mask of horror. She gave him a hard, furious look as he fell to his knees in front of her, taking her hand and staring at the drops of blood now forming on the cut.

"You don't understand," he said quietly, looking up at her, "This is the only way. I will never be free of the poison. I'll never be free of the ones I've lost. I just want it to stop." He blinked up at her several times and then looked back at the cut on her arm. It was not deep, but he reached for her and stared at the thin line of blood that trickled down into her palm.

Gieva felt her entire body surge with anger and a sadness so wrenching she was sure it would tear her apart, but when she spoke her voice was quiet and dangerous. "Before you turn that sword on yourself, you are going to have to put it in my heart first."

"I never want hurt you," he said, touching her face. "But I have. You ought to let me go so that I can't hurt you anymore."

"How can you say that you don't want to hurt me, and yet you would take away one of the only things that I have left?" her voice was rising, "I have lost everything, over and over again. I lost my sister. I lost my parents. I lost my cousin and my friends and all of my kin, and I lost my husband, who will never know his child. I cannot lose you too."

"You are better without me," he said.

"I would have burned to death in that hall without you," she hissed, "I would have frozen to death with my child inside of me on the edge of my husband's grave, without you. I would never have been able to bring my daughter into the world, without you. And you think that is better?"

He closed his eyes, and a tear rolled down his cheek. "I can't keep doing this. I am not strong enough."

Gieva was crying now, bitter, hot, angry tears that made his face blurry. She tried to say something, but she could not arrange a coherent thought. She fell to her knees in front of him, gripping the sides of his face and staring into his eyes.

"Then I will make you strong," she said, her voice grating with the fire that was blazing in her heart.

*****

Sunniva clenched her fist as Godomar patted her arm looped through his. His head was lifted high, his fingers curling gently over Sunniva's arm to show his ornate rings, his cloak thrown back to reveal a violet coat over burnished mail.

They turned west, and Sunniva felt a slow swell of unease that had nothing to do with getting her blood. She turned her eyes away from the stakes that stood sentry outside the west gate. The skulls were picked clean now, and one had toppled off to shatter on the stony ground below. She did not know whether to weep, or scream. She might not be able to give them proper burials, but anything was better than this disgrace.

She waited silently while Godomar said some words to the crowd that Sunniva did not listen to, and he kissed her chastely on the mouth before he mounted his horse. The train of men aligned themselves behind him, and though it seemed to take a hundred years to depart, eventually she saw their figures disappear around the stand of trees to the North. The few remaining villagers turned and headed for home, but Sunniva waited, her eyes downcast as if in worry.

Once everyone had gone, she would gather the skulls and bury them, she decided. It would not take long. She could at least give them that dignity while she was free of Godomar.

Sunniva felt a hard hand clasp her upper arm, and she wrenched it away. "I know how to walk," she said acidly, and the hand tightened. Walaric stared ahead, steering Sunniva back into the village.

She scowled, but walked in stately dignity despite the dull pain where his fingers gripped her. She felt the edges of the iron amulet between her breasts, and focused on the weight of it. She would fight, but any warrior knew that he should not start a battle he had no chance of winning.

They passed the blacksmith's open-sided workspace; its childless, unmarried owner was absent, following Godomar grudgingly with half a hundred others like him. The forge was cold, but heavy hammers lined the thick wooden table and racks, awaiting their master's return.

"Let go of me," she hissed at him.

"I am escorting you back to the hall," Walaric said dully, "To protect you."

She nearly spat in his face, but spat a harsh laugh instead. "Protect me? The only one here who has ever laid a hand on me was you."

He pulled her again, and she resisted.

"What will you do?" she asked derisively, "I'd be surprised if you could walk and talk at the same time without Godomar giving you permission. Are you going to beat me? You can see I am quite unprotected."

"You are indeed unprotected," he said dully, "And you had best heed my instructions."

"Yes, you got rid of my protection, didn't you?" she spat, "Afraid that my brother might break those ugly teeth of yours, so you had him killed, didn't you?"

Walaric rolled his eyes, tugging her again but she resisted even harder, wiggling her arm out of his reach.

"I know you have taken my brother, and you will tell me where he is," Sunniva spat. "Otherwise, it will be the worse for you."

Walaric ignored her, yanking her to round the corner past the blacksmith's house.

"You know," she mocked, "It says a great deal of a man to be so afraid of a coward and a liar like Godomar. Do you think he will give you some reward for beating a helpless woman? You are as spineless as a worm."

"A worm I might be, but I am still at liberty to discipline you if you put a toe out of line." It was the most words she had ever heard him string together, and his fist tightened even harder around her arm.

"Where is he?" she spat, "Where are you keeping –"

She felt a sharp blow across the side of her face, and she glanced back up, grinning. "My dear husband won't like it much if you damage my pretty face," she said, turning the other cheek toward him, "But if you really feel that I need to be taught a lesson..."

Walaric did not raise his had again.

"Come now," she said, "I've just called your master a coward and a liar," she cooed, "Dogs do not like when people insult their masters."

Fool girl, she thought dully as she nearly bent double, his fist in her stomach, *stupid, stupid girl. You don't goad a wolf when you have a feather as a weapon...*

She knew vaguely that he had pushed her into the blacksmith's house, back toward the single wall. The anvil and table and racks of tools screened her vision to the outside.

"Where is he?" she hissed.

Her knees were knocked out from under her, and she felt his boot on the back of her lower leg, pinning her to the ground. He had a hand around her neck, the other clenching her wrist so tightly that her fingers began to turn purple.

She spat in his face and he pressed harder on her leg with his boot. Sunniva ground her teeth together, but did not cry out.

"My brother would not grieve at your death," Walaric hissed at her, leaning into her ear. "He would not weep if an unfortunate accident happened to befall you while he was away; no more than he would mourn the loss of a ring."

Perhaps he had been waiting for her to weep, but she grinned instead. "Except he will not have the chance, as he will be trampled like the piece of *swines scitte* that he is and his enemies will not leave him a ring to adorn his shallow grave."

The blow after that remark sent stars into her vision, but she cleared them in a moment.

"I look forward to spitting on his corpse." She said when the stars had cleared.

Walaric thrust his left hand forward against her neck, slamming the back of her head into the plank wall behind her. She blinked, but the stars did not disappear as quickly this time.

Bloody fool, she thought dully as her head struck the wall again.

"I will be happy to finally kill you," he said with the closest thing to a grin she had ever seen him wear as he tightened his fingers. The stars reappeared, and she felt something scraping in her neck as he said, "Before I kill you, though, you deserve the punishment that is owed to –"

He released her suddenly, roaring in pain. He spun round, and Sunniva saw the wooden hilt of a belt-knife protruding from between his shoulder blades; the attacker hidden by his mass. Sunniva sprang to her feet, reaching out and grabbing the first thing her fingers could find. She leapt forward, swinging the heavy object to collide with Walaric's head.

The first attacker sprang back as Walaric's weight fell forward, and Sunniva glanced up to see Hilde's white face staring back at her, hands raised as if to fend off blows. Sunniva had fallen atop Walaric, who was now stirring slightly as Sunniva stared wide-eyed at Hilde. Without thinking, Sunniva brought the hammer down on the man's temple.

A satisfying and sickening crunch rent the air and Sunniva heard the dull thud of his legs as they twitched against the packed dirt floor. He bucked wildly, nearly knocking her off of him. She slammed the hammer down again, and then once more, unsure if it was the rage built up in her, or the shock and horror that he was still shaking even with half of his brains clinging to the iron hammer's head.

Hilde yanked her arm and pulled her away from the jerking body, and Sunniva threw her arms around the other woman, though she was still gripping the handle of the blacksmith's hammer so tightly that her fingers might have broken.

"I came looking for you when you did not return to the hall, and –"

"Are you hurt?" Sunniva choked.

Hilde shook her head, staring past Sunniva at the pool of blood now seeping into the packed dirt floor. She closed her mouth abruptly, shaking her head again.

Sunniva glanced back down to the now-stilled man's body, nausea spreading into her very bones as she looked at the featureless mass of crunched bone and blood and hair where his head ought to have been. She staggered backward, clutching the heavy anvil for support.

She had scoffed when Ecgric had talked about the sound of a man's body hitting the ground, but the scraping of Walaric's boots still screamed in her mind. She swallowed with difficulty.

"Hilde," she said slowly, dragging her eyes away from the scene and up to the other woman.

Hilde's mouth was hanging open again, and she closed it with a snap as she took a step backward.

"You have to leave," Sunniva said, "Go back to the church."

"And then what?" Hilde asked, "Wait there while someone finds you and throws you in a cell?"

Sunniva felt the weight of the hammer in her hand, the weight of the hammer against her chest. They were heavy, but a power was growing in her limbs and in her heart as she felt the weight of her fear and her pain being lifted from her.

"Come with me, then," Sunniva said.

Hilde's eyes widened in shock, though Sunniva knew that something more lay hidden beneath that Hilde was trying to keep secret.

"Come with you?" she asked, "Where?"

"Anywhere," Sunniva felt a twisting of her mouth that she had not felt in months. She looked to her right, out of the open front of the blacksmith's house toward the West Gate.

"We can't," Hilde said faintly, but the hint of something like hope filled her quiet voice before she snapped back into fearful seriousness. "Sunniva, we are just girls! We can't just –"

"Just girls?" Sunniva snarled, "Does that look like a bloody sewing needle to you?" She jabbed a finger toward the short dagger still protruding from the dead man's back. She lifted the blood-caked hammer, "Does this look like a flaming spindle?"

"No, but –"

"That piece of filth can never hurt me again, and I'll not give his *wearg* of a brother the chance to try." Sunniva said with a glance downward, the strange twist of her mouth returning.

What was it? It was the same shape she forced her face into when Godomar had told her to smile, but this...

"I am taking my chance. Are you with me?"

Hilde's eyes filled with that peculiar solidity of determination and hope once more. "They will come after us," she panted, though the corners of her mouth were twitching upwards just as Sunniva's did.

"Then it is a good thing that I am a fast runner," Sunniva said. She clenched the hammer in one hand and took Hilde's in the other, and for the first time since she had stepped foot in this land, she knew that the smile on her face was her own.

*****

Several days passed, and Gieva had not left his side for a moment. As long as she was there, firmly beside him with Lytling in her arms, he knew that he could keep fighting. He had to keep fighting.

Messengers had gone out a few weeks before, and the fruits of their errands were beginning to appear at the Bricgweard. Dozens of *ealdormen* and hundreds of their retainers had flooded into the area, and soon the kings began to arrive as well.

Eorwald was unsure what the king had planned to do, bringing so many powerful men together. He knew that the previous attempt at forging alliances had not gone according to plan – if he had been able to win the esteem of the kings of Mercia or of the Eota, he would not have been obliged to marry Sunniva off to the Franca. Father did not seem keen to explain his actions to Eorwald, though he spent long hours in conversation with Edwin and with Ricbert and Ecgric. Eorwald felt a slow glug of poison in his blood when he thought of their whispered meetings. He knew that his father did not have faith in him, but seeing the proof of it was more than he could stand.

He did not speak much to anyone during the feast, but he sat in long observation of the kings of the Eota, the Eastseaxe, Mercia, and the Hwicce. They seemed to be surveying him as well, as if deciding if his silence was meant to intimidate them.

"I have heard much about you," Eadbald, the son of the former *heahcyning*, told him, "and of your exploits. It rather sounds like some story out of the old days, doesn't it?"

Eorwald did not say anything immediately, and Ecgric spoke instead. "Eorwald is one of the fiercest fighters I have ever seen. His deeds at the River Idle will not be forgotten." Some of the others nodded appreciatively. Eorwald held Gieva's hand under the table as Ecgric related the story. He kept his face blank, and perhaps they thought it simply made him look fierce, for they seemed to be in awe of the tale of his escape from the Northumbrians' camp and his vengeance at the River Idle. Eorwald could feel his hand shaking in Gieva's as Ecgric spoke, but her breathing was deep and slow and he matched it with his own.

"I should be proud to have such a son," said Sæwine, the king of the Eastseaxe, raising his horn to Rædwald.

"Very proud indeed," said Rædwald. Perhaps he meant it, but Eorwald did not feel as though he could believe him.

Eorwald had little appetite, and drink only ever made the horrors worse, so he ate and drank little. He focused on Gieva's presence next to him, and she gave him courage. "I learned from the best," he said. "My father is the finest warrior and *dryhten* in the world. Men will sing of his victory for years to come." Someone shouted in approval of his words, but Eorwald fell silent and focused on Gieva's slow breathing.

"It was a formidable foe," said Ecgric. "No one could have believed that Athelfrith's men would be so cowardly and so cruel. They needed a true leader, and not some spineless worm hiding in his northern hole."

"And now they have a proper *cyning*!" said Eadyth, who was grinning fiercely. She raised one of the gilded wooden cups to Edwin. "And long may he rule our northern allies in peace."

"All thanks to Rædwald Cyning," said Edwin. "Happy was my fate when I found my way through the lands of my enemies," he gave a long, hard look at Cearl of Mercia, and back to Rædwald, "to find myself in your keeping, my Dryhten."

Sæwine of the Eastseaxe looked mildly amused at the lavish and blatantly extravagant praise being heaped upon Rædwald, though the other kings did not seem to share his pleasure. Eadbald kept glancing over his shoulder to look at a knot of women who were listening intently to the conversation, while the surly old kings of Mercia and the Hwicce and some of their *ealdormen* shared dark looks.

They were all silent for a moment, but Edwin rose from his seat. "I owe my crown to you," he said. His voice was stately and solemn, the voice of a king. He waited until every mouth in the hall had closed, and every eye was upon him.

Edwin passed his fellow kings and knelt in front of the high seat, where Rædwald loomed over every other person in the hall. His beard and hair were woven with gold rings, his massive gold belt buckle gleaming at his waist, his ring-covered hand wrapped around the gold-fitted drinking horn. Eorwald felt very small as he looked at his father the king, and he knew he was not the only one. Only the queen, who had a fiery look in her eye and a hard grin on her lips, seemed to match his majesty.

"Rædwald, great *cyning* of the Engla people," Edwin had dropped to one knee and spoke in a slow, carrying voice, "I, Edwin, *cyning* of Deira and Bernicia and the Islands, and *ealdorman* of Lindsey, wish to place myself under your protection and your guidance. I hereby swear my fealty and my love to you from this day henceforth, as I take you for my *heahcyning*." It was expertly done, Eorwald thought, and wondered if this was what his father and Edwin had been speaking about in all those long hours of conversation. Edwin beckoned to a servant, who brought forth something long and thin as a spear, but very heavy.

Edwin took the covered thing from the servant and removed the wrapping to reveal a very old, rusted ring, topped with a stag and attached to a long iron pole. "This," he said, holding it up for everyone to see, "is the standard born by the ancient ones who ruled this land, the symbol of their high chief. The mighty stag, the ruler of the wild woods of this land. The Breattas of old united themselves under this standard, the symbol of the *brytenwalda*." He paused, looking around. "Only three men, only three *cyningas*, have united our people under this banner since the time of Hengest and Horsa, since our ancestors came over the sea to take this land in glorious conquest. Only three before now have been worthy of uniting the Engla and the Seaxe, the Gyrwas and the Hwicce and the Eota, and all of the people of this land in peace and plenty. Only three in the history of our folk have shown their worth and their strength in glorious battle. Here sits the fourth!" He shouted at the crowd as he waved his hand toward the king, and glared at everyone in the hall, challenging them to gainsay him.

Eorwald felt Gieva's hand slip into his as his breathing quickened. He knew what was coming, and his heart raced.

"I take you as my *heahcyning*," said Edwin, turning again to Rædwald. "I offer you the standard of the ancient *brytenwalda*, that you might unite the kingdoms. I would have you as my *dryhten* forevermore, and I urge my fellow *cyningas* and every man of worth in this hall to swear their love and fealty to you now, before gods and men."

Rædwald held up his hand. "I accept your service and your love," he said. "But I will not bear this standard unless the *cyningas*, the *ealdormen*, and all men of worth are united behind me." Rædwald blazed with a fire that Eorwald only ever saw during battle, but he was silent.

Edwin was still holding the standard as Ecgric stood. He may have been only an *ealdorman*, but the kings respected him, and he shot them all a look of challenge as he knelt before Rædwald's seat. "I stand by my oaths before you, Rædwald Cyning," he said loudly, offering the hilt of his sword to Rædwald with a flourish, "And I renew them now. I swear by my sword and by my axe that as I live and die, you will ever be my *dryhten*, and I will serve you in this life and in the next." There was a ripple through the silence in the hall, and Eorwald saw the kings sharing glances at one another.

Eorwald got to his feet before he realized what he was doing, though he knew it was the right thing to do, and half-fell to one knee before his father's seat. He drew Weargbana, tucking the blade under his arm as he offered the pommel to the king as Ecgric had done.

"On my honor will I fight for you, my Cyning," he said, his voice steady and confident despite the weakness in his knees, "I take you now not only as my *dryhten* but as my *cyning* and *heahcyning*, to lead me in honor and glory. By my life, if you should fall, I will fight in your place until my last breath. This I swear with the gods and these worthy men as my witnesses."

"And thus I swear in front of these worthy men and the gods that I shall lead you faithfully, as you honor me with your trust, my son," Father took the sword; his face filled with something Eorwald hoped was pride.

Eorwald swallowed once, hoping that the taste in his mouth was simply the aftertaste of sour beer. He took the hilt as it was offered back to him, and slid Weargbana back into her sheath.

Eorwald saw the king of the Eota glance behind him to where a dark-haired, hard looking woman was watching him. She gave him an arching glare, and Eadbald rose from his seat, his mouth twisted into something half scowl and half bemused grin.

Eorwald took his seat, seizing Gieva's hand under the table. She squeezed it, asking a silent question with her eyes that he answered with a minute nod. He matched his breathing to hers, slow and steady as he swallowed the foul taste in his mouth.

"I know the joys of being in the service of one such as you," Eadbald said with a seemingly forced grin. "I swear my loyalty and my love to you, my *heahcyning*, with these assembled folk and all the gods as my witnesses. Long may you live and well may you lead us!"

The word *"heahcyning"* rippled around the room. Eadyth had a hard look on her face as Sæwine of the Eastseaxe stood and offered his allegiance as well. Eorwald was overwhelmed by the flurry of excited muttering erupting throughout the hall now.

Eorwald's teeth felt like they might break and he knew that if he were not clenching his muscles so tightly they might have given out and he would have fallen to the floor. He fought it, fought the slow swell of poison as it found its way upward.

"You are strong," Gieva whispered in his ear. She was only one of half a hundred women leaning over to their friends to mutter quiet words together, and went unnoticed.

Eorwald was able to gather a breath as he felt her fingers tense and release in time with her breathing. He pushed the poison down. He could let it have him later. He had to be strong now. He was strong. She made him that way.

Silence fell as every eye fell to the last man who had not given an oath. The ear-piercing silence swelled. At last, Cearl of Mercia stood and bent the knee before him. His oath was less pronounced than the others, perhaps owing to his extreme age, but he spoke the words nonetheless.

Just a few moments and he could let it take him. He could let it spread its foulness into his heart and his mind and his guts. He just had to be strong. Gieva's hand tugged his as everyone rose to their feet.

Rædwald got to his feet as well, and Edwin beamed as he handed Rædwald the standard. "I accept this honor gladly," he said in a deep, carrying voice, "I will do my best to serve you, my brothers, as your lord and as your *dryhten*. May our lands thrive and prosper under our newly-won peace."

He let Gieva's gentle pull on his hand lead him back several steps toward the door behind them. He just had to breathe, and then they would be outside. He could let it take him, and she would be there.

"Hold on," she whispered, half-supporting him as he stared directly ahead.

He could hold on. She would be there. She *was* there. She made him strong.

"I ask the blessings of the gods as I earn your trust and your love," Rædwald intoned with finality. Eorwald noted that his father refrained from using the word "*heahcyning*," but Edwin did it for him.

"*Hægel Rædwald, sunu Tytila Wuffingas! Hægel ure heahcyning!* Hail, Rædwald, Tytila's son of the Wuffingas! Hail to our *heahcyning*!" he shouted to the world, and the symbol of the stag flashed in Rædwald's hand.

A Sneak Preview of *Wycing*, Book Two of the Sutton Hoo Stories

There was no sound here. Sometimes it seemed as if there had never been language, as if men had never spoken in the first place. Sometimes he had to speak aloud to the emptiness, just to remind himself that sounds existed.

Suddenly, the silence was shattered. He could hear someone screaming. It was a man's voice, and the man was in pain. The screaming sang of hatred and grief and loss; of someone's heart being torn out. He wanted to help, but he could not see where the man was being tortured. He tried to stand but he could not move his arms or his legs; something was coiled around them and he could not break free.

He breathed in deeply, trying to ignore the stench of battle; of blood and iron and shit and death. The screaming would stop for a moment, but as he tried to call out to the tormented one his voice was drowned in the sea of renewed anguish.

It was a long time before he realized that the screams were his own.

Appendix A – Pronunciation Guide & Glossary

Pronunciation Guide for Old English Characters

Old English	Pronunciation	As in...
Æ/æ	[æ]	Cat, black, ash
Þ/þ or Ð/ð	[ð] or [θ]	thing OR there
cg	[dʒ]	edge
sc	[ʃ]	ship, shield
g	[g] or [j] or [ɣ]	grave OR year OR [ɣ] (as German or Dutch 'g' sound)

Glossary of Old English Words

Old English	Pronunciation	Definition
ætheling	ah-the-ling	prince/princess, son or daughter of a king or high nobleman
ceorl	churl	Free servant
cwene	kway-n	Queen
cyning	kyoo-ning	King
dryhten	drick-ten	chieftain, warlord, commander
ealdorman	ay-al-dor-man	earl, nobleman
flyting	fly-ting	a verbal competition of wits, often involving poetic insults
gedriht	ye-drickt	professional trained warriors
heahcwene	hay-ah-kway-n	high queen
heahcyning	hay-ah-kyoo-ning	high king
hilderinc	hill-deh-rink	warrior
hlaford	hla-ford	lord, chief, leader (archaic form of "lord")
huscarl	hoos-karl	household guard, bodyguard, retainer
moot/-mot	moot	meeting, gathering
pening/ peningas	pen-ing/pen-ing-as	unit of currency, equivalent to about £15-20
scylling/ scyllingas	shilling/shilling-as	unit of currency, equivalent to about £100

symbel	sim-bel	a highly ritualized drinking ceremony in a mead hall
thegn	thane	retainers of a king or lord, similar to the later knight
wergild	ware-gild	Fine for an offense against a person (lit. "man-gold")
witenagamot	wi-tana-ga-mot	council

Appendix B – Characters

Name, Title and Birth Year	Pronunciation
Eadyth of the Eastseaxe, Queen of the Engla (born c. AD 575)	Eah-dith
Ecgric, son of Ricbert, Ealdorman of Gipeswic (b. AD 590)	Edge-rick
Eorwald son of Rædwald, *ætheling* of the Engla (b. AD 599)	Eh-or-wald
Gieva, daughter of Cynhelm of the Gyrwas (born AD 598)	Yee-ay-vah
Godomar, *Graf* of Heldergem (born c. AD 587)	Go-doh-mar
Rædwald, King of the Engla (born c. AD 560)	Red-wald
Rægenhere (Rægen), son of Rædwald, *ætheling* of the Engla (born AD 597)	Rah-gen-hair-eh (Rah-gen)*[1]
Ricbert of the East Engla (born c. AD 557)	Rick-bert
Sigebryht (Sige), son of Sigeweald of the Eastseaxe (born AD 591)	Sig-eh-brickt (See-gyeh)
Sunniva, daughter of Rædwald (b. AD 601)	Soo-nee-vah

[1] [g] as in "go," not as in "generation"

Appendix C – Places and Peoples

Old English	Pronunciation	Modern Equivalent
Cantwareburh	Kent-war-uh-berg	Canterbury
Ealdham	Eld-um	Fictional, near Bury St. Edmunds, Suffolk
Elge	Ee-ley	Ely, Cambridgeshire
Eoforwic	Ever-wich	York, Yorkshire
Gipeswic	Yip-switch	Ipswich, Suffolk
Grantabricge	Grant-uh-bridge	Cambridge, Cambridge-shire
Heldergem	Hel-der-yem	Fictional, near Tournai, Belgium
Lundenburh	Lun-den-burg	London (the fortified settlement of London)
Mæduwic	Med-uh-wich	Fictional, near New-market, Suffolk
Northwic	North-witch	Norwich, Norfolk
Northumbraland	North-umbra-land	Northumbria (northern England/southern Scot-land)
Witunceastre	Weet-un-chee-ast-ra	Winchester, Hampshire
Wuffingham	Woof-ing-um	"Home of the Wuff-ingas," near Wood-bridge, Suffolk
-bricg/bricge	-bridge	Settlement near a bridge
-burh	-burg	Fortified town
-ham	-hum	home/dwelling of
-wic	-witch	Market town

Old English	Modern English Equivalent
Cantware	People of Kent
Ealdseaxe	Old Saxons (Continental Germanic Tribe)
Eastseaxe	East Saxons
Engla	East Anglians
Eota	Jutes
Franca	Franks
Hwicce	West Saxons
Gyrwa	People of Jarrow
-isc, -ian	-ish (adjectival form - English, Frankish, etc.)

About the Author

S.T. Sonntag holds a master's degree in Archaeology with a focus on the Migration Period and Early Medieval Anglo-Saxon culture, and the Anglo-Saxon and Viking conversions to Christianity. She reads and speaks Old and Middle English, Latin, French, and Swedish.

She lives in New Mexico with her partner and her two cats, Boethius and King Arthur. She loves swimming, knitting, going for adventures, social justice, reading, and having long discussions about how to dismantle the patriarchy while drinking ungodly amounts of tea.

Acknowledgements

This book was immensely satisfying for me to finally write, and I have to offer my loving thanks to those who helped me along the way:

Goose, my wingman forever.

My siblings, who are sometimes jerks but usually pretty awesome, and also my amazingly supportive parents who never stop believing in me.

Amber Murray and Eric Mix, for reading my terrible first drafts and giving me amazing advice and notes.

Amber Cannon, Matt Makofske, Sarah Obenauf and Melissa Valenzuela for putting up with my nonsense and listening to me talk about my characters over obscene amounts of tea.

Dr. Helen Damico and Dr. Jonathan Davis-Secord for making me rage-quit and then fall in love with this ridiculous and gorgeous ancestor of our language.

Dr. Timothy Graham for causing, and then enabling and encouraging, my Anglo-Saxon obsession.

Printed in Great Britain
by Amazon